IN THE PROPHETIC REALM . . .

A force like a blow snapped Rosarion's head back. Flames rose up to obscure his vision, and for one terrifying heartbeat he feared the Living Flame was coming to devour him. Then the vision steadied as the fiery tree rose up. The tree exploded, the flames about it became a sea of crimson waves, and the Shadow Catcher loomed above him, Its net cast forward. Bodies began to rise, drawn up from the depths of death. They carried the scars of recent battle and their colors were the colors of Branion.

Rosarion stood in the past and watched the dragon of Essus screech as four figures drove their knives into the body of the Living Flame. The statue of an Essusiate Saint covered their escape and began to bleed, and the blood became flame.

Then the vision changed again. The fiery tree exploded in flame once more and one shoot began to grow. The dragon of Essus, perched upon its trunk, screamed, and one clawed foot came down to smash it. It went up in a cloud of cinders. From the base of the tree another flame began to grow. It weaved about the old tree's trunk, and the dragon turned. With its front claws clasped around the shoot, it wrapped itself about the tiny flame as the cinders fed its strength. As the dragon melted away before the fully reborn Living Flame, Rosarion glimpsed his own death and his vision shattered. But just before the seizure took control of his mind and body a face leaped into his vision. The surprise of it was so shocking that he spat out the word before he could stop himself.

"Kassandra!"

THE
PAINTER
KNIGHT

Fiona Patton

DAW BOOKS, INC.
DONALD A. WOLLHEIM, FOUNDER
375 Hudson Street, New York, NY 10014

ELIZABETH R. WOLLHEIM
SHEILA E. GILBERT
PUBLISHERS

DAW TRADEMARK REGISTERED
U.S. PAT. OFF. AND FOREIGN COUNTRIES
—MARCA REGISTRADA
HECHO EN U.S.A.

PRINTED IN THE U.S.A.

This book is dedicated to the memories of:

Harold Preston Patton
1929–1991
My Father

and

Mary Robertson Ross Treacher, née Cheape
1908–1996
My Grandmother

Wallace and Bruce give us a call!
Give us an answer or nothing at all!

Leave all!

BRANION
737 DR

THE BRANION REALM 737 DR
and Surrounding Countries

THE COLUMBAS

NORDANGER

DANELIND

Bryholm

BJERRE SEA

STORVICHOLM

HEATHLAND

SORLANDY

Caerockeith

FENLAND

Yorbourne

KORMANDEAUX

BACHIEM

GWYNETH

MIST

Branbridge

ANVRE

GALLIA

BRANION

Kempstor

ROLAND

QUILLIARD

EIRION

TIBERIA

PANISHA

Shaded outlines indicate lands
within the Branion Realm
in 737 DR

©97Gilbert

The Painter Knight
Principal Characters
In Order of Appearance

Simon of Florenz: An Essusiate artist raised in Tiberia.
Marsellus III/Leary: The Aristok and friend of Simon's.
Fay Falconer: Branbridge Town Watch and Simon's mother.
Hamlin Ewer: Stained glass artisan and Simon's father.
Dani Ashwood: Hamlin's apprentice.
Luis: Fay and Hamlin's server.
Ellisander DeMarian: Duke of Yorbourne, Marsellus' brother-in-law and cousin.
Rosarion DeLynne: A Seer Flame Priest and Herbalist.
Kuritus DeMarian: Ellisander's Grandfather, now dead.
Lysanda DeSandra: Earl of Surbrook, follower of Ellisander.
Hadrian DeSandra: Viscount, Lysanda's brother, follower of Ellisander.
Gawaina DeKathrine: Hierarchpriest of Cannonshire, Captain of the Knights of the Sword and Marsellus III's Regent in his minority.
Jordana DeLynne: Earl of Wiltham and Captain of the Shield Knights.
Evelynne DeMarian: Duke of Lochsbridge, Admiral of the First Fleet.
Kassandra DeMarian: Prince of Gwyneth, Marsellus' daughter and Heir to the Throne.
Gabriella of Branbridge: Auxiliary Companion and Kassandra's Nurse.
Cyterion DeLynne: Rosarion's father, now dead.
Saralynne DeLynne: Rosarion's sister, Ellisander's intended, now dead.

Kathrine DeMarian: Marsellus' Consort and Ellisander's sister, now dead.

Willan: Rosarion's apprentice.

Anne: An independent Assassin known as a Traveler.

Carlita: A Branion Assassin's Guild member known as a Cousin.

Julianus DeKathrine: The Archpriest of the Flame and a Seer.

Drusus the Pretender: The last Essusiate Aristok, 656–657 DR.

Kade: Marsellus' valet.

Jeri: Ellisander's vallet.

Bronwynne DeLlewellynne: A Flame Priest and Seer.

Beryl: An Essusiate merchant from Bachiem.

Warrin Fire-Eater: A tumbler and juggler.

Ballentire of Briery: The leader of The Spinning Coins Tumbling Troupe.

Tamara of Moleshil: A tumbler and Ballentire's partner.

Turi of Moleshil: A tumbler and Tamara's brother.

Terrilynne DeMarian: Duke of Kempston, Marsellus' fourth cousin.

Eddison Croft: Terrilynne's Lieutenant of Foot.

Alexius DeMarian: Terrilynne's squire and cousin.

Lauren of Cambury: Terrilynne's Second Companion.

Gerron Reed: Terrilynne's Quartermaster.

Icarus Haven: Terrilynne's Stable Master.

Wrendolynne: A Herald.

Moll: An ex-Flame Temple Guard.

Marc: A tumbler and Ballentire's cousin.

Gladys DeLlewellynne: Earl of Radnydd and one of Terrilynne's knights.

Sean Cailein: Battle Captain of the Cailein family of Heathland.

Amanda DeKathrine: Earl of Guilcove and Terrilynne's Cavalry Commander.

Elanna Lowe: A Flame Temple Herbalist and Rosarion's teacher, now dead.

Adrianus: Companion to Ellisander.

Talisar: A Flame Priest and Interrogator.

Seth Cannon: A Flame Priest and Seer.

Atreus DePaula: A Flame Champion and follower of Ellisander.

Zavier DeMarian: Duke of Lanborough and Marsellus' fourth cousin.

Albion DeMarian: Earl of Wakeford, Terrilynne's brother.

Nathaniel DeKathrine: Viscount of Dunmouth, and Albion's current lover.

Reb Tanner: A bandit leader in the Kenneth Forest.

Hartney: A tumbler.

Mina: An Essusiate Healer.

Shannon DeYvonne: Earl of Berford and follower of Ellisander.

Jennet Porter: Flame Priest at Caerockeith.

Rhian Cairn: Terrilynne's Steward.

Tee Hanover: Terrilynne's cook.

Yvonnia of Cambury: Terrilynne's First Companion.

Joan Cailein: Chief of the Cailein family of Heathland.

Moraq Cailein: Nominal Chief of the Cailein family and Joan's daughter.

Jade Asher: One of Terrilynne's soldiers and the mother of Simon's son.

Bessie Cheape: One of Terrilynne's archers.

Kalidon DeKathrine: Knight of the Sword.

Holly DeKathrine: Kalidon's squire and niece.

Innes Eathan: A Flame Priest and Seer.

Serus DeYvonne: Knight of the Lance.

Crowitanus: A Herald.

Elias Maple: Knight of the Bow.

Sam Pallaton: Knight of the Bow.

Hywellynne DeLlewellynne: Archpriest of Radnydd.

Bennie: a tumbler.

Alec Hanson: One of Terrilynne's soldiers.

Briar Stone: One of Terrilynne's soldiers.

Jael Asher: Simon and Jade's son.

Carrie Croft: Eddison's daughter.

Bella Croft: Eddison's daughter.

Ross Haven: Icarus Haven's son.

Maggie Haven: Icarus Haven's daughter.

Aggie Haven: Icarus Haven's daughter.

Arren Potter: Serves in the castle.

Kate Potter: Page for Jennet Porter.

Willie Cheape: Bessie's son.

Davin Cheape: Bessie's son.

Marri Cheape: Bessie's daughter.

Nan Guilcove: the Physician at Caerockeith.

Tarn: A Fourth Bryholm Mercenary Company Lieutenant.

Bill: A Bryholm Assassin or "Cousin."

Suzy: A Bryholm Physician.

Arnet Chandler: A messenger from Yorbourne.

Alida Asher: A weaver, Jade's mother and Jael's grandmother.

Jem Roth: A weaver, Alida's partner.

Eleanor mac Mairi: Prince of Eireon and Commander of the Eireon troops in support of Terrilynne.

Eagleynne: A Herald attached to Terrilynne.

Fionn Griffith: One of Terrilynne's scouts.

Camerus DeSandra: Earl of Austinshire.

Sasha Lamb: One of Terrilynne's scouts.

Ptarmiganna: The Head of the Heraldic College.

Ploverian: A Herald attached to Gawaina DeKathrine.

Ospreyan: A Herald formerly attached to Marsellus III.

Wrenassandra: A Herald attached to Ellisander.

Edrud DeLlewellynne: One of Terrilynne's soldiers.

Tomlyn Martin: Lieutenant of the Flame Champions, Seer Archer and follower of Ellisander.

I. Simon of Florenz

Winter, Mean Gearran, 783 DR

The storm raged beyond the palace walls. In a southern suite, an old man dozed fitfully in his chair, now and then muttering some long-ago name before sinking back into deeper slumber. As the thunder built, his sleep grew more restless until finally he awoke with a start.

The room was dark. Groaning, he fumbled for the poker with damp-stiffened fingers, then rose and prodded at the fire. Coaxing a thin wisp of flame from the coals, he spent the next few minutes building up the blaze until it threw a comfortable warmth over the hearth before sitting back again.

The rain beat against the shutters like the ticking of a clock. It made him restless, but beyond his door he knew the palace slept soundly. It was late, or early. No time to be tottering about the halls. No time to be sitting, staring at the flickering images in the firelight either.

He grunted as he fished beside the chair for his jug. *You're getting too dependent on this swill, old man,* he chided himself. *You should give it up, eat properly, work hard until bedtime, then sleep soundly as your father did. That's the key to a long life.*

He snorted as he filled a cup. *I'm seventy now. At what age can you call a life long?*

"Twenty-two."

The old man turned to peer into a shadow-draped corner.

"Ah, no, Leary, twenty-two is no age to die."

The shadows chuckled. *"I packed a lot of living into*

those twenty-two years. More than you did with your decades of moldy walls, cheap paint, and faded dreams."

The old man's expression grew affronted. "Cheap paint indeed! I bedecked your Realm in the loveliest colors in all the world!"

"Heretic. You never stopped to live."

"Nonsense. I've seen and made more beauty than you ever knew. That's living to me."

The old man pulled his robe more tightly about him and poked at the fire again. *Faded dreams. Ha! What did Leary know about dreams?*

"What do you know about dreams, old ghost?"

The shadows gave no reply.

"Fine. Sulk. See if I care."

He swung his attention back to the fire. Leary had been hanging about more and more often lately, nagging, scolding; tempting him to lay down his brushes, but he couldn't. He had so much work to do. So much work, and no time to finish. The hand of the Shadow Catcher groped ever closer, searching for him amidst the maze of immortal images he'd built up around him. It would find him soon, and then there'd be nothing left of Simon of Branbridge save the paintings and the murals. But they were so few, so few of the many he'd dreamed.

Patting at the large silver locket lying against his chest and grunting with the effort, he pushed himself up, squinting out the open shutters at the darkened sky. It would be a dull day with little light to paint by, but he was used to that. The brilliant sun of his boyhood only invaded the skies of his old age on the end of his brush.

The bells of Dorian's Tower tolled four. Two hours until dawn. He was waking earlier and earlier this last year. Soon he'd need no sleep at all, and then maybe he could get some real work done.

Running his hand through his hair, still thick despite his years, he tugged at a bit of dried tempera.

"Oh, Simon, you've paint in your hair!"

"I know, Ma."

"Have you finished for the day?"

"Not quite."

*"Well, there's a pie in the oven for you and your father.
I'm going down to the Red Duck."*

"Thanks, Ma."

The pie was always rock hard when he was finally
driven from his studio by the onset of dusk. His father,
his own hair and beard sprinkled with the powders that
gave his windows such vibrant colors, would be there as
late, for the same reason.

*"Simon, I'm out of cobalt. Run down to Lenarti's and
fetch me some."*

"Yes, Pa."

The old man sighed and closed his eyes. The bright
image of the dye powder vied in his memory with the
sparkling cobalt of the Florenzian waters where he'd first
learned to paint. Lenarti's shop was by the harbor, and
he'd loved to run errands there as a boy. Past the docks
with its fish markets and bustling crowds, past the small
boats and the great ships to the little street where you
could buy powders and paint and glass and lead and
canvas and brushes.

*"Old fool, you never bought canvas in Florenz. You
haven't been back in fifty-two years. Not since 731. You
meant to go back, but you were so busy . . . so busy. . . ."*

*"So busy since you were commissioned by an Aristok
to paint a library."*

"Yes."

"You never finished it."

"No. You wanted your coronation recorded in the
main wing of the palace. And then you wanted your new
chapel decorated. You always were the most impatient
patron I ever had, Leary."

"I was the greatest patron you ever had."

"Not true. The Pontiff himself commissioned me to
paint his daughter's portrait the year before I came
home."

*"Heretic. I commissioned you to paint my daughter's
birth, and it was the greatest fresco in history."*

"Yes. But these new ones will be greater still."

"You'll never finish them."

"I will!" Half rising, the old man shook his fist at the

shadows. "I'll finish it," he shouted, "If you'll just bugger off and let me work!"

Rising, he lit a candle and shuffled over to a table strewn with sketches. "Here! It's all here! Every panel, every scene, right here!" He slammed his fist against the table, then snatched up a ragged drawing. "Here, Leary, look at this one. It's finished. The first one in the story. This one, do you remember that terrible day? It's done. It's right above the altar at Holy Triarchy, right in front of you as you come in."

The shadows seemed to lean toward the torn piece of paper in the old man's hand.

"It'll do. I hope it's suitably bloody and dramatic in execution."

"Of course it is." The drawing slapped onto the table. "It's beautiful!"

"Then I'll come see it today. I've a friend who wants to see it, too."

The sketches jerked under the old man's hands.

"No! Don't come today. It's . . . it's not finished yet."

"My scene's finished. You said so yourself."

"But the rest of the story's not finished yet. You can't appreciate the single piece outside the context of the whole. Don't, Leary, you mustn't! When it's finished, come when it's finished."

"By then you'll have started something else," the shadows admonished. *"You can't put it off forever, Simon. You'll always have dreams unrealized. Eventually you'll have to hand the brushes over to someone else."*

"But not yet, not now. Please, Leary," the old man begged. "Let me finish this one last vision. My final masterpiece. Hold the Shadow Catcher back one more time. You can, I know you can. All I need is a little more time."

He peered anxiously into the darkness.

The shadows were silent for a long moment while the old man held his breath, sketches clutched to his chest. Finally, he heard a whisper so faint it might have been the wind outside, or his own imaginings.

"Very well, Simon, one more time."

Spring, Mean Marta, 737 DR

"Simon!"

The morning sun streamed through the chapel's empty window frames, pooling over the flagstones. A large scaffold dominated the far end of the nave, and the auburn-haired man who'd just entered, strode angrily toward it.

"Simon! Torch you forever, you Essus-fornicating son of a dog, answer me!"

When he reached the maze of wood, he kicked it viciously. There was a muffled curse and a long, drawn-out sigh from above.

"Yes, Your Most Regal."

"Where, by the Flame, are you!?"

"I'm up here with paint in my face, thanks to Your Majesty's most ungentle greeting."

"Well, get down here. I want to talk to you."

"If Your Majesty would just wait one minute . . ."

"If Your Artistship would just move his arse. I didn't ascend the throne to wait on a poxy, bearded, bastard painter!"

The sigh was repeated, and then a thin-faced man, beard and hair spattered with red peered over the edge. "I'm coming."

When the other man's feet touched the ground, Marsellus the Third, thirty-fourth DeMarian Aristok of Branion, Heathland, Kormandeux, Aquilliard and Roland, Gracious Sovereign of the Triarchy, Most High Patron of the Knights of the Sword, Vessel of the Living Flame, handed him an embroidered handkerchief. Simon accepted it wordlessly and swiped at the splatters. Regarding him critically, Marsellus leaned against the scaffold.

"You look like a murder victim."

"Your Majesty is too kind."

"You're right there. I've just spent an hour with the flaming Hierarchpriest, all because Simon of Continental flaming Florenz and his holier-than-thou, I know everything because I'm an artist, blistering attitude."

"Cannonshire?"

"Who by the Flame else would the Hierarchpriest be?"

Simon shrugged dismissively. "They all look the same to me."

"Well, you can have her face carved on your tombstone to help you remember it. She came to me this morning demanding your balls on a biscuit. Demanding! Me! Arrogant old harpy." Marsellus threw himself onto the first level of scaffolding and pulled out his pipe.

"I can't imagine why." Simon leaned against the frame and rubbed at his left knee, stiff from a childhood injury. "We haven't even spoken since last fall when you forced me to do that battle piece for her."

"Well, she spoke at length today. She finally visited Cambury and saw the mockery you've made of her grand ballroom."

Simon bridled. "That's one of the greatest frescoes in Branion! There's not another piece on the island to match it!"

"Maybe so, except that it was saturated with bloody Essusiate imagery!"

"What imagery?"

"All those buggering dragons, what blazing imagery do you think?" Marsellus shouted, dropping his pipe in a shower of sparks. "And what was all that foreign olive leaf, fig leaf, star-covered bordering supposed to represent?"

"That's not Essusiate imagery."

"Well, if it's Triarctic, I'm the son of a pig and an ass!"

With a shrug, Simon retrieved the pipe and handed it back. "It's not Essusiate imagery. It's Eastern mythological imagery."

"I don't care if it's Northern bloody knickers imagery! It's totally, scorchingly inappropriate!"

"It's entirely appropriate within the context of the whole," Simon huffed. "It links the panels together in perfect symmetry."

"In Florenz, maybe. Not on the walls of the burning Hierarchpriest of Cannonshire's private bloody residence, you imbecile!"

"Art transcends religion."

"Bollocks! Repaint it!"

Simon grew very quiet. "I'm afraid I can't do that, Majesty."

"You bloody can and you bloody will, if I have to drag you there and tie you to the scaffolding myself!"

Simon regarded his sovereign gravely. "I'm sorry, My Liege, truly I am, but I can't."

"You mean you won't."

"As Your Majesty wishes."

"His Majesty wishes that the Hierarchpriest and the Court Painter would savage each other and leave him alone."

"*I* didn't bring the argument to you. Gawaina knows where I am. If she's dissatisfied, she should come here and discuss it with me rationally."

Marsellus jerked a hand through his hair, his flame-pooled eyes—the legacy of his family's pact with the Living Flame—flashing dangerously. "She doesn't want to discuss it with you rationally. She wants you thrown in the darkest dungeon to be devoured by rats, and if you pull this kind of nonsense again, I'll do it, by all the Flame in the Land, do you hear me, Simon? I know you did it on purpose to rattle her, and I won't have it." He slammed his fist against the scaffolding. "I need her cooperation if I'm going to win this campaign against Panisha!"

Simon looked away. "Of course, Your Majesty. I'm sorry."

The Aristok snorted in disbelief. "No, you're not. You're not sorry for anything you do. You think your talent is shield enough for the worst behavior. You're a flaming disrespectful bastard, you know that? Aren't you afraid of anything at all?"

Simon regarded the other man gravely.

"Mediocrity," he said at last.

"Liar." Jumping down, Marsellus changed the subject. "And why isn't my chapel finished? You've been at it for months?"

"It's close. I've just the one wall left to complete."

"So you've said before. And what about my windows?" Marsellus shook his fist under the other man's nose "If I hear one more excuse from that father of yours, I'll tip him into prison next to you."

"The first one's being fitted tomorrow."

"It'd better be. And there'd better not be any heretical imagery from him either. Why I waste my money on the pair of you . . ."

Simon smiled. "Because Your Majesty has exquisite taste."

"Balls!" Pacing the length of the room, the Aristok turned and squinted at the other man through a shaft of sunlight.

"*I* will speak with Cannonshire and calm her down. *You* will come to the banquet tomorrow evening, *and* you'll behave yourself, *and* you'll meet with her afterward and apologize and explain there was no insult intended *and* you'll use every ounce of charm and dissembling tact you possess, which is flaming little. You'll grovel, acquiesce, or kiss her holy arse if necessary."

Tipping his head to one side, Simon studied his patron's face, then shrugged. "If you wish, Majesty."

"I burning well do wish. Now I'm leaving. Are you going home tonight?"

"Yes, Sire."

"You tell Hamlin I want my windows. And be at the Broken Sword at six sharp."

"Yes, Sire."

Marsellus left as explosively as he'd arrived, and Simon leaned against the scaffold and grimaced. Reaching behind him, he pulled out a small jug. "No insult intended? Well, at least Gawaina's no Seer."

Uncorking it, he took a long swallow.

Gawaina DeKathrine, Earl of Cambury, Hierarchpriest of Cannonshire and Head of the Knights of the Sword, was indeed no Seer; however, she was a powerful and ruthless woman. "And a bloodthirsty fanatic," the artist muttered under his breath.

Raised in the open atmosphere of the Florenzian capital, Simon viewed all religions, east or west, as fodder for artistic imagery, period. A symbol held international truth or nothing at all, and those who adhered blindly to one philosophy irked him no end.

Chuckling, he replaced the jug and climbed back up to his perch. Marsellus was right, though. He had *begun* the dragons to bother Gawaina, but as he'd worked, they'd blended with the overall theme to produce a beautiful, flowing collection of imagery. Usually quite capable of seeing genius in his own work, even Simon had been awed by the final effect.

And he'd be buried in goose dung if he'd change a brush stroke.

"It's perfect," he muttered, "perfect."

But Gawaina was a powerful woman and jealous of her influence over the Aristok. Simon frowned as he stirred a paint pot with the end of his brush.

Marsellus the Third had been a year past his majority when the artist and his family had returned to Branion after almost a two-decade absence. The seventeen-year-old Aristok was a lavish patron of the arts and, armed with his Continental reputation and the belief he was the greatest painter alive, Simon had quickly caught his attention. Only two years older, and able to defuse the Aristok's quick temper, they'd become close friends. Gawaina DeKathrine believed the artist harbored dangerously seditious beliefs and had not approved of the relationship.

Wiping the paint from the brush handle on his shirt, Simon stretched out on his back and gazed up at the half-finished figure of a magnificent white dragon crouched in a fiery oak tree, above him. "Seditious, my arse," he muttered. After a moment's scrutiny, he began a dappling layer of creamy shadow over the creature's back in wide, even strokes. "It's a lovely beast."

Gawaina DeKathrine was used to power, Simon's thoughts continued. Having overseen the education of two child rulers; Kathrine the Fifth, and when she committed suicide at age twenty; her brother, Marsellus the Third, the Hierarchpriest had ruled the country in all but name for almost two decades. She was power hungry, unscrupulous, and hated Essusiatism with a passion that was almost obsessive. That she was unable to completely rid her Faith of its Continental influence was the fracture in an otherwise imposing power structure.

The Triarchy was a complicated entity. Its followers worshiped three minor geographical Aspects: Sea, Wind, and Earth; and one major Aspect: Flame, personified by a ruler whose eyes carried the evidence of a pact made by the first of their number, Braniana DeMarian, with the primordial power known as the Living Flame over seven hundred years ago. It was a practical, agrarian philosophy colored by a century of Continental Essusiate rule just eighty years past.

Gallian-raised Dorian the Third had set Essusiatism above the Triarchy in 543 DR; Atreus The third had restored the Triarctic beliefs one hundred and fourteen years later, keeping numerous Essusiate teachings to ease the transition. Simon approved. The Essusiate Pontiff in Tiberia had not.

"Greedy old fart," the artist muttered through his teeth as he ran his brush lightly along the dragon's tail.

The Essusiate Pontiff had ordered a crusade against the Triarctic Realm. It had failed. His successor had done the same not a decade later. It had also failed. The most recent crusade, waged seventeen years ago when the young Kathrine the Fifth had been only fifteen, had come close to succeeding. When the invaders were finally thrown back, the Branion dead numbered in the thousands. Gawaina DeKathrine had never forgotten nor forgiven, and the Essusiate population of Branion had borne the brunt of her rage.

Marsellus the Third had been willing to continue his tutor's policies until his budding friendship with a foreign-influenced, Essusiate painter had softened his attitude toward his less influential subjects.

Simon paused, chewing reflectively on the end of his brush. The fresco commissioned for Gawaina's demesne of Cambury had been Marsellus' attempt to mollify the Hierarchpriest; an uncharacteristic gesture that Simon had known wouldn't work.

With a snort, he added a shimmer of golden yellow to the dragon's wings before his mind wandered back to the problem of Gawaina. If she decided to get ugly, the Hierarchpriest could cause trouble for the young Aristok, so, as much as it irritated him, he would do as his friend asked. He hoped Marsellus appreciated it.

Gazing lovingly up at the completed dragon, Simon turned his brush to the next figure.

*   *   *

Some hours later, as the spring breeze snapped at his clothes, the painter turned down Harper's Lane just north of the capital's West Gate. The late afternoon sun shone off the brightly painted signs of the Glazier's and Glass Maker's shops that shared this tiny artisan's street with his father's trade and squinting, Simon could just make out Hamlin's cobalt ewer hanging beside the golden bottle and rose of the neighboring business at the end of the lane.

Whistling tunelessly between his teeth, he scanned the familiar surroundings, adding a color here and texture there, building up his mind's representation of the buildings and streets for some painting he might do . . . some day. Around him, people stepped easily from his path, used to the artist's faraway gaze. Simon rarely noticed.

He reached his parents' home moments later and, after returning the wave of the Glass Maker next door, he strode down the close between the two workshops, emerging into the shadowed courtyard beyond. Enclosed by the living quarters of both buildings and the ancient west wall of Branbridge, it was a small, comfortable space. A stone kiln and smelting furnace dominated one side, with a well pump in the center, a small privy at the back, and a roofed stall, protecting stacks of neatly piled wood and coal, built against the workshop. The courtyard spoke of tidy industry and moderate wealth, and Simon smiled as he reflected on his own cluttered and chaotic palace suite, so unlike the sparse rooms he kept here.

Popping his head through the workshop's rear door, he saw Hamlin and his apprentice absorbed at the cutting table, so he made his way back through the courtyard and into the kitchen.

The warm smell of baking made his mouth water even before he entered, and the heavyset woman bending over the table, rolling dough, never saw him until he snuck up behind her and planted a kiss on the top of her head.

Fay Falconer, late of the Earl of Guilcove's Personal Guard and now a member of the Branbridge Town Watch, spun around and caught him a crack across the ear that made him yelp.

"Knave!"

Rubbing his ear reproachfully, Simon grinned down at her. "Hullo, Ma. Your turn to cook tonight?"

"Mm-hm. Your father made a roast yesterday. Here, sit down and be useful." She handed him a bowl of apples.

Glancing at the bowl in mock horror, Simon picked up a knife. "Where's Luis?"

"At the Fishmonger's. It won't kill you to help your mother."

"I suppose not." With a smile, Simon made himself comfortable at the table and picked up an apple.

Fay returned to her baking.

"How's the chapel coming?" she asked over her shoulder, as she lifted the rolled dough quickly into a pan.

"Fine, good. I've only the one wall to complete."

"And then what? Don't take so much flesh off with the peel, Simon."

"And then maybe I'll have a chance to finish that library piece." Running his thumb along the apple's skin, he glanced slyly at his mother. "They're a bit soft, aren't they, Ma?"

"They're not! They've been in the cold cellar since fall, and they're as crisp as the day they were picked. There, see for yourself."

Scooping one up, she took a bite and tossed him the rest.

Simon tasted it critically, then smiled. "You're right; they are a bit mouse-chewed, though."

"I'll mouse chew you. Here, tip that cat down there, if you think there's mice in the cellar."

Simon turned toward the large, orange cat asleep by the oven. The cat opened one yellow eye to observe him, flexed a taloned paw, then went back to sleep.

"I suppose they're fine," Simon admitted, stilling the urge to tweak its tail. Popping a piece of skin into his mouth, he tossed the peeled apple into the bowl.

"So, how's—what's her name—Dani, working out?"

"Very well. She's a hardworking girl, and your father's quite pleased with her progress," Fay answered primly. "He enrolled her at Centerhall yesterday."

"Has it been a whole year, then?"

"It has. As you might remember if you visited more often."

Simon squirmed a little. "I've been busy."

"Because you insist on doing everything yourself. That's not how Lorenzo taught you." She turned, hands on hips. "When are you going to get an apprentice of your own, Simon?"

He shrugged. "I don't know. In a year or so, maybe. I haven't time to teach anyone right now. Why?"

His mother gave an identical shrug. "I've one or two talented youngsters in mind."

"I'm sure." Reaching for another apple, he paused. "I was thinking I might wait until Jael was old enough," he said. "You never know, the boy might want to be an artist."

"Last I heard, he wanted to be a juggler."

"That's because Jade took him to see Ballentire and the Troupe."

"Oh, yes. Did you get a chance to see them when they were in town this week?"

"No, I was busy."

"Oh, Simon!" Shaking her head, Fay turned back to her pie. "That reminds me. We had a tinker stop by this morning with a message from Jade. She say's she's started Jael on his letters as you requested, though she doesn't see the sense in it and neither do I. The lad's too young to sit at lessons. Besides, hard work'll make his fortune, not a lot of book learning and Triarctic nonsense."

"It'll increase his chances for a good trade," Simon explained patiently. "Most of the major Guilds these days demand some reading and writing."

"It's a load of rubbish. Here, I'll take those." Accepting the bowl of peeled apples she began cutting them into smaller pieces. "Jade says the Aristok has the Earl of Kempston and the company holding Dunleyshire again this year," she continued.

Simon shook his head. "That's bad country, especially since the Elliot business. I wish Jade would request a transfer to Kempston itself. The Earl would probably say yes; she's served her long enough.

"Worried?"

"For Jael's sake."

Fay tipped the apple pieces into the pan and dusted them with nutmeg. "Jael's fine. Jade's a good soldier, and her service in Heathland will ensure the boy's future."

"What kind of future will he have if she dies?"

"Simon, stop fussing." Fay turned, hands on hips. "You knew Jade's trade when you agreed to father her child. Now, what's really bothering you?"

"Nothing." Glancing up at his mother's stern expression, Simon smiled ruefully. "All right, maybe I miss him a little. I never thought I would when he was born, you know. He was all red and squalling and squashed looking. But now . . . maybe I'll visit him when this piece is finished. You never know, we might even take a trip, see Florenz together."

"That would be nice." Fay smiled as she turned back to roll the top crust. "Oh, and that reminds me," she said casually a moment later. "That tinker brought along a bit of a letter from the boy as I recall. Now where did I put it?"

Simon's face lit up. "A letter from Jael? Why didn't you tell me?"

"It slipped my mind, dear. I wonder if I left it in the buttery."

"Ma!"

"Don't tease the boy, Mother. Hullo, Simon. I thought I saw you go by."

Hamlin Ewer stooped as he entered the kitchen and, after kissing Fay on the cheek, stole a piece of apple before dropping down on the bench beside their son.

Simon shook his father's hand, then turned back to his mother.

"Ma!"

"What, child? Oh, yes, the letter." Smiling, she reached inside her tunic and pulled out a folded piece of parchment. Simon took it eagerly and went to the window for more light.

Running his finger along the seal, his thoughts turned to the memory of a five-year-old imp stealing raisins from his grandmother's cupboard in Mosswell. "I've got to go and see him," he murmured as he broke the seal. "After I finish this piece."

"Yes, you do," Fay agreed. "Now what does he say?"

Simon held the careful printing up in a shaft of sunlight.

"Dear Da. I am well. I have a dog named Soot. Come to see us soon. Love to Gran and Granda. Jael."

Hamlin beamed when Simon finished. "Not bad for such a small lad, eh, Mother?"

Fay snorted.

"Well, he probably had help," Simon admitted.

"He did not!" Fay snatched the letter back and replaced it in her tunic. "That tinker said the boy wrote it out all by himself, the dear lad, while the man waited."

Simon shared a smile with his father.

"Don't you tell me my grandson needed help," she continued. "Why, you were writing the same at his age yourself!"

Hamlin grinned widely. "Didn't you say it was rubbish, Mother?"

"It is rubbish. It was when Lorenzo wanted it for Simon and it is now that he wants it for Jael, but that doesn't have anything to do with how well my boys do it." She turned back to the pie. "Now disappear both of you, I've work to do and here comes Luis with the fish."

She shooed them both from the kitchen as the young server entered carrying a leather bucket of trout.

Hamlin snuck an apple while her back was turned, and the two men ambled back to the workshop. In the courtyard, Dani was busy adding copper oxide to a smelting pot of molten glass. Hamlin stopped to watch for a moment, then grunted his approval. She smiled quickly without taking her eyes off the work, then her face grew serious again.

Hamlin gestured Simon into the shop. Perching on the end of one worktable, the painter glanced over at a pile of neatly packed frames and glass.

"The Aristok sends his regards, Pa," he began, "and was wondering when the windows'd be ready."

With a chuckle, Hamlin moved a pile of leads from a chair and sat. Tapping his pipe on the edge of the table, he filled and lit it before answering.

"Sends his regards, did he?"

Simon smiled. "Well, he threatened to throw us both in prison. He's eager, you see."

"The first one's ready to go. We should have it in place by tomorrow night. It has the most red in it; he should be pleased."

"That's what I told him."

His father nodded without speaking. They sat for a time in companionable silence, then the older man stirred.

"Did you know that Ballentire and the Troupe were in town?"

Simon nodded. "I heard. Did you get a chance to see them?"

"Two nights ago. They were at the Wind Temple Theater doing *Braniana's Quest*. We had supper with them afterward. Bal and Tam asked after you."

"I was busy. You know how it is."

"Mm hm. How *is* the piece coming?"

"Fine, good. There's just the one panel to go. If I can get some peace, it should be done in a fortnight, maybe sooner."

"Good lad."

Silence descended again as the light cast ever darkening shadows throughout the shop.

This was Simon's favorite time of day; after the work was done and supper was almost ready. It was a time to sit and think, to maybe mention some problem of context or lighting to his father, or toss a new concept around and see where it led. The familiar confines of the workshop, smelling of metallic salts and heated glass, with the muted sounds of the city filtering in through the open shop front was just the place for quiet contemplation. It had been so ever since he was a child in Florenz.

The stacks of glass infused with their brilliant reds, blues, and greens had taught him his first lessons about color, and the quiet man who'd set a stir stick in his hands to mix the potash, later soda and limestone that made his glass had taught him his first lessons about craft. They were lessons of the spirit, and Simon valued them above all other philosophies, religious or political.

Lighting his own pipe, the painter leaned back, content to let the silence stretch.

A short time later, Dani came in to lower the shutters, and the three of them went in to supper.

The kitchen smelled of roasting fish when they entered and, as was the Essusiate custom, there were two strangers of less fortunate circumstance as guests. Luis raced around serving and then took his own place on the bench beside Dani.

Already dressed in her Watch uniform, Fay spoke the evening prayer as the others held hands around the table.

"May Essus cast blessings on this food and on this company for health and prosperity to all."

"Essus be praised," the others answered.

For a while the only sound was that of eating. Finally, after the apple pie had been devoured, and the guests had thanked them and called down Essus' blessing on the house, Hamlin lit his pipe again with a sigh.

"That was a fine supper, Mother. I always love a good trout on Di Gwener."

Fay nodded, as she took a taper light from the candle and lit her own pipe. "Better than a vegetable stew, that's true. And there was many a time in the old days that we were glad to have that."

"Hm. We're fortunate, Essus be thanked."

Luis rose and began to clear the table as Fay turned to Simon.

"Are you staying tonight, Son?"

Lighting his own pipe, Simon shook his head. "No, I have to be at the Broken Sword by six."

His parents shared a worried frown.

"With Leary?" his father asked.

"Yes."

Fay opened her mouth to say something, then just shook her head.

"Well," Hamlin continued, stroking his beard, "be sure you don't get too carried away with your reveling, Son. Your mother's on Shield Gate tonight and she just might haul you both in."

Simon laughed. "Ma wouldn't do that."

"Don't be too sure," Fay retorted. "It's lucky for us

that Leary confines his revelry to Taverners' Row and not on some quiet merchant or chapel street. Make sure it stays that way, Simon."

The artist rose and kissed her on the cheek. "Worried?"

"Always. I don't like it when you drink, you know that. The fifth tenet of Essus is, *'Do not drink wine or smoke fenweed to excess, for when the mind is blunted, the spirit of Essus is weakened.'* "

"I'll be fine. I never lose control."

"Perhaps not, but Leary does. You protect him, you hear? Keep him out of trouble. A dozen cracked skulls and broken furniture with no one to pay for them; or worse, Leary lying knifed in some alley or brothel room would end your prospects in Branion pretty quick."

"I'll be careful."

"Make sure you are. Now, help me with this hauberk, please."

After it was in place, Simon tapped his pipe clean in a brass bowl and replaced it in its pouch. "I'll walk you over, if you like."

"That would be nice." Kissing Hamlin, Fay then turned to Luis. "Don't forget the fire, it's supposed to turn cold tonight, and never mind that cat if he won't come in. I won't have you chasing him all night. He can sleep at the neighbor's. Hamlin, don't take your pipe to bed, and don't be too late. Dani, you can read in the parlor, not in your room, we're almost out of candles. Luis, run along to the Candle Maker's first thing tomorrow and buy half a dozen. Here's a helm, that should be enough. I'll be home just past two. Love you all. Come along, Simon."

Taking her halberd from its stand by the door, Fay glanced around the room, nodding her satisfaction, then left, Simon in tow.

A quiet peace settled over the house as the sun set and the lamplighters began their rounds about the capital.

A dozen streets away, the Broken Sword was already bustling with trade as the city bells tolled six. An inn of modest means, it stood halfway along Taverner's Row below the Shield Gate; far enough west to serve imported wine on demand, and far enough east to afford some excitement for the nobility who crowded its taprooms.

When Simon arrived, Leary was already well into his second bottle, his face flushed with drink and his flame-filled eyes marking his kinship to the half-dozen De-Marians gathered around him. He spotted the painter immediately.

"Simon! Over here! Come and drown your passion in the sweet bowl of the Triarchy's most blessed fruit!"

Overbalancing, he stumbled against another patron, who caught him under the arms and deposited him gently back in his chair. The company around him laughed, and Leary made an exaggerated, seated bow at his rescuer as Simon joined him at the table.

"Someone find me another cup! Server, another cup here!" Leary shouted.

A boy appeared at Simon's elbow, deposited the cup, caught the crested helm Leary flung at him, then disappeared just as swiftly. Leary tipped well, the more so as the evening wore on, and the proprietors of the Broken Sword were very attentive to his needs.

Simon laughed as his friend slopped wine down the front of his tunic. "Are you drunk already?"

"I am marvelously, swillingly drunk and I intend to remain so all night, so come and play skeans with me while I still have some dexterity left." Rising, Leary wove his way unsteadily across the room, shoving a larger man out of his way. The man cursed and made to swing his fist at the back of Leary's head.

"I wouldn't do that, brother." Catching the fist, Simon slid easily between the two men, his voice coldly polite.

The man pulled his arm away with a curse and Leary turned, a dark smile of anticipation on his face. The taproom grew very quiet.

"Simon," Leary admonished, "you're being ungracious to our . . ." He squinted in the firelight at the man's face, noting the short goatee and mustaches. " . . . foreign friend. Gallian?"

The man glared. "Bachiem."

"Of course. They say the Bachiems are some of the

fiercest fighters on the Continent, and that they never run from a conflict, did you know that, Simon? And yet they did run two years ago at the Battle of Brescburg, didn't they? Of course, they were outnumbered then."

Leary's voice had dropped to a purr. "And I think you're outnumbered here, too, friend." His gaze tracked across the room and several patrons rose, their flame-touched eyes glowing in the firelight. "Will you run away again?"

The man turned a fierce look toward a nearby table and its occupants stood uneasily, the cut of their clothes and beards marking them as his associates.

Leary smiled. "Even odds. I like that." His fingers danced on the pommel of his sword.

Leaning negligently against the bar, Simon turned toward the man. "You're in over your head, brother."

"Simon . . ." Leary warned."

The painter shook his head. "I thought you wanted to play skeans."

"Later. When I'm finished playing Bachiem."

Simon turned to the man's associates. "You're facing DeMarians, cousins of the Aristok. Even if you win, you're bound to be arrested. I'd get your brother out of here, while you still have your liberty and valuables intact."

The man's compatriots inched toward him. "We don't want any trouble," one of them said in Leary's direction. "We came to trade, not to fight. We're merchants, not soldiers."

"Remind your friend."

"He's drunk. He means no harm. Come on, Werner. It's time we left."

The man allowed himself to be bustled out the door, his eyes never leaving Leary's face. When they were gone, Leary turned on Simon with a frown.

"You ruined my fun," he growled. "I wanted to kill him."

"You'd get blood on Nell's floor," the artist answered absently. "Besides, I thought we were going to play skeans."

He set the small throwing knife in his friend's hand,

and Leary glared at him resentfully. "You never are afraid of me, are you?" he asked in a sullen tone.

Simon met his eyes. "Do you really want me to be?"

They regarded each other for a long moment, and then Leary laughed. "No. No, I want you just the way you are, with bigger balls than a bulldog."

Raising his hand, he sent the skean flying off in the vague direction of the board. It stuck in the second layer of cork and he turned with a sloppy grin. "Beat that if you can, you cocky bastard. You, give Simon a skean!"

The DeMarian woman in question handed him one with an inviting leer, and Leary laughed. "Thank you, Eve. I knew you scorching lot of ill-conceived royal brats would be useful for something tonight. A fine lot of menacing brutes you all are. Now bugger off, I want to play."

Pausing to check his aim, Simon nodded toward the door as the rest of the taproom returned to its own business. "That Bachiem man's an enemy we may see more of in a dark alley tonight. That is, if some well-meaning stranger doesn't tell them who you are," he added. "We should be cautious."

"Nonsense. I don't need caution. I have you and your silver tongue to extricate me from any irksome altercation."

Simon smiled and threw his own knife. It struck the center of the corkboard triangle and he turned to his friend and smiled. "Yes, you do. And you owe me a drink."

Leary glowered. "You're too burning sober. Boy! Another cup of wine for my friend to destroy his aim and get him drunk, though not too drunk." He waggled his finger at the artist. "The night is young and we have a lot of pleasure to pack in before morning." He laughed as he picked up another skean.

By midnight, the Broken Sword was too dull for Leary's taste, and after a boisterous farewell, they left in search of less cultivated entertainment. As the night wore on, Leary grew louder and more belligerent until the tapster of the Wild Stoat, the fifth alehouse they'd visited, respectfully asked Simon to take him home. As the Bran-

bridge bells tolled three, the two men began their
weaving path westward.

They passed through the West Gate without incident,
refusing the Watch's offer of an escort, and turned onto
Collin's Road. After a time, they came to the small
bridge that crossed the River Swift.

Leary leaned across the rail, the moonlight bleaching
the color from his face and darkening the fire in his eyes.
He sighed.

"This is marvelous, Simon. I don't want the night to
ever end."

The artist frowned as he peered into the gloom behind
them, the wine in his system making his vision swim.
"Then, I've some news for you that should make you
happy," he replied. "We're being followed."

Leary grinned. "Those from the Broken Sword?"

"Mm-hm."

"How nice. I've been far too civilized all day. Time for
a little fun. Shall we have at them here, or farther on."

Simon shrugged, his eyes tracking across the bridge,
from the line of oak trees that marked the beginnings
of Collin's Park and the Royal palace, to the last few
buildings behind them that hid the three figures he'd
spotted. "Whatever you like," he answered distantly.
"One place is as good as another for defense here."

"Then let's get things trotting along!" Throwing his
head back, Leary let out a whoop into the quiet night.

"All Continentals are cowardly dogs and all Bachiems
are the most cowardly lot of all!"

Stumbling, he righted himself, his sword snaking out
from its scabbard just as three burly men appeared at
the end of the bridge.

"Come to me, my pretty ones," he crooned. "Come
to me."

They came in a rush.

The big man from the bar swung a knife at Leary's
head, but it was obvious he was expecting him to be far
more drunk than he was, for his stroke went wide as the
other man danced away. With a laugh, the DeMarian
feinted right, then snapped his sword up to slice a ragged
gash through the other man's sleeve and into the flesh

below. The Bachiem man grunted in pain, and for the first time his expression showed fear.

Grinning crazily, his eyes bright with heightened fire, Leary pressed the attack.

The other two assailants split up. One raced to join his comrade against Leary, while the other swung his own blade at Simon.

The painter, leaning nonchalantly against the bridge, seemed almost to ignore the man's swing, then at the last moment he caught his attacker's wrist and knocked it against the rail. The knife went spinning down into the river, and with a negligent gesture Simon tipped the man over the edge to join it. When he turned, the second assailant was engaged against the DeMarian and raising his blade to strike.

"Leary!"

His friend turned, his sword making one path across his attacker's midsection and the man went down, screaming and clutching himself. As Simon came to join him, Leary turned to the first assailant, lying moaning on the bridge.

"You really haven't been much fun at all," he scolded, weaving his blade point back and forth in front of the man's face. "I expected more. I'm afraid I shall have to invade your burning country now, you're so scorching pitiful."

He raised the sword.

"Leary."

The weapon came down, met resistance, and then came up bloody.

"What?"

With a sigh, Simon shook his head. "Nothing."

The run to the royal apartments left the artist little time to speak. Exhilarated by the combat, Leary laughed aloud as they raced through the orchard and cultivated garden portions of Collin's Park. The chill air seemed to have sobered him somewhat, for he didn't slow down until they reached the main entrance to the palace.

Sweeping through, Leary barely acknowledged the Palace Guard snapping to attention. Striding down the blue-and-black-tiled hall, he shouted for wine as he slammed open the oaken door to the Royal wing.

The Shield Knights on duty, forbidden to follow their Sovereign on his nightly adventures, sighed with relief as Marsellus the Third, thirty-fourth Aristok of Branion, disappeared into his suite, the Court Painter in tow.

Moments later, they lay sprawled across the huge royal bed, their clothes scattered about on the floor. Running his fingers through the other man's dark, auburn hair, Simon turned one lock toward the firelight.

"Like flames reflected in blood," he murmured. "How could you ever mix such a color? You couldn't, not truly. You could only experience it firsthand, and always be in danger of burning or drowning in it."

"Pig's balls," Leary retorted comfortably. "You think too much, that's your problem."

"And you take too many risks."

"I don't either. *I'm* the Vessel of the Living Flame. *'The amphisbane of true prophecy speaks these words: A fiery tree explodes into flames, growing larger until it becomes a sea of flame. Into this sea floats the Shadow Catcher in an ash-gray boat, harvesting a great catch of the dead. The sea covers the whole world and then transforms into a lush, green garden.'*

"My Archpriest of the Flame told me that in prophecy this afternoon. Pretty words, aren't they?"

"A bit over the top."

"No more than your last attempt at poetry."

Simon chuckled. "Maybe, but then I'm drunk." Folding his hands behind his head, the artist made himself comfortable. "So what do they mean, then?" he asked.

"They mean I'm immortal, all-encompassing Flame, and I can't lose."

"Can't lose what?"

"Anything." Leary smiled sleepily. "Anything at all." He grew quiet. Just as Simon thought he'd fallen asleep, the other man stirred.

"Gawaina thinks it means I shall invade the Continent."

"Shall you?"

With a yawn, Leary pulled the blankets up around his

chin. "I expect I shall. We're already at odds with Panisha's fleet. That's the sea of blood, no doubt."

"Flame."

"Whatever. Seems a pity to waste such a gory prophecy on long-winded negotiations."

"Maybe. It could mean something quite different."

"Well, Julianus thinks the same, and if you can't believe the Archpriest of the Flame who can you believe?"

"The Aristok?"

"Hm. Well, I'll decide tomorrow. The roads are still too wet for an invasion, anyway. Besides, now I want to go to sleep. Good night."

The artist chuckled. "Dream well, Leary."

As his friend's breathing deepened immediately into slumber, Simon lay on his back, watching the painted figures above his head dance in the firelight; the figures he himself had painted for Leary just last summer. They waved their tiny golden swords at him, and he shivered. Gawaina wanted a war, so did Julianus. It would increase the already sizable Branion territory on the Continent, and more territory meant more taxes, for the Crown and for the Triarchy. Simon shook his head. It also meant more risks, for Leary and for anyone he took with him.

"Which won't be me," the artist muttered, settling down beside the other man. But he would be here when Leary returned triumphant from his new war against Panisha or Bachiem, or whoever; triumphant and rich and demanding a new fresco to commemorate his victories. Simon smiled. Leary was right. He couldn't lose anything at all, and with his patronage, Simon of Florenz could win all that he desired.

His mind filled with designs and colors, the Court Painter slowly fell asleep beside his Sovereign.

2. Rosarion

Branion's High Temple of the Living Flame was situated to the west of the Royal Palace. Begun by Bran Bendigeid, brother to Braniana DeMarian, in the year 31 DR, it had been expanded over the years until the original structure was almost obliterated, save here and there where there could be found the odd piece of first century architecture. The Flame Temple Herbarium was one such section; a small, round building, made from stones quarried from the temple's own foundations. It had served many purposes over the centuries; however for the last few years it had housed the Temple Herbalist. Situated at the extreme eastern end of the grounds, it was far enough from the main areas to afford some privacy while still retaining the protection of the temple walls. The surrounding garden plots and drying sheds made it a quiet and peaceful place, the perfect home for the Seer Priest whom everyone knew was dying.

The copper-haired man who strode purposely through the beds of new peas and onions was neither interested in its past nor in its present, but was well satisfied with its remote location. Sweeping his gaze across the landscape, he marked the escape routes and the shadowed places that might hide an eavesdropper, then entered the herbarium workshop without knocking.

The sunken-eyed young man who stood coughing before the hearth, turned at the sound of the door.

"You're early," he said shortly, bringing a handkerchief to his mouth.

"And you're insolent." Ellisander DeMarian, Duke of Yorbourne, cousin to the Aristok, and second in line to the Throne of Branion, seated himself at the long worktable. "But useful.

"Julianus spoke Prophecy for the Aristok yesterday."

Rosarion DeLynne, Temple Herbalist and Priest of the Flame, measured a jug of water into an iron pot before answering.

"I know. I read his account of it. It was unclear and inconclusive. I had a wet dream of more detailed prophecy last night. He's getting old."

Ellisander dismissed the comment with an impatient wave of his hand. "You will speak Prophecy more clearly for me today."

"Yes." Rosarion took a finger full of dried blossoms and added them to the water before he turned. The dark shadows around his eyes dulled their feverish glint, but his gaze was still glazed and unfocused. "The signs all speak of great changes on the wind, but Julianus in his darkest dreams doesn't dare surmise what those changes might be. I'd guess you're less than a month away from acting out your plan."

"Perhaps." The Duke crossed his long legs at the ankles. "How long will your apprentice be gone?"

"All morning." With practiced ease, Rosarion added handfuls of dried leaves and grated root into the water. Then, leaning against the hearth, he coughed into the handkerchief again. "The potion should be ready in a few minutes, but I should warn you, it's more powerful when most of the ingredients are dried." He prodded at the fire with a poker. "I had an attack this morning," he said calmly. "I could have a seizure or try to injure myself. You may have to intercede."

"Don't I always?"

The Duke's voice was soft, and the herbalist looked away. "It has to boil a few minutes, then cool."

"An amphisbane standing on its tail speaks the words of prophecy!"

Rosarion collapsed against the herbarium table. A pot of dried leaves went flying as he threw one arm out to catch himself, then fell heavily to the floor. He began to cough, a thick, ragged bray that shook his thin frame. After several minutes, he managed to catch his breath, holding onto the table leg for support. Raising his head, he stared into the distance, seeing nothing.

Ellisander leaned forward.

"The amphisbane was revealed by Julianus yesterday," he said icily. "I expect you can do better than this."

Rosarion's eyes grew heavy and then closed. "I have drunk from the Potion of Truth," he murmured, his voice a ragged whisper. "And the prophecy will do your bidding."

"Then do it!" Catching the younger man by the tunic, Ellisander hauled him to his feet. "Pull yourself together before I throttle you!" He pushed him into a chair. The herbalist began to cough again, and the DeMarian jerked back in disgust. Even knowing that the other was in the third, noncontagious stage of his illness did nothing to soften the Duke's expression as he wiped the spittle from his dark blue sleeve with an embroidered handkerchief.

After a time the attack passed, and Rosarion looked up, his hazel eyes red-rimmed and unfocused.

"The East Wind is blowing across the Land," he whispered, "harboring dark and deadly changes.

"It blows through the branches of a fiery tree and the tree glows red."

He reached out his hand toward something only he could see, moving his fingers as if running them over some misty curtain.

"Below the tree a wyvern sleeps with its tail coiled tightly about its body."

"A wyvern?" Ellisander's flame-sparked green eyes narrowed. "Julianus said it was a dragon."

Rosarion shook his head drunkenly, then dropped it onto his arms. He murmured something, and the DeMarian grabbed his head and thrust it up.

"Speak clearly. You were trained better than that!"

The priest nodded blearily, and Ellisander released him.

"The wyvern awakens," he continued dreamily. "It climbs the trunk of the fiery tree . . . its claws digging deeply into the bark. The tree . . . the tree begins to sway.

"The tree explodes!" Rosarion surged to his feet,

knocking his chair to the floor. "It bursts into flames and is devoured!"

He made a lunge for the hearth and for the first time, Ellisander showed alarm. Leaping up, he caught the other man by the shoulders and jerked him backward. The young priest unbalanced, his arms flailing out, and both men fell to the floor. Twisting in Ellisander's arms until he could see the fire, Rosarion reached out as if to grab it.

"Tongues of flame spring up from the trunk," he spat out. "One tiny shoot stabs toward the darkness, but it's overtaken by another! This other is strong, a pool of flame that grows and grows until it becomes a sea!"

"A sea of flame," Ellisander repeated, his fire-touched eyes glowing.

Rosarion nodded, then his eyes went wide.

"The Shadow Catcher! Wait, no! I'm not ready yet!" He swung his fist, tried to jerk away, but the DeMarian held him immobile, his arms about his chest.

"The Shadow Catcher touched you four years ago, Rosarion," he replied harshly. "You're only living on its suffrage now. You're its messenger, here to speak its prophecy in your final days. So speak it!"

"I . . ." Rosarion convulsed, spittle flying from his lips. "I see the Shadow Catcher cast its net from an ash-gray boat! It draws up a great catch of the dead!"

"Whose dead?" Ellisander hissed.

Shaking his head, Rosarion shuddered. "I can't see . . . just . . . the dead." He passed a hand over his eyes.

"The sea grows," he continued in a whisper. "The sea grows and grows, covering the whole world with fire." His hands traced a weak pattern in the air. "And now the wind picks up, though not . . . not the East Wind. The *West* Wind sweeps across the Land and the sea becomes a garden . . . a . . . a green garden." Rosarion stiffened, choking. "More? I can't . . . I can't . . . see more, not yet. It's hidden. The amphisbane . . . is covered in flames!" He jerked forward, his head cracking against the table. His eyes rolled back in his head, and he went limp in Ellisander's arms.

*   *   *

It was some time before he regained consciousness. The Royal Duke held him patiently, mulling over his words until he felt the herbalist stir groggily.

"Is that all?"

"All."

The DeMarian nodded. Rising, he caught Rosarion under the arms and hauled him up. Pulling a chair upright, he dropped the younger man into it and brushed at his own clothes.

"When will you be coherent enough to discuss this?"

The priest's head drooped until it was pillowed on his arms. "All," he murmured.

Shaking his head, Ellisander dropped a blanket over Rosarion's shoulders. "I shall return in one hour. Be ready." Turning, he strode from the room.

When he returned, Rosarion was stirring a pot of boiling water, his eyes deeply sunken and his face gray and wet with perspiration. He still clutched the blanket around him with his free hand. Glancing up as Ellisander entered, he turned back and picked up a bowl of dried herbs. Slowly shaking them into the water, he nodded toward a chair.

"I'll attend you in a moment," he said hoarsely.

When the decoction had boiled, he poured the water through a strip of cheesecloth into a cup and came to join the other man, moving stiffly as if his limbs pained him. "Wine?"

"No."

Sipping at the cup, Rosarion wiped his face shakily, and then folded the handkerchief and laid it beside him. He looked up.

"The amphisbane is crucial," he said, his voice still thick from the vision.

"How so?"

"It was the first prophet. One head looking into the past, the other into the future. It's said Braniana DeMarian consulted it before she made the pact with the Living Flame."

"I know what's said," Ellisander answered coolly. "Why is it crucial?"

Rosarion coughed and pulled the blanket more tightly

about him. "The amphisbane represents true prophecy and in this case it represents a specific prophet, me." He laid one pale hand against his chest.

"Modest, aren't we? It showed up in the Archpriest's vision as well. I was with Marsellus when Julianus frothed and screamed and capered before him yesterday, much as you did today."

His voice held disgust and Rosarion shrugged. "The Potion of Truth's a harsh drug. Convulsions are common. It takes a strong prophet to withstand the strain."

"Strong?" Ellisander snorted. "Mad. You're all a pack of insane charlatans."

"Then why listen to us?"

"Because Marsellus listens."

The young priest shook his head. "No. You listen to Julianus because Marsellus listens to him; you listen to me because you believe. You believe you're destined to be Aristok."

Ellisander leaned forward, his flame-tinged eyes narrowed. "And am I, Seer?"

Rosarion nodded. "You're the pool of flame that grows to devour the entire world."

"And you *know* this?"

"I have *Seen* it. The fiery tree explodes when a wyvern climbs its trunk. You're the Duke of Yorbourne, symbolized by a fire-wolf and a *wyvern*."

"Julianus said it was a *dragon*."

"A wyvern is a two-legged dragon."

"Then why didn't Julianus make that connection?"

"Because he never saw it clearly. And he won't," Rosarion added, forestalling the Duke's next question. "My prophecy is greater than his, and more detailed."

"Because you're the stronger prophet?" Ellisander's voice was sarcastic.

"No, because I take a much stronger dosage of the Potion of Truth than he dares to. You said it yourself, I'm only here on suffrage. My death is already written on my lungs. I've nothing left to fear."

"Really? I thought you'd piss yourself when the Shadow Catcher made its appearance."

Rosarion looked away. "I always urinate before I

speak prophecy," he answered vaguely. "There was never any danger of *that*."

"A little trick of the trade?"

"Yes." Taking a swallow from the cup, the younger man pressed the handkerchief against his lips. After a time, the gray pallor began to leave his features. "Most face death with less composure than they'd imagined," he continued, "even a Royal Duke."

Ellisander gave him a cold smile. "I made a good choice when I brought my own people in to save your life, I think," he said casually, ignoring the remark. "After your whole family had died in the last white lung epidemic and the physicians said you had maybe six months to live. Even you'd given up on yourself. There you were, lying on that bed in the temple infirmary, too delirious and too weak to even wipe your own arse when I found you. Do you remember?"

"How could I forget?"

"I knew you were a tenacious little prick even then," the DeMarian continued. "And here you are, almost four years later, testing my patience."

Rosarion met his eyes.

"Most of the Temple Seers have been having visions similar to Julianus' for some time. This change has been brewing as long as your ambition. Your patience will last at least that long. Afterward I'll likely be dead."

"Likely. Or wishing you were. I'll have that wine now."

They locked eyes for a long moment, Ellisander's green, flame-touched stare boring into Rosarion's shadowed gaze. Finally the priest broke contact and looked away. Rising, he fetched a bottle and a goblet. Placing them before the other man, he resumed his seat.

The DeMarian simply looked at him, and with a sigh, Rosarion filled the goblet. "You don't have to remind me of your power," he said. "I know what I owe you, and why."

"Just so you don't forget." Ellisander touched the dark liquid to his lips, then set the goblet down.

"Julianus says the prophecy speaks of Marsellus and his army exploding outward to war against Essusiatism and bringing the Triarchy to the known world."

"Julianus is wrong."

"He's the Archpriest of the Flame. What makes your interpretation more accurate than his?"

"Why don't you ask him?"

"Because I'm asking you." The Duke's eyes flashed dangerously. "You've pushed me as far as I will allow you to this morning. Now answer my question."

Rosarion closed his eyes a moment, then rose. Taking up the cheesecloth, he emptied it back into the pot. "The wyvern brings about the downfall of the fiery tree, then transforms into the greater flame," he answered. "Julianus didn't see this because he doesn't dream of your intentions. How could he? You're Marsellus' closest kin and councillor, but Marsellus is a dead man. You've told me so yourself. With that knowledge the vision can only mean one thing. Yorbourne takes the throne. Whether you then make war on Essusiatism afterward to fulfill the prophecy or your own desires is your own business. The whole thing is actually quite simple and self-explanatory if you know what to look for."

Pouring the last of the water through the cheesecloth, he emptied the cup in one swallow.

"So that's all?" Ellisander asked.

Rosarion nodded. "All."

The DeMarian rose. "Good enough." He placed a golden crown on the table. "Here. Buy yourself a bottle."

The priest shook his head. "It interacts badly with the cough remedy."

"Then put it by. One or two more and you should be able to afford your own funeral. Sell that," Ellisander noted, indicating the cup, "to others so afflicted and you might even be able to pay a Herald to say a few words at your tomb."

His voice had an air of mock concern, and Rosarion matched the tone. "It's too dangerous," he answered simply. "It causes hallucinations. Who knows what others might See."

Ellisander's expression grew dark. "Who indeed." He came forward, making use of his extra three inches to loom over the other man. "Tread very carefully, my little dying priest," he said, lifting the other's man's face up with two fingers. "If you don't cough your lungs into shreds before my patience finally frays, you may find yourself with an enemy instead of a patron, and if this has been no more than some drug-induced hallucination, you'll wish the Shadow Catcher had taken you peacefully before it delivered you into my debt."

Rosarion looked away, his face flushed. "I know the difference between delusions and visions," he said quietly. "Besides, your plan was in motion long before my prophecy. All I'm doing is confirming its success. You don't really need me for anything save confidence."

"Not even for that," the DeMarian answered softly, stroking one finger along Rosarion's jaw. "I'm simply giving you the opportunity to make some mark on history with what's left of your life because I cared for your sister."

He dropped his hand and turned away before the priest could answer. At the door he paused.

"Oh, one more thing. Kassandra, the Aristok's daughter, who will, of course, inherit the Throne on her father's death. Where does she fit into your prophecy?"

Rosarion kept his attention on the hearth. "She's the tiny shoot of flame that's overtaken and devoured."

"But when is this to occur?"

The young priest shrugged. "It's not clear, though obviously not now. You told me yourself that she was pivotal to your plans."

"She is pivotal," the Royal Duke agreed. "For the balance of power to remain stable, Kassandra the Sixth must remain on the Throne until she is grown." When Rosarion turned with a confused look, Ellisander explained impatiently. "The only person truly strong enough to challenge my authority is Terrilynne DeMarian, the Duke of Kempston."

"Your cousin."

"Third cousin. She will not contest my candidacy for the Regency, but she would for the Throne, therefore Kassandra must take the Throne in order to avoid civil war."

"Won't Kempston contest when you finally decide to *take* the Throne?"

Ellisander made a dismissive gesture. "By that time

she will no longer be a threat." His flame-filled eyes caught and held the other man's gaze. "What I want from you now, Rosarion, is a guarantee that the shoot that is Kassandra will not be overtaken too quickly."

Gripping the back of his chair, Rosarion sat down carefully. "How can I promise you that?" he asked. "The Shadow Catcher comes for everyone eventually. For all I know she'll die of a fever next week."

"But you doubt it."

The herbalist snorted, and then his expression grew sad. "If she's as pivotal as you say, then I expect you'll protect her as long as she's useful to you," he answered. "At least as well as you've protected me," he added. "You could hold the Shadow Catcher off by will alone."

His voice was grudgingly admiring, and Ellisander came back into the room and laid his hand lightly on the back of Rosarion's neck. Leaning down, he whispered into his hair. "And I shall continue to protect you at least as well as I shall her, little priest. As long as you also remain useful to me, so don't fail me."

The Duke's breath was warm against his skin and Rosarion closed his yes. "I won't. The amphisbane always speaks the truth." He began to cough again. Groping for his handkerchief, he did not look up as Ellisander stroked his hair once more and then departed.

Moments later, striding down the dark paneled halls of the palace's south wing, the Duke of Yorbourne acknowledged the bow of a passing courtier and smiled to himself. Events were moving along perfectly. Rosarion would continue to provide him with the information he needed as long as he perceived that it was Ellisander who was keeping him alive.

Accounted the most influential man in Branion behind his cousin-cum-brother-in-law Marsellus the Third, Ellisander DeMarian knew the value of cultivating such a belief.

Glancing over at a row of DeMarian portraits on the wall, Ellisander idly named off each celebrated ancestor as he passed them until he came to the flaming-eyed, copper-haired visage of his Grandfather Kuritus.

*   *   *

"All people are motivated by one thing, and one thing only, boy: power. You might be fooled at first into thinking that it's duty or love or altruism, but trust me, when the shit hits the stable door, as sure as it'll stink up the entire building, it always comes down to power. Who has it, and who doesn't."

Those words had been spoken by Kuritus on his deathbed; one last piece of cynical wisdom imparted to the sixteen-year-old grandson he knew would follow in his footsteps.

Himself the grandson of Drusus the Pretender, exiled to the Tiberian Continent by Atreus the Third, Kuritus DeMarian had systematically set out from an early age to tie his issue back into the ruling line of Branion and reclaim the power of the Living Flame. At sixteen he'd wooed and wed his cousin Claudia, the daughter of Tristan DeMarian, who'd died fighting his half brother Atreus in 657 DR. Amenable to his intentions, she'd agreed to move to Danelind, the ancestral home of the DeMarians, and return to the Triarctic faith, turning her back on Essusiatism, as Kuritus had. Twenty-five years later, in 703 DR, he'd married their firstborn daughter, Klairinda, to the DeMarian Aristok, Marsellus the Second and, twelve years after that, he'd stood with the Continental dignitaries at Bran's Palace as his own granddaughter ascended the Branion throne as Kathrine the Fifth.

It was a heady day; however, Kuritus DeMarian was not finished. In 710 DR he'd married his other daughter, Kethra, to her second cousin, Quinton, grandson of Kuritus' Uncle Evenon. Kuritus' only stipulation was that Quinton return to the Triarchy. An alliance with the Branion Royal Line was well worth the heresy to the politically motivated young DeMarian, and the marriage plans had been sealed at once.

Thus, when Kethra's and Quinton's children, Kathrine and Ellisander were born, they were heir to three Continental DeMarian lines. The power of the Flame was rising in the eyes of Kuritus DeMarian's descendants.

He lived just long enough to see his granddaughter Kathrine engaged to his grandson Marsellus the Third.

He did not live long enough to see her brother reach for the Throne, but he would have been proud.

Ellisander had his own theories about what motivated people. They were not driven by power, he'd concluded, but rather by needs, power being only one. They would reach for what they needed, and therefore their actions were predictable. Once you knew what people needed, you could control and manipulate their actions by providing or withholding those needs.

And in order to do that, you also needed an intimate knowledge of what you yourself needed so that your actions would not be manipulated in turn.

Ellisander had given it a great deal of study, and as it turned out, Grandfather Kuritus had been right this time. What Ellisander DeMarian needed was power, pure and simple.

This decided, he'd accompanied his sister Kathrine on her betrothal journey to Branion seven years ago with no particular strategy. He'd simply begun amassing power through whatever means seemed appropriate, building his influence up as one builds a castle stronghold, from the foundations of servants and retainers to the battlements of nobles and priests, to the high turret of the Aristok himself. He quickly became, not only Marsellus' closest adviser, but also the chief buffer between the unstable Aristok and his ministers. By the time Kassandra DeMarian was born, bringing four DeMarian lines together, as Kuritus had hoped, Ellisander DeMarian had reached as high as he could go.

It might have been enough. He'd met and fallen in love with a young noblewoman, Saralynne DeLynne, and in her company his ambitions had cooled. But then she'd died, as had his sister Kathrine; Marsellus the Third had fled his royal obligations for the Branbridge taverns, and the country had turned to Ellisander. When the Aristok was able to return to his duties, the Duke of Yorbourne discovered that he did not want to relinquish them.

Ellisander guessed that his wily old grandfather would have told him that had he been alive.

As he wasn't, Ellisander DeMarian, Duke of Yorbourne, second in line to the Throne of Branion, decided to take the advice the old man would have given him if he had been. He decided to reach for it all.

Rosarion DeLynne, the sickly brother of his dead love was an important factor in that decision. Driven by the belief that somehow he should have saved Saralynne's life, he needed the Duke of Yorbourne to stand between himself and his consuming guilt personified by the Shadow Catcher. In exchange, he offered his vision of the future to Ellisander alone. By doing so, he deflected the vision of his fellow Seer Priests away from the Duke and his assignation. He was Ellisander's eyes. The Duke had others to be his hands.

Lysanda DeSandra, Earl of Surbrook, and her brother, the Viscount Hadrian DeSandra, fit that bill perfectly; the one was ambitious, the other weak. Both were willing to do whatever was necessary to maintain the Duke's patronage, including commit regicide.

The two DeSandras were waiting in Ellisander's audience room and jumped up eagerly as he entered.

Dismissing the servant who'd followed him in, the Royal Duke indicated the wine decanter and Hadrian moved forward. Ellisander's look of disdain was mirrored in Lysanda's cool blue eyes.

The Duke of Yorbourne took his place on a small dais and waved one hand toward her. "Have a glass, if you wish, Lysanda."

She shook her head. "No, thank you, My Lord. Perhaps later."

"Well, I'd like one," her brother said. After a nod from the Duke, he poured himself a goblet.

"That will be the last one, Hadrian," Lysanda said with a frown as she took a seat before the Duke. "You've had too much today as it is."

"I haven't."

"Enough." Ellisander's icy tone cut off the impending argument. "We've more important things to discuss today."

They both turned expectantly as the Duke steepled his fingers.

"The prophecy has been confirmed. The Living Flame shall abandon the branch of Marsellus the First and be reborn in the line of Drusus," he said. "The time is almost upon us."

"Did it reveal the one who would strike the blow?" Lysanda asked eagerly.

"Essus."

The two DeSandras glanced at each other in confusion.

"The prophecy speaks of a sleeping dragon at the foot of the tree that is the Aristok," Ellisander explained patiently. "The dragon is the symbol of Essusiatism. Therefore it appears that the followers of Essus shall be the hand of fate."

"A sleeping dragon at the foot of the tree," Hadrian murmured. "That could be the Branion Essusiates, My Lord, lying beneath the Branion throne."

"And their lives and lands forfeit to that throne." Lysanda smiled greedily.

"Exactly."

Hadrian took a deep swallow, then stroked one finger along his jaw, his lean face wearing a pensive expression. "The Essusiate merchants have been agitating for freer trade legislation, and the Bachiem Ambassador has been making supportive noises. A delegation petitioning the Aristok might get ugly if their pleas were ignored."

"Possibly." Ellisander met his eyes. "I want you to investigate this aspect of the prophecy personally, My Lord Viscount," he said. "I trust no one else with such an errand."

"Of course, My Lord." Hadrian smiled ingratiatingly.

Ellisander turned to Lysanda. "Now, as to the time . . ."

Drumming her fingers against the padded leather of her chair, she shrugged eloquently. "Evening? On one of his drunken adventures outside the palace?"

The Royal Duke shook his head. "Too public."

"Perhaps in his bed, then? The Companion's Guild will no longer contract to him, due to his violence, so he often sleeps alone."

"Or maybe on returning from some function along an empty corridor," Hadrian added.

Ellisander considered it. "Perhaps. When the Living Flame chooses to bring his spirit into Its service forever, a guard or two to escort him on his final journey would not be untoward. However, if he meets his fate in his bedchamber fewer instruments would be necessary." He grew thoughtful.

"I will need an itinerary of his every move in the next month, My Lord Viscount. In fact, I believe it is necessary for you to enter upon this errand immediately."

Hadrian opened his mouth to say something, then closed it again, recognizing the dismissal. "Of course, My Lord. Are you coming, Sanda?"

The woman didn't bother to turn. "Presently."

"You are dismissed, My Lord Viscount."

After a quick glance from one to the other, Hadrian bowed and made to go.

"My Lord Viscount?"

Hadrian turned back at the Duke's summons.

"Yes, My Lord?"

"I have smoothed over your little difficulty with His Lordship Kalidon DeKathrine. He no longer requires that you give him satisfaction by the sword, and you may consider your debts to him paid in full."

Relief crossed the young DeSandra's face. "Thank you, sir," he stammered. "I . . . don't know how I shall repay you."

"Just insure that you carry out my wishes with all possible speed and confidentiality."

"Of course, My Lord. I shall do my utmost."

"I have every faith that you shall."

His face flushed, Hadrian bowed once again and withdrew.

Ellisander shook his head. "He is not a strong tool, I'm afraid, My Lord of Surbrook," he murmured sadly.

"He's a fool," Lysanda growled. "And a weak fool at that."

"Hm. I fear he may not survive the coming trials." The DeMarian rose and came around the desk to stand above her. "Would you mourn for him?" he asked, sweeping her hair from the back of her neck and touching his lips to the warm skin beneath.

Lysanda tipped her head to one side and smiled. "No, My Lord. I don't believe I shall."

"You surprise me, My Lord Earl. I thought you loved him."

She met his gaze evenly. "I may have once, long ago, but I've become a woman now, with a woman's passions, and he's still a child."

"And I am a man."

"Indeed, My Lord," Taking his hand, she guided it to her lips, as she stood. "A very powerful man. A man of fate. And of action?" Her dark eyes bright with anticipation, she glanced toward the Duke's inner chamber door. Ellisander smiled.

"As always, my dear, you get directly to the point.

She returned the smile. Leading him inside, she threw the bolt and turned.

"Just so we aren't disturbed," she whispered."

Some time later they lay in the Duke's bed, the blankets in disarray about them. Lysanda ran her tongue lightly along his lips. "When is it to be, My Lord?" she asked.

"Hm? Soon." Ellisander, the fire in his eyes damped by the aftermath of passion, smiled in contentment. "Hadrian must provide me with his movements and a plausible explanation to gain the Essusiates entry into the palace."

"So you will use my brother, the weak tool, then, My Lord?"

"In all that he may be useful for."

"And with your own hands untouched by an Aristok's blood, the Flame Priests would be hard-pressed to link you to the deed."

"As you say."

"And the child?"

"Greedy."

She smiled. "If you're to become Aristok, the child must be removed."

"And for me to name you Lord over all your family's holdings, the child must also be removed."

"The one follows the other, My Lord."

"Well, don't fear, the child shall join her father as soon as her death cannot be linked back to his. A decade perhaps."

"With her Uncle-Cousin acting as her loving Regent in the meantime?"

"As you say."

"And Hadrian, My Lord?"

He shrugged. "Shall meet with an accident," he answered brutally.

"And shall I also fear for my life, My Lord?" she asked with a tone of mock fear, and the Duke raised himself on one elbow.

"No. Your loyalty, as we both know, My Lord Earl of Surbrook, is based upon payment and assured upon blackmail. Few DeSandras would follow a matricide, no matter what other unsavory action they might ignore."

"As few Branions would follow a regicide, My Lord."

He returned her smile with a chilly one of his own. "As you say. We are equally bound to silence, so you need fear no violence from me. In the meantime, I want you to find a suitable candidate to insure the success of this little expedition. Hadrian is a fool, therefore his own tools will likely be fools as well. Once begun, the deed must be completed."

She pursed her lips in thought. "I may have one or two that might do. However, be assured, My Lord, my own hands shall not be so stained as my idiot brother's."

"Whoever's hands are stained so long as the deed is accomplished," he growled.

"As you command in all things."

Pressing up against him, her hands snaked under the covers and she smiled as he gave an involuntary jump. "Shall we return to more pleasant tasks, My Lord? We have a little time before Council."

His answer was lost in the weaving of her hands.

"There's a plot against the Throne!"

The Privy Council turned in shock as Marsellus the Third entered the hall.

"Well, that shut you up," the Aristok muttered. Crossing the length of the Council Chamber, he acknowledged the somewhat shaky obeisance of his Ministers before throwing himself into his chair.

Ellisander, his face suddenly pale, took his seat to the Aristok's left. "My Liege?" he asked in a tight voice.

"A plot—what, are you all deaf—spearheaded by the Bachiem merchants in Branion."

"Bachiems, Sire?" Gawaina DeKathrine frowned.

"Yes. Burning, bloody Bachiems! I want them all tossed out! All of them!" He pounded his fist against the table and the gathered Ministers jumped.

Ellisander rose smoothly, his natural color returning to his cheeks. "Sire, how can this be? The trade agreement with Bachiem has only just been signed and all parties were content with its terms?"

There were murmurs of agreement around the table and Marsellus scowled.

"The trade agreement be scorched! Three of them tried to murder me last night!"

"I'll send out the Guard for their arrest at once, My Liege." Jordana DeLynne, the Captain of the Shield Knights jumped up, but Marsellus waved her back into her seat.

"Don't bother, they're all dead. I want the rest of them out of my city by Calan Maitide and out of the country by Mean Ebril!"

"The Bachiem Ambassador may protest, Sire," Gawaina DeKathrine noted carefully.

"So toss him out, too. He's a burning spy anyway!"

"As Your Majesty wishes. However, it is my duty as your First Minister to warn Your Majesty that there may be political ramifications."

"Good. Julianus has prophesied that there's to be war. Yes?" He turned to the aged Archpriest of the Flame.

"Yes, Most Holy."

"Then let there be war. We have a mandate from the Living Flame and I, as Its Vessel, shall carry out its wishes. I want a Parliament in three weeks' time. You," he waved at a Herald seated in the south gallery. "Write the proclamation and send it out to all my nobles. We're for war on the Continent. I want soldiers, money, and arms."

"Against Bachiem, Majesty?" The DeMarian woman from the Broken Sword asked uncertainly. "This year?"

"This year, My Lord Admiral Duke of Lochsbridge. We'll go through Gallia or, better yet, right across the Bjerre Sea."

"But what about the Panishan Navy, Sire," and our response to their presence in our waters?" she persisted.

"You and your First Fleet are going to deal with them while Icarian and the Second Fleet deal with the Bachiem."

"But, Majesty . . ."

"Eve," the Aristok looked disappointed. "Are you telling me that your people are not capable of engaging the Panishans without aid from Icarian DePaula?"

The woman glared across the table at her celebrated relative, then shook her head sharply. "No, Your Majesty."

"Excellent. We should leave after spring planting and be back by harvest. A simple, one-season campaign if everyone cooperates." He glared around the table. The Council all made acquiescent noises, and he sat back again.

Gawaina DeKathrine cleared her throat. "And what of Heathland, Majesty?"

"Heathland be scorched."

"Yes, Majesty. However, they may take this opportunity to rebel."

"Bah!" Marsellus snorted. "Not after the drubbing we gave their so-called Royal Family two years ago. They'd not dare raise their noses from the manure piles they've hidden themselves in. Besides, I've sent Terrilynne to Dunleyshire again this year. She can hold that rabble."

"Of course, Sire. Your Majesty's cousin is a fine Commander. Although if I might suggest . . ."

"Papa, I'm bored!"

The imperious little voice cut off the Hierarchpriest's reply as all turned to the south gallery. An auburn-haired child in the DeMarian colors sat pulling the ears of a toy horse. When she saw she had her father's attention, she stood, the Royal fire-wolf and Gwynethian gryphon crest on her little tunic glittering with the movement.

"I'm bored and I want to leave now."

Smiling broadly, Marsellus crossed the room and swung the little girl into his arms while the Councillors rose. "So, you find my Council tedious, do you, little Gwyneth?"

The child turned her flame-touched black eyes on her father's face. "What's tedious?" she demanded.

"Boring."

"I just said that. So, yes. I want to leave. Call my nurse, please."

Marsellus turned. "You! Get the Prince Kassandra's nurse!"

The young man in question leaped up, then paused at the door. "My Liege?"

Both royal heads turned.

"Um, where might I find her?"

"How the blazes should I know? Wherever she is!"

"She's waiting in the hall solar," Kassandra answered regally. "Bring my guard, too. *He's* outside the door."

The man bowed and disappeared.

Shifting his daughter to one hip, Marsellus returned to his chair and set her on the table beside him.

The Council resumed their seats.

"Where's Spotty?"

"Right here, Kasey." Reaching down, Ellisander retrieved the toy horse from the floor.

"Thanks, Uncle Sandi. Papa made me drop her."

Marsellus and Ellisander shared a grin at the accusatory tone, and then the Aristok turned to his daughter. "I did, did I?"

"Uh-huh. 'Cause you knocked her against the table. When do I get my own *real* horse, Papa? I picked out a stall and everything."

"When did I say last time?"

"When I was five."

"Then you'll have one when you're five."

"But the stall's all empty, and the stablemaster's awful lonely. You could get me one now, if you really wanted to." She looked up at him expectantly, and even Gawaina smirked.

"Are you five now?" Marsellus gave her a mock scowl.

"I'm almost five now," she answered, ignoring his expression with perfect disdain. "I'll be five real soon, maybe even tomorrow, and the horse won't be there." Her voice took on a petulant tone.

"You'll be five the twelfth of Mean Ebril. That's . . . how many days?"

"Forty-eight, Sire," Ellisander offered. Kassandra shot him a dark look.

"A whole forty-eight tomorrows to wait," Marsellus carried on. "And the *pony* will be there when you wake up the morning of the forty-ninth. Have I ever failed you?"

She made a show of thinking about it, then laughed when he looked affronted. "No."

"Good. Now, before I let you leave, My little Lord Prince of Gwyneth, what have you learned about Councils today?"

"Um." She stuck her finger in her mouth, then quickly pulled it out when he glared at her. "That Ministers, um, talk a lot."

The Council smiled politely while Marsellus laughed. Finally, he calmed enough to notice the woman standing quietly by the door.

"There you are, Gabriella. Her Grace wishes to leave now. You may take her."

"I want to see the carriage horses," Kassandra demanded.

"So go see them."

The woman cleared her throat.

"What?"

"Excuse me, Your Majesty, but Her Royal Highness always naps about this time of day."

"Is that true?" Marsellus turned a frown on his daughter.

Picking at the ribbons on her tunic, Kassandra shrugged. "Sometimes. Oh, all right, always. But I'm a Prince! I should be able to see the horses first and then nap if I want to! Snowmane and Firestar are s'posed to be groomed today, and I'll miss it!" Her eyes threatened tears, and Marsellus threw up his hands in resignation.

"Horses first."

"Oh, Papa, I love you!" She threw her arms around his neck, and he choked.

"Yes, I know. Here, take her."

He passed her to Gabriella. "Now. Half an hour at the stables and then to bed. Agreed?"

"Uh-huh. Will you come and have supper with me?"

"I don't know. What am I doing?"

"You're attending a banquet at the Temple of the Flame, My Liege, with myself and the Hierarchpriest," Ellisander answered evenly.

"Oh, bugger it. Well, I'll stop in before I go."

Her face fell. "Never mind. You'll be busy, and you'll forget."

"Well, then, we'll have breakfast together tomorrow. How about that? I'll have your Uncle Sandi come to remind me so I won't forget."

The smile returned. "That would do! I'll order it! We'll have all kinds of the best stuff!"

"I'm sure of it. Here, don't forget the horse."

Tucking it into the crook of her arm, Marsellus kissed her cheek, then turned back to his Council as Gabriella took Kassandra, Prince of Gwyneth, Earl of Kraburn and Briery, and Heir to the Throne of Branion out to inspect the carriage horses before her nap.

Some hours later, the Privy Council adjourned with two major events decided upon. The first was that Branion would go to war against Bachiem. The Hierarchpriest was to find a plausible political excuse, and the rest were to throw their support behind their Aristok. The grave misgivings over this rash and untenable plan were not voiced by the Council, who'd learned after the bloody decision to wipe out the Royal Elliots of Heathland that Marsellus the Third would not be deterred.

The second decision was made privately by Ellisander DeMarian. Marsellus the Third would not live to set foot on the Continent. He would move now. This decision was cemented by Hadrian DeSandra, who came to his Ducal Lord late that night, carrying the Aristok's itinerary and a list of Essusiate militants. His sister arrived later with the name of one Essusiate professional. The three debated for several hours before the final decisions of the day were made: who, when, and where.

As Bran's Bell tolled two, the conspiracy was set and all the conspirators resolved. Ellisander DeMarian retired with his Companion, Adrianus, content that each puppet on his stage would play the parts assigned, Lysanda and Hadrian DeSandra returned to her townhouse to iron out one or two private details, and the man who'd begun it all with an unsanctioned prophecy to the Duke of Yorbourne lay, coughing and dreaming, in the Flame Temple Herbarium.

"This is my youngest boy, Rosarion.
"Son, the Duke of Yorbourne is here to see Saralynne. Entertain him while I send for her."

His father's words echoing in his dreams, Rosarion DeLynne turned fitfully in bed and shivered. High above, the narrow windows allowed a steady stream of fresh air in to chill the room. The air was good for his condition and spring was on the wind, his fourth since contracting the disease that had taken his father to his grave at age fifty-two, but the nights were still cold. Sometimes he wondered if frostbite would deliver him to the Shadow Catcher before the white lung did.

". . . Entertain him while I send for her."

The old man seemed closer than ever these days, standing just beyond Rosarion's waking sight; waiting and watching, a reproachful frown on his misty features. He had something to say, and as usual he would not be deterred until it was said.

Pulling the woolen quilt more closely about his shoulders, Rosarion followed the Lord Cyterion DeLynne's voice down into dreaming.

". . . Entertain him while I send for her."
"Yes, Father."
The sixteen-year-old acolyte looked suspiciously at the DeMarian Duke and tried to assume an air of polite welcome.
"Will you, ah . . . have a drink while you wait, sir?" he inquired.
Ellisander Demarian nodded and seated himself on the hall's divan.

After fetching one of the family's precious glasses, Rosarion stood uncertainly to one side. He wasn't sure why he disliked this tall, Continental-born cousin to the Aristok. Named Duke of Yorbourne when his sister Kathrine had wed Marsellus the Third, Ellisander DeMarian was so far above Rosarion in rank that it was both ludicrous and dangerous to harbor such feelings. Had they not been introduced when the Duke had escorted the boy's sister Saralynne to a court ball, the DeMarian would not even have been aware that the boy existed at all.

Rosarion scowled. Maybe the fact that Saralynne had been spending far too much time mooning over the Royal Duke lately had caused him to cast a jaundiced eye over the other man. Maybe because he seemed to be returning her interest.

"Your father tells me you entered the priesthood this year." The DeMarian's cultured, Continental accent was strange to Rosarion's ears, but the underlying steel in his voice made the younger man stir nervously.

"Yes, My Lord," he answered with stiff formality. "I assist master Elanna, the herbalist."

"Interesting." Ellisander's flame-touched eyes looked him up and down. "I also hear that you've great promise as a Seer."

Drawn by the compliment despite his suspicion, the boy colored slightly. "I am studying the prophetic skills, My Lord."

The Duke nodded to himself. "Good. That's very good. I expect you will be of great value to the Throne." He rose. "Ah, Saralynne. You look lovely this evening."

Thunder, rolling across the sky to the west, woke the herbalist, and he sat up with a groan. His nightshirt was damp with perspiration, as were the sheets beneath him. One more reminder of his condition. Coughing, he fumbled for his cup and gulped at the cold infusion, before lying back down.

"Is there something wrong, Your Grace?"
Ellisander spoke without turning as he watched Saralynne run up the stairs to change out of her riding habit. The Duke had been calling for six months now and court

*gossip whispered that he had eyes only for Saralynne.
Cyterion and Dorotea DeLynne were ecstatic. Their
youngest son, Rosarion, was not. Even the Duke himself
had finally noticed the boy's displeasure.*

*Having entered the hall from a side room, Rosarion
paused.*

"No, sir."

"Really? You seem disturbed." *Ellisander fixed his
fiery gaze on Rosarion's face.*

"I . . . heard voices, My Lord. I just came to see who
it was."

"And didn't like what you saw?"

*The younger man looked away. The DeMarian Heir
Presumptive had been spending far too much time with
Sara lately, and only Rosarion seemed to realize that his
ever-increasing attention was dangerous. The kiss he'd interrupted had confirmed his worst fears.*

*He met the Royal Duke's eyes. There was really only
one answer, and the DeMarian knew it already. He might
as well admit it.* "No, My Lord," *he answered, a faint
quaver in his voice.*

*Ellisander's expression showed mild surprise, and then
he smiled.*

"You are bold," *he said, bemused, removing his gauntlets and laying them on the table by the door.* "But honest. Honesty has its place. Now and then." *He came
forward.*

*Rosarion took one step backward, and Ellisander
raised his hand.* "Stay a moment. We should talk. Your
father has invited me for supper before Saralynne and I
go to the theater. We shan't return until well past midnight, so you and I will not have the opportunity to
speak later."

*The boy glanced up the stairs, fighting to keep his fea-
tures even.*

Ellisander came forward. "Your family is welcoming
this interest from the royal line," *he said softly.* "You are
not. Why?"

*Moving to put some more distance between himself and
the hot gaze of the DeMarian Duke, Rosarion's heels
bumped into the wall.* "It's not for me to say, My Lord."

"It is for you to answer my question."

The young priest swallowed. "My sister is a very gentle person, sir," he said finally.

"And I am not."

"I didn't mean that, My Lord."

"Yes, you did, Your Grace. You fear for her safety, for her honor, is that it?"

The boy met the older man's gaze, then shrugged carefully. "Just for her happiness."

Just for her happiness. Rosarion lay, staring at the beams above his head and listening to the wind pass through the Temple orchard outside. What an idiot he'd been. She had been happy, and as the weeks had passed and spring had warmed the country after the cold embrace of winter, the jealous little brother he'd been had slowly thawed toward his sister's intended. Due, to the greater degree, he had to admit even now, to the surprising patience of the Duke of Yorbourne.

Three months after their conversation the expected announcement was made at the Festival of Oimelc. Ellisander DeMarian and Saralynne DeLynne were to be married that summer. Rafael, Vairius, and Rosarion DeLynne were to stand in their Honor Guard, Marsellus the Third would officiate; the rulers of the Triarctic nations would all be in attendance, as would representatives from four Essusiate countries. It would be the finest event since the marriage between Marsellus the Third and Kathrine DeMarian, two years previous.

But that spring the white lung struck Branbridge.

It swept through the capital like a scythe. Many of the nobility fled the city and were spared, but the DeLynnes, with their close ties to the merchant traders and shippers of Branbridge were decimated. The entire family of Cyterion DeLynne fell ill. One by one they died. Saralynne took to her bed the day before they buried her mother and joined her three weeks later. Finally only Rosarion was left, growing steadily weaker in the temple infirmary.

Finally the dry months of summer arrived and the disease began to abate. The city breathed a little easier, believing that the worst had finally passed, and then disaster struck the Royal Family.

Kathrine DeMarian collapsed in Council. For twelve days she lay, feverish and racked by the thick, choking cough that marked the white lung. Marsellus canceled his appointments, sat by her bedside night and day. She called out deliriously for her husband and daughter, and did not recognize the distraught Aristok as he sat clutching her hand. The Court Physician braved his Sovereign's frantic wrath by forbidding the ten-month-old Prince Kassandra's entry to the sick room and was banished from the palace. He remained despite the order, though there was little he could do. Kathrine DeMarian was dying. On the thirteenth day, a kind of hazy peace settled over her, and she sank into unconsciousness. Finally as the afternoon sun cast a warm glow about her wasted face, she died.

Marsellus, already reeling from days without sleep, staggered from the room, weeping. He disappeared into the taverns which had not seen him since his wedding day, and there he stayed.

The country turned to Ellisander. Mourning for his sister and his intended, he turned away at first, then at the insistence of the Hierarchpriest of Cannonshire and the Archpriest of the Flame, he emerged to take on the burdens of duty. After seeing to the immediate demands of Royal Obligation, he went in search of his cousin Marsellus.

He found him, fought him, brought him home, sobered him up, and stood by his side as they consigned Kathrine's body to the Royal Necropolis. Marsellus was to rely on his cousin in all things from that day forward.

Meanwhile, Rosarion DeLynne, last of his family, lay delirious and weakening in the Flame Temple Infirmary. He hadn't eaten in forty-six hours, hadn't kept even water down for over twenty-four. The physicians had given up hope and gone, only the priest who stood watch over the dying remained. The Shadow Catcher paused to gather one more spirit and was turned aside by the flame-born will of Ellisander DeMarian.

From his bed, Rosarion had stared blankly up at the tall, copper-haired man, and slowly his eyes had cleared.

*　　*　　*

"She's dead." His voice, barely a ragged whisper, was cut off by a bout of congested coughing.

"I know."

"Sara . . . I tried . . . everything I knew . . . but she died . . ."

"I know."

Rosarion's feverish gaze searched the gaunt features of his sister's lover. The Duke's face was impassive, although his flame-touched eyes were dark with barely controlled hatred.

Running his tongue along lips cracked and bloody, the boy tried to speak again, choked, and began to cough. "I'm sorry," he managed to say finally.

"I know." Ellisander rose.

"Can he be moved?"

The old priest shuffled forward. "Oh, no, My Lord." She shook her head vehemently. "He's dying."

"How long?"

"Only the Shadow Catcher knows for certain, My Lord, but soon. A matter of hours I'd say."

"Then it won't change his fate if he's moved." The DeMarian turned to a heavyset man hovering to one side. "Take him up, Nole."

"Sir."

The man came forward, lifted the wasted form, blankets and all, and headed for the door.

Ellisander returned his attention to the priest sputtering by his side. "Tell Archpriest Julianus that the boy Rosarion is being taken to the Duke of Yorbourne's wing of the palace where he shall be cared for until his recovery."

"But, My Lord . . ." she gasped.

"Tell him I shall return him to the temple when that recovery is assured."

"But . . ." she glanced uncertainly from the Royal Duke to his retainer, then bowed. "As you wish, My Lord."

Alarmed consternation marked their progress, though none dared interfere as they left the Temple of the Flame and entered Ellisander's private coach. The driver snapped the reins, and they set off toward Bran's Palace.

Inside the coach, the young priest began to shake and

*the Duke of Yorbourne pulled the blankets more closely
about him, his expression unreadable.*

As dawn slowly brought activity back to the Temple
of the Flame, Rosarion lay, contemplating the night's
dreaming. It had been four years since Ellisander had
taken him from his deathbed. Four years, and in that
time the DeMarian Duke had changed. Outwardly he
was still the same charmingly dangerous man he'd always been, but the hatred Rosarion had seen blaze forth
in the Temple Infirmary still smoldered behind his eyes.
It had been some time before the herbalist had realized
it was not directed at him. Very soon that hatred would
take the form of regicide.

The herbarium door opened, interrupting his thoughts,
as his apprentice Willan entered to build up the fire and
make breakfast. Rosarion rose, the vague form of his
father's face remaining in his mind like the afterimage
of lightning across his vision. Cyterion mouthed one silent word at his last remaining son, then faded away.

Shivering, Rosarion pulled on his robe, pausing to
cough into his handkerchief as he looked up into the
gray dawn. Very soon, maybe today, history would be
made in some dark and bloody corner of the palace and
the world would be turned upside down. Few of those
suspected would survive the following days of hysteria,
although most of the true conspirators would not even
be considered.

Certainly no one would suspect Rosarion DeLynne,
herbalist of the Holy Order of the Flame. As the white
lung sucked the life and strength from his body, he had
passed off the symptoms of prolonged exposure to the
prophetic herbs to his condition. *The fatigue was caused
by his bouts of continuous coughing, the seizures, by the
medicine he drank to alleviate the congestion in his lungs.*
He was dying and the rest of the Priesthood had drawn
back from him in respect for his need to face the Shadow
Catcher alone.

And in his isolation he chased that elusive Captain of
the Dead with an almost frantic urgency. One day the
prophecy would reveal Its misty face and he would know
his final hour. In the meantime he would deliver up the

future to the man who'd stayed Its hand. What Ellisander did with that knowledge was his own business.

Crossing to the hearth, Rosarion took up a jar. Willan had set the iron pot on its hook, and as the herbalist measured out the herbs that would give some small alleviation to his strained lungs, he tried to banish his father's scowling face from his mind, but the word Cyterion had spoken repeated over and over in his thoughts.

Traitor.

Reaching for his handkerchief, Rosarion began to cough.

3. Anne

14 Mean Boaldyn

The assassin sat on the terrace of the Dog and Dou-
blet Inn and stared out across the River Mist. Far in
the distance she could see the outline of the Flame Temple, the copper turrets blazing in the late afternoon sun.
Her eyes narrowed.

A server, setting a jug of wine at her elbow, shivered
at her expression and withdrew quickly. The stranger
had paid for a week's lodgings and made it plain she
wanted the service to be discreet and silent. The server
was more than willing. The stranger made him very nervous. Her pale gray eyes seemed to look right through
him.

The assassin, known only as Anne, although she sometimes took other names as the situation demanded it,
filled her own cup, her gaze never leaving the temple
across the river.

A fortnight ago she'd been sitting on a similar terrace
in Bryholm when the message had arrived; word of a
possible Visit in Branion and a fat purse of silver for
expenses. The instructions had been short and specific.
She was to join a Bachiem merchant train, non-Reform-
ist if possible, no later than two days from that date,
make the crossing in their midst, take a room at a speci-
fied inn on Branbridge's south bank, and wait.

Anne had not questioned the odd instructions. The
man who'd contacted her worked for a shadowy Patron
in Branion's capital city, that much she knew, and had
employed the assassin twice before. Both times on Branion soil, both times with curious details that made little
sense to anyone unfamiliar with the Triarctic Flame

Priests and their prophetic abilities. Anne merely assumed that the seemingly meaningless details were meant to cast a shadow across the Sight of the Temple Seers and cloud their vision. As that also shadowed Anne's own identity, she was satisfied to comply with the instructions. Raised Essusiate in the ancient Triarctic land of Danelind, she had a wary respect for their prophets. Besides, her Branion Patron paid well. One more Visit might be enough to retire on.

Draining the cup, the assassin's thoughts drifted to the journey from Bryholm. The crossing had been an easy one. The Bachiem merchant she'd befriended had kept up a steady stream of conversation all the way and had even offered her a place to stay while in Branion. Anne had declined. She was staying with her cousins, she'd explained. They served in the House Guard of a minor noble family in Oaksend and had promised her a job. At her age, such work was hard to come by and she'd jumped at the chance.

The woman had been vaguely sympathetic. Her family were wealthy wool merchants and she herself had never been without, but Anne had the look of someone who'd seen the harder side of life, so the merchant woman had nodded and clucked her tongue and wished her well. They'd parted with a promise to keep in touch.

In a way, Anne had told her new friend the truth. She had come to meet her "Cousins," although they shared no blood tie and served under no family save their own; their common oaths a much stronger bond than any kinship or country could impose. The Branion Assassin's Guild did not insist that all independents, or Travelers as they were known, serve under their orders; however, certain formalities had to be observed. A message must be sent informing the Cousins of her presence, a fee paid in advance—the sum determined by the rank of the Host—and an indication of possible ramifications that might endanger the Guild. They did not expect to be told the name of the Host or the details of the Visit but were open to such information and were willing to be of assistance for a further sum.

As soon as she'd obtained her rooms, Anne had sent

messages to both her Branion contact and to the Cousins. Then she'd settled down to wait.

The contact was the first to reply. A boy arrived to request that she take a walk down by the docks and did not wait for an answer. Pushing aside the remains of her dinner, Anne pulled on her cloak and wandered down to the river.

Walking slowly, she kept her gaze on the water, though little in the surrounding area escaped her attention. She noticed the figure crouched in the shadows by a dilapidated dock before she passed it, and pausing to scoop up a handful of pebbles began to toss them idly at the waves without looking around.

"No one followed you here?"

Anne shook her head and lobbed a stone high into the air. She recognized the thin, reedy voice with its underlying inflections of the Branbridge merchant class as her Branion contact.

"You're wanted for a very sensitive Visit," he began. "Very dangerous, but very lucrative. Are you interested?"

"I could be." The assassin selected another stone and tossed it toward the same spot. "The message said I would be paid twenty coronets in advance for just coming to Branbridge."

"It'll be on the dock when we finish speaking."

"Good enough. What's the invitation?"

"It's political. There'll be three others with you. You're to lead the attack."

Anne frowned at a seagull perched on a half-sunken coracle.

"I work alone."

"Not this time."

"I said I work alone."

"This is not negotiable!" The man's voice was shrill and edged with panic. "The deed must be done exactly as instructed, exactly, or we'll find another agent."

On the verge of refusing the Visit, Anne paused, the words unspoken. She had come this far; she would hear him out.

"Anyone I know?"

"No."

"Professionals?"

"Professional enough."

Amateurs.

"Who are they?"

"You don't need to know."

"I think I do." The man made to answer, but Anne cut him off. "Amateurs have no place in political assassination. Who are they?"

The contact was silent for a time and when he spoke his voice was resentful. "Essusiate militants."

"Oh, perfect. Fanatics."

"They're absolutely reliable, and trained for just this type of situation!"

"Then what do you need me for?"

"Insurance. You're the professional, but if you feel you aren't up to it, then say so now, and we'll find someone else who is."

Her every instinct warning that she should walk away, Anne lobbed another stone at the waves and considered his words.

"Where's it to be?" she asked finally.

"The palace. The Royal wing. Any problems?" His tone was sarcastic now. She merely shrugged.

"It's easy enough to crack."

"It must be done in broad daylight, five days from now at four in the afternoon. The others will meet you at a designated point. You're to guide them to the site, coordinate the attack, return them safely, and get back to the Continent with all possible speed. There must be no misunderstanding about that part. A ship will be made available for your departure, and you must be on it and gone before the alarm spreads and they close the harbor."

"That sensitive, is it?"

"You have no idea. Are you interested?"

"Maybe. What's the offer?"

"Four hundred golden sovereigns."

Anne gave no reaction, but inside she was staggered. *Four hundred?* She could retire into luxury on that much money, and perhaps that was the idea. That, or a quick voyage to the bottom of the ocean, her mind supplied. She tossed a stone at the gull, and it rose, squawking indignantly, into the air.

"Who's the Host?"

"You'll make the Visit?"

It was insanity. Too many stipulations, too many risks, too many details left to chance, and three others of uncertain reliability, but . . . But. *Four hundred* golden sovereigns. If she survived, she would be comfortable for the rest of her days. And there was something about this Visit, something urgent in the air that set the hair on the back of her neck rising. She nodded slowly, knowing the man was watching.

"With all its stipulations?"

The assassin shrugged. "They're easy enough to incorporate." How, she would determine later. "Who's the Host?"

The man was silent for a long time. "You must understand the perilous nature of this Visit," he continued instead. "Once the name is spoken aloud, it can never be spoken again. You've already agreed, so you cannot change your mind, or your own life will be forfeit."

With a short jerk of her hand Anne dismissed the badly delivered threat and growled out her former question. The answer was not the one she expected.

In shock, she turned and stared in the direction of the crouched figure.

"Is there a problem?" The panic was back in his voice, and Anne returned her attention to the waves, tossing another pebble at the seagull while she collected her thoughts. *Sensitive, indeed.*

"Just surprised. Where will he be?"

"In his private chapel on the second floor of the Royal wing. His guards will be waiting at the bottom of the stairs, far enough away so they won't hear anything.

"You're to go in the night before and wait in the Consort's suite. It was closed up after Kathrine De-Marian's death, and no one ever goes near it. Your three associates will be led there by one of my people, and you'll return them to his keeping afterward."

Her mind already occupied with the problems posed by these three "associates," Anne listened with only half an ear as he outlined the topography of the Royal wing.

"And it must be done swiftly and quietly, for the Flame's Sake," he finished.

"An interesting turn of phrase."

"What?"

"Nothing. What about the money?"

"Half will be waiting for you under the statue of a hippogriff in the Consort's training room. The other half will be paid on board once you're out on the Bjerre Sea."

"And the name of the ship?"

"The *Ptarmigan*. It's berthed down at the Graywark Docks."

Anne nodded. "Done."

"I cannot impress on you how important the details are. It must be done quietly, and you must evade capture at all cost."

Anne was growing tired of the man's pretentious little voice. He sounded as if he were reading the lines of a bad play. Avoid capture at all cost? She snorted inwardly. Of course she would avoid capture. She had no wish to die at the end of a Branion rope after prolonged torture at the hands of the Branion priests, yet she simply nodded and tossed another stone at the river.

"Very well," the man continued. "I shall tell my employer that you accept." There was a rustle of cloth and then silence.

Anne waited another five minutes, staring out at the river and mulling over his words. Finally she tossed the last pebble into the water, watching the tiny waves ripple out from its impact, then turned and crossed to the dock. At the base of one post she found a leather bag. She counted the twenty silver coins inside, stuffed it into her shirt, and without a second look, returned to the inn to order more wine.

An hour later, a representative from the Cousins joined her table. The woman made a quick sign with two fingers across her side and waited until Anne responded before dropping into a chair. Catching the server's eye, she crooked her finger.

Minutes later they were tucking into a mutton stew. The server refilled Anne's jug, set an extra cup beside it, and departed with a crested helm and instructions that the two women were not to be disturbed. He took his money with a short bow, gave the owner her cut, and the two withdrew to the bar to serve their less reticent customers.

The woman filled her cup and raised it in the air. "Greetings in prosperity, Cousin."

"And to you also."

"The Continent's been good to you. We heard of your successful Visit in Florenz last summer."

Anne shrugged. "The Duc had poor security for a man so powerful. It was a simple task."

The woman dipped a chunk of bread into the stew. "So what brings a Traveler of your renown to Branion?"

"A Visit."

"With the same Patron as before?"

Anne nodded. "And with the same puffed-up little prick for a contact as before."

The woman smirked. "You know, for a small fee we could identify this puffed-up little prick for you." She made an obscene gesture with the bread and Anne grinned.

"Maybe later. His anonymity is always part of the deal." She leaned forward. "This is a big one, Carlita, one to retire on if I live long enough to enjoy it."

"You suspect your Patron might have other ideas?"

"Maybe. This time it might be more politic to send me to the bottom of the ocean instead of trusting my silence. They've provided a ship for the journey home. The *Ptarmigan*."

"I don't know it. Do you want us to look into its . . . seaworthiness?"

"If you would. I'd hate for it to spring a leak in mid-voyage."

"As would the Cousins. Our relationship has always been most cordial."

They sipped at their drinks.

Finally Anne set her cup down and pushed the bag, minus half its contents toward the other woman. Carlita peered inside.

"An exceptionally large fee," she noted. "Anything you'd care to tell us about this Visit?"

Anne sat back. "Only that it's more ambitious than any Visit you've ever made, and when it's discovered, the world will be turned upside down."

"The response will be very public, then?"

"*Very* public. I'd look to your own security in the next four days if I were you and keep your alibis handy on the fifth."

Carlita cocked her head to one side. "Most intriguing. We've not heard of any political move of such magnitude. Your Patron's security must be very tight. You wouldn't care to divulge the name of the Host?"

"Not this time, Cousin, the stakes are far too high."

"How thrilling, a mystery to uncover. In the meantime, is there anything else you need our assistance with?"

"A detailed map of the palace."

"Easy enough."

"And a DeKathrine House Guard's uniform carrying the Earl of Snowdon's crest. Will that run me extra?"

Hefting the purse, Carlita smiled. "Tell you what, I'll throw it in for old time's sake. Anything else?"

Anne shook her head. "Just check on the ship and its Captain for me if you would."

Carlita dropped her spoon into the empty bowl and rose. "I'll see to it personally. The Wind blow success on your enterprise and keep you safe, Cousin."

Acknowledging the Triarctic phrase with a solemn nod, Anne returned her attention to the north bank as the other woman departed. Looking past the Flame Temple turrets to the great bulk of Dorian's Tower, she frowned.

The identity of her Host did not concern her. She carried no superstitious fear of religious leaders, either Triarctic or Essusiate. Everyone died, some by disease, some by age, and some by the hand of an assassin, professional or amateur. It was the price the rich and powerful paid for their luxuries. What did concern her was the Visit itself. She drained the cup and called the server over to refill the jug.

Getting in was simple enough. She would enter through the unused southeast section, go over the roofs to the Royal wing and down the wall's elaborate stonework to the inner balcony. The DeMarians believed that, buried deep in the center of their ancient palace, the Royal wing was secure, but Anne knew that no building was truly secure to rats or to assassins. So getting in was taken care of. Getting out was more complicated, although she had a fairly simple plan to cover that aspect as well. It was the deed itself that presented the greatest danger. She grimaced.

Wait for some stranger to bring her three amateurs, take them in charge to murder the Vessel of the Living God of Branion, get them back safely, and only then to make her own escape? It stank of a hidden agenda.

Anne ground her teeth. She did not work well with others, neither as a leader nor as a subordinate, which was why she had never joined the Cousins, and trusting others, strangers, with her life did not appeal to her.

For a moment she contemplated solving her problem with three well-aimed crossbow quarrels in the backs of her supposed compatriots, then dismissed the idea. There was a lot more here than her contact was telling her, and until she knew more, she was groping about blind. She would wait and see what Carlita turned up.

Glaring through narrowed lids, she stared out across the water as the sun set over Bran's Palace.

On the north bank, a mile from where the assassin's gaze rested, a handful of men were meeting with a similar purpose. Gathered by Hadrian's contact, a Cleric of Essus, they'd come to strike a blow for their Faith. Each man was Essusiate by birth and each was dedicated to the prosperity of their people in this Triarctic land; dedicated enough to brave palace security and the outrage that would follow in order to kill the Vessel of the Living Flame.

The cleric outlined his plan. Five days from now, at three in the afternoon, representatives of the Essusiate Merchant's Coalition had been granted an audience with the Chamberlain, Hierarchpriest Gawaina DeKathrine; their safety assured by the Bachiem Ambassador. These three men would enter the palace as part of his entourage. At a designated moment, they would be spirited from the public areas to the empty Consort's wing and, with the aid of a *professional,* make their way to the Aristok's private chapel where Marsellus was due to spend an hour in meditation. They were to strike as Bran's Bell tolled four, then exit the palace as they'd come with the ambassadorial party held up on some pretense until they returned. They had an hour's grace, plenty of time to make it to the cellars of St. Thomasino's in the Weaver's Quarters where they would be hidden.

The men were agreed, and one by one they moved off to wait for the appointed hour.

Half a mile away Hadrian DeSandra's most loyal retainer outlined the details of a proposed Visit to a representative of the Branion Assassin's Guild, the Host to be an Essusiate cleric, minister to the faithful of St. Thomasino's in the Weaver's Quarters. The Cousin named his price. The retainer agreed. The fee was paid, and the retainer departed in good spirits. With the cleric's fate secured, the three others could be dealt with more prosaically.

Meanwhile, Ellisander DeMarian, Heir to three De-Marian royal lines, sat in the Flame Temple Library, deep in conversation with the Archpriest Julianus De-Kathrine. The Festival of Calan Mai was just a fortnight away and they had much to arrange. As Archpriest of the Knights of the Sword, the Royal Duke had officiated at many such religious functions and as Julianus had grown older and more infirm, those duties had increased.

In the course of their conversation Ellisander allowed the Archpriest to convince him to spend the afternoon, five days from then, at the temple to continue their discussions and have dinner with Julianus and his priests. After a show of some deliberation, Ellisander agreed. He would meet with the Archpriest at three that afternoon.

And so it was decided.

Returning to the Palace, the Duke went over the itineraries of his fellow conspirators as he made his way toward his suite.

Hadrian would be hosting a group of his fellow Knights of the Bow at his town house. Lysanda would be testing the mettle of her Guard with that of Rosemary DeKathrine at the Branbridge tournament fields. Rosarion, as Temple Herbalist and friend to the Duke of Yorbourne, would be closeted with Ellisander and the

Archpriest, to advise them on the festival, but really to gauge the old man's reaction to the terrible news.

The Duke nodded to himself. Everything was in readiness. Entering his suite, he ordered a bath and settled into a chair before the fire. All they had to do now was wait five days, at which point history would be reforged. He smiled, his flame-tinged green eyes mirroring the fire in the hearth.

Five days later, the early morning hours of the nineteenth day of Mean Boaldyn, 737 DR, were shrouded in storm clouds, as a lone figure ran swiftly through Collin's Park. She carried her crossbow lashed to the back of her pack, and now and then she crouched to avoid tangling it on any low-hanging branches. At the edge of the kitchen gardens, she paused.

The empty herb pots showed up as darker smudges between the rows of mounded earth and she weaved her way through them carefully until she reached the base of Adrianne's Tower. The bulky structure had once housed the personal guard of the Aristok Adrianne DeMarian some seven centuries previous; for the last hundred years, however, it had been used simply as a dovecote.

Anne scaled the outside wall, careful not to disturb the sleeping birds. A second-floor window provided easy access, then up a crumbling flight of stairs and across a wooden floor, soft with age and rot, and she stood before the door to the southeast wing. It was locked.

Running her fingers along its length, Anne grinned in the darkness. One of her first lessons had been that a lock was only as strong as the doorjamb it was attached to. One tug, and the old wood splintered; she carefully eased the door open. The rusty hinges made less noise than she expected, and soon the space was wide enough to slip through.

The corridor beyond was dark and quiet. Keeping the map of the palace before her mind's eye, she made her way down its length. A turn, a quick run through several empty rooms, down another passageway and up a flight of stairs, and she stood behind a dusty tapestry. The assassin moved it gently aside and peered past. The hall beyond was quiet.

She traversed another wing, this one showing signs of more recent occupation, before she judged that she should now take to the roofs. Easing out a window, she leaped to a stone wyvern and, using its head as a springboard, jumped for the roof overhang. Pulling herself onto the tiles above, she paused to listen. In the distance she heard the harsh cry of a gryphon, and then silence. A moment later she was picking her way along the moss-covered slate, moving steadily northwest.

Soon she came to the more populated areas of the palace. The roofs here were in better condition, and she made good time, only slowing now and then to creep under a darkened window. Leaping a narrow gap between two tower turrets, she paused for breath on the edge of the central wing, then continued on. Skirting the main conservatory, she sprinted across a spanning archway, and dropped onto the crenellated roof of the Royal wing's main entrance hall. As Bran's Bell tolled three, she started silently along its length. A scramble over the throne room's steep roof, a cautious descent down an iron trellis, and she stood on the Royal wing's inner balcony.

It was deserted.

Anne nodded to herself as she crept along. The first floor had no windows and the only occupant of the second floor was Kassandra, Prince of Gwyneth. The assassin glanced across at the Heir's suite, noting the position of the various rooms, then continued on her way toward the Consort's wing.

The diamond-shaped pane of glass before the window latch was easily removed, and without pausing for breath she had the latch turned up and had swarmed over the sill. Seconds later she stood inside. The Royal wing was silent. She had not been observed. After easing the glass back into its leaden frame, she turned to survey her surroundings.

The Consort's suite had an air of abandonment, the rugs and tapestries undisturbed since the day of Kathrine DeMarian's death. Making her way to the training room,

Anne halted before the statue of a great hippogriff, its wings tucked around its body as if in slumber.

Kneeling, she felt about its base. At the back, her fingers brushed against wood and she pulled out a rough, unadorned box.

Crouching beside the statue, the assassin opened the lid, and counted out the coins inside by touch, running her thumb along their engraved faces. Then she replaced them, tucking the box in her pack and began a silent exploration of the second floor. When she was sure she was alone, she settled with her back against the statue, loaded and cocked her crossbow, laid it close to hand, and forced herself to relax. After a time, she slept.

When dawn came, she made a more thorough search of her temporary quarters. The second floor housed a midden, a training room, an upper gallery, and an outer chamber. It was at the far end of the latter that she found the door she was looking for. It was locked, but posed little problem; moments later, she felt the tumblers give way. Easing the door open, she was reassured that it did not squeak unduly, and leaving it open, she crept along the passageway to the Aristok's chapel.

Without touching the door, she studied it in the pale light. It had no lock, and she grinned to herself. Of course it had no lock. Who would dare enter the chamber where the Vessel of the Living Flame communed with his God? Who indeed? She peered around the corner. At the far end of the corridor she spotted a set of stairs leading down. The stairs the Aristok would ascend that afternoon.

Decided, she returned her attention to the door, and after only a moment's hesitation, pushed it open and slipped inside.

The chapel was a small room, the single candle on the altar bathing it with a soft, golden light. It had an air of sanctity that even she could not ignore, and she paused to still the chill that ran briefly up her spine. This was not her faith, she reminded herself firmly, and the Branion Aristok was not a God, merely the Vessel of a primordial power, no matter what the Triarchs believed.

Returning her thoughts to the Visit ahead, she noted

that the candle wick had been trimmed recently, then made a careful study of the furnishings. Rich tapestries covered the stone walls around a small hearth and drapery hung before the two window alcoves. Anne pulled each aside, measuring the space between. They were fairly wide, and could easily hold two people each.

Drumming her fingers against her chin, she considered her options, then decided. Three would be positioned inside to do the deed; one would wait outside in case, despite her contact's assurances, the guards needed to be dealt with. Simple.

Returning to the training room, she sat with her back against the wall. Taking her flask from her pack, she went over her plans. The four of them had to be in place well before the Aristok arrived, but she needed at least ten minutes to brief the others and gain some idea of their skills and reliability. The Visit itself should take no more than another ten minutes from the time the Aristok arrived to their return to the Consort's suite. After that the others were on their own, and that was what worried her. Even assuming they managed to avoid capture, her route across the roofs would take much longer than she had, even in daylight. She would not be off the palace grounds before the deed was discovered, and there was no guarantee she would not be seen. So the roofs were out. Uncorking the flask, she took a deep swallow.

She'd considered this problem back at the inn while waiting for Carlita. She had two alternatives, she'd surmised. The first was to hide in one of the disused areas of the palace until dark—only to be routed out by the Flame Priests who would be as thick as fleas on a dog's arse as soon as the deed was discovered—the second was to walk out in plain sight, and the best way to do that was to appear to belong there. And that posed no problem at all.

Bran's Palace permanently housed approximately two hundred members of the nobility and the Triarctic hierarchy. They were served and cared for by four times that many servants, guards, and apprentices. In the chaos that would follow, no one would notice one more armed retainer hurrying from the palace. A simple case of misdirection.

Pulling out the uniform Carlita had furnished her with, she held it up to the light. It was of a simple design, black under-tunic and breeches, black belt with knife sheath and harness for the crossbow, and a surcoat of forest green emblazoned with the DeKathrine bear, enfield, and heron design of Bessalynne DeKathrine, Earl of Snowdon.

Anne ran one finger along the crest. It was a good choice. The Earl was old and cantankerous and kept a large, rotating House Guard to serve her, mostly stolen temporarily from the Guard of her many children. One more unfamiliar face in her entourage would not be unexpected.

Satisfied, she laid it out on a trunk, then pulled a wrapped package of bread and cheese from her pack. After a light breakfast, she curled up and caught some more sleep.

She awoke to the sound of Bran's Bell tolling one. After finishing the food in her pack, she made a quick visit to the midden, then returned to her place below the window. She still had two hours to wait, so she took the wooden box from her pack and made a more thorough count of her money.

The thick reddish gold, mined in the hills of Gwyneth, gleamed in the sunlight, and she arranged them idly into piles by ruler. Seventy-four showed the head of Marsellus the Third, the current Aristok; thirty-seven depicted his older sister, Kathrine the Fifth.

Anne scowled. Kathrine had committed suicide on the tenth anniversary of their father's death. Her coins were considered ill luck, and most had gone to the Triarchy in the form of anonymous donations years ago. That so many of such a high denomination were found in one place, pointed an accusing finger toward someone with access to Triarchy funds.

With a frown, she set the last sovereign on top of the pile. The coins presented a problem as they could not be spent in Branion and would not go unnoticed in any Triarctic nation. Any other country's coinage could be melted down, but Gwynethian gold was used only for

Branion sovereigns or for Triarctic ornaments. They would have to be exchanged by a broker, and she would lose severely on the deal. She glared at the coins, thinking dark thoughts about her Patron.

Turning her attention to the other piles, she studied the profiles of Marsellus the Second, fifty-eight coins, Kassandra the Fifth, twenty-one coins, and Atreus the Third, nine coins. They would be easy enough to spend or exchange for silver if she went to half a dozen different places.

There was one coin left.

The assassin squinted down at the unfamiliar face. It was of a young man dressed in the style of seventh century royalty and bearded. Anne frowned. Triarctic men went clean shaven to honor the first Vessel of the Flame, Braniana DeMarian. Beards were an Essusiate custom. The name came slowly. Drusus, the last of the four Essusiate Aristoks.

She turned it back and forth in the light. The engraving was still sharp, the face shiny and untarnished. This piece had not been in circulation long, which wasn't surprising. Drusus the Pretender had held the throne for less than a year. His nephew, Gwynethian-born Atreus the Bastard, son of Drusus' older brother Marsellus the First, and a Gwynethian Lord, Llewellynne ap Rowena, had deposed the Essusiate ruler and forced him into exile on the Continent. All the coins which bore his face had been recalled and melted down to make candlesticks for the chapels of the newly reinstated Triarchy.

Anne rubbed the coin between finger and thumb. This had to have come from a private collection, added to the box to complete the payment. Who in Branion would risk heresy to keep such a coin?

The assassin shook her head, her earlier suspicion growing. This coin presented a much greater problem than Kathrine's. It could never be exchanged in a Triarctic Land. She would have to journey to Gallia or Bachiem, and even then it would cause enough of a stir that the Flame Priests might hear of it. Her Patron must know this, so why pay her in useless coin?

Tipping up the flask, she took another swallow, then

glared at the coin once more, remembering Carlita's
words last night.

"*The Captain of the* Ptarmigan's *a man named Danus
Arden. He's a Triarch, though not particularly devout.
He usually runs small cargo from Danelind to Branion
and back, so there's nothing unusual there. He dabbles in
smuggling from time to time, usually in banned Essusiate
goods, and occasionally runs fugitives out of the country.*

"*The word on the docks is that he's got a very lucrative
job coming up. He's filling his holds and has reported to
the Harbormaster that he'll be making his usual run to
Danelind in a few days.*"

Anne leaned back on the bed and helped herself to a
chicken leg.

"*Sounds like it's legitimate enough,*" she mused.

Carlita frowned. "*Maybe. From what I hear he's spending more money than usual. Of course, if he's running a
desperate and dangerous Traveler,*" she waved her own
chicken leg at Anne, "*then the sum would not be untoward. However, he's taken on two new sailors, known to
be willing to do anything for money, and the Captain has
the same reputation, so . . . I'd stay on my guard. If it* is
*a betrayal, it's being played very close to the vest.
Sorry, Cousin.*"

Anne shrugged. "*You did the best you could. Maybe
it's just as it seems, an expedient way to leave the country.*" But she didn't believe her own words.

With a shake of her head, the assassin slipped the
sovereign into her belt and returned the rest of the
money to the box.

Thirty-eight coins either impossible or extremely difficult to spend, provided by someone obviously powerful
enough to keep them without censure, an unfamiliar ship
provided to return her home, and a Visit so politically
explosive it would be far more expedient to remove the
Traveler than pay her off.

Cocking her head to one side, she considered the list
and finally came to a decision. She could not risk taking
the *Ptarmigan* home, but did that mean she couldn't take
whatever money might be aboard it? With a sigh, she

put it out of her mind. Time enough to consider piracy later.

She spent twenty minutes loosening up for the Visit and then pulled on a hooded tunic and gloves. Snapping the quarrels into their quiver, she began to check her crossbow.

Bran's Bell had just tolled three when her preparations were interrupted by a small sound outside. Turning in a crouch, she rose cautiously and peered outside.

Across the courtyard, on the second floor of the Prince's wing, a small, auburn-haired girl was climbing out a window. The child carried a toy horse and was dressed in a loose-fitting dark blue tunic that fell past her knees. As she turned, the sun shone off the red-and-golden fire-wolf crest emblazoned on the tunic's front. It could only be the Prince Kassandra.

"Well, now," the assassin breathed, "and where do you think you're going?"

The child dropped lightly to the balcony, crouching down until she was assured no one had seen her departure, then made her way along its length until she reached an iron trellis similar to the one that Anne had used earlier that morning. After pausing to gauge the distance to the courtyard below, she dropped the toy horse. Satisfied that it had landed without harm, she swarmed down the trellis, reaching the ground a moment later. Picking up the horse, she glanced around and then opened a small door and slipped back inside the palace.

With a grin, Anne wondering what mischief the Royal Heir was up to, but sobered quickly. If the child's absence was discovered, it might disturb the Aristok.

Placing her pack behind a tapestry, she left the training room and tucked herself into a corner of the gallery where she could see the main doors of the Consort's suite. She hoped for all their sakes that her "associates" would be on time.

Minutes later, the door opened and three armed and bearded men entered the Consort's outer chamber behind a smaller, clean-shaven man dressed in the livery of a palace servant. Eyes narrowed, Anne drew closer, moving along the gallery on her elbows.

The men glanced about as the servant closed the door behind them. One leaned against a trunk, and taking a knife from his belt, began stropping it against a small whetstone.

"How long do we wait?" he growled in the direction of the servant.

"Not long." The man rubbed his hands nervously. "You have to be in place by four, and it's only just half past three now." His voice was high-pitched with tension and Anne frowned.

"How're we to get from here to there? There's an occupied wing in between," another, younger man asked, a whine in his voice.

"We wait for this *professional* of theirs," the man with the knife answered. "Don't worry." He grinned in the murky light. "The God's with us on this one, that's for sure. We're instruments of Fate in the hands of Essus, sent to strike down the Aristok for his villainy."

"And send his rotting heart into the cold darkness," the third man intoned.

They all nodded, although Anne noticed the servant inch warily toward the door.

"We should take them all out, every stinking one of them," the younger man snarled.

The first man chuckled. "One at a time, boy. The Aristok first, and then who knows, maybe we'll be called upon to deal with the rest of them."

"In the meantime," the third man interrupted, "where's this professional of yours?"

"Above you."

The men spun around as the assassin rose, the crossbow pointed in their direction. Keeping the weapon trained on them, she crossed the length of the gallery and moved down the long flight of stairs. Once she reached the bottom, the servant bowed nervously.

"Good," he said, attempting an air of command. "We're all here, then. There's, huh, been no change in the Aristok's itinerary, so I'll leave you to it." He edged toward the door.

"I don't think so." The crossbow swung to cover him. "You." Anne jerked her head at the younger man. "Find something to truss him up with until our return."

When both men made to protest, she turned to the man with the knife. "Do you trust a Triarch to remain steadfast to our cause, Brother?" she asked. "Do you trust him with the success of our mission and the lives of your men, because I don't, and I'm prepared to put a bolt through his eye right now to insure my own safety."

The man met her steady gaze and then gestured at the younger, who turned to obey with a scowl. As he passed her, Anne stepped in front of him. "Some advice, Brother, *I* lead this little company. You do what I say, and you do it immediately or they'll be the last words you ever hear."

He glanced down at the loaded weapon held negligently under her arm, and then up into her pale eyes and nodded. Anne turned back to the first man as the others took hold of the protesting servant. The look that passed between them was measuring.

"You're a Sister of the True Faith?" he asked.

"As I was born. I may not follow the same path as you, Brother, but we both serve Essus today."

"True enough."

"Then let's get to it, we don't have much time."

He nodded.

On the other side of the central wing, the thirty-fifth Heir to the Throne of Branion slipped through the door of the newly built Marsellus Chapel. The room was deep in late afternoon shadow, the only illumination coming from the lanterns set up at the far end. As the child made for the light, she glanced about proprietorially.

"Simon! Simon, where are you?" Her piping voice echoed through the chapel.

The painter turned in surprise. "Highness?" Jumping down from the scaffolding, he came forward quickly and knelt before her. "What are you doing here?"

"I came to see you." Kassandra's voice was nonchalant and looking past his shoulder, she spied the pots and brushes. "Whatcha' painting now?"

"A forest. Aren't you supposed to be napping? Where's your nurse?"

Kassandra shrugged. "Back in my rooms. She doesn't know I'm gone."

"Then you should go back." The painter tried a frown which the Royal child ignored.

"I'm not sleepy," she answered. "I wanted to see your pictures, and they never made any time for them. Lessons, lessons, lessons! I told them I wanted to see you today and they never listened!" She stamped her foot. "So I left."

"Who never listened, Highness?"

"My nurse and my tutors, so now they will just have to get a scare when they find me gone. That'll teach 'em." She scowled fiercely and Simon laughed.

"Yes, I dare say it will."

"You won't tell Papa?"

The painter shook his head. "I live only to serve Your Highness."

"Good. I want to paint trees like I did on the back wall." She waved one small hand in the direction of the door. "They looked good, didn't they?"

"Of course they did. You're not really dressed for it though," he added dubiously.

"I am, too!" Her tone was indignant. "This is an *old* tunic of *Papa's,* Simon!"

"Ah, my mistake. Well, then, Your Highness, if you're to be my apprentice today, we'd best get you up here."

He lifted her onto the scaffolding, then joined her.

"And if I'm your 'prentice, then I'm not a Highness, right?"

"Right. Do you remember your apprentice name?"

"Um . . ." She put her finger in her mouth and thought a moment. "Sparky!"

"That's right. Well, then, Sparky, take the brush and scoop up some paint like this."

"Can Spotty help?"

Simon made a show of considering it seriously. "Can Spotty actually hold a brush?"

"Well . . . not actually."

"Then she'd better just watch."

The Prince nodded and placed the toy carefully to one side. Then she picked up her brush again. The painter took her hand and guided it toward the stylized outline of a large oak tree.

"There. Now in wide, even strokes."

They were just standing back to admire their work when the bells of Bran's Tower began to toll in the distance.

In the private chapel of Marsellus the Third, the Vessel of the Living Flame knelt before the altar as Bran's Bell tolled four. He never noticed the figures in the shadows around him.

The first assailant struck poorly, his knife digging into the Aristok's left shoulder instead of his back as planned. With an exclamation of pain and surprise, Marsellus jerked around.

"Simon?"
"Yes, Sparky."
"I feel hot."

The second assailant leaped forward, drove her own blade into the Aristok's chest, while clamping her other hand over his mouth to silence him. Spinning him around, she held him out for the others.

Simon turned, a concerned expression on his face. "Are you getting a fever?"
"I dunno. My head hurts."
The painter laid his hand on the child's forehead.

The third assailant struck as well, the combined force of the attack lifting the Aristok's body and spraying his blood across the altar. The others moved in.

"I knew I shouldn't have let you pad around in your bare feet. If you've gotten sick, your father's going to kill me."

The Aristok fell, his flame-filled eyes blank and staring, and in the chapel named for a dead man, his only daughter jerked forward. Her own eyes blazing suddenly red, she shrieked in pain as the Living Flame claimed its thirty-fifth Vessel.
"Highness!"
The painter barely managed to catch hold of the

Royal child as she tried to throw herself from the scaffolding. Her back arching with the force of the Flame's
passing, she screamed again and flung her arms out,
catching him a sharp blow across the temple. He reeled,
but kept his arms around her as she began to convulse.
Somehow, he managed to half sit, half fall onto the
boards, pressing his back against the rough wood of the
scaffolding frame. Unable to climb down with the
screaming child in his arms, he began to rock her back
and forth, babbling whatever comforting words he could
think of, his eyes wide with alarm. After a long time,
she began to cry.

In the corridor beyond, the assassin paused. She'd led
the others back to the Consort's suite after the Visit and
had then taken her leave, returning to the gallery as
they'd untied the servant. What they did with him was
their concern, although she had a pretty good idea what
it would be. Stripping quickly, she'd stuffed the blood-
soaked clothes down the midden and then, using the last
of the ale in her flask, she wiped her face and hands
clean of blood.

Minutes later, wearing the disguise and carrying the
pack and crossbow, she crept along the balcony and up
onto the roofs once more.

This time she went only a short distance before reen-
tering the palace. Feeling horribly exposed, she made
her way through the corridors of the central wing, ignoring the few palace servants and guards she passed as
they ignored her. She was making for the new Marsellus
Chapel, the closest unguarded exit to Collin's Park, for
if what Carlita had said was true, most of the long windows had yet to be installed. If there were workers inside, she would move on to her next choice; if not, she
would be safely off the palace grounds in minutes.

Opening the door carefully, she slipped inside.

The great vaulted room was deep in shadow, and it
was some time before she realized that she was not
alone. Voices came from the far end, and creeping forward, she saw two figures crouched on a maze of scaffolding by the altar space; an Essusiate man and an
auburn-haired child crying in his arms.

Anne felt a superstitious tingle run up her back. The child was dressed in the same blue tunic she'd seen on the Prince Kassandra earlier. This could only be she, and her state meant only one thing. The Flame had passed.

Stories of child rulers, driven mad by the power of the Flame, came to her mind. The tales had meant nothing to her then, but now, watching the child's weeping and the helpless way the man patted her shoulder, the assassin felt . . . she studied the new feeling curiously . . . pity. She shook herself. She was delaying. The girl must take her own chances as she must. The man and child were too absorbed to notice her if she moved quietly, and the first of the great window alcoves was only three feet away and swathed in shadow. She moved determinedly forward.

As she came to the edge of the lantern light, her eyes were suddenly drawn to a painting of a magnificent oak tree on the side wall. Its leaves were painted in fiery reds and golds, and it stretched its limbs toward the arched ceiling in a tangled maze of color. Wrapped about its trunk, as if embracing the rough bark, was a luminescent white figure; Merrone, the dragon Guardian of Essus.

The assassin gave an involuntary gasp as the room suddenly darkened around her. The dragon's sapphire eyes grew bright with so deep and feral an intelligence that she felt frozen in its stare. The hairs on the back of her neck rose as the air grew chill around her and, as she stared, the white dragon, the most ancient symbol of Essus, turned, its tail slowly unwinding from the tree and one golden clawed forelimb stretching out as if beckoning to her.

Its predatory gaze holding the assassin's own, it climbed slowly down the tree's trunk, using its sharp claws to grip the bark. When it reached the bottom, it paused. Its tongue darted out from between its teeth and a sibilant whisper went through her mind.

You are the instrument in the hands of Essus.

She shuddered, feeling the power of her God, a power she had not known since her earliest childhood, touch her.

You are the instrument in the hands of Essus.

Slowly she brought her own hands up to unbuckle the crowbow from its harness. It could only want one thing. As if in a dream, she brought a quarrel forward and snapped it into the breech. Something made her pause.

The dragon, still crouched at the bottom of the fiery tree, was moving again. Around it tongues of flame crackled and grew, and as she watched, it wrapped its scaly forelimbs about one tiny shoot of fire. The light from it bathed the dragon's face, softening its jagged features, but when it looked back at the assassin, its gaze was as sharp as a knife blade, and her mind became suddenly clear.

The Aristok was dead, his only daughter a child, little prepared to take on the heavy mantle of the Living Flame, and the next in line was Continental-born Ellisander DeMarian. Descended from Drusus the Pretender, he would have the motive, and as Archpriest of the Knights of the Sword, he would have the means, and access to gold no other would dare keep in their possession. The golden coin of Drusus seemed to burn into her side, but she was frozen, unable to remove it from her belt.

The dragon's soft whisper echoed in her head once again, and she stared into its fierce gaze, seeing all she had done in the past, and all she might do in the future. She saw a purpose she did not understand, and a command she was to follow regardless.

She stepped forward into the lantern light.

Kassandra had cried herself into hiccups, and Simon was holding her tightly and stroking her hair when he noticed the armed woman stepping out from the shadows. He jerked, his eyes going wide, and drew his arms more protectively about the weeping child.

"Who are you?" he demanded.

"Don't be afraid." The assassin's voice echoed deeply in the vaulted space. "I won't hurt her."

Simon's expression cleared as he recognized the DeKathrine uniform. "You have to help me," he began. "The Prince is ill. She needs a physician."

Anne shook her head. "A physician can't help her now. Something terrible has happened. More terrible than you can possibly imagine, by a hand unlooked for."

"Wha . . . what are you talking about?"

Anne glanced at the Prince, no—her mind amended—the Aristok, the Vessel of the Living Flame, the leader of the Triarchy. Her mind grew cloudy for just a moment in confusion, and then it cleared. The God's reasons were the God's. She had her orders. Seeking a way to tell the man without telling the child, she finally dropped into religious vernacular.

"The Flame has passed."

"The Flame?"

"Has passed." The assassin's tone was heavy with meaning, and the painter's eyes grew even wider as the realization hit him. "But . . ."

Anne shook her head. "Look into her eyes if you doubt my words."

Reluctantly Simon took his eyes off the woman and looked down.

"Sparky," he whispered, "it's all right, you're going to be all right, just let me look at you." With one finger under her chin, he lifted her head. The Flame blazed forth from her fevered gaze, and he closed his own eyes from the heat of it.

"Please, no."

"Yes. And you have a decision to make."

Simon looked up, his face blank with shock.

Anne frowned. "There's no time for hesitation. Believe it and act. The deed's been done, and there's nothing you can do for him."

"For him? For . . . ?" *Leary.* Simon shook his head. "How? Who . . . ?"

"There's no time for explanations either. The hand that planned the deed . . ." she glanced nervously at the door, suddenly mindful of the situation beyond, "is he who will gain the power of the Flame if Its passing destroys the child."

The painter began to shake, all this knowledge too much to assimilate so quickly. "I can't . . . how do you know all this?"

"Because I was hired to ensure the Flame's passing." Her expression was meaningful, and the painter cast an involuntary glance down at the child who'd buried her

head in his tunic. Her hot, little face almost burned his
flesh, and he frowned uncertainly.

"But you serve the Earl of Snowdon . . ."

"A disguise only."

"A . . ." Simon raised his head and his eyes caught
sight of the crossbow still clutched in her hand. "I won't
let you harm her."

The assassin raised one eyebrow, but did not reply,
her silence answer enough. She saw the realization hit
him that if she'd wanted to hurt the child, Kassandra
would be dead already. Simon's shoulders tensed a fraction, then his expression grew uncertain again.

"The one who would have gained the power . . . ?"

"Yes."

"But the Duke of Yorbourne? He's her uncle." He
glanced down quickly, but Kassandra gave no indication
that she'd heard him. He turned back. "I can't believe
it. You know this for certain?"

The assassin plucked the sovereign from her belt and
tossed it forward, the gold gleaming in the lantern light
as it spun.

Simon caught it and frowned down at the engraved
face. "Drusus," he whispered.

She nodded. "There's other evidence, though no time
to tell you, but my information is true. Soon the deed
will be discovered, and I've no wish to be scooped up
in the mass arrests that will follow. Keep the coin. It
may help to prove his guilt one day." She paused. "And
there's more. The hand of the God is at work here,
Brother."

"The . . . ?"

"Essus led me here. The God protects the child. I
don't know why, don't ask me. I've never been particularly devout, and I've done things that would have me
executed as an apostate if they were ever known. Why
I was chosen, I don't know either, but there it is."

"The God uses what tools are at hand," Simon murmured, quoting a passage from his own childhood's faith.

"As you say." She turned to leave abruptly, and
Simon threw his hand out.

"Wait!"

At the door, she turned.

"What do I do?"

She shrugged. "I've no idea how far-reaching this conspiracy is. I will tell you this, trust anyone in Branbridge and you risk handing the child over to her father's murderers, and Essus does not want that. I suggest you do exactly what I'm going to do. Run."

"Run?"

She nodded. "Take the child and run and keep on running until you find somewhere safe. That's my advice to you." She paused. "Essus keep you, Brother," she said almost as an afterthought. "If we both live through this, maybe we'll meet again."

She disappeared through the door.

In the now silent chapel, Simon rocked Kassandra gently, his mind in shock. "Run?"

He glanced down. The child's breathing was ragged, and she didn't respond when he called her name. He felt a moment's panic. "Run where?"

Shaking his head, he stood, pulling his cloak from the scaffold and drawing it around her. "It doesn't matter, Simon," he told himself sternly. "Just go." Tucking the toy horse into her arms, he searched the child's features for some reaction. Her face was wet with fever and her auburn hair, so like her father's, was plastered to her brow. She made no response and he choked.

"Oh, Leary."

He pulled himself together roughly. If what the woman said was true, and the evidence of his own eyes told him it had to be, then Leary was dead and beyond his help, but his daughter was alive and in danger.

Decided, Simon of Florenz took up the unconscious body of Kassandra the Sixth, thirty-fifth DeMarian Aristok of Branion, Heathland, Kormandeux, Aquilliard, and Roland, Gracious Sovereign of the Triarchy, Most High Patron of the Knights of the Sword and Vessel of the Living Flame, in his arms and turned to go.

As he eased them both down from the scaffolding, his gaze fell for a moment on his fresco of the white dragon of Essus crouched at the bottom of the fiery oak tree. His mind, distracted with the momentous events of the day, barely registered the position of the beast, the position he had not painted it in.

4. Marsellus III

In the Aristok's inner chamber the mantel clock ticked away and Kade, Marsellus' valet, turned and glanced at it nervously. His Majesty was supposed to return to his suite to dress for dinner at five, and it was now ten past that. If he didn't arrive soon, he would be late for supper with the Admiralty, and that would make him angry. The valet swallowed. He'd served under Marsellus for only six months, but he already lived in terror of the Aristok's temper. If His Majesty's schedule was disrupted, he would blame whoever was handy, and his valet was handy.

His eyes traveled to the clock once more as he chewed at one fingernail. He would wait five more minutes.

Five more minutes passed.

Finally decided, he made his way through the Royal wing and asked the page on duty in the outer office to bring the Duke of Yorbourne's valet to the Aristok's inner chamber. Jeri'd been with the Duke since before he came to Branion. He would know what to do.

A few minutes later the older man entered the room with a questioning look and Kade spilled the problem out in a rush of words.

"Jeri, you've got to help me find the Aristok. He was due here at five to dress for supper and receive the Prince Kassandra. If he's not here, she'll throw a fit, but he isn't and she will be, any minute. I don't know what to do." He wrung his hands. "I don't dare go to his chapel, but . . . maybe I could send someone else?"

With a skeptical look, Jeri caught Kade's arm as he made to leave and pushed him into a chair. Fishing a small pouch from the other man's pocket, he filled two pipes with fenweed and thrust one into Kade's hand.

"That won't do," he answered as he lit his pipe from a nearby candle. "If the Aristok's still at prayers, we can't disturb him. Besides, your duty is to *be here* when he returns, not *make* him arrive."

He scowled at the younger valet in mock ire from under his brows and provoked a nervous smile in return.

Satisfied, Jeri puffed at his pipe as he glanced at the clock. "It's almost half past now. If nothing else, Gabriella will arrive with Her Highness soon and *she* might have some idea where the Aristok is, so light up and calm down."

Kade obeyed, drawing in a shaky puff of smoke before looking back at the older man.

"So it's not my fault?"

"Oh, please!"

Reassured by Jeri's rough comfort, Kade sucked at the stem of his pipe, as together the two valets waited for the Prince Kassandra and her nurse.

Gabriella's sole arrival did nothing to alleviate their fears. She had no idea where the Aristok was, and the Prince was also missing, spirited from her bed while the nurse sat in the next room. She was not, however, intending to merely sit and wait until they were found. Crisply telling the valets to stay put, she made her way to the Aristok's private chapel.

The door was slightly ajar.

"Majesty?"

There was no answer.

Mindful of the Aristok's temper, she counted to three and then pushed the door open.

Auxiliary Companion Gabriella of Branbridge had seen death before. Trained as a political bodyguard, she'd been contracted to the Royal Family as a nurse through two generations and had protected her charges by whatever means were necessary. She'd seen death before, caused by both her hand and by others. All that did not prepare her for what she found on the chapel floor.

Marsellus the Third, thirty-fourth Aristok of Branion, lay on his back before the altar, blood staining the auburn of his hair a darker red. The ugly pooling across the stones beneath him, and the gore-clotted wounds in his throat and chest told her, as much as his staring visage, that he'd been dead for some time. After standing, frozen, in the doorway for what seemed like an eternity, she placed one hand upon her breast to still her pounding heart, then stepped inside. The chapel was quiet, but she made a quick, visual search of the room anyway. Marsellus' blank gaze seemed to follow her, making the flesh between her shoulder blades crawl, but she completed her survey with as much professionalism as she could. Only after she was certain that she'd missed nothing, did she allow herself to look down at the dead man at her feet. Her expression grew sad.

There was no trace of the haughty, high-strung little boy she'd known in Marsellus' blood-covered features. His expression was one of pained surprise, although the cruel upturn of his lip suggested that even at the moment of death, he'd held nothing but contempt for his murderers.

Resisting the urge to push the matted hair from his face, Gabriella drew a handkerchief from her sleeve and pressed it to her eyes. It blocked out the terrible sight, and she used the moment to pull herself together. There was nothing she could do for Marsellus now; he lay in the arms of the Living Flame, but his daughter was missing and must be found. This terrible new development made finding her even more imperative. Closing the chapel door, Gabriella hurried back to the Aristok's inner chamber.

Once there, she told the two valets what she'd found in as few words as possible, and began to issue orders. Kade, almost fainting with fear, was sent to find Gawaina DeKathrine; Jeri was to bring the Duke of Yorbourne and the Archpriest Julianus to the scene and to send several pages back. Neither was to say anything to anybody else.

When the pages arrived, she sent one with a sealed message to the Branbridge School of Companions and the other to the Captain of the Shield Guards. Then she sat, trying to bring her scattered thoughts into some order. Hopefully Master Ursulynne would send a Senior Master to advise her quickly. Some very bad times were about to occur and she feared they might all be caught in the crossfire.

Rubbing arms grown suddenly cold, the Companion stared about her unseeingly until the portrait of a young woman dressed in the rich dark blue and black of the DeMarians, caught her eye. The Consort Kathrine had been only sixteen when the portrait had been rendered. Commissioned to convince the Aristok to rejoin the splintered DeMarian lines of Marsellus and Drusus, it had captured his heart as well. They were married a week after her eighteenth birthday, and by the next spring, Kassandra, Heir to seven centuries of DeMarian rule, had been born. Less than a year later, her mother was dead.

Gabriella wondered if the young Consort had had any inkling of the bloody future awaiting her small family so few years after the portrait had been painted. Kathrine dead at nineteen, Marsellus dead at twenty-two. And Kassandra . . .

Companions were not taught any official religion. Nonetheless, Gabriella of Branbridge prayed that Kassandra DeMarian, thirty-fifth Aristok of Branion, would be found playing with her toy horse in some out-of-the-way corner, oblivious to the terrible deed that had suddenly placed too many adult responsibilities onto her young shoulders.

She prayed, though she didn't really believe.

"But, Ma . . ."

"Don't you Ma, me, Simon Ewer Falconer! That child needs a physician!" Kneeling by the parlor divan where the artist had placed Kassandra, Fay shot her son a withering glance.

Simon groped for a chair and dropped his head into his hands. "If she's found, they'll kill her," he said thickly.

"And if this fever isn't broken, *it* may kill her." Holding up a cup of warm catmint tea, Fay raised Kassandra's head. "There now, my little one, you drink this up like a good girl."

Kassandra whimpered feverishly, pushing the cup away. Fay persisted, and after a time, the child obeyed.

Fay then turned with a businesslike air to the two youths hovering hesitantly by the parlor door. "Luis, bring in the wash tub. Dani, you go find Hamlin. He went to Centerhall today, so he's likely at the Cock's Tail with that drunken artisan crowd. Bring him, but in Essus' name, don't tell anyone else what's happened. Just tell him I need him to come home immediately."

Dani nodded and ran from the room as Luis wrestled the large tub in from the kitchen.

"And take your cloak! It's cold outside!"

The slam of the kitchen door was her only reply.

Shaking her head, Fay dipped a cloth into a bowl of water and after squeezing it, laid it onto Kassandra's forehead. Then she turned to her son. He hadn't spoken more than a dozen words since carrying the unconscious child into the house, and his minimal explanation of the danger she faced had been uttered in a tone of near panic that was very unlike him. Fay wanted to nip that in the bud right away.

"Now, Simon," she said sternly, tucking Kassandra into the crook of her arm, "from the beginning."

Raising his head, he stared blankly at her for a moment, then, in a distant voice, he narrated the events in the palace and the strange woman's words.

"I got out through one of the empty window frames," he finished. "You know how the chapel looks out onto Collin's Park. Then I just ran."

Kassandra clutched tightly to his chest, his only plan had been to get as far away from the palace as possible. He might have kept running blindly if an unseen oak root hadn't arrested his flight. He'd stumbled to his knees beside an overgrown hedge maze and finally begun to think. Making his way inside, he'd dropped onto a stone bench to catch his breath and come to some kind of rational decision.

All he was sure of was that the child had to have help, and soon. Since leaving the chapel, she'd been a dead weight in his arms. Fearfully he moved the flap of his cloak aside and peered down at her. Her breathing was shallow, her eyes tightly closed, and he hugged her close, his initial fear of the unspeakable calmed for the moment.

"It's all right, Sparky. It's going to be all right."

He'd whispered that every step of the way since leaving the chapel, and now he repeated it, pressing his face into her hair as if the words themselves could bring her back to consciousness. He had to get help, but from where?

In the distance, the copper turret tops of the Flame Temple poked out from above the trees and he almost set out that way, then stopped, the strange woman's words ringing in his ears.

"I've no idea how far-reaching this conspiracy is. I will tell you this, trust anyone in Branbridge and you risk handling the child over to her father's murderers."

He shivered. Surely the Flame Priests would not be in league against their own Avatar?

". . . I was hired to ensure the Flame's passing."

A dull throb began to beat at his temples.

". . . was he who will gain the power of the Flame . . ."

He shook his head. If Ellisander were truly guilty, then anyone could be, and there was no one he could trust, not her family and not her priests.

"The hand of the God is at work here."

But why?

Sitting uncertainly in the midst of the hedge maze, the unconscious daughter of his closest friend in his arms, Simon had never felt more helpless in his life. There was no one he could trust and no place he could go, except one. He stood.

A boat had been easy enough to find, tied up on a small dock at the edge of the park. The oars were missing, but one well-placed kick at the door of a nearby shed discovered them and minutes later they were heading down the Mist.

Thankfully they met no one on the water nor as Simon carried the child, her bright hair concealed in his cloak, up Fishmonger's Row from the river bank. Most of Brainbridge's citizenry were at supper, the streets deserted of all save a few late patrons who paid them scant notice. When a passing collier, smiling maternally, mentioned something about sleeping children being Essus' blessing, he realized that somehow Kassandra's disappearance had not yet been discovered. Breathing a prayer of thanks, he turned quickly onto Harper's Lane.

He reached his parents' home as the bells of the city rang half past five.

Fay was shaking her head when he finished.

"And you trust this person's words?"

He looked up defensively. "It's the only answer, Ma. She was fine until four when she suddenly took some kind of seizure. Then that woman appeared. I didn't dare wait to see if her words were true. I just ran."

"I didn't know what else to do," he finished woodenly, staring at the floor.

Fay frowned. After wiping the cloth across Kassandra's cheeks, she turned and gave her son a stern look. "You did right to think of her safety first, Simon," she said firmly. "Even if none of it were true. However, that being said, if it's not true and something else is afoot, like poison for example, the child must have a physician."

Simon dropped his head into his hands again. "You didn't see her eyes, Ma," he answered softly. "The Flame has passed."

Pursing her lips in disapproval of the Triarctic phrasing, Fay turned back to the child as Luis finished filling the wash tub.

"Help the boy, Simon," she said shortly. "We'll discuss this again once her fever's been brought down."

They'd just finished and were slipping Kassandra into one of Luis' old nightshirts when they heard Hamlin's footsteps in the kitchen. Minutes later he stood in the parlor doorway, Dani at his heels, an expression of questioning concern on his broad face. As he opened his mouth to ask for some explanation, the alarm bells of Branbridge began to ring. As one, the household turned in the direction of the palace.

It took only moments for the news to reach the city. The Aristok had been murdered, and a house-to-house search was beginning for his killers. A junior member of the Town Watch cornered Hamlin outside his workshop where he'd gone to discuss the shocking news with the neighbors. Fay was ordered to the Shield Gate with the rest of her company. Hamlin said he would tell her and returned inside.

Fay and Simon were still in the parlor, sitting like two bodyguards, the child between them. Hamlin fished out his pipe and observed them gravely before speaking.

"I'm afraid that woman was right," he said sadly. "The Aristok's been murdered. I'm so sorry, Son."

The painter nodded, suddenly unable to speak.

"You have to report to the Shield Gate, Mother," the artisan continued. "They're searching the city and everyone's wanted, but perhaps we could tell them you're not well?"

Fay rose with a shake of her head. "I haven't missed a shift in four years, Ham, you know that. I must go, or it will seem odd, particularly today. You'll have to guard the child without me. Her fever's down, so she should be fine." She closed her eyes a moment, her lips moving in silent prayer, but when she opened them again, her expression was businesslike. "Simon, you take her to the upstairs solar and stay there with her. Luis, carry the bowl and a bucket of water up with him." Turning back to her husband, she took his arm and guided him out of their way. "It'll probably be the West Gate Company searching this area, Ham. They're all friends, so don't worry, they won't tear the house apart. If they get as far as the solar door, tell them the key's been lost for years. Remember, they'll be hunting for killers, not for . . . well, for rescuers."

She surveyed her little family and then smiled reassuringly. "Everything will be fine, with Essus' Grace, you'll see," she said. "Now, Luis, you make up a calming tea for everyone, and I want you all to drink it. Dani, you look after Hamlin."

She kissed them all and then knelt before Kassandra again.

"Don't be afraid, my little poppet," she murmured. "My family will take good care of you."

She kissed the sleeping child's brow, then waved her

son forward. "You stay up there with her until I return, Simon."

He nodded.

"Luis, take the candle and light his way."

"Yes, ma'am."

Simon took Kassandra up and followed the server from the room as Hamlin helped Fay into her hauberk.

"Be careful," the artisan said with a worried frown. "There's more than drunken sailors and petty thieves out there tonight. There's killers who wouldn't hesitate to add more blood to today's business."

"I'll be fine." Cupping his cheek affectionately, she then tugged at his beard. "Protect the child, Ham."

"I will. But what about those Temple Seers? Do you think they'll scry out where she is?"

"I don't know. I do know, however, that Essus would never let harm come to a little child with the faithful guarding her door, no matter what her religion. Besides, Simon has told us that the God is involved here, and we must believe him."

The artisan nodded doubtfully, waving at his wife's back as she hurried from the house, the limp from an old wound more pronounced than it had been earlier that day. After a few minutes of aimless pacing, he sat down, pipe in hand, to wait for the West Gate Watch.

Up in the solar, Simon settled on a makeshift pallet, his back against the wall and Kassandra in his arms. Arranging the blankets around her, he laid her head gently against his shoulder while Luis set the candle on an upended trunk.

"I'd better take the light when I leave, Simon. If the Watch sees it through the shutters, they'll know someone's up here."

The painter shrugged. "I don't need it."

Pouring some water in the bowl, Luis set the cloth by Simon's elbow. "Do you want anything else?"

The older man shook his head.

"You don't want some tea?"

"No."

Taking up the candle, Luis hesitated by the door. "Simon?"

The painter looked up, his face in shadow.

"Will Her Majesty be all right?"

Her Majesty.

"I don't know."

"Simon?"

"What, Luis?"

"Will *you* be all right?"

Simon's eyes were pinched, but he gave the boy a twisted half smile.

"Yes."

After another moment's hesitation, the server left and the room dropped into darkness. Simon heard the sound of the key in the latch, the boy's footsteps receding down the stairs, and then silence.

Tears burned at the back of his eyes, though they stubbornly refused to fall. Why couldn't he cry?

Memories, released by the darkness, came unbidden and he squeezed his eyes shut as they played out before him. Memories of a drunken friend holding court in the Broken Sword, his head thrown back and his flame-filled eyes bright with laughter; memories of an Aristok, arrogant and selfish, the centuries of Royal Privilege backing up his demands for more and greater images to bedeck his halls; and memories of a gentle and indulgent father leaning down to listen with all seriousness to the lisping words of a child so like Simon's own in so many ways.

They'd shared so much, and now it was all gone. Why couldn't he cry for them? Why couldn't he cry for Leary?

Laying his cheek against Kassandra's head, he closed his eyes. This is stupid, he told himself with little conviction. He'd harbored no real illusions about his friend. He'd known he was violent and dangerous, given to wild impulses and fits of rage. Many people had believed him to be mad, and Simon supposed they'd been right, although that had never mattered to the Florenzian-raised artist whose only fear was that his visions would not find true form. They'd been closer than lovers, closer than brothers. Leary had given him the means to bring life to his dreams, and Simon had been the only one able to look the Aristok in the eye without fear since his wife's death had taken away his stability.

A sob catching in his throat, Simon held the child close.

"I'll keep her safe, Leary," he whispered. "I swear to you."

As he sat in the darkness, he heard the sounds of soldiers in the street below and then the expected banging on the workshop door.

In the corners, the muted shadows stirred sluggishly, drawn to his grief.

"Two hours!"

The Captain of the Shield Knights, the traditional guard of the Royal Family, paced across the Royal wing's main hall, slamming one mailed fist into the palm of the other. The palace had been sealed off minutes after the deed was discovered, and both the Shield Knights and the Palace Guard had been sent searching for the Aristok's murderers and for the Prince Kassandra.

The *Aristok* Kassandra.

The Captain grimaced, one hand drumming on the pommel of her sword.

"Two bloody, burning hours," she repeated.

Glancing in through the chapel door, she closed her eyes briefly, resisting the urge to cover up the body of her dead Patron. The lump in her throat belied the angry scowl on her face and she turned to pace the length of the hall once more. Marsellus could not be moved until His Grace the Archpriest of the Flame arrived to study the scene with his prophetic sight; until then the indignity of his state must be borne.

Leaning a moment against the doorframe, she took a deep breath, then gently closed the door.

Captain Jordana DeLynne, Earl of Wiltham, had served the Royal Family all her life, and had seen more death in the DeMarian line than anyone alive. She had marched as a Squire in the funeral procession of Atreus the Bastard, had guarded the battlefield corpse of his daughter Kassandra the Fifth, had stood by the bedside of Marsellus the Second as he fought the Shadow Catcher hour after hour; and had carried the rain-soaked body of the young Kathrine the Fifth from the courtyard where she'd plunged to her death on her little brother's tenth birthday. Now that brother lay alone on the cold stones of his private chapel, and his only daughter was missing and either dead or held captive by her father's murderers.

The Captain passed a shaking hand over her eyes. So many deaths in so few years, all fated to be, she'd believed. This time, though, it was different. This time it was murder. The guarding hand of the Shield Knights had failed their royal charge. *She* had failed him. During all those nights of drunken reveling, with the Shield Knights forbidden to follow their Liege, she'd paced the halls of the palace knowing there was nothing she could do to protect him if an assassin had lain waiting in the shadows. The one time she'd disobeyed him and sent her people out to follow him at a discreet distance had almost gotten the entire Order of the Shield exiled. Now the assassin's hand had struck in the palace itself where they, where she, should have been vigilant.

Closing her eyes a moment, she allowed herself to feel the full weight of the responsibility. When the murderers were caught, she would offer her resignation to Kassandra's Regent if she herself was not arrested first. In the meantime she must do her duty as best she could.

As the bells of Branbridge began to ring out the alarm, she ran over the details of the last half hour.

"Send riders out on all roads. Search Collin's Park and the Flame Temple grounds, and seal off the harbor and all the city gates. Begin a house-to-house search."

Her Lieutenants, given their orders, saluted and hurried from the room as the Captain turned her attention to those remaining.

"Has the Archpriest of the Flame been sent for?" Her question was aimed at the Aristok's valet and he quailed under her dark gaze.

"I . . . I don't know, My Lord," he stammered.

"Well, who *has* been sent for?"

"The Duke of Yorbourne's valet has gone to fetch his Master, My Lord," Gabriella interceded smoothly. "He was visiting the Flame Temple this afternoon. The valet *has been told to request the Archpriest's presence as well."*

"Fine. Now, about . . . the Aristok Kassandra. You heard nothing from her room?"

"Nothing, My Lord, and there was no sign of a forced entry or of a struggle."

"And you never thought to check on her sooner?"

The Captain's voice was dark with suspicion. Gabriella chose not to notice. "Her Grace is a light sleeper," she explained. "If she is disturbed before the hour is up, she often wishes to rise immediately, so it is my custom to listen, rather than to see her sleeping."

"And she sleeps alone? She has no . . ." The Captain searched for the right words, acutely conscious of the Companion's eyes on her. ". . . child-friend to keep her company?"

"No, My Lord. Her mother believed in a Continental upbringing, and her father chose to continue that course after her death."

Mention of the Consort Kathrine's untimely death brought the Captain back quickly to the subject.

"Has she run off before?"

"Once or twice, My Lord, yes."

"So it's possible that she might have been lured away from her bed by some promise of adventure made earlier in the day?"

Gabriella tipped her head to one side. "You mean by someone with ransom or blackmail designs on the Throne, My Lord?"

"That's exactly what I mean."

After some consideration, the Companion nodded. "Yes, I suppose that's possible."

"I want a list of everyone she's spoken with today, and anyone she would trust enough to accompany.

"You checked everywhere she might have gone?"

"Yes, My Lord."

"We will check again. See to it." The Captain jerked her head at a squire who darted off, then returned her gaze to the Companion, "I must advise you now, Your Grace," she began formally, "that until the Flame Priests have examined you, you are under suspicion of conspir-

acy to commit regicide and possible kidnapping. You are not to leave this room."

Gabriella inclined her head. *"I am at the service of the Flame whenever they wish to send for me,"* she answered evenly.

"Good. Have you informed your Guild of what's happened?"

"I have."

"They may not speak with you until after I have the report from the Flame Priests."

"As you wish."

Somewhat nonplussed by the Companion's calm demeanor, the Captain turned to the valet and repeated her words. She was rewarded by a near faint from the young man and, feeling somewhat petty, but better nevertheless, she gestured a junior knight forward. *"Turlin, these two are to remain here. I'll stand guard myself over the late Aristok. Send the Archpriest to me when he arrives."*

Now, standing before the chapel door, the Captain of the Shield Knights, protectors of the Royal Family for four hundred years, bowed her head and asked her Lord's spirit for forgiveness as the alarm bells continued to toll.

In the city the search was under way with a growing number of arrests and the rumblings of resentment beginning in the Essusiate quarters. When Gawaina De-Kathrine took personal control of the search, the arrests increased dramatically. However, the killing was begun by another's hand.

In the Weaver's Quarters a Cleric of Essus was murdered in the manse of St. Tomasino's. When the church was searched by a company in ill-fitting Town Watch uniforms, three men who'd believed themselves safe were also set upon. Then the company quietly left the area and returned to Hadrian DeSandra's town house to the west of Branbridge.

Two of the Aristok's murderers were now dead, and one lay as still as his compatriots, the blood from the deep gash in his forehead making a convincingly gory pool beneath him. However, they were not the first.

* * *

That morning, out on the Branbridge tournament fields, a terrible accident had occurred. One of Lysandra DeSandra's guards missed his swing and hit a retainer standing by the lists. As Anne's Branion contact fell, his last sight was of his Lord's face, and he knew his death had been no accident. Lysanda made a note to send a purse to his surviving partner, had the body removed with a show of regret, then ordered the melee to continue.

Nor were they to be the last.

On a ship tied up at the ocean side of Bran's Bridge, a Captain and crew awaited a passenger who was not to reach the Continent alive. They were confident she would be no trouble and eager to share out the reward locked in the Captain's cabin.

And so the conspiracy was secured and the conspirators protected.

At the Temple of the Flame, the news had shocked the gathered priests. Still, many of the elders nodded their heads, the day's events suddenly made clear. At four that afternoon the Duke of Yorbourne, walking with the Archpriest through the Temple galleries, had suddenly collapsed. They'd carried him to Julianus' study and called for the Temple Physicians, fearing he'd been poisoned. Now they knew the truth. The Flame had passed.

When his valet arrived and imparted the terrible news, the Duke had gone pale, but left immediately for the palace, supported by Rosarion DeLynne on one side and the Captain of the Flame Champions on the other. The Archpriest followed more slowly with a detail of Champions and Seers, and within minutes the Palace Guard at each entrance was replaced by a scarlet-clad Champion of the Flame. Their heavy, ax-topped pikes barred the way of any not on Flame Temple business. Rumors from the palace were immediately cut off.

In the Royal chapel, looking down at the bloody corpse of his dead kinsman, Ellisander swayed and covered his face with his hands. When he raised his head, his gaze found the Shield Captain and everyone present could see the heightened flames in his eyes. Standing stiffly at attention, she awaited his orders. He merely turned away, his expression one of grieving disbelief.

"Julianus?" The Royal Duke groped blindly for the older man and the Archpriest took his arm.

"How could this have happened?"

"I don't know, My Lord, but we will discover it. You have my assurance."

"And Kasey . . . missing. We have to find her. She'll be ill with the Passing. We must find her."

"We will, sir. The Champions are combing the palace and the city. I have Rosarion here and Bronwynne De-Llewellynne, the Order's most powerful Seers. I swear to you . . ." The old man's voice caught in his throat. "I swear to you, My Lord, the ones who did this will be caught and punished."

Drawing in a shuddering breath, Ellisander nodded. "I know they will, Julianus." His eyes caught Rosarion's gaze and held it. "I have *every* faith in you." Sinking down on the velvet bench inside the chapel door, he passed one shaking hand across his eyes. "What shall we do without him," he whispered. "How can we go on?"

"We must do our duty, sir," the old man answered.

The Duke shook his head. "I can't. Julianus, I can't. Not again. First Kathrine and now . . . now Mars. I can't bear it."

"You must." The Archpriest's voice was strong, and almost unwillingly, the Duke raised his head to meet his stern gaze.

"The Realm needs your strength, Ellisander," Julianus continued. "It needs your protection and your guidance more than it's ever needed it in the past. You must stand and be a buttress against the chaos this news will incite. You must."

His words had a visible effect on the shaken Duke and he straightened, his expression embarrassed. "I will. I'm sorry.

"Captain?" He turned. "The Shield is dismissed. You may retire to your chapterhouse. Captain Devrana of the Flame Champions will inform the Palace Guard of who may remain on duty."

"Sir!" The Shield Knight Captain turned to go, then paused at a weary gesture from the Royal Duke.

"I know you're feeling responsible for this tragedy, My Lord Earl," Ellisander said slowly. "But I'm assigning no blame as of yet. I'll take a complement of Flame Champions as guard for now, because tradition demands it, and your people must be questioned. That notwithstanding, as soon as possible, they'll be returned to their rightful place. I hold only respect and honor for the Shield Knights and their order."

"We are at your command, sir," she answered thickly. At the Duke's nod, she saluted and withdrew.

Ellisander returned his attention to the Archpriest. "I shall attend to my duty, Julianus, but I need to be somewhere quiet for a time. I'll be in my study, if there's any news."

"Of course, My Lord."

Rosarion stepped forward. "Uh, sir, a moment before you go."

"Yes?"

The herbalist's expression was uncertain, but he faced the Royal Duke regardless. "The Flame has passed, My Lord. How far we don't know yet . . ." He paused at the sudden pain in the Duke's face and coughed uncomfortably. Pulling a handkerchief from his sleeve, he pressed it to his lips, then continued. "What I mean to say, sir, is that you'll need something to ease Its passing. I'll send my apprentice to you with an infusion."

"No, I'm fine."

"But, My Lord . . ."

"I said no. It's unnecessary." The Duke's voice brooked no argument and Rosarian turned to the Archpriest.

With a sigh, Julianus laid a restraining hand on Ellisander's shoulder. "We can't risk it, My Lord," he said sadly. "We must face the possibility that you may be the new Vessel of the Living Flame. Its passing is perilous and we must protect your body as well as your mind. I know this pains you, yet, Sandi, we must do our duty."

Ellisander slumped. "Always duty," he whispered.

Julianus' thin hand gripped the younger man's shoulder with surprising strength. "Yes, always duty. Those that can carry its burden must do so for the sake of the Realm." He motioned the Champions forward. "Escort His Lordship the Duke to his study and remain there with him.

"I shall send Rosarion's boy to you with the infusion, My Lord."

With a weak nod, Ellisander rose, and without looking back, left the chapel, the Flame Champions grouped protectively about him. He seemed to those left behind, to be suddenly older than his twenty-nine years.

The Archpriest watched him go, then turned, his expression stern once again. "Now, my priests, to this bloody business. Bronwynne, I want a scribe for each of us and two assistants in case the visions become violent, which they very likely will. Rosarion, you will make up enough of the Potion of Truth for two hours' vision for three priests, and one extra should one of us fall before the vision is complete."

The herbalist nodded. Wiping the handkerchief across his brow, he returned it to his sleeve.

The old man frowned. "Are you strong enough to withstand the Prophecy today? It will be hazardous. Perhaps Seth or Innes should take your place."

Rosarion shook his head. "I'm no worse than always, Your Grace," he answered dismissively. "And the Prophetic Realm will be in chaos with what's happened. You'll need my Sight today."

"Too true." The Archpriest bowed his head; when he raised it, they could see his eyes were bright with tears. "How many more will fall before this business is through?" he murmured.

"The criminals, Your Grace."

The old man looked into Bronwynne's inflexible countenance and nodded. "See to your duties, then, my priests."

They bowed and left quickly, while the Archpriest of the Flame entered the chapel and began the preparations for the visions that would pierce the future and give up the names of those who had slain a God.

Meanwhile, in a warehouse on the Essusiate wharf of St. Fatima, an assassin paused to wipe a sleeve across her brow. She'd arrived just over an hour ago with the story of a job fallen through and had been hard at work helping her merchant friend prepare for yet another sea voyage, one the woman had promised Anne a berth on, and never mind the cost if she would help load the cargo.

It was hot work.

"Still happy to see me?" the older woman asked with a laugh as she tossed her a wineskin.

Catching it, Anne poured a stream into her mouth before answering. "Happy enough to see *you,* Beryl, but next time I help you load stock, you can heft the rotting bundles onto the carts and *I'll* tally them.

"Well, there's only a dozen more to go, and then we'll break for supper."

Anne's rather obscene reply was cut short by the appearance of a Sword Gate Sergeant and four guards. The two women turned as the leader approached them while the others fanned out across the warehouse.

"How long have you been here," the Sergeant asked without preamble, eyeing the Essusiate cut of the two women's aprons with suspicion.

"All afternoon," Beryl answered evenly. "We're loading up for a shipment to Bryholm."

"The name of the ship?"

"The *Kilnmach.* It's the three master down at the dock." She pointed past him, and the Sergeant turned to squint into the setting sun.

"Bachiem?"

Beryl raised one eyebrow. "You have a good ear, Sergeant. Yes. We have a residence in Branbridge, my husband and I, and one in Bachiem. Hello, Julian."

She smiled at the Corporal, and he raised his hand hesitantly in reply.

The Sergeant coughed, and she returned her attention to him.

"Have you seen anyone suspicious around lately, any strangers?"

Beryl shook her head and behind her Anne mirrored the movement.

The Sergeant opened his mouth to ask another question, and Beryl cut him off. "Is there any news from the palace?" she asked. "The little Prince, have they found her yet?"

He shook his head in disgust at how fast gossip traveled and turned without answering as his people finished their search.

"Everything's in order, sir," the Corporal reported, and the Sergeant scowled in discontent. His eyes tracked across the warehouse suspiciously, but finally he grunted.

"Well, if you see anyone, notify the Town Watch immediately," he told the two women curtly.

"We will, Sergeant." Nodding, Beryl turned. "Oh, Randi, you can pick up that bolt of wool for your mother any time."

The youngest guard nodded with an embarrassed smile and when the others trooped from the warehouse, he lingered behind. "Be careful, Beryl," he said in a low, anxious voice. "They say the killers are Essusiates, maybe even Bachiems, a response for the Aristok's latest restrictions. It could be dangerous for you and yours."

"We'll take care. Thank you, you're a sweet boy."

He turned to go, then paused at the warehouse door. "When do you leave for Bryholm?"

"We were planning on tomorrow morning at high tide, but now with the harbor closed, I couldn't say," she answered in a resigned voice. Hearing the false ring in her friend's tone, Anne watched the other woman curiously.

Oblivious, Randi nodded. "I could talk to Uncle Deverne, see if he can get you on tomorrow's roster for cleared ships. I'd hate to see anything happen to you, and things are liable to get ugly before they get better."

"Oh, that would be so kind of you, Randi. Are you sure it won't get you into trouble?"

He straightened visibly, pushing his hair from his eyes. "Oh, no. Uncle Deverne knows I like . . . I mean . . .

um, it'll be all right. I'll bring word tonight when I come for Mum's cloth.

"Will, um, Karla be home?"

Beryl smiled. "I think she just might be. We're having supper in about an hour. Why don't you join us?"

"Could I? I mean . . . thank you, I will. I should be off by then, we've just two more streets to search."

"Have they found anything yet?"

"A few possible suspects." He dropped his gaze. "All Essusiate, I'm afraid. The Hierarchpriest has sent the Sword Knights into Church Row."

"Oh, dear."

He nodded. "Well, um, I'll see you tonight." He smiled sympathetically, then, suddenly remembering his mission, darted off to rejoin the rest of his company.

Beryl chuckled. "He's sweet on my youngest," she explained in response to Anne's questioning look.

"I see."

"Yes. He's a good boy. Pity he's a Triarch. Ordinarily that wouldn't be a problem, but with all this tension . . ." She clucked her tongue. "I hope Karla's not too serious about him." Turning back to her roster, she then set it down with a shake of her head. "A bad thing this murder; bad for relations and bad for business. I hope Randi can get us cleared. I'd like to get the children away from Branion until things settle down."

"I'm sure he can."

"Hm." Beryl stared into the distance and then shook herself. "Well, the stock won't load itself. A dozen more and then we'll go in to supper. Will mutton stew and fresh bread be payment enough for a couple hours of shoving?"

"More than enough." Anne turned back to the bundles of wool as Beryl picked up her roster again. The assassin set a load onto the cart by her side, her eyes traveling casually past the door to the ship berthed at the dock. The Guard Sergeant was gesturing at Klaus, Beryl's husband, while the others went aboard to search the ship's holds.

Her hands busy with the next bundle, Anne's mind slowly went over the night's itinerary. Initially she'd sought out Beryl for a loose alibi and a safe place to spend the night. Now, with the woman's offer of passage back to the Continent and even Anne's alibi provided with her words to the Guard Sergeant, it looked like she might be on her way home. She'd originally planned on approaching the Cousins for aid in escaping the city and in obtaining the rest of her promised payment. Now another idea began to emerge, one that would not place her Branion associates in added danger. She would sup with Beryl and her family and linger until she heard if the *Kilnmach* was cleared to leave the next day. Then she would pay a late night call on the *Ptarmigan*, not four wharfs to the west, and be back in time for breakfast. If all went well, she would be out on the open sea by noon.

Expecting no difficulty in carrying out her new itinerary, her thoughts turned to the Sergeant's response as she hefted the next bundle. No sign of the child. That was good. The painter must have had more sense than she'd believed of him. With luck, they'd all be safe from Ellisander DeMarian's ambitious clutches by the next nightfall. Satisfied, she put all thought of the day's Visit from her mind.

At the Palace, three Priests of the Flame made ready to enter the Prophetic Realm. Two prepared to stretch their abilities to the limit to discover the identities of those who had murdered the Vessel of the Living Flame, the other had a more complicated agenda.

In the chapel hearth, the Potion of Truth bubbled in an iron pot, and Rosarion DeLynne gestured at his apprentice to take over as it finished boiling. Removing the pot from its hook, Willan poured the contents into three deep bowls while the herbalist added the final two ingredients. When it was done, he accepted a small cup from a side pot and downed the contents with a grimace. Made mostly from red-and-white clover, the infusion should suppress the constant coughing that kept his lungs clear until after the vision was complete. Then he would need a fairly potent expectorant, but he would worry about that later. Behind him, Willan clipped a leather brace about the herbalist's chest, there to protect his ribs from the damage the coughing and seizures had caused. After shifting it so it sat more comfortably, Rosarion accepted the apprentice's arm as he eased himself to the floor before the royal corpse, his back pressed against his assistant.

Beside him, Julianus and Bronwynne also made ready, the Archpriest giving last minute instructions to the scribes who would record the words each priest was able to dredge up from their individual visions.

To calm the sudden nervous fluttering in his stomach, Rosarion went over the talents and weaknesses of the others as they joined him on the floor. Bronwynne DeLlewelynne was the pragmatist, pushing past symbolism and metaphor to the faces and deeds of those she sought in vision. It was primarily her Sight which the conspirators had labored so long to confuse, for they knew she was capable of discovering the identities of every conspirator who'd raised a hand against the Living Flame that day. She was relentless in her pursuit of clarity, yet this very intensity could also work against her. The conspirators hoped that by setting the Essusiate connection out in plain sight, she would miss the hand of kin working in the shadows. Knowing her politics as he did, Rosarion had assured Ellisander of just that result.

Beside him, an acolyte placed a pillow behind the Archpriest as he settled himself against her. Both Rosarion and Julianus would need the added support of an assistant, the herbalist because of his condition, and the Archpriest because of his age. It was for just this reason that Rosarion believed that Julianus represented no great threat. He was old, his vision failing, and his Sight obscured by the terrible deed which had severed the Living Flame's link to Its priests, and by the chaos the Prophetic Realm would predict.

The Triarchy had been dealt a serious blow, and Its Ecclesiastical leader's vision would rock with the effects as Essus and those in competition with the Living Flame flocked to take advantage of Its weakened state. The Archpriest would see only the greater repercussions. The lesser would be lost in the flood.

This left Rosarion DeLynne. Although weakened by the ravages of the white lung and the medicines he took

to keep his failing body alive, he was still a powerful
Seer, strong in both symbolism and clarity and trusted
as completely as any who wore the red robe of the
Flame. The others were relying on him to discover the
motives behind the deeds and the identities of anyone
hidden in the shadows.

And he could have done it. He could have named
every conspirator from the Royal Duke of Yorbourne
down to Hadrian DeSandra's most lowly retainer had
his own name not been counted among the first of their
number. Instead he must protect them, obscure their
identities and mislead his fellow priests, twisting the
meaning of his own vision and theirs until they followed
the path Ellisander DeMarian had laid out. Rosarion
DeLynne could do that, too.

The only risk was that he might speak some suspicious
detail in vision, but his higher tolerance of the Potion
of Truth would keep his self-control strong and only reveal
what he wanted them to hear. This was what he'd told
Ellisander, and this was what he believed with absolute
conviction as he accepted the first bowl from his
apprentice.

Breathing deeply of the Potion's bitter scent, he tipped
the bowl forward. The familiar acrid taste made his
tongue and mouth go dry and he mentally ran over the
ingredients and their proportions as he drank: ratroot,
three handfuls, to delve into the Prophetic Realm,
nightbloom and holly berries, one cup each, to make the
visions clear, wild lettuce, one bunch, to bring the symbols into focus, and wormroot, one handful, to help subdue the seizures that often accompanied large infusions
of the Potion of Truth; all boiled in two quarts of sap
from a young birch, the traditional Tree of Prophecy.

The proportions were important, for most of the ingredients were poisonous, but he knew them as well as he
knew his own name, and he finished the bowl with confidence. Moments later, the others did the same.

Beginning the rapid breathing that would attune his
Sight, the Temple Herbalist emptied his mind as the Potion took effect. His head grew heavy. Pressing his back
against the strong support of his assistant, he took one
deep breath to steady his Sight as his mind began its

decent through the layers of the Physical Realms. Beside him he felt without having to see, Julianus and Bron-wynne do the same.

The world about him was gray and misty now, features indistinct. Warmed by the closed confines of the chapel, he let his mind float downward for a time, then, as the vision took hold, he felt his inner Sight open. The amphis-bane, the symbol he had taken for his own, rose up and slipped about him like a second skin. Looking out at the Prophetic Realm through its tawny-colored eyes, he reached out his hand in the physical world and touched his dead Sovereign.

The reaction was immediate, a force like a blow that snapped his head back and drew an explosive cough from his injured lungs. Flames rose up to obscure his vision, and for one terrifying heartbeat he feared the Living Flame was coming to devour him. Then the vision steadied as the familiar sight of the fiery tree rose up.

His throat worked with the effort to speak. Finally training took hold and he spat out the description of his earlier vision, one clear part of his mind noting silently that the wyvern had now merged with that of the dragon of Essus. Faintly, he could hear a voice whisper, "Clarity, clarity," and knew it was Bronwynne, the word, her personal mantra, spoken to bring her vision into sharper focus. He used his own word, "Down, down," to sink deeper into the Prophetic Realm as his earlier vision unfolded before him. The fiery tree exploded, the flames about it became a sea of crimson waves, and the Shadow Catcher loomed above him once again, Its net cast forward. Bodies began to rise, drawn up from the depths of death, their features much clearer now. They carried the scars of recent battle and their colors were the colors of Branion.

He passed this information along, knowing that it symbolized civil war so the Archpriest would surely see it, too.

The vision continued with scenes of battle. Faces swam before his eyes, some he knew, some he would know. The Royal standard with its red-and-golden fire-wolf above the three oak leaf clusters was raised high and then torn suddenly down the middle. Rosarion jerked forward. A sudden coughing fit took him, obscuring his Sight. He felt his assistant hold him steady and wipe the spittle from his face, and he pushed him away impatiently as the vision began to buck his control. He stood in the past and watched the dragon of Essus screech as four figures drove their knives into the body of the Living Flame. The statue of an Essusiate Saint covered their escape and began to bleed, and the blood became flame. He found himself in the sea once more as a boat carried a woman whose face was obscured by a bright white light away from the Island Realm. Then the waves rose up to cover his mouth and nose, and he began to choke.

His body jerking with his efforts to breathe, he began to thrash, and once again, his assistant's arms cut through his prophecy. His breath came in one explosive gasp and the world before him spun in a kaleidoscope of colors. The amphisbane turned in on itself, and he looked suddenly into the eyes of its other self. A sense of familiarity took hold of him as if he should know the intelligence that looked out from its scaly visage, and then the vision changed again. The fiery tree exploded in flame once more and one shoot began to grow. The dragon of Essus, perched upon its truck, screamed, and one clawed foot came down to smash it. It went up in a cloud of cinders, then from the base of the tree another flame began to grow. It weaved about the old tree's trunk, and the dragon of Essus turned. With its front claws clasped around the shoot, it wrapped itself about the tiny flame as the cinders fed its strength. As the dragon melted away before the fully reborn Living Flame, Rosarion glimpsed his own death waiting in the wings and his vision shattered. He felt his self-control leave him and just before the seizure took control of his mind and body a face leaped into his vision. The surprise of it was so shocking that he spat out the word before he could stop himself.

"Kassandra!"

5. Essus

"Where is she?"

In the Duke's study Ellisander caught Rosarion by the collar and hauled him half out of his chair. "You tell me where she is!"

"I . . ." A spasm of coughing, caused by the sudden movement, cut off the herbalist's words. Finally, he managed to loosen the fabric of his collar enough to gasp out a few words. "I don't know."

"You don't know!"

"I wasn't . . ." He began to cough again, spittle flecked with blood spraying from between his teeth. "I wasn't searching for the Heir," he gasped out. "I only saw her face at the end of the vision."

With an exclamation of disgust, the Duke shoved him back into the chair. "The *Heir* is now the *Aristok* and the *Aristok* is now missing," he snarled. "I told you how important she was. For Terrilynne to remain in Heathland, the child must take the Throne."

Choking, Rosarion fumbled for his handkerchief, and pressed it against his mouth. "I'm sorry," he said, his voice muffled by the linen, "but I didn't take her. Did you ask the DeSandras? Maybe something screwed up at their end . . ." He broke off as the Duke's expression grew dark.

"They haven't reported in yet." Turning his back on Rosarion, Ellisander stared out the window. A light rain was falling, and mist had begun to cover the ground of the enclosed courtyard beyond. He returned his attention to the younger man, his emotions under control once again. "You're the Seer," he said. "You saw her face. You tell me what happened to her."

"There were no details around it."

"But you did See it. So tell me, Seer, what did you See?"

The Duke's tone had calmed, but the words, words of ritual used to invoke a Seer's interpretation as well as his vision, made Rosarion shudder. "I told you . . ." he began, then sighed and closed his eyes. Calling up the final image, he frowned as he tried to bring the hazy memory into clearer focus. "I See her face," he said. "There's nothing around it, only a . . . a white mist." He opened his eyes. "It was only for a moment. It probably means nothing."

"You cried out her name. It means something."

"I was surprised. It was unexpected."

"So was her disappearance."

"Maybe Julianus and Bronwynne saw something more."

"The great prophet," Ellisander sneered. "Julianus is old, Bronwynne is blinkered. Neither can hold a prophetic candle to the great Rosarion DeLynne . . . until now."

He bent down, his face inches from the other man's. "I need to know why she wasn't in her room when she was supposed to be, Rosarion. I need to know where she is now and who has her, and I need to know before anyone else does and you're going to find out and tell me. Do you understand?"

The herbalist held his eyes for only a second before the Duke's heated expression made him avert his own gaze. He nodded. "The others and I still have to meet to compare interpretations first, though," he said. "The Archpriest is letting me rest here for a while, but he'll want to begin the investigation of the Aristok's death as soon as possible. Seth Cannon and Innes Eathan are already preparing to go into Vision to look for Kassandra."

Ellisander's eyes narrowed, and Rosarion quickly raised his hands. "I can't brew up another batch of the Potion so soon without exciting suspicion. I have to be alone, and it takes time, so does the Seeing, and Julianus is going to want me back on the investigation of the Aristok's murder as soon as I'm able."

"Then send a message telling him you're ill and to

begin without you. He has the written report. That will have to suffice for now."

"I can't just . . ."

"I'll corroborate your story. Return to the herbarium, prepare another dose, and wait for my arrival."

"But . . ."

"This discussion is at an end."

The Duke's flame-washed green eyes were dark, and Rosarion looked away. "All right." He touched the handkerchief to his lips and glanced down at the blood staining the linen. "I'll go as soon as I can stand."

"Good. Now in the meantime, what of these first visions?" Ellisander picked up the rough reports the Archpriest had given him. "You said you saw the country torn apart by civil war. Julianus concurs, but that was not in your original prophecy."

Relieved to be discussing something concrete, Rosarion pushed himself up. "It was, but not in detail. It's only just now becoming clear that the Shadow Catcher brings up a net of *Branion* dead. It could only mean civil war." He grew thoughtful. "Precipitated by the Aristok's death, and . . . taking advantage of the ensuing political instability . . . a number of small forces rise up and grab what power they can. No, wait, the image was torn in half. That suggests two equal or nearly equal adversaries. So, someone with enough power to move quickly makes a play for the Throne; someone who isn't involved yet."

"Someone who might have already moved with the abduction of Kassandra?"

Rosarion shook his head. "I don't think so. It corresponds too neatly with the Aristok's death. That would suggest prior knowledge, possibly the defection of a compatriot and that would've shown up in the earlier visions. At least in mine. It's too important an event."

"So you're suggesting that Kassandra's disappearance is not too important an event?"

Rosarion gave a cautious nod. "Essentially."

"And yet you believe this torn vision and catch of corpses to be a play for the Throne?"

"It's the most fitting interpretation at this time."

"Even though you don't know who this person might be?"

"No. Not yet."

"You didn't *See* Terrilynne DeMarian?"

"No."

"But she is the most logical choice?"

"Yes."

Ellisander dropped the reports back onto the desk. "If it's not her, there are few others with power enough to challenge me. They can be identified and dealt with. If it is her . . ." The Duke returned his attention to the courtyard. "We must follow the most likely assumption; that it is her," he said almost to himself. "I will send to Yorbourne to begin preparing for a military strike from the north." His flame-pooled eyes returned to Rosarion. "Any other sudden bursts of clarity that I should know about?" he asked with deep sarcasm.

"No."

"You're sure? I don't think I shall permit any more surprises from you today."

"I'm sure."

"Does Julianus agree with this interpretation?"

"I think so, but I've only had a cursory glance at the other reports. I'll know more when we meet again."

"Which will be after you speak prophecy for me."

"Yes."

"And that will be . . . when?"

"Uh, now." Rosarion tucked the handkerchief away. "I'm better now."

"Good. I'll follow presently. And, Rosarion?"

"Yes."

"Search at least as well as I shall. Remember that."

The herbalist nodded, and Ellisander waved his dismissal.

With a faint groan, Rosarion rose. His last glance saw the Royal Duke staring out the window again. Watching the growing blanket of fog that was rising to obscure the courtyard.

Sending the page on duty outside the Royal wing to Julianus with the Duke's message, Rosarion then summoned Willan to help him home. The boy was surprised at the decision, but said nothing as he accepted the herbalist's weight on his shoulder. After all, everyone knew

Rosarion DeLynne was dying. He'd nearly killed himself prophesying for the Archpriest this evening. It was only right that he should rest for a while.

Leaning on the boy more than he was willing to admit, Rosarion tried to push his legs into a steady pace, but his knees kept shaking, and he had to stop every twenty paces or so to rest. When they finally exited the palace and set off through Collin's Park, bloody saliva began to fill his mouth, and he paused to spit it out onto the ground.

You aren't up to this, he warned himself as he pressed his handkerchief against his lips. *You're shaking, you're feverish, your lungs are full of blood and mucus. You need to rest.*

Shivering as the evening air cooled the sweat on his face, he scoffed at the idea. *Rest? You gave up the right to rest when you made your first interpretation for El-lisander DeMarian,* he chided. *You can rest when all this is over.* Stuffing the bloodied cloth back into his sleeve, he gestured for Willan to keep walking.

Cutting through the wooded copse that marked the far western edge of the palace grounds, they reached the temple wall a few minutes later. Rosarion leaned against the rough stone while Willan opened the gate, then accepted his shoulder once again. The herbarium was only a few steps away. He thought he could make it that far.

Once there, he could barely stand and collapsed into a chair while Willan bustled about wrapping blankets around him and building up the fire, then set a pot of water on to boil and pulled out a plate and bowl.

"There's bread and cheese ready now," the boy said, "And I could make some broth if you wanted it."

"Bread and cheese will do."

"I'll brew up your expectorant."

"Thank you."

Setting the food by Rosarion's elbow, Willan prepared the dry ingredients and opened a small jar.

"We're almost out of honey," he said, a tinge of accusation in his tone and Rosarion gave a guilty shrug.

"I suppose I've been using too much lately," he said, "but everything tastes like goat's piss these days."

Reminded of his Master's condition, Willan ducked

his head and cast about for some other subject. "I remember the first day I came here," he said a little self-consciously. "You were making up something for Brother Devarian's toothache and you said, 'I've put some burrberry leaves in it to make it sweet,' as if that would actually help the taste."

"Burrberry leaves *are* sweet."

"Not very."

"Well, not compared to honey, but compared to calenwort they're as sweet *as* honey. And besides . . ."

Rosarion paused as the temple bells began to toll. "Well, anyway, there's the call for evening prayers. You'd better go or you'll be late."

"I should stay. You might need me."

"I'm fine." Raising his hand, he cut off the boy's protest. "There'll be too many of us missing prayers tonight as it is, Willan."

"But . . ."

"No buts." Turning, he caught the boy's hand. "Willan, listen to me," he said seriously. "The Flame has no Consecrated Vessel tonight. Do you know what that means? It will be weakened, vulnerable, and Essus has already appeared in the visions. We need as many priests as possible at the rituals to maintain Its strength and ours. Remember, we serve the Living Flame. It needs you far more then I do tonight."

Reminded of his duty, the boy reddened, but obeyed only after tucking the blankets more tightly about Rosarion's shoulders.

"You're sure you can manage the pot?"

"I'm sure."

"And you won't exert yourself?"

"No." Rosarion's answer was made through gritted teeth and Willan made a conciliatory gesture.

"All right, I'm going. I'll be back right after prayers."

"You'll be back after the Lightning."

"But . . ."

"Just do as I say, Willan."

Rosarion's voice was weary, and the boy closed his mouth on another protest. With one last worried glance, he left the herbarium.

After he'd gone, Rosarion rubbed his temples, a look

of disgust growing on his face. "We serve the Living Flame. You burning hypocrite," he whispered.

Rising with a groan, he placed the herbs Willan had gathered into the pot, then began assembling those necessary for the Potion of Truth.

I do serve the Flame, he argued with himself, as he measured out the nightbloom. *The Flame is not the Vessel.*

His ecclesiastical training remained unconvinced. *The Flame and the Vessel are one,* it countered.

And the Sight is the Gift of the Flame and the vision is Its illumination of the future, he shot back, reaching for the ratroot.

Yet the future is now uncertain. And that means . . .

A wave of dizziness made him lean heavily against the table until it passed.

And that means?

And that means your interpretation may be wrong.

He began to cough again as the words took form. If his interpretation was wrong, then . . . No. The interpretation was not wrong, and if it was, it was far too late to turn back now. The final image came into his mind then, and for the first time since he'd drunk the Potion of Truth as a raw acolyte, he was afraid of what he would See.

He shook himself. "Don't be stupid," he muttered. "The vision is the message. It does not involve the messenger."

Taking an earthenware jar from the shelf above him, he poured a small amount of dried holly berries into his palm, staring at the dark red fruit as if they alone could reveal the future to him.

If the vision were truly the illumination of the Living Flame as he'd been taught, his reflections continued, then something had gone badly awry because Kassandra DeMarian's face had been shrouded in the white light of Essus, and he had no idea what that meant.

Grunting with the effort, he filled an iron pot with water and set it on its hook to boil. He would find out soon enough, he told himself. Searching for the child would be relatively easy now with the deed done and most of the unprotected conspirators revealed, and once her whereabouts were discovered, the Duke could move forward with his scheming and he, Rosarion, could rest for a while.

Everything now ready, he poured the expectorant into a cup and sat down shakily to wait for Ellisander DeMarian.

Half a mile away in a tiny upstairs solar, Simon of Florenz slept sporadically, the thirty-fifth Vessel of the Living Flame held tightly in his arms.

Around them, the shadows grew darker and more substantial. They flitted over the sleeping forms of the man and the child, wrapping them in a protective pall of mist. As the night deepened, the latter dreamed of her father while the former dreamed of Essus.

In his dream Simon was running through the streets of Branbridge, Kassandra clutched tightly to his chest. A fog had risen, obscuring the street, but a huge, white dragon flew above them, illuminating the path he was to take with a light that emanated from its outstretched wings. Its voice, sibilant and insistent, drove him through the streets and down toward the river, and he knew if he could only make the Mist, they'd be safe. With the urgent voice of Essus and the overloud beating of his heart pushing him forward almost in a panic, it was with weak-kneed relief that he finally saw the river appear between the buildings before him. An army of shadowy figures, flames about their heads like crowns, stood upon the opposite bank, beckoning to him, one so familiar that he almost spoke the name aloud before the fog obscured his sight again. With one burst of speed he staggered out onto the riverbank.

In the herbarium, the potion was ready and the priest prepared. By the time Ellisander arrived, Rosarion had managed to clear some of the accumulated phlegm and blood from his lungs, but his legs still felt uncertain, and his throat throbbed painfully. Sitting on the floor with his back pressed against the DeMarian for support, he raised the bowl to his lips and, with only a moment's hesitation to check the steadiness of his hands, he drained it.

The residue of the first potion still in his system mingled quickly with the new dose, and he gasped as the vision took control almost immediately and jerked him back into the Prophetic Realm. This time there was no flaming tree, no sea of flame nor Shadow Catcher looming above him, only the white light of Essus. He passed this information along, acutely aware of the Duke's arms about his chest, despite the strength of the vision. His proximity to the Living Flame pulled him ever deeper and he reached out, his Sight fully open.

"I see the child," he whispered, "Kassandra, surrounded by the light. I see . . . I see . . . the light is blocking my . . . I can't . . ." He waved a hand in front of his face as if to push the light away. "Down, down, go down," he murmured. "I see a face . . ."

The voice of Essus was all around him now, merging with the beating of the dragon's wings. It pushed him onward, warning of a danger just behind. Simon risked one backward glance, saw a red-robed figure stretch out clawlike hands to catch him, and fell.

Rosarion jerked forward, his eyes wide, his fingers clutching at Ellisander's arm. "I see a face!"

"Whose face?" Ellisander hissed in his ear, and the herbalist shook his head as the words drew him from the vision. He waved at the Duke to be silent, then delved back down in search of the features he'd almost identified.

A shadow passed before his Sight.

"I can't . . . I . . . I . . ." He sighed as the image melted away, leaving only a ghostly imprint on the background of white light. Deepening his breathing, he forced himself to relax and reached out again. "I see the Flame," he said. "I see it rise from the light of Essus. The light . . . the light dims, and . . . I see a man! He holds the child!" He flung one arm forward, trying to seize the figure he could barely make out.

"Who is he?"

"Not now! I see him, I see . . . down, go down. He's bearded; an Essusiate. Colors swirl about him like tree

branches in a high wind. They obscure his face, but . . ."
the herbalist grimaced with the effort to bring the vision
into sharper focus. "I see . . . He's the hand of Essus."

"His name!"

"I can't . . . I see . . . the man is covered in a cloak
of merging colors. I see the amphisbane. I see the Flame
surrounded by the light of Essus. Down, go down. I see
a woman wearing many faces, and another with many
faces lined up behind her. The latter is . . . auburn-
haired with flaming eyes. A DeMarian. I see painted
figures of battle flags and horses, of people and . . .
it's . . . it's . . . I see him. I see his mind, his, his . . .
thoughts."

The Duke relaxed his grip slightly as Rosarion twisted
in his arms. The herbalist reached out his hand as if to
touch someone, and his fingers brushed against the
Duke's face. "I see . . . Saralynne?" he said, his voice
confused.

Ellisander's expression softened into one of sadness,
and he allowed the other's fingers to remain against his
cheek for just a moment before gently moving his
head away.

"I see the man again," Rosarion continued almost in
a sigh. "He's sleeping and dreaming, dreaming of Essus.
He's not far . . . to the east, I think . . . I see . . .
Saralynne? Why are you here?"

The red-robed figure reached out. Simon saw his face,
felt his fingers brush against his cheek and saw a woman
he didn't know appear beside them in a swirl of shadows. She passed a cloak of deep purple and red before
the figure's eyes. He heard someone call to him, saw the
shadows suddenly rose up in the shape of a snarling
fire-wolf.

The dream shattered.

Rosarion cried out as the sudden loss of contact
knocked the vision from his control. It sent him spinning
down into a vortex of colors; purple-and-red light swirling about a core of fire. The only image he could maintain was that of his sister's face, and he held onto it as
the seizures began.

*   *   *

"Son!"

Simon awoke. Shrinking back, he stared wildly about him and then relaxed as he realized the figure in the doorway was not the red-robed menace of his dream.

Seeing he was awake, Hamlin entered the room and crouched down beside the pallet.

"Son," he said again. "Are you all right? You were calling out in your sleep."

Rubbing at his face with one hand, Simon squinted up at him.

"What time is it?"

"Just after ten."

Glancing down at Kassandra, the artist was relieved to see her sleeping peacefully, her face smooth of pain. "I had a nightmare," he explained.

"About the child?"

"Yes."

"And Essus?"

"Yes."

"So did I."

They stared at each other and Simon shook his head slowly. "There was a shadowy figure. I thought I knew it; and I heard a voice."

"Telling you to run?"

"To the Mist."

Hamlin nodded.

"And there was someone wearing red robes . . . trying to catch me. I almost didn't make it past."

"The Flame Priests wear red robes."

"I know."

Hamlin set the candle down carefully. "I don't like this. Any of it. Essus, the Living Flame. I wish your mother were here."

"They're still searching?"

"They must be. She's not home yet, but a fog's risen. I can't imagine they can see very much."

"A fog?"

Simon eased Kassandra gently onto the pallet, wrapped the blankets around her once again, then rose. Opening the shutters a crack, he peered out.

Nothing was visible. The streetlamp below was a faint glow in the distance and the moon managed only to illuminate the rolling bands of fog.

"A white fog," Simon whispered. "A white light." He turned to stare at Hamlin. "I think we have to leave, Pa. I think we have to follow the dream." The image of the army of flame-crowned figures came to him then, and he nodded slowly. "And I think I know where we have to go."

In the corner, unobserved, the shadows sighed.

Dani and Luis were confused, but obedient when Hamlin roused them. He sent the server into the pantry to fill a pack with food, then turned to his apprentice.

"I want you to tell Fay what's happened. Explain about the dreams and tell her where we've gone."

"But where *are* you going?"

"Dunleyshire." Simon spoke the word from the parlor where he'd taken Kassandra. The child murmured peevishly, but did not awaken, and Simon brushed a strand of hair from her face.

"You three are to follow us as soon as Fay comes home." Hamlin added.

Dani's eyes widened. "Dunleyshire's in Heathland."

"I know." Simon came into the kitchen. "But that's also where Jade is."

And where Jade was, so was Terrilynne DeMarian, and Terrilynne DeMarian had an army, an army big enough to place Kassandra on the throne and deal with the Duke of Yorbourne; if she would do it.

This was what he'd explained to Hamlin as they'd hurried from the solar. Hamlin had agreed, and together they'd cobbled together a basic plan to get them there, if the prophetic hand of the Flame Priests didn't catch them first, but Simon had an idea about that, too.

In the Flame Temple Herbarium, the one priest who could have caught them then was writhing in the throes of a violent seizure. His head had hit the wall when the convulsions had first struck, and blood matted his hair, and trickled down his collar. The Duke of Yorbourne had managed to hook a blanket off the bed and had used this to secure Rosarion's arms close to his body, but his legs continued to drum against the floor. There was nothing Ellisander could do about that, so he simply held him tightly, bracing his own legs against the bed, while the younger man fought his control. All the while, Rossarion's words ran through his mind.

He had no idea what most of his babbling meant, although he was certain of one thing. The auburn-haired, flaming-eyed woman with the faces at her back could only be Terrilynne DeMarian.

His face twisted in annoyance. He'd believed Heathland far enough north to keep her from interfering with his plans, but obviously not. Still, he considered, she was in Heathland and whoever it was who'd taken Kassandra must travel north on the main road for at least two weeks to reach her. They could be easily intercepted.

But Rosarion had said that the man was to the east, sleeping, his musing continued. This either meant he was still in Branbridge, surely a foolhardy risk, with the Triarchy Knights and the Town Watch searching every house; or he was taking ship, equally foolish as the harbor was closed. So he was trapped either way. Ellisander smiled. He would have him soon enough. He would set Hadrian on it when he returned to the palace. Glancing down at the man in his arms, he tried to gauge how long these convulsions were likely to run.

Rosarion's breathing was congested and ragged, but the tremors had begun to ease a little. Ellisander shifted his weight more comfortably, then stared up at the herbarium widows, listening to the scratch of tree branches against the shutters.

"Colors swirling about an Essusiate man like tree branches in a high wind," he murmured.

Seven years of listening to the Aristok's Flame Priests had taught the Duke something of their methods, and he tossed these two descriptions about. Rosarion had mentioned them at the same time and the color reference had been repeated, so they represented the same man, yes?

Yes.

Idly he pressed a hand against the herbalist's forehead as if to delve into his mind from the outside.

"Colors . . ." he murmured.

Julianus had once said that a symbol's strongest association was usually its representation in vision. So, colors. Each noble family wore individual colors . . . No, Rosarion had not mentioned any specific combination, just colors.

Rosarion jerked suddenly, and Ellisander dropped his hand and clasped the younger man about the chest again.

Who would be represented by many colors?

Someone who had power over all the noble families and therefore all the noble colors?

No. Rosarion had said the man was an Essusiate, and no Essusiate had that kind of power.

Someone with no affiliation, then? The Duke shook his head in frustration. Everyone had an affiliation to something, either to a noble house or to a religious order or to a Guild: even the Heralds who might claim impartial jurisdiction over the noble colors. And besides, all Heralds were Triarchs.

The Duke glanced down, but Rosarion was still slumped, twitching in his arms.

All right. So who had no affiliations but could be represented by all colors?

The image of the new Marsellus Chapel suddenly came into his mind, its paint-decorated ceiling stretching out before him.

A painter.

Realization made his teeth snap together. A painter. The Court Painter. Trusted by Marsellus and Kassandra both. A man with no affiliation but with the power of influence over the highest Triarchs in the land.

"An Essusiate painter named Simon of Florenz." The Duke grated the words in a harsh growl.

Once the identity of the man was clear, the rest fell into place; the colors, the colors of an artist, the light of Essus, that God's protection of his servant and Terrilynne's involvement? He searched his memory. Marsellus had once told him that Simon had sired a son off a soldier, a soldier in Terrilynne's company. That would be why he was running to the Royal Cousin. He was connected with her, and he knew she would take advantage of this sudden rift in Ellisander's power structure. And his father was the stained-glass artisan commissioned to provide the windows for the new Marsellus Chapel.

His hands balling into fists, Ellisander grinned savagely. "Now I have you, you meddling little shit," he whispered. "Now I have your name. Soon I'll have your parents, and if I can't find you, I'll have your son, and then I'll have you, Terrilynne or no Terrilynne."

Rosarion had slowly quieted during this time and now he lay, sleeping deeply, his breath coming in ragged whispers. Ellisander rose, lifted the herbalist's limp form like a child's and placed him gently on the bed.

Staring at him for a long time, the Duke took in the other's pale, sweat-covered face with its darkly shadowed eyes and sunken cheeks, his almost translucent skin, and his wasted form. This last vision had drained his strength, and the DeMarian wondered how long it would be until he was reunited with the sister who'd brought them together. Not long, he expected. Then they would both be gone, and Ellisander would no longer know the future, but he would also no longer see the woman he'd loved in the face of the man he'd saved for her memory.

Bending down, he pushed the fair hair, so like Saralynne's, away from Rosarion's face. "Sleep well, little Seer," he whispered. "Gain back what strength you can, for I still have need of your insights for a time."

He covered him with a blanket and then turned away. The wound on Rosarion's head was shallow. It should staunch with the pressure from the pillow, and could be explained away by the herbalist himself. All that remained for the Duke was to clean up the Potion of Truth. He picked up the bowl from where Rosarion had flung it and began to collect the scattered ingredients.

When he was finished, he left the herbarium, a strategy already formulating in his mind. He would remember that he had not seen Simon of Florenz since before the Aristok's death, and that Kassandra was often in the habit of stealing away to spend an hour or two with him at his work. He would tell Julianus, and with this information the old man would be easily convinced to return to the Prophetic Realm if Seth Canon or Innes Eathan had not already Seen the painter in vision. With this new information Julianus would surely See him, and armed with that, Ellisander would go to Gawaina.

"And if you're still sleeping peacefully, as Rosarion says you are, you're going to have a rude awakening. And if not, Gawaina will send the Sword Knights to chase you down and drag you back to Branbridge in chains," he said with a smile. The Hierarchpriest hated Essusiatism and hated Simon of Florenz most particularly for his influence over her former charge. She was just the person to see to his arrest and questioning. Kassandra would be safely returned to her uncle's care and his plans could continue undisturbed.

His decision made, the Duke returned along the route Rosarion and Willan had taken earlier that evening. The rising fog completely obscured his path and he had to grope his way along, moving from tree to tree before he emerged at the far western entrance. By the time he realized the fog's significance, it was too late.

Simon and Hamlin were at that moment creeping through the streets of Branbridge. Without a lantern or even a candle to light their way the journey was a series of scares and false alarms, as unreal as the dreams that had prompted it. Hamlin went in front, alert to any sound of the Watch; Simon followed, carrying Kassandra wrapped in a blanket.

His breath caught in his throat at every noise. It was so like his dream that Simon kept glancing up, expecting to see the white dragon of Essus flying above them, but the fog was so thick he could barely make out Hamlin. Twice they had to press up against a building as the sounds of marching feet passed them, but they went unseen, and after what seemed like an eternity, they were moving downhill toward the river. When the ground beneath their feet told them they'd reached the embankment, Simon allowed his breathing to return to normal. Hours later, it seemed, he barked his skins against the rough wood of the dock where he'd left the boat.

Miraculously, it still lay where he'd left it, the oars hidden beneath. Simon climbed in, mindful of the child, still deep in sleep, then Hamlin pushed off and clambered in himself. Crouched in the bow, the painter let his father take the oars and navigate them out into the center of the river.

They heard no one else. The fog muffled all noise around them, and Simon had the sudden fear that they were the only people left alive in Branbridge, the muted splash of the oars dipping into the water the only sound left in the whole world.

He shivered, pressing his cheek against Kassandra's hair. There were plenty of others out tonight, he told himself firmly, no matter what his overactive imagination said, and none of them were people he was eager to meet. Breathing a silent prayer of thanks to Essus for the concealing fog, he tucked Kassandra into the crook of one arm, and shook the other, trying to bring some life back into it. When it began to tingle painfully, he did the same with the first. Kassandra made no sound.

He knew that her sleep must be unnatural, but whether it was from a physical or metaphysical cause, he had no idea. The painter turned aside the blanket to peer anxiously down at her, but she made no motion. His face tight with worry, he bundled her up again. He was doing everything he could for her already. He'd just have to trust that was enough. Imagining what his mother was going to say about this escapade gave him little comfort, so he put it out of his mind. Leaning against the gunwale, he stared into the mist, watching intently for signs of other craft.

They traveled steadily westward, pushed along against the current by Hamlin's powerful strokes on the oars. At one point they heard the distant peal of Bran's Bell tolling twelve and knew they were passing Collin's Park and Bran's Palace. Soon they would be passing the Temple of the Flame.

Simon found himself holding his breath and forced it out slowly. They would either make it past or they wouldn't, he counseled himself. It was in the God's hands.

The ringing bells faded into the distance, and they pressed on with the same eerie, unreal sense as before. Simon began to count slowly, ticking off the seconds in his head as if it were the only thing making time move forward. After half an hour's counting he judged they'd passed the Temple grounds, and he told Hamlin, whispering to keep his voice from moving out across the water.

They both began to relax a little. Shifting Kassandra into a more comfortable position in his lap, Simon tried to get some sleep.

Hours later he raised his head to Hamlin's whispered call and saw the hazy outline of the Westonborough docks. The artisan picked one at random and tied up the boat, then helped Simon out.

They stood a moment on the grassy bank, stamping their feet to bring the blood back into circulation, then set out walking. Soon the fog began to burn off and they could make out the outlines of dwellings and trees. They quickened their pace.

Dawn found them at Westonborough's north market fields. Six brightly painted wagons were parked in the center, with a dozen draft horses tethered nearby. A number of people were already up seeing to morning chores, and they stared warily as the two men approached. One, a tall, burly man, with muscles bulging beneath his leather jerkin came forward with a frown. Simon and Hamlin recognized Warrin Fire-Eater, the Troupe's most gentle player. The artisan waved.

Warrin's fierce expression changed to one of confused pleasure, which remained as Hamlin explained their presence briefly, significantly not mentioning the bundle in Simon's arms. Scratching his head, the big man didn't ask, but led them toward the lead wagon, a picture of three spinning coins painted on its side. Simon recognized his own work with a distracted glance.

Warrin knocked, then stuck his head in through the door and called out the name of its owner.

After one shared look of apprehension, Simon and Hamlin marshaled their expressions to ones of exaggerated innocence as Ballentire of Briery emerged, a blanket wrapped loosely about her shoulders. She glared at the two of them in sleepy suspicion.

"What, by the Flame, are you two doing here?" she demanded.

The Spinning Coins Tumbling Troupe were a mixed group of Panishan and Branion Players, traveling in the Triartic Kingdom for the last two years. Simon had become acquainted with them in Gallia and had traveled with them for two seasons, making sketches and drawings of their lives on the road. He and Ballentire, their leader, had been through a number of scrapes and adventures together that neither her partner Tamara nor Simon's parents were aware of, but they were good memories of risk and camaraderie, so when he'd awakened that night in Branbridge knowing that he must make a run for safety, he'd known exactly who to turn to.

Now, the Troupe Leader stared at them in horror as Simon lifted the flap of the blanket aside and revealed Kassandra's bright auburn hair in explanation for their presence.

"Have you both completely lost your minds?"

Simon gave her a tired smile. "No, Bal, we haven't."

"That's the Aristok. The *Branion* Aristok."

"We know. Calm down and we'll explain everything, but we need to do it somewhere privately."

"And the child needs a quiet place to sleep," Hamlin added. "Can Tam look after her while we talk?"

"Tam's asleep."

"Bal."

"Oh, all right, just a minute." Ballentire disappeared back into the wagon and a moment later followed her sleepy-eyed partner from the wagon. Wrapping a robe unhurriedly about her, Tamara of Moleshil glanced quizzically at the two men, but despite being roused from slumber with no explanation, she smiled as Simon handed Kassandra over to her.

"Does Jade know about your newest offspring, Sy?" she asked the painter, then laughed as Simon opened his mouth to protest. "Never mind, talk to Bal first. I'll be at Turi's wagon, he's better with children than I am. Bal, you'd better put some clothes on."

She headed off, shooing away the crowd of tumblers

that had gathered, as Simon and Hamlin entered the wagon behind the Troupe Leader.

Once inside, Ballentire tossed the blanket onto the bed with casual indifference and reached for a pair of breeches.

"Pass me that tunic, Sy."

The artist fished it out from a pile of clothes on the floor and handed it over.

Pulling it on over her head, Ballentire gestured at the chairs. "Sit, talk, and it better be good."

After half an hour's explanation, she cut off Simon's words with a stab of her finger.

"No," she said firmly. "No, no, no, and no."

"Bal . . ." the painter made to rise, but she glared him back into his seat.

"Don't Bal me, you lunatic. Do you know what you've done? Does Fay know it? And now you want me and my people to be a party to kidnapping?"

"I told you, we didn't kidnap her."

"Oh, sorry!" The Troupe Leader threw her hands dramatically into the air. "How could I forget! Essus led you to commit treason! That'll go over wonderfully well at your *Triarctic* trial!"

Simon rose, eased past her and opened her wall cabinet. "Bal, you're becoming hysterical," he said soothingly. "Have a drink."

"It's five in the morning. I haven't even had breakfast."

"Breakfast sounds good, too. I'm starved." He fished out a jug of apple jack. "This'll do. Don't you have more than two cups?"

"No. And give me that!" She snatched the jug away and slammed it down on the small table. "I always knew you were flat-out mad, Sy, hanging around with the Aristok and his like, but I assumed your father had more sense."

"Apparently not." Hamlin smiled and accepted the cup Simon held out to him. "Didn't you mention something about breakfast?"

Ballentire's answer was extremely rude, but she went to the door and called out to one of the children lingering by the fire to bring some oatmeal.

*   *   *

After they'd finished and the bowls had been pushed aside, Simon turned back to his old friend.

"We need your help, Bal. *She* needs your help."

"To do what, fool, get killed?"

Hamlin smiled as he filled his pipe with fenweed. "Not at all. We have a idea that just might do the trick. Son?"

Simon explained. When he was finished, Ballentire uncorked the jug wordlessly and took a long swallow.

"You're insane, and it'll never work."

"What's happened to the Ballentire I used to know?" Simon asked. "The woman who would jump at the chance for an adventure like this?"

"She grew up."

He leaned forward. "Will you help us anyway, Bal?"

"No. It'll mean the gallows for every one of us."

"It'll mean fame and glory for every one of you and the greatest story in history," he replied. "Think of it, Bal. The Aristok flees the wicked treason of an uncle's hand. With danger at every turn . . ."

"That's right, Sy, danger, the danger of capture, imprisonment, torture, and death."

". . . aided only by two courageous . . ."

"Insane."

". . . artists and a gallant troupe of tumblers, and disguised as a common juggler's apprentice, she makes her way north. Past the guards and soldiers of her enemy, her loyal people bring her safely to the arms of her cousin, who places her at the head of a mighty army and returns her home in triumph. The enemy is defeated, the Aristok seated on her rightful throne, and the faithful and steadfast tumblers go on to riches and fame. Think of the story it would make, Bal."

"One the minstrels would sing of for years," Hamlin agreed.

"Maybe even for centuries."

They were leaning toward her now, one on either side. Ballentire glared at them both, and muttered a comment about carrion birds, but they could see their words had sparked her interest. She sat back, passing the jug absently from hand to hand, a reflective expression on her face. Finally she set it on the table.

"Neither one of you knows when to quit layering it on, do you?" she growled.

"But you'll do it?"

"I'll do it. But not for any badly told, melodramatic story," she added quickly as the two men traded a triumphant glance. "For the child. I can't have the two of you dragging her around the countryside; you'd get her killed in the first mile."

"Exactly my thought, Bal," Simon answered easily.

"Sure." The Troupe Leader looked skeptical, but after a moment she sighed in resignation. "All right, well, her disguise will be easy enough," she said. "A little walnut stain in her hair and on her face to darken them, and a tumbler's tunic should be enough, as long as strangers don't get close enough to have a good look at her eyes, but you two . . . it won't be long before those Triarchy Seers sniff you out. We're harder to nail down in vision, something about wearing too many hats or too many faces or some such nonsense, and maybe, just maybe, that might be enough to hide *Her* whereabouts, *if* we keep moving, but they'll eventually pinpoint you two, and then your descriptions will be all over Branion. We'll have to change those descriptions as much as possible. So . . ." She grinned evilly, "it's to the barber for you, my Essusiate friends."

She began to laugh at their furious protests, and continued to laugh even after a girl came to tell Simon that the Aristok was awake and demanding to see him.

6. Kassandra

Mean Marta, 783 DR

In the main sanctuary of the Holy Triarchy Cathedral, the old man heaved himself up to the top level of scaffolding with a groan. *You won't be able to do this much longer,* his aching joints warned him, *and then what will you do?*

Have myself hoisted up with a block and tackle, he answered, *do shut up.* He glared at his left knee as it popped noisily and eased himself down onto the planks with another groan. Then, fishing through the canvas bag at his shoulder, he pulled out his jug, uncorked it, and drew in a deep mouthful.

All was quiet this morning. The sun pouring through the windows left a rippled pattern of reds and blues across the stone floor and he regarded them sadly, remembering the windows of another time and place. The Holy Triarchy boasted some of the most magnificent stained glass in the DeMarian Realm, but they weren't Hamlin's, so they never seemed as bright or as beautiful to the old man.

He tipped up his head, his gaze traveling across the ceiling above him. The finished panels were a maze of color, somewhat misshapen at this angle. From the floor, however, he knew they'd be magnificent. In comparison, the breadth of unpainted ceiling mocked him in its emptiness. He'd completed the sketches over a year ago, and the work was progressing, but far too slowly. The sweeping majesty of cities and armies had yet to be realized in true form. He had so much to do, and so little time in which to do it.

Sighing, he took another swallow. He could have given

the background paintings over to his apprentices along with the uncomfortable job of applying the day's plastering, but he'd never liked having others involved in his visions, and besides, they had work of their own to accomplish.

Critically, he eyed the nearest pillar. Twisting vines chased each other up its length and he grunted in satisfaction. Kora was coming along fine. She'd be finished before Shale by a week at least, and the boy'd lose the better part of a month's wages to their bet.

And if he didn't get to work soon, he reminded himself, they'd be in here fussing and arguing and asking questions long before he was ready for them.

He set the jug to one side and fished a handful of new brushes from the bag. Laying them out in a neat row, he glanced out the nearest window, judging it to be about half past six. He'd have at least two hours of uninterrupted work before they descended on him. How he was expected to get anything accomplished with all these distractions was a mystery, but at least he had his mornings. The others all knew that this was the time of day he liked to work alone and left him in peace to do it, out of respect and because—he admitted to himself—he might be a little . . . well, cantankerous in the morning, but if a man of seventy wasn't allowed a few . . .

"Shouldn't you be getting on with it?"

A cloud passed over the sun, the shadows inside the cathedral growing suddenly darker and more substantial.

"When I get my breath back, old ghost," the artist replied. "I'm not as young as I once was, you know."

Cracking the wax seal on the first pot of tempera, he scooped out a measure of yellow ocher with his knife, humming tunelessly to himself. "Good for at least another day," he muttered as he slapped it down onto his pallet, and reached for another jar, "Still, Shale will need to mix more tomorrow. Must remember to tell him so."

The sun began to peek from the clouds, causing the shadows to flit from one image to another while the old man pretended not to notice. When they came to rest by the first mural over the altar, he chuckled.

"You like that one, don't you?" he asked. "You always come back to it."

"Well, it's about me," the shadows retorted. *"It's the only one about me . . . ungrateful wretch."*

"Not true." The artist waved a brush at the thinly outlined figures. "This panel's about you, too."

The shadows loomed above him, and for the space of a heartbeat the old man felt cold. Then the sun returned, flooding the sanctuary with warmth and light.

"Hardly enough," the shadows pronounced in a petulant tone from a still-darkened corner.

The artist shook his head. "It's not your story, Leary," he admonished. "It's hers."

A snort came from the corner.

"Now don't sulk. Look at this." The old man held out the panel's cartoon. "See how I've represented you here, with all these swirling reds and yellows. You'll like that."

"You were pissing buckets that day," the shadows retorted impolitely, refusing to be mollified. *"Without me, you'd have bungled the whole thing and she'd have been scarred for life."*

"I know." The old man patted the silver locket about his neck and then began to apply color to the outlines of three giant coins, moving the brush delicately over the damp plaster with the ease of long familiarity. "I didn't know how I was going to tell her," he said. "She loved you so much."

"She still does!"

"Of course she does, Leary. We all do."

"Better not forget it," the shadows muttered peevishly, and the old man smiled. The movement of his brush was soothing and soon all the stiffness began to leave his limbs. As the images took form, one part of his mind remained on the work, while another wandered to that day long ago when he'd had to tell a five-year-old child that her father was dead and that all she loved in the world was in danger of being destroyed by an uncle's hand.

Beside him, the shadows hovered quietly now, hushed into silence by the hypnotic pattern of the old man's brush strokes and by the strength of the old man's memories.

Mean Boaldyn 737 DR

The morning had turned warm as Simon followed a girl across the field to Turi's wagon. Hamlin had asked if he'd wanted him to come along, and the artist had shaken his head. Kassandra was his responsibility, and it was up to him to answer the questions she was bound to ask. Questions like: where was she, where was her father, and why had Simon dragged her away from her home to this strange place surrounded by strange people? He wondered what he was going to tell her.

Tamara's brother Turi met him at the wagon door, his dark eyes amused. He looked quite similar to his twin sister, the same wavy blond hair, the same trim, muscular tumbler's body. Only the neat goatee on his chin told them apart. He gave Simon a quick update on Kassandra's condition, informed him that he was going to get her some tea, and that Tamara was sitting with her now. Simon thanked him, and the other man brushed the words away with a dismissive motion of his hand.

"My pleasure, Sy." Opening the door with a flourish, he stepped back. "She's a sweetie."

A sweetie? Simon shook his head as he bent to pass under the lintel. *Only Turi would describe a DeMarian child as a sweetie.*

He paused a moment for his eyes to adjust to the darkened room, and soon made out Tamara sitting in the wagon's one chair. She smiled when she saw him and gestured dramatically toward the bed where a small figure wrapped in shawls peered up at Simon with alert, fire-splashed eyes.

Kassandra DeMarian had awakened from her long fever, hungry and demanding to know where she was and why her head hurt. She'd accepted Tamara's assurance that Simon would explain all and Turi's promise of broth with the easy majesty of a child who'd only known obeisance from those around her. Now, with the broth warm in her stomach, she regarded the painter expectantly, her face pinched-looking and pale, but her fiery gaze unmarked by illness.

At first Simon was so relieved to see her awake that

his knees buckled, but he held onto the doorpost until the spell passed and then entered the wagon shakily.

Tamara smiled at his reaction as she tucked the blankets more securely about the child. "Now then, you see," she whispered to her. "Here's Sy. I told you he'd be right over."

Dropping to his knees beside the bed, Simon took Kassandra in his arms. Unable to speak, he merely held her until she began to squirm.

"My throat hurts," she said in a hoarse voice after he'd released her.

Still not trusting himself to speak, Simon nodded.

"I've sent Turi for some camomile tea," Tamera answered. "Would you like that, little one?"

"With honey?" Kassandra asked with deep suspicion and the woman laughed.

"Of course with honey."

The child nodded.

"How about you, Sy?"

He shook his head.

Kassandra glanced from one to the other, then tugged at Simon's sleeve. "Am I sick? I don't feel good."

The painter sat down on the edge of the bed. "You were sick," he answered gently.

"Will I be better soon?"

"I think so. Yes, you will."

"Good, 'cause Tam says that she an' Turi are tumblers, an' that they'll show me a human pyramid when I'm better."

"I'm sure you'll really like that."

"Uh-huh." The child stared, wide-eyed, around the wagon, then returned her dark, fire-washed gaze to his face. "Tam says you brought me here an' you'd tell me why, 'cause I don't remember. Is it a surprise?"

Squirming a little, Simon looked away. "Not exactly, Sparky," he answered evasively.

"Where's Nurse?"

"Uh . . ." Rubbing his beard, Simon cast about for a harmless answer. "She's back at the palace," he said finally.

"Why?"

"Because we . . . didn't have time to bring her with us."

The answer was no real answer at all, and the child frowned at him. Simon could almost see her next question forming, but when she spoke her words were a surprise.

"Where's Spotty?"

"Spotty?"

"Spotty." For the first time her voice held the imperious tone he was used to. "My horse," she explained with labored patience. "Spotty. Where is she? You didn't leave her behind, did you?"

She glared at him reproachfully as he searched his memory for the toy's whereabouts. He hadn't left it behind, had he? He hoped not. Finally he smiled in relief. "It's in my pack, Sparky. I was afraid we'd drop it. Shall I go and fetch it for you?"

"Yes."

Simon made to rise, and Tamara waved at him to be seated again.

"I'll get it, Sy. You'll want to talk alone, anyhow, won't you."

She gave him a meaningful look as she left the wagon, and Simon returned reluctantly to his place on the bed. Absently stroking the child's hair, he stared at the light filtering in through the shutters.

"Sparky," he said, unable to meet her eyes, "I have something to tell you. Something bad . . . has happened."

"Bad to us?"

"Yes. And . . . bad to your father." He glanced down at her finally and saw her watching him with eyes so like Leary's that it made his chest constrict. Closing his own eyes, he took a deep breath and was startled to feel a light touch on his cheek. Opening them, he saw Kassandra regarding him seriously.

"It's all right, Simon," she said gravely. "You don't gots ta tell me really, 'cause Papa told me already."

"Papa told you already?" The artist looked down at her in confusion.

She nodded. "I was sleeping an' Papa came an' said

that he was with the Living Flame now, an' that I had to look after you, 'cause he couldn't no more."

"You had to look after me?"

"Uh-huh."

"He told you this . . . in a dream?" Her words made no sense to him and he shook his head to clear it.

"I guess." She shrugged. "I was asleep, an' he came, like I said. His face was all . . ." She frowned, trying to find the right word. "Misty, you know, shadowy."

Unsure of how to respond, Simon just stared at her blankly. *Her father came to her.*

Well, his mind offered up sluggishly, *her father was the Avatar of a God. Who's to say what he was capable of. Not you. You're an Essusiate painter, not a Triarctic priest.*

Another tug at his sleeve interrupted his thinking.

"Simon?"

He refocused on her face. "Yes?"

"Why did Papa go?"

Why did Papa go?

Why did Leary go?

He felt a lump begin to grow in his throat and pushed the sudden image of his friend's laughing face from his mind. She was waiting for an answer.

"What did he tell you?" he asked instead.

"Jus' that he had to go an' that I was Aristok now, an' that you'd be real sad, so I had to take care of you."

"Oh."

"Anyway, why did he go?"

There was that question again. If he didn't answer she'd only keep on asking, and who was there to tell her the truth except for him?

He decided to be blunt. Jade had always said that children were simpler than adults and wanted simple answers, not elaborate explanations.

"He didn't want to go, but some bad people came and killed him," he said.

"But he was the Aristok," she protested, her eyes wide. "No one's *ever* s'posed to kill the Aristok. Papa said."

"I know."

"Is Uncle Sandi one of the bad people, too?"

Caught off guard by her unexpected insight, he could only stare down at her again.

"How did you know that?" he finally managed to choke out.

" 'Cause Papa was real mad at him. He said his name an' these big fireballs shot out his eyes." Kassandra tipped her head to one side. "I wonder if I could do that?"

For a moment her own eyes grew hot, and Simon had the sudden fear that she'd do just that.

Get a grip. This is a five-year-old child, he told himself. *This is the Avatar of a living God, you fool,* his mind responded. *Her age only means she's more likely to do it.*

Rubbing his beard, he tried to think of something to distract her, but after a moment her expression cleared.

"Simon?"

"Yes?"

"How come Uncle Sandi wanted to kill Papa?"

He sighed. At least her questions were easier to deal with than the possibility of her setting the wagon on fire.

"I don't know, Sparky," he answered truthfully. "I guess he wanted to be Aristok instead."

"But he can't be, 'cause I am. I'm the Heir, I mean, I was the Heir, and now I'm the Aristok. Is he going to try an' kill me, too?"

"I . . ." Simon took a deep breath. "I don't know. I think so. I was too scared to ask him in case he does, but that's why we're here. I found out about him and the bad people, and I ran away with you so you'd be safe."

A noise outside the wagon made him jump, but it was only Tamara bringing Spotty and the tea. Relieved by the interruption, Simon tucked the horse into bed beside the child, then fluffed up her pillows as the woman placed the cup on the table.

"I'm going for breakfast, Sy," she said. "If you need anything, just shout for Turi."

"Thanks, Tam."

The tumbler gave his shoulder a squeeze and after winking at Kassandra, left the wagon.

Simon picked up the cup. "Why don't you drink this for a bit." He held it out. "And we'll talk some more later."

Helping her steady the cup, he waited until she'd finished most of it before letting her take hold of it herself.
Finally she looked up at him from over its rim.

"Where're we gonna go now?" she asked. "Are we
gonna stay here for always, an' be tumblers?"

Stretching his legs, he winced as his left knee popped,
and took the now empty cup. "We can't stay here for
always and be tumblers," he answered, "because you're
the Aristok, remember, and we both have work to do
back home."

"Oh, yeah." She looked disappointed for a moment,
then her expression cleared. " 'Course, now that I'm Aristok everyone has to do what I say, right?"

"Right." *As if anyone had ever denied you before,* he
added sardonically, although he kept that to himself. "I
thought we'd go to your Cousin Terrilynne and ask her
for help," he answered instead.

Kassandra considered this.

"Are you sure Terri's not one of the bad people,
too?" she asked.

"Pretty sure. She's kind of a long way away."

"An' Terri an' Uncle Sandi hate each other," she
added. "They couldn't even have supper together last
Braniana's Day without fighting."

"I remember." As he recalled, the argument had been
over Heathland and might have ended in bloodshed had
Marsellus not intervened.

"But I get to see the tumblers first, right?"

"Right."

She nodded, satisfied. "Simon?"

"Yes?"

"I'm tired."

"Why don't you sleep for a while, then?"

"Will you stay?"

"I'll stay until you fall asleep, but then I need to get
some sleep, too. Turi or Tam will look after you then,
all right?"

She nodded her agreement and snuggled under the
covers, the toy horse peeking out from beside her chin.
Simon bent down to kiss her forehead, now relievedly
cool, and moved to the wagon's one chair.

"Simon?"

"Yes?"

"When we get to Terri's, it will be almost my birthday."

"I know."

"Will I still get my own pony?"

"Yes."

"How will Terri know what pony Papa was gonna get me?"

"I'll tell her."

"Did Papa tell you?"

"Of course he did. He told me about all his surprises for you." *Except this one.* He felt his throat constrict again.

"Simon?"

"Yes?"

"I miss Papa."

"I know. But if you go to sleep now, maybe he'll visit you in your dreams again."

"Do you think he might visit you, too?"

"I wish he would. I miss him, too."

"Simon?"

"Weren't you going to go to sleep?"

"I am in a minute." Her tone was imperious again and he smiled.

"Promise?"

"I said I was."

"All right, then, what do you want to ask?"

"I don't wanna ask nothin', I wanna tell you somethin'."

She paused and after a time he indulged her, "Well, what did you want to tell me?"

"Jus' that you don't gots ta *ask* Terri for help, you know."

"I don't?"

"No, you don't 'cause I'm the Aristok now. You *tell* her to help and she will."

A chill eased up his spine. This was a five-year-old child with all the powers of the Triarctic God at her youthful command. He had the sudden feeling that Kassandra the Sixth, thirty-fifty DeMarian Aristok of Branion, was going to be a much more dangerous adversary than the Duke of Yorbourne had expected she'd be.

"Yes, Your Majesty," he answered.

The child smiled sleepily at his words, and after a time her breathing deepened. When he was sure she was asleep, he rose.

Turi was waiting outside and he took the other man's place, promising to send for him should anything new arise. Closing the door softly behind him, Simon of Florenz went in search of a drink.

Hamlin and Ballentire were waiting for him when he got back to the Troupe Leader's wagon. The artisan knocked his pipe clean against his hand and laughed at Simon's expression.

"You look a little green, Son," he noted.

The painter dropped into a chair and groped for the jug. "I just had my first audience with the new Aristok," he answered wryly.

"As bad as all that?"

"You have no idea." He narrated their conversation and Ballentire snorted derisively when he finished.

"It may not be as easy as all that, you know."

"Oh?"

She gave him a sarcastic look. "What if the Duke of Yorbourne gets to Terrilynne first, which he very likely will, and she claps you in chains and sends the kid home again?"

Pouring a cup of apple jack, Simon shook his head. "She'd never just give Kassandra up to Ellisander, especially with suspicion of regicide. They hate each other. At the very worst, she'll clap us in chains and then set Kassandra up under her own protection. Either way she'll be safe."

"Either way it doesn't change the chains bit. What happened to the fame and glory part?"

"I'm working on it."

"Well, work a little harder, I don't think much of your ending."

"Neither do I, but right now I'm too tired to care. Is there anywhere we can catch some sleep, Bal? I'm done in."

She motioned toward the bed. "Right here, but first you both have to visit the barber, no arguments!" she barked as he opened his mouth to protest. "If your God's so keen on interfering in the doings of the Living Flame, a little hirsute heresy should be easily forgiven. I don't want the buggering Flame Priests descending on us before we get halfway to Heathland. That's my price for helping you, Sy."

The painter glanced at Hamlin who shrugged in glum resignation. "She's been working on me since you left," he said. "And I'm afraid she's right."

"Kassandra'll never recognize me," Simon grumbled.

"With luck your own mother won't recognize you," Ballentire retorted.

"Oh, she'll know him easily enough," Hamlin said in a woeful tone. "It's me she won't recognize."

"You never know, maybe she'll fall for you all over again."

"Maybe she'll kill me."

"If she hasn't yet, she's not likely to now."

"Sure. That's easy for you to say." Tucking his pipe in his pocket, the artisan rose and allowed himself and Simon to be pushed from the wagon.

In Branbridge Fay had other concerns. The morning had seen continued arrests and sporadic bursts of resistance easily quelled, but it wasn't until Gawaina De-Kathrine's Sword Knights came to arrest her when she returned home that the resistance turned violent. Fay would not be taken so easily by the enemies of her son, and when their neighbors came to her aid, the fighting on Harper's Lane quickly became bloody. The Sword Knights eventually managed to win free with their prisoner, but they left two of their number behind.

Still enraged by the death of their Aristok, the Triarctic population rose up in retaliation. Essusiate businesses were looted and their proprietors attacked. The Essusiate Merchants' Coalition mobilized to protect their property, and riots broke out all over Branbridge, quelled only when the Flame Champions were sent out to restore order. Meanwhile Fay Falconer was hustled out of Branbridge, and by the time the sun rose fully over the Sword Tower turrets, she was secured in the Flame Temple dungeons exactly where Ellisander DeMarian wanted her.

* * *

Later that morning as the Royal Duke made his way to the Sword Tower, a dozen Shield Knights about him as an escort, he surveyed the damage to the city with little interest. There would be much more destruction before the end of this, he surmised. Branbridge could afford to sacrifice a few shops and streets.

He stifled a yawn. He'd awakened early that morning, the nearness to the heart of the Living Flame making him restless. It was a feeling he'd been quite comfortable with before Kassandra's birth, and was one he knew he'd get used to again. Until then, it left him with a surplus of energy, so when the Hierarchpriest of Cannonshire's message had arrived, asking for an audience, he'd sent the messenger back with word that he would attend her.

He was ushered into her office with much ceremony, and after bringing wine and wafers, her people left them alone.

Without preamble, Gawaina passed a document over for the Duke's perusal.

"The Flame Priests have Seen the light of Essus covering the deed," she said. "They have over a hundred Essusiates in custody now. They've made little headway in their investigations of conspiracy; however, they have interrogated the wounded Essusiate found in the cellars of St. Tomasino's. It's confirmed now that he was one of the murderers. He broke immediately." She sniffed in disdain. "He claims that he and his compatriots had been assured of safety only to be set upon by the Town Watch. He thinks they were betrayed and so gave up the Cleric who'd recruited them. Innes Eathan has Seen her in vision already dead. Her body was dragged from the Mist an hour ago. She'd been garroted. Very professional."

"Hm." Ellisander kept his face impassive. He'd learned of the botched cleanup job from his own Guard Captain that morning. It was one of the details Hadrian and Lysanda had to explain later that day.

"I've sent my Lieutenant to speak to the Watch Captain," Gawaina continued. "It's most probable they resisted and the Watch responded with excessive force. It's also possible they were silenced before they could give up their superiors. I want those involved questioned in either case."

"Quite right." Ellisander's eyes scanned the page, then stopped. He looked up, his face showing shock. "It says here that they were led to the Royal wing by a palace servant . . . a Triarctic servant."

She nodded, her face grim. "So Seth Cannon says also. The priests are even now combing the Royal wing, and they've begun questioning the servants, but it will take time. The palace is overflowing with people." She clicked her tongue. "Five hundred guards and pages; priests, heralds, retainers, twice that many palace and personal servants. It's a security nightmare."

"It's always been so," Ellisander answered vaguely. "I trust that our Flame Priests will find this person, regardless." *In the Shadow Realm,* he added silently.

The Hierarchpriest leaned forward. "In the meantime, they *have* uncovered one vital piece of information, My Lord. Our prisoner claims that he and his compatriots gained access to the palace with the help of the Bachiem Ambassador."

"Brenburg?" The Duke's eyes narrowed. "That puts a new twist on the matter." *Although not a dangerous one. The old fool had no idea who used him. He could be thrown to the wolves.*

"It does indeed," Gawaina agreed. "I have him in custody now." She laid her hand on another document. "I'd like him interrogated. I'd like him hanged, but these are decisions that can only be made by the Aristok."

"And?"

"And I can't order it without your permission, My Lord. As next in line to the Throne or to the Regency, it's your decision alone."

The Duke met her gaze. Gawaina DeKathrine had regented both Kathrine the Fifth and her brother Marsellus the Third. She would be a dangerous ally, and an equally dangerous adversary, but she was a strict observer of the law, and it was his right to sit as either Regent for Kassandra, or as Aristok. Gawaina DeKathrine would not contest that right as long as she believed him uninvolved in his cousin's death. If she ever suspected, she'd have to be removed. He had a plan in place for that contingency also, but for the moment, she did not suspect him. And would not if he could get the child back in the capital as quickly as possible.

He inclined his head. "I rely on your counsel always, My Lord of Cannonshire, but let us not speak of the Throne, for Julianus assures me that he and his Flame Priests have Seen her unharmed."

"Yes, My Lord. He's informed me of their vision also." She glared down at a document bearing the seal of the Flame Temple. "They've Seen her unharmed, but they haven't actually located her." Her voice was frustrated.

"Julianus tells me she is hidden by the light of Essus," Ellisander answered. "Since it is clear now that Essusiates are to blame for the late Aristok's death, it seems equally obvious that they are also responsible for Kassandra's disappearance."

"But why haven't they pierced through this . . . light of Essus to find her?"

Her tone was angrily suspicious, and Ellisander sighed. "We're all worried about her, Winna," he replied in a gently admonishing tone. "The Flame Priests are doing all they can. I know they'll find her. Julianus is certain she'll be returned unharmed. We must keep the faith."

When the Hierarchpriest nodded reluctantly, he continued. "The Knights and the Watch are still out searching the city?"

"Yes, My Lord."

"Then all we can do is wait for their reports. In the meantime, we must think of what's best for the Realm. I agree that Ambassador Brenburg should be questioned, but as for hanging . . . that may create a political situation we're not yet prepared to deal with."

The Hierarchpriest leaned forward again. "The late Aristok was planning war with Bachiem, My Lord," she pressed. "The declaration of war had already been drafted. It only awaited his signature. What better way to seal it than with the Ambassador's blood?"

"I know what Marsellus was planning," Ellisander answered sharply. "War with Bachiem is inevitable, especially with this new evidence, yet I believe that the Count of Brenburg would be better as bargaining leverage at this time . . ." He smiled thinly. ". . . than as sealing wax.

"Request that he come in himself. He'll oblige. He doesn't want an international incident right now either. Then send me the report as soon as you have it, and I'll decide what's to be done with him. In the meantime, Winna, he's to be treated with all due respect."

"As you wish, My Lord." The Head of the Knights of the Sword did not mask her disappointment and Ellisander made a conciliatory gesture.

"A response to the Essusiate involvement does need to be made, however." He paused as if in thought. "All Continental Essusiates are to be deported immediately and their goods seized. All Branion Essusiates of name are to be summoned and made to swear immediate fealty to the Throne with financial assurances equal to their status, or they're to be stripped of lands and titles and exiled."

Gawaina showed her teeth in an approving grimace. "There're a few DeCarlas remaining in Branbridge worthy of such notice, My Lord," she said, "and numerous merchants and traders."

"Start with them."

"It shall be my pleasure."

"Good, now to other business, did you receive the Archpriest's report on Terrilynne?"

"I did, My Lord. Based on Julianus' latest vision, it's certain that the Duke of Kempston is involved to some degree. With your permission, I'd like to send a contingent of Sword Knights to Dunleyshire, Julianus wants to send Flame Champions and Seers, and Captain Jordana of Wiltham wishes to go herself with a company of Shield Knights."

"We can't all go, My Lord of Cannonshire."

"As you say, My Lord. However, I think a show of strength is warranted."

"Agreed. I will draft her a letter, one Royal cousin to another. We have no real proof of her guilt so far, just evidence that this Simon of Florenz will try to contact her. I shall request that, if and when he appears, she bring him and the Aristok back to Branbridge with all possible speed."

"What if she refuses?"

Ellisander gave a shrug. "The Realm is weakened without Its Avatar. She knows this. To resist would be treason. The messenger should be a Herald, I think, accompanied by a strong enough company to impart this; a company composed of troops from all four militant orders and the Flame. This will make our intent, and our solidarity, plain. I suggest we send Crowitanus. He's known to her. One of Julianus' senior priests, Seth Cannon or Innes Eathan," *which will take them away from Kassandra's investigation,* he thought silently, "will accompany him with two Flame Champions, and two each from the Sword, Shield, Bow, and Lance. That will make twelve, ten of whom will be heavily armed. That should suffice."

Gawaina nodded. "I agree, My Lord, but may I suggest that the militant arm be led by Captain Jordana. She believes her honor has been stained by the deed and wishes to make personal amends."

"Acceptable. She'll be most diligent, I'm sure."

"That leaves only one detail, My Lord," the Hierarchpriest held up another document. "This foreign artist. He wasn't in his palace suite, nor at his family's house in Branbridge. His mother's in custody and under interrogation as we speak. Did you know she was a member of the Town Watch?"

Ellisander made his expression go dark. "No, I didn't. This Essusiate conspiracy is growing more twisted every day."

"We may find she's linked to the removal of the Aristok's murderers, My Lord. I'll send you a copy of her confession as soon as it's obtained. His Grace, Rosarion DeLynne has been assigned to her interrogation."

Ellisander frowned. "Rosarion? I assumed he was too ill to enter the Prophetic Realm."

The Hierarchpriest shrugged. "Julianus chose him because of his earlier vision when he saw the Aristok Kassandra. Still, I could request that he assign another priest to the duty if Your Lordship wishes?"

After a show of some consideration, the Royal Duke shook his head. "No, I trust that the Archpriest knows what he's doing." *Once the idea had been stuffed into his senile old head.* "In the meantime what of the rest of the artist's family?"

"The father wasn't home, My Lord. Possibly he fled with the artist—I've left a guard at his door in either case—The two youths who I'm told reside with them, were seen fleeing the area. My people were under instruction to let them go. They may run to tell Simon of Florenz of his mother's capture, so if the Duke of Kemston doesn't give him up, he may return on his own for her sake."

"An insightful plan, My Lord of Cannonshire. I'm sure it will be exactly as you say." He rose. "Now, if that's all, you must excuse me as I have other business to attend to."

Rising with him, the Hierarchpriest bowed. "Of course, sir, and thank you for coming. I'll have the company assembled and sent forth within the hour."

"I have every faith that you will."

The Duke took his leave quickly.

As he headed back toward the palace, Ellisander DeMarian, Nominal Regent of Branion, allowed himself one chilly smile. The Essusiates were bearing the blame for Marsellus' murder, Gawaina had been aimed toward Terrilynne—it wouldn't be long before his dear cousin fell under suspicion as well—and as soon as Rosarion made his report on Fay Falconer, she could be held out as bait for Simon of Florenz and the Aristok. Everything was moving smoothly.

Tossing a coin to a beggar crouched in the lea of the West Gate, Ellisander led his company onto the Palace Road, well satisfied with the morning's work.

In a cell in the Flame Temple dungeons, Rosarion DeLynne sat rubbing his temples. After a full night's sleep he was feeling fragile but functional, and after speaking with the Duke about his vision of the day before, he'd gained some badly needed clarity. None of this had prepared him for the woman he now faced. Every attempt he'd made to glean what she knew about Kassandra's kidnappers had met with frustrating defeat. It was giving him a splitting headache. Usually there would be two priests conducting such an interrogation,

one working while the other observed, but Ellisander
had wanted Fay questioned by Rosarion alone, in fear,
likely, of what Simon of Florenz had told her. It had
taken some time for the herbalist to convince Julianus
to let him interrogate her "undistracted" by another, but
so far she wasn't talking. Drumming his fingers on the
arm of his chair, he considered how best to proceed as
he studied her.

Short and stocky, she had gray hair and gray eyes that
stared into his own without the least hint of fear. In
fact, her expression showed more disgust than any other
emotion and it made him uneasy. Her Town Watch uniform was torn and dusty and there was blood on one
sleeve which he'd been told wasn't hers; all telling re-
minders that she was a dangerous prisoner; as telling as
the chains about her wrists and ankles.

Rosarian grimaced as a tickle in his throat threatened
to bring on a coughing spell. He'd taken the Potion of
Revealing—a slightly different version of the Potion of
Truth, used to enhance a Seer's ability to pierce the
thoughts of others—before entering the cell. It had a
powerful effect on the mind and body, and he'd been
unable to take his expectorant with it. Now his chest felt
thick and congested.

He should have risked it, he reflected, as the tickle
became an itch. It was distracting him, and he needed
all the concentration he could muster because there was
more than met the eye behind Fay Falconer's stubborn
strength.

Rather than protest her innocence in words that could
be sifted through and turned about for the truth, the
woman had simply refused to speak at all. Neither bait-
ing, nor reasoning'd had any noticeable effect, and, to
his surprise, he found he could not penetrate her
thoughts with his Seer's abilities.

At first he'd surmised that she might be a latent
Prophet, except that her strength of will carried no sign
of a Seer's defenses. In fact, her shields were unlike any
he'd ever encountered before. Not being a true interrogator, he had little experience with bending another's
will, and he was unsure if—in his present condition—he
could break through hers at all. He was sure, however,

that Gawaina DeKathrine would have no such trouble. She used rather less sophisticated methods.

He pointed this out to the woman and was met with a haughty stare. So much for threatening. There wasn't much left. Coughing hard to clear his lungs, he wrapped his arms about his aching chest and reached out with his mind to try and penetrate her thoughts once again.

Unable to move due to the chains about her, Fay stood and stared defiantly back at this young Priest of the Flame, throwing up her own will against the pressure on her mind. When it eased, she used the moment to marshal her forces and think about her situation.

She'd returned home closer to dawn than to two, and found the house in chaos, with a company of Sword Knights waiting. Knowing what she did had given her plenty of reason to resist them, and the sight of Luis' pale features staring out at her from behind the courtyard wall had given her added strength. Two had fallen to her halberd before they'd finally overwhelmed her.

The last sight of her home had been of Dani's arm pulling Luis down from his perch and away and a great weight had lifted from her shoulders. At least the children were safe. What had happened to Hamlin, Simon, and their Royal charge, she didn't know, but it was obvious her captors didn't either, so she assumed they were also safe. That left only herself in the clutches of the Aristok's murderers. With Essus' help, she prayed, she'd have the strength to resist them.

Pressing her lips together in an expression of scorn, she made her own study of the priest across from her as he studied her.

What she saw was a young blond man, thin and frail, with a sickly air, and dark circles under hazel eyes that were cloudy and unfocused. He frequently pressed a handkerchief against his mouth, and he coughed often. He'd entered the cell as if every muscle in his body ached, and it was clear that he'd not be able to stand for long. A guard had brought him a chair and once he was seated, he and Fay'd had a good, long look at each other. He was not what she'd expected in a Flame Priest and hadn't believed him strong enough to question anyone, until his eyes had met hers. The force of his mind had almost knocked her over. Her own eyes narrowing, she'd thrown up an image of Essus' servant, the white dragon Merrone, to defend her, and it was the priest who'd flinched. Fay won their first encounter. The second was not long in coming.

As the morning wore on, the priest alternately questioned, reasoned, and pressed at her mind with his own. Determined to give him nothing, Fay ignored his words, refusing to be drawn into argument or baited into anger. She couldn't help the occasional reaction to his mention of Simon or the child, but she steadfastly remained silent, and since images of Essus obviously disturbed his concentration she filled her mind with prayers, passages from the Books of Law, and the likeness of each saint she knew.

Sometimes strange, foreign images entered her thoughts. Each time, they seemed to give her strength, so she allowed them to form, believing them to be gifts of Essus. When a particularly fiery impression slapped his mind away, she used the respite to catch her breath. So far she'd won, though that wouldn't last forever. The boy was flagging fast, and she knew that soon enough a stronger priest would replace him. Then she would have to withstand torture both mental and physical, and she prepared herself to face it.

The priest spoke to her again, threatening just that, and she gave him a superior look. Years of guard service had taught her something about guilt and innocence and she sensed something in this young man's demeanor that suggested the weakness of a shameful secret. Since she already knew the Royal Duke was involved, she assumed the same about this ill, young priest, so when she felt his mind thrust at her again she formed one word and spat it back at him with all the power of her faith.
TRAITOR!

Rosarion jerked as if he'd been struck. His eyes went wide, and his mouth opened to form a question; then a serious coughing spell took him and he was unable to speak for a long time. When he finally looked back into her eyes, he saw what she suspected and found himself unable to continue. Ellisander would have to find a different way to gain the knowledge he sought, Rosarion knew then. He, Priest of the Living Flame, and follower of the Duke of Yorbourne, the murderer of Its Vessel, could not penetrate the thoughts of one of Its protectors. It was that simple.

Calling to the guard on duty, he left the cell, the woman's scornful gaze burning a hole between his shoulder blades. Willan was waiting for him and together they returned to the herbarium. Rosarion had a lot to think about, and he wanted to do it in the privacy of his own workshop before the Duke demanded an explanation for his failure.

An hour later he faced Ellisander's fire-washed stare. "You failed?"

Rosarion nodded. "Her mind's too strong for me. I can't breach it."

"You told me you were the strongest Seer in Branbridge."

Expecting this, the Herbalist shrugged. "I am," he answered, "the strongest Seer, not the strongest Interrogator. They're different abilities. I can't get in. I don't have the skill."

"Did you learn anything besides this?"

The question, although sarcastic, was not rhetorical, and, rubbing at his temples, Rosarion took stock of what little he'd been able to learn from Fay's reactions.

"She obviously knows something. She refused to go with the Sword Knights and fought them every step of the way. She even attacked a Flame Champion. When I questioned her, she refused to speak at all, although when I mentioned the child, she couldn't help but react. I don't think she knows where they've gone, though."

"That's of little importance." Ellisander steepled his fingers. "*I* know where they've gone."

Pressing his hand against his mouth, Rosarion stifled a cough. "Have Lysanda and Hadrian turned up anything?" he asked after a moment.

"The professional remains at large. Apparently she boarded the ship, took the Captain's payment, and vanished. Later I want you to scry for her, unless that, too, is a *different* ability?"

"No."

"I shall expect a greater degree of success, then."

Rosarion kept his expression even, though he had little hope that would be the case. The Gods had become involved, that much he was certain of now, and that meant anything was possible.

"As for the others," the Duke continued, "Hadrian's guards botched their job, and one of the murderers is now in custody."

"I know." Rosarion had heard the man's screams two cells away. Fay Falconer had reacted less than he had.

"He knows nothing. As soon as Julianus' people have wrung him dry, he can be given to the mob as a spectacle."

Rosarion shuddered, and the Duke smiled in disdain. "It's all right, you needn't attend."

"Thank you. I've never liked executions."

"No? I find them stimulating."

The herbalist said nothing as a worm of unease began to grow in his stomach.

Ignoring his expression, The Duke steepled his fingers again. "Terrilynne is about to be visited by a contingent from the greatest in the Realm, and Simon of Florenz has a surprise in store for him, too. All the stray chickens will soon be brought back to the roost. I think we're in very good shape. Your Prophecy is coming true, Seer."

Shivering at the cold tone in the other man's voice, Rosarion dropped his gaze and wiped away the beads of perspiration that had sprung up on his face and neck. The image of the fiery tree that Fay Falconer had used to defend herself from his Sight came to mind then and would not be banished. The Prophecy was indeed coming true, he surmised, but what was the Prophecy now?

On the Covenham Road, one of the Prophecy's main players was rubbing at his bare chin in irritation. The skin was sensitive, and the light application of walnut stain Ballentire had dabbed on to darken the pink flesh underneath had caused a rash. With a grimace, Simon lay down beside his father, equally clean shaven for the first time in Simon's life and, ignoring the swaying of the wagon, tried to get some sleep.

Dusk found him up and answering Kassandra's imperious commands. Her reaction to his appearance was surprise, but with the practical selfishness of childhood, she was more interested in when supper would be.

He assured her they'd be stopping soon and that he imagined they'd be having stew. Satisfied, she allowed herself to be tucked in again and soon fell back to sleep.

Sitting by her bedside, Simon stared out the window, and thought of his family. Knowing the itinerary of the Spinning Coins Troupe, Hamlin had arranged with Dani and Luis to bring Fay as soon as possible to Albangate, a town twenty miles north of Branbridge. The largest market town in Branshire, Albangate was the crossroads for three Royal post roads, and was always bustling with visitors bound for the capital or leaving it. The Coins would remain at least two days, plying their trade. It was a good place to meet fellow travelers and listen for rumors.

Staring out at the passing fields, Simon tried to shake off a growing sense of unease. He'd awakened with an anxious feeling that he'd hoped was just motion sickness, but as they reached the outskirts of the village of Barnlow, he began to believe it wasn't. Something very bad had happened.

He left Kassandra's side quietly, and opening the door, climbed out of the slowly moving wagon. Stepping off the road to avoid the last two wagons, he turned and stared back the way they had come. Trees obscured the horizon, but his mind supplied the sight of the spires and towers of Branbridge. The streets would be emptying shortly as dusk sent the citizens to their suppers, but soon enough the taverns would be bustling and the Town Watch would be waiting for the fights to begin. Despite the political upheavals of an Aristok's death, life would go on.

Would things be different now that Leary no longer brightened the night with his fiery gaze and his dangerous smile, Simon wondered? And would he ever be able to walk into a Branbridge public house again without expecting to see the other man playing skeans with some cousin or shouting belligerently at another patron?

He remembered his parents' words to him that last night. Well, he'd kept Leary safe in the streets, but nobody had expected he'd need protecting in his own chapel. Obviously the Living Flame was not so omnipotent as Its priesthood told their parishioners.

A faint rumble of thunder to the east made him glance up at the darkening sky. It looked like a storm was coming. Behind him the last wagon was disappearing around a bend in the road, and Simon hurried to catch up with them.

The feeling of unease remained. As he fell into step with the few Coins still walking, Simon prayed all his family would be safe under cover before the storm broke, but feared that, somehow, it was already too late.

Miles ahead, Luis and Dani, worn out from running, were hiding in a shearing shed just north of the village of Endowne.

They'd barely escaped the knights sent to arrest Fay, darting out the kitchen as the knights were hammering on the workshop door. They'd scrambled over the back wall just in time. They'd watched as Fay returned home to find it occupied by the enemy and knocked down two of her opponents before the neighborhood had erupted into violence. Luis had wanted to join the fight, and it had taken all of Dani's strength to keep him hidden as the Flame Champions scattered the crowd. There were too many of them, she'd hissed in his ear, her fists balled up in the fabric of his tunic. They had to find Hamlin and Simon. The boy had finally agreed.

Their last sight of their home was of their neighbor, Fay's cat held tightly in her arms, cautiously approaching the broken kitchen door. Together the two youths slipped out of Branbridge, clambering over a crumbling section of the city's west wall. Then they'd simply run until they couldn't run any more.

They left the city's outlying villages about noon, keeping mostly to the side of the road and scurrying behind whatever cover they could find when they heard horses or carts approaching. Twice it had been Royal Heralds, once a huge company of armed knights, but they'd remained unseen and had continued their journey when the dust had settled.

They'd eaten eggs stolen from a dovecote and drunk from a stream, but dusk found them shivering and too nervous to travel farther at night. Unwilling to risk sleeping in Endowne in case their descriptions were known, Dani broke a shutter on a shearing shed outside of town, and they'd buried themselves in the bales of soft wool.

Luis began to sniffle and Dani held him close, whispering that they would find Hamlin and everything would be all right. They were only ten miles from Albangate. Surely the Coins would be there when they arrived tomorrow.

She tried to believe it herself, ignoring the little girl inside who wanted to cry, too. She had to be strong for Luis, she told herself firmly. She was older.

Tucking him into the crook of her arm, she began to sing a lullaby her mother had taught her, and after a time, they both slept.

The night brought a cold, spring storm. Lightning flashed across the sky in streaks of white and red. Street Seers and Hedge Seers said the Gods were walking in the clouds and predicted dire results in the future. Those who believed shut themselves into their homes, invoking whatever charms they held dear to preserve themselves from danger. Those who didn't believe locked themselves in as well, either from fear of the storm, or of the wrath of Triarctic Knights.

Cradled in its protective cover, Dani and Luis slept undisturbed all through the night and awakened early to a beautiful dawn.

After a short walk, they came upon a farm, and Luis stole them a breakfast from the pig's trough while Dani held its owner off with a stick. They barely managed to outrun the angry swine, but the food saved filled their stomachs and they set off walking again.

Simon and Hamlin, hidden in Turi's wagon, spent the morning trying to distract the new Aristok, rested and rapidly growing bored with her bed. And in the dungeons of the Flame Temple, Fay Falconer ate the bread provided and wondered about the dream she'd had. The white dragon, Merrone, holding her family in its claws, had swooped over her and headed into the warmth of the sun.

It gave her comfort after the long night, so lifting her head, she spoke the morning's invocation, her voice loud and confident, the blessed words of Essus, her challenge to her Triarctic captors.

In the cell two doors down, another prisoner heard her through a haze of pain and drew strength from the ancient ritual. He'd served his God. That would have to be enough for his life. With a long, drawn-out breath, he died.

Mean Marta 783 DR

In the chapel of the Holy Triarchy Cathedral, the setting sun cast multihued reflections through the west windows, and the old man wiped a surreptitious tear from his eye as he finished the figure of the lone murderer. After a moment's pause, he painted a series of white droplets around him to represent Essus, then scrutinized the day's work. The three coins spun above the figures of himself, Hamlin, and the child, while a dark cloud hovered above Fay and the others. The reds and whites of the two Gods made a cradling form about them all, and he nodded in satisfaction.

The second panel was finished, depicting the first day of Kassandra the Sixth's reign. Almost all the principal players had been ready that day, poised to take the stage for Act Two. There'd been only one missing. Terrilynne DeMarian.

Turning, the old man cast his gaze over the blank wall to his left. That was tomorrow's work, he told himself. Before dawn, Kora would be hard at work laying the plaster for him, but for now, it was time to quit.

Carefully easing himself down from the scaffolding, he stared up at the day's panel again. The light was fading, bringing up some colors and muting others. Like his memories, he reflected; some remembered as brilliantly as if they'd happened that day; others soft and worn like an old quilt.

Oh, go to supper, he snorted, *you're getting maudlin.*

Groaning with the stiffness in his legs, he rubbed his locket between finger and thumb, then turned and hobbled from the chapel. With luck Kora and Shale had saved him something to eat, although he hadn't much hope.

Left behind, the shadows flitted about the newly painted images, and in the corner by the altar a deeper shadow waited patiently for the story to continue.

7. Terrilynne

Spring, Dunleyshire, Heathland, 737 DR

On the roads, Branion patrols began to make their presence known again, and in the towns, Heaths—Armistones and Crosers mostly—met in secret in barns and taverns to plan this season's response to the invaders of their land. At Caerockeith Castle masons and carpenters swarmed about the keep, repairing the winter's damage, while the garrison shook off the winter's lethargy with widened patrols and extra guard duty.

In a disused corral to the west of the castle's main gate, two figures did battle, the sound of their swords ringing against each other echoing in the still afternoon air. The one figure was gray-haired, heavyset, and muscular, the scars on his arms and torso betraying his long familiarity with the sword. The other was of a height, but slimmer and younger, with copper hair and flame-washed eyes narrowed in concentration.

The veins standing out on his neck, the man brought his sword whistling down toward his attacker's head. The other met the blade with her own, using the strength in her wrists to bring the heavy two-handed broadsword up in a tight arc.

The weapons met with a crash that reverberated down the blades, and both combatants grunted from the force of it. The woman was the first to recover. With a leftward cut, she brought her sword sweeping around, her blade catching the other's and knocking it almost effortlessly from his hands. In a moment it was over. As the sword went spinning off, the man stepped back, and the woman dropped her point.

"A good bout, Eddie."

Lieutenant Eddison Croft grimaced in reply and went to retrieve his fallen sword.

Terrilynne DeMarian, Duke of Kempston, cousin to the Aristok, now second in line to the Throne of Branion, grinned at his sour expression and gestured to her squire.

The girl came running with a bucket.

The Duke fished out a ladle of water and drank thirstily as she squinted up at the bright sun.

By the Flame, it was a warm one today, she reflected.

Refilling the ladle, she poured it over her head, then after tossing it back into the bucket, held out the sword.

"Alex, take this over to Piper and have him sharpen it."

The squire, her own copper hair and flame-touched eyes marking her as a DeMarian, accepted the broadsword with a grin of anticipation. She turned to leave immediately, then stopped at a gesture from the older woman.

"Just deliver it and come right back."

"But, Terri . . ."

"No." The Duke's hand chopped down. "I need you this afternoon. You can watch Eli work later."

"Yes, Cousin."

"Find Amanda and get her patrol reports. I'll be in the keep . . . somewhere."

"Yes, Cousin."

"And tell Maia I want Lightfoot and Dusty saddled in an hour for Dunley Vale. Wear light armor. Have Lily lay out mine."

"Yes, Cousin."

Alex was anxious to be gone, and finally the Duke dismissed her. The girl left the corral at a dead run, and Terrilynne watched her go with a smile. Eli Haven was her Stablemaster's oldest son and the Armorer, Piper Oakes' apprentice. Blond, sixteen, and well-muscled, he was the focus of a number of the youths' attentions, and if Alexius DeMarian was missing, you could lay odds that she was seated on a barrel in the smithy watching him work. Terrilynne shook her head. Even when she'd been that young, she'd never been that young.

Turning, she accepted Eddison's salute, then leaned against the fence.

"The Flame's passing has left its mark," she noted.

Wiping the sweat from his face, Eddison tossed his tunic onto the fence before fishing a ladle of water out for himself.

"You're stronger, Captain, yes," he acknowledged, "but you're also more distracted. I almost had you there a couple of times."

"It takes some getting used to."

"We should practice again later."

"Tomorrow. I have to go to Dunley Vale this afternoon to threaten the Mayor. Sasha reports a group of cloaked figures skulking about the town last night."

"Heaths?"

"Who else? It's springtime, and sedition's sprouting as fast as the crops."

Eddison snorted. "The Mayor's in it up to his arse, you know."

"It hardly matters," she answered with a shrug. "He's a cowardly dog. I'll rattle my sword at him, and he'll behave for a while."

"But for how long, Captain?" The Lieutenant asked gravely. "With the Aristok dead and all this uncertainty over the Ascension, the Heaths are bound to take advantage."

Terrilynne made a dismissive gesture. "We'll do what we can. We may not even be here next season anyway. If Ellisander takes the Throne this summer, we'll be guarding the middens at Midges Castle in Kormandeux a month later."

"Migard."

"Whatever."

Pulling his tunic over his head, Eddison grimaced as the damp cloth settled against his skin. "You think the child is dead, then, Captain?"

"Don't you?"

"Yes, I suppose I do," he sighed. With three small children of his own—who had him wrapped about their little fingers—Eddison was known to be a soft touch.

Running a hand through his graying hair, he glanced sideways at the Duke, trying to gauge her mood. Terrilynne DeMarian's feud with her Continental cousin was well known, and most of the company was laying odds they'd be marching on Branbridge this summer. So far, though, she hadn't made her plans known to them.

"It does seem suspicious," Eddison commented. "The Aristok *and* his Heir dead or missing at the same time and only the Duke of Yorbourne there to take command."

"It does at that."

They stood quietly for a moment, the silence broken only by the sound of children's laughter in the distance. Finally Eddison stirred.

"Do you think Yorbourne engineered it, Captain?"

Tipping up her head, the Duke of Kempston stared at the castle walls for a long time before answering.

"Yes."

"What are we going to do?"

"Nothing." She continued to stare up at the walls, her expression pensive. "Nothing for the moment."

"But . . ." Eddison paused, unsure of how to voice the company's fears. "If Yorbourne's plotted murder once, he's bound to again, Captain."

Terrilynne nodded absently, her attention obviously focused elsewhere.

"Captain?"

The Duke's eyes cleared.

"Shouldn't we at least plan for defense?"

She nodded. "Of course; against both Ellisander and the Heaths, as always, Lieutenant."

He looked unconvinced but accepted his Lord's words with a resigned nod, recognizing the dismissal as Terrilynne was already moving away.

"If you see Amanda, tell her I'm in the keep," she said over her shoulder.

"Yes, Captain."

He saluted automatically, but the Duke was through the corral gate and striding toward the castle without looking back.

Eddison watched her go with a worried frown.

He'd known the young DeMarian Duke all her life. He'd served her mother before her, and like her mother, Terrilynne was a deep one, thinking through a problem thoroughly before acting and keeping her thoughts to herself until the last minute. She rarely asked for council or advice, and when she did, she rarely responded to the giver. She simply made her decision, gave her orders, and expected them to be obeyed.

Usually her strategies were sound. Eddison had fought with her in Roland two years ago and marched beside her into that province's capital city less than a month later. This time, however, she was up against an older, wilier opponent, a DeMarian himself. The most dangerous of the family, Eddison believed.

Scratching at a scar that only acted up when he was worried, the Lieutenant frowned. Terrilynne would move in her own good time, and no amount of advice, nagging, or worrying would change that. Her officers would still try, though, until that fiery gaze grew dark, telling them all that they pushed too far. Then they would back off, waiting impatiently for their Lord's slow progress toward action. It had brought them victory in the past. Eddison hoped this time would be no exception. But he supposed they would find out soon enough. Worrying would do no good and he had work of his own to finish. With a sigh, he, too, left the corral.

As she walked across the outer compound, the Duke of Kempston kept half an eye on the work going on around her. Making for the castle drawbridge, she absently noted the industry of each of her people, but her mind was elsewhere.

Her conversation with Eddison had made her thoughtful. She'd had much the same words with Amanda De-Kathrine and Gladys DeLlewellynne, her two senior knights, and with Yvonnia and Lauren, her Companions. Ellisander would move, they all knew it, and they all wanted to face him now, but now was not the time. Terrilynne knew her cousin as much as she disliked him. He would move, but not now, not yet. He had to consolidate his position in Branbridge first, allay any suspicions, and bring the noble families under his command.

Terrilynne glared at nothing, and a passing guard ducked nervously out of her line of sight. As Eddie had said, it was strange about Kassandra, she reflected, noting the man's movement without comment. The child's disappearance so soon after the father's death put suspicion on Ellisander, and if he was guilty—as all of Terrilynne's people believed him to be—it was poor strategy. That wasn't like him. As much as Terrilynne despised her Continental cousin, she had to admit he was thorough, as was Terrilynne herself. That no one in the capital seemed to be as instantly suspicious as she and her company was not surprising. They'd always sucked up to Ellisander in the past. But he'd want to be certain. He had Branbridge at his back as she had Heathland, and both must be secured first.

Her gaze moving automatically to the hazy hills in the distance, she wondered how many eyes were turned in Caerockeith's direction now that spring was here. There would be little action until the planting was done and the roads had hardened, but after that, with the Aristok dead and the Living Flame without a consecrated Vessel, the Essusiate Heaths would take advantage of Branion's weakness, as would the Gallians, the Bachiemens, and the Panishans. It would be a smaller Realm, no doubt, by the end of the year.

An idea began to make itself known in its slow way, and Terrilynne let it grow, neither dismissing it, nor scrutinizing it too closely. Passing under the raised portcullis, she accepted the salute of the gate guards and moved toward the storehouse, a low, stone building across the inner compound.

Moments later, her thoughts were interrupted by a band of screaming children led by Jael Asher, Jade Asher's six-year-old scamp of a son. They came racing out from the west barracks and barely managed to avoid running her down. Rocking to a halt, Jael mouthed an apology as the others piled up behind him.

The Duke held the boy in a long, steady stare, then jerked her head in dismissal. As one, the children disappeared through the gate, and Terrilynne allowed herself half a smile. Jael had spirit. He'd make a good soldier some day if he wasn't drowned in the moat or crushed by a horse first. Chuckling, she continued on her way, ducking under the storehouse's low doorway a minute later.

It was dark and cool inside and the Duke paused to

let her eyes adjust to the light and listen to two upraised voices coming from the far room. Lauren, her Second Companion, and Gerron Reed, the Company Quartermaster; from the sound of it, arguing forcibly.

They broke off as Terrilynne entered.

"Problem?" she asked pleasantly.

Gerron scowled and shoved one finger under the patch over his left eye to scratch at it. "No *problem*, Capt'n," he said stiffly, "jus' no buggerin' tile to fix the buggerin' stable roofs, and Icarus has been on my buggerin' arse all morning."

Terrilynne snorted. Icarus Haven was the most unobtrusive of men. He'd likely only mentioned it to Gerron once over breakfast, however, that would have been enough to send her touchy Quartermaster off into a rage.

"Don't we have spare tile in the west tower?"

"We did," Lauren interjected smoothly before Gerron could reply, "but we used it repairing the roof of the main hall last autumn."

"Waste of buggerin' tiles!" The Quartermaster spat at the wall.

"Hm." Terrilynne took the offered supply roster and glanced over it. "Any in Dunley Vale?"

The others shook their heads simultaneously.

"Then send to Carisley for some. Zavier owes me. In the meantime, take some from the west barracks and move people into the east until you can patch the holes with wooden tiles temporarily."

Gerron gave a crooked-toothed grin. "Guilcove won't like it. Puttin' archers an' their ilk in with her precious Knights."

"I'll speak with Amanda. Just do it."

"My pleasure, Capt'n. Kyle! Kyle Terron Reed, get yerself in here! Drat him, he's always underfoot when I don't want him and gone when I do."

While Gerron went in search of his missing son-come-assistant, Terrilynne leafed through the supply roster.

Lauren made a show of moving a few jars around, then looked up.

"Any new word from Branbridge?" she asked casually.

"Not since the first Herald."

"It's odd that you weren't summoned."

"It's not at all odd." Terrilynne glanced over at the other woman. "The last thing they need is another De-Marian cluttering up the place."

"Shouldn't the priests have learned who murdered the Aristok by now?"

"I don't think it's that simple."

Noting the mouse droppings beside the grain bags, Terrilynne turned with a distracted frown. "It could have been anyone," she continued. "Plenty had cause to wish him dead, and any number might have had the means. He never took proper precautions."

"Neither do you," Lauren pointed out.

"I haven't needed to."

"You're next in line."

"*After* Ellisander."

"And that makes you even more vulnerable now than you were before."

"Nonsense. Ellisander will probably hold power this summer, and he'll want me as far away from him as possible. That could mean Gallia, Danelind, anywhere."

"The Shadow Realm," the Companion said quietly, her brown eyes concerned.

"I'm not that easy to kill."

"What if he orders you to Branbridge without the company?"

"He has no reason to." Terrilynne's voice was becoming annoyed. "Listen to me, Lauren. He has *no* authority. When I go to Branbridge, I will go in state as befitting my rank, and that means with a large, armed escort." She took the other woman in her arms. "So stop worrying."

"He'd have the authority to strip you of that escort if he were Aristok," the Companion answered stubbornly, "and you just said he'll soon hold power in Branbridge."

Terrilynne released her. "What would you have me do, Lauren? Accuse him of regicide? We have no proof. Challenge his right to the Throne? He's next in line, and he has the Knightly Orders and the Flame Priests backing him up. We'd lose."

"He murdered the Aristok and probably the Prince Kassandra."

"We don't know that."

The Companion merely glanced at her and the Duke gave a resigned shrug. "All right, we have a pretty good idea, but we still have no proof," she repeated. "Nobody's going to believe me if I start shouting regicide. Everyone knows Ellisander and I hate each other. They'll just see it as a play for the Throne."

"Well, maybe you should *make* a play for the Throne."

"Enough. Without proof it's treason."

Returning, Gerron caught the Duke's last words and grimaced. "Easy enough to get proof," he offered.

"What?" Terrilynne turned a scowl on her Quartermaster.

"I said, it's easy enough to get proof . . . Capt'n."

"And how do you plan on doing that, pluck it from the Shadow Realm?"

"No." He scratched beneath the eyepatch again. "We was thinkin' of something a little more practical."

"We?"

"Well, me an' the others, yer Commanders, an' yer Companions, Capt'n."

The Duke stared at him a moment, then shook her head, more bemused then angry.

"So you're all in league against me, are you?"

Recognizing the tone, he grinned slyly at her. "Not as such, Capt'n, no, but most of us figure if Yorbourne takes the Throne, he's gonna move against ye sooner or later. He hates ye, an' yer a threat to him."

"And your suggestion?"

Ignoring the sarcastic tone, he waved toward Lauren. "Get some of her an' Yvonnia's Guild to snoop about for ye. Yorbourne has a Companion hisself, don't he?"

Lauren nodded.

"I'll think about it," the Duke answered. "In the meantime, before you start planning to get me executed, do you mind if we get on with the business of securing Dunleyshire first?"

Recognizing that he'd get no further, Gerron nodded his acquiescence. Lauren also agreed to leave the subject for now, although the set of her jaw suggested that it would be pursued again later.

That settled, the three of them then turned their attention to the meager supplies of food stores left over from the winter.

An hour later, armed and armored, the Duke of Kempston left the castle flanked by two mounted knights and followed by Alexius. Lightfoot had been exercised regularly that week by Dane Haven and was in a placid mood, so Terrilynne pointed the bay toward town and let her mind turn to the problem of her cousin. Beside her, the others recognized her mood and kept silent.

In the past, the DeMarian line had been straight and true, Terrilynne reflected. These days the family was larger, covering several branches, the main split being the lines of Marsellus the Second and Drusus. Brothers over one hundred years before, Drusus had ascended the throne at Marsellus' death, bypassing his elder brother's firstborn, as was the Essusiate custom concerning bastards.

He hadn't held the throne long. Gwynnethian-born, Triarch-raised, Atreus the Third had knocked him from the Throne and sent him running back to the Continent where he'd sired the line that had culminated in Klairinda and Kether DeMarian, mothers of the late Aristok and his Consort Kathrine. And of Ellisander.

The Living Flame flowed through the truest DeMarian line. Ellisander DeMarian, progeny of several of those lines brought together through marriage and intermarriage, had the strongest claim next to his cousin-come-niece, Kassandra, and after that came the other descendants of Marsellus the Second and his various lovers. The Flame Priests had assured Terrilynne this was so, and to be honest, she'd never quite cared. Descended from Flairalynne DeMarian, daughter of Marsellus the Second and Jessandra DeLynne, a Knight of the Sword, the Duke of Kempston had inherited her great-grandmother's tenacity, pragmatism, and practicality. Holding Dunleyshire had been enough to content her, even though she knew it had been an appointment made to keep her and Ellisander apart.

She'd recognized the wisdom of the move even then,

for the two third cousins had hated each other on sight. Ellisander had seen her as a threat to his power base and she in turn had mistrusted his motives, but he was the beloved brother of Marsellus' beloved wife and he could do no wrong. Keeping them apart had probably saved one of their lives.

Crossing the red sandstone bridge that spanned the narrow River Nyth, the Duke glared at the passing scenery as the afternoon sun caused red spots to dance before her flame-touched gray eyes.

She was still getting used to the new sensations she'd inherited with the passing of the Flame. Four days ago, she'd suddenly become unaccountably flushed and irritable. She'd just assumed her flows were coming early. Yesterday evening when a Royal Herald had arrived, worn out from fifty straight hours in the saddle, she'd learned the truth. Marsellus the Third was dead.

Seated in the castle's main hall where she'd received her, Terrilynne had stared silently at the mud-spattered woman.

"Dead?"
Breathing heavily, the Herald nodded.
"Yes, My Lord. Murdered three days ago as he communed with the Living Flame in his chapel."
Even flat from fatigue her voice still carried an undercurrent of outrage, and Terrilynne nodded as she gestured to Alexius.
"Fetch our guest a drink, Your Grace."
The girl moved to obey, her eyes wide.
"Please go on . . . uh . . ."
"Wrendolynne, My Lord."
"Wrendolynne."
"The Flame Priests have uncovered an Essusiate plot, My Lord, and many arrests were being made when I departed. Also, I am charged with telling you, My Lord, that Prince Kassandra, now the Aristok, is missing, believed kidnapped and perhaps murdered by the selfsame plotters.

Terrilynne's face had betrayed none of the suspicion that had suddenly leaped to mind upon hearing these

words. The Herald's features had also been professionally impassive, so the Duke had merely indicated politely
that she continue; however, that had been the end of her
message. The Duke of Kempston's presence was neither
required in the capital, nor was any reply expected. The
Parliament that Marsellus had called had been canceled.

Officially sent by the Hierarchpriest of Cannonshire,
Terrilynne had sensed Ellisander's influence behind
these words. She'd made no reaction to either statement,
merely thanked the other woman and ordered a meal
and a bed prepared for her.

The Herald had left this morning before dawn on a
new mount accompanied by Eaglelynne, Terrilynne's
own personal Herald. Rhys DeLlewellynne, Gladys'
nephew and squire had left five hours earlier, charged
with discovering as much as possible in as little time as
possible and returning immediately. He would be several
days. Sent officially, Eaglelynne would be a good deal
longer as the College of Heralds would determine what
information he returned with.

Drumming her fingers on her saddlehorn, Terrilynne
let Lightfoot find her own way through the collection of
small cottages that made up the village of Mosswell
where the families of most of her people lived. Absently
accepting the salutes of those off duty, she then turned
her mounted party onto the north road to Dunley Vale,
and letting the bay have her head once more, she returned her thoughts to Branbridge.

Like the Herald, her anger was directed more at the
perpetrators of heresy than of regicide. She'd been no
closer to Marsellus than any other of his DeMarian vassals and had not been particularly grief-stricken upon
hearing of his death. She'd sworn her oath of fealty to
him when she'd reached her majority, then gone on to
bring him victory in Gallia and Panisha. It had earned
her more lands and a seat on his Council, but when
Marsellus had married his Cousin Kathrine and met her
brother Ellisander, all those in Branion had been forgotten, slighted, or ignored.

Terrilynne had watched Ellisander coldly use the
power the Aristok's favor had brought with it to place
himself between Marsellus and all his Councillors. Then

after Kathrine's death of white lung, the Aristok would take solace from none save her brother, and Ellisander's coup had been complete.

Terrilynne had managed to ignore most of his machinations with the pragmatic patience she was known for until last Braniana's Day when she'd finally lost her temper. It had shocked everyone except those who'd known the young Duke well. Unfortunately it had also warned Ellisander that he had an enemy in his Cousin Terrilynne.

The Duke of Kempston had regretted that outburst. It gave the Duke of Yorbourne an edge.

A change in Lightfoot's walk brought her up from her reverie, and Alexius took the opportunity to point out the spires of Dunley Vale's Essusiate Church just visible over the trees. Terrilynne nodded and returned to her musing.

She had approximately forty-five troops she could put into the field immediately, mostly foot soldiers with some archers to support her six mounted knights, and she could raise another seventy-five from Kempston. The difficulty was that her coastal Dukedom was far to the south, making troop movement awkward and time-consuming. If she were going to challenge Ellisander, her people would have to be summoned soon and brought secretly by ship. Terrilynne had ships, what she didn't have was much time.

Her younger brother, Albion—just come into his knighthood—could, if convinced, bring another fifty from his Earldom of Wakeford which was closer. That made approximately one hundred and seventy-five altogether. Nowhere near enough to make a serious assault on Ellisander, whose Dukedom of Yorbourne was between herself and his base at Branbridge, although a preliminary attack against Yorbourne itself was an enticing option. But first she needed more troops. There were a number of Branion Lords, like her cousin Zavier, who might throw in with her if they were approached properly, and there were always paid mercenaries from Danelind or Sorlandy who could be hired. The most audacious idea presenting itself with several problems, although none that couldn't be ironed out in time. It was worth considering, so Terrilynne tucked it into the back of her mind to study later.

Now, as they passed the first houses of Dunley Vale, she urged Lightfoot into a gallop. It was time to make a show of might.

Scattering chickens before them, the four Branion riders reined up in the center of town. The Mayor was waiting for them on the steps of the town hall, having been warned of their arrival, and with a warmth he did not feel, and they did not believe, ushered them inside.

Three hundred miles away, on the banks of the Green river, east of Albangate, the Spinning Coins Tumbling Troupe went about the afternoon's performances. Some fought mock battles with various oversized kitchen utensils, others did acrobatics or practiced snatches of bawdy poetry or songs. The village children raced around them, refused admittance only to the six wagons parked in a tight circle off to one side.

In the center of the wagons, Ballentire was juggling with a set of unlit torches and arguing with Simon, while Warrin Fire-Eater kept a close watch on the surrounding area.

"We can't move any faster, Sy. This is our livelihood you're talking about," the Troupe Leader said irritably.

"Twenty-one stops between here and Dunleyshire? It'll take all summer." Seated on a blanket, the artist was sketching in an old book he'd left with the Coins last year. Kassandra was standing beside him throwing a pair of small red balls into the air. Now and then one would bounce off into the grass and Warrin would fetch it back for her.

At first Simon had been afraid of letting her out where she might be seen, but the child would not be confined and in the end, he'd given up.

Now, with her auburn hair cut short and dyed brown with the same walnut stain that darkened his own features, a nondescript gray tunic, and a liberal smearing of dirt, Kassandra the Sixth looked no different than any other grubby tumbler's child. The only concern was her eyes. Simon hoped he could keep strangers at least far enough away that they'd not see them.

Kassandra had been enchanted with the disguise and had immediately demanded to be taught the trade of tumbler's apprentice. So far she'd learned how to somersault backward and forward in a muddy field, how to steal treats from Turi's wagon—where she'd gone to be patched up after somersaulting into a nettle bush—and how to avoid being kicked by a horse under whose belly she'd crawled to retrieve one of her juggling balls.

The whole thing was giving Simon palpitations, and it was only their second day with the Troupe.

Still concentrating on her juggling, Ballentire shook her head, her black hair flopping over the strip of cloth she wore bound about her temples.

"The itinerary's bare bones now," she retorted. "Some of those stops are major towns. It would look burning strange if we just raced on through them."

"Hayward?" Simon's opinion of the small hamlet as a major town was obvious and she grinned.

"It's traditionally generous."

"And Moleshil?"

"That's Tam's birthplace. Listen, Sy, it's the best I can do. If you don't like it, strike out on your own."

"Bal, they won't juggle proper!" Kassandra banged one of the balls down on the blanket in frustration and glared up at the Troupe Leader.

Ballentire laughed. "Patience, Your Majesty. You won't learn it overnight."

"But I've been practicing forever an' it hasn't got any better!"

"Well, I suppose I should tell you the truth." She looked furtively about. "It's because you don't know the ancient trade secrets."

"What?" Kassandra's expression became affronted. "Do you know them?"

Flipping the torches rapidly through the air without watching them, Ballentire grinned. "I might know one or two."

"Then teach me!"

"Teach you?" The Troupe Leader fell back in mock horror, the torches tumbling to the ground about her feet. "Teach the Aristok the most guarded secrets of my profession? The secrets that have been passed down from one master to another since the time of Jamarchanderian the Dextrous of Shammeria? The secrets that no outsider has ever been privileged to learn, not even Atreus the Second, the greatest patron of the Arts in the history of Branion?"

Kassandra laughed. "Yes, teach me! I wanna juggle, too! I won't tell anyone else. Not even Simon. An' I'm gonna be a greater patron then ever Atreus was, really."

"Well . . ." Ballentire looked troubled. "There are occasional exceptions to every rule, I suppose. And if you were going to be an extra special great patron . . ."

"Bal . . ." Simon said warningly.

"You must promise the most serious promise ever to never tell anyone what we show you," she continued, ignoring him.

"I promise," Kassandra said eagerly. "I promise on . . . uh . . ." She sucked one finger for a moment. "I promise on the pony Terri's gonna get me!"

She smiled triumphantly. Ballentire gave a dramatic bow, and Simon rolled his eyes.

"Then your wish is my humble command, Your Majesty." Stooping to pick up the torches, the Troupe Leader gestured for Kassandra to come and stand beside her.

"Now you must place your feet like so . . ." She crossed her feet at the ankles.

"No, you don't!"

"You don't?"

"No!"

"Oh, yes, that's right, you place them like so . . ." Ballentire untangled herself and planted her feet on the grass. The child copied her promptly.

"Now you close your eyes . . ."

"You do not!"

"You're sure?"

"Yes!" The child scowled up at her fiercely. "Wait, I know why you're not teaching it right. Simon?"

The Artist looked up from his sketchbook where he was adding Kassandra into the picture. "Yes, Your Majesty?"

"Go away."

"Go away?"

"Yes. Bal can't teach me the ancient trade secrets if you're here, so go away."

With the Troupe Leader smirking beside her, Kassandra waited as Simon rose.

"I guess I'll leave then, I mean, if I'm not wanted," he said woefully.

"You are wanted, jus' not right here, an' not right now." Chewing on her finger, she smiled suddenly. "I'm thirsty. Please be so good as to fetch me a drink, Your Grace."

He grinned despite himself. "Your Grace?"

"Well, that's what Papa always said when he was trying to be nice, an' I'm trying to be nice." She stamped her foot, her tone suggesting that she wouldn't be trying for much longer.

He hid a smile as he bowed. "Of course, Your Majesty. I shall leave at once. You'll keep an eye on things here, Bal?"

She nodded, and Simon headed off, his sketchbook tucked under one arm, his eyes scanning the area for strangers.

As he passed between two wagons, he turned to watch as, with much silliness, Ballentire attempted to teach the impatient, five-year-old head of the Branion Realm to juggle without knocking herself on the head with a wooden practice ball. With a chuckle, Simon went in search of her drink.

At the far end of the field, two youths emerged from the trees. They were tired and dirty and seemed somewhat disoriented until they spotted the brightly painted wagons. Then they stumbled forward, the one supporting the other.

At the sight of them, a player came forward suspiciously, but when they made themselves known, he brought them to Ballentire's wagon at a run.

Moments later, Hamlin, his face white, found Simon who was trying without success to find a jug of unfermented cider.

"Son," he said, his voice thick. "They have your mother."

The three cloaked figures paused at the edge of the Flame Temple grounds, the one in front holding up a hand to halt the others. When she was sure the area before them was empty of guards or priests, she motioned them forward.

It was high summer 731 DR. Marsellus the Third was to wed Kathrine DeMarian of Bryholm in less than one week; Simon of Florenz had been in Branbridge for four months and Leary DeMarian was in his prime, sixteen years old and able to drink and carouse until dawn, night after riotous night.

This particular night the moon was a glowing crescent in a cloudless sky, and after an evening at the Fattened Goose Tavern in Westonborough, Leary decided he must see the preparations for the wedding at the Holy Triarchy Cathedral.

Simon was not at all sure this was a good idea, but his friend was adamant. They'd be accompanied by a drinking comrade of Leary's, a Flame Temple guard—retired after one too many drunken nights on duty—who knew the surroundings well. It must be done in secret and it must be done tonight.

Holy Triarchy was situated on the grounds of the Flame Temple and they came upon it from the north where the border between its lands and Collin's Park was marked by a line of young oak trees. Their horses were tethered here, far enough behind to keep them from being heard and close enough for a quick escape should the adventurers be discovered. All part of Leary's dramatics.

The unfinished Cathedral was entered easily enough; one small side door was always left unlocked for the faithful. Deserted at this time of night, however, it provided little sport.

Leaning against the main altar, Leary expressed his disgust with characteristic bluntness.

"This is a buggering bore! Don't you have anything better to offer, Moll?"

Simon snorted, easing himself down into a seated position, his back resting against the multihued Pillar of

Flame. *"You were the one who wanted to see it,"* he reminded the other man.

"Don't be impertinent, or I'll have your head on a trencher. I want some action."

"Perhaps you'd like a tour of the Flame Temple, sir," Moll said, a sloppy grin on her face. *"I know a secret way in."*

"A secret way in?" Leary's expression was doubtful, and she nodded eagerly.

"Well, more a secret way out," she amended. *"Some of the others and I used to use it to, uh, leave now and again, to facilitate the, uh . . ."*

"The, uh . . . desertion of your post?" Simon offered.

"Yes. That's right." She smiled carelessly.

Leary gave a barking laugh and waved his hand. *"Then lead on, Moll. It sounds like fun."*

The Flame Temple was an ancient structure, built on the ruins of an even older, pre-Triarctic site. Begun by Bran Bendigeid in the last years of his life, it had taken thirty years to complete, and been overseen by a dozen different architects. Thus, the front was magnificent, the four great wings somewhat sprawling, and the adjoining areas haphazardly cobbled together.

In one such alcove, overgrown with weeds, there was a small, bricked-up doorway. They halted as Leary, cursing roundly, decapitated a thistle head stuck to his breeches. Then Moll began to quietly remove the bricks one by one, bits of mortar falling away as she worked.

"You're sure this way is unguarded?" Simon asked.

"Of course I'm sure," Moll retorted with drunken confidence. *"Almost no one knows about it anymore. Most think it's bricked up, and those that did use it are all gone now."* She wiped away a tear. *"Ah, here we are."*

With the removal of one last brick, she'd cleared an area about two feet around, and one after another, they squeezed through.

It was very dark inside and Moll opened her lantern a crack.

"The infirmary's up there," she said as they began to descend a crumbling set of stone steps. *"This used to be*

the entrance to the dying room in Octavia's time. It was closed up after the plague outbreak in 344."

"Plague?" Simon's voice was unimpressed.

"Well, it was over four hundred years ago," she answered. "I'm sure there's no plague left."

"But there are rats." At the bottom of the steps, Leary kicked out and connected with one of the small, red-eyed creatures. There was a resentful squeak and the sounds of scrambling, then silence.

Turning, Simon could just make out his friend's own eyes, burning crimson in the lantern light, and looked away, suddenly uncomfortable with the comparison.

Sensing his thoughts, Leary gave an amused chuckle, before gesturing for Moll to keep going.

They followed a dank-smelling passageway, past the barred doors of the old dying room and around a sunken area that dripped with moisture from above. Easing between the base of two large pillars, Moll placed a finger to her lips and pointed up as she gestured them through.

Leary didn't bother to look, but, glancing up, Simon saw a dim light spilling through a rusted grate above their heads.

After turning a corner, Moll crouched on a pile of rubble and pulled out a hip flask.

"What was all that about," Simon asked.

"The Temple dungeons," she answered with a shudder. "Nothing to recommend them unless you like the sound of screaming."

"Does that happen often?"

"Oh, yes." She tipped the flask up and took a long swallow. "The Seer Priests can just reach in and . . ." She made a yanking motion. "But torture softens 'em up, especially if the prisoner's Essusiate. I stood guard in the dungeons for years. Lousy duty. Enough to drive you to drink."

"As if you needed an excuse," Leary snorted. "Retiring was too good for you. You should have been hanged."

"The Aristok pardoned me," she answered smugly.

"You groveled well."

"Can we get on with it, please."

The two turned to Simon. "I'm cold," he said. "And this isn't much of an adventure."

"True," Leary admitted. *"Lead on, Moll. I expected to peek in on at least one fornication this night, and so far I am highly disappointed."*

"The sleeping quarters are above us now," Moll answered, *"but the walls and floors are too thick to hear much. The middens are this way, though, and they're a different story altogether."*

She led the way down a tight corridor which became increasingly pungent as they went. Just as Simon was about to suggest a retreat for air, they came to a crumbling wall.

"If you place your ear just here," Moll whispered, *"you can hear people talking, or doing . . . other things."*

She grinned as Leary tipped his head up.

"Other things?"

"Use your imagination, sir."

"You're not going to touch your face to that, are you?" Simon asked in disgust. *"You'll get some hideous disease."*

"Of course I'm not.' Leary retorted indignantly. *"I'm going to use Moll's hat."*

Later, after standing there for an hour, eavesdropping on the Flame Priests bodily functions, Leary pronounced himself bored and they made their way back past the dungeon grate, the dying room, and out.

Simon was relieved to see the stars again. Quiet most of the way back to the palace, he turned over Moll's words concerning the Essusiate prisoners and wondered how he could broach the subject later so that the Aristok might do something to change that.

"No, Son. I won't allow it."

Gathered in Ballentire's wagon, the others had just heard Simon's shortened narrative of that evening's adventure and Hamlin was shaking his head vehemently.

"You need to stay here and protect Kassandra. I'll go."

It was Simon's turn to shake his head.

"You don't know the way, Pa. I do."

"You can give me directions."

"It was pitch-dark *five* years ago. I might be able to

find the way again, maybe, if I walked it, but I couldn't tell someone else how to find it.

"It might be bricked up by now, anyway" he added.

"I don't care." Hamlin was adamant. "It's too dangerous, and the child needs you."

"Ham's right, Sy," Tamara added. "What if you get caught?"

"What if Pa does?" Scratching at his chin in frustration, Simon caught sight of Luis' worried expression and took a deep breath. "Look," he said in a calmer voice, "It's a risk we have to take if we're going to get Ma out of there."

"It's not a risk *we* have to take at all. It's a risk *I* have to take. She's *my* wife," Hamlin answered.

"And she's *my* mother."

They were on their feet now, glaring at each other, and Ballentire banged her fist against the table, causing them all to jump.

"She's also my friend Tam's Church-Mother, Luis' Master, and Dani's mentor, so give it a rest and sit down!"

When they were both seated again, the Troupe Leader stood.

"Do you really think this is a coincidence, Sy?" she asked. "What if this ex-guard talked and *they* know that *you* know this *secret* way in? We've already agreed that Fay's likely in the hands of the Flame Priests; the *Seer* Flame Priests, so even if she didn't talk, it's *got* to be a trap; and even if it isn't, known route or no known route, it's going to be burning hard to get her out of there, maybe even impossible. Fay wouldn't want either of you to put yourselves or Kassandra in jeopardy, and it *will.* That's the hard fact of the matter. If either *one* of you goes and gets caught, they'll scoop you out like a melon and be onto us before we get five miles. Finished. You dead, the Coins destroyed, and the child back in the hands of the Duke of Yorbourne."

She sat down. "Is that what you really want?"

Outside, Kassandra could be heard peremptorily ordering Warrin and Turi about, and the two men looked away. Finally Hamlin met Ballentire's eyes, his expression serious.

"We have to try," he said bluntly. "We can't leave her there."

Simon nodded his agreement. "*One* of us is going."

Ballentire looked steadily from one to the other, then threw up her hands. "All right," she answered. "If you've made up your minds, but," and she stabbed a finger at them, "you come up with a plan that'll protect Kassandra at the very least. I didn't take you in and place my people's lives in danger just to have you bugger off and leave her to the mercy of the man who killed her father."

They accepted this without argument, and Ballentire moved to the cupboard and brought down the jug. She thumped it down on the table, then returned to her seat. "Start talking."

Two hours later they had the rough outlines of a plan. Simon would go. Knowing the route, he had a better chance of getting in and out unseen. Ballentire would provide him with a costume that, in dim light, would look more or less like a temple guard's uniform, and Marc, Ballentire's cousin, would come with him and wait outside the temple grounds. If Simon wasn't back with Fay by a certain time, or any alarm was given, Marc would make for Albangate as fast as he could. If Simon were caught, he would try to hold out as long as possible. Meanwhile Hamlin would stay with Kassandra. If a given time elapsed without word, he would take her and leave the Troupe, making a run for Heathland by a route undiscussed.

It wasn't much of a plan, and Ballentire said so in no uncertain terms, but it was the best they could come up with on short notice.

And so it was decided.

Half an hour later, dressed for travel, a cloak concealing a red-and-brown surcoat, Simon said good-bye to his father. They stood quietly together, unsure of what to say until Hamlin took the younger man in his arms and hugged him fiercely.

"You get your mother out of there," he said with mock gruffness.

"I will."

"And . . . take care of yourself, too."

"I will."

"It really should be me going."

"I know, Pa. Thanks for letting me do it."

"Well. You're welcome." Hamlin stared into the trees for a moment. "I'm not as good at this as your mother is."

Simon smiled. "You do fine. Oh, here." He placed a coin in Hamlin's hand and the artisan squinted down at it.

"It's the sovereign of Drusus that woman gave me. If anything happens . . . you know, to me, you can still use it against Yorbourne."

"Nothing's going to happen to you."

"Yes, Pa."

"That's better. Well, go in Essus' Grace, Son."

"You too, Pa."

Taking the reins of his horse, Simon led it to where Marc was waiting at a discreet distance. As he mounted, he turned at Hamlin's call.

"What about the child? Did you tell her?"

Simon nodded. "She said to go save my Momma."

"Good. Well, that's everything, then."

They both paused a moment. Simon took in his father's worried frown and slumped posture against the backdrop of trees, professionally freezing the scene in his mind as if for a portrait, then turned his mount's head. As he and Marc made their way through the trees and onto the road toward Branbridge, a shiver made its way up his spine. He ignored it.

At Dunley Vale, as the setting sun cast long red shadows across the face of Caerockeith Castle, Lieutenant Croft led an older Heathland man into the main hall. The man's hair and beard were a fine, soft gray, but they were long and braided with pieces of cloth torn from his enemies' clothes as was the custom among the western Heaths. He walked with a confident stride, and his sharp eyes quickly took in the room and its occupants. Two exits, eight thin windows too narrow to climb through, a central fire pit; three knights, a squire, and the trooper who walked beside him, all Triarchs.

At the far end of the hall, Terrilynne sat with her two Earls. She waited until the man paused before the table, then motioned for him to be seated. When he obliged, Eddison took his own place beside Gladys DeLlewellynne, Earl of Radnydd.

In the center of the table was a heavy leather bag. The man glanced at it, then showed no more interest.

Terrilynne gestured at Alexius, standing off to one side, and the squire came forward to pour them each a cup of beer. When she was done, the Duke lifted hers and took a swallow.

"Good of you to come, Sean."

He grunted. "I hadn't much choice in the matter, had I?" He gestured at Eddison and Terrilynne shrugged.

"You wouldn't have come if I'd just asked."

"True. What do you want?"

The DeMarian Duke leaned forward. "I want you, you and your family."

"For what?"

"Insurance for the moment. Some sword rattling later. A battle, maybe a war."

"Where?"

"Branion."

He smirked. "Moving against Yorbourne, are we?"

Terrilynne showed no reaction, although she wasn't surprised that he'd guessed her decision. News of Marsellus' death had traveled fast.

"Interested?"

"Maybe." Taking up one of the cups, he studied the fiery pattern etched into the glaze. "Why would a Branion Duke need the help of a Heathland family?"

"Could I find better fighters?"

He grinned, showing a gap in one side of his teeth. "No." He glanced at her slyly. "You've no need of us in Heathland, then?"

"Maybe."

"We can't move against Lindies or Taggens right now. We've a treaty."

The Earl of Guilcove snorted, and Terrilynne allowed

herself a half smile. "You'd move against your own mother for enough money, Sean."

He smirked. "Maybe. It'd have to be a whole lot of money, though. She wields a mean pike. I'd hate to cross her alone. But as we're on the subject of money. How much?"

"A fair price."

"Fair for who?"

"Fair for both of us." She indicated the bag. "There's that for inducement. More will come later. If we win, there's power and position, and the Cailein lands confiscated by Marsellus the Third returned to you."

"And if you lose?"

She shrugged. "You'll still have the money. Run to the hills until the dust settles, like you always do. You're small pickings to the Duke of Yorbourne. Hardly worth chasing."

"And what are we to the Duke of Kempston?"

"Extra troops," she answered bluntly.

"How many do you have lined up now?"

"As many as I need."

He dropped the subject with a shrug. "When do you need an answer for?"

"Within the week."

Finishing the cup, he made a show of considering it as he stroked his beard. "I'm the Cailein Battle Captain," he said, "not its Chief. Joan would have to consent."

"Yes, I know." Terrilynne emptied her own cup, and Alexius refilled both. "And I'd be speaking with her now, except it seemed rude to send an armed guard to interrupt her supper."

"But not to interrupt mine."

"You're not a seventy-eight-year-old woman."

"What about Morag?"

"I understand she's at Braxborough. Naturally she needs to be consulted, but her mother's still Chief. Besides, that's your problem, not mine. Mine is to enlist your interest."

Nodding he drained his cup and stood, scooping up the bag. "I'll speak with Joan and with Morag. Send Eddie in three days. I'll have an answer for you by then.

Tell him to knock first; I don't need my door broken down again."

Eddison showed his teeth.

Terrilynne merely nodded. "Lieutenant, show our guest the way out."

He bowed. "Yes, My Lord."

When the two men had left, Amanda turned to the Duke.

"I don't trust him," she scowled.

Terrilynne shrugged. "He'll give good enough service as long as the money keeps flowing, and he'll keep quiet to ensure I don't turn to anyone else."

Gladys sipped at her cup and made a face at the inferiority of the brew. "The Caileins are a powerful family," she said. "They should be able to keep the other Heaths at bay."

"And provide a few extra troops to help deal with Ellisander," Terrilynne added.

"So we're making a move, then?"

"We are."

"Good. I never could stand that arrogant little prick, anyway."

Outside, the sun dipped below the horizon. Eddison escorted Sean to the edge of Mosswell where the older man was met by three of his children, heavily armed. Waving sarcastically at the Lieutenant, he tossed the bag to his eldest, and the four of them moved away. Eddison remained until they were out of sight, then he turned back toward the castle.

In the field outside the village, a hawk circling high overhead gave a long shriek and the Lieutenant stopped to watch it plummet to the ground. It rose a second later, a rat dangling from its claws, and Eddison smiled in appreciation of its skill.

There would be war this summer, he mused. That was good. The company needed a war to keep its own skill as sharp.

Above him, the hawk suddenly veered and the rat twisted from its grip. Eddison watched the rodent fall as the hawk shrieked its outrage.

"Very funny," he muttered to the Wind, the most ironically personified of the four Aspects. Turning his back on the obvious ill omen, he returned to Caerockeith.

In the main hall, as servants began setting the table for supper, Terrilynne DeMarian sat deep in thought, planning the campaign against Yorbourne that would place Kempston on the Throne.

8. Flame Priest

"*Ratroot.*"
    "*To delve into the Prophetic Realm.*"
"*Nightbloom.*"
"*To clear the Sight.*"
"*Holly berries.*"
"*To clear the vision.*"
"*Wild lettuce.*"
"*To bring the symbols of prophecy into focus.*"
"*Wormroot.*"
"*To subdue the seizures caused by the ratroot and the wormroot.*"
"*Birch sap.*"
"*A sacrifice to the Triarchy meant to plead admittance to the Shadow Realm.*"
"*A what?*"
Her Grace Elanna Lowe, the Flame Temple Herbalist paused in her list and stared at her apprentice.

Rosarion blushed, suddenly tongue-tied by her expression. "*I mean . . . ah . . .*" He stumbled over the words and fell into an awkward silence.

"*Who told you that?*" she demanded.

"*The Archpriest Julianus, Your Grace, in yesterday's reading.*"

Her nostrils flaring in irritation, Elanna closed her book with a snap. "*Meddling, little . . .*" she muttered under her breath. "*Now you listen to me, Rosarion,*" she said. "*This is Herbalism.*" She indicated the book. "*These are herbs.*" With a wave of her hand she took in the bowls of greenery on the table. "*They have chemical properties which cause metaphysical reactions when*

*mixed in the right proportions. Anyone can do it if they
know how. Anyone. Sacrifice to the Triarchy, indeed."
She snorted angrily.*

*Rosarion looked down at his hands in confusion. "But,
Your Grace," he asked hesitantly, "isn't prayer and sacrifice essential for the True Vision?"*

*Elanna closed her mouth in a tight line, breathing
deeply through her nose. "Of course, child," she replied
in a slightly more modified tone, although her expression
was still one of fierce disapproval. "For the priest entering
the Prophetic Realm, faith, discipline, and prayer are essential for purity of spirit which brings the True Vision
but they have nothing to do with herbalism!"*

*Her voice had risen at her last words, and Rosarion
winced.*

*"Now," she said in a more businesslike tone, "birch
sap if you please, sir."*

"Uh . . . to, uh . . . for purity of vision?" he offered.

"Why?"

"Because . . . it contains less contaminants than water?"

"And?"

*"And . . . because its . . . dampening effect smooths the
transition of individual herbs into a concentrated whole."*

"Good. Now doesn't that make more sense?"

"Yes, ma'am."

Elanna had been nearing seventy when Rosarion had
served his apprenticeship under her. She'd been at the
Flame Temple sixty years, and had known and bullied
every high-ranking priest within its walls. Her sharp,
hawklike stare and no-nonsense approach to their faith
had terrified Rosarion at first, but as his studies and his
knowledge had increased, he'd found her views much to
his own way of thinking, and they'd gotten along surpris-
ingly well.

She did not believe in training more than one new
Herbalist at a time, so Rosarion had shouldered all the
duties of acolyte, Herbalist, Seer, and servant to a tyran-
nical old woman. It was hard work, but it had its re-
wards. In the evenings, after prayers and after the
Lighting, they'd sat together in the herbarium doorway,
watching the sun cast the red light of the Triarchy across

the gardens and talking about their day. Often, Elanna's expression would soften with memories, and she'd tell Rosarion stories of her long life in the service of the Flame and any bits of knowledge or lore she could remember.

He would fetch her shawl or her cane or her medicine, fussing over her as Willan now fussed over him.

They'd been close.

Unbeknownst to the others at the temple, Elanna's health had been failing rapidly. Rosarion had watched her take increasingly strong doses of the remedies she'd developed; doses well beyond the safety range she herself had taught him.

"I'm dying," she'd said bluntly. "These will keep me alive long enough to pass on what knowledge you'll need to succeed me. After that it doesn't matter."

She'd died four months before Rosarion had contracted the disease which had placed him in the same position as she, fifty years younger. True to her stubborn, individualist teachings he took what remedies he needed, ignored the consequences as she had, and did what he had to do.

Does that include catching pneumonia, fool?

Wrapped in a blanket, Rosarion sat in the herbarium doorway, watching the rain fall on the gardens beyond. His thoughts, drifting here and there, had settled into an accusatory tone that was all too familiar of late. Too much time with nothing to do except think, he speculated. Ignoring the voice, he pulled the blanket tighter about his shoulders and remained where he was. He wanted the fresh air, pneumonia or no.

He'd been bedridden since his interrogation of Fay Falconer. The dampness of the Flame Temple dungeons had entered his lungs, and for a time the Shadow Catcher had seemed closer than ever. He'd recovered, though his mind had remained unfocused and sluggish.

He rubbed his eyes. He'd better find some clarity soon. Ellisander wasn't going to wait forever.

The Duke had not yet demanded the Herbalist's services. He'd sent pages with food, blankets, and books to speed Rosarion's recovery and seemed to be waiting patiently, but that wouldn't last. As soon as he was well enough to risk another vision, the Duke would want him to go in. And Rosarion would go. Elanna had also taught him to honor his debts.

Hypocrite. Elanna didn't teach you to commit heresy, his mind accused.

Didn't she? he answered.

No. You came to that all on your own.

She taught me that the ends justify the means.

Horse shit. She taught you only to make your own choices.

Isn't that heresy for a Triarchy Priest?

His mind was silent, chewing that one over, and Rosarion used the respite to sip the infusion Willan had made him before leaving reluctantly for prayers.

The Herbalist frowned. Had he taught him all he would need to know? He supposed it didn't really matter. Willan would muddle through somehow, as he had. If Rosarion lived to complete his training, the boy could take over from him as he had from Elanna; if not, they would have to send for someone to finish his apprenticeship. Either way the Flame Temple would not be without an Herbalist.

Just because you feel responsible to them doesn't make you any less a heretic, his mind pronounced. *And if they ever find out what you've done they'll hang you from the main temple gate until you rot.*

Shut up.

He slept. His dreams were vivid, the residue of potion and medicinal herbs in his system causing him to fall into a light prophetic trance. One image kept repeating over and over; a figure riding through a storm, leading a line of warriors carrying the fire-wolf and tyger banner of the Duke of Kempston. Rosarion could see the wounds on their bodies and the blood on their weapons and knew there would be war.

The lead figure came closer and suddenly the Herbalist saw him in detail. He was riding a bay gelding and was dressed in the red-and-brown uniform of a Flame Temple guard, though it fit him awkwardly. As Rosarion watched, he reached the temple gates and passed within.

A boy with many faces, held in sway by the light of Essus, awaited his return. Crossing the temple common, the figure fetched up by the infirmary doors and reached forward.

Suddenly Rosarion knew the future. Simon of Florenz was coming to rescue Fay Falconer, just as Ellisander'd said he would.

Waking with a start, the Herbalist stared about him, the last shreds of the prophetic trace causing him to blink dazedly around. He half expected to see the artist bearing down on him, but the rain and gathering darkness obscured his view of the gardens. He knew he was coming, though, and coming soon.

Rosarion rose too quickly. The room spun around him, and he fell, cracking his knuckles against the chair. With a curse, he grabbed the doorjamb for support and hauled himself up again. He had to get to Ellisander. The Duke had to know about this. Frantically, he stumbled across the workroom to his bed alcove.

His mind was in a whirl. He wasn't even sure why it was so important that the Duke know right now, but the urgency of it drove him on as he dressed with frenzied haste. In the corner of his wardrobe was Elanna's old cane, and he used it now as he made his way back to the door and out into the storm.

He staggered to the gate, the rain pelting against his head and face. He hadn't remembered to bring a cloak. By the time he'd gotten the gate opened, he was soaked through, but he scarcely noticed as, leaving it swinging free, he plunged into Collin's Park.

The Duke of Yorbourne had retired early with his Companion, Adrianus. They'd just finished a tumultuous lovemaking and were enjoying a cup of hot wine when a page tentatively entered to say His Grace Rosarion DeLynne was in the Duke's outer chamber in a fearful condition and demanding to speak with His Lordship.

The Duke left his bed in a state of cold anger, but the whispered words of the coughing, bedraggled Herbalist were enough to change his mood instantly to one of triumph. Sending the page to fetch the Hierarchpriest of Cannonshire and the Archpriest of the Flame, he helped

Rosarion into his study where the younger man collapsed into a chair.

In the dull glow of the firelight the Herbalist looked ghastly. He was dripping wet, his face gaunt and gray, and he was shaking uncontrollably.

Fearing a seizure, Ellisander pried the younger man's mouth open and poured his own cup of wine down his throat. Then, stripping him unceremoniously of his wet clothes, he wrapped him in a blanket and turned to order the fire built up and some dry things found.

After a while the pallor slowly left Rosarion's features, and he was able to stop shaking. Blinking up at the Duke, he coughed, dribbling some wine out onto the blanket. "What are you going to do?" he asked weakly.

His eyes sparkling in the firelight, Ellisander smiled. "Prepare a fitting welcome for our guest," he answered. "And when you're well enough, we'll go and meet him and have a little chat about Kassandra."

"What about Gawaina and Julianus?"

"What about them?"

"Suppose Simon accuses you of the Aristok's death in their presence?"

Ellisander shrugged eloquently. "Why would he?" He leaned over the younger man. "Just because you know I'm involved, doesn't mean he does," he whispered.

Rosarion kept his eyes on the fire. "He's running to Terrilynne. I Saw it. Why would he run all the way to Heathland if he didn't suspect?"

"What if he does? He can't possibly have any proof." Ellisander straightened. "It will simply be seen as a desperate attempt to save his own life by falsely implicating others. Remember, *he* has been seen in vision. I have not." He stroked the younger man's hair softly. "So stop worrying."

Rosarion nodded, still uncertain, but too exhausted and too distracted by the force of the Duke's presence to argue.

Minutes later the Hierarchpriest arrived. Ellisander made the Herbalist repeat his words while he sent for more wine. When Rosarion was finished, the Duke turned to Gawaina.

"This is the opportunity we've been waiting for," he said. "We must move immediately."

The predatory gleam in the Hierarchpriest's eyes was much the same as the Duke's, although she held up a cautionary hand. Turning to Rosarion, she caught him in a firm stare.

"You're sure that this is a True Vision, Your Grace, and not just a dream?"

He nodded. "I'm sure. He's coming, My Lord. I have Seen it."

"But this is madness. How can he hope to steal her out from beneath our very noses?"

"Perhaps he has compatriots among the guard," Ellisander replied impatiently as he paced across the room. "What does it matter? He's coming and we must be ready. Only Kassandra's safety matters now."

"Of course, My Lord, but he may have planned to use her as a hostage in case of capture," Gawaina replied smoothly. "We must move with some caution."

"Did you see anything of the Aristok's whereabouts, Your Grace?" She returned her sharp gaze to the Herbalist.

Rosarion shook his head. "The dream was fragmentary, My Lord, but he is coming."

"And we will be ready to meet him." Ellisander checked his pacing at a knock on the door. "Come."

A page entered. "The Archpriest of the Flame, My Lord."

"Ah, Julianus." Ellisander came forward and took the older man's arm. "We have good news, a breakthrough. Come." After guiding the older man to a chair, the Duke seated himself as well.

"Simon of Florenz is within our grasp."

On the border of the Flame Temple grounds it was still raining heavily as two riders pulled up to the line of oak trees. Dismounting, Simon handed the reins to Marc, then turned as the Westonborough bells tolled nine.

"Two hours, no longer," he said, returning his attention to the boy. "If I'm not back by then or any alarm is given, return to Albangate as fast as you can."

Marc nodded. Pulling his hood farther up over his

head, he huddled down into his cloak. "Uh . . . Essus protect you," he said awkwardly.

Simon smiled. "And the warmth of the Triarchy keep you safe as well."

They shook hands, and then Simon turned and plunged into the trees. Within a few seconds he was lost from sight.

The way was more laborious than he'd remembered. The night was dark and a fog had risen, making it difficult to see very far. Every sound was distorted by the rain, the flashes of lightning only causing the afterimages of trees to dance in front of his eyes. More than once he stumbled over rocks or branches, but trusting more to luck then he wanted to admit, the artist pressed on. Soon he was soaking wet. After what seemed like an hour, he finally stepped onto the Flame Temple common. Mouthing a silent prayer to Essus, he ran across the open ground to the Flame Temple proper, then moved quickly around to the west wing.

The alcove was just as he'd remembered it. Running his fingers along the wall, he found the loose bricks and, prying them free, flung them aside without caring where they fell. Time was the most important factor now.

Soon the opening was a dark, man-sized hole and he squeezed through.

It was eerily silent after the sound of the rain outside. It was also as black as pitch. Belatedly realizing why they'd had a lantern the last time, Simon cursed his lack of foresight, but it was too late to turn back now. Groping his way down the steps, he tried not to shudder as his fingers passed over the damp, moss-covered wall.

At the bottom of the stairs, he heard a noise and froze. Minutes passed. Straining to hear past the overloud beating of his heart, he stood squinting into the darkness. Had it been footsteps or just movement from above filtering down through the stone? The echoing drip of water along the passageway was his only answer.

Simon inched slowly forward. His foot came down on something soft and he almost shouted in surprise as he stumbled backward. Crouching down, he felt around and touched cold fur. A dead rat. Rubbing his hands against his breeches, he called himself a few choice names and pushed on, ignoring the growing sense of fear.

His reaching fingers found the old door to the dying room exactly as it had been. Passing that quickly, he negotiated the open area by memory alone and fetched up against the pillars. He was almost there. This might just work after all.

Allowing himself a deep breath of relief, he glanced up at the light spilling weakly across his face. The grate had had an additional five years to rust away. With luck he should be able to pry it free. Standing on a pile of rubble, he grasped it in one hand, and supporting himself against the pillar with the other, he pulled.

The grate came free much faster than he'd expected. Suddenly off balance, he lost his footing and fell, knocking his head against a pillar. The lights bouncing across his vision momentarily concealed the two figures who stepped out from behind him. One swung his arm and the lights abruptly went out.

On the borders of the Flame Temple Marc listened to the Westonborough bells toll, counting off the chimes on his fingers. An hour and a half to go. It was still raining.

The darkness was total for a long time. Slowly a faint glimmer of light became apparent, but on its heels came a throbbing headache. Simon groaned. He tried to turn his head away, and the pain grew suddenly worse, making him cry out. The darkness rushed in again.

After a time he heard voices murmuring somewhere above him; voices he thought he recognized. He opened his eyes again, this time being careful not to move. His head felt like it was on fire, and he could feel cold metal on his wrists and ankles. Chains.

The light moved closer, and he squinted painfully as several faces came into focus; faces above the red and brown of the Flame Temple guards and one above the black and green of the DeKathrines.

Gawaina DeKathrine, Duke of Cannonshire, Head of the Knights of the Sword, Hierarchpriest of the Triarchy, and enemy of Essusiatism, looked down at him and smiled.

*   *   *

Alone in the Duke of Yorbourne's study, Rosarion clutched the blanket more tightly about his shoulders as he tried not to think about what was happening.

After planning Simon's capture, the others had hastened to the Flame Temple to await him, agreeing that the Herbalist was too ill to accompany them. Rosarion had not argued. The journey across Collin's Park in the rain had taken the last of his strength.

He was so cold. Even dressed in a warm woolen tunic and leggings of Adrianus', he still shook uncontrollably. His face was hot and damp, and his chest was painfully congested. Wiping the sweat from his forehead, he eased aside the blanket, letting the warmth of the fire move across his legs and feet.

The fire crackled, and he stared dazedly into the flames, watching them weave themselves into patterns. The center of the Triarchy, Flame was also the Aspect of Prophecy, and Rosarion knew the future was as much in its ever-changing motif as in the Prophetic Realm itself. If you knew what to look for. Rosarion knew, although he no longer wanted to See.

Before him the DeMarian fire-wolf rose up from the burning yew logs. It danced above the grate for an instant, was destroyed, was reborn, and was transformed into a myriad of serpentine phantoms; each one taking shape for an instant before merging into the next. Reluctantly Rosarion counted off the symbols as they wove through their intricate designs, noting their meanings and their context as if he were once again an acolyte reciting his lessons before Julianus.

Wyvern, symbol of Yorbourne, the richest Royal Dukedom in Branion. Created for the Consort Julian by Kathrine the Second as a marriage gift in the year 105 DR. Ellisander.

Gryphon, the Royal beast of Gwyneth, added to Branion heraldry by Atreus the Third, formerly Prince Rhys ap Llewellynne ap Owain of that great western realm, and held by each firstborn heir ever since. Kassandra.

Dragon, the four-legged manifestation of Essus, the Triarchy's ever watchful rival. Merrone.

And finally the amphisbane, the two-headed Speaker of Prophecy and messenger of the Living Flame. Himself.

Rosarion closed his eyes, letting the flames reflect through his lids. Wyvern, Yorbourne, Ellisander. Gryphon, Gwyneth, Kassandra. Dragon, Merrone, Essus. Amphisbane, prophecy, Rosarion himself. All entwined with the illusive fire-wolf of the DeMarians. There were so many symbols and so many interpretations. Which was the right one?

Opening his eyes, the Herbalist stared into the flames again. Once, the Prophecy had been clear and easy to understand. Now, everything was confused and out of sync. Simon of Florenz was the key, the pivot on which all the fates turned in this age, but how did he fit in and where?

One thing was clear enough: In seeking the future, he'd lost sight of the present, and by chasing his death, he'd run from his faith. Perhaps it was time to stop running.

Easing himself down onto the floor, he made the sign of the Triarchy across his breast then, whispering a prayer he hadn't spoken since he was a child, he reached out to the Living Flame hidden deep in the burning yew of the Duke of Yorbourne's fire.

"Where is the Aristok?"

The question was asked politely, even kindly. Through a haze of crimson Simon blinked up at the Hierarchpriest. Her expression was mild, but behind her stood three Temple Guards, their fists already red with his blood.

His own hair was matted with it. It flowed down his face from a cut on his forehead and filled his mouth where a blow had driven his lips against his teeth. He was continuously coughing it out onto the floor so he could breathe because early in the interrogation they'd broken his nose, but he had to buy time for Marc to get away. That was all that mattered.

He sensed that he'd been conscious for about an hour. After the first few moments, things had fallen into a routine, blows coming after each repetition of the same softly asked questions. Where was the Aristok? Who were his accomplices?

Without looking up, he answered the first question as he had each time before.

"Safe."

"Safe where?"

"Just safe."

The Hierarchpriest gestured, and two guards lifted him up, supporting his limp weight between them. The chains on his wrists clanked and Simon winced as the noise sent pain shooting through his head.

"You know," Gawaina said conversationally, "you can't hold out forever. Sooner or later you'll tell me what I want to know. The question is only how much of you will be left when you do."

He said nothing.

She stood aside, and the third guard moved in, using his fists to batter Simon to his knees. The others let him fall, waiting for a signal from the Hierarchpriest. She nodded, and they dragged him up again.

"Who are your accomplices?"

Simon shook his head groggily. "No one."

"Who is your leader?"

"No one."

"Why did you kidnap the Aristok Kassandra?"

Spitting blood from his mouth again, he coughed weakly. "Didn't. Ran. Made her safe."

"From whom?"

"Killers . . . her father's killers."

"Who are?"

"Yorbourne."

"Yorbourne. The Duke of Yorbourne. I see." She shook her head in disgust. "I've been trying to understand why you aren't as afraid as you should be," she said. "Maybe it's because you're too stupid to understand the trouble you're in. Do you know what the penalty for treason and regicide are in this country? They disembowel you and throw your guts into the fire before they hack you into pieces." When he made no answer, she cocked her head to one side. "Or maybe you think your God will protect you. Don't count on it." She leaned forward until their faces were only an inch apart. "You're in the *Flame* Temple dungeons now. Only the *Living Flame* has dominion here, and you have sinned against the Flame."

"No."

She stood. "Where is the Aristok?"

"I . . . won't tell you. You'll give her up to him."

"Him?"

"Yorbourne."

She sighed. "I'm a patient woman, Simon, but this is becoming stale. I'll ask you one last time. If I don't get a satisfactory answer from you, I'll leave you to the mercy of these very loyal men, and then I'll send the Flame Priests in to tear your mind apart, piece by piece, and leave you a babbling idiot. Where is the Aristok?"

Simon was quiet for a long time. The pain in his head warred with the pain in his body, and he couldn't think straight. What could he tell them? Only one thing would satisfy them. Only one would make the pain stop. But he couldn't betray the Coins and the child. He'd walked into this place knowing what would happen if he were caught, and he would accept the consequences now that he had been.

He shook his head groggily. "Safe," he repeated.

Gawaina moved to the door. "Beat him," she said over her shoulder, "but don't let him lose consciousness. If he wants to talk, I'll be with the Archpriest Julianus."

"Yes, My Lord."

The Hierarchpriest left the cell while the three guards returned their attention to their prisoner.

Ellisander was pacing impatiently in Julianus' study, when Gawaina entered.

"Well?"

Accepting a cup of wine from a young initiate, she sipped at it before answering.

"He's a stubborn one," she said, "but he'll break."

"We should send in the priests," Julianus said.

"Why waste their talents? He's a weak-willed fool."

"Because Kassandra may be in danger while you wait," Ellisander snarled. "You can take your revenge on him after she's rescued, as we all will."

"Of course, My Lord," the Hierarchpriest said, bowing. "Forgive my enthusiasm. Send in the priests if you wish, Julianus."

The old man nodded and sent the initiate to summon them. Then he leaned forward. "Did he say anything at all, Gawaina?"

She glanced over at the Duke of Yorbourne. "He accused His Lordship of conspiracy," she answered.

Ellisander's eyes narrowed. "Did he?"

"Yes, My Lord."

"Well, after he's answered for the murder of Marsellus and the kidnapping of Kassandra, if there's anything left of him, he can answer for that, too."

Rosarion was dozing before the fire when a page woke him gently to tell him that His Highness, the Duke of Yorbourne, was requesting his presence at the Flame Temple.

He stretched gingerly, testing each limb. The shaking had subsided and he felt groggy, but better, after his sleep.

"Is it still raining?"

"No, Your Grace."

"Well, that's good news anyway. Help me up."

The page took his arm and, holding onto the back of the chair with his other hand, Rosarion rose. He felt a little dizzy, although after a moment it faded. He thought he could make it to the temple if he had someone to help him. Leaning heavily on the page, he left the Duke of Yorbourne's study.

In his cell Simon of Florenz was pinned to the floor between two guards. The other held his head still as three priests of the Living Flame stood over him. The combined force of their will slammed against his mind, smashing at his self-control like a battering ram.

He screamed, the sound forced out of him by the strength of their attack. His head felt as if it was on fire. He couldn't think, couldn't speak. Words and thoughts were torn from him as he struggled to hold onto them, images from his life swirling about him in a maelstrom of colors and sounds.

Bit by bit, the priests drove through the layers of self, tearing each one loose, then flinging it aside as they searched for the answers to their questions.

He had nothing to throw up against them. Early in their assault he'd tried to pray, to use Essus as a shield between the priests and his mind, but Gawaina's words had shaken his belief and he could not call on the Flame, a lifetime's worship of Essus held his tongue.

He tried to hide behind the brilliant colors of his work, yet inexorably, they hammered this down as well. Every fear of obscurity or mediocrity he'd ever felt was systematically ripped free and held up as truth to weaken him.

Finally, all he had was the pain of his body to focus on, but as the agony in his mind grew unbearable, he could feel that slipping away, too.

Sensing him falter, the priests came at him again. Forming their might into one blazing bolt of fire, they flung it at the center of his mind. It hit him with the force of a hurricane, and something shattered in his head. Shards of thoughts, flying like pieces of broken mirror, went spinning away. Shadows rose up with a roar and he fell into a rushing vortex of white and red light.

When he screamed, he was too far away to hear it.

Bronwynne of Branbridge, Seer and Holy Interrogator of the Flame, disengaged abruptly, causing the other two priests to stagger forward. Grinding her teeth in frustration, she snatched a cup of the Potion of Revealing from an acolyte and downed it in one swallow.

"Something's blocking us," she snarled, flinging the cup aside.

"He has a strong will," one of the others offered.

"No, Talisar. It's that scorching white light. It's covering him, just like it's covered the visions ever since the Aristok's murder. Bloody Essus!" She spat. "Without it, he'd have broken by now."

"He will."

"Yes, he will." She nodded, feeling the added potion begin to build the power of her mind back to a frenzied height. It sizzled through her body, causing her hair to stand on end and a familiar buzzing to begin in her ears. "Yes, he will," she agreed, gesturing to the guards. "Get him up. We'll go again."

When the attack came, Simon was too weak to fight it. They hit him one solid blow and knocked an image of Kassandra free. He cried out, and with one last shred of will he hadn't known he had flung an image of Leary up in its place.

They fell on it like dogs on a bone, sure that it meant more than it did, and he was able to snatch the image of the child back up and hold it tightly to him. It worked for just an instant, and then they were on him again and he was flung back into the maelstrom of pain and light.

Moments later, her face wet from the effort, Bronwynne disengaged again and kicked out at the artist in frustration.

"That's it," she panted. "I've had it screwing around with this little piece of Essusiate shit. You," she pointed at one of the guards. "Go find me something heavy. You two, get him up and bring him over here."

Taking him by the arms, the guards dragged Simon forward.

"Tell me when he comes back to himself."

They waited, Bronwynne pacing back and forth, the others using the respite to catch their breath. Finally Simon groaned. Bronwynne smiled grimly.

When the other guard returned, he handed her a brick and she pointed at the small table. "Put his right hand on that." They obeyed and she grasped him by the hair, pulling his head up. "Look at me," she commanded. When his pain-clouded eyes focused on her face she held the brick for him to see. "I hear you're an artist," she said. "A muralist, am I right? Well, listen well, muralist. In one minute I'm going to take this brick, and I'm going to smash all your fingers. Are you listening? I'm sick of playing games with you. You have one minute to talk."

The importance of her words took a moment to penetrate the shattering of his reason. By the time he realized what she intended to do, it was too late.

Rosarion entered Julianus' study on the arm of one of the younger initiates. A palace page had helped him through Collin's Park, then the temple guard on duty at the main doors had found an acolyte to help him to Julianus'. The girl took him to a chair, remaining by the door at the Archpriest's gesture.

Ellisander handed the Herbalist a cup of wine.

"How are you feeling?"

"I'm better, My Lord, thank you."

"Well enough to assist Bronwynne and the others?"

"If My Lord wishes, although I don't know how much help I can be."

Julianus reached over and patted him on the arm.

"We know you're unwell, Rosarion, but in these times we must all make sacrifices. We felt that since you saw him in such detail in vision, you might be able to glean some clue about the Aristok's presence that the others might miss."

"I'll do my best, Your Grace."

"I know you will. Janek will accompany you and give you any assistance you need."

When her arm came down, the pain was unbearable. Choking back a cry, Simon tried to jerk away, but the guards held him immobile as the priest raised her arm again. This time the blow tore a scream from him as the pain and the crack of bones scattered his self-control. The shadows erupted. He broke.

Descending the stairs to the dungeons, Rosarion stumbled. Falling against the railing, his hand flew forward to keep him from falling as the sudden sense of anguish and despair made him stagger. Janek grabbed his arm, holding him still until the sensation passed. Then, sweat forming on his face and neck, Rosarion signaled that he was all right and began his descent again.

The dungeons were damp and cold, causing his chest to tighten almost immediately. The first emotion had been so strong and so sudden that he was off balance and unprepared when, upon reaching the dungeon floor, all physical sensations were swept aside by the force of the psychic beating going on. It doubled him over, nausea threatening to spill the wine he'd had out onto the floor. The acolyte held him, pushing his head down, and it was some minutes before he could make himself continue.

The guard before the cell area seemed wholly unaffected. He unlocked the gate, waited for the two priests to go through, then closed it again with a shrug, but as he passed, Rosarion could smell stale wine on his breath. It didn't surprise him.

Wishing he'd had more to drink himself, the Herbalist inched forward. The feelings of torment and despair were much stronger here, so close to the cells. Rosarion stumbled forward like a man in a windstorm, falling against the door to the artist's cell before Janek could reach it.

The door, unsecured, fell open and Rosarion took in the scene in an instant. Blood splattered the walls and the floor. Three temple guards restrained a man over a small table while three priests stood over them. One of the priests, Bronwynne, had something large in her hand. Their prisoner, Simon of Florenz, was crying and pleading with them to stop.

Bronwynne turned when Rosarion entered, her expression even.

"Ah, Rosarion," she said. "You're just in time. Janek, go and tell the Archpriest that Simon of Florenz has decided to be reasonable."

"Yes, Your Grace." The acolyte helped Rosarion to the cell's one chair, then withdrew.

The Herbalist looked down at the broken, blood-covered man before him, trying to bring the sight into alignment with the towering figure he'd Seen riding toward them with an army at his back. The man was choking and gasping in pain, his one hand, still held in the grip of the guards, bleeding badly. When he raised his head and looked into Rosarion's eyes, the Herbalist felt a sudden blow of recognition.

An amphisbane standing on its tail speaks the words of prophecy.

Simon of Florenz was almost unrecognizable behind a mask of blood and swelling, but the eyes which stared into his were as familiar as the Herbalist's own.

The amphisbane turns in on itself and looks into the eyes of its other half.

Eyes he recognized, eyes he stared into now and saw their torment and their defeat, and eyes that saw in him all that he had done.

The firelight blending, merging, becoming the two-headed Speaker of Prophecy, the messenger of the Living Flame. The amphisbane, Rosarion and . . . Simon.

In one rushing moment Rosarion saw the answer he'd

been seeking, the true interpretation that had eluded him ever since his first version for the Duke of Yorbourne. He started to speak, but Bronwynne was moving forward, was jerking Simon to his feet, and was asking the first of the questions they'd been asking without success most of the night.

"Where is the Aristok?"

Simon opened his mouth and coughed, blood spilling out from between his battered lips as he continued to stare, mesmerized, at Rosarion.

"Where!"

The cell grew almost perceptibly darker, the shadows crawling forward as if to hear his answer. Simon tried to speak, coughed again, clawed at his throat with his one good hand. He managed a few halting, unintelligible syllables.

The Priest shook her head and growled a threat. Rosarion turned away.

The artist began to shake. Coughing a mouthful of blood onto the cell floor, he gasped out, "Albangate."

Once released, the words spilled out in a rush, desperate to be believed, desperate to stop their attack on the one thing he treasured above all else.

When he finally grew silent and the shadows rushed forward to claim him again, Bronwynne stood back with a grim smile. She let him fall.

Silence. Time has passed, Simon didn't know how much time, although it hardly mattered. He'd failed. He'd failed Kassandra, he'd failed Leary, he'd failed everyone. Ballentire had been right. He'd broken.

Now they were gone. Having gotten their answers, they'd left him alone. Dragging himself as far into a corner as the chains about him would allow, he pressed his head against the cool stone wall, cradling his ruined hand against his chest. That was it. There was nothing left. He'd betrayed them all and soon they'd be joining him here and Kassandra would be in the hands of her mortal enemy and Ellisander would win.

The worst of it was that he'd told them everything, and they still didn't believe them. They'd be back soon, and the beatings and the mental attacks would start again. He had nothing more to tell them, but they wouldn't listen. Next time it would be his other hand, not that the damage hadn't already been done. He would never hold a brush again, even if he got out of this alive.

You won't, his mind said harshly. *They're going to kill you, you blind, stupid fool.*

Pressed against the wall, he cried out for Leary just once, and then slipped into unconsciousness.

In an empty cell two doors down, the shadows moved to the flickering of the torches on the walls outside. They ebbed and grew and flowed over the man crouched in their midst. Rosarion DeLynne sat with his back pressed against the wall, his handkerchief bunched up against his mouth. The mental barrage had faded with the priests' leave-taking; now there was only the lingering residue of old torment in the air.

He'd stayed and listened to the halting confession of Simon of Florenz for as long as he could, then, sick, he'd staggered from the room. Even in the passageway, he could hear the other man's gasping words and Bronwynne's angry replies.

Simon had told them of his flight from the palace, of his dream of Essus and the white light that had covered his escape from Branbridge; of his return through the old dying room entrance to rescue his mother, and of his plan to have his father run with the child by a secret route to the Duke of Kempston, their hope that she would return the child to the capital with an army to protect her.

And he'd spoken of something else, although Rosarion had been unable to hear him as all sound in the cell grew suddenly muted. Attuned to the prophecy of the amphisbane, the Herbalist had perceived the shift, although no one else in the room seemed to have noticed. When the spell passed, the artist was telling them of the assassin, of the coin she'd given him and her words about Ellisander DeMarian. This had triggered another beating, and after that there'd been only silence.

When Bronwynne and the others had left the dungeons, Rosarion was crouched in the darkness of the next cell, his mind awhirl with what he'd learned and the new interpretation it conveyed.

One tiny shoot stabs toward the darkness, is overtaken by another which grows and grows until it becomes a sea of flame.

He'd always believed the first shoot to be Kassandra, the second Ellisander, but what if their positions were reversed? The shoot that was the Duke of Yorbourne rises in attempted coup and is engulfed by the True Flame that is Kassandra the Sixth?

One shoot begins to grow. The dragon of Essus screams and one clawed foot comes down to smash it. From the base of the tree grows another and with its front claws clasped around it, the dragon wraps itself about the tiny flame, and then melts away before the fully reborn Living Flame.

Essus in the form of Simon of Florenz defies the power of Ellisander DeMarian and protects Kassandra until she's able to take on the mantel of the Living Flame.

Staring into the darkness Rosarion began to rock back and forth. What had he done? He had Seen the True Future, but, entangled in Ellisander's plotting, he'd interpreted it falsely. He'd misrepresented his vision, deliberately setting Essus in the place of Yorbourne, and somehow he'd come to believe it himself. In doing so, he'd missed the genuine hand of that God at work, at work in tandem with the Living Flame to bring Its True Vessel out from the hands of apostatical murder.

Staring at the light spilling through the open door, Rosarion began to shake. The cold and damp of the stone wall was seeping through his clothing, causing his chest to ache, and he let it build. What had he done?

Coughing, he pushed the thought away. What was done could not be undone, it could only be paid for. Fate and the Gods had chosen their Champions. He closed his eyes, arms wrapped tightly about his chest. They had chosen their Champions.

The firelight blending and merging, becoming the two-headed Speaker of Prophecy, the messenger of the Living Flame. The amphisbane, Simon.

And Rosarion.

He raised his head suddenly. He had always Seen himself in the Prophecy. Identifying with the amphisbane, however, he had interpreted his part as that of observer, nothing more. Yet, if Simon of Florenz was also the amphisbane and one of the Gods' Champions, what did that make him?

The shadows grew suddenly more substantial.

He stood.

"What does it make me?"

It makes you an addlepated idiot, his mind shot back at him as he suddenly bolted from the room. *Hurry up before they come back.*

The key to Simon's cell was hung on a peg by the door. Using it now, Rosarion entered the room quietly and looked down at the other man.

The artist was curled into a tight ball in a far corner. He made no movement and gave no sign that he sensed another's presence. Rosarion had seen what they'd done to him and knew he'd never be able to get him out of there alone.

The shadows darkened.

Standing there uncertainly, Rosarion had a moment of panic, then an idea. He'd never be able to get him out of there alone, so he needed help. Crossing the passageway, he opened the door to Fay Falconer's cell.

Fay had spent the last four hours on her knees, praying to Essus to save her son. She'd heard them bring Simon in, had heard the sounds of blows, of cursing and screaming, had heard the questions and his answers and had heard him break, his voice almost unrecognizable from pain and despair. Fay had cried then, pleading with their God, offering any bargain or service for just one miracle.

Then her door had opened, and the sickly young Triarchy Priest had stood there, looking as if he himself had been in the hands of the torturers. When he unlocked the chains about her, she didn't ask the reason why, merely breathed a thanksgiving to Essus and followed him out.

Simon was just as Rosarion had left him. On seeing him, Fay swayed, but recovered quickly. This was no time for weakness. While the priest unlocked his chains, she squatted down beside her son, trying to get him to uncurl. He did not respond. She called his name, quietly at first, and then with more urgency. Beside her, Rosarion glanced nervously at the door.

In the midst of the shadows, Simon felt something tug at him, but the movement sent ripples of pain running up his arm, so he ignored it. The shadows were safe. He would stay with the shadows.

He heard his name called. He ignored that, too.

"Simon you have to move."
"No. I can't."
"You have to. I'll help you."

The artist uncurled just enough to let Fay get her arms about him. Then, with almost superhuman strength, she lifted him gently and carried him from the cell, much as she'd carried him onto the boat that had taken her small family to the Continent so many years before.

Simon was a dead weight in her arms. She stumbled when she passed the threshold, and Rosarion leaped forward to help her. They laid him on the passageway floor, and the Herbalist closed and locked the door, setting the key ring back on its post.

When he turned back to them, Fay was smoothing Simon's hair from his face, his injured hand cradled gently in hers. She looked up at the Herbalist as he crouched down beside her.

"Help him."

Reluctantly Rosarion looked down. "I can't. I'm not a physician."

"You're a priest. You got him into this. Help him."

Her stare was intense, and he swallowed as he broke eye contact and looked down at the terrible injury.

"I . . . I don't know what to do. We have to . . . protect it, bind it, but we also have to get out of here before they come back."

"So bind it."

Rosarion looked frantically around, then bent and

began to tear at Simon's disguise, starting at every sound around them.

It took a few precious moments, but soon Simon's hand was wrapped in a bulky makeshift bandage. Rosarion stood.

"Now what?" Fay asked.

"Now we leave. Quickly. I had a vision of a boy and a pair of horses waiting on the temple border. A white light is holding him there, but it won't last forever. We have to hurry."

"How?"

"We go out the same way he got in. I'll show you—it's this way."

Lifting Simon up, they carried him down the passageway until they came to a hole in the floor. Kneeling, Rosarion peered through it.

"Here. He never made it this far, although he managed to take the grate out from below. We should be able to squeeze through, then follow his path back to the place where he came in."

"You know this path?"

"I have Seen it."

Fay eyed the hole's dimensions with misgivings, but nodded. "Very well. Essus knows our needs—and our size. You go first. I'll pass Simon down to you and then follow."

"Are you sure?"

"Just do as I say, boy," she snapped.

Her voice was so like Elanna's that Rosarion found himself obeying without hesitation. Lowering himself through the hole, he hung from the lip for a moment, then let go. He dropped a few feet, stumbled, righted himself and whispered, "I'm here."

With much maneuvering, Fay managed to guide Simon through the hole. "When did you get so tall," she murmured into her son's hair, then with one whispered warning to the priest, she released him. There was a thump and a curse, but after a moment, she heard him call up to her again.

"It's all right, I have him. Come down."

"Easy for you to say," she muttered as she sat and swung her legs into empty air. "Skinny little . . ." Pushing forward, she eased herself down slowly. After a moment's consternation, she managed to twist and wriggle enough to squeeze her hips through. Then she, too, hung from the lip for an instant before letting go. She hit a pile of rubble, fell painfully to one knee, and pushed herself up.

It was very dark after the torchlit corridor, and she peered around before making out the outline of the priest crouched beside her with Simon in his arms.

"Are you all right?"

"I'm fine," she grated. "Where are we?"

"Under the Temple, in the foundations of a pre-Triarctic site. The entrance to the old infirmary dying room is that way," he whispered, touching her left arm. "You can just feel a breeze. If you take his shoulders, I'll take his legs and guide the way."

Fay gripped his hand in agreement, and together they rose and lifted the artist between them.

It seemed to take forever. It was much darker than he'd expected, and Rosarion floundered about in the open area, swearing as water splashed up into his boot. There was a squeak and a scuttle beneath his feet, and the Herbalist nearly dropped Simon in his surprise, but, after a hissed threat from Fay he righted himself and carried on.

The breeze grew steadily stronger. At the end of the corridor, they paused to catch their breath, and Rosarion mentally tallied up how long they'd taken and how long it might be before Bronwynne and the others returned and found their prisoners missing.

They'd have to give their report to Julianus and the others—twenty minutes maybe—then another twenty to digest the information, plan the next interrogation, and send an armed company after Kassandra. Ellisander would be fuming in mock rage at Simon's accusations, and the others would be busy trying to calm him down; ten maybe fifteen minutes there.

Rosarion shuddered as he imagined what the Duke's true rage would be like when he discovered Rosarion's defection. Hopefully he would be nowhere near to feel it.

His heels bumped against the stairs, interrupting his

thoughts. With care, they carried Simon up and guided him through the hole he'd made in the alcove entrance over four hours before. Once outside they allowed themselves a moment's rest, relieved to feel the cold wind on their cheeks.

The rain had stopped, and the crescent moon gave off just enough light to see by. With Rosarion in front they crossed the common in good time, then slowly negotiated the tangle of trees and bracken until they came finally to the place where he'd Seen Simon arrive in vision. They heard the soft whicker of horses, then suddenly a small form knocked the artist from Rosarion's grip and sent the Herbalist tumbling to the ground. An explosive cough was driven from his lungs, cold metal was pressed against his throat and he froze.

"Don't move," a young, quavering voice commanded. "I'll cut you, I will."

"Don't." Rosarion swallowed and felt the knife dig into his throat. "Wait. I'm a friend."

"Who's that?" Fay demanded from the darkness and the arm with the knife quivered.

"Fay? Is that you?"

"Who else would it be? Marc?"

The knife was withdrawn and a boy stood up in the faint moonlight. "Fay? I'm sorry, I fell asleep. I was supposed to only wait two hours. I'm sorry."

"The hand of Essus is on it," she replied simply. "Do you have horses?"

"Yes, ma'am."

"Then help me. Simon's badly hurt, and your little acrobatic act didn't help him any."

"I'm sorry. I mean, yes, ma'am."

He hurried to help her with Simon's limp form as Rosarion moved aside. Fay mounted quickly, then leaned over and reached for Simon. "Now pass him up here. You, too," she gestured impatiently at the Herbalist. "The boy can't do it himself."

Rosarion came forward, and between them, he and Marc muscled the unconscious artist up onto the saddle in front of her.

"Now come along, Marc, we have a long ride to make."

She was about to start off when Rosarion caught her bridle.

"Let me come with you."

She looked down at him with a keen stare that was so penetrating, even in the faint moonlight, that he dropped his own gaze.

"Have we decided whose side we're on?" she asked.

"Yes." He raised his head. "I have. Let me come with you. I have nowhere else to go now, and I can help. I See things."

Fay considered it a moment. "Very well," she said finally. "Ride with Marc."

Feeling as if he'd been granted a Royal Pardon, Rosarion got up behind the boy as Fay led the way onto the road. Then, as fast as the two burdened horses could ride in the darkness, they set off. It was twenty miles to Albangate and they had to be there before dawn.

Bronwynne of Branbridge was admitted to Archpriest Julianus' study without delay. Her report that the Aristok was being held in Albangate by Hamlin Ewer and that they had just under three hours to make it there before he was to take the child and run by a secret route to Caerockeith had sent a Triarchy page scuttling to fetch the Captain of the Flame Champions. Within half an hour a large company was sent out, three Seers in their midst. Their orders were simple. Find Hamlin Ewer and the Aristok. If the artisan eluded them in Albangate, they were to split up, taking the Royal post road to Leiston, the north road to Middlesford, and the west coast road to Barrowness. Seth Cannon, the Senior Seer, was to concentrate on the north road which led to Essusiate Vervickshire after the Kenneth Forest. Both Gawaina DeKathrine and Ellisander, Duke of Yorbourne, believed that Hamlin Ewer would likely run that way for help. Bronwynne agreed with them.

Standing by the fire, her hands still bloody from Simon's questioning, the Seer Priest watched dispassionately as the three most powerful nobles in the Realm discussed her report, waiting patiently and answering any questions they directed toward her. The Potion of Revealing still moved within her system, and her head buzzed with the force of it. Words took on new timbre, colors and forms twisted into new shapes. Bronwynne observed it all with the stolid detachment she was known for.

Ellisander was speaking on some point. He paced across the room, locked eyes with Bronwynne for a second, then moved past her. Wisps of flame traveled along behind him, visible to her drug-enhanced Sight. Bronwynne watched his back and considered Simon's words.

The artist had accused the Duke of Yorbourne of complicity in the Aristok's murder. Bronwynne had not believed him then, and the gathered nobility had not believed him when she'd made her report. The Royal Duke was above suspicion, cleared by the True Vision of the three most powerful Seers in Branbridge. It was subterfuge to cloud the issue, nothing more. But Simon had broken, of that she was absolutely certain. In such a situation his continued accusations were unusual.

Bronwynne was looking forward to solving this mystery in his next interrogation, and with that in mind, when the discussion turned to more prosaic topics, she asked to be excused and made her way back to the dungeons.

On the road to Albangate the sounds of approaching hooves caused Fay and Marc to guide their mounts quickly into the covering trees. Moments later a large company thundered by, the moonlight glinting off the embossed flames on their breastplates.

"Flame Champions and Seers," Rosarion whispered in answer to Fay's hissed question, "heading for Albangate."

Marc fidgeted uneasily. "What're we going to do, Fay?"

"Follow them."

Rosarion squinted at her in the faint light. "Follow them? It's not safe."

"It's not safe regardless."

"But the priests will know we've gone north, and . . ."

"No." She chopped one hand down. "If you want to leave us, then you do so, but we're going to Albangate. That's where Hamlin is, and that's where the child is;

end of discussion." She pressed her knees into her horse's sides. "Walk on."

Returning to the road, she did not look back and after a glance at the priest, Marc followed her. Behind him, Rosarion swallowed against the coppery taste of fear that filled his mouth. The company had made much better time than he'd expected. Clutching at his tunic with one hand, he shivered in the cold and wondered if their absence had been discovered yet.

At that moment, Her Grace Bronwynne of Branbridge was standing in the Flame Temple dungeons, staring at the empty cell that had contained Simon of Florenz. Her face working in a combination of surprise and anger and her Sight, still wide open from the effects of the Potion of Revealing, streaked out to seek the answer to this sudden question. It hit the mind of another Seer with explosive force.

Where are you?

Rosarion convulsed in sudden pain as the force of the question cracked through his mind. His hands flew up to clutch his head, and as another bolt of power hit him, he was flung from the horse. Simon cried out also as a brilliant red light pierced the darkness all around him. He would have fallen had Fay not kept one arm held tightly about his waist. Still he jerked backward, crying out as his injured hand slapped against the saddle.

Coughing and gagging on the ground, Rosarion struggled to his knees and looked up to see the misty image of a Triarchy Priest rise up before him. She pointed one accusing finger at the young Herbalist, then turned and reached out for Simon. Rosarion tried to rise, to drive his own power between them, but a fit of coughing threw him back to his knees. The image stretched out one ghostly hand, the fingers drawn up into claws, and then a shadowy figure rose up to cast a cloak of flames before it. It pulled Simon down into the darkness, leaving Rosarion to face the priest's image alone. As she turned, her eyes bright with the red glow of prophecy, he used the last of his own will to call up the amphisbane and fling it at her, breaking contact.

It was quiet on the road. After a moment Marc helped Rosarion rise. Fay looked down at him, her face pale in the moonlight.

"What happened?"

"Seer Priest," he gasped. "Bronwynne of Branbridge. She knows .. about our escape."

"Does she know where we are?"

"I don't think so, but she'll try again . . . so will the others."

"Can you hold them off?"

"Maybe. But the attacks will grow in strength as they coordinate. I don't think I can keep them at bay and ride at the same time."

"What if Marc holds you in the saddle?"

He shook his head helplessly. "I don't know."

"Rosarion."

He looked up.

"I know your mind is strong. I felt it in the dungeons. We need you to shield our whereabouts. No one else can do it. Will you?"

Rosarion swallowed. *Not can you, will you.* Unable to turn away from the unexpected trust inherent in the question, the Herbalist nodded.

Fay smiled. "Thank you. Now, Marc, you must hold him steady."

"Yes, Fay."

The boy reached down and helped Rosarion mount in front of him. Once they were settled, Fay gave a nod and they headed up the road again.

In the Flame Temple dungeon, Bronwynne of Branbridge had not Seen the fugitives' whereabouts, but she had Seen enough. When she came back to herself, she went immediately to Master Julianus with the news. Simon of Florenz had escaped and Rosarion DeLynne, Priest of the Flame, was on the road with him. After a shocked silence, Ellisander DeMarian stood, the green of his eyes obliterated by the rising Flame.

9. The Spinning Coins

"**E**nough work! I'm going to the Broken Sword and you're coming with me if I have to toss your brushes into the fire. It's too blistering dark to paint anyway."

"I'll just be a moment."

"You'll just be now. I've waited all the moments I'm planning to wait."

All right, Leary, I'm coming now."

The shadows swirled about him, covering him like the waves of the ocean. Now and then an image or a memory would surface, only to sink back down into the murky shadows.

"We want the walls of Our Octavia Library to depict the life of Its Most Illustrious Patron. And we want it to be more beautiful than anything the Continent might boast of."

"Yes, Your Majesty."

The feel of the brush in his hand was as familiar as his mother's touch; the smooth wood against his palm, the heaviness of the paint-coated bristles. He raised his hand to begin the first stroke, and pain drove the memory away.

Lorenzo says he'll take you on as an apprentice, Son, if you're sure that's what you want."

"I'm sure, Pa. It's all I've ever wanted."

He remembered. It was all he'd ever wanted: the forms, the colors; the way he merged into the work, losing all sense of self or time; painting until the failing light drove him from the walls and toward the drawing table and the candles that burned low night after night; filling sketchbook after sketchbook, never quite satisfied, always reaching, always perfecting his visions. But not anymore.

"What's that, Pa?"
"It's lead, Simon."
"What's it for?"
"To hold the glass pieces together."
"Why do you use lead?"
"Because it's soft, but it's strong. Everything needs something like that to hold them together. Even people."
"Even me?"
"Even you. Look at your skin. It's soft, but it's strong, too."

The memory showed him a hand, childishly soft and round. As he watched it changed, growing longer, stronger, then a weight came down, smashing against it, and the image shattered.

"Leary!"
"I'm here."
"It hurts, I can't use it. Help me, Leary, it hurts. Make it stop. Make it stop!"
"I will, Simon."

The shadows flowed in, and the pain was swept away down a hazy tide of unconsciousness.

On the road, Simon slumped in the saddle, and Fay held him close, her eyes moist.

The trees were the wrong color.

That was the first thing Kassandra noticed when she opened her eyes.

She'd gone to sleep by the main fire, dressed in her tumbler's clothes, a small pack containing Spotty, her father's tunic, and Luis' nightshirt used as a pillow; in case she and Hamlin had to leave quickly in the night. Simon had told her his plan before he'd left to rescue

his Momma, and Kassandra had given her permission
for him to go. Now she waited for them to come back,
wrapped in Hamlin's strong arms and surrounded by the
watchful members of the Troupe.

Then suddenly, she was awake. Something had disturbed her dreams, but she couldn't tell what. And the
trees were the wrong color.

She squinted up at them. The trees had been brown
when she'd gone to sleep. Now they were . . . red. She
glanced around. Everything was red. She stared into the
fire. It was also red, but then she'd expected that. Fire
was supposed to be red. The shadowy figure crouched
beside it was as familiar as the fire itself, although she
couldn't see his features. Squirming a little to disentangle
herself from Hamlin's arms, she rose and padded over
to her Papa.

He seemed not to notice her at first. His flaming eyes
stared unblinkingly into the fire, but when she sat down
beside him, he put one misty arm about her shoulders.
She pressed into his side, breathing in his familiar smell
of leather and metal, and sighed.

Before he'd gone away, Papa used to visit her at bedtime, back at the palace. The two of them would sit in
the big chair by her hearth and stare into the fire, making up stories about the shapes they saw. Papa said it
was important to *consult the Living Flame*. He said that
she was strong and that the Flame *liked* to talk to her,
and that she should always listen when it did, 'cause the
priests weren't always real smart. Then he'd call her his
Little Gwyneth and smile.

So now, Kassandra looked deep into the main campfire and saw two little fiery horses with two little fiery
riders each weaving back and forth over the logs. It reminded her of the pony Papa had promised to give her
and she turned to him then, but he shook his head and
pointed back at the flames. With a small pout, she
obeyed.

The little figures grew bigger.

"Is that Simon?" she asked after a time.

"*Yes.*"

"An' his Momma?"

"*Yes.*"

"An' that's Marc, there. I recognize him, 'cause he gave me a star on a string."

She reached into her tunic to pull out the wooden gift she wore about her neck.

Her father leaned down politely to admire it.

"Who's that other man with Marc?" she asked after she'd returned the star to its place.

With a negligent shrug that she remembered meant he didn't want to talk about it, her Papa looked off into space. Kassandra returned her attention to the fire.

"Are they a long way away?" she asked.

"Yes."

"Will they be back soon?"

"No."

"But Simon told me that if they wasn't . . . I mean if they weren't back soon, we'd have to run away, me and Hamlin, to Terrilynne's."

"You can't. Simon's hurt, and he needs you to wait."

"Is he hurt real bad?"

"Real bad."

"Oh." She studied the figures, trying to see where Simon was hurt. "Should I tell Hamlin?"

"Only that I told you to wait. If you tell him Simon's hurt, he'll try to go to him, and I want him here. Waiting."

"All right."

They sat in silence for a few minutes.

"Papa?"

"Yes, Little Gwyneth?"

At the sound of her pet name, Kassandra pushed her face into his side. "I'm not a Little Gwyneth any more, am I?" she asked sadly.

"No. You are the Aristok."

"Papa?"

"Yes?"

"I miss you," she whispered.

"I miss you, too, Kassandra."

Half an hour later, the thirty-fifth Aristok of Branion stood with her feet planted firmly apart, glaring up at Ballentire and Hamlin. She had *told* them her Papa's words, but they weren't listening. *They* thought she'd dreamed it, as if she wouldn't know a dream from real life. *She* was almost five. Feeling her eyes grow hot, she marshaled her fiercest stare and looked Simon's Papa right in the eye. She was the Aristok. He *would* obey her. A nimbus of red light rose up between them.

Dawn touched the eastern sky. Hamlin stood silently by the south road, his pipe cold in his hand, his eyes squinting up the road into the early morning gloom. Beside him, Ballentire stamped her feet, trying to bring some warmth back to her toes. When she turned to face him, her expression was resolute. Hamlin gave a sigh and shook his head.

"Not yet, Bal."

"They're long overdue."

"I know, but we agreed. We give them until dawn."

The Troupe Leader glanced pointedly past the artisan's left shoulder to where the sky was turning the horizon a pale pink. Hamlin shook his head again.

"The sun's not fully up yet."

"Something's happened. You know that."

He nodded. "But we agreed," he repeated. "We wait until dawn."

Ballentire glowered at him, then swung her attention back to the road.

The two of them had been there ever since Kassandra DeMarian had refused to leave the camp, citing a father's ghostly visitation as cause. Both he and Ballentire had tried to explain the very real need to leave the area, but the child had been adamant. When they'd pushed the argument, her eyes had gone hot and a misty aura of red light had risen to turn her already auburn hair the color of blood. The Troupe Leader had never seen Marsellus the Third. Hamlin had, and the sudden manifestation of Kassandra's power had caused him to back up a step, reminded of just what her inheritance was.

Her demands had prevailed. She'd told them to wait; all of them, so wait they would, but Ballentire was nervous and worried for the safety of the Coins. Hamlin doubted she would stay much longer despite the Royal command.

Beside him, the Troupe Leader blew on her hands and glanced back at the inexorably rising sun. They'd all had an anxious night. Imperative that the Coins maintain a normal facade, it was also necessary that they keep a constant watch for troops sent from Branbridge. Some of the players had ringed the woods about the camp while others had lain awake by fires strategically placed around the wagons. To the nervous Troupe Leader they'd resembled a badly-laid-out army encampment, but it was absolutely necessary if they were to get the Aristok away safely.

If she could be convinced to leave.

"Papa said Simon needed us to wait, so we're gonna wait!"

"The Flame save me from child rulers," Ballentire muttered as she returned her attention to the road. It remained stubbornly empty. "What happened, Simon? Tell me it just took longer than you expected, so you sent your old friend Leary to keep us here until you made it back.

"Right. The dead Aristok just happens to trot up here to deliver your message as a favor from the Shadow Realm. If you believe that, you'll believe dragons can talk."

Stamping her feet again, she blew on her fingers and squinted back down the road. "Fame and glory, my arse," she muttered. "More like frostbite and ghosts."

Slowly, the trees took on their daylight appearance, trunks and limbs standing out against the lightening sky. As the townsfolk of Albangate rose to start their day, it began to rain. Ballentire cursed.

"Bal!"

The Troop Leader turned quickly as Turi came running forward.

"Katie's just come from town. She says a company of Flame Champions are searching every home and arresting anyone who tries to stop them!"

"What?"

He nodded. "They have Seers with them; three of them!"

"That's torn it! We leave now! Turi, get the Troupe up and moving! Ham, get Kassandra out of here fast! I don't care how you convince her!"

"What about Simon?"

"I'll take care of it. Just go!"

With one last glance up the road, Hamlin turned and raced back toward camp.

The Troupe were barely two miles gone when a company of Flame Champions, led by a thin, wild-eyed Triarchy Priest, caught up to them. They lined the tumblers up along the road and searched each wagon, pulling up floorboards and emptying trunks and bedding out onto the road. Then the priest, his pale eyes lit with the eerie glow of a drug-induced trance, began questioning each Troupe member; asking, as Ballentire feared he would, after Hamlin, the Aristok, and Simon. Two other priests stood behind him, lending their power to his, and the air above them crackled with the intensity of their abilities.

Most of the Troupe dropped instantly into Panishan, indicating through awkward pantomime that they did not understand the priest's words. It was masterfully done, the more so because it gave the Seers little information to sift through, but when the priest's sharp gaze turned on Ballentire, she felt a sudden stab of uncertainty. As leader, she would be expected to speak Branion. She almost blurted out the truth, then at the last moment, recognizing the compulsion for an external pressure and, reminding herself sternly that the Living Flame was on their side, the Troupe Leader looked the Triarchy Priest firmly in the eye and lied through her teeth.

Above them the clouds grew thicker, sending a patter of rain to follow the sudden shadows. The priest squinted, then, after what seemed an eternity, turned away, signaling the others to mount up.

Ballentire gave a sigh of relief as the company moved off. When they were well out of sight, Tamara came up to her.

"That was too close," she breathed.

The Troupe Leader nodded. "He's suspicious," she said.

"But not enough to arrest anyone."

"Maybe. We stay on guard, though. You never know, they might be back." She turned to the others. "Let's clean up and move out. You all did very well. I half believed you myself."

The Coins began to pick up their scattered props, while Tamara fished a wooden practice ball from a nest of weeds and studied it.

"I hope Ham and the child are all right, Bal," she said quietly.

"Me, too."

"I don't like the thought of them out there alone. It's not safe."

"I know." Glancing down the road, the Troupe Leader watched intently, but the Flame Company did not reappear.

From a high vantage point between two hillocks, Hamlin and Dani crouched behind a rock, watching the company of red-clad riders move out. Kassandra stood beside them with Luis, staring down at the Coins and kicking idly at a patch of moss. She had seen the clouds move in, covering the image of her father's face in the sky and was not at all surprised that the riders had gone away. When her Papa got mad, most everyone but Simon went away.

She glanced up at the sky. Her father's face was gone, but she knew his spirit was still here. She could feel it. Pressing her hand to her chest to feel the warmth inside, she leaned against Hamlin's leg.

The artisan absently put his arm about her.

Kassandra had agreed to leave the Coins as long as they didn't move too far away. Willing to grant her anything as long as they left, Hamlin had acquiesced quickly. Dani and Luis had been pressed into service as well, in case they were recognized, and now the four of them watched as the Coins began to pick up their scattered belongings.

Kassandra looked up.

"Were those bad people?" she asked Hamlin.

The artisan nodded.

"They didn't look like bad people. They looked like Papa's .. I mean my Flame Champions. Why are we running from my Flame Champions?"

Avoiding her gaze, the artisan made to pull at his

beard, remembered that it was gone and scratched at his chin instead. He wished Simon were here to answer her questions. Her fire-filled gaze made him distinctly nervous.

Seeing the dilemma of her reticent master, Dani turned to the young Sovereign. "Because they don't know the Duke of Yorbourne is one of the bad people, Majesty," she answered. "And they'd have taken you back to him and arrested Warrin and the other Coins. Until we get to the Duke of Kempston's, it's not safe for anyone to know where you are."

Kassandra considered this. "Where do you s'pose they're gonna look now?"

"I don't know," Dani answered truthfully.

"Do you s'pose they'll come back?"

"They might."

"But if they don't, we go back to the Coins tonight, right?" Kassandra returned her fierce gaze to Hamlin.

"Of course, Majesty."

"Good, 'cause I don't want Warrin to worry. He might do something dumb like come looking for me an' get lost an' die in the woods. An' besides, Simon's gonna need me, Papa said."

Before Hamlin could ask her what she meant, Luis touched his arm. "Uh, it's raining," he noted.

The artisan nodded. "We'd better go down, Majesty."

"Very well."

With one proprietary glance back at the Coins, Kassandra took Luis' hand and began to pick her way down the hill, the server obediently holding her steady. Hamlin and Dani followed, relieved that the child ruler had been placated, but still concerned about her words.

None of them saw the company of Flame Champions pause, while one of them dismounted. Handing his reins to another, he listened intently to the instructions of the Senior Flame Priest, then saluted and made his way into the trees along the road.

Kassandra and her self-appointed bodyguards followed the Coins at a discreet distance for most of the morning, keeping to the woods and hills along the road. The Troupe was moving deliberately slowly, and it was just before noon when one of the back riders sang out that two burdened horses were making their way through the sparse woods toward them. Hamlin beat the others to the spot.

The artisan's joyful greeting of his wife was cut off by the sight of their son. He stopped so abruptly that Ballentire, coming up swiftly behind, almost collided with him. The Troupe Leader spared him one exasperated glance.

The Spinning Coins quickly gathered around the two exhausted mounts. Shocked into silence by Simon's appearance and by Fay's grim expression, they said nothing. Finally Hamlin reached out his arms, and wordlessly his wife let him take their son down from the saddle. Fay then stiffly dismounted herself.

They stood and stared at each other for a long moment, until Tamara brought a blanket to wrap around the other woman's shoulders. Then Fay sagged and allowed the tumbler to escort her to Turi's wagon, while Hamlin took charge of Simon. One by one, the Coins returned to the wagons.

Warrin came to stand beside Kassandra and the two youths. The child gave him a quick glance, but her attention was fixed on the young man who stood coughing and shaking with fatigue behind Marc. Her flame-filled eyes narrowed as she stared at him, trying to see what it was about him that had caused her father such angry indifference. Finally, aware of her regard, the young man turned, his sunken, fever-tinged eyes meeting hers.

Almost against his will, Rosarion met the fiery gaze of the new Aristok. He had seen the child come out of the woods with the man he'd assumed to be Hamlin Ewer. She looked more like a grubby little urchin than the nation's Sovereign, but when her fiery gaze had fallen on him, he'd felt an overpowering compulsion to look at her. He'd obeyed, unable to withstand a lifetime of training. The Living Flame flowed freely behind her dark eyes. Untainted by madness or weakness, It shimmered all around her like a second skin, held in check by a will as strong as any adult DeMarian's. And It was very close to the surface.

The child seemed to see right through him, and as she continued to stare at him, Rosarion DeLynne, heretical Priest of the Flame, sank to his knees before her.

Hidden behind a stand of trees, Atreus DePaula, Junior Champion of the Flame and paid follower of Ellisander Demarian, Royal Duke of Yorbourne, watched as the young Aristok of Branion reached her hand out to place it on the head of the renegade priest.

Ballentire set flankers ahead and behind the wagons as makeshift guards, and once they had Simon and Rosarion safely stowed in Turi's wagon, the Coins set off again. They had to continue toward Caerockeith, but at such a pace that they didn't catch up to the Flame Company ahead of them. It was an intolerably unsafe situation and Ballentire called a meeting in the lead wagon to discuss it as soon as they were underway.

Convinced to leave Simon's side for a few minutes, Fay gave them a shortened version of his questioning at the hands of the Flame Priests, narrating the events in a flat monotone that showed no hint of her reaction. When she was finished, Hamlin put his arm about her while the others sat, unsure of what to say. Finally Ballentire shook herself.

"You're sure he didn't give up the Troupe, Fay?" she asked dubiously.

The other woman nodded grimly. "I asked the priest to be certain. He said, *"the power of the Flame passed over the cell, muting his words."*

"The power of the Flame?" Ballentire shook her head.

"That's what he said."

"And you believe him?"

"Yes."

"But who is this priest, and why did he help you escape?" Hamlin asked with a frown.

"He is the Hand of Essus. He's been shielding us from the Temple Seers who've been seeking us ever since our escape."

"A Triarchy Priest?" Ballentire's voice was incredulous.

"Yes." The look Fay shot the other woman suggested that she wasn't going to maintain her temper much longer, and with raised hands, Ballentire let it drop.

"Well, we can't stay on the main road, regardless," she said. "Not with this company from Branbridge sniffing around, and that means taking secondary roads."

Tamara frowned. "There aren't that many going north, Bal," she said.

"I know, and most are no better than cow paths. That's going to mean a serious loss of time, and if the wagons get bogged down or break an axle, we'll really be in trouble."

"Just how much lost time are we looking at?" Hamlin asked.

Ballentire silently ticked off the stops on her fingers. "It's twenty-five days to Heathland on our regular schedule," she said finally. "Eighteen, maybe twenty, on the main road if we avoid populated towns and limit the time we spend in each one when we do stop. That's assuming we aren't found out by this Flame Company. Taking a secondary route would be safer, but it would add . . . six maybe even ten days, especially if it rains."

"We have to get to Caerockeith as soon as possible," Hamlin said, shaking his head. "It's not safe in the open, no matter what route we take. I say we stay on the main road. The Company already questioned you and carried on. They should be halfway to Vervickshire by now."

"And Simon needs a physician, which we won't find on a secondary road," Fay added.

Her husband turned to her with a worried frown. "Isn't Turi looking after him?"

"Turi's not a physician," Tamara replied for her. "He can clean him up and stitch his wounds, but Sy's hand's going to need professional healing."

They all fell silent. Everyone in the room had seen the blood and fluid seeping through the crude bandage on Simon's painting hand and knew what it foretold. If it got infected, he could die, or lose the use of his hand, which would be almost the same. They had to find him a proper physician.

"The only one I'd trust under these circumstances would be Maggie back home," Tamara said.

Ballentire shook her head. "It's six days on the main road to Moleshil, even if we move quickly, which we can't do without arousing suspicion."

"What about Graveswood? Can we risk speed on the road that long?"

"Graveswood." The Troupe Leader scratched at a scar on the back of one hand. "There might be someone there who'd do, but it's four days' travel at least. Can Sy wait four days if Turi keeps on top of that injury?"

They all turned to Fay.

She pursed her lips grimly. "He'll wait if he has to," she said finally. "But not a day later."

Hamlin looked unhappy. "Are you sure there's no one between here and there?"

"No one of the caliber we need," Tamara answered. "Hempsbridge is too small and I wouldn't trust anyone in Toweford not to sing to the authorities. We need to get through the Kenneth Forest and into Graveswood in Vervickshire first. It's still a DeCarla stronghold. The folk are predominantly Essusiate and much less likely to cooperate with Branbridge than they are here in Berfordshire."

"And if we change course after Graveswood," Ballentire added thoughtfully, "we could make for the west coast on mostly good roads. Port Ellsey's pretty big. You could probably find a ship there that could take you to Caerockeith. The Flame Champions wouldn't expect a move like that. We could be there in nine, maybe ten days, then, say, two days by ship. You'd be there in just over a fortnight."

The others glanced at Tamara. To change course after Graveswood would mean missing Moleshil, her and Turi's hometown, but the tumbler's expression was even. Obviously, she and Ballentire had already discussed this.

"It seems the best plan," Hamlin said finally.

Fay nodded. "As long as we get Simon to a physician first. Without help . . ." she choked, unable to finish the sentence. Hamlin put his arm around her shoulders.

"We're agreed, then." Ballentire stood. "We'll keep the flankers out until we reach Denstead. The town should be buzzing about the Flame Company, so we can find out how far ahead they are and if it's safe to carry on to Graveswood. In the meantime, Fay and Hamlin need to keep out of sight and so does the child."

The others agreed and, with the important decisions finally made, they returned to their own wagons.

While the others discussed strategy, Rosarion watched Turi of Moleshil cut Simon's bloody clothes away. Unsure of where to go when the Troupe had begun to move out, he'd followed Hamlin and Simon. Turi had taken one look at the Herbalist's pale, sweat-covered features and put out a hand.

"Are you all right? You look faint."

Rosarion had nodded. "I'll be fine," he said weakly. "I just need to sit down a moment."

Turi had indicated the chair and Rosarion had sunk into it gratefully, pressing one hand against his temple. When Hamlin and Fay left to meet with Ballentire and the others, he looked up to see the young tumbler watching him with a worried expression. "I have white lung," he said simply. He'd found that in the past being totally honest about his illness was the best line to take. He didn't mention the constant psychic attacks by Bronwynne and the other Seers of Branbridge. Speaking their names would give them strength, and he was barely able to hold them off now as it was.

The other man's eyes widened.

"I'm in stage three," Rosarion continued. "Noncontagious."

Turi regarded him with a serious expression. "Most people don't make it to stage three," he said.

"Most people don't make it to stage two."

The tumbler nodded. "I'm Turious. People call me Turi. I'm sort of the unofficial healer."

"Rosarion. I'm an Herbalist and . . . a Flame Priest."

"Essus greet you."

"Uh . . ."

Turi shrugged self-consciously. "Sorry, force of habit. I mean, I'm glad to meet you." He turned back to Simon, then looked up. "You say you're an Herbalist?"

"Yes."

"Know anything about healing?"

Rosarion nodded slowly. "A little." He rose wearily and moved forward to help.

By the time Fay returned, they'd washed and bandaged the artist's wounds, but the sight of his crushed hand had given them both pause. Finally Rosarion had begun to gently clean the caked blood away from his fingers, trying to repair some of the damage his associates had caused. Simon had groaned once, then fallen silent.

Together they'd wrapped each finger and covered the hand with a clean piece of linen from an old nightshirt. They'd forced a cup of hoodweed tea down his throat and hoped for the best. Rosarion would try to find enough ingredients to make some kind of a salve, but he'd left the Flame Temple with nothing and already his own hands were beginning to shake. Privately neither man believed Simon had much of a chance.

Fay took charge of his other needs. Refusing all help, she sent the two men away, and they went without an argument. Without a proper physician they could do no more for him now than she could. Turi took Rosarion to his cousin Hartney's wagon and, at the end of his strength, the Herbalist fell into a deep and exhausted sleep, lulled by the quiet darkness and the gently swaying wagon. The shadows grudgingly covered his mind and for a while he drifted in silence, the Branbridge Seers momentarily thwarted.

Meanwhile the Spinning Coins Tumbling Troupe trundled down the road, trying to put as many miles between themselves and the capital as possible before nightfall.

They did not make as many as Ballentire would have liked. They were all tired after their long vigil, and when Warrin Fire-Eater fell both asleep and off his wagon five miles past Denstead, she called a reluctant halt for an hour. Most of the Troupe simply stretched out on the grass by the side of the road and fell asleep.

Later that afternoon, somewhat revived, they came to the small village of Brickham. There they received some good news. The Flame Company was at least a day ahead of them and had split into three, one group heading west, one east and the third north. The news that they now faced only one Triarchy Priest raised everyone's spirits. They gave a single performance in town and were ready to move out as soon as Ballentire gave the word. If they pushed it, they might make Toweford before dark.

The Troupe Leader herself was waiting for Fay. Standing on the banks of the Bricklin River, she silently watched as the older woman washed out a piece of bloodstained cloth for the third time.

Without acknowledging the other woman's presence, Fay dipped the cloth into the water, wrung it out, then dipped it in again.

Decided, Ballentire made her way down to the riverbank and took the older woman by the arm.

"C'mon, Fay. They're clean. We have to go now."

The other woman rose woodenly.

Picking up the cloths, Ballentire led her back to the wagons, and after giving the bundle to Turi and setting out the flankers once again, she signaled to her partner.

Tamara nodded.

"Walk on." Snapping the reins, she guided the lead team across the bridge and onto the road.

Ballentire tucked Fay's arm into hers and set off at a brisk gait that kept words to a minimum. They walked in silence for a long time until finally the Troupe Leader glanced over at the other woman.

Fay was walking heavily, her familiar limp more exaggerated today, and her expression was unfocused.

Ballentire slowed. "I've been meaning to ask you, Fay," she said after a time. "Are *you* all right? I mean, they didn't .. hurt you, did they?"

"They?"

"The Flame Priests?"

The older woman shook her head. "I believe I was there as bait to trap Simon." She sighed. "It worked. He's a foolish man."

Scooping up an empty acorn shell, Ballentire tossed it absently from hand to hand. "I tried to tell him that," she said quietly.

"And he wouldn't listen."

"No." She glanced up at the trees then, turned back, an uncertain expression on her face. "Fay, I know this is going to come out wrong, but I'm glad he went anyway. It got you out."

"Yes, but at what cost?"

"At whatever cost. Look, I'm not an Essusiate. I leave all that Fate-God stuff to Tam. All I know is that what's done is done, for whatever reason. We just have to live with it and carry on."

"And I'm not?" Fay gave her a rueful half smile.

"No, you're not. You're dwelling on it. Thinking too much. Or not thinking enough. Simon's going to be all right. You have to believe that. I know you've been through a lot, but you usually bounce back better than this. It's got everyone worried."

"Worried about me?"

Ballentire looked embarrassed. "Well, sure. You're usually a lot . . . tougher. I'm not saying this right, am I?"

"No." Fay smiled at the Troupe Leader's expression. "But it's all right." She patted her arm wearily. "I appreciate the thought." She took a deep breath. "Essus has a plan for us. I know that. We'll just have to carry on and trust that the God knows what's best. Now I have to go to my son."

Her expression firm, she unhooked her arm and strode purposely toward Turi's wagon.

Ballentire stood watching her go with a dubious expression. "Trust in Gods?" she muttered. "Not likely." The Troupe Leader had seen too many plays about the fickle habits of divine beings to have much faith in them, but Fay's words were reassuring.

"One down, one to go," she said quietly. Watching the older woman catch up and enter Turi's wagon, she sighed. "Hopefully one down."

"How long were you on the Continent?"

Simon glanced down from the scaffolding that covered the west wall of the Octavian Library. The young Aristok was looking up at him, his black eyes bright with the Living Flame.

"Eighteen years, Majesty."

"But you were born in Branion?"

"Yes, in Guilcove."

"And yet you call yourself Simon of Florenz?"

Simon set his brush down. *"Eighteen years is a long time. It's where I trained, where I made my reputation."*

"Some might consider it an insult."

"Some?" The artist raised one eyebrow and Marsellus grinned.

"All right, the Hierarchpriest of Cannonshire. She says you're a heretic."

"I'm an Essusiate."

"It's the same thing to Gawaina."

"What is it to Your Majesty?"

The Aristok smiled seductively. *"A challenge."*

The memory was a peaceful one, full of promise and youthful pleasure, so Simon let it flow over him. Far away, a familiar touch on his forehead filtered down to him, but on its heels came the nightmares of blood and pain that the shadows were keeping at bay. The painter turned away from his mother's hand and plunged deeper into insensibility.

"Spend the night with me."

"Majesty?" Simon looked over at Marsellus in surprise.

The two of them had, at the Aristok's insistence, left the library at dusk and gone alone to a tavern in Branbridge. The regular patrons seemed used to the appearance of their Sovereign dressed as a common tinker and had paid him little mind. Marsellus had shouted for wine and had settled into a chair, kicking one forward for the artist.

That had been several hours ago, and now the Aristok was happily drunk.

"Call me Leary, for the scorchin' Flame's sake! How many times do I have to tell you!" The Aristok knocked over a tankard which was quickly retrieved by a server.

Simon regarded him quizzically. *"If you like, but I still don't understand why."*

"Because it pleases me! I'm in disguise. What are you, simple?"

"Oh." The artist glanced around at the other patrons

*who were studiously ignoring them. "In disguise. I'll try
to remember that."*

"See that you do."

When Simon drifted back up, it was dark all around
him. Somewhere he could feel pain, but it was mercifully
distant, and as he floated, something touched his head,
raising it up. Cool water flowed down his throat. He
tasted bitter herbs and honey and swallowed reflexively,
then the shadows rolled back in and he drifted off again.
He was a long time returning.

The Coins were in Toweford the next day, their last
stop before the Kenneth Forest. They arrived in mid-
morning and immediately set up the pennants and tents
for a Day Fair. Hamlin was against it, but Ballentire was
adamant. It was essential that they act naturally here,
she said. Nobody traveled the Kenneth in anything save
full daylight and no company of traveling players would
lose the opportunity to ply their trade while they waited.
The area was heavily reliant on the Earl of Berfordshire's troops to protect them. The citizens of Toweford
were grateful and loyal, and the Earl was one of the
Duke of Yorbourne's supporters. If there were spies
anywhere, it would be here, and one suspicious move
and a dozen people would run for the constable. Reluctantly Hamlin acquiesced.

The Troupe set up a makeshift stage at one end of a
rocky field and settled in for a day of tumbling, singing,
and staged mummery. The town, eager to enjoy this unexpected holiday, threw itself into the act, and before
long booths and tables were set up all around the field
with drinks, sweets, and other wares colorfully displayed.

"Besides," Ballentire said to the artisan after they'd
bought a couple of meat pies from the local butcher,
"we need this. Everyone's getting way too jumpy."

They began to walk casually around the perimeter.
Before them the crowd called out its admiration as Warrin Fire-Eater, his face, arms, and chest painted in a
series of fiery designs, placed the flaming tip of a short
spear into his mouth. Grinning furiously, he pulled the
blacked tip out, then shot a bolt of fire into the sky.

Several of the more sensitive citizens cried out in alarm, but most began to applaud and throw money.

Hamlin nodded, recognizing the wisdom of Ballentire's words. The Coins had relaxed in the familiar atmosphere of their trade, forgetting the sword that hung over all their heads in the haste to milk as much money from Toweford as possible. So far, no one was acting nervous except him.

His gaze stole to the wagons parked at the edge of the trees. Two heavyset players loitered by the door to the smallest of the six. Apparently resting, they were, in fact, guarding its most valuable treasure. Hamlin wondered idly how long that treasure would be willing to stay guarded.

Thinking of Kassandra made him think of Simon, and his gaze moved automatically to the young man they'd pinned all their hopes on for their son's recovery.

Temporarily relieved of sick duty, Tamara's brother was dressed in his gaudiest finery, his long blond hair bound in a loose braid. He stood poised on a rope, tied taut between two trees, and held a set of brightly painted clubs aloft. After a dramatic pause, he began to dance lightly along the rope, the juggling clubs becoming a blur of color around him.

Hamlin and Ballentire watched for a moment and then continued their walk around the fair.

In Turi's wagon, Tamara and Fay were having just the problem Hamlin had predicted.

"I want to go outside and see the fair!"

Kassandra, her young face red with fury, stamped her foot and glared up at the two women.

"But, poppet, it's too dangerous," Fay explained to the furious little Sovereign.

Tamara nodded her agreement. "If someone was to see you, Majesty, we'd all be in a lot of trouble."

"But I'm in disguise!"

"Yes, dear, I know, but one look at your eyes and everyone would guess who you were."

"I don't care! I'm sick of staying in here when everyone else is having fun outside!"

There was a knock at the door.

Relieved by the interruption, Tamara opened it warily only to see Warrin Fire-Eater, his large hands filled with sweetmeats, standing on the step.

"Oh, hello, Warrin. Have you finished your set?"

He nodded. "I wanted to bring Kasey some sweets," he replied slowly.

Early in their travels Kassandra had adopted the big man as her personal bodyguard. As such, he was permitted certain familiarities by the young ruler, such as using a pet name and lavishing attention and sweetmeats on her.

Now, as he ducked his head to enter the wagon, its wheels creaked loudly in protest and the room suddenly seemed much smaller.

He held out his offering to the child.

Kassandra had thrown herself into the wagon's one chair and was sitting with her arms crossed defiantly over her chest. Now she unbent enough to graciously accept one of the sticky treats, then fixed him with an imperious stare.

"I want to go outside and see the fair, Warrin," she said forcefully.

"All right, I'll take you."

"Warrin . . ."

The warning tone in Tamara's voice brought a confused look to the big man's face and a scowl to Kassandra's.

"What?" he asked.

"It's too dangerous."

"Why?"

"Why? Because she's the Aristok, fool," the woman hissed at him.

He scratched his head. "Isn't she in disguise?"

"That's what *I* said," the child agreed peevishly.

Tamara shook her head in exasperation.

"Her eyes," she said with exaggerated patience.

"Oh." He looked from the tumbler to Fay to Kassandra, then back to Tamara. "Well, why can't we disguise them, too?"

"With what?"

"Um, a hat?" His broad face suddenly lit up. "We

could pretend she's blind," he said triumphantly. "She could wear that cloth thing we use in the plays?"

Seating herself on the bed and taking Simon's good hand in hers, Fay looked up. "Cloth thing?" she asked.

Tamara nodded, her own expression thoughtful. "We sometimes use a Blind Chorus to introduce the plays from the Continent. It's part of the Panishan theatrical tradition. The actor wears a fine muslin tied about the eyes to show blindness, but can still see and move about." Her expression firmed again. "It's still too dangerous, Warrin. She couldn't run around on her own; she'd need a guide."

"I could guide," he answered. Crouching down beside the still angry child, he smiled at her. "Would you like to do that, little Lord, pretend like you're blind an' Warrin'd carry you about an' we could both watch the shows, an' get more sweets?"

She gave him a calculated look. "Would I ride on your shoulders so I was above everyone else?"

"Sure would. An' up there you can see for miles. I know, 'cause my head's up there, too, an' it's right empty."

Tamara couldn't help but snicker and Warrin gave her a haughty look.

"I mean there's few other heads in my way," he growled as she tried to work her expression back into one of seriousness.

Kassandra stood up, decided. "We will do that." She pointed at Tamara. "You may get the muslin now, an' Warrin an' I will go out to see the shows, an' I will ride on his shoulders an' he will protect me, an' you will not fuss, but go an' get Fay an' Simon some food."

With a resigned gesture, Tamara gave up. The child would be as safe with Warrin as anywhere. Besides, she had tumbling of her own to get to. Making a dramatic bow, she left in the direction of the props wagon and Kassandra favored Warrin with a sunny smile.

Now, with the advent of night, torches lined the makeshift stage as the Aristok and her faithful retainer stood at the back of the crowd watching the players file on stage.

"My most generous patrons!" Ballentire shouted. "May I present to you the Spinning Coins Tumblers in a most dramatic and bloody rendition of the Gwynethian ballad, 'The Greedy Merchant and the Gray Gryphon!' "

Each player took up a pose and froze as the Troupe Leader began to introduce the various characters.

Dressed in a loose-fitting cloak and hat with the strip of muslin tied about her eyes, Kassandra finished a piece of candied apple and squirmed uncomfortably on the big man's shoulders. "It itches," she complained in a fierce whisper. "An' I can't see now it's dark."

Warrin shifted the foot that was digging into one shoulder blade and nodded his sympathy. "Tip yer hat down then," he whispered back, "an' push the cloth up a bit. No one's lookin' at us. It'll be all right. Jus' don' tell Tam, or she'll kill me."

" 'Kay." Relieved, the child did as he suggested, then wrapped her arms about his forehead, her chin resting on his head.

"What're they doing, Warrin?"

"They're tellin' a story 'bout a merchant that wanted all the gold in the whole Realm jus' for hisself," he answered.

"How come they're not moving?"

"They will in a bit."

Ballentire began the story, each player acting out their part as they were pointed to, then freezing again as she moved on. In the end the gryphon tore the merchant to pieces—symbolized by bits of red cloth being flung into the air from various pockets in his clothing. He died theatrically after a long speech in which he repented of his greed and selfishness, and the crowd began to toss coins on the stage in appreciation of his bloody demise.

Warrin backed up into the shadowed corner of a taverner's booth and Kassandra tucked the cloth back over her eyes as, the night's entertainment now come to an end, the townsfolk began to drift away. When the area was empty of people, Warrin began to make his way back to the wagons.

Kassandra sat quietly on his shoulders, her cheek resting on his head and her arms wrapped loosely about his neck. As they passed the first of the Troupe's small camp fires, she sighed.

"Is it all over now?"

He nodded. "All done. Time for bed."

"I really liked the play."

"Me, too. Hartney makes a good merchant, doesn't he?"

"Uh-huh. Warrin?"

"Yeah, Kasey?"

"I'm thirsty."

"Oh, uh . . ." He looked around. "Pollie, have you got anything to drink?"

The woman in question held up a cup and the big man passed it over.

Pulling the cloth down, Kassandra emptied the cup slowly, wrinkling her nose as she drank. When she was finished, she gave the cup to Warrin who tossed it back.

"Warrin?" Kassandra asked again as the big man headed for Turi's wagon.

"Yeah, Kasey?"

"I gotta pee."

"Oh." With a sigh, he took the child over to the make-shift latrine tent they'd set up. He stood outside, whistling tunelessly through his teeth while he waited.

When the child emerged, she held up her arms, and he replaced her on his shoulders.

"What should we do now?" she asked innocently.

Warrin scratched his head. "Well, we really oughtta go in," he answered. "It's getting late. Aren't you sleepy?"

"No."

"Oh. I am. All that fire-eating makes me very sleepy."

She giggled. Drumming her heels against his chest in time with his footsteps, she bounced a little as he walked.

"Warrin?"

"Uh-huh?"

"How can you eat fire without burning up?"

"Well, it's really just a trick."

"Oh. So you don't actually eat it?"

"No. Not actually. My stomach would get awfully sore if I actually ate it."

"I guess."

She laid her cheek against his hair for a moment, then pulled on his ears.

"Warrin?"

"Yeah, Kasey?"

"Do you s'pose Braniana ate the Living Flame?"

He made to scratch his head, found her arm laid across his usual spot and contented himself with scratching his brow.

"I dunno," he answered after a minute. "Didn't they kinda come together like?"

"Yes, but the Flame went inside her."

"That's true. I guess maybe she did, then. They say her Momma was a giant, so maybe it didn't hurt her stomach."

"The Flame's inside me now, an' my stomach doesn't hurt."

"No?"

"No. Jus' my head sometimes."

"Maybe there's a trick to it, too."

"I guess, but I don't know what it is. My Papa died before he could tell me."

She snuffled a bit, and Warrin reached up to stroke her hair as they came up on Turi's wagon.

"I don't want to go in yet,' she said as he made to knock on the door.

"But it's late."

"I know, but I'm tired of staying in the wagon. Simon's all sick, an' it makes me scared for him."

"Do you want to sleep in a different wagon?"

"No, I wanna sit outside with you."

He smiled. "Well, I guess we could for a little while." Reaching up, he lifted her off his shoulders and, wrapping her securely in her cloak, sat down on the wagon's steps with her on his lap.

They sat there quietly for a while, Warrin looking up at the stars and Kassandra burrowed into his tunic. Just when the big man thought she was asleep, the child stirred.

"Warrin?"

"Yeah?"

"Is Simon gonna die?"

"No."

"Are you sure?" The child looked up into Warrin's face, seeking reassurance, and he smiled at her.

"I'm sure."

She settled back, but after a moment, looked up again.

"Warrin?"

"Yeah?"

"Why did they hurt Simon like that?"

He sighed and rubbed his cheek against her hair.

"I dunno, sweetie. Why does anyone hurt other people?"

"Do you figure Uncle Sandi did it?"

"Probably. I guess. I dunno, Kasey, I'm just a player, I don't know anything about stuff like that. I'm sorry."

"That's all right, Warrin." She patted his arm and laid her head against his chest. "I like that you don't, cause it makes you more like you an' less like everybody else."

"Thanks."

"Warrin?"

"Yeah?"

"Do you s'pose what happened to the merchant will happen to Uncle Sandi?"

He considered it for a minute. "Probably," he said finally. "He did a real bad thing, killing yer Papa, an' trying to hurt you, you know, but I guess it'll be up to yer cousin Terrilynne."

She stuck her fingers under the cloth and played with it a moment before shaking her head.

"No," she said emphatically.

"Huh?"

"It's not up to Terri, Warrin. It's up to me. I'm the Aristok, an' Papa said the Aristok has the final say in everything."

"Oh. Then I guess it is up to you." He paused. "Do you *want* to do that to your Uncle Sandi?"

Her finger in her mouth, the child leaned against the big man's chest again, listening to the thump of his heartbeat.

"I dunno," she answered, suddenly sleepy.

"Well, you've got a while to decide," he said, his voice relieved. "An' you'll probably have a bunch of councillors to help you make up your mind, anyway."

"I guess." She yawned. "But Papa never listened to his councillors much."

"No?"

"Nope. He usually called them bad names an' then did what he wanted. All 'cept for Simon. He always listened to Simon."

"Yeah?"

"Yeah. Simon's special."

"He sure is."

Kassandra's breathing deepened.

"Yer gettin' awful sleepy," Warrin said to the top of her head. "Don't you want to go in now?"

"No."

He smiled. "Well, I guess we can sit for a bit longer."

Shifting her so she was tucked into the crook of his arm, he began to rock her gently back and forth.

She yawned again. "Warrin?"

"Yeah?"

"Sing me something."

He smiled into the darkness. "Sure."

He began an old sea song, his rich, baritone voice making a comfortable rumbling in his chest.

"Sleep little babe, in the arms of the Sea.
Sleep and be safe in the waves.
Your net is your blanket, your catch is your dreams,
Your cradle the ship that shall bring you to me."

Pressed against him, the child smiled dreamily and closed her eyes.

In the wagon, Fay's expression softened at the sound of the ancient lullaby she herself had sung to Simon so many years before. Stroking away the tight lines on his face, her gaze moved to the ugly bandage on his hand, and she was suddenly very tired. Lying down beside her son still lost in his world of pain and shadows, she slowly fell asleep, lulled by the soft voice of the gentle man outside.

Outside in the field the Coins quickly cleared away the remains of the fair, then sought their own beds. When Warrin Fire-Eater finally carried the sleeping ruler into Turi's wagon, all was quiet around them. He laid her gently down beside Simon and Fay and the child wrapped her small arms about the artist. Warrin draped a blanket about the three of them, and then, quiet despite his size, he left the wagon and stretched out before its door.

In the darkness the Living Flame stirred in the breast of Its young Vessel. Instinctively drawn by the need of Its chosen Champion, It reached out and, wrapping Simon's wounded mind in layers of warmth, It cradled it like a child. The shadows swirled jealously around It, but were inexorably pushed back by the surprising strength of Its new Avatar.

Touching by the divine, a part deep inside Simon's mind relaxed and he slept without dreaming.

The field grew still. The only movement was the rustle of those players on guard around the small fires, lighting pipes and settling down to watch the shadowed woods around them.

And, in the darkness, unseen by those watchers, Atreus DePaula stood, studying the sleeping camp. Folk with many faces had been Seen in vision and even Atreus knew that could mean actors or tumblers, and His Grace, Seth Cannon's orders had been specific: watch the tumbling troupe. If they did anything suspicious, get to the nearest authority and have them all arrested, then get a message to the company's main body. Ellisander DeMarian's orders had been equally succinct. Find Rosarion DeLynne. Bring him back.

Atreus was not a particularly devout young man. The fifth child of the Viscount of Bercombe, he had tested as a Seer at thirteen and this discovery had set his life out for him. He'd entered the Flame Temple as squire to a second cousin, learned to use his Gift in battle, was knighted as a Flame Champion five years later, and took his place in that exalted company as a junior knight just as he was expected to. His family was proud of him in the absentminded way one is proud of a child whose actions had never prompted a strong response.

He'd been in the paid service of Ellisander DeMarian since before his knighthood; courted and won by the

Royal Duke who recognized an ambitious but lazy
young man when he saw him. The Duke had offered
him patronage, paid his gambling debts, and gifted him
with presents of money when the youth's allowance ran
out. He'd used his influence to smooth over an embar-
rassing incident or two and had asked nothing in return
until now.

Atreus had almost balked at his request. The Duke
could be a frightening man, and his involvement in present circumstances did not bear looking at too closely.
Plus Rosarion DeLynne was one of the most powerful
Seers in the Realm. He was sure to know he was being
hunted. And how was he—Atreus—to get away from
the Company he'd just been assigned to? Seth Cannon
was to command it, and he was accounted almost as
powerful a Seer as Rosarion.

The Duke had listened politely to Atreus' concerns,
then casually mentioned his debts—to both Ellisander
and certain gaming houses in the capital that wouldn't
look too kindly on a sudden decrease in payments—and
suggested he use his initiative. Atreus may have been
lazy, but he wasn't stupid. He caught the gist of the
Duke's threats immediately, assured the other man of
his loyalty, and got out of his presence as fast as possible.

In the end, absenting himself from Seth Cannon and
the Company had been easy enough. He'd simply suggested that the tumbling troupe seemed to be acting suspiciously and should be watched. He'd intended to leave
at the first opportunity. Then the Triarchy dropped Its
greatest gift into his lap.

Rosarion DeLynne had linked up with the tumblers,
bringing Simon of Florenz and Fay Falconer with him.
Then Hamlin Ewer had come out of the woods with the
Aristok herself by the hand. Every person Ellisander
DeMarian desired to have within his grasp once more
were together in one group, and only Atreus knew their
whereabouts. If he could think of some way to bring
them all to him, the Duke would pay handsomely,
maybe even a Barony or an Earldom.

Chewing on a twig, Atreus considered the problem.
He would need troops to take them all, but if he went
to the Earl of Berford, she might take the credit and

there would go his Barony. He frowned. The troupe was heading for Vervickshire and there was a Sword Chapterhouse in Graveswood. With his status as a Flame Champion he could commandeer some junior Knights, take the whole troupe, and bring them back to Branbridge. That was the answer; he would wait until Graveswood.

His mind filling with images of wealth and power, Atreus curled up under a tree and, pulling his cloak tightly about him, slept.

10. Ellisander

"**S**he's coming today."

Leary paced back and forth across the empty conservatory, tugging anxiously at the silver filigree on his tunic sleeve. The sunlight, pouring in through the glass doors, highlighted his hair in streaks of dark auburn fire.

Simon smiled in appreciation of the sight, then returned his attention to his work. He'd brought a pad of Florenzian watercolor paper to the palace today and was busy stroking pale green paint across the top sheet in preparation for a depiction of the Atrean gardens.

"Who's coming?" he asked absently, dipping his brush in a crystal glass of water. "Kathrine?"

"My Cousin Kathrine. My betrothed Cousin Kathrine. My betrothed soon-to-be Consort Cousin Kathrine."

"And you're nervous?"

Leary turned to stare at the other man. "What a stupid question," he barked. "Of course I'm nervous! Who wouldn't be nervous? Weren't you nervous?"

"When?"

"When you first met Jade!" The DeMarian threw his arms wide, knocking a vase of roses off its stand. It fell to the floor with a crash, and a servant appeared out of nowhere to clean it up.

With a sigh, Simon set his brush down. "No, but then we weren't betrothed. It wasn't until after she told me she wanted a child that I admit I felt a little . . . pressure."

"Fine," Leary grated out. "That's what I'm feeling. A little pressure. I'm about to be married to a woman I've never met, and I'm feeling a little pressure!"

"You're overreacting."

"Am I?" the DeMarian asked almost hysterically.

"What if we hate each other? It's important that we get along, you know, important for the Realm."

Simon studied his friend's face and made the correct assessment.

"Don't worry. She'll like you."

Leary glared at him. *"How do you know?"* he asked accusingly.

"What's not to like?"

The DeMarian studied the other man's face, searching for sarcasm, but Simon's expression remained neutral.

"Her brother's coming, too," the DeMarian announced instead, changing the subject.

"So?"

"So? So what if I like her, but hate him?"

"Send him home."

"Oh, just like that?"

"Just like that."

"Well, what if I hate her and like him?" Leary's voice was petulantly challenging, and with a sigh, Simon returned to his painting.

"Then marry him," he answered.

"You're not so funny."

Simon filled his brush with color. *"Will you relax? You will like them both. They will like you. You will all live happily ever after together."*

"You know this, oh, great prophet?"

"I do. I have spoken." Simon flourished the brush in the air, splattering the floor with paint. The servant reappeared with a cloth in his hand.

Leary laughed, his mood suddenly brightening like the summer sky. *"I'll believe you,"* he said. *"At any rate, I'm tired of thinking about it."* He came forward. *"Let's go riding and make love in a field one last time before my marriage."*

"Can I finish my painting?"

"No."

"Leary . . ."

"No!"

"Very well." With a sigh, Simon set his brush aside again and allowed Leary to drag him out the glass doors and into the sunshine beyond.

* * *

The memory disintegrated so quickly that he almost gasped aloud. Darkness surrounded him, blocking out the warmth of that long-ago summer's day. He was lost and in pain, the comforting shadows nowhere around him, and he cried out in sudden fear.

"Leary!"

The shadows stirred weakly. *"Simon."*

"Where are you? It's dark. It's . . . hot. I can't feel you. I'm so hot."

"Something terrible's about to happen. I can sense it. She can sense it."

"What?"

"I don't know." The shadows grew faint. *"It's Ellisander. He's done something."*

Simon reached out, sensing nothing. *"I can't see you!"*

"I can't see you either."

"Don't go, Leary! Please don't go."

"I'll try. Simon . . . help me."

The shadows disappeared, and without their support the artist sank into fever-induced unconsciousness.

In Branbridge, the Duke of Yorbourne sat in his outer chamber, his steepled fingers pressed against the bridge of his nose. The morning was overcast, the clouds outside his window causing the room to drop into a precipitated gloom, matching his mood. Earlier Jeri had entered to ask after breakfast, but had departed after his hesitant inquires had brought no response from his Royal Master. Exasperated, Adrianus had left the suite with him. Ignoring them both, Ellisander sat staring into the fire, his thoughts in the recent past.

After hearing Bronwynne's and Talisar's reports on Rosarion's disappearance, the Duke had returned to his own suite, too overcome by the young priest's sudden treason—or so he'd told Archpriest Julianus—to remain. In actual fact, the fury at hearing of Rosarion's defection had threatened to spill over into violence. He'd barely made it to his suite where the broken pieces of pottery scattered about the floor were a mute testimony to his rage.

They remained there three days later, untouched by order of the Duke, glittering accusingly in the firelight.

A reminder that a lack of control could ruin everything. His servants were too frightened to question his actions, his Companion was too pragmatic.

Taking a deep breath, Ellisander willed the still seething power of the Flame, lessened by only one degree, back behind the battlements of his self-control. Now was not the time to allow anger to cloud his reason. Now was the time to sit quietly and think before all his carefully organized plans came unraveled. Later, when Rosarion was returned to Branbridge, that would be the time to let anger and betrayal have its due.

Ellisander stared into the fire, his eyes narrowing. He'd believed that, motivated by guilt and by the love they'd both shared for Saralynne DeLynne, Rosarion had been unable to betray him. That had been his first mistake. That he had not planned for it was his second. There would not be a third.

The Duke's hands clenched into fists. He had taken Rosarion from his sickbed, saved his life, given him a reason to live, and held off the Shadow Catcher. And for what? To be betrayed. His vision grew red.

Forcing himself to breathe deeply, Ellisander opened his fists and stared curiously at the eight red crescents pressed into the palms. *"Control,"* he chided himself. *"Remember, people are motivated by needs."* Laying his palms flat against the arms of his chair, he returned his gaze to the fire.

So what had Rosarion needed that he hadn't anticipated? Punishment for his part in regicide? The Duke passed that estimation back and forth. Possibly. But due to his belief in a predictable future, Rosarion had been a willing participant, guilt or no guilt, until his visit to the Flame Temple dungeons. So, what event had caused that guilt to override his commitment to what he saw as a True Vision of the future? The recognition of a shift in power brought on by some new vision at the time? Again, possibly.

The Duke shook his head in impatience. Of all those involved in Marsellus' death, only Rosarion would be believed, and only he had so little to lose that the consequences of regicide would not frighten him into silence. So, conjecture aside, what he, Ellisander, needed was

real answers or Rosarion dead before anyone else discovered them.

He stood, suddenly unable to keep still, his fingers
curling up into stiff claws. No, this had become personal.
What he needed was Rosarion, here, under his control
once again.

To that end, he'd sent for Atreus DePaula as soon as
his rage had cooled enough to let him think clearly. The
Flame Champion was to be part of the Company sent
looking for the fugitives, and Ellisander had one simple
order for him. Bring Rosarion back. The Duke did not
care how he did it.

That had been three days ago and Atreus had not
returned, but he would and then everything would be
back as it should be.

Forcing himself to return to his seat, the Duke took
a deep calming breath. When he felt his anger dissipate,
he turned his mind to less personal matters. When had
events begun to slip from his control? he asked himself.

When Kassandra DeMarian had disappeared from her
bedroom, obviously, his thoughts answered.

Could he have planned for that? Should he have foreseen it?

Grinding his teeth, he started sightlessly across the
room. Rosarion should have foreseen it, he thought, his
anger returning. The child was pivotal to his plans, he'd
told the Herbalist that. And she must be returned to
him before Terrilynne DeMarian moved on the capital.
He closed his eyes, watching the tiny flames lick at the
back of his lids.

The Duke of Kempston was most certainly amassing
troops for an assault against Yorbourne preparatory to
marching on Branbridge itself, he speculated. To counter
such a move, he had sent word to his Steward and to
those Lords under his influence to prepare for war and
had taken steps to insure the Branbridge nobles remained firmly on his side. Julianus' Flame Champions
were scouring the countryside and his priests were con-
stantly in the Prophetic Realm seeking a way past Essus'
scorching interference, to pinpoint the Aristok's whereabouts. It was only a matter of time before they found
her, and after she was returned, Terrilynne could not

move against him without incurring the wrath of the Realm.

The room darkened perceptibly, and Ellisander looked up with a frown, but it was only the gathering clouds. He took a deep breath.

Eyes narrowed, he glared at the small fire in his hearth, willing it to reveal Kassandra's location. The flames remained obscure as they always had. Only the Seer Priests could view the Prophetic Realm in fire.

Only the Seer Priests and the Vessel of the Living Flame, a tiny part of his mind added.

He'd ignored it. Soon he would be that Vessel. First, however, he must cloud the minds of the Seer Priests once more. Without Rosarion it would be tricky, but he had taken steps to insure that as well.

He had sent for Hadrian after his meeting with Atreus. The DeSandra Viscount was to deal with the problem of the Seer Priests and their Vision. The Duke's orders had not been specific; his only imperative was that it be taken care of immediately.

Hadrian had required very little persuasion. Unlike Atreus, he was far too involved to balk now.

The Duke sat back, satisfied that his arrangements were back on track. Hadrian and Atreus would come to him when they'd completed their tasks. Julianus would come to him when the Aristok was found. Marsellus was dead, and Rosarion and Simon of Florenz would soon be in his hands. He was still going to win.

In the corner of the room, the shadows stirred uneasily, then fled as Ellisander DeMarian's mind suddenly exploded in flames.

It flung him up from his seat and tore a scream from his lips as the room burst into fire before his eyes. In the distance the alarm bells of the Branbridge Flame Temple began to sound.

FIRE!

The force of the sudden contact slammed into Rosarion's mind, snapping him out of sleep in an instant. He fell out of bed, crying out and slapping at his clothes as his sight filled with scenes of fire. Flames were everywhere, blocking every avenue of escape, and as he spun about wildly, people crowded into his vision. Bronwynne, Julianus, Devarian, most of the priests he'd lived and trained with shrieked in agony as, trapped, they stumbled about their fire-engulfed sleeping quarters.

THE FLAME TEMPLE IS BURNING!

The Herbalist jerked backward, cracking his head against the wagon's small table. He had a brief vision of Warrin Fire-Eater's face, and then the burning temple rose up before him again.

HELP ME!

Smoke filled Rosarion's lungs and he began to panic as his vision grew dizzy. Clawing at his throat, he began to cough, and then a noise above him made him jerk his head up. The ceiling was on fire, the beams outlined in traceries of red. It cracked, sagged, and suddenly fell with a great gout of smoke and flames, trapping him beneath the burning rubble. He screamed as he felt the heat against his flesh, and all around him, people echoed his cries.

Dying in agony, the honed Gifts of the Flame Priests snapped together in one great bolt of energy and streaked out, making contact with any who might save them. As one they cracked against Rosarion's mind, disintegrating his defenses, and sending him spinning into a maelstrom of death and torment. Unable to contain it, his own Gift fled to the mind of Seth Cannon not ten miles away. But the Senior Seer was also trapped in the death throes of his fellow priests. Together, the traitor and the loyal priest began to scream.

FIRE! BURNING! HELP US!

All across Branion, the desperate cry went out.

In a troop of Berfordshire guards, Atreus DePaula jerked as if he'd been struck and fell unconscious, his small Gift overcome by the force of the agony that slammed into it.

In Vervickshire, a whole company of Flame Champions collapsed, leaving only their servants standing to tend to them and to their Senior Seer who convulsed in agony, screaming that he was on fire.

On the roads to Leiston, Barrowness, and Caerockeith, it was the same. And in Branbridge, the center of the psychic blast was like a white-hot conflagration. People with even the slightest sensitivity fell screaming; those with more convulsed and died, their spines snapped by the power of the dying priests. Their need spread out in waves, catching every Street Seer, physician, and priest in Branion.

The Royal DeMarians no matter how distant, were caught up by the cry to the Flame within them, and flung, convulsing to the ground.

In conference with Sean Cailein at Caerockeith, Terrilynne DeMarian suddenly collapsed, her mouth bloody where she'd bitten her tongue. As her people leaped to her aid, she went into a seizure.

Her young cousin, Alexius DeMarian, was knocked off her feet in the castle stables and barely avoided an upraised pitchfork as she fell.

In Carisley, Zavier DeMarian suddenly choked on his breakfast and would have died if his Companion Octavian hadn't been there to help him.

In Wakefield, Albion DeMarian began to seizure in bed. Frantically, his latest lover, Nathaniel DeKathrine, rang for a servant, then held him, trying to keep him from throwing himself to the floor.

In her town house in the capital, Evelynne DeMarian also began to convulse in bed, held by her two Companions.

And in his suite in Bran's Palace, Ellisander DeMarian, Duke of Yorbourne, was beyond his people's aid. The passage of the priests and the answering rise of the Flame within him had sent him careening across the room, his mind on fire. He hit the far wall of his outer chamber and collapsed like a broken puppet. When his servants found him, they managed to get him into bed, but there was no one to tend to him. All the Court Physicians had been struck down as well.

The blast reached the borders of Branion and arched

across the waters toward Eireon and Danelind. All over the Triarchy, the followers of the Living Flame added their pain to that of their senior priests, and in Turi of Moleshil's wagon, It heard and responded to their need.

It swelled and grew within the breast of Kassandra the Sixth, and the child was swung into the air above her bed by the force of it, held up by the power of the Flame. Her eyes aglow with an incandescent light, power danced over her arms and legs. Soon it was too much for the small Vessel to contain and with a crack of displaced air, the Living Flame spewed out into the sky. It surrounded the small wagon in a halo of red-and-orange light, pulsing outward as the need of Its followers still called to It. It began to spin, radiating outward like a giant whirlpool. It reached the already flayed mind of Rosarion DeLynne and knocked it into darkness, catching up its share of energy as it passed. It sucked up the pain of Simon of Florenz and the power of the ragged shadows still clinging to his mind. It widened to engulf Berfordshire, felling people as It collected their thoughts and feelings like sheaves of wheat. Then, swollen with power, it moved on.

By the time It hit Branbridge, the Living Flame finished what the burning of the Flame Temple had begun. All through the capital, people collapsed, the weak and young dying before they hit the ground as, out of control, It sucked up the energy of their faith and left them empty.

Within the place where the Gods dwell, the balance of power shifted over Branion and, like one end of a pendulum, Essus turned to respond.

The High Essusiate Abbot of Branbridge awoke from a dream of fire and fear. The God's voice echoed in her mind, demanding she rise and give aid to the followers of the Triarchy. She did not question Essus' motives, but rose at once and began to gather her followers. By the time they were ready, their mission was clear. The eastern sky glowed with the ugly orange of buildings on fire.

The followers of Essus ran for the source of the blaze, gathering others as they went. They formed a human

bucket chain down to the banks of the Mist, and one by
one, they passed its waters up to the Flame Temple.
Those not within the chain roused others of their faith
to help pull the priests and acolytes from the outer buildings not yet on fire, and tend to those who'd managed
to escape. In the city, Essusiate Clerics and lay people
moved quickly to tend to the Triarchs struck down by
the passing of their priesthood, bringing many of them
into the Essusiate churches for care. Numerous Triarchy
Priests and citizens awoke hours later, blinking up at the
painted face of Merrone staring down at them. It was a
sobering experience.

Above them, the presence of Essus rose to meet the
power of the Living Flame. The two Gods merged, grew,
and calmed, as the one channeled the wild power of the
other into the earth beneath them. The roaring above
the capital grew quiet, and in Toweford, Kassandra De-
Marian eased slowly down to her bed and began to cry.

There was silence in Branion.

Slowly, throughout the country, those able to, began
to pick themselves up and glance fearfully around. Their
towns looked like a hurricane had blasted through them.
Trees had been uprooted, houses and barns had had
their roofs torn off and people littered the ground.

Crouched by her brother's wagon, her clothes in
shreds, Tamara of Moleshil, stared at the red patina engraved on it, her mind too shocked to truly grasp what
she'd seen.

Around her, groaning, the Coins began to pick themselves up and, ever practical, one thought slowly made
its way into Tamara's mind. When they recovered, everyone in Toweford was going to know exactly where
the destructive power had come from. The Troupe was
in danger. They had to get out.

She turned and with much slow maneuvering managed
to get the Coins stumbling sluggishly toward the horses.
The Essusiate members were a little better off, so Tamara set them to helping the others. They found Ballentire in the branches of a fallen tree, where she'd been
knocked when the Living Flame had exploded from
Turi's wagon. She was groggy and barely responsive, but

alive. They got her to the lead wagon, and when she was sure every member of the extended Troupe was alive and accounted for, Tamara got them moving. There was only one place to go now, as dangerous as it might be.

By the time Toweford began to pull itself together and somebody from the Duke of Berford's Estate was found to take charge, the Spinning Coins Tumbling Troupe were well into the Kenneth Forest. They were shaky, without the guidance of their Troupe Leader and without guards, but at least they were out of Berford-shire, where too many questions were about to be asked. That was all Tamara could do right now. The rest she would deal with later.

In Turi's wagon, Fay held Kassandra, sleeping peacefully despire her ordeal.

In Branbridge, Lysanda DeSandra had been in her stables when the alarm bells of the Flame Temple began to toll. Moments later it seemed the whole world had been turned upside down. Her stable master and half her grooms had fallen screaming to the ground, three others had crumbled, their faces lined with pain. The Earl herself had felt suddenly dizzy, but the spell had passed. Across the city other bells began to ring the alarm as the capital rocked from the sudden loss of its Priesthood.

Lysanda had wasted little time. When the worst of the effects had ebbed, she'd seen to her own household, then left her Companion Larista in charge, and called for her riding horse. Moments later, she was clattering down the cobbled streets of the city, four guards keeping pace around her. By flagging down a passerby, she managed to learn what had happened. The Flame Temple was on fire, its priesthood trapped within.

Branbridge was in chaos. To the west there was an ugly orange glow to the sky that confirmed their words. To the east the effect was spreading. Those not affected and not already running with anything that could carry water, were either caring for the wounded, or were adding to the confusion by panicking or looting. Lysanda watched a man exit a tavern, unimpeded, a huge keg in his arms. It gave her an idea.

Turning onto Morian Street, she headed toward her brother's house.

She found his household in turmoil. His steward's heart had failed, and his servants were beside themselves. Through a judicious use of force, Lysanda managed to calm them down enough to learn that Hadrian had become hysterical and, screaming, had locked himself in his bedroom. Her face expressionless, the Earl of Surbrook took charge. Ordering Hadrian's servants to begin cleaning up, she went in search of her brother, pulling out the key to his inner chamber that she carried from force of habit.

She found him already reeling drunk and weeping by his hearth. Two empty bottles lay on the floor by his feet, and he raised another to his lips. Growling in disgust, Lysanda crossed the room and snatched it away from him.

Hadrian goggled at her sudden appearance and made a grab for the bottle. Overbalancing, he fell heavily to the floor.

Grabbing him by the tunic, Lysanda hauled him to his feet and shoved him into a chair.

"What's the matter with you?" she hissed. "You're acting like a five-year-old afraid of a thunderstorm. Get a grip! Your people all think you've taken a fever that's addled your wits!"

Hadrian dropped his head into his hands.

"Perhaps that's it, then," he moaned. "Yes, maybe it is, maybe it's not my fault," He looked up at her, his eyes glassy. "It's not my fault, Lys. I didn't know, I didn't know he'd . . . I didn't think he'd go that far. I mean, who would?"

"What are you babbling about?"

Hadrian swallowed and glanced about for his bottle. Lysanda set it firmly on the table beside her, out of reach. "Well?"

"I didn't think he'd . . . burn it," he whispered, "and kill all those people. They're the scorching Flame Priests! How could I have known! Who would have dared?" His voice rose hysterically, but his sister gave him a disgusted look and he subsided a little.

Lysanda's eyes narrowed. "Burn it?" she asked. "You mean burn the Flame Temple?"

He nodded.

"*You* did that?"

"I didn't mean to," he wailed. "I assumed he'd just do something to distract them or . . ." he trailed off.

His sister was still staring at him. "*You* ordered the burning of the Flame Temple?"

"Stop saying that! I didn't order it! The Duke did. He told me to do something about the priests! I just passed the message along!"

"To whom?"

"The man, I don't know his name. He said he could do anything, solve any problems. He said he was a mirror, you know, someone the Seers can't See. I just told him to do it, you know, get them out of the way, cloud their Prophecy. I didn't know he'd do that."

Lysanda took a swallow from the glass.

"You know Aunt Bretna was at the Flame Temple?" she asked him reflectively.

"I know. Scorch it, Lys, it's not my fault!"

Lysanda wasn't looking at him. "It's all right, Ryan," she murmured, using his childhood name absently. "I never liked her anyway. And I never would have believed you had it in you," she added with a smile. Then her expression grew disdainful again. "So what are you howling about?"

"What do you mean what am I . . . ? He burned down the scorching Flame Temple, Lys! *The Flame Temple.*"

"Yes. You already told me that."

"But when they find out, they'll kill me, they'll torture me and tear me apart and throw my body into the Mist!"

"Who will?"

Hadrian sputtered at her. "The Hierarchpriest of scorching bloody Cannonshire for a start!" he shrieked, infuriated by her lack of concern.

She raised one eyebrow. "How? From what I hear, most of the Seer Priests are dead, and the others are so incapacitated they might never recover, so how's Gawaina to find out you had anything to do with it?

Unless you're planning on confessing?" she added sarcastically.

He glared sullenly at her. "Very funny." Then he straightened. "You're right. The Prophecy is blinded." He stood. "They can't See it, they can't See anything. This is wonderful!" He laughed. "I'm saved!"

"Hooray," his sister answered dryly. Standing, she went in search of a glass, and once found, poured herself a drink. "So, now that you're not going to die, we have to decide what to do next."

"What do you mean?"

"I mean, stupid, that this is a golden opportunity for us."

When Hadrian's face remained blank, she closed her eyes and counted to ten. "Who's in charge right now?" she asked slowly.

"Well, the Duke of Yorbourne."

"Wrong. Word from the palace is that he got the shit kicked out of him from your little incident."

Hadrian winced. "Gawaina?"

"Very good. And she's going to need all the help she can get when the Essusiates realize that Branion's Prophetic strength has been crippled. So who's going to help her?"

"Well, the Privy Council . . ."

"Who are all either Priests or DeMarians, and . . ."

He blinked. "Are all in the same shape as the Duke?"

"That's right. So if we make ourselves available, we won't just come out of this healthy, but wealthy besides, whoever ends up in charge later."

He began to grin. "I like it."

"I thought you might. Now, are you sober?"

" 'Course. Well, mostly, why?"

She sighed. "Because we have to go find the Hierarchpriest and offer her our services. Remember?"

"Oh. Right."

Rolling her eyes, Lysanda crossed to the door and called Hadrian's valet to help him dress. The man came on the run, his face relieved and, an hour later, the brother and sister were on their way into the city in search of Gawaina DeKathrine.

*   *   *

At that moment, the Hierarchpriest of Cannonshire was standing on the water-soaked stones of the Flame Temple's main courtyard, staring up at the building's soot-grimed facade. The fire, which had quickly spread from the sleeping quarters to the other, more open areas of the temple, had finally been quelled, and a steady stream of people, mostly Essusiates, were beginning the mammoth task of clearing away rubble and unearthing the dead. The Hierarchpriest shook her head, both the personal and political ramifications too overwhelming to contemplate.

A bearded man carrying the body of a young acolyte moved past her, and she stared at his retreating back for a long time, unsure of what to make of it.

Gawaina DeKathrine had been fighting Essusiatism all her life. Born during the reign of Atreus the Bastard, she'd lost her father during the First Tiberian Crusade. She herself had fought in the Second and led troops in the name of the young Kathrine the Fifth in the Third. The De-Kathrine name was synonymous with militant loyalty to the Triarchy, and this generation had been no exception. Dozens had fought and died to preserve Its place in Branion. But now . . .

She gazed dazedly about, unable to fathom the blow the Triarchy had taken. At first she'd thought to convene the Privy Council to help deal with this catastrophe, but most were either dead or incapacitated. The Triarchy Knights were in a like state. Finally she'd begun to gather what nobles were still standing and sent them into the city with their retainers to bring what order they could to the capital. They found it in the very capable hands of the High Essusiate Abbot of Branbridge who was busy organizing relief and care for the wounded. Unsure of how to deal with this sudden change of circumstance, most of the Branion nobility had simply placed themselves under her direction.

Gawaina DeKathrine was not sure how to deal with this either, but had decided to leave it alone for now. She had other problems.

Julianus was dead and Ellisander was unconscious, as was every DeMarian of rank in the city. This left her and her alone to hold the country together. Very slowly, her years of training took control of her dazed senses. First she must ensure the capital's safety. That meant getting the army and navy up and moving. Second, she must find out how widespread the devastation was and whether it had been part of a larger attack. And third, she must get the investigation of the blaze moving. But how? So many of her people had fallen.

Her gaze moved to the blackened facade of the Flame Temple. How had they not known? Branion's eyes had been plucked out in one blow. It stank of conspiracy, and it stank of Essus. First the Aristok and the Heir, and now the Flame Temple with its Seer Priests and Triarctic hierarchy. In one week they had become frighteningly vulnerable.

She swayed, then brought herself back under control as the steely will for which she was famous began to reassert itself. They had been crippled, but they had not and would not fall. She would send messages to Eireon and Danelind immediately, asking for help. Branbridge must be sealed off from potential attack and the Branion army mustered. She had neither the time nor the true authority to call a Parliament, so it must be circumvented. The call must go out. All loyal Branions must rise to their country's defense, for whether the Branbridge Essusiates were involved or not was unimportant. The Continental Hierarchy along with their allies in Gallia and Panisha would not hesitate to take advantage of Branion's weakened state. As for the investigation . . .

She glanced around and saw two young nobles approaching. Her mind quickly supplied their identities. Lysanda DeSandra, Earl of Surbrook, and her brother, the Viscount Hadrian, members of the Duke of Yorbourne's circle. They would do.

Galvanized now, Gawaina waved the two forward as she turned and headed for the palace, issuing orders as she went.

Slowly, the capital moved out from under its blanket of shock as its leaders began to take charge once again.

In the Kenneth Forest, the Spinning Coins made their way along the narrow path. Branches scraped against the wagon tops and more than once those players still on their feet had to battle the encroaching undergrowth to push the wagons free from muddy holes churned up by previous travelers. Everyone was on edge. The Troupe children were all confined to the wagons and the adults walked sluggishly, their eyes dull.

Tamara kept her eyes on the path, resisting the urge to glance through the trees, praying that the power which had decimated Toweford had also hit the bandit haunts. The days when the infamous marauder Kenneth the One-eyed had ruled this area virtually unchallenged were long past, but those journeying through its depths usually traveled in large groups for the forest was still a favorite haunt for footpads and criminals.

Around her the forest was ominously silent.

The Coins staggered into the first clearing around noon. Drawn up in a tight circle in the middle, they paused for breath then took stock of their situation. At least half the adults were unable to rise. All had minor injuries. Tamara and the other able-bodied Troupe members busied themselves with tending to the wounded and comforting the children while Warrin and Hartney kept watch on the woods around them. Turi and Fay did what they could for Rosarion and Simon, but both were out of their depth. After a moment's hesitation, the tumbler moved on to see to Ballentire, and Fay took Kassandra in her arms, rocking her back and forth.

A few yards past the trees three figures crouched, invisible in the thick bracken. The leader, a heavyset, black-bearded man known as Reb Tanner, studied the six wagons with a quizzical expression; the other two waited on his word.

Most of those in Tanner's encampment had been asleep when a storm like a hurricane had suddenly raged through their makeshift homes. Those not asleep on guard had sworn they'd seen a pillar of fire rise over the trees to the south. They'd been jeered at, but Reb had to admit something deuced-odd had happened. And now, here was this troupe of actors, obviously the worse for wear, come into their territory without so much as a single guard.

Tanner frowned. Actors were notoriously small in the pocket and were often better able to defend themselves than the heavily guarded merchant trains that passed through the Kenneth, but those moving about the wagons looked as if a strong breeze would knock them over.

His gaze swept across the clearing. First to go would have to be the big man, then the blonde woman giving orders. After that, the others should fall without a whimper.

Beside him, one of the others stirred impatiently and he jerked a threatening hand in his direction. Not normally a cautious man, it still rankled him that such an easy prize should have dropped into their laps on such a strange morning. What were they doing here? People just did not travel the Kenneth alone in such a state.

Unless they were running from something worse, his slow thoughts added.

His gaze found the smallest of the wagons. It had a fiery pattern painted across its wooden sides, unlike the decoration on the other wagons. The sight made the hair on the back of his neck rise. He almost decided to leave the troupe be, then changed his mind. He'd never be able to justify it to his people, and Zender was already testing his leadership. But he would bring the others. No sense taking foolish risks, whether the actors were healthy or not.

Gesturing to the others to follow, he slipped back into the forest.

An hour later, crossbows cocked and ready, they stepped out of the trees. Those in the clearing froze.

Tamara turned, feeling the silence and knowing instantly what it foretold. Armed figures surrounded the camp. A quick tally put them at fifteen, all with loaded crossbows in their hands. The Coins had maybe seven to put against them, so fighting was out. The tumbler knew a moment of panic and then made herself be calm. What would Ballentire do in this situation, she asked herself.

The answer was simple. Ballentire would fleece the fleecers. With a nod, Tamara put a smile on her face as a tall, black-bearded man came forward, holding his crossbow negligently under one arm. Obviously the leader, his gaze traveled briefly over the wagons, then his dark eyes came to rest on Tamara.

"Had some trouble," he said simply.

"Some, Brother," she agreed pleasantly. "It's been an unusual morning and you find us not at our best, but if you will give us a moment, we shall endeavor to provide you with such entertainment as we are able. The Spinning Coins Tumbling Troupe at your service!"

She waved her arms dramatically, and realizing what she was doing, the others truck up comic poses. Tamara smiled.

"And who do we have the pleasure of performing before today?" She looked expectantly at the bandit leader, who frowned.

"Reb Tanner," he said finally. "These are my people."

Tamara bowed. "Tamara of Moleshil, your most humble servant. Will your company sit, Brother, or do you wish to return with provender and make a picnic of it, or will you have us follow you to your village so that all might enjoy our feats of dexterity and skill? I admit we may need a moment or two to sort ourselves out, but we are at your most gracious disposal."

Tanner shook his head in confusion. Around him, his people stirred uncertainly, as the few actors began unpacking instruments and props with every intention of putting on a display right there.

Beside him, Zender was grinning. Reb shrugged. He supposed it wouldn't hurt to take in some entertainment first. There'd been little enough of it in past years.

"I 'spect you'd best come back to the . . . village," he answered. "You can . . . perform there."

"Certainly, Brother." With a brilliant smile, Tamara turned to the Troupe and gestured for them to pack up and make ready to follow the brigands. The tumbler herself fell into step with the bandit leader, chatting amiably.

"In truth, we're glad to meet up with you, Brother," she said conversationally as the wagons began their awkward trek off the main path.

"Oh?"

"Indeed. This morning's happenings were very unsettling. The wind came up so suddenly it caught us all off guard. Many of us were injured. We were barely able to leave town."

"Why didn't you just wait?" Reb asked, drawn into conversation despite himself. "A caravan was bound to set out sooner or later. And you could probably have found a physician there for your wounded."

"Yes, but as you know, Toweford is a very anti-Essusiate town," Tamara answered sadly. "We're a mixed Troupe, you see. We follow no single truth and so are sometimes despised by everyone. We were afraid that once they got back on their feet the good citizens of Toweford would look for someone to blame for this morning, and that someone just might be us. The town took an awful beating."

Reb's eyes suddenly brightened with interest. "Did it now?" he asked casually.

Tamara nodded, ignoring the avaricious sound in the man's voice. "I think it is the God's curse on them," she added.

"Oh?"

"From what I saw, only Triarchs were affected, so it had to be."

Reb nodded, the gleam growing in his eyes. "Could be so," he agreed. "How long you figure it'll take for 'em to sort 'emselves out?"

Resisting the urge to completely throw Toweford to the wolves, Tamara made a show of considering the question. "A couple of days at least," she answered. "There was a lot of damage."

"Pity."

Tamara sniffed. "At least the troupe is safe now," she said with exaggerated relief.

Reb couldn't help casting her an incredulous glance. "You sure 'bout that?"

She nodded. "Of course, I've heard about the bandits of the Kenneth," she said, "but we have nothing save our skills in this world, plus a few battered props with which we ply our trade. What sport could robbers possibly gain by taking what little goods we have? And we can provide much better entertainment unhindered. When was the last time you had a festival day, isolated as you are?"

He grunted. "Long time, I guess."

"Exactly. And who can say, if we suit each other and the Kenneth turns out to be a profitable stop, the Troupe could perform for you and yours whenever we pass this way."

He paused. "You want *us* to pay *you?*"

She laughed. "It is the usual arrangement, Brother, but I can see how it might be difficult under these circumstances."

"It might."

Tamara ignored the heavy sarcasm in his tone. "Perhaps we could take payment in kind, then, instead. A day's entertainment for safe passage through the Kenneth, for example."

Reb shrugged. "Maybe."

"It's settled, then." Tamara smiled brightly at him and tucked his arm in hers as they walked.

"Oh, good," was all he could think to answer.

"There is only one problem," Tamara said after a time.

"Oh?"

"As I told you, some of us were injured this morning. Do you have a physician in your village? We can't pay in coin, of course, but we could stay an extra day in exchange for food and medical care."

Reb considered it. "We can give you bandages and the like," he said finally.

"That's very kind, Brother, but I was hoping you might have someone with greater skill. You see, one of our people was . . . well, detained by the authorities and questioned. He's in a bad way."

"Questioned?"

"Tortured."

He nodded, suddenly understanding. "That's why you risked the Kenneth," he mused out loud. "You're running from the Triarchy authorities."

Tamara nodded. "Yes," she said grimly. "We are."

They continued to press through the woods. The wagons had some difficulty, but drawn into the game with Tamara, the Coins put on their brightest professional faces and laughed and joked with their "hosts" until everyone was put at ease.

So it was in a festive mood, however false, that the Spinning Coins Tumbling Troupe entered the bandit settlement.

It was a rough looking place, consisting of a dozen makeshift huts and corrals. The few adults who emerged stared at the Troupe, openmouthed, and the fewer children were equally amazed. Those Troupe members not driving the wagons began to tumble and play on pipes and drums, and with one swipe, Warrin scooped up a little girl and set her on his shoulders, while her mother gawked at them with the rest of the brigands.

No one had ever willingly entered their camp before, and all eyes turned to Reb. He just glowered in answer to their questions as the Troupe stopped in the center of the encampment. Tamara bowed to all and then began issuing orders. In moments a makeshift stage was set up, and Warrin began the festivities with a juggling display.

Meanwhile, Reb made good his promise of care, by sending several confused bandits to help tend to the Troupe's wounded.

In their wagon, Ballentire listened with a proud but weak smile as Tamara explained their situation. She did not interfere, just took the care offered, and later came out to help assist the performers.

Tamara also sent Luis with food for Fay and Simon and, confident of their situation, even agreed to let Kassandra, who for some unknown reason, was feeling fine, out to act as chorus in her blind disguise. Surrounded by the actors just in case, and with Warrin hovering nearby, the child performed admirably.

The day passed without violence. Music, juggling, tumbling, and acting were all performed, and for a time, everyone, criminal and tumbler alike, forgot the desperation in their lives. Ale and whiskey were passed around and food was brought out. The Coins were invited to join the feast, and they did so, encouraging their hosts to eat, drink, and be merry. Turi and Tamara began to play a reel and the Troupe pulled the brigands to their feet for a wild bout of dancing. Soon everyone was drunk and exhausted.

Meanwhile, Ballentire had set Warrin and Hartney to

surreptitiously paint over the effects of the Living Flame splashed across Turi's wagon. They made a reasonable job of it and were ready to put on a show of fire-eating and torch juggling with the Troupe Leader before any of their hosts could become suspicious.

Tamara, meanwhile, continued to press Reb for a physician, and at dusk one of the youths came to the wagons leading a tiny, wizened old woman, clutching a hawthorn cane and a large canvas bag.

"This is Mina," he said. "Reb's auntie. She's a midwife and a hedge healer. She should be able to help your friend."

Tamara bowed and led the way to Turi's wagon. The old woman allowed her to help her up the steps and peered inside.

The wagon was crowded with people. Fay and Hamlin sat on either side of Simon who lay still insensible upon the bed, and Turi stood by the door with Rosarion, pale and unsteady, but up, beside him. The young priest had managed to give them some idea of what must have happened, and that had made Tamara even more confident that the Kenneth had been a better choice than Toweford.

Fay stood up as the old woman hobbled in, and the tumbler craned her head around the door.

"A good thing Warrin's not here, too, or the whole wagon'd collapse. Everyone, this is Mina. She's a healer."

The old woman squinted suspiciously at them in the dim lantern light. Her hair beneath her kerchief was white and her face was a maze of wrinkles, but her birdlike black eyes were still bright with intelligence.

"Where's the patient?" she demanded in a quavering but imperious voice.

Tamara pointed at the bed. "Simon of Florenz."

Mina nodded. "Everyone else get out," she said. "You, boy," she jabbed one arthritic finger at Turi. "Get these shutters open. You, what's your name?"

"Fay. I'm his mother."

"You can stay, then. Get these blankets off him and have them aired out."

She set her bag on the floor, then removed her shawl

and kerchief. "You, young thing," she turned a penetrating stare on Tamara, "you know anything about herbs?"

The tumbler shook her head.

Rosarion raised one hand shakily. "I do."

"You?" Mina swiveled her head and looked him up and down. "You look like Death's Church-Son. You sure?"

"Yes, ma'am."

"Then here." She fished a pouch from her bag and tossed it at him. "Prepare the sachet inside for me and the leaves for him. Make sure you boil the water for at least five minutes before you add the ingredients and leave the sachet in the cup. I'll take it out myself."

He opened the bag and peered inside. "Firethistle?" he said doubtfully.

"Your point?"

"It'll bring him up."

"Of course it will," she snapped. "I don't want him under, I want him awake. How else am I going to talk to him?"

"Uh . . ."

"Get going!"

"Yes, ma'am."

Rosarion pushed past Tamara, his face red, and Turi took his arm to help him from the wagon.

Mina now turned her belligerent stare on Hamlin. "Who're you?"

The artisan gave her a deliberately pleasant smile. "Hamlin Ewer, his father," he said evenly.

"Good, you can lift him while your wife . . . wife?" she looked questioningly at Fay who nodded, too impressed by the old woman's commanding presence to be affronted by the question.

"Never could see the sense in marriage myself," Mina snorted. "In my day we figured it was a foolish idea. Good enough for them that has property, maybe, but a waste of time for the rest of us. Now the Bastard, he had the right idea to outlaw it. Hasn't been an Aristok like him since and won't be again, I shouldn't wonder, for all he was a Triarch. Anyway, you lift him up while your wife gets them blankets out from under him. Young thing . . ."

"Tamara."

"Whatever. Get me some rags—clean rags, mind—and a bucket of warm, not hot, water." The old woman turned her attention to her patient as the others moved to obey her orders.

Outside, Rosarion slowly set up an iron tripod over the nearest fire. Turi filled a small cauldron with water and hung it on its hook for him, while the herbalist laid Mina's pouch to one side.

The tumbler leaned against the wagon. "What is that stuff?" he asked.

Crouching, Rosarion opened the pouch and pulled out a serrated green leaf. "This is firethistle," he said, holding it up. "It's a stimulant. This . . ." he removed the sachet, "is probably a potion of Healing Sight." He brought it up to his nose and sniffed. "Yes. Holly, nightbloom, probably silverseal and . . . peppermint?" He shook his head and coughed weakly. "Physicians use it to enter the Second Physical Realm."

"To do what?"

"To commune with the injured body to see what it needs."

When Turi looked skeptical, Rosarion sat back, feeling dizzy.

"There are three Physical Realms," he said patiently. "The First is the world," he gestured about him, "where the physical exists in concert with the mind and the spirit; the one we all live in consciously." Pulling out his handkerchief, he wiped his face, then folded it and set it in his lap. "The Second is the place where the physical resides without mental awareness, but with a spiritual presence. The Realm where the Gods exist and where an unconscious person may be trapped because of great pain or injury."

"And the Third?"

"Is where the four Aspects commune within the physical state."

"Wha . . . ?"

"Where Flame, Sea, Wind, and Earth combine as both spiritual and physical manifestations. You know," he said as Turi continued to stare at him, mystified, "rocks, trees, rain?"

"Isn't that the First Realm?"

"No, the First Realm includes awareness of one's place within the world, the Third does not."

Turi shook his head. "Forget I asked. What about the other stuff, the firethistle, what does it do?"

Rosarion frowned. "I told you, it's a stimulant. She wants Simon conscious so she can talk to him, but I think it's a bad idea. If she brings him up, he'll be forced to face certain realities that I don't think he's ready for."

"Like his hand?"

Rosarion nodded. *Hypocrite,* his mind breathed. *You're just afraid he'll recognize you.*

That's not true, he answered silently.

Unaware of this internal dialogue, Turi glanced toward his wagon.

"Are you going to tell her that?" he asked.

The Herbalist stared into the cauldron of boiling water. "No," he answered.

In the wagon, Mina waited while Hamlin and Fay stripped away the bedding. Simon was pale and sweat-covered beneath the blood-encrusted wounds and bruising. He moaned feverishly once, and when his father gently raised him up for Fay to put down new linen, he gave a small whimper. Her mouth drawn into a tight line, Fay helped Hamlin lay him down again, smoothing the hair from his face with a gentle motion.

Clicking her tongue, Mina sat down on the edge of the bed and took Simon's uninjured hand in hers.

"Well, laddie," she said quietly. "You've been done good and proper, haven't you? But don't you worry. Old Mina'll fix you up. Old Mina's seen it all."

Fay came forward. "Can you fix his hand?"

Mina looked down. "Hard to say," she answered noncommittally.

"He's an artist."

"Ah, well, I'll do my best."

By the time Rosarion returned with the first infusion, the old woman had examined each of Simon's wounds individually, his parents standing nearby ready to assist her when she asked. Averting his gaze, the Herbalist handed her the cup.

"You want the firethistle after you finish tending him?" he asked.

"Not going to give it to him before, child," she muttered. "What, did you think I wanted him writhing and screaming while I patched him up?" She looked at him, and he backed up a step without answering. "Stay," she continued. "I might need you. Hamlin, you've done good. You can leave now. I never let the fathers hang about, they're too sensitive. Fay, you can stay if you want to."

"Thank you, I will."

Mina nodded, and after Hamlin had left, she returned her sharp gaze to Rosarion. "I hear you and the other boy did the first healing?"

He nodded.

"You did all right." Not waiting for an answer, she seated herself on the bed and plucked the sachet from the cup. Raising the cup to her lips, she drained it in one quick swallow, then set it carefully aside. She closed her eyes. After taking several deep breaths, she grew very still and Rosarion could almost see her descending through the Physical Realms.

When she opened her eyes again, they were dark and fathomless, the pupils dilated almost fully. She stared fixedly down at Simon, then reached for the bowl of water.

It took less time than Rosarion expected. Deep in trance, Mina washed, treated, and bound each wound with professional speed, all the while muttering to herself and to the unconscious man on the bed. Now and then she would tip her head to one side as if hearing an answer, then nod sagely. At one point her eyes grew wide, and then narrowed in concentration, then she pressed on. When she came to his wounded hand, she slowed. Each motion was carefully made, as if even the lightest touch might cause some new injury. Rosarion stood there as long as he could, then left the wagon.

Fay watched him leave with a neutral expression on her face.

When Mina finished salving and dressing Simon's

hand, she sat back and stared down at him for a long time. The artist shivered and muttered feverishly, and she motioned for Fay to pull the blankets over him. Then she turned, fixing her with the same unfocused stare. Fay looked fearlessly back at her.

Mina gave the other woman a toothless smile.

"You've come through a dark place," she said, her voice still thick from the potion's influence. "The lad's still there. I'm going to bring him out soon, because it's no place for true healing, but he's going to need your strength to help him stay out."

Fay nodded.

"I've Seen a lot while I was down there," the old woman continued. "I Saw two men, this one and that one that was just here. They're linked somehow in God business. That's never healthy, but there's not much that can be done about it."

"No?" Fay asked darkly.

Sucking in her lips, Mina gave her an understanding look. "I know it's hard," she said. "I had ten myself, and I've outlived all but four of them. You love 'em, but you can only protect 'em while they're babies. After that, you've gotta let 'em go."

"I know."

"Good." The old woman looked back at Simon. "I Saw a child, too, with hair all in Flames and the Gods as thick as fleas about her. He was holding thoughts of her like a treasure he was afraid of losing. She's woven right through the Physical Realms." She paused, then shook her head. "I'm not going to ask you who she is, but I got a pretty good idea."

Fay stiffened.

"Don't worry. I won't be tellin' Reb," Mina continued. "He's not a bad fella, as footpads and murderers go, but this'd just make him ambitious and get most of his folk killed, I don't doubt. He's better not knowin'."

She turned at a knock on the door.

"Come."

Rosarion entered. He took in the bandaged artist and the two women seated comfortably on either side of him, and held out a cup. "Your firethistle," he said noncommittally.

"Bring it here." The old woman waved him forward, then turned back to Fay. "I want you to go and get some rest now. And don't you worry, everything's going to be just fine. Reb and his folk won't hurt you. Most of 'em are too drunk to see straight right now, anyway. That was well done. You can tell the young thing I said so."

Fay smiled. "Thank you, Mina."

"No charge." The old woman gave a toothless bark of a laugh. "Now get along, I want to speak to the boy alone."

After she left, Mina turned and fixed the Herbalist with a penetrating stare.

"White lung," she said bluntly.

He nodded.

"That why you're all out of sync with the Flame, little priest?" When his eyes widened, she snorted. "It's as plain as the nose on your face; if you know what to look for."

He looked away. "No," he answered stiffly.

"Didn't think so. Feels more like a simple case of juvenile behavior to me, what do you think?"

He shrugged. Dropping down on the edge of the bed, he stared at the unconscious artist. "He save my life," he whispered to Simon after a time. "What else could I do? I only told him what I Saw, I never told him to go out and murder him. I never told him to hurt you."

"Who?"

He looked up at the old woman, his gaze unfocused and just shook his head.

She shrugged. "Have it your own way, child. In the meantime, you know you're linked to this one here, probably all the way down to the Shadow Realm?"

"I hope not, for his sake. I'll reach it long before he does."

"Don't be a smart mouth," she snapped. "All right, I'll make this plain because his drink's getting cold, and I want to get home to my bed. He needs your help to recover. I want you to give it to him. It's important, understand?"

"Why me?"

"You're a priest, and you know about herbs."

"He won't want me."

"I don't care. He needs you. Now, I'm going to bring him up and have a talk with him. He needs to know where he stands with his health and his future. He won't like it, and I'm too old to fight with him over it, so that's where you come in."

"What if he sees me?"

"What if he does?"

Rosarion turned away. "I was there. I was . . . part of . ."

"His questioning?"

"How did you . . . ?"

"I told you, I See things, too, boy."

"He'll react."

"Of course he will. I want him to."

"I don't think it's a good idea."

She snorted. "I didn't ask you." Fetching the cup, she raised Simon's head and pressed the rim against his lips. Muttering under her breath, she began to pour it, drop by drop into his mouth.

Something was pulling at him, dragging him away from Leary as inexorably as a fish caught on a line is pulled from the water. Leary fought it, Simon fought it, but, little by little, he was forced upward into consciousness.

Light was the first thing he was aware of, then sound, then pain.

He groaned.

A voice commanded him to open his eyes, and reluctantly he obeyed as best he could. His vision swam dizzily for a moment, and then he was looking blearily into the wizened face of an old woman. He squinted.

"My name is Mina," she said. "I'm a physician."

He was a long time answering. Finally he croaked out, "I . . . can't see."

"Black eyes do cause that."

"Where . . . am I?"

"You're with friends, actors."

"The . . . Troupe? The . . . Coins?"

"That's them. You've been hurt, laddie, hurt bad. Do you remember how?"

". . . No."

"Yes, you do."

Simon closed his eyes as an expression of grief crossed his face.

"Come back, laddie."

He opened his eyes again, staring blankly up at her.

"You're alive. That's important to remember. And you'll heal, most of you anyway. That hand now . . . maybe not."

"No."

"I'm sorry, lad. You may get control of it back, you may not."

"My . . . work."

"I've heard. Of that I can't say. But what you can do is use it when it heals. It'll hurt like mad, but you have to use it or it'll freeze up, you understand? Simon?"

"What if . . . I can't?" His voice had dropped to a ragged whisper, and Mina leaned forward.

"We all have a destiny, boy," she answered not unkindly. "If you were meant to paint, that's what you'll do. If not," she shrugged, "you'll find something else."

"No."

Pursing her lips, the old woman gave him a keen stare, but said nothing. After setting the bowl and spare bandages aside, she laid her palm against his forehead. "I want you to sleep without drugs tonight," she said. "And tomorrow I want you to eat."

He said nothing.

She frowned. "There's too much at stake for you to behave like this, laddie. You've a fever and infection in that hand. You have to fight it."

When he made no answer, she shook her head. "It's what I figured," she said, bending over him to study his face. "Something's got quite a grip on you, boy, but not so strong as me." Her voice had grown hard. "To that end . . ." She took a deep breath. "This is Rosarion. He's here to help you. Say hello."

Drawn by the strength in her voice, Simon obeyed, gazing blearily at the man standing behind her. His face swam in and out of focus and then steadied. When he recognized him, the artist jerked from the bed, throwing his good arm up over his face.

"Leary!"

His cry brought Fay into the wagon at a run.

Rosarion was backed up against the wall, his face white. Simon was crouched in the far corner, shaking and keening hoarsely. Shooting a furious look at the older woman, Fay ran to her son. Kneeling down, she took his head in her hands.

"Simon! Simon, it's me, you're safe." She pulled him into a tight embrace and glared at the others in the wagon. "Get out," she hissed.

Rosarion obeyed, stumbling out the door. Mina, her lips pressed tightly together in a disapproving line, sat stiffly on the bed.

Fay began to rock her son back and forth while he continued to cry out, murmuring assurances into his hair until he calmed. Finally she looked up.

"How could you?"

Mina returned her glare with an even expression.

"He needed to face reality," she said.

"He didn't have to face it now."

"Yes, he did, Fay." The old woman leaned forward. "There's something there, something in the Second Physical Realm with him that was keeping him from healing."

Fay glared at her, unwilling to believe her words. "Something? What do you mean?"

"A presence," Mina answered. "A very strong and familiar presence, made of fire and power. It doesn't want him to leave, and he doesn't want to go.

"Has he ever lost someone very close to him? Someone who might want to keep him safe and free from pain? Someone who'd be willing to let him fade, just to keep him close?"

Fay nodded, beginning to understand. "Leary," she whispered.

"He said Leary. Who was it, a brother, a lover?"

"A friend." She looked down at her son's tormented features. "And a lover. Leary was keeping him away from me?" Her expression grew hard.

Mina nodded. "I'm not saying he means him any harm. It probably feels very safe and comforting to them both, but Simon can't heal there. If he stays, he'll eventually weaken and die. He has to come out, and he has to stay out. This Leary doesn't want him to, and he won't want to either. He won't want to face the pain, but he has to. You don't like my methods. Trust 'em anyway. He had to be shocked out. And once out, you have to keep him out, do you understand?"

Fay slumped. "Yes."

"Good. Now, the floor'll do him no good. Best get him up."

Between them, the two women convinced Simon to rise and stumble back into bed. Fay sat down beside him, holding his good hand in hers.

"How will I know when he's slipping back?" she asked wearily.

"He'll start to fade out. That's why you have to keep talking to him and get him to talk back. Get him to notice the world again. He can sleep, but only for about an hour at a time, then you've got to wake him up and bring him back for a few moments."

Fay nodded. "What about Leary? Will he fight back?"

"Probably. Are you stronger than a ghost?"

Fay looked up sharply, her expression dark. "I am," she said tightly.

"Then don't worry about this Leary."

Fay nodded.

"Good." With a last glance at her patient, the old physician rose and left the wagon.

Rosarion was crouched, coughing by the fire. He looked up, his face drawn and tight, as she hobbled toward him. Mina chose not to notice.

"You go in and help Fay," she said.

He shook his head. "I'd just make him worse."

"Horse buttocks! You're just what he needs."

"You've Seen that?" he asked sarcastically.

"Watch your mouth." Draping her bag over one shoulder, she took a firm hold on her cane. "I'll tell you what I told him, child. We all have a destiny. We can embrace it or deny it, but we can't escape it. The healthiest thing to do is make the best of it." She shook her head. "You think you're the only one who's done wrong, boy? There's folks here who could give you a run for your money. Some have committed such crimes as to make your blood run cold. Some even regret 'em, but they keep on livin'. It's all they can do. It's all you can do, too." Without another word, she turned and hobbled away.

Fishing his handkerchief from his sleeve, Rosarion pressed it against his mouth. His shoulders shaking with the effort to still the coughing which welled up, he held it there for a long time, then rose and returned to Turi's wagon.

He and Fay sat with Simon far into the night. Sometimes Fay held him, sometimes she merely sat by his side, stroking his hair and singing quietly to him, while he cried out for Leary. Sometimes Hamlin joined her, sometimes Dani or Luis. All through the night, Rosarion sat at the foot of the bed watching and saying nothing as the candle burned low.

In the corners of the wagon, the shadows crouched. Sometimes they overcame the forces arrayed against them and returned to cling to Simon's spirit, sometimes they were driven back, but they always returned.

The next day it stormed. The rain began just before dawn and came down in torrents throughout the morning. The Coins huddled in their wagons, passing the time playing cards and telling stories. Most of the bandits, hung over and miserable, remained in their own homes. Mina arrived wet and in a dreadful mood, shooing everyone from Simon's sickbed. Fay and Hamlin left to crowd into Ballentire's and Tamara's wagon. Warrin brought Dani and Luis to his to help him amuse Kassandra. The four of them spent the morning digging through trunks of costumes and props while the rain pelted against the roof.

Noon saw no abatement in the storm. Reb was up and fuzzily agreed that there would be no performance that day. With real reluctance and a great deal of difficulty, the troupe managed to return to the path, and press on through the Kenneth.

It took the rest of the day to make Vervickshire. A thick fog had risen, and it was a wet and bedraggled group of players that made their splashing way into the town of Graveswood just past dusk. The events of the day before had hit the town almost as hard as Toweford, and there were only a few people about to mark their arrival. Ballentire brought the Coins to the east fields, and they bedded down for the night.

They were up and gone long before dawn could bring the crowds of curious townspeople wondering why they had risked the Kenneth so foolishly the night before. They turned onto a narrow packhorse trail leading northwest and began the journey to Port Ellsey on the coast. It was no longer safe to linger on the main road. Whether suspicion was roused on the way or not, they had to get to Caerockeith as quickly as possible.

11. Judgments

Atreus DePaula awoke on a makeshift pallet in a small temple in Toweford with a splitting headache and a bandaged brow. Around him, others lay groaning and thrashing, and from the limited number of caregivers, he assumed that whatever had hit him had also hit the town. He tried to remember.

FIRE! BURNING! DYING!

Vision spinning, he slammed the psychic door closed on his Sight, and fingers gripping his temples, waited until the pain had subsided. Then he glanced cautiously upward.

The sun which shone weakly through the window seemed to be high above the buildings. It must be almost noon, or just after.

He tried to rise, and the room suddenly spun around and he fell back. Drawn by the movement, a woman in a cream-colored smock came forward.

"You're not to move for a while yet, My Lord," she said, pulling the blanket over him again. "You took a nasty crack on the head. You just lay back now."

"What happened?"

"All we know is that a God-power manifested; strong enough to knock down most of the Triarctic Priests in town and many of the citizens. The Earl has sent her retainers in to help with the wounded." She hesitated. "By your garb, sir, we recognized you as a Triarchy Knight, a Flame Champion?"

"That's right."

"Her Lordship wants to be informed the moment you regain yourself. I expect she hopes you'll be able to shed some light on what happened. Can you?" she asked hopefully.

"I . . . don't think so."

"Well, perhaps it will come to you later. I'll be sending word to the manor now that you're awake, and they'll likely take you up to see her. The beds are much softer at the manor than here, I expect. Would you like some broth while you wait?"

His stomach heaved at the idea, and he shook his head.

"Maybe later, then. I'll be back to check on you in a bit."

When she'd gone, Atreus tried to bring his scattered memories back into some order. Before the . . . whatever it had been, he'd arranged to make the journey through the Kenneth with a merchant caravan. He'd been talking to the Earl's Guard Captain when . . .

The pain threatened to return with the onset of memory, and he quickly changed the pattern of his thoughts.

He'd arranged to make the journey through the Kenneth in the same caravan as the tumbling troupe.

The tumbling troupe.

He made to rise again and once more fell back, his vision spinning. Leaning forward with his head bent until the spell passed, he forced himself to think clearly.

Where was the tumbling troupe?

He closed his eyes. The blast seemed to have decimated most of the town, so it had probably affected the caravan as well. That being likely, it was also likely that the troupe was still in Toweford. But . . .

His head began to pound, and he breathed deeply for a few minutes. But if they'd been injured like the others around him, they'd need medical attention and that would lead to their discovery and the ruin of all his plans.

He almost rose again, but caught himself at the last minute. Think, he told himself firmly. It was past noon. If they had been discovered, it would have been before now and the healer woman would have told him. People didn't keep that kind of news to themselves. So the troupe must still be at large.

Memories of the morning flitted through his mind, despite his self-control. He winced as it sent a line of pain across his temples, then his eyes widened. If the force of the blast had affected his small Gift so dramatically, what must it have done to the Vessel of the Living Flame? If she were injured or even ...

He left the thought unfinished. Moving very cautiously, he got groggily to his feet and stumbled to the temple door.

The scene which met his eyes was like the aftermath of a major battle. Trees had been uprooted, houses ravaged, and people were staggering blindly about the streets. A company of soldiers from the Earl of Berford marched by, giving orders and assigning people to the cleanup. Atreus pulled back inside the doorway until they had moved on, then stumbled outside.

Moving carefully from building to building, the Flame Champion made his way to the outskirts of town and the edge of the north fields. Once there he stared sightlessly down at the deep rows of wagon tracks leading away. The Spinning Coins Tumbling Troupe had gone.

The world grew very pale.

When he awoke again, it was to the observation that he'd done this before. The same, dark-beamed ceiling loomed above him, the same people lay on the same makeshift pallets around him. But now it was darker, almost dusk. He groaned. This time an older woman responded. She got the young Flame Champion sitting up and spoon-fed him some broth, then waved to the armored man standing by the door. Atreus glanced up at the Earl's Guard Captain and winced.

Despite his protestations, they brought a litter to carry him up to the manor house. From there he was able to look down on the town, and it was just as he feared. There was no sign of the six wagons and their troupe members anywhere. He fell back with a moan. They reached the manor house quickly, and two guards helped him alight. Leaning more heavily on them than he would have liked, he was ushered into the Earl's study.

Her Lordship, Shannon DeYvonne, the Earl of Berford, was an older woman, her graying hair worn short in the style popular twenty years before. She had a hard, no-nonsense look about her, and Atreus stilled a shiver as he was announced. She gestured to a chair and he was helped over by the guards who then left silently. An equally silent Steward got him a cup of wine, and then also departed. After a moment, she turned her penetrating gaze on the young Knight.

"I see that you're unwell, My Lord," she said, "so I won't keep you long. I understand from my priests, those that are still able to make themselves understood, that something terrible has happened in the capital, but they are unable to tell me what. I hope that you'll be able to."

"I can tell you what I felt, My Lord," he answered, "But I'm not sure how useful it will be."

Shaking, he allowed a tiny bit of the memories to surface. It brought a faint headache along with it, although not as bad as he'd feared it would be. Slowly, he told her what he'd experienced. When he was done, the young Knight was bathed in sweat and the Earl's expression was dark. She rose.

"Thank you, My Lord. I shall send troops to the capital at once. In the meantime, my Steward has prepared a bed for you. No doubt, you'll want to rest."

He shook his head. "I can't. I'm on a mission," he began and then paused. How much should he divulge? Enough to gain her cooperation, but not enough to have any of her people detain the tumblers. He looked up at her, allowing some of his anxiety to show through. "A mission from his Grace, Seth Cannon, and from His Royal Highness, the Duke of Yorbourne. I can't stay."

She frowned. "This mission is imperative?"

"Yes, My Lord. I was to follow a troupe of traveling players who were in the capital at the time of . . . of the assassination, keeping them in sight without giving them suspicion of my presence. But now they've gone." He slumped. "I've lost them. I've failed him." He didn't bother to explain which him he meant and she didn't ask—Berfordshire had been gifted to her by the Duke of Yorbourne and she understood about such obligations.

"They can't have gone very far, My Lord," she said in a more reassuring tone. "I shall send some of my people into town to search for them."

He grew alarmed. "No, please, My Lord. If they become suspicious . . ."

"My people will be discreet."

Atreus was dubious, but eventually accepted her offer with weary resignation.

She waved aside his mumbled thanks dismissively. "In these times we need to know whom we can count on, My Lord," she answered stiffly. "I'll have you informed of what my people discover. In the meantime, you should rest. You'll do the Duke no service if you're too ill to stand."

"Of course, you're right, My Lord."

Atreus stood and allowed the Steward to help him from the room. He didn't realize how tired he was until he sank into the soft feather bed, and despite his fears for the future he fell soundly asleep.

The next morning he was greeted by the appalling news that the tumbling troupe had actually braved the Kenneth alone a mere hour after the blast had ebbed. Cursing, he rose, despite the sudden headache, and went immediately to see the Earl.

She was sympathetic, but pointed to the storm lashing rain against the windowpanes. No one was going anywhere today. When he protested, she grew impatient. She would not send her people through the Kenneth in the teeth of a storm. If the tumblers were foolhardy enough to attempt it, they would be bogged down by now.

Chafing at the delay, Atreus managed to get her promise of an armed escort as soon as the storm passed and spent a long day staring moodily out a north window, watching his prosperity fall with the raindrops.

Fortunately, the sun was shining the next day, and he was up at dawn, feeling almost back to normal. The Earl provided him with ten armed guards and a horse out of her own stable. After hurried thanks, he was on the road.

The way was muddy and slow going. The rain of the day before had wiped away any possibility of tracks, but there was only one path and one destination; Graveswood.

They arrived at dusk, soaking wet and no closer to finding the troupe than before. They bunked down in the barracks used for such purposes, and the next morning Atreus started asking questions.

After a frustrating morning he was ready to believe the unthinkable, that the players had not made it out of the forest. But in a nearby tavern, a gnarled old man told him that two nights before a God-born mist had fallen. With what had happened that morning most of Graveswood's residents had hidden in their homes, but he'd had to relieve himself, and peering around a tree, he'd seen a troupe of faerie folk leave the Kenneth and disappear into the west. Naturally, he'd tried to follow, because everyone knew that faerie horses crapped out solid gold, but he'd gotten lost and ended up in the brook. By the time he'd extricated himself, they'd vanished.

Tossing the old man a silver coronet, Atreus left the tavern. He thanked the Guard Captain, dismissed the company as casually as he was able, and was on the trail alone half an hour later. The troupe had a day's lead, but he had a good horse and strong motivation. He would catch them. Passing the outskirts of Graveswood, he set his horse to a trot and headed west.

Miles ahead, on the road to coastal Samlinshire, Rosarion DeLynne huddled in a thick blanket on the wagon seat beside Turi of Moleshil. He'd managed to get enough ingredients in Leamston to make his expectorant, but his head still felt heavy, and the thick, braying cough that shook his slight frame made his chest ache. Yesterday, Turi had wrapped his ribs in strips of leather and the support had helped a little. He'd forced himself to rise and dress, even though he'd needed the tumbler's help to shave; his hand shaking too hard to hold the razor.

He was up against the other man's advice, but Hartney's wagon was too dark and close. He needed air and light to prove to himself that he wasn't already half in the Shadow Realm. His head still ached from the effects of three days ago, and his vision faded in and out alarmingly. Also, five days without the Potion of Truth was making him nauseous and faint. He couldn't just lie still and wait for the withdrawal to sap the life out of him.

Turi had shaken his head but hadn't pressed the argument.

The two men had been riding together for the last hour, talking herbs and healing, concentrating on Simon's treatment. The artist was still weak and feverish, his hand oozing liquid into the bandaging. Rosarion had next to no hope that it would heal properly, but Turi remained positive, and the Herbalist found himself drawn to that belief despite himself.

Now Turi guided his team behind Hartney's wagon as they followed along one of the interminable streams and rivers that crisscrossed this part of Austinshire.

"So, hoodweed's a neutral blue bile nervine you take with water?" The tumbler gave a confused laugh as the wagon lurched over a small brook.

Rosarion gave a weak smile. "Not exactly. It's a sedative predominantly. You can smoke it or, in Simon's case, drink it, with birch sap or water."

"So where does all this other nonsense come into it?"

"It's *Triarctic* signature, you mean?" Rosarion used his most pompous voice and Turi chuckled. "Hoodweed is a neutralizing herb: neutralizing the conflicting humors in the body. It's Bi-Aspected, meaning it belongs to both Wind, since you use the leaves, and Sea because it's blue."

"Because it's blue?"

"Because it's blue."

"And the bile?"

"There's no bile." The Herbalist was becoming exasperated. "Why do you keep coming back to bile?"

"Doesn't all Triarctic healing came down to bile?"

"You're out of your head."

"At least I don't link a meadow herb with the ocean because it's blue."

"And at least I don't consider valerian holy just because dragons eat it."

"It's the sacred food of Merrone, Guardian of the Faithful," Turi replied smugly.

"It smells like stinky feet and cures flatulence," Rosarion shot back.

"Exactly. You've never heard a dragon fart, have you? Holy creatures don't because they eat valerian; that's the secret."

Rosarion's retort to this latest piece of eccentric theology was cut off as the wagon shifted.

"Feels like Fay's come back," Turi said. The guardswoman had been splitting her time between Warrin's wagon, where Kassandra now stayed, and Simon's bedside here in Turi's wagon. "I hope she'll be all right. She seems so tired these days, yet she won't rest."

"I know. She's a remarkable woman."

"Yes, she is."

The memory of Fay staring down at him on the boundaries of the Flame Temple caused Rosarion to drop into silence. He had told her what had transpired in Branbridge and her look had been the same measuring stare. The Herbalist couldn't shake the feeling that she blamed him, although she hadn't said it. He was certain, however, that Ellisander was somehow behind it, and the thought that the Duke could have called up enough rage to murder that many important people so horribly caused him to grow faint.

Pulling the blanket more securely about his shoulders, Rosarion huddled down, purposely shoving Ellisander out of his mind. Ever since his sudden decision to leave Branbridge he'd let others carry him along, refusing to deal with the possible consequences of his numerous defections. Sooner or later, he knew, he'd have to face them, probably in Caerockeith, for Terrilynne DeMarian was just as likely to hang him without pause for treason and regicide as Ellisander was to kill him for betrayal, but for now he was warm and safe. That was all he could ask for. He closed his eyes.

The swaying wagon lulled him into a slight doze, and for a while he drifted without coherent thoughts or dreams. Then the wagon lurched and he awoke, Kassandra DeMarian, her eyes red-hot coals in her pale face, staring at him from beneath a ring of trees. He shivered.

Ever sensitive, Turi made an inquiring noise. Rosarion shook his head, and the other man returned his attention to his team. The Herbalist pressed his handkerchief to his lips and stared at the passing scenery, willing his chest to relax.

"It probably means nothing."
"You saw her face. It means something."

He turned to the other man.

"Why haven't you learned more healing?" he asked, changing the direction of his thoughts as they followed the other wagons off the road away from the stream and onto a narrow, dirt path.

Turi shrugged. "There's usually no real need for it," he answered. "We're never too far away from a town or village to make it necessary. Until now."

He paused as one wheel splashed into a flooded badger hole, dipping the wagon precariously to one side. "Stupid idea, this,' he muttered, after urging the horses to pull them free. "I suppose you could teach me a bit if you wanted to," he offered. "It would pass the time while we all try to get bogged down in a turnip patch." He gave the other man a smile. "If you can keep the ocean-wind-bile stuff to a minimum."

Rosarion snorted as Turi began to laugh.

In the wagon Simon listened without expression as the free sound of Turi's laughter drifted in to him. His fever had broken in the night, bringing him a deep healing sleep without dreams. It had strengthened him, and he'd managed to stay awake most of the morning. Suffering both Fay's firm and Rosarion's hesitating ministrations without comment, he'd eaten when they'd brought food and voided when they'd brought the pot, but he would not speak of his injuries. The overwhelming sense of loss and despair with which he'd greeted the sight of his bandaged hand had mercifully faded to a dull disbelief, and he found that if he did not dwell on the past, it stayed that way. And it would stay that way.

Beside him, Fay misinterpreted his sudden grimace and reached for a cold cloth, while deep in the recesses of his mind Leary's shadowy manifestation stirred uneasily, drawn up by the artist's thoughts. Simon closed his eyes, so Fay would not notice, and drew Leary close to him, soothing his friend's disquiet until he lay quiescent beside him.

The painter did not question his friend's ghostly presence. Leary had come to him on that dark, pain-filled ride from Branbridge, had shielded him from the searching minds of the Flame Priests, and had dulled the pain in his body and mind until he was able to bear it himself. When he'd inexplicably disappeared just before the entire world seemed to burst into flames, it had felt as if Simon had lost him all over again. Now that he was back, weakened and vulnerable, he would not lose him again. He knew what Fay and Mina believed, but they were wrong. Leary would never hurt him. And he would not let them hurt Leary.

Willing himself to sleep, he followed Turi's laughter down into lighter memories.

The free sound of Leary's laughter floated over to him as Simon stretched out on the grassy bank, a glass of wine in one hand, a charcoal stick in the other. The Aristok and his Consort were feeding the Collin's Park swans, and every now and then one would take liberties. Soon the Royal Couple were surrounded by white-winged marauders.

It had been just over two years since Kathrine DeMarian had arrived in Branbridge. The Consort-to-be had charmed the capital and had completely besotted her Regal Cousin. They'd held a swift courtship, then married in the ancient Temple of the Wind. Marsellus had begun building a cathedral beside the Flame Temple in her honor, and Simon had promised to bedeck it in the most beautiful images under the sky. His sketches were moving slowly however as the Royal Couple had demanded his presence on most of their excursions that summer and there had been many.

Today they were picnicking by the River Mist with Kathrine's brother Ellisander and his intended, Her Grace Saralynne DeLynne. Leary had offered to find someone to accompany the artist, but Simon had gracefully declined. He would bring his sketchbook and continue to work on his ideas for the Cathedral. Marsellus had acquiesced easily.

Kathrine's presence had calmed the high-strung young ruler, and the birth of their daughter Kassandra this spring had peaked his happiness. The three-month-old Prince had accompanied them today, in the arms of her nurse. Staring up at the bright blue sky, she was gurgling happily, the warm sun making her fire-touched black eyes sparkle.

"Bring more bread, for the Flame's sake, before we're eaten alive!"

The Aristok's shout brought Simon's head up, but Saralynne was rising to rescue them, so he returned his attention to his drawing.

Beside him, Ellisander DeMarian leaned forward.

"Water rushes?" he asked politely.

"Yes, My Lord."

Simon had been introduced to the newly made Duke of Yorbourne at the court ball held in honor of his sister's arrival. The DeMarian was handsome and charming, as arrogantly confident as his Royal Cousin but without the chaotic overlay that marked the Aristok's personality. He had managed to become close friends with Marsellus without alienating his other friends. Simon liked him in a guarded way.

Now the DeMarian Duke lay back.

"Did His Majesty tell you that Saralynne and I are to be married?" he asked, allowing Kassandra to hold onto his finger.

"Yes, My Lord. Congratulations."

"Thank you. I should like to commission you to paint the main hall at Yorbourne Castle to commemorate the wedding."

"I should be only too honored, sir."

"Ellis! Ellis, help!" Saralynne's laughing cry interrupted their conversation. With an easy smile, the Duke rose to rescue the others, leaving Simon to his sketches.

In Turi's wagon, Simon's face grew distant, and despite her own wishes, Fay shook him gently. He awoke, anger flashing in his eyes for just an instant before being covered over by a guarded expression. Fay held up a cup of water and slowly, the artist raised his good hand and took hold of it.

"Are you feeling a little stronger?" she asked, ignoring the sudden stab of worry.

Simon nodded his head.

"I'm fine," he answered.

The next day the Troupe passed the boundary stone for Samlinshire. The way slowly flattened out and the roads improved as the stream-bisected moors of Austinshire gave way to fields of cattle and sheep. Warrin and Hartney went out that night, and there was goose for supper. No one asked where it had come from, though the speed at which they passed the nearby farms spoke volumes. Fay accepted a portion for Simon but refused any for herself, glaring sternly at the two men who grinned back sheepishly. But the warm meat helped the artist and the next day, at his own insistence, he took his first steps from the wagon.

Walking slowly, and supported by Hamlin and Dani, he joined the Coins at the main campfire for breakfast. He didn't speak, but Kassandra and Bennie brought a faint smile to his face when they put on an impromptu juggling performance for him. He almost looked his old self again, for he and Hamlin were letting their beards grow back, but his eyes were still shadowed behind the bruising and he held his bandaged right hand tightly to his chest. He suffered Rosarion's presence with stiff silence, only willing to relax when the Herbalist, equally uncomfortable, left to help Turi and Hartney bring water.

For his part, Rosarion came to Turi's wagon each day to tend to Simon's needs because Mina had told him to and because Fay held him to his word. After each session, the young priest grew morose with guilt and even Turi could not pull him from his mood.

He was taking strong infusions of burnet, wormwort, and clover these days, picked along the way to alleviate the congestion in his lungs. He'd managed to find enough ratroot, the one visionary herb that he needed to maintain a constant level of, and had taken to smoking semidried wolfweed and wild lettuce to calm the shaking in his limbs due to the withdrawal of the Potion of Truth. It gave him a constant headache and made him feel depressed and anxious, but it was better than the alternative. He felt terrible most of the time but bore it without comment like a self-induced penance.

This day, when the Troupe paused for supper beside a small brook, Rosarion gently refused Turi's company and headed downstream to look for more burnet.

He surprised Kassandra and Warrin standing in the shallows hunting minnows with Simon sitting on the bank, an old blanket wrapped around his shoulders. The big tumbler shot him a warning glare, and Rosarion was about to turn away when Kassandra looked up.

"You, come here." She waved the priest forward.

Her imperious little voice was enough like her father's to cause a superstitious tingle to move down his spine, but he obeyed her, nonetheless.

"I want to ask you something," she said, sitting down on a tussock. "No, Simon, you stay, too."

The artist looked about to refuse her demand, but after a moment his face grew hard and he looked away.

With a gesture from the young Aristok, Rosarion hesitantly seated himself on the other side of her. Behind them, Warrin hunkered down, glaring at the Herbalist like the bodyguard he'd become, although Rosarion couldn't be sure which one he guarded. He tried with some success not to look at him.

Kassandra stared up at the priest. "My Papa came to me," she said without preamble. "He was real mad at you. Why?"

This was the line of questioning he'd been dreading, and he looked away, caught the glimpse of shadows in Simon's disinterested gaze, and dropped his eyes. "Most Holy," he began, digging into the soft bank soil with the toe of his boot. "It's . . . uh . . . it's complicated."

Warrin snorted.

Picking up a blade of grass, the Aristok placed it between her two thumbs. " 'Splain it to me, then."

"Well, uh, Most Holy . . . You know how your Papa had priests who had visions to serve him?"

"Uh-huh." She blew on the grass and produced a faint whistling sound before it broke. With a grimace, she picked another piece. "The Living Flame showed them stuff to tell Papa an' they would, an' then he'd run the country. It coulda told him, but It didn't always 'cause usually he was too busy. Papa said I would be the strongest Vessel ever 'cause it was already talkin' to me." She blew on the new blade of grass and produced a very satisfactory shriek before staring up at him again.

"Yes . . . Well . . . I Saw something . . ." Rosarion paused, then plunged ahead. "I Saw your Uncle Sandi kill your Papa, but . . . then I didn't tell him."

Simon stiffened.

"Why," the child asked.

Why.

"I . . . uh . . ." He looked away, raising one hand in a helpless gesture. "At first I wasn't sure that's what it was, Most Holy. I Saw your uncle and I told him, that is, I told your uncle, and . . . the rest just kind of . . . grew," he finished uncertainly.

"So why didn't you tell Papa when you were sure?"

Why hadn't he?

Forced to study the question he'd never actually asked himself, Rosarion stared at his boots. *Why hadn't he?*

Things had just flowed along, and before he knew it, he was involved in a plot to murder the Aristok.

No, that wasn't right. He'd known right from the start what telling the Duke of Yorbourne would mean.

Because the future was set and so he wasn't truly to blame.

Tempting, but no again. The future could be changed, was always changed, True Vision or no. That was why the Aristok took council from the Flame Priests. And it had been his duty to inform the Aristok, or at least Master Julianus.

So why hadn't he?

The repeated question brought the faint throbbing of a new headache, but behind that the rumblings of a sullen anger.

He'd been taking the Potion of Truth alone against the rules for a year, chasing the Shadow Catcher and the elusive timing of his death, afraid to face the future without knowing. He'd gone to Ellisander to make sense of his first vision because the Duke had saved his life, such as it was, and because he couldn't tell Julianus about his unsanctioned vision. Ellisander had wanted details, and he'd gone into the Prophetic Realm again, relieved that someone else was bearing the responsibility for the decision. He hadn't cared about much of anything in those days, and by the time Rosarion realized the seed he had planted in the Duke of Yorbourne's mind, he was already committed to his service. And to be honest, the ramifications had not truly bothered him at all.

It felt good to be needed again. Julianus had stopped asking him to speak Prophecy for the priesthood, mindful of his illness, and the others had drawn back from him, unsure of what to say. He also knew they were getting many of the potions they needed from the temple at High Wyford. They didn't need him.

Ellisander had given him purpose again, a purpose to distract him from the fear and self-pity that shadowed his life. Besides, he was going to die, why shouldn't Marsellus? What was it to him? It happened to them all sooner or later. What had Ellisander called him? The Shadow Catcher's messenger?

But that wasn't all of it. His life had been destroyed, and angry with Fate and suffering from the need to be special, to be important just once before he died, he'd willingly joined with Ellisander DeMarian and committed treason to strike out at the one man above such things, the Vessel of the Living Flame. The discovery of the petty reasoning behind such an act made him redden.

He glanced up. Kassandra was still waiting patiently for an answer, and even Simon was watching him with a guarded expression. But how could he explain all that to a child. "I guess . . ." he said slowly. "I guess . . . Have you ever done anything bad, I mean really bad, and you weren't sure why you did it at the time, you just did it?"

The child cocked her head to one side. "I broke a window once 'cause Nurse wouldn't let me stay up an' I'm a Prince, so I got mad and threw a candlestick at her an' she ducked an' it hit the window. 'Member, Simon?"

The artist nodded.

"I guess I did that too sort of," Rosarion admitted. "You see, Most Holy, I'm very sick."

She nodded. "Hamlin told me. You've got white lung. My momma died of white lung," she added quietly.

Instinctively Simon put his one good arm around her. She leaned into his side and for a moment the shadows over his face softened.

"So did mine," Rosarion answered. "My whole family died and . . . well . . . I guess I blamed . . ."

"You blamed Papa."

He stared at her. "Wha . . . I mean, pardon, Most Holy?"

She sat up. "Papa is the Vessel of the Living Flame, see," she explained. "An' so he takes care of everybody, but you didn't think he took care of you an' your Momma an' Papa, so you got mad an' said, there I won't help him so there!"

"Uh . . ."

"But that's still real bad," she went on. "'Cause he's, I mean, he was the Aristok an' he knows best even if you don't think so, so you musn't question him, just do what he says."

Her voice had taken on a singsong cadence like she was reciting something she'd been told. Rosarion dropped his gaze.

"I guess I should have," he admitted.

"I guess so." She gave him firm stare. "But now I'm the Aristok, an' I know what's best an' you'd better listen to me, 'cause I won't let you get away with not tellin' me stuff."

He looked up, half amused despite the seriousness of the conversation. "No, Most Holy?"

"No. You're my priest an' you're s'posed to help me, so's I can run things an' if you don't I will have your head lopped off."

Rosarion swallowed, knowing the truth of her words despite the lisping tone. Child or not, Kassandra De-Marian was the Realm's True Sovereign and the Vessel of the Living Flame. If she chose to order his death, even in a fit of childish pique, there were many who would leap to obey. And it was just as likely to happen later—when someone explained his part had been a bit more than just not telling the Aristok—as now. "Yes, Most Holy," he said quietly.

"Good." She plucked another blade of grass. "So is there anything you oughta tell me about right now?"

He glanced at Simon, who looked darkly away, but Warrin was glaring pointedly at him. He took a deep breath.

"Just that it was really more than just not telling your Papa about your Uncle Sandi. It was, well, treason, and heresy, and that's punishable by death."

Kassandra gave him a shrewd look incongruously adult on her young face. "I know," she answered.

"You do?"

"Uh-huh. Papa used to take me to Court with him sometimes an' he would tell me about his judgments. Being a traitor's the very badest thing you can be. Papa says you kill traitors."

He'd been expecting this line of reasoning. "Are you going to kill me?" he asked.

She thought for a moment. "I oughta," she answered finally, "cause it was really bad what you did, but Papa also said that for some things there are 'stenuating circum . . . something, that means they might have had a reason that you could kind of forgive them for if they promised real hard to never do it again, an did something to make up for it."

"Do you think it might be that way for me?"

"Maybe. But you'd have to make up for a lot."

"I know. But, there's still more." He glanced quickly at the artist, and then, unable to meet his eyes, looked away. "I was one of the ones who hurt Simon," he said softly.

She grew very still. "No one told me that." She turned to the artist. "Simon, why didn't anyone tell me that?" Her voice was young and scared and he felt a stab of pain in the place where Leary touched his mind.

"I don't know, Sparky," he said after a moment, his own voice weak from his experience in the Temple dungeons. "I think they didn't want to upset you."

"But I was already upset."

"I know."

Kassandra turned back to Rosarion. "Why did you hurt Simon?" she asked.

He dug another trench in the bank with the toe of his

boot. "Because Gawaina believed that he'd hurt you and she wanted answers, and if I didn't help her get them, she'd have known I was one of the traitors," he answered in a low tone.

Simon closed his eyes as the child's fire-filled eyes narrowed. "That's real cowardly," she said.

"I know, Most Holy."

She was silent for a long time.

"So how come you helped him an' Fay get away then?" she asked finally. "That must have made them think you were a traitor, at least to them."

"To start making up for it, Most Holy."

She thought for a long moment. "Well, that's better. It was getting really hard not to kill you."

Her gaze was still pensive, so Rosarion remained silent.

"But it was awfully bad an' you gotta be punished, but are you really, really sorry for what you did?"

Rosarion ignored Warrin's sudden dark expression. "Yes, Most Holy."

"An' you'll help Simon get better an' 'pologize to him an' let him be mad at you if he wants?"

"Yes, Most Holy."

"So do it."

"Most Holy?"

She gave an exasperated snort. " 'Pologize."

Rosarion's eyes widened in alarm, but Simon simply looked away. "Uh . . ." he swallowed."Forgive me, Simon," he whispered.

The artist was quiet for a long time, staring past the stream at the distant hills. The others said nothing, waiting, listening to the gurgling water and the peep of swallows hunting in the sky overhead. Finally the artist shrugged. "You're forgiven," he said stiffly, the set of his shoulders belying his words.

Rosarion dropped his gaze.

"Do you promise never, *ever* to *ever* do anything like that again or no forgiveness or nothin'?" Kassandra asked.

"Yes, Most Holy."

She gave him a hard stare. "Promise, cause you're mine now, cause Papa said all citizens are vassals of the

Aristok an' that makes you mine, an' have to do what I say, an' serve me right always."

He looked into her fiery gaze, saw the Living Flame staring back at him and stilled a shiver. "I promise, Your Majesty," he said seriously, "to be your true liege man. I swear to follow you in all things and make such atonement as you demand. And may I attain no mercy in this Realm or in the next if I break this, my sacred vow." He bowed his head, and the child placed her hand on it again.

"Good. What is it, Warrin?"

The big man whispered something into her hair and she nodded impatiently.

"I was comin' to that." She turned back to Rosarion. "I can't think of a punishment yet, but I will an' I'll let you know, an' if I forget, Warrin'll remind me."

Rosarion glanced at the fire-eater, who showed his teeth in response. Kassandra clapped her hands imperiously and the two men returned their attention to her.

"That's all now," she said. "Court is, uh, done an' I want to catch minnows. You must help us. Go find something to carry them in, while we catch 'em."

"Yes, Most Holy."

Rosarion rose, and not looking at the small group on the bank, went in search of a jar for the Aristok to put minnows in.

Crouched on an escarpment above, too high to hear what had just transpired, although close enough to recognize the child ruler, despite the walnut coloring of her hair, Atreus DePaula breathed a sigh of relief. It had taken all this time to catch up with the troupe and he had feared for a while that his search was in vain. Then he'd crested this last hill and seen the wagons below, the figures of the troupe moving about preparing a meal, and his heart had risen. He would be rich after all.

Returning down the escarpment, he made a cold meal while he deliberated on what to do next. At first he'd just wanted to find them again, but now he was going to have to capitalize on that find quickly before something else went wrong. The troupe was moving due west. That meant they must be planning to follow the coast

road north to Caerockeith. Atreus had intended to take
action nearer to the Duke's demesne of Yorbourne,
however, it was obvious now that the troupe was going
to travel as far from that county as possible. He chewed
at one knuckle.

The nearest town was Stanbeck. There might be
troops there that could help him arrest the tumblers and
take them back to Branbridge, and if not there, then
there was a Lance Chapterhouse in Eagleston a few
miles south.

Caught up in his plans, he never saw the man come
up behind him until his shadow fell across his camp.

Hartney dumped the unconscious man at Ballentire's
feet and there was silence about the fire.

"He was hidin' in them bushes back there beyond the
bank," he said with a scowl. "Spyin'."

Ballentire glanced down at the young man at her feet.
The late afternoon sun gleamed off the red of his cloak
and even without helmet or breastplate it was clear what
his rank was.

"Flame Champion," Tamara said.

"Shit," the Troupe Leader answered.

"Hartney caught a what?"

Rosarion looked up from the rock he was grinding
burnet leaves on and blinked at Turi.

"A Flame Champion. Hartney say's he was hiding in
the woods, watching us; watching Kassandra. Bal wants
you to come and see if you can identify him."

"Ah, shit."

"That's what she thinks."

When Rosarion and Turi got to the main campfire,
Tamara and Hartney were arguing furiously. Simon was
seated between Fay and Hamlin, his face white, staring
at the unconscious body of the young man in question.
Ballentire was pacing back and forth. Finally she stopped
and threw her hands into the air.

"What do you want me to do," she said angrily in no
particular direction. "He's a *Flame* Champion. One of
the elite of the Flame *Temple*. You know, the ones who
swear loyalty to the *Living* Flame. We can't just truss

him up and make a run for it, and we can't keep him; it's kidnapping, and we can't kill him. All right, I suppose we could kill him, except that it's murder and probably heresy, but . . . oh, there you are, Rosarion. Do you know this . . . person?" She nudged the Champion with her toe.

Rosarion looked down at the man at the Troupe Leader's feet and his face grew serious. "It's Atreus DePaula," he said quietly, pressing his handkerchief against his mouth as his throat began to tighten.

"A Flame Champion," Ballentire added. "One of Seth Cannon's."

The Herbalist shook his head. "One of Ellisander DeMarian's." When the others looked confused, he explained. "He's been in the Duke's pocket for a couple of years now. Owes him a lot of money." He looked down. "The Duke must have sent him to find Kassandra or to find us."

Ballentire spat at the fire. "That's just great!"

Hamlin looked grim. "Well, he's found us, the question is, what do we do with him now? Any ideas?"

"How much has he seen?"

Ballentire shrugged. "We don't know, although Hartney's pretty sure he saw the child. She and Simon were sitting out by the brook right below where he caught him."

"Then he's also seen me."

"But he wasn't making for the authorities. Hm." Ballentire considered it a moment. "You say he's in Yorbourne's employ? Like you?"

Rosarion bridled. "No, not like me. He serves him because Ellisander pays his gaming debts. I . . .." he remembered his conversation with Kassandra. "I used to serve him for more complicated reasons," he finished lamely.

Ballentire raised an eyebrow, then shrugged. "Whatever. Does he know you? Know you used to serve the Duke?"

"Yes."

Hartney pulled a knife from his belt and began to strop it against a rock. "We have to kill him," he said simply.

"He's a Flame Champion," Ballentire repeated.

"He's a traitor."

"That's not for us to say."

"Why not? It's him or us, and *us* is also Kassandra."

Fay stood. "He's right," she added grimly. "We have to protect the child."

Hamlin joined her. "Essus knows, I don't believe in bloodshed, but the child's safety comes first, Bal. We have to do what we have to do."

"No, we don't."

The quiet ragged voice made them all pause, and they turned in surprise to see Simon looking up at them.

"No, we don't," he repeated.

"Son . . ." Hamlin began, but Simon shook his head. "No more killing," he said. "It's wrong."

Fay made to argue, but Rosarion touched her elbow gently. "He's right," he said. "Atreus DePaula is a Flame Champion, sworn to the Vessel of the Living Flame, no matter who else he serves, and only the Vessel has the right to pass judgment on him."

"The Vessel is a five-year-old child," Ballentire reminded him through gritted teeth.

"I know, and no Aristok in his or her minority has ever passed a death judgment. It's practically a law."

"So we're right back where we started from."

"Not quite," Simon answered slowly. He turned a reluctant look on the Herbalist.

"You say this Flame Champion serves Yorbourne for money? He's not a . . . vassal?"

"No." Rosarion frowned, wondering what the artist was thinking.

"And he has debts?"

"Yes."

"Is he a traitorous man or a weak man?"

Rosarion turned the question over in his mind. "I'd say weak. Ellisander likes weak men. They're . . . we're," he admitted, "more easily controlled."

Ballentire frowned. "Where are you taking this, Sy?" she asked.

Simon smiled thinly. "If he's a weak man, he can be bought."

"With what?"

The artist shrugged. "His life."

The Troupe Leader nodded, beginning to understand. "Bought into changing sides?"

"Would it stick?" Hartney asked dubiously.

"Oh, it'll stick," Ballentire said darkly. "Trust me. It'll stick. I have an idea. Warrin told me what you and Kassandra talked about on the bank, Rosarion," she said, turning to the Herbalist.

He grew still. "Did he?"

"Yes. And if it worked on one, it might work on another."

"What are you saying, Bal?" Hamlin asked.

"That we let her decide."

Rosarion shook his head. "This isn't a play, you know," he said dubiously. "She takes her duties and her responsibilities very seriously."

"You think I don't know that?"

"What if she gets angry and demands we kill him? We'd have to do it or face the consequences when she's placed on the Throne."

Ballentire shrugged. "You're the Flame Priest, adviser to Royalty," she said sarcastically. "Talk her out of it."

"But . . ."

Simon looked up. "*I'll* talk to her," he said.

When Atreus DePaula regained consciousness some time later, he found himself bound to a rock in the center of a ring of armed players. His head felt as if it were splitting and the sight of all those confidently held weapons made his mouth grow dry. But he was a Flame Champion and so he mustered a haughty look.

"What's the meaning of this?" he demanded. His voice came out as a frightened squeak, and he scowled and cleared his throat as the gathered Troupe smirked. "I said, what's the meaning of this?" he repeated. "I'm a Champion of the Flame Temple. Release me at once!"

Ballentire stepped forward. "I'm afraid we can't do that," she answered. "Matter of national security."

"National sec . . . Now, look here, I'm on official Temple business."

"Really?" The Troupe Leader looked surprised. "My

information suggests that you were sent here to spy on us."

Atreus drew himself as far up as his bonds would allow. "I travel on the orders of His Grace, Seth Cannon, Priest of the Flame."

"You travel on the orders of His Highness, Ellisander DeMarian," a new voice said. "Murderer of the Aristok."

Atreus looked up, startled, as Rosarion came into the firelight. The Flame Champion jerked forward. "You . . ." he sputtered. He turned. "You travel with a known traitor and a heretic," he spat at Ballentire. "He's wanted by the Flame Temple."

She nodded. "I know. His activities have only recently been made known to me."

Atreus smiled with a certain amount of relief. "Release me," he said, "and I'll take him into custody. Your names don't have to be mentioned. You can just carry on with your business."

"All of us?" she asked sweetly.

He nodded, made to speak, and then paused.

Ballentire nodded in return. "You see how it is," she said almost sympathetically. "We're sort of all in this together. We know what you've seen and that means we can't let you go. We also know whose pay you're in and that means we can't trust you enough to keep you. You see what a bind that puts us in."

Hartney came forward carrying a large knife. Atreus shrank back against the rock.

"You wouldn't dare," he breathed.

"Yes, they would. They've only one concern, and it's not for you." Rosarion crouched down in front of the Flame Champion.

"I know you, Tray," he said quietly. "I've Seen you. I've Seen your deeds, and I know your thoughts."

His tone made the other man shudder. "You couldn't have," he said, his voice rising. "I haven't done anything."

"Haven't you? You serve the Duke of Yorbourne, and he murdered the Aristok."

"No! That's not true! I don't believe you!"

"Yes, you do. Remember, Tray, I'm a Temple Seer. I know the future, I know the past. I can see your lies written on your face. You know. You serve him. That makes you a conspirator in regicide. That's punishable by death."

"I'm not! I didn't know! I just suspected, but I had no proof! What could I have done?"

"You could have gone to Gawaina or Julianus."

"They wouldn't have believed me, and besides, I didn't know for sure."

"And it's so much easier to just go along, isn't it? After all, you calculated that you couldn't be linked to the deed through him. And he pays well. It was a bad mistake to follow his orders this time though. He sent you here, not Seth Cannon, didn't he?"

"No! I . . . mean, yes, sort of. He sent me to find you because, because you broke from the Temple and helped Simon of Florenz escape. And anyway you served him, too. You're a Seer, right? So you're probably in it farther than I am!"

Rosarion nodded. "I am in it farther than you are," he agreed. "But my fate has been averted for now. Yours is at hand."

He stepped back and Ballentire came forward. "Who did you see on the bank this afternoon?" she asked politely.

"Nu . . . no one. That is . . . no one except Rosarion." Hartney moved forward and Atreus swallowed.

"All right, I saw the Aristok, but you can't kill me, I'm under the protection of the Flame Temple!"

"Not out here."

"It's murder!"

"Self-preservation."

"No, he's right," Rosarion said. "He's a Flame Champion, sworn to the Vessel of the Living Flame. Only she can decide his fate."

Ballentire nodded. "Then we'll let her decide," she answered.

Atreus looked suddenly worried. "But the Vessel is just a child. She can't possibly understand what she's doing."

Ballentire grinned. "We'll explain it to her."

The Troupe moved forward.

* * *

It took only a moment to truss Atreus' arms to a tree branch and drag him to Turi's wagon. The seat had been covered in black cloth and torch holders had been set up to either side. Warrin Fire-Eater and Simon of Florenz, dressed as guards, sat on logs to either side and between them on the wagon seat sat Kassandra DeMarian, thirty-fifth Aristok of Branion. Her flame-filled eyes glittered in the torchlight, as did the Royal crest on the tunic she wore as a robe. Rosarion bowed and came forward to stand before her as Hartney and Ballentire dragged Atreus forward.

The bedraggled Flame Champion gaped at the child, and then, with a well-placed shove to the back of one calf, Ballentire knocked him to the ground.

Atreus managed to get shakily to his knees without the use of his hands and looked fearfully up at the young head of his faith.

Kassandra stared back at him.

Rosarion came forward. "Most Holy," he bowed. "The Viscount Atreus DePaula, Champion of your Flame Temple," he said. "And paid minion of Your Majesty's Uncle Ellisander. In league with him to find and return Your Majesty to him and arrest those who have labored to keep you safe." Rosarion stepped back.

Not daring to speak, Atreus merely stared mutely at Kassandra. The last time he had seen her she'd been a harum-scarum child of four, not this regal, frightening Vessel to the Living Flame's power. He remembered the touch of the Flame on his small Gift and shivered.

Kassandra cocked her head to one side. "What shall we do with you, My Lord Champion," she asked very formally.

Atreus opened his mouth and closed it again. This was a nightmare. In his worst moments he had never imagined this. But the Aristok looked as if she were waiting for an answer, and so he said the first thing that came into his head.

"Mercy, Most Holy."

It turned out to be a good answer.

The Aristok pursed her lips. "Maybe. But you serve Uncle Sandi, an' he's a traitor," she said matter-of-factly. "He killed my Papa, *the Aristok*."

He nodded fearfully. "I didn't know, Majesty. I swear it."

"Maybe," she said again. "How come you're a Flame Champion an' you take orders from Uncle . . . from the Duke of Yorbourne? You're s'posed to be sworn to the Vessel of the Living Flame only."

He wet his lips. "They . . . they didn't seem to be at odds, Majesty."

"They are now."

He swallowed. "Yes, Most Holy."

"You know that now that my Papa is dead, I'm the Vessel of the Living Flame, so you're s'posed to be sworn to me, so anything you do that I don't like is treason, right?"

"Y-yes, Most Holy."

"So for followin' Uncle Sandi, I ought execute you, an' I can, you know." She peered down at him with narrowed eyes.

Atreus stilled the urge to glance about at the heavily armed players around him. The child's gaze held him like a snake's, and he began to tremble.

"Spare me, Most Holy," he whispered. "I beg you. I'm not a traitor. I swear it."

"An' what would you do if I did?"

"I'd serve you well, My Liege," he answered almost eagerly. "I'm trained in Seer combat and in strategy."

"What about Uncle Sandi?"

He dropped his gaze. "I'm sworn to the Vessel of the Living Flame, Most Holy," he said. "And only the Vessel."

She nodded. "An' don't forget it. But my advisers say that maybe you can't be trusted, cause you took money. So I think I oughta punish you so you'd remember later not to do it again." She cocked her head to one side again. "It's gotta be good so it makes you never want to be bad ever again . . ."

She grew thoughtful as she tried to come up with something suitably dreadful, and Atreus began to tremble. Rosarion, too, looked uneasy, and the gathered players cast somewhat apprehensive glances at Simon. The artist's expression was even, but shadows from the fire played across his face, bringing a frown to Fay's lips. Finally the child looked up.

"I command you to eat worms," she said firmly.

There was silence all across the clearing and then Ballentire grinned. Kassandra looked over at her.

"Your Grace, Ballentire of Briery, come forward."

"Majesty!" The Troupe Leader marched to within nine paces of the makeshift throne and slammed to attention dramatically.

"You an' Hartney go an get eight, no ten, really big worms."

"Yes, Majesty!" The Troupe Leader executed a perfect salute and left briskly, Hartney in tow. The others waited, trying to keep serious expressions.

The deed took less time than most of the Coins had bet on. Untied, Atreus had been made to eat the ten earthworms the two tumblers had dug up. He'd done a reasonable job of it, managing to keep from vomiting until after the last one. Then he'd been made to swear his loyalty to Kassandra, and that done, she'd allowed Turi to take him off and get him something for his stomach. Then she'd formally closed the court and ordered supper.

The Troupe moved to obey, leaving Warrin, Simon, and Rosarion alone with the young Sovereign. Kassandra looked down at Simon.

"How was that?"

He smiled weakly. "Very good, Majesty. Your father would have been proud."

"I know. Was everyone worried, like you figured they'd be?"

"I think so."

When Rosarion gave him a questioning look, Simon explained stiffly. "Her Majesty knew that his crime wasn't punishable by death. So did Atreus. It was the Troupe that had to be convinced."

Kassandra nodded. "Papa says it's the leaders you gotta punish hard, not the followers. They just need a good reason to follow a new leader."

"And mercy is a good reason?" Rosarion asked.

Simon nodded. "Tempered with justice."

Remembering the look on the young Champion's face, Rosarion swallowed. "Beg pardon, Your Majesty, but I pray that when my turn comes to stand before you, you don't pick such a punishment for me."

"Just you remember it though," she said ominously.

"I will, Most Holy."

"He got off easy," Warrin muttered.

"You don't question the judgments of the Aristok," Kassandra admonished him almost absently. "Simon?"

"Yes, Majesty?"

"Am I gonna have to do this with *all* Uncle Sandi's people?"

"Probably."

She sighed. "It's gonna take such a long time."

"I know, but you'll have people to help you."

"I wish Uncle Sandi hadn't done it."

"So do I."

He put his arm around her, careful of his one hand, and the four of them stood watching the fire without speaking until Luis came to tell them that supper was ready.

12. Plans

Dawn, Di Jerdein, the twenty-third day of Mean Boaldyn

Terrilynne DeMarian stood on the top of the south tower looking north past the castle's red sandstone gate-house, up the Nyth River to Mosswell and beyond that to Dunley Vale. Her people in town had informed her that Morag Cailein had arrived late last night and was staying with her mother, Joan. Terrilynne had sent a message via Eddison, inviting the nominal Captain and Sean to Caerockeith for the noon repast to discuss their alliance. The returning message was brief. They would come.

Morag Cailein's reputation was one of mistrust and intractability toward her sometime Branion allies, but Terrilynne wasn't concerned about the Nominal Captain. The Cailein family was for sale, their loyalty in direct proportion to the price. And she was about to offer a very large price. More importantly, they would keep to themselves and provide their own supplies, something which would relieve Terrilynne's Quartermaster this spring. Little else would.

A small flock of starlings suddenly took flight off the roof of the great hall, and Terrilynne watched them wheel toward the south. It was a cold, clear morning and she could easily make out the Branion hills of her Cousin Zavier's Dukedom of Lanborough across the Banngate Estuary.

Zavier was descended from Gaby DeMarian, half sister to Atreus the Bastard and offspring of Marsellus the First, as was Terrilynne's great grandmother Flairilynne and Ellisander's great grandfather Tristan. He was on fairly good terms with his Kempston cousin Terrilynne, but even so, his reply to her request for support had been disappointingly neutral.

The Duke frowned. She needed Zavier. Well, mostly she needed provisions from his ample fields in Lanborough, she amended.

Drumming her fingers against the side of her chin, she stared sightlessly across the water. It looked as if she might have to head the negotiations herself. Zavier was always easier to intimidate in person. She'd invite him to stay awhile now that her brother Albion was here. He'd know it was a trap, but he'd come anyway. The two men had been lovers as youths and were still close friends.

She smiled, the thought of her incorrigible brother lightening her mood. A tall, pleasant-looking man, with dark red curls, and fire-filled blue eyes that flashed more often with merriment than with anger, Albion DeMarian was less than two years younger than his sister Terrilynne. They'd been inseparable as children and knowing that he stood beside her in this new adventure raised her spirits immeasurably, despite his easygoing habits. He'd arrived yesterday evening with a handful of troops and half his household, including his recent lover, the Viscount of Dunmouth, who was more than willing to throw in with them; his lands bordered Yorbourne to the west and Ellisander was an arrogant and domineering neighbor.

Albion would have come sooner, he'd explained, but the psychic blast that had knocked Terrilynne down in her main hall six days ago had kept him off his feet for a few days. His very capable Steward had taken charge, however, and so, when the young Viscount had been able to travel, four mounted troops and six archers had been ready to follow him. More were on their way. Albion was still a bit wobbly on his feet, but then, who wasn't.

Rubbing a scratch across her right cheek, caused by falling against the main hall table, Terrilynne squinted up at the bright morning sun. Her Grace, Jennet Porter, Caerockeith's Priest of the Flame, had told her that something terrible had happened in Branbridge, although it wasn't until two days ago when Rhys DeLlewellyne had returned to them from his mission in the capital that they'd learned the whole story. Someone had torched the Flame Temple.

The garrison of Caerockeith had been shocked and outraged when they'd heard, and every last one of them had blamed Yorbourne. Even Rhys' word that the Duke was practically in the Shadow Realm as a result had little effect. They knew in their bones that it was his doing, as did their Captain; and they wanted vengeance.

The Duke of Kempston leaned against the upper parapet. Well, they'd get it, she mused. She'd sent riders both east and west to Danelind, Sorlandy and to Eireon, asking for troops from whatever source she could get them. Most of her messengers should have arrived by now and begun negotiations. She'd also sent two of her precious pigeons flying home to Kempston with Alexius following by ship. With luck and good weather holding, the girl should arrive today, although it would be some time before she would return with troops.

Terrilynne counted off the days necessary. A fortnight maybe. That would put Alexius back in early Mean Ebril, with the other commissioned troops trickling in both before and after.

Her first target would have to be Yorbourne. She didn't want Ellisander's demesne behind her. Still, he must have known that would be her first decision and would have prepared for it. However, if he were truly as crippled as Rhys said he was, then Yorbourne's defense would be carried out by his Steward, Manderus Greydove and not by the Duke himself. That gave her the advantage.

Terrilynne grinned as the wind brought the faint taste of salt to her lips. Three weeks was all she needed to assemble an army large enough to move on Yorbourne, prepared or not. In the meantime, she'd finished the repairs on Caerockeith itself in case they needed a fortified headquarters, and was laying in as much provender as her people could scrounge. They were going to need it as Albion's retainers had already swelled the garrison and there were going to be many more before they could move. Gerron Reed was already in a frothing bad mood with the extra mouths to feed.

Terrilynne mused over the ever pressing problem of provisions. She really needed those supplies from Carisley. She'd send the invitation this morning with Edrud DeLlewellynne. The big man was hard to refuse, and, her mind added, if the bulk of his presence alone wasn't persuasion enough, then his twinkling blue eyes and thick, ebony hair would be. The Earl of Carisley had a weakness for beautiful men. She would send him directly.

Glancing up at the sun, Terrilynne noted the time. It was almost noon. Morag and Sean would be here soon. If she hurried, there'd be time to send Edrud and have a brief council meeting with her garrison commanders before meeting the Caileins.

With one last glance at the misty hills of Branion, she turned and made her way down into the shadowy recesses of the tower's spiral staircase.

She collared Alex Potter at the bottom and sent him to bring Albion and the Viscount of Dunmouth to the main hall. Her exact words were, "Drag my brother out of bed if necessary, but be polite to our guest." The boy saluted with a grin, knowing he couldn't really carry out the threat, but enjoying the idea anyway. Terrilynne continued on down the corridor.

When she reached the main hall, her three Commanders rose and bowed. Without preamble, Eddison began the first of the morning's reports.

Albion and Nathaniel joined them some time later, looking as if they'd both tumbled out of bed, which, in fact, they had. Terrilynne greeted the Viscount of Dunmouth with a nod, and he smiled brightly if somewhat vacantly in return as he accepted the offer of a chair. Albion took one beside him, grinning in response to his sister's mock frown.

The morning's business was barely finished and the keep servants just beginning to rebuild the hall's central firepit when Rhian Cairn, the Castle Steward, came to announce that Joan Cailein and party were approaching the keep. The Branions glanced at each other quizzically.

"Joan Cailein?" the Viscount of Dunmouth asked.

"The Head of the Cailein family," Terrilynne answered with a puzzled frown. "She's very old and rarely leaves her home."

"She must consider this meeting to be of extreme importance," Amanda observed.

"Yes. Rhian, have Lily fetch my good tunic, the black one with the crest on it."

The Steward bowed.

The Duke thought a moment. "How big is the party, Rhian?"

"Six, My Lord."

"Are Yvonnia and Lauren about the keep?"

"I believe they are in the library, My Lord."

"Ask them to join us and have a new keg of beer brought up."

"Yes, My Lord. I've taken the liberty of asking Tee to make up a lech lumbard. Captain Cailein is quite partial to it, I'm told."

"Does Tee even know how to make lech lumbard?" The thought of the hulking garrison cook making anything so delicate was hard to believe.

"Oh, yes, My Lord."

"He's never made it for me."

Nothing cracked the Steward's precise stance. "No, My Lord? Perhaps he felt My Lord preferred less . . . ostentatious fare."

Eddison frowned. "Where does he get the dates from?"

"I have never asked him, sir. Will that be all, My Lord?"

"Just show them in when they get here, Rhian."

"Certainly, My Lord." The Steward bowed again, her face expressionless, and withdrew.

Pulling a lace handkerchief from his sleeve, the Viscount of Dunmouth dabbed it against his lips, and then turned to his host.

"Will you have all six to dine then, My Lord?"

Terrilynne nodded absently.

"Surely most are mere . . . retainers." His voice was disdainful.

"The others will all be family," Terrilynne explained

patiently. "Sons or daughters or cousins. It would be a serious insult to refuse any of them at table."

"How exotic."

"If exotic's your taste, Nate, we should go into Dunley Vale," Albion invited, holding his cup out to be refilled. "The men hold tests of strength in the nude." He waggled his eyebrows at the other man.

"Really? Don't they catch cold?"

"They're very hairy. I expect that's how they keep warm."

"Albion." Terrilynne's admonishment was cut off by the arrival of her Companions. The Duke stood to allow Lauren to slip the stiffly embroidered dark blue and black formal tunic over her shirt, while giving them a quick update on their new dinner company.

"I understood that Joan Cailein was too ill to travel," Yvonnia said.

"Apparently not."

"This changes things somewhat."

"Not really." The Duke returned to her seat. "Joan won't interfere with Morag's negotiations. She knows she'll barter a good deal for the family."

"So why come herself?" Gladys asked.

"To show me that the Cailein leadership is still strong and to warn me not to try anything."

"That would be in character," Yvonnia agreed.

"The cheek," Nathaniel DeKathrine huffed.

"Maybe." The Duke shrugged. "But effective enough in its own way."

The sound of a horn winded from the gatehouse interrupted their conversation as Rhian appeared in the doorway. "The Cailein party is entering the castle, My Lord."

The Duke nodded. "Show them in as soon as they arrive."

"Yes, My Lord."

They were not kept waiting long. A few minutes later Rhian ushered six Heathland warriors into Caerockeith's great hall.

"My Lord, Captain Joan Cailein, Captain Morag Cailein, Battle Captain Sean Cailein, Kerry, Jock, and Arren Cailein."

Terrilynne stood to honor the old woman who hob-

bled into the main hall, and almost as one, the Branions
at the table followed the Duke's lead.

Joan Cailein was in her late seventies now, but in her
youth she'd been one of the greatest fighting Captains
of Heathland. Always shrewd and dedicated to the prosperity of her own family above all things, she'd taken
the Caileins in whatever direction that goal had led,
fighting both for and against five DeMarian Aristoks.
Age and ill health had forced her to give up much of the
daily workings of the family's leadership to her daughter
Morag, but she still held the strings when she wanted
to. She walked bent over, a cane in one hand, the arm
of a burly young man gripped in the other, but her white
hair was still thick and braided with battle trophies, and
her eyes were still clear and sharp with intelligence.

Behind her, Morag Cailein walked with a stiff-legged
stride. She was a stocky, brown-haired woman in her
early thirties, with a look of haughty confidence. Her
hawklike gaze tracked across the great hall, marking
each exit and each occupant with a cool stare. A worthy
Battle Captain in her own right, Morag was willing to
wield what power her mother released, but was fully
capable of taking initiative when needed. If she had one
fault it was arrogance, which tended to cloud her judgment at times, but she had Joan's complete confidence,
and in public they were united in all things.

Beside her, Sean Cailein, Joan's brother and Morag's
uncle, was exactly as he'd been the last time he'd been
a guest in Caerockeith. His expression suggested he was
enjoying the Branions' surprise at their unexpected
guest.

The three others in the party all had the look of sib-
lings or cousins, as was expected.

Terrilynne stood until Joan was seated, then took her
own chair, gesturing to the others at the table to follow suit.

"Captain Cailein, welcome to Caerockeith Castle.
Your presence is an honor."

"I was here often in my youth," the old woman answered, her voice a ragged whisper. "Not so much
these days."

Terrilynne nodded. In Joan's youth Caerockeith had

been held by the Cailein family, but it had been lost first to the Ramsens and then to the armies of Kassandra the Fifth. Terrilynne was banking on Caerockeith being a fat prize, one well worth dealing for honorably.

"May I introduce my brother, Albion DeMarian, Earl of Wakeford," she said smoothly, showing none of this in her expression, "my guest, the Viscount of Dunmouth, Nathaniel DeKathrine, my Commanders, Amànda DeKathrine, Earl of Guilcove and Gladys DeLlewellynne, Earl of Radnydd, my Lieutenant of Foot, Eddison Croft, and my Companions Yvonnia and Lauren of Cambury."

Joan acknowledged the assembled Branion nobility with a regal nod. "My daughter, Captain Morag Cailein," she whispered. "You know Sean here, and these are my nephews and my niece."

"They're welcome at my table." The Duke gestured, and servants began to come forward with plates of meat while in the recesses of the upper balcony a harper began to play quietly. "We'll eat first," she said. "Business always moves more smoothly on a full stomach."

The meal passed pleasantly enough with little talk. Unused to the ways of Heathland, the Viscount of Dunmouth couldn't help but stare at the Cailein style of dress and eating habits. Out of politeness to their host, they chose to ignore what might have been taken as a challenge. Finally Albion whispered something to him and he swung his gaze away with a blush. Arren Cailein grinned invitingly at the young DeMarian Lord and Albion gave him a warm smile in return. There were, after all, several arts of diplomacy. Ignoring protocol, Joan kicked her nephew under the table and he quickly schooled his expression.

Finally beer and wafers were served after the lech lumbard and Terrilynne turned to her guest.

"I expect Sean has told you of my offer," she said.

Joan nodded. "My voice is not what it once was," she replied. "Morag will negotiate for me."

"Certainly, Captain." Terrilynne swung her attention to the younger Cailein woman. "I need a minimum of fifty Heathland hill fighters in alliance against Yorbourne," she said bluntly. "They'll maintain their own camp and provide their own weapons, mounts, and provender. For that I offer a half cornet to each of them for the duration and a crested helm each to you for their use."

Morag drained her cup before answering. "Duration of one month."

"I need them for at least two."

The nominal Captain shook her head. "We have planting to consider."

"Two months at one crested helm, two after that. That should more than make up for any crop loss."

"One month at the crested helm, the second month two, and then they go home."

"Two months is no good for me. I need them longer. I'll meet your price if I get the option of keeping them another two months."

Morag considered it. "Three."

"Done. I'll need them in Dunley Vale as soon as possible."

"They'll be there as soon as as you deliver the money."

"Eddison will see to it before you leave."

"Good enough." Morag leaned forward. "But we take orders from our own Captain only. That will be me. And I will not suffer the orders of any Branion Commander but yourself or we go home."

"Agreed." Terrilynne gestured for more beer. "Sean tells me you've a treaty with the Taggens and the Lindies."

"That's right."

"Would that be the Lindies of Falkeith?"

"It might be. Why?"

"I need an open route from the east coast for troops."

"A route behind the Gildarock Hills?"

"Maybe."

"Pennineshire not part of this, then?"

"Pennineshire is my concern."

Morag's eyes narrowed. "There're Armistones between us and Falkeith, you know," she said. "They'd be your concern as well. They'll never deal with De-Marians." The last word carried a sneer which Terrilynne chose to ignore.

"No, but they might deal with Ramsens who are a wed family to the Taggens who you have a treaty with."

"Maybe. But they won't hold to any agreement that helps DeMarians."

The Duke of Kempston leaned forward. "I need a route through Heathland to the Bjerre Sea, Captain Cailein. I'm willing to pay for it, but I *am* going through."

Morag sipped her drink. "So there's the threat, then?"

"There's the threat," the Duke agreed. "You know what's going on in Branion. Right now, it's a lot more important to me than what's going on in Heathland. My lands are to the south. If you come down from the hills against us you'll either hit Pennineshire, which is Brandius DePaula's problem, Yorbourne, which is Ellisander's, and good for me anyway, or Lanborough, which is the Duke's and his ample cavalry's. You can't hit them all, because you're not unified, and you can't do very much damage for the same reason."

Morag folded her arms, her expression belligerent. "My thanks for the lesson in strategy, Captain DeMarian."

Terrilynne showed her teeth. "I'm offering you and the other border families the chance to make some money and kill a few Branions, Morag. I don't need the cooperation of all of you."

"Just the Caileins," Joan added darkly.

"Just the Caileins."

Morag glanced at her mother, then returned her belligerent stare to the DeMarian Duke. "You want us to negotiate your route to the sea through our territory? To openly ally with Branion in negotiations with Heathland?"

"I do. The Caileins have been openly siding with Branion since 674, so it's nothing new. However, I do have an offer for your services; one that will put you in a position of strength. Caerockeith Castle itself."

The Heaths around the table grew silent. Joan sucked on her gums and gave the Duke a shrewd look.

"The castle itself?"

"That's right. I don't have the troops spare to leave a

garrison here, and since it was once a Cailein stronghold, I offer it to you again."

Morag leaned forward. "You do realize that once it's in our possession you won't be getting it back?"

Terrilynne shrugged. "I don't need it back. As I said before, Branion is my concern right now, not Heathland. Of course, you don't have to accept it," she added casually. "We both know that if you do you'll be marked as a Branion ally to your fellow Heaths, but then, you'll be a Branion ally with a border castle."

"And what if we use it as a base to raid into Branion territory?"

"Then the armies of the Aristok will have to come back north when we're finished and pound it into rubble."

Morag snorted but Terrilynne could see her point was well taken.

She called for more wine as Joan, Morag, and Sean held a whispered conversation. Finally the nominal Captain returned her attention to Terrilynne.

"What about Mosswell?"

"It will be evacuated when the army moves south."

"Done. The money and the castle."

"Agreed."

Morag leaned back and considered the younger woman. "By the time this is over, you're going to be bankrupt," she observed.

Terrilynne shrugged. "Or Yorbourne is."

Morag showed her teeth. "Good point."

The party broke up after another hour with most of their business settled. The Caileins would fight on Kempston's side and would negotiate with the other border families. Terrilynne escorted them to the gate and Eddison handed Kerry Cailein the first payment they'd agreed upon. As the Heathland party trotted down through Mosswell, he turned to his Captain.

"Do you trust them?" he asked.

Terrilynne shrugged. "As far as I need to. They're insurance, Eddie, extra bodies, nothing more."

He grunted.

"Besides," the Duke added, as they made their way

back to the keep. "As long as they're squabbling over the best way to milk us, they won't be plotting for the best way to betray us."

"Captain!" Terrilynne turned to see Jade Asher running toward them. She rocked to a halt and saluted. "Our scouts in Falltrees reports a party of Branion Knights have passed through town and are headed this way!"

"Captain!"

The sentry on the gatehouse battlements flung his arm out eastward.

"A huge mounted party is approaching from Rossway!"

The Duke and the Lieutenant shared one look before they both ran for the stairs.

"I'd say thirty, wouldn't you, Eddie?" Terrilynne asked as she squinted down at the figures in the distance.

"At least, Captain."

"Bessie?"

"More, Captain." Accounted the best archer for distance, Bessie Cheape leaned over the parapet, gripping the standard pole for support. "I see a lot of banners flying; four Knightly orders, the Flame's Branbridge Temple, six noble families, and the Royal Standard."

"DeMarians?" Eddison asked.

Bessie shook her head. "It's carried at the front of the company and it's . . . triangular . . . it's a Herald's standard. There's a . . ." she squinted. "A red pennant above it, I think."

"Crowitanus," Eddison said.

Terrilynne nodded. "He's a Senior Royal Herald. No official Ducal affiliations, but leaning toward Yorbourne like most of Branbridge.

"What else can you see, Bessie?"

"A lot of DeLlewellynne standards, Captain. Bothsyde, Porth Wells, and . . . Radnydd."

"Radnydd?"

"Red field with golden flames, crossed with a green bar, three white blurs in the middle that are probably owls and hawklets, Captain."

"Archpriest of Radnydd," Eddison supplied.

"Gladys is going to be pissed. She can't stand her cousin Hywellynne."

"I see the banners of Wiltham and Dorsley as well, Captain," Bessie added.

"Jordana DeLynne and Xaviana DeKathrine."

"That's a lot of armed nobility in one place, Captain."

"True." Terrilynne smiled grimly. "I wonder what they want?"

Eddison ignored the sarcastic tone. "Not to wish us well."

"But probably to eat our provisions, scorch it."

"What are you going to do, Captain?" Bessie asked.

Terrilynne shrugged. "We can't close up like frightened chickens. I'll meet them as befits a DeMarian Duke, welcoming, but armed. Jade, get down to Mosswell and put them on alert. All troops to the castle."

"Captain!" the woman took off down the stairs.

Terrilynne turned to Eddison. "Lieutenant, I want the archers on the walls, most concentrated here at the front, just in case. Have Amanda and Gladys suit up and assemble the troops in the main common."

"And your brother, Captain?"

She considered it. "Ask him if he brought his battle armor."

"Do you think they're planning an assault, Captain," Bessie asked worriedly.

"Probably not, but it doesn't pay to take chances."

"Yes, Captain."

"Shall I stay up here, Captain?" Bessie asked.

Terrilynne nodded as she headed for the stairs. "I'm going to need your eyes, Bess. Sing out if you spot anything unusual."

"Yes, Captain."

The archer returned her gaze to the mounted company in the distance as the Duke of Kempston and her Lieutenant made their way downstairs. Meanwhile, the garrison readied to meet their uninvited guests.

"Uncle, wood pigeon!"

Kalidon DeKathrine, Senior Knight of the Sword, thrust his arm up in response to the cry, releasing the peregrine falcon perched on his wrist. The hawk shot into the sky after the other bird. There was a burst of feathers and the peregrine returned to the knight's wrist, the bloodied wood pigeon in its beak. His squire pried the body away and held it up proudly. Her uncle beamed at her.

"Well spotted, Holly!" Kalidon roared with a hearty laugh. "We'll make a falconer of you yet!"

The squire gave a short bow in the saddle as Kalidon turned to the woman riding beside him.

"No dry stores tonight, aye, Eathan? At least not for me and the girl. There might be a touch left if ye'd care to join us."

Innes Eathan smiled thinly, her face pale beneath an encircling bandage. "No thank you, My Lord," she said with tight-lipped politeness.

"Oh, that's right, I'm sorry, you're on medicinal rations for that thingy . . . your head wound still, aren't you?"

"Yes, My Lord."

"Well, more for me and the girl then. Proper game bird tonight, Holly!" He swung his attention back to his squire. "We'll get someone at Caerock . . . whatever-it's-called to cook it up for us, maybe in a nice parsley and onion sauce. That'd put some meat on your bones!"

"Yes, Uncle!"

"I doubt we'll have time for much feasting at Caerock-eith, My Lord Kalidon," Innes said stiffly. "Especially not with the Royal Duke's household."

"Oh, come now, Your Grace!" The Knight turned his beaming countenance back on the Flame Priest. "We're not an arresting party. There's always time for feasting!"

"I think Her Grace is right, Kalidon," Captain Jordana added from behind them. "We'll likely be camped outside the walls or in Mosswell, not at the keep."

"Oh, fiddle swabble! The whole thing'll be sorted out long before bedtime if not suppertime, you'll see."

"Care to bet on that, Kal?" Serus DeYvonne, a Knight of the Lance, called out to him from the back of the party.

"Ten crowns says I'll be sleeping in a proper castle bed this night no matter what the rest of you lot do," the Knight retorted.

"It's a bet."

Innes Eathan made to say something and then snapped her mouth closed, returning her attention to the road. Kalidon laughed.

Stretching in the saddle, the Knight grinned happily to himself. He was a simple man with simple tastes, he'd often remarked. He liked riding, hawking, fighting, and feasting, in no particular order. The adored fifth child of the Duke of Exenworth, Kalidon lived a happy life spending his substantial allowance. He was big, blond, and red-faced, with twinkling green eyes, a broad sense of humor, and a wide smile that usually charmed whoever he directed it at, even his more conservative comrades like Innes and Jordana. Later in life he was going to have trouble with his weight when age curtailed his active habits, but for now he made a formidable sight on his big roan, falcon on one wrist and iron-studded, DeKathrine embossed shield at his back. Little affected his easygoing nature, and serious mission or no, he was determined to enjoy the journey.

The company had been sent out the day after Marsellus the Third had been murdered. Kalidon didn't think much of rattling their swords at Terrilynne DeMarian; he liked the Duke of Kempston and she was going to take serious offense at their attitude. Besides, the idea that she was a traitor was absurd. But there was plenty of riding in the open air and a tolerable amount of hawking to be had along the way, so Kalidon kept his opinion of their mission quiet after the first few miles.

They'd made good time, although Kalidon knew they'd been a burden to every manor house, keep, and town they'd stopped at.

"Well, what do you expect?" he'd asked Jordana De-Lynne in a booming voice that had carried easily to their host of the first night, after that man had stared open-mouthed at their call for provisions. *"A bloody great lot of Triarctic brutes, over thirty strong, clatter into your dooryard demanding what little food you have left from the winter. I'm surprised the poor fellow doesn't drop dead at the very suggestion."*

Jordana had not appreciated the humor of the observation, but then Kalidon wasn't really trying to be funny, he was being accurate.

Captain, the Earl of Wiltham, Jordana DeLynne and Kalidon DeKathrine were old friends despite their difference in temperament. He could usually draw a smile from her, and he repeatedly tried to pull her from the funk the Aristok's death had put her in over the course of their journey, but had met with little success. He was determined to win, however. Kalidon DeKathrine always won, usually from sheer determination.

He glanced across at the Flame Priest riding silently beside him. Now there was another in need of a sense of humor in the worst way, he reflected, but she wasn't likely to get one on this journey, not with last week's events still ringing in her ears.

A shadow passed over the Knight's usually bright countenance. That was ill done. Whoever was responsible was going to pay dearly when what was left of the priesthood caught up with them.

He shook the mood off. Maybe then Innes would smile a little. He'd like to see that. She was a fine-looking woman and would be beautiful if only she'd lighten up.

Leaning back, Kalidon glanced around at the others in the company. Ahead of them, Senior Herald Crowitanus rode, stiffly straight in the saddle, his eyes never leaving the hills in the distance. Unused to traveling with so many, the Herald was ill at ease in so large a company. He'd kept to himself during their stops and had pressed them to make as many miles as possible. Beside him, the heraldic standard of the Royal DeMarians snapped in the breeze as the young apprentice Herald who carried it tried valiantly to keep up with his master and hold it aloft.

"Poor little beggar," Kalidon thought sympathetically. The Knight glared at the back of the Herald's head. *"Cold fish that one, and no sauce on him to cover up the taste either."* He grinned at his own joke. He supposed Crowitanus could be forgiven for his stiff demeanor. Not everyone had had the benefit of Kalidon's rambunctious upbringing, but that was no reason to fly his standard all the livelong day and exhaust the boy riding behind him. *"We'll share the pigeon with him,"* he thought gener-

ously. *"Holly won't mind. Getting him away from old stick-in-the-mud for an evening would do him some good."*

He sighed dramatically. There'd been few in the company willing to travel in the spirit of adventure that Kalidon met each day with. There was young Serus, of course. Kalidon had already rooked him for most of his purse. And the Bow Knights, Elias Maple and Sam Pallaton, neither one of them nobility, could be counted on for a joke and a game of cards now and again. The rest were all far too stuffy.

Kalidon began to whistle, and then broke off as the sun glinted off a metal turret in the distance.

"That'll be Caerock . . . thingy now," he boomed. "At last. We'd better shake a leg, Crowitanus, or we'll likely find the gate barred against us and the hot tar ready on the battlements!"

There was the faint sound of trumpets in the distance.

"Oh! Too late!"

Crowitanus gave no sign that he'd heard but urged his horse, and therefore the company, into a gallop.

With a laugh, Kalidon pushed the roan into a matching stride as Jordana's squire pulled out a horn and gave it wind.

Yes, the Knight thought silently. *That's how it should be done. Let them know you're coming so they can meet you face-to-face.*

He glanced over at the Earl of Wiltham. He liked Jordana a lot. Perhaps when this was all sorted out they might try and make a go of it again. In the meantime, they had an impression to make.

With both the present and the future accounted for, Kalidon DeKathrine began to sing happily as the red sandstone walls of Caerockeith came into view.

On the upper battlements, Terrilynne squinted down at the huge company splashing their way along the north shore of the Banngate.

"A pretty sight." Albion leaned over the parapet to get a better view. "Look at all those colorful pennants and banners. They look like they're coming to a joust."

Terrilynne just grunted.

"Is that Kalidon DeKathrine?"

The Duke followed his gaze. "I'd say."

"Oh, well, that's all right then, Kal's a good sort. He wouldn't be in Ellisander's pocket."

"Maybe not, but the Archpriest of Radnydd could easily be, and that's Innes Eathan down there. She is not a *good sort*."

"She's just stuffy."

"Whatever." Terrilynne turned away. "We'd better get down there."

Albion nodded. Together the two DeMarians descended to the main castle common.

An hour later they heard the horn call of a Royal Herald. Eddison shouted for attention and, as the company crossed the castle's wooden bridge and passed under the gatehouse, the assembled garrison slammed their pike shafts against the ground with a unified crash.

Dressed in formal battle attire, the fire-wolf and tyger crest of Kempston glittering on her surcoat, Terrilynne was waiting for them on the steps of the main keep. She nodded as the first riders reined up in front of the gathered troops.

"Welcome to Caerockeith, Your Grace," she said, greeting the Herald first. "It's been a long time."

Children ran forward to take their horses' bridles, and Crowitanus dismounted and bowed, handing his reins over to Jael.

"I bring a message from Her Lordship, the Hierarchpriest of Cannonshire, My Lord," he announced.

Terrilyne cocked her head at the company. "You come very heavily escorted. Are the roads of Branion so unsafe these days?"

He made a sour face. "Of those with me, My Lord, they may speak for their own mission. I am sent only with a message from Hierarchpriest Gawaina DeKathrine."

"And I shall hear it. If you'll follow my Steward, she'll lead you to a place where you may wait in comfort. I'll come as soon as I've greeted my other guests."

"Thank you, My Lord." Crowitanus bowed again and,

without a glance at the others, followed Rhian Cairn into the keep.

Terrilyne turned her gaze to the others crowded into the common.

"My greeting to you also, My Lord Earl of Wiltham," she said. "And to you all. You are welcome to Dunleyshire."

Jordana dismounted. "We come to speak with you on a matter of grave urgency, My Lord," she said stiffly.

Terrilyne nodded. "It must be so if so many are sent to the far reaches of the Realm when there is so much unrest in the capital. But we will speak of it later," she added before the Shield Knight Captain had a chance to answer. "You'll be tired from your long journey. My people will see you all bestowed and then we will meet for supper. Lieutenant!"

Eddison came forward and saluted. "My Lord!"

"Have the garrison see to our guests."

"Yes, My Lord!"

"My Lords of Guilcove and Radnydd, if you will come with me."

"Of course, My Lord." The two Earls came forward and together they followed the Duke of Kempston into the keep as Eddison took charge of the company despite their protestations.

Meanwhile, Terrilynne entered her private audience hall and took a seat on a low dais, Amanda and Gladys to either side of her. Guards took positions before the doors and windows and, when they were all in place, she signaled to Rhian. The Steward left to bring the Herald to the Duke's presence.

Crowitanus entered swiftly, came to within nine paces of the dais and bowed.

He was a thin, ascetic-looking man without his muffling traveling attire. White streaked his dark hair and lines traced patterns down either side of his mouth. It was said that he was soon to retire to teach at the Herald's College, and his presence here was a statement as much as the memorized words he was to impart.

Terrilynne acknowledged his bow with a short wave of her hand.

"What message do you bring me, Herald?" she asked formally.

"My Lord, I am charged to tell you that you have been Seen in Vision with the Aristok Kassandra the Sixth."

Amanda and Gladys exchanged a glance, but Terrilynne's face remained impassive.

"It has been discovered that Simon of Florenz, the Court Painter, is responsible for her kidnapping," the Herald continued, "and is making for Caerockeith, with the hope that the Duke of Kempston will shelter him from justice due to her difficulties with the Duke of Yorbourne. My Lord, it is requested that as soon as he makes himself known you turn the Aristok and her captor over to the authorities in Branbridge immediately."

Amanda bridled at the Herald's words, and Terrilynne held one hand up to calm her.

"In what state was Branbridge when you left, Your Grace?" she asked in a tone of simple curiosity.

"In a state of tension, My Lord. However, I understand that things have since become worse."

"I've heard that also. Is the Hierarchpriest certain that the Court Painter is responsible for Kassandra's disappearance?"

"Yes, My Lord."

"Do they know why?"

"They have not imparted that knowledge to me, My Lord."

"And what of her father's murder? Do they think he's responsible for that, too?"

"Of that I cannot say, however, I was told that it was imperative that My Lord, the Duke of Kempston, remembers her oaths and returns the Aristok to her rightful place in the capital as soon as he appears with her."

"And who is it that reminds me of my oaths?" Terrilynne's tone was flat, and the Herald kept his expression carefully respectful.

"His Lordship, the Duke of Yorbourne, My Lord."

"I see, and this company of armed Knights and Triarchy Priests is here to see that I do so, is that right, Your Grace?"

"It is, My Lord."

"And how long are they planning on staying?"

"I don't know, My Lord. I am charged with returning immediately, however."

The relief in his tone was obvious and Terrilynne made a show of reflection. "You are, of course, welcome to make your stay with us as long as you need to, Your Grace, and fresh mounts for you and your squire will be made available upon your request."

"Thank you, My Lord."

Terrilynne nodded. "When you return to Branbridge," she continued, "you may tell the Hierarchpriest that Kassandra the Sixth is not here, nor do I have any idea of her whereabouts, but I shall be certain to bring her back to her capital if the Aristok requires it of me. You may also assure my Cousin, the Duke of Yorbourne, that when I come, I shall do so accompanied by an honor guard of at least as many as have accompanied you on your journey here."

"I shall, My Lord."

"In the meantime, you are welcome to join us at supper or take your repast alone. My own Herald Eaglelynne is away so you may use her quarters. My Steward will show you the way."

The Herald bowed. "My thanks again, My Lord. With your permission I will take my supper quietly with my apprentice and be gone tomorrow morning."

"Of course."

Terrilynne waved Rhian forward and the Herald left with her.

When the door closed, Amanda slammed one fist into the palm of the other.

"Bloody Yorbourne!"

"Hm." Terrilynne motioned to one of the guards at the door. "Briar?"

"Captain!"

"Have Eddison join us and then tell Kalidon De-Kathrine I'd like to speak with him."

"Yes, Captain."

When Eddison arrived, Gladys filled him in on the Herald's message.

Eddison frowned. "Jael's father?"

"That's right."

"*He*'s supposed to have kidnapped Kassandra?"

"Apparently," Terrilynne answered.

"But why?"

"If you ask me, the Seers have been dipping into too much Sabat Wine," Gladys answered.

Amanda snorted. "I say it's another one of Yorbourne's slimy plots."

Terrilynne made a dismissive gesture. "Maybe. Let's wait and see what Kalidon has to say."

Some moments later there was a clatter of metal outside the hall and Briar announced Kalidon DeKathrine.

The big man entered with an easy stride. He, too, stopped nine paces from the dais and bowed, but there was a grin on his face and a twinkle in his eyes when he straightened.

Terrilyne smiled in return. "Bring a chair for His Lordship, Briar."

When this was done and Kalidon was seated comfortably with a cup of wine, she nodded at him. "Good to see you again, Kal."

"And you, My Lord Terri."

"How's your mother?"

"In excellent health as always. Father's got the gout, though."

"Sorry to hear it."

"Yes, it puts him in the foulest mood. He can't hunt, you see."

"Hm. Crowitanus tells me you've come to drag the Aristok and myself back to Branbridge."

He nodded pleasantly. "Have her about, do you?"

"No."

"Didn't think so, otherwise you'd have been flying the Royal Standard, I expect."

"Possibly. Quite a large party to make the point."

His broad face grew serious. "It was ill done and I told them so. 'It'll put her back up,' I said, but nobody listens to me."

"It'll only put my back up if they eat me out of house and home," Terrilyne replied with a sour expression. "How long do you think they'll be staying."

He shrugged. "You'll have to ask Innes or Jordana,

My Lord. Me, I plan on staying until you throw me out. But I, at least, can pay my own way. I prefer to hunt Heathland birds and deer, not Branion Aristoks. And I'm willing to share."

"Then you're welcome to stay as long as long as you like."

Kalidon stretched with a smile. "Spring is a poor time for company, that's for sure," he noted. "And your garrison looks to have pretty healthy appetites. Grown some since the last time I saw it. Planning a few military exercises?"

Terrilynne shrugged. "Wouldn't you be?"

"Me? You know I have no ambition. But then the Aristok isn't likely to come knocking on my door and provide me with a convenient rallying cry."

"Are you sure she'll come knocking at mine?"

He shrugged. "The priests are sure, but the whole thing's all muddled what with the Flame Temple set alight and their Herbalist's defection."

Terrilynne blinked at him. "Herbalist?"

Kalidon snorted. "You are out of touch."

He made himself comfortable.

When he was finished, he knocked back the wine as Terrilynne considered his story.

"A great deal going on," she observed.

"It is that." He looked keenly at her. "So what are you going to do about your guests, Terri? The Flame knows, I'm not one to get involved in political squabbles, but I'd have to defend this lot if you decided to pop them all into dungeon cells. After all, they're only acting in the best interests of the Realm."

"What if they weren't?"

He looked confused. "How do you mean?"

"What if the best interests of the Realm involved allying with me against Yorbourne, not posturing before my gate?"

"What, you mean a civil war? How could that possibly be in the best interests of the Realm?"

"If Ellisander were a regicide."

Kalidon grew very quiet. He knew the two DeMarian

Dukes hated each other, but he also knew that Terrilynne did not make idle accusations.

"Do you have proof?" he asked finally.

"No," she admitted. "But I'm willing to act on my suspicions, anyway. I won't suffer Ellisander on the Throne."

"What about Kassandra? Once she's found, it will be her on the Throne, not Yorbourne."

"If Ellisander killed her father, then he'll move against her sooner or later. Either way, I'm already committed." She leaned forward. "Will you support me, Kalidon?"

After a moment's contemplation, the knight shook his head. "I couldn't be a party to bringing violence to Branion now, My Lord," he said, all traces of his earlier humor gone.

"I'd hate to see you fighting against me on the battlefield, Kal."

"As would I, but the Realm's too vulnerable after this attack on the Temple Seers. We can't risk civil war. Now if you had proof, that would be different. We could take it to the Hierarchpriest."

The Duke snorted. "We'd never get near Gawaina. Ellisander would see to that. No, Kal, the only answer is to knock Yorbourne off his power base."

"Well, I can't help you there, I'm sorry."

"So am I."

"Going to warm up the dungeons?"

The twinkle was back in his eyes, and Terrilynne smiled.

"No, just my powers of reason. I'll have you on my side sooner or later, Kalidon DeKathrine."

He grinned. "Good luck."

With a returning smile, Terrilyne waved Briar forward. "Supper should be ready soon. I'll let you get some rest. But I'd rather you didn't mention this conversation to the others, Kal. I'll speak with Jordana and Innes myself later."

"As you wish, My Lord." Kalidon rose, bowed once more, and allowed Briar to lead him from the hall.

When the door closed, Eddison turned to the Duke.

"A good man," he noted.

"What he said made a lot of sense."

"We're still moving, though, right, Captain?"

"As I told Kalidon, I'm committed now, proof or no proof. I know Ellisander's guilty."

Scratching at an itch under her vambrace, Amanda turned.

"Do you think Simon is really bringing Kassandra to Caerockeith?"

"Why would he?" Eddison answered.

"Why would he steal her away in the first place?"

"Who knows."

"It would be something if the Aristok did come here," Gladys mused.

Amanda gave a feral grin. "Yorbourne would have fits."

"I expect he's having fits already if they suspect she's on her way."

Terrilynne chopped a hand down impatiently. "It doesn't matter."

"Captain?" All three stopped the discussion to look at her.

"Our immediate problem is this Triarctic Company. They are here, so we might as well try and make use of them if possible. My Lords of Guilcove and Radnydd, I want you to speak with the Knights, see what they think and where their loyalties lie. Eddison, I want you to speak with the others. Find out the same thing. I'll work on Jordana and Innes."

"I don't envy you, Captain," Gladys snorted.

"Don't be so sure. I want you to talk to your cousin Hywellynne."

The Gwynethian Lord made a face, and the others chuckled.

"What if the Aristok does come here, Captain?" Eddison asked.

Terrilynne made a dismissive gesture with one hand. "*If* she's coming here, she'll have to go back to Branbridge eventually, and she'll need an army to escort her." She rose.

"That's all, people. I'll see you at the banquet."

She turned and strode from the hall. The others stood

a moment, considering their various orders, then they, too, made their way out.

Later that afternoon, on the west coast of Branion, the Aristok Kassandra the Sixth sat on a high embankment overlooking the town of Port Ellsey where Hamlin and Fay had gone to find a ship that would take them north to Caerockeith. Below, oceangoing vessels and smaller fishing craft crowded into the harbor, and out to sea the waves sparkled in the orange sunlight. The air smelled like salt and fish. Off to one side, Luis climbed nimbly along the cliff face, searching for gull nests. Warrin Fire-Eater stood silently behind Kassandra and after a moment, she turned to him with a woeful expression.

"I don't wanna go, Warrin," she said.

The big man crouched down beside her. "How come, Kasey?"

"Papa didn't like boats. He said they were as likely to tip you in the scorching drink as look at you."

Warrin pondered her words a moment. "How can a boat look at you?"

Kassandra gave an indifferent shrug. "I dunno, but that's what he said, anyway."

"I came to Branion on a boat."

"Did you?"

"Uh-huh. From Panisha."

"Was it a big boat?"

"It was a very big boat. The whole Troupe came on it, wagons, horses, and all."

"So how come you can't come with us on this boat?"

" 'Cause it would look too suspicious. Players travel on land so they can perform in towns, an' make money.

"We'll catch up to you, though."

"When?"

The big man scratched at his beard. "Uh . . . a couple of weeks, I think."

"You'd better be there in time for my birthday." The child scowled.

"We will. Uh . . . when is it?"

"The twelfth day of Mean Ebril."

"Oh, that gives us lots of time."

A sound behind them made them turn to see Simon

climbing laboriously up the hill. His face was pale, and he still cradled his one hand tightly to his chest. He made himself smile when he saw them although his face was tight with pain.

"Didn't you come up here to search for gulls' eggs?" he asked a little breathlessly when he reached them.

"We were, but they are too crafty for us," Kassandra answered. "They make their nests too far down the cliff, so Luis is looking an' we are watching. You can come an' watch, too."

Simon joined them and sat staring out to sea.

Kassandra tipped her head up to peer up at him. "Are you gonna draw the boats?" she asked.

He shook his head. "Not today, Sparky."

The child plucked a tiny red clover from the grass and held it to her nose. "Why?"

"Because I didn't bring my sketchbook."

"Why?"

Simon closed his eyes briefly, and the shadows tensed. "Because I couldn't climb and carry it with one hand," he said. The shadows subsided.

"You coulda put it in a bag over your shoulder." Kassandra's voice was reproachful. "Fay says you gotta exercise your fingers."

"My fingers are fine."

"Hamlin says you should start practicing with your left hand like Lor . . . Lor somebody taught you."

"Lorenzo."

"That's right."

"I don't need to practice with my left hand, Sparky. My right is healing."

"What if it doesn't?"

Simon glanced down. The child's fire-washed eyes gazed up at him frankly, expecting an answer.

"Then I'll use the left," he answered grudgingly.

"When?"

"When we get to Caerockeith."

She considered him a moment. "All right." She returned her attention to the harbor.

"Will we go on a very big boat?"

He squinted down at the ships. "Probably not."

"Is it likely to tip us in the scorching drink?"

He smiled weakly, recognizing Leary's words. "I don't think so, Sparky," he answered.

At that moment there was a shout, and Luis scrambled up from the edge, a bird's nest in one hand. "Majesty, look! I found four!"

Kassandra favored him with a sunny smile of regal approval.

Fay and Hamlin returned later that evening. After hearing of Kassandra's triumphant expedition to find supper, they accepted a cup of catmint tea, some stew, and the bit of boiled egg the child had saved for them.

The others gathered about the fire, and after a time Fay looked up.

"We found a ship," she said without preamble. "The *Osprey*. It leaves at first tide tomorrow and can carry eight people north to Kirkwald, that's only five miles from Caerockeith."

The others were silent a moment. "First tide," Ballentire said slowly. "That's soon."

Hamlin nodded. "Just past dawn."

"We'll miss you," Tamara said, resting one hand on Fay's arm.

The older woman smiled. "Are you sure? We caused you all a lot of worry."

"It was an adventure," the tumbler answered loyally.

"Well, the adventure's not over yet," Hamlin answered. "You promised to come to Caerockeith. We'll hold you to that."

Tucked into Simon's side, a warm blanket around them both, Kassandra nodded.

"We'll be there," Ballentire promised.

Beside the fire, Atreus stirred. "Eight?" he asked. "So you are taking me, then?"

"We are, boy." Fay nodded and Kassandra turned to glare at him indignantly.

"You're mine now," she said. "I told you that. You go where I go."

He smiled shyly. "Yes, Most Holy."

She gave him a regal nod and tucked herself back into Simon's side. He made to stroke her hair with his right hand, caught himself, and just hugged her with his left.

The Troupe sat quietly, staring into the fire. Above them, the stars slowly came out, and the children lay back in the grass.

"Look, Bal," Dani said, pointing. "The Players are out tonight."

As one, the Troupe craned their necks up to gaze at the collection of stars named for their trade.

"So they are."

"Where?" Kassandra demanded.

"Do you see those stars over there?" The Troupe Leader pointed. "The ones that look like a group of three people?"

"Yes."

"Do you see how the upper stars make them look like they have their arms up in the air?"

"I guess."

"They're called the Players."

"Why?"

"Because of the way we bow." Ballentire stood and motioned. As one the whole Troupe rose and turned to face the Branion Aristok. Ballentire raised her arms and the rest followed her lead. They stood frozen for an instant, silhouetted against the moonlit sky, then they bowed from the waist, sweeping their arms down.

Kassandra laughed and applauded.

"I wish I had a star," she said wistfully when they were seated again. "I mean besides the one you gave me, Marc," she said quickly as the boy's face fell. He smiled.

"But you do," Simon answered. "Do you see that bright reddish star to the north?"

"Yes."

"That's called the Flame."

"Really?"

The child twisted around to stare at him, her fire-touched eyes wide."

"Really. In the Triarctic scripts it says that star was the birthplace of the Living Flame."

"So how did it get all the way down here?"

"I don't know."

Hamlin lit his pipe, the red glow mirroring the coals in the low fire. "Why don't you ask Rosarion," he offered.

They glanced around. "Where is he?" Fay asked, tak-

ing the stem of her own pipe from between her teeth.
"Atreus, have you seen Rosarion?"

The Flame Champion looked startled to be addressed.
"Uh, no, ma'am."

"He was here at supper," Luis offered. "He and Turi
were sitting together."

Bennie snickered. Ballentire glanced over at him. He
gave her an innocent look, and she narrowed her eyes.
"Benedito-Ximenes of San Valeville," she intoned,
"what do you know?"

He giggled. "Just that he and Turi went off that way."
He jerked his head in the direction of the cliffs.

"Are they going for more gulls' eggs?" Kassandra
asked.

Most of the Troupe attempted to keep a straight face.

"No," Simon told her finally, after she'd repeated the
question. "They're uh . . ."

"Saying good-bye to each other," Fay finished sternly,
glaring at the tumblers who were still snickering.

"Oh." The child twisted in Simon's lap until her head
rested against his chest. "Show me more stars," she
demanded.

Some distance away, Turi and Rosarion stared up at
the stars as the others did. They'd made love quickly
but gently, and now lay wrapped in their cloaks, just
holding each other. Rosarion coughed, and Turi raised
himself up on one elbow.

"We should go back to the fire," he said with a worried frown.

"Not yet. I'm fine. It's just the damp." Rosarion
pulled the tumbler back down. "It'll be a long time until
we see each other again. I want to make the most of it."

"It'll be at least two or three weeks," Turi agreed.

"I hope everything goes well at Caerockeith."

"Worried about the Duke of Kempston?"

"Yes." The Herbalist shivered. "It's funny. Before, in
Branbridge, after my family died, I had nothing to live
for. I didn't want to live, but I did anyway. Then I had
the Visions, and . . . well, Ellisander, but I still didn't
care if I lived or died. Now . . ."

"Now?"

"Now I do care, because now I have something to live for."

Turi smiled. "And what would that be?"

Rosarion looked up into the other man's gentle face. "You."

They kissed, and after a while they made love for a second time on the cool grass.

The next morning Kassandra the Sixth and her entourage took leave of the Spinning Coins Tumbling Troupe. There were a lot of tears and promises to rejoin as soon as they could. Ballentire and Tamara gave Kassandra a set of bright red juggling balls and Warrin gave her a small tinderbox. The whole Troupe had pooled their money, and Ballentire handed the small leather bag to Simon. When the artist started to argue, the Troupe Leader called in Fay. Simon pocketed the money with a grimace.

Off to one side, Turi and Rosarion shared a suddenly shy embrace before the Herbalist went to stand beside Fay.

Everyone had to say good-bye and wish them well, but eventually everything was said, and they parted company. The Troupe stood on the cliff's edge watching Kassandra and the others make their own way down the cliff path to Port Ellsey.

Kassandra continued to turn and wave long after she lost sight of them.

The *Osprey* was waiting for them. The Captain, an Essusiate woman, took their payment without comment and ushered them aboard.

As the new sun rose over the waves, Kassandra De-Marian could just make out the forms of six wagons perched on the cliffs above. She waved as the ship slowly put out to sea, and she was sure she saw one large form, towering over all the others, waving back.

Simon came to stand beside her and, as the cliffs melted into the horizon, they turned their faces to the north and Caerockeith three days away.

13. Caerockeith

Three days after Captain Jordana DeLynne's company arrived in Caerockeith, Terrilynne DeMarian stood on the upper parapets once again, staring out across the hills of Heathland. It had been raining most of the day, and the castle was damp, stuffy, and crowded with people driven inside by the storm. Forced into close company, the two groups of nobles did their best to avoid stepping on each others' toes, but tempers were short.

Ordered to remain inside the castle to maintain an armed presence, the mood of the garrison wasn't much better. Eddison had begun a leave rotation yesterday, so most were able to visit their families in Mosswell for few hours, but resentment against their guests was still high. Today's group had headed off despite the rain.

The Duke herself had made for the upper parapets as soon as the storm had abated, and now, with the cloud cover finally lifting, the sun shone down on the distant fields with a beautiful, almost magical, glow that was particular to Heathland. Terrilynne took in a deep lungful of the fresh, new air.

Below, people were beginning to emerge from the keep, moving to take advantage of the afternoon's reprieve. Hooves clattered on the castle cobblestones, and she glanced down to see Kalidon and a party of falconers trotting through the gate house tunnel and out, heading for the east fields. He'd invited her along, but she'd declined. It was peaceful up here, and Kalidon was anything but peaceful. She needed time to think and decide on her next move.

The Duke of Kempston had spent the last three days subtly sounding out the other members of the Triarctic Company as to their political loyalties. Most were fairly neutral regarding herself and the Duke of Yorbourne, although the contingent of DeLlewellynnes—following the lead of their kinswoman Hywellynne, Archpriest of Radnydd—seemed to be leaning toward Ellisander. All were angry over Marsellus' death and Kassandra's disappearance, but had no one to direct that anger toward. It made them brittle and mistrustful, and Terrilynne was heartily sick of the lot of them.

She watched as a wild hawk flew lazy circles over the west fields, oblivious to the tame birds some distance away.

The Duke had done her best to be a reasonable host for her guests, holding banquets and entertainments at night and tourneys and hunting parties during the day. Kalidon had become her strongest ally in the latter, dragging off as many of both the garrison and the company as he could out hunting every day. Yesterday, Terrilynne had joined him, Jordana, and Xaviana DeKathrine, the Viscount of Dorsley, and the four of them had taken down a roebuck. Fresh venison had done a lot to ease the tension between the two groups, although each remained suspicious of the other's motives.

The wild hawk screeched angrily. Kalidon's party was out of sight behind the low hills, so, wondering what had occurred to upset it, Terrilynne leaned forward and peered over the edge of the parapet.

Below, a single figure moved purposefully over the west fields. Probably a child from Mosswell seeking ground nests, the Duke assumed.

She returned her thoughts to her military plans. It was still too early to expect troops from Eireon or Danelind, but she'd received a message from Zavier today.

Her Samlinshire cousin would come. Although he still promised nothing, Terrilynne was satisfied. If he came, Zavier would stay. Albion would see to that.

As for her Heathland allies, Terilynne hadn't heard from Morag, although her scouts reported a number of Caileins filtering into Dunley Vale. It was a beginning.

She swept her gaze across the landscape. The fields were awash with red-and-white clover. Soon the roads would dry and the pasture lands would be dotted with sheep and cattle.

To the west the figure had left the fields and was coming swiftly down the road to Mosswell. To the east the sun was beginning its own descent, fingers of orange light spreading across the land. Already half the castle was in shadow and Terrilynne tilted her head, letting the last few rays of warmth caress her face.

The figure reached the village and disappeared behind the rows of thatched-roofed cottages.

The sun touched the horizon.

Terrilynne considered returning downstairs, but hesitated. She'd get little enough quiet tonight. There was another banquet to attend. Gerron Reed and Tee Hanover were having seizures about the amount of food being wasted, but it couldn't be helped. The Triarctic Company would be staying at least a week before the lack of political activity made Innes Eathan edgy and she took them back to Branbridge.

The Duke leaned against the parapet, her chin resting on her hand. When was the last time she'd been in the capital, she wondered. It had to be last Braniana's Day. Had it really been seven months?

A sudden surge of homesickness welled up, surprising in its strength. Terrilynne had been born in Branbridge. A Knight of the Sword, her mother had given birth to her in the Sword Tower's private meditation chamber, believing, as many did, that the place of a child's birth would affect its future. Danielle DeMarian had prayed for strength and success for her first born. The former had come to pass; the latter was yet to be decided upon.

Due to an untimely arrival, Danielle had not made it to the Sword Tower for Albion's birth. Her son had been born in a Public House on Taverners' Row, where she'd been forced to stop on her way. All things considered, Terrilynne judged it ironically appropriate. Albion himself often joked that when his firstborn was due, he and his wife were going to take up residence in a dung heap to insure the child's success at Court. Terrilynne felt that it couldn't hurt.

A figure emerged from behind a hedgerow, moving away from Mosswell toward the castle.

The Duke watched idly, wondering if it was the same person whose progress she'd marked through the fields. One of her people's children, perhaps? Her interest sparked, she leaned forward, squinting against the shadows. The figure could be an adult, she supposed. Maybe a messenger from the Caileins.

The unknown person continued toward the castle, unaware of the Duke's scrutiny from above. Terrilynne continued to watch as the figure drew nearer, some features becoming more distinct. A youth, wearing nondescript breeches and cloak. Not a Cailein, then, and not one of her own people's. She knew every youth in Mosswell; Nicholas Orren, her Guard Sergeant, was training most of them in the castle common.

The figure glanced up at the walls, hesitated for an instant, then carried on. Terrilynne caught sight of a determined frown on an otherwise smooth brow. A young woman. She reminded the Duke of Ianna Reed, Gerron's firstborn, although she could see that it wasn't her.

The figure reached the common, spoke with the guard on duty and was motioned onward. A messenger of some kind, definitely. She disappeared behind the bulk of the castle, out of Terrilynne's view.

Intrigued now, the Duke descended the tower and made for the gatehouse.

The youth was speaking urgently with the gate guard. He turned at the sound of the Duke's approach and saluted.

"Who is she, Alec?"

"She says she comes with a message from Atreus De-Paula, Champion of the Flame, Captain. She won't tell me what it concerns. Just says it's important and only for the Duke of Kempston's ears." He rolled his eyes.

Terrilynne smiled at the dramatics and glanced over at the youth. She saw a stocky, serious-looking young woman with light brown hair and brown eyes, tensely twisting an iron apprenticeship ring on her finger. The youth met the Duke's gaze frankly until she realized who she must be, and then gave an awkward bow. Terrilynne gestured.

The youth came forward.

* * *

Dani had been walking most of the morning, stalwartly refusing to wait until the storm had passed. If she could make Caerockeith before dusk, they might all be under cover that night. Now she was wet and cold, but tried to show none of this to the Duke of Kempston as the older woman looked her up and down with a fire-sparked stare. Her message was too important to get lost in nervousness. Kassandra the Sixth was coming to Caerockeith.

The Aristok and her company of protectors had made an uneventful trip up the coast and, three days after setting out, had docked at the Heathland town of Kirkwald. It wasn't a true town by Branion standards, although it was big enough to have a small Sword Tower which caused them some consternation. Only Atreus had ever been to Heathland before, and he reluctantly took charge, finding them an inn on the edge of town.

A few of the patrons had stared at the strange mix of Triarchs and Essusiates traveling together, but the size of the party had kept their interest to mere curiosity. Branions were not their concern unless they could be swiftly dealt with without retaliation, and eight people were a bit too many to handle easily.

They took a large room, ordered up some supper, and sat down to discuss their next move. Terrilynne DeMarian would have to be contacted in such a way that the messenger wouldn't immediately be arrested by the first person they met. After much argument it was decided to send Dani. She wasn't known and could easily make the five miles to the castle quickly. She was to say she carried a message from Atreus DePaula, Flame Champion in the entourage of His Grace Seth Cannon. That would get her in to see the Duke of Kempston without suspicion.

Dani had been proud to be chosen and had set out as soon as she'd been able to convince Hamlin she'd remembered what they told her to say.

She ought to remember, she said dryly to herself, they'd run her through it a dozen times.

Once free, she'd made for the red sandstone castle, obvious even at that distance, and had arrived in plenty of time. The two guards she'd spoken with had accepted her words and sent her on and now she faced the person whom she'd come to see. Terrilynne DeMarian, Duke of Kempston, Cousin to the child they'd protected for the last two weeks. Dani studied her shyly.

She saw a tall, confident-looking woman, with bright, copper hair, and strong hands. She was the first De-Marian Dani had ever seen other than Kassandra, and the apprentice tried not to stare at the red fire which shone from the Duke's blue eyes. It made it hard to look at her anyway, and Dani averted her gaze.

At the Duke's gesture, she came forward and, suddenly unsure, she gave an awkward bow.

Terrilynne looked her up and down.

"You are?"

Dani took a deep breath to calm the sudden pounding of her heart. She'd rehearsed this speech a dozen times, she told herself firmly. She knew it. "If it pleases you, My Lord," she began. "I'm Dani Ashwood, apprenticed to Hamlin Ewer, the Royal Stained-Glass Maker. I come with a message from Atreus DePaula, Champion of the Flame." She hesitated. "It's very urgent, My Lord, and very, um . . . private. It concerns the Aristok."

The Duke raised one eyebrow. "Then I'd better hear it right away, hadn't I?" she said. Gesturing at the guard, she waited as he opened a door in the side of the gatehouse with a large set of keys. The door creaked loudly, as if it hadn't been moved in some time. The Duke entered and Dani followed.

They ascended a flight of worn spiral stairs and came into a small room, seats cut into the stone of the barred windows and a large, cold hearth set in one wall. Sunlight streamed across the floor, and the Duke crossed to the far end and sat. After a moment she tipped her head to one side in a motion that reminded Dani suddenly of Kassandra. "Well?" she asked.

Dani twisted her apprenticeship ring around her finger. "Um . . . My Lord, I'm to tell you that the Aristok is in Heathland, safe among loyal followers and she requires My Lord of Kempston to provide her with sanctuary from her enemies." She took a breath. There, it was said.

The faint widening of her eyes was the Duke's only outward reaction. Catching Dani in a crimson stare, she scrutinized her for a long moment. "Where is she?" she asked finally.

"Awaiting you to the west, My Lord." Here was the tricky bit. Dani straightened her shoulders. "I am to tell you that Her Majesty requires transportation to Caerockeith for herself and seven others, some of whom will be known to you. I am required to ask you to suspend judgment of their actions until Her Majesty can avail you of certain facts regarding her father's death."

Terrilynne's face remained expressionless.

"And these seven others are whom?"

"His Lordship Atreus DePaula, um . . . Simon of Florenz and his family, and Rosarion DeLynne, My Lord."

Rubbing at a scratch on her knuckles, Terrilynne regarded the young woman quizzically. "Simon of Florenz and Rosarion DeLynne have been named traitor," she said in a neutral voice.

The youth stirred in discomfort but met the Duke's eyes bravely enough. "Yes, My Lord," she answered, "but there are extenuating circumstances that we beg you to consider first. I am to tell you that we are at your command regardless, asking only that you protect the Aristok Kassandra and take her under heavy escort back to her capital and there right the wrongs done to her."

"Wrongs done by whom?"

"Uh, My Lord, I am told to tell you that all of that will be explained when the Aristok arrives."

"I see. And how am I to find the Aristok and this eclectic entourage of hers."

Despite the sarcastic edge to the question, Dani gave an inaudible sigh. It was almost over. "I'm to guide you there, My Lord. I'm told to request a cart of some kind, as the Aristok is young and will not be able to travel the distance on foot."

The Duke gave a crooked half smile. "Of course," she murmured. She looked at the youth for a long time, then stood. "There are those in my keep at the moment, Dani Ashwood, who may interfere with the telling of your tale. So, if the Aristok pleases, I will wait for full darkness before responding. Then you and I will go to Her Majesty and convey her here in secret."

Dani bowed. "Thank you, My Lord." She was suddenly very tired.

Terrilynne nodded. "In the meantime, I think it safest that you remain here. I'll have a fire built and food sent over."

"Thank you, My Lord."

"Hm." The Duke gave her one more penetrating look, then crossed the room and left, the door closing solidly behind her.

Dani listened for the sound of a key in the lock, but heard nothing. She took a step toward the door, then stopped. What was she going to do if it was unlocked? She stood a moment in uncertainty, then finally sank down on one of the window seats with a long, drawn-out sigh. She'd done her best. The Duke seemed like she would be reasonable, but they wouldn't know until the others got here.

Stripping off her cloak, she laid it on the bench across from her to dry and, breathing a quick prayer to Essus that they would all soon be safe, she settled down to wait.

"It's a trap!"

Eddison paced across the Duke's study, his face twisted into a frown.

Terrilynne had sent for her Council as soon as she'd returned from the gatehouse. When they'd arrived, she'd explained in as few words as possible and let the news sink in. Eddison had been the first to react.

"How do you know that?" Yvonnia asked. Seated next to Lauren on a low divan before the fire, she returned the Lieutenant's glare with a smooth smile.

He snorted. "Well, who is she? One of Innes' spies, I'd wager."

"Trying to do what?"

"Lead the Captain into an ambush," Amanda answered for him.

"For what purpose?"

"To leave us without a leader and at the mercy of the

Duke of Yorbourne." Eddison paced across the room again.

"Don't be so paranoid, Eddie."

"I'm not paranoid. I think it's too burning convenient that they say she's coming here and then some stranger arrives saying she's arrived, but the Captain has to go off in the dead of night alone to find her." He slammed one fist into the palm of the other to emphasize his opinion.

"I concur," Amanda added.

"It was my idea to go at night," Terrilynne reminded them both calmly from the window.

"Why couldn't they just bring her here?"

"Would *you* just march up to the front gate?" Yvonnia asked. "I think it's very wise that they sent a messenger to scout out the land first."

Eddison snorted. "What about this Atreus DePaula? What would a Flame Champion of Seth Cannon's be doing with Simon and Rosarion DeLynne?"

"When I find them, I'll ask them," Terrilynne answered.

"But, Captain . . ."

"If you're so concerned about my safety, Lieutenant, you can come along. I'll also take Edrud and Fionn— they're both of an impressive size—Eaglelynne can accompany us to make it official, and Jade can drive the cart since she and Simon were close in the past."

Eddison looked unhappy. "Where are we going to hide eight people so Innes Eathan doesn't find out about them?" he asked, trying a different tack.

"I'm not going to hide them."

"But, Captain . . ."

"No." Terrilynne chopped one hand down as everyone in the room began to talk at once. "The Aristok has every right to go where she pleases and expect to be welcomed. Innes Eathan is a Priest of the Flame, sworn to Its Vessel; she can in no way compel Kassandra to do anything, and she can in no way compel me."

"I hope Innes knows that," Gladys commented dryly.

"Enough. When we find her . . ."

"Assuming she's really here," Eddison broke in.

"Yes, assuming." Terrilynne glared at him, and he

stiffened to attention, realizing he'd gone too far. "Then I'll speak with her and discover what happened in Branbridge and what she wants from us at Caerockeith.

"In the meantime, the youth—Dani's her name—is safely tucked away in the gatehouse, and we have a banquet to dress for. When it's over, we'll leave. That's all, Eddie."

"Yes, Captain." The lieutenant looked glum, but gave a halfhearted salute as the Duke and her Companions left the study for Terrilynne's inner chamber. Amanda and Gladys gave identical shrugs before taking the other door. With a growl, Eddison followed them out, pointedly not slamming the door behind him.

This night's banquet proved to be a short one even with its host's hidden agenda. The rain had put everyone out of sorts, and the musicians and tumblers went mostly unnoticed. After an hour, Terrilynne rose, and the gathered gratefully retired.

The Duke spent some time going over supplies with Gerron Reed, then made her way to the stables with her Herald. Eddison and Edrud joined them a few minutes later, and once the crescent moon had risen above the castle walls, they saddled up and met Fionn and Dani on the outer common. Jade had brought Tee's supply wagon and Terrilynne indicated that the apprentice was to sit up with her and the guardsman.

"By the way," the Duke said casually, leaning down from her mount to peer at the youth in the weak moonlight. "If this is a trap of any sort, Fionn will kill you first."

Dani swallowed, unable to take her eyes from the Duke's illuminated gaze. "It's not a trap, My Lord."

"Good."

Terrilynne gave a signal and they moved off the common and onto the road.

At the Crooked Cock Inn outside Kirkwald, Simon and the others had been waiting most of the day. They'd paid to be undisturbed, but even so, they were nervous, jumping at every sound filtering up from the taproom below. Their room—the only one large enough to hold the seven of them—was at the back of the building, so they could not keep watch from upstairs. Once Dani had been gone a good three hours, they decided it was safe enough to take turns waiting on the bench beside the front door. Hamlin went first, so he could have a smoke, and then Fay for the same reason. Rosarion, having used most of his limited store of energy just getting there, sat by the fire, wrapped in blankets, his eyes dull. Simon, too, was worn out, and he spent most of the day asleep, the shadows much closer than Fay and Hamlin suspected.

The afternoon passed into evening. No one felt much like talking or playing with the worn pack of cards Bennie had given Luis. The adults were still wary in each other's company and, after exhausting her limited supply of patience, Kassandra sat sulkily smacking one of her juggling balls on the window seat, refusing to be drawn into any distracting games.

Finally there was the sound of footsteps coming up the stairs and they all sat up tensely.

There was a knock at the door.

Hamlin set his pipe down and opened it, and Luis, whose turn it was, put his head in to say Dani and the Duke of Kempston had arrived.

Exchanging an apprehensive look with Rosarion, Simon rose with his parents' help, and Kassandra turned from the window as Dani ushered Terrilynne DeMarian inside.

The Duke took in the room's occupants in a second. Four men and a woman, dressed in traveling clothes, the two youths who'd followed her upstairs, and one child; a child with short, brown hair, but the fiery black eyes and eerily adult expression of a DeMarian; the Aristok, Kassandra the Sixth of Branion. The Duke crossed the room, stopped nine paces before her, and after a searching look, dropped to one knee and bowed.

Kassandra tipped her head to one side as Dani carefully closed the door behind them.

"Cousin Terrilynne," the child said formally.

"Your Majesty." The Duke stood up. "Welcome to Heathland."

"Thank you. I am pleased to be here. This is Simon."

She gestured at the artist who came forward possessively. "He rescued me, an' this is his family. They're under my protection." An imperious wave of her tiny hand took in Hamlin, Fay, Dani, and Luis. She turned. "An' this is Rosarion, an' this is Atreus. They're under my protection, too." Her flame-washed eyes were challenging as she returned her attention to her Cousin.

The Duke passed her own fiery gaze over the two men, who averted their own eyes.

"You sent me the message," she said to the Flame Champion, who nodded.

The Duke glanced about.

"But you're not in charge."

"No, My Lord."

Simon met her flame-sparked eyes defiantly. "I am," he said, "by the Grace of Her Majesty, Kassandra the Sixth."

"I see. There have been many rumors regarding your whereabouts, Majesty," the Duke said dryly, returning her gaze to her young Cousin. "Rumors about kidnapping and the like."

Kassandra made a dismissive gesture. "I was on my way here, 'cause you're the only family I can trust," she said regally.

"I'm honored, Majesty."

"I know." The child's expression grew suddenly wrathful. "Uncle Sandi's a traitor," she announced. "Did you know that?"

Taken aback by the sudden question, Terrilynne could only nod. "I had my suspicions, Majesty, but no proof."

"I've got proof. Simon?"

"Majesty?"

"You tell Terri, I mean, the Duke of Kempston, what happened, an' then Rosarion, you tell her what you know, too. Never mind about being bad. You're under my protection, so you can tell her."

The Herbalist nodded, his eyes red-rimmed and his hands shaking in his lap. "Yes, Most Holy," he said hoarsely.

The child returned her fiery gaze to her Cousin's face. "You can sit down, Terri," she said graciously. "This is gonna take a long time."

* * *

When they were finished with their story, the Duke of Kempston sat, turning Drusus' coin over and over, a thoughtful expression on her face. "Most of the high-level Flame Priests died in the fire," she noted, almost to herself. "But Innes Eathan is at Caerockeith, and Seth Cannon is on the road somewhere. They should be enough to add weight to your story once they're strong enough to enter the Prophetic Realm."

Rosarion stirred. "Innes Eathan is at Caerockeith, My Lord?" he asked weakly.

"Yes. She and a large company of Triarctic Knights arrived three days ago, suggesting strongly that I *give the Aristok back*." The Duke's tone was sarcastic.

"Give her back, My Lord?" Fay asked.

"They assumed you would bring Her Majesty to me because of my dislike for Ellisander."

"They were right," Kassandra broke in imperiously. "It was Simon's idea, an' I approved it. Innes Eathan don't, I mean, doesn't, tell what to do. I'll go home when I say an' not when anybody else does." She scowled and Terrilynne gave her an approving half smile.

"Quite right, Majesty, but might I suggest that you at least wait until I can assemble a proper armed escort for you."

"How long is that gonna take?"

"I can have eight hundred troops here in a fortnight."

Simon looked startled. "So soon?" he asked, although Atreus was nodding his understanding.

Terrilynne shrugged. "Most are already on their way. As I said earlier, I don't like Ellisander, especially now." Her voice had grown dark. "In sixteen days we could be in Yorbourne."

"My birthday is in sixteen days," Kassandra said quietly. "Papa promised me a pony."

The adults grew silent. Terrilynne rose and came over to kneel beside the child.

"I'll get you a pony, little cousin," she said softly. "And on your birthday you'll set out in the center of an army that will carry you home and punish everyone who had a hand in killing your Papa. I promise."

The Aristok sniffled. Terrilynne held out her arms, and the child allowed herself to be taken up and hugged, burying her face in her cousin's neck.

Simon looked away, unable to watch his charge take comfort from someone else.

"I'm not cryin'," the child said in a muffled tone.

"I know," her cousin answered.

"I'm the Aristok. Aristoks don't cry."

Holding her tight, Terrilynne began to rock her gently back and forth. "Sure they do," she answered. "Your Papa cried for your Momma."

"Did he?" The child looked up at her.

"Uh-huh."

"Then it's all right for me to cry for Papa?"

"Yes."

Kassandra reburied her head.

After a time she grew still, and Terrilynne rose with her in her arms. "Do you want to go to Caerockeith now?" she whispered.

The child nodded and the Duke turned to the others in the room. "Thank you for bringing my Royal cousin safely away from her enemies," she said, her fire-sparked eyes burning brightly behind a sheen of moisture. "You may consider yourselves under the protection of the Duke of Kempston as well as in her debt."

The men shuffled awkwardly, but Fay smiled back at the DeMarian Duke. "It was no more than we would have done, My Lord," she said thickly, her own eyes wet. "She's a sweet child. The sweetest child."

Hamlin smiled and touched his wife's arm.

"And what are you looking at, you great oaf?" Dabbling her eyes with a handkerchief, Fay pushed him gently away. "Let's be going before it gets any later. Lead on, My Lord.

"Luis, you open that door."

The youth obeyed and the Duke of Kempston led the way downstairs, still carrying Kassandra. The others followed, Atreus supporting Rosarion, who began to cough as soon as he stood, and Hamlin supporting Simon whose expression was unreadable.

The few patrons in the taproom gaped as the party left the tavern, the identity of the little girl suddenly obvious. As one, half a dozen people left by the back door as the Aristok was carried out the front. Heathland would know about Kassandra's reappearance before Branion would.

Edrud was sent galloping back to ready the garrison. The others were crowded into the wagon, as Terrilynne set Kassandra in front of her in the saddle. Simon barely had a chance to say hello to a bemused Jade before they were off, setting a brisk pace for Caerockeith Castle.

Their arrival was tumultuous. Knowing how Innes Eathan and Jordana DeLynne were likely to respond, Terrilynne had told Edrud to go to Amanda and Eddison. The latter called out the garrison and the former bullied the Triarctic Company into their midst. The Aristok was arriving in Caerockeith and expected a proper welcome from all her subjects.

Sputtering with surprise, their guests found themselves mounted in the midst of the castle garrison.

They didn't have long to wait.

Briar was standing watch on the gatehouse tower and, as soon as the wagon came into view, she gave the signal and the horn notes for visiting Royalty echoed from the top of the castle, Eddison gave a shout and the Royal Standard was hoisted up the main flagpole. The red fire-wolf and golden oak leaf clusters of the DeMarian Sovereign glittered in the light of dozens of torches that had been hastily lit all over the castle parapets.

Alerted to the event by runners sent to Mosswell, people lined the road. Many also carried torches and it was almost as bright as midday as their Duke came into view, the Branion Aristok perched on the saddle before her. As one, the people began to cheer.

Kassandra smiled majestically and waved her hand at the crowd as they came up to the castle common.

Eddison marched forward.

"Garrison is dismissed!"

There was pandemonium on the common. Innes Eathan struggled to reach the gatehouse, but was hemmed in on all sides by excited troops.

Waiting by the wall, Kalidon DeKathrine grinned and

poked his squire in the ribs. She smiled excitedly back at him.

Terrilynne got Kassandra into the castle's private audience room without incident. Rhian expertly shoved the Aristok's comrades in behind them, barred the door, then turned, awaiting instructions.

"Now what?" Kassandra asked curiously as Terrilynne set her on her own chair and collapsed into another.

"Now we catch our breath, Majesty," the Duke answered. "And then, if I might suggest, we send for wine and cider, and you receive the oaths of your vassals at the castle before anyone has a chance to think."

"Think about what?"

"Anything, Majesty."

"Oh." The child considered her cousin's words a moment and then nodded. "Will it take a long time?"

"Are you getting sleepy?"

"No." She yawned.

"It won't take a long time. There are eight in the garrison at the moment who need to swear their oaths to Your Majesty, including myself, and ten in the Triarctic Company, plus three Flame Priests, Innes Eathan—who it would do well to remind just who's in charge around here anyway—Hywellynne DeLlewellynne, and our own priest, Jennet Porter. You could take the common oaths of the garrison tomorrow, if you want."

Kassandra swung her feet back and forth. "All right. But I gotta change into my proper Aristok's clothes first. I have a tunic of Papa's in Simon's bag."

"That would be perfect, Your Majesty."

"I thought so, too."

The change was made quickly, which was just as well, as Innes Eathan had finally reached the door, and was demanding to see the Aristok. Rhian was sent to tell her she would have to wait and to assemble the eight members of the garrison nobility left in the castle—most had been sent out with Terrilynne's request for troops.

When they arrived, Terrilynne DeMarian, Duke of Kempston, was the first to kneel before her young cousin and speak her oath, followed by Amanda DeKathrine, Earl of Guilcove, and Gladys DeLlewellynne, Earl of

Radnydd. When they were all finished, they fanned out behind the dais and Terrilynne signaled for the company to be brought in.

"Wait!"

The Duke turned at the Aristok's command.

"Yes, Majesty?"

"I want Simon an' the others beside me. Simon?"

Moving stiffly, the artist came forward from the far corner where he and the others had gathered.

"Yes, Your Majesty?"

"I want you to stand next to me, an' then Fay an' then Hamlin. An', Rosarion, you an' Atreus stand next to Cousin Terri, an' then Dani an' Luis. You all rescued me, an' I want you all here."

Simon gave the Duke a swift, questioning glance before bowing.

"Of course, Majesty."

With Terrilynne on one side, and Simon on the other, with those who had brought her to Caerockeith lined up dutifully beside them, and a member of the College of Heralds present as recorder, the thirty-fifth Aristok of Branion, Heathland, Kormandeaux, Aquilliard and Roland, Gracious Soverign of the Triarchy, Most High Patron of the Knights of the Sword, and Vessel of the Living Flame, was ready to receive her more recalcitrant subjects.

They were allowed into the room as a group, Innes Eathan in the lead. Her expression suspicious, she quickly sized up the armed group behind the child, pausing briefly to glare at Rosarion, her eyes narrowed. Advancing to within nine paces of the dais, she bowed.

Terrilynne whispered her name in Kassandra's ear.

"Your Grace, *My* Priest, Innes Eathan," the child said.

"Most Holy." The woman stared searchingly into the face of her Avatar, her own expression moving from suspicion to worry. "We feared you were dead or taken captive."

"No."

Her face working through a number of emotions, Innes shook her head. "But, Most Holy, your sudden disappearance so soon after . . ." She trailed off. "What became of you?"

Kassandra swung her legs back and forth under her chair. "I went to see Simon paint Papa's chapel," she explained in an offhand manner. "I climbed out the window an' down the rose trellis."

The priest was still shaking her head. "How could you leave the Royal wing without being seen by the Guard, Most Holy?"

"Oh, that was easy. There's a hall behind Papa's bedroom, an' it's got a door an' that leads round to a buncha' rooms an' past a really big room an' down some stairs an' through another hall an' round a . . . a round room an' that goes to the hall by Papa's chapel. I found it exploring one time."

The Flame Priest could only stare at this long explanation.

Behind her, it was Jordana DeLynne's turn to shake her head. "A door," she said weakly. "Marsellus the First's door into the north wing, but it was boarded up years ago."

"There's a hole in it," Kassandra answered, unconcerned. "Just big enough for me to get through. The wood around it's all soft." She tipped her head to one side. "I think the roof leaked on it."

"Anyway, I went to see Simon an' we painted an' then I got real sick, an' Simon's Momma made me better an' then Simon an' Hamlin an' me all ran away, so Uncle Sandi wouldn't get me, 'cause he killed Papa, an' then Uncle Sandi hurt Fay an' Simon, but Rosarion helped them get away an' come back to me."

Later Terrilynne would have to admit she enjoyed the looks that crossed the faces of the entire Triarctic Company, shock mixed with disbelief rapidly turning to stony-faced anger and back to shock. Innes Eathan could not speak for some moments, and when she did, her voice came out as a squeak.

"How do you know this, Most Holy?"

The child's face grew serious, and her black, flame-filled eyes flashed dangerously. "Because Papa came to me an' told me so," she said, her voice suddenly deep.

Her eyes widened and she sat up very straight as the room seemed suddenly filled with shadows.

"He plotted to take over the Regency and then the Throne, first by the murder of his Royal Cousin and then by the murder of his own niece."

Everyone in the room felt the hair on the back of their necks rise. Those who had known Marsellus the Third made the sign of the Triarchy across their breasts as his voice issued from the mouth of his daughter. Beside her, Simon swayed and would have fallen if Hamlin had not grabbed his arm.

Kassandra slumped as the shadows ebbed, then straightened, shaking herself with an annoyed frown. She looked at Innes Eathan. "I am not kidnapped," she said firmly in her own voice again. "Not by Simon an' not by Terrilynne, so don't you think this is just some plot to get Uncle Sandi an' I'm being made to say stuff I don't want to just 'cause I'm little. I know what's right an' what isn't an' I know that's what you were thinkin'."

The Priest started guiltily.

At the back, Kalidon DeKathrine smirked.

"Anyone who tries to make me do *anything* is gonna get blasted right outta this room," Kassandra added darkly. "I can do that, you know."

Innes could only nod, her expression alarmed.

"I want you to help cousin Terrilynne take me home," Kassandra continued in a more even tone. "She's my Regent now. But first, I'm hungry, so you gotta swear loyalty to me like everyone else did, an' then I want some bread an' milk."

Innes Eathan shook her head dazedly as a look of confused wonder slowly crossed her face. "You're really safe, Most Holy?" she asked in a small voice.

Kassandra nodded. "An' I'm gonna make everyone else safe, too," she declared.

Innes slowly went down on her knees.

She spoke her vows in a tone of weary relief, and then waved her acolyte forward to help her rise as Jordana DeLynne came forward next.

It took over an hour, for Terrilynne omitted no one, not even the youngest squire. When the entire Triarctic Company had finally sworn their separate oaths, either ecclesiastical or secular to their new ruler, the Aristok regally dismissed everyone and allowed herself to be taken up to bed in Terrilynne's inner chamber with the promise of bread and milk to follow. At her insistence, Simon was allowed to stay with her. Rosarion was supported to Jennet Porter's rooms, and Simon's family and the others were housed in guest quarters nearby. Innes Eathan and Jordana gave up their rooms without a word and soon everyone was placed in a bed somewhere in the keep.

As the midnight all clear was called from the gatehouse tower, the Duke of Kempston met quietly in Amanda's outer chamber with her three Commanders and her Companions.

Pouring each of them a glass of wine, Lauren took a seat beside Yvonnia, and picked up a small harp. With the familiar strains filling the room, everyone began to relax a little.

"Quite a momentous night," she observed.

Standing by the fire, pipe in hand, Eddison looked to the Duke. "What do we do now, Captain?" he asked.

Terrilynne stared out the window at the cloudy night sky. She could hear the rumblings of thunder in the distance.

"We continue building the army," she answered.

Eddison exchanged a look with Amanda and Gladys.

"But haven't things changed with the Aristok's arrival?"

"No." She turned. "Ellisander will never just stand aside as we march into the capital and proclaim him a regicide, even with Innes' and Jordana's support." She stared out the window again. "He'll have planned for this."

"What can he do?" Amanda asked caustically. "He's caught. We have the Aristok; we have the proof."

Terrilynne shook her head. "It's not that simple, Mandi. He'll have planned for this," she repeated, then turned away from the window. "We raise the army and march on Yorbourne. The only difference now is that we march in the name of Kassandra the Sixth and not in the name of Terrilynne of Kempston. If Yorbourne surrenders peacefully, we'll carry on to Branbridge. Either way, the army goes with us. I don't trust Ellisander, and I don't trust anyone who deals with him."

"What about the others, Innes and Jordana and Hywellynne?" Gladys asked.

"What about them?"

"They're going to be trouble," the Earl of Radnydd predicted darkly.

"How do you mean, My Lord," Yvonnia asked. "They've sworn their oaths."

"Sure, but they'll have their own ideas about what we should do."

Terrilynne made a dismissive gesture. "They can advise if they wish, but I'm Kassandra's Regent as of tonight, as you recall. It's my army and I make the decisions. In the meantime, I'm hungry, too. That will be all for tonight, people. Lauren, would you have the kitchens send me up a plate of something?"

As the others rose in a somewhat subdued manner, the Auxiliary Companion smiled. "Would that be bread and milk, My Lord?" she asked gently.

Terrilynne looked at her, caught her meaning, and began to smile ruefully. "Unsubtle point taken," she said. She looked to the others. "Thank you all for your support tonight, but it's still past midnight and we have a lot to do tomorrow. The politicking hasn't ended with the Aristok's arrival; it's only just changed timbre."

Eddison groaned, and Terrilynne chuckled. "Gladys is right; we need Jordana's and Innes' cooperation—and Hywellynne's," she added as the Gwyethian Lord smirked.

Gladys made a sour face.

"Tomorrow we have to convene the Aristok's first War Council," the Duke continued. "And if we're lucky, it will be without the Regal and Sacred, but very young, presence of the Aristok herself. If she insists on being present, the Flame alone knows how much we'll get accomplished, so we're all going to need some sleep."

Eddison came crisply to attention. "Yes, Captain." He led the way out. With a kiss, Lauren went to find some food, leaving the Duke and her first Companion alone together.

Terrilynne dropped into a chair by the fire and Yvonnia came around behind her with a smile. Massaging her Lord's shoulders, the Companion began to hum a quiet song.

Terrilynne let the familiar touch relax her. Finally she laid her hands over the other woman's.

"Life has suddenly become very complicated," she observed.

The Companion nodded. "Are you disappointed that you won't be wrestling the Throne from Ellisander," she asked quietly.

The Duke closed her eyes. "No," she answered truthfully. "Kassandra's the rightful leader, and I'm relieved she's alive and safe. I've never wanted to be Aristok; I just wasn't about to let Ellisander be either. Besides," she smiled, "I still get to wrestle with him, only now it's for the Regency. And I will wrestle with him, right down into the Shadow Realm if that's what it takes."

The Companion brushed her hands through the Duke's thick copper hair, then came around to sit beside her. Laying her head on the other woman's shoulder, she gently touched the scratch on her cheek.

"You shouldn't say such things," she admonished gently. "It's bad luck."

Terrilynne smiled. "Nonsense. DeMarians aren't subject to luck. We make it."

"Arrogance."

"True."

The two women sat staring into the fire. After a time Lauren returned with a plate of cold chicken and the three of them had a small bite to eat and then retired.

In the Duke's inner chamber, Simon lifted the milk cup from Kassandra's unresisting fingers and tucked the heavy, goose-down quilt under her chin. He sat for a moment, studying her profile in the flickering candlelight, looking unconsciously for some sign of her father, and finding it, before rising.

"Simon?"

He turned. "I thought you were asleep," he said in a whisper.

"I was, but I woke up. Where's Spotty?"

"Right beside you."

"Oh." The child tucked the toy horse more firmly under her arm and looked sleepily up at him. "We're safe now, right?"

"Yes."

"An' we're gonna stay until my birthday?"

"Yes."

"Are you gonna start drawing again?"

He looked away. "Yes," he answered, but his tone made her frown.

"You promised you would when we got to Cousin Terri's," she reminded him.

"I know."

"You could paint me coming to the castle in the hall by where I sat. There's a big blank wall there."

"I could."

"An' I could help."

"Yes."

"Promise?"

He stared at the ugly bandage on his hand, his expression hard. "I promise."

"Good." She yawned. "G'night, Simon."

"Good night, Sparky."

"Say g'night to Spotty, too."

"Good night, Spotty."

The child snuggled down in the bed and soon her breathing deepened. Simon stood watching until he was sure she was asleep, and then took the candle over to the cot the servants had made up for him before the fire.

Sitting, he looked down at his right hand, still wrapped in bandages. The hand ached horribly, despite the strong infusions Rosarion had been giving him for the pain. It throbbed up his arm and across his neck. Sometimes, when it was especially bad, his vision seemed to twist and he thought he saw Leary standing in the shadows, no longer held to the times when he was asleep. And then he would be gone, so quickly that Simon was sure he'd imagined it. It had been like that when he was talking to Kassandra, one minute the late Aristok was leaning over the bed, the next minute the room was empty.

Blowing out the candle, Simon lay down, too weary

to keep looking. After a few moments spent staring into the fire, he slept.

The shadows stirred. They swirled about him, seeking entry to his thoughts. As the thunder began to rumble in the distance, Simon's dreams spiraled slowly into nightmare and the shadows surged forward.

Lightning flashed across the sky as patrons of the Broken Sword scattered before the Aristok's madness.

"Get away from me, all of you!" Leary stumbled against the bar, his sword weaving drunkenly before him.

"The first person to come near me gets dragged out of here as a headless corpse! You want it to be you?" He darted toward Evelynne DeMarian who backed quickly away. "Or you!" He swung the weapon toward Simon. The artist held his place, and after a moment, Leary turned away.

"A drink! Get me a drink, or by the Flame, I'll burn this place to the ground!"

Servers scrambled to do his bidding as most of the patrons of the Broken Sword fled.

It was spring; Mean Boaldyn, 733 DR. The white lung had decimated Branbridge. Three thousand citizens had died, including the Consort Kathrine DeMarian, and the Aristok had gone mad.

"A toast!" Leary threw up his arm, wine slopping down his arm. "To the Shadow Catcher, a right Royal bastard!"

He finished the wine in one swallow and threw the cup at a server. "Get me another! No, wait, I'll just take the bottle! Why waste a cup when a bottle's just as good! Get me a bottle, blast you all! You!" He rounded on Simon. "What are you still doing here? I told you to get out!"

The artist looked at his friend sadly. "I know."

"Then get out!"

"I won't leave you."

"Then I'll kill you!"

Leary suddenly leaped at him, knocking the painter to the floor. Standing over him, he raised his sword. Simon lay at his feet, looking up at him, refusing to defend himself, and Leary's face crumpled. Stumbling away, he

snatched up the bottle and sank down against the bar
with a choking sob.

Simon made to rise, and then a hand came into his
vision.

Ellisander DeMarian stood above him, his own expression grieving, his hand held out to the artist.

Simon took it and allowed the Duke to help him rise.

Ellisander gestured. "How long has he been like this?"
he asked.

"Three days."

"Has he done himself any injury?"

"He tried to yesterday."

"You stopped him?"

"Yes."

"Thank you."

Simon shrugged.

The Duke glanced over at his Royal cousin.

"You should get some sleep."

Simon shook his head. "I won't leave him."

"He's going to get some sleep, too."

"He won't listen to you."

The Duke's eyes were suddenly dark fire. "Oh, he'll
listen to me," he grated. "But it will get ugly. You
should go."

Simon shook his head again. "I won't leave him," he
repeated.

The shadows weaved back and forth before the battlements of Simon's recovery.

"Don't leave me."

"Leary?"

"Simon. It's dark, I need you."

Drawn to his friend's need, Simon reached out, fighting
against his own health to reach the other spirit.

"I can't . . ."

"Try! Please, Simon, don't leave me!"

Leary's voice was frantic, and with a huge effort, Simon
threw himself back into the darkness. They touched, em-
braced, and merged around each other once again.

"I won't leave you."

*   *   *

At Caerockeith, Simon of Florenz slept, Leary's memory held safe once more, despite all Fay's and Rosarion's ministrations.

As the early morning hours of the twenty-sixth day of Mean Boaldyn began, all that moved at Caerockeith Castle were the sentries on guard, and the Royal Standard flying from the main flagpole.

14. Capt'n Kasey

Kassandra the Sixth perched on a high pile of baled hay in the Caerockeith stables. Jael Asher stood below her, a crowd of children around him.

"C'mon, Kasey, he said encouragingly. "I'll catch you."

The Aristok jumped.

It had taken very little time for Kassandra to establish herself as ruler of the local children as well as the adults. After taking the oaths of the castle garrison, in an interminably long ceremony, she'd changed back into her tumbler's outfit and demanded a tour of the keep from Terrilynne. Simon had also accompanied her at her insistence. When she'd spotted Jael staring out at her from behind a pillar, she'd commanded him to come out where she could see him.

Simon introduced his son to the Aristok, prompting him to give a short bow. Kassandra took a long look at the boy, her flame-washed eyes tracking up the length of him.

"You look like Simon," she said.

Jael nodded. "That's cause he's my Da. You look like your Da, too."

"How do you know?"

The boy shrugged with casual eloquence. "I have his picture on a sovereign that Da sent me for my birthday."

"You still have it?" Simon asked with a bemused smile.

" 'Course I do." The boy scowled. "Ma wouldn't let me spend it. She made me give it to the Captain for safekeeping for when I was older."

"I want to see it, Terri," the Aristok interrupted, turning to the Duke. "I want to see Papa's picture on Jael's coin."

Terrilynne bowed. "Certainly, Your Majesty," she said evenly. "Did you want to do that now or wait until after Council?"

"How long will Council be?"

The Duke made a show of considering it. "Several hours, Majesty, and you'll probably be tired afterward and want a nap, so it wouldn't be until after supper at least."

The child frowned. "I don't want a nap an' I don't want to go to no several hours of Council. You're my Regent. You go, an' later you can tell me what happened like Gawaina used to tell Papa when he went out to have fun instead. I want to go and have fun like he did." She tipped her head to one side. "Papa used to go with you, Simon, didn't he?"

The artist nodded, stilling the sudden stab of memory. "So I will go with Jael."

"Go where, Majesty?" Terrilynne asked uncertainly.

The child waved her hand in a dismissive gesture. "Wherever. Jael will show me fun things to do," she pronounced.

"Very well. I shall assign guards to your service."

"I don't want guards. Papa never had guards."

"He did, Majesty," Simon answered gently.

"Not when he went out to have fun. He told me so."

Shooting a mental jab at Leary, Simon carefully knelt down until he was the same height as the indignant child.

"Things are different now, Sparky," he said. "It's not safe for the Aristok to go out alone any more."

"What if we stay in the keep?"

The artist looked up at Terrilynne who considered it.

"If you stayed in the keep, I think it would be safe enough for now." She turned to the boy. "You're responsible for Her Majesty's safety, Jael. I want you to take care of her. Stay in the castle and don't do anything dangerous. And if anything happens, you sing out for an adult right away. Understand."

"Sure, Captain."

"Well, go on, then."

The two children hesitated a moment, then took off at a dead run. Terrilynne watched them go with a smile.

"This is *the Company*. Mine, not Capt'n Terri's."

Perched on a hay bale in the keep's stables—one of the garrison children's special places—Jael's wave took in the crowd of ten grubby children. Beside him Kassandra regarded her new subjects with fire-sparked interest.

"This here's Carrie and Bella Croft," the boy said, beginning the introductions. "They're Lieutenant Eddie's. The kitchen staff really likes them 'cause their mother's dead, so they can get treats for us just about any time."

Two chubby little girls bowed awkwardly and Kassandra gave them a regal wave of her tiny hand.

"These are Havens," Jael continued. "They're Icarus the Stablemaster's. Ross, he's old; he's nine, but he has a limp so he can't keep up to the older ones so he stays with us. He can make whistles."

A sandy-haired boy holding a crutch in one hand smiled shyly at the Aristok.

Kassandra scrutinized him. "I want a whistle," she commanded.

He nodded. "I could make you one today, uh, Majesty," he said.

"Good." She returned her attention to Jael.

This here's Maggie an' this is Aggie," he continued. "They're half sisters. Maggie's good at tellin' stories an' Aggie's good for a lookout when we don't want grown-ups around 'cause she's little so they don't spot her, an' she's good for gettin' us out of trouble 'cause it's hard to yell at her. They have three older brothers an' sisters who're all squires at the castle. Their real names are Maggria and Aggria, but we call 'em Maggie an' Aggie."

Kassandra accepted the greetings of the two sisters. "My real name is the Aristok Kassandra the Sixth, Your Majesty, but you can call me Kasey when it's just us," she said graciously.

"Is it a special secret name for only us to use?" Maggie asked, her eyes wide.

"Yes. Well, you an' the Spinning Coins Traveling Troupe, but they're not here yet, but they will be here soon an' when they come, they're gonna put on juggling an' tumbling an' fire-eating just for us."

The children murmured their appreciation of this show of regal patronage and Kassandra indicated that Jael should continue his introductions.

"This is Alex Potter," he said, indicating a dark-haired boy in a tunic and leggings two sizes too big for him. "He's seven an' does stuff mostly in the keep, so if we need to hide someplace, he can get us in just about any room. This is his sister, Kate." He waved toward a girl dressed much the same, chewing on the end of a dark blonde braid. "She's five an' can read an' write the best. Her Grace Jennet Porter has kinda taken her on an' wants her to be a priest maybe, but Kate wants to be a groom."

"I'm gonna get a pony soon," Kassandra said to the girl. "An when I do, you can look after it for me whether you're a priest or not."

"Thank you, Majesty, I mean Kasey," Kate said happily, and Kassandra smiled back.

"An these are all Cheapes." Jael pointed at three children with very similar features. "There's Willie, he's the oldest, that's Davin an' that's Marri. Davin an' Marri are good at finding eggs an' stuff. If you see one, you see the other 'cause they always do things together, an' Willie can reach high things, 'cause he's the tallest.

"An' this is Soot, my dog." A scruffy, black puppy put its front paws up on Kassandra's knee. She patted its head and it licked her hand.

"And what about you?" She fixed Jael with a fiery stare. "What do you do?"

"I'm the Capt'n. I give the orders."

"Oh?" Her voice became dangerously sweet.

Jael scuffed his foot into the stable floor. "Well, I guess you do now, but Capt'n Terri says that a leader is more than just rank, a leader has to inspire people."

"I can inspire people." The Aristok's voice was indignant. "I inspired all sorts of people to take care of me an' bring me to cousin Terri's. 'Sides, it's different with the Aristok, everyone has to take my orders whether they're inspired or not."

Jael scratched at a scab on his nose. "I guess that's true."

The others looked from one to the other, fascinated by this shift in power.

"So I'm the Capt'n, then," Kassandra said, "but I'm gonna need a General 'cause I can't do all the ordering myself, so you can be my General."

Jael's face cleared, although Willie looked puzzled. "But isn't a General higher than a Capt'n?" he asked.

"Oh." Kassandra considered it. "So what's just under a Capt'n?"

"A Lieutenant," Carrie answered promptly. "Like Papa. He's a Lieutenant under Capt'n Terri."

"Sure, but he's not just under her," Willie answered.

"He is, too!" Carrie took a swing at him and Willie moved easily out of her way.

"No, he isn't, Carrie," he said patiently. "The Earl of Guilcove's just under Capt'n Terri."

"That doesn't count, she's a noble!"

"That's right, Willie," Jael agreed. "You don't count nobles."

"Why?" Kassandra looked from one to the other.

" 'Cause they're, well, nobles. They're not like regular people."

"Cousin Terri's a noble."

"No, she's not, she's DeMarian. That's different."

"Why?"

" 'Cause she's got the Livin' Flame in her," Kate answered promptly.

"So do I."

"Uh-huh. You've got it more than anyone else in the whole world. Jennet said so."

"That's 'cause I'm the Aristok. So what I say goes, an' I say that I'm the Capt'n an' Jael's my Lieutenant, like Eddie is cousin Terri's, so I give him orders an' he gives everyone else orders. 'An that's the way it's gonna be."

"Right," Jael agreed.

After a moment's thought, the rest of the children nodded. Jael'd had to give Willie a bloody nose to take over the original Captaincy; it was one of the Company's favorite stories, but they were willing to accept this new pecking order without a fight because, after all, Kassandra *was* the Aristok.

"So what're your first orders?" the new Lieutenant asked.

"I want to have fun like my Papa did."

"What did your Papa do?"

"Um." Kassandra put a finger into her mouth and tried to remember. "He went into town and got drunk with Simon," she answered.

"Yeah?" Jael looked interested in pursuing the topic of his father getting drunk, but Maggie shook her head.

"We aren't allowed on the road without a grown-up," she explained. "But if we found one to take us to Moss-well, we could play there."

"No grown-ups," Kassandra declared emphatically. "I already tol' Terri that. 'An 'sides, they aren't part of the Company, so they can't play with us."

The children all murmured their agreement of this truism.

"You wanna play 'follow me'?" Jael asked.

"What's that?"

"That's where I go places an' everyone follows."

"No. 'Cause I don't follow anyone, not ever. Papa said."

"Oh. We could follow you."

"I don't know the castle well enough yet, an' I might fall in a midden like this acolyte did once back home."

"Ew," they all chorused.

"Yeah. He smelled awful for five whole days."

This led to an animated discussion of nasty smells they'd all encountered, but finally Kassandra silenced them.

"I want to go play now," she said.

Jael went over their various pursuits in his mind, discarding the more obviously dangerous games. "You wanna jump off hay bales?" he asked finally.

Kassandra considered it. "Yes."

"Great. There's a really big one back here."

He led the way.

In the inner common, Simon and Jade walked slowly around the walls. The artist's face was haggard, and he still held his hand tight to his chest. He'd risen early this morning against Fay's wishes, curtly telling her that he was fine. He'd stubbornly stood by Kassandra's side during the oath taking, despite the heat and the long hours, and then had willingly accompanied her on her tour of the castle although his head and hand were aching fiercely. Afterward, he'd managed to avoid the worried frowns of his parents and escaped to the castle common to get some air, where he'd met Jade.

They walked for a time in silence, and then the guardswoman cleared her throat.

"So," she said.

"So."

"It's good to see you, Sy."

"You, too."

"I wasn't expecting you so soon."

"I know."

"And with the Aristok."

"Yes."

They paused, unsure of what to say next.

"I'm sorry about Leary," Jade ventured finally.

The shadows stirred in the far corners of his mind and Simon looked away. "You know it's been over a fortnight since he . . . died," he said quietly. "In some ways it seems like it's been forever since I've seen him, and in other ways it's like I can't believe it's only been . . . seventeen days."

Jade said nothing. Finally she glanced up at him, saw the sheen of exertion on his face, and indicated a stone bench. "Do you want to sit? she asked.

He shook his head. "I'm fine."

They made another slow pass around the common.

"Did you get Jael's letter?" Jade asked, changing the subject.

"Yes. He's doing well."

"He's a smart boy; takes after his mother."

Simon smiled weakly. "I haven't had much time to spend with him yet. Maybe later."

They reached the bench again and this time Jade simply sat down, forcing Simon to join her.

He leaned against the cool stone of the castle wall with an inaudible sigh.

After a time, Jade looked over at him.

"Fay told me about what happened in Branbridge, Sy."

He stiffened. "Oh?"

She chewed at her lip uncertainly. "How bad is the hand?"

Simon said nothing as the sun went behind a cloud.

"Sy?"

"It's fine. It's healing."

"Really?"

"Really."

"When can you take the bandage off?"

"Turi and . . . Turi took it off every day to clean it. Now . . . I guess I can ask Nan to do it."

"Did Turi say if he thinks it will heal fully?"

"I didn't ask him."

Jade made to ask another question, then closed her mouth, uncertain in the face of Simon's unwillingness to talk. They sat in awkward silence for a long time until the sound of the stable door banging open caught their attention.

Alex Potter skidded into the common. He slipped and fell, righted himself, and came pounding over to them, his brown eyes wide.

"Jade!"

"What is it, boy?"

"It's uh . . . it's uh . . ."

"It's uh what?"

"It's uh . . . the Aristok. She uh . . . she fell."

Simon grabbed his arm. "Where?"

"In the stables."

The two adults ran, Alex panting behind them. When they reached the stables, they found the children crowded around Kassandra and Jael. The Aristok was sitting on the stable floor, being comforted by Maggie and Carrie. She had a large bump beginning to swell on her forehead, and she looked dazedly up as Simon and Jade ran forward.

"Sparky!" The artist knelt before the child who allowed him to look her over frantically. "Are you all right? What happened?"

"I jumped off those hay bales there," she said a little breathlessly. "An' I landed kinda on Jael."

Jade rounded on her son. "Jael Falconer Asher, what have you done?"

The boy shook his head, blood running from his lip. "Nothing, Ma, honest. We were just jumpin'."

"Jumping! You let the Aristok jump from that height?"

"Well, all the others can."

"She's only four years old! You don't expect Aggie to make a jump like that, do you?"

"No." He dropped his gaze.

"I'm almost five," Kassandra interrupted indignantly. "An' I coulda done it. Jael was gonna catch me, but I kinda missed and kinda whacked him when I fell."

"You kinda of whacked yourself, too, Sparky," Simon said gently, gingerly examining the bump on her head with his good hand.

"Oh, yeah. It hurts."

"I'm sure it does."

Jade turned to Alex. "Go and get Nan right away." As the boy ran off, she returned her attention to her son. "I'm very disappointed in you, Jael. You were supposed to look after the Aristok, and the first time we leave you alone with her, you almost get her killed."

The boy hung his head.

"I think I'd better tell the Captain that you're too young to keep an eye on her and that she'd better have an adult with her."

"Ma!"

"No!" Kassandra made to rise and then half fell into Simon's lap. "You can't do that!" she said imperiously. "It wasn't Jael's fault. I said I could do it!"

"He should have known better than to let you try in the first place, Majesty," Jade answered, still glaring at her son.

"He couldn't have stopped me. I'm the Aristok."

"Yes, I know, but I'll bet it wasn't your idea to jump off the hay bales, was it?"

Kassandra paused. "Well, no," she admitted.

"It was Jael's idea, right?"

"Well, yeah."

"And he should have known better."

"Maybe. But he's just a child."

Simon couldn't help but smile as his son vehemently denied this claim. Finally Kassandra drew herself up and told him to be quiet. Jael subsided, muttering.

"You can't take him away, he's my Lieutenant," she said.

Jade suppressed a smile. "He's my son, Majesty," she answered. "And Mother outranks every other title."

"Not the Aristok."

"Even the Aristok."

Kassandra stared up at her. "Really?"

"Really."

"Papa never told me that."

"That's because he was a Papa, not a Momma."

Kassandra turned an incredulous gaze on Simon. "Is that true?"

The artist tried his best to look serious. "It's true, Sparky."

"So Fay outranks you and Hamlin?"

"By a mile."

"Oh." She tipped her head to one side and winced. "I kinda figured that, you know," she said after a minute.

At this point, Nan Guilcove, the garrison physician arrived, carrying a satchel. After examining Kassandra, she put a cold compress on her forehead and pronounced her all right. Then she turned to Jael. Her verdict was more dire.

"He's going to need a stitch in that lip," she declared. "Let's get him to the infirmary."

Jade nodded grimly as the boy turned pale. Kassandra put her hand on his arm.

"Don't worry, Jael," she said. "I'll come with you."

The stitch took less than a minute. Jael held Kassandra's hand very tightly and she murmured encouragement to him as Nan worked. When it was over, the young Aristok turned to Jade.

"You mustn't pull Momma rank," she said. "He won't do it again, an' I need him. I never had a friend my own age before." Her eyes began to well up, and Jade tried, without success, to keep a stern expression on her face.

"I won't take him away from you, Majesty," she said gently. "But one more incident like this and I'll have to request an adult bodyguard for you. Your safety's just too important. Do you understand me, Jael?" She turned to her son.

"Yes, ma'am."

"Good." Jade opened the infirmary door, surprising the Company who were pressed up against the keyhole.

After an awkward moment, they pushed Aggie forward instinctively.

"Is the Aristok killed?" she asked, her eyes wide.

Jade sighed. They were all just too good at this. "No, Aggie, she is not killed."

"Is Jael?"

"Not yet, but next time he just might be."

She gestured and the others crowded into the infirmary. "The Aristok has a bump on the head," she explained. "So I want you all to take care of her and play quietly and I want you where you can be seen. You can sit in the common and Maggie can tell you a story."

"Yes, ma'am," they all chorused.

"Go."

The two wounded leaders of the Company were surrounded, and they headed outside.

"Did you get a spoonful of honey, Jael?" Aggie asked.

" 'Course not. That's for babies."

"Oh. Can I have your spoonful, then?"

"No."

"Oh."

As they settled themselves into a far corner, Simon smiled.

"You have a way with children," he noted.

"I manage. You wanna make another one?"

He started. "I . . . not . . . are you serious?"

"I suppose not. At least not right now with war looming and everything. But I'd like to have another one before too long. Come back in a year; without the Aristok this time."

He smiled awkwardly. "Don't Alida and Fay have enough grandchildren to fight over already?"

She snorted. "They'll live. So will you."

"Don't be so sure."

"Stop it." She turned on him, hands on hips. "I don't want to hear any predictions of doom and gloom, you understand me?"

He looked away.

"Sy?" she growled.

"Yes, ma'am."

With a snort, she tucked his arm in hers again. "Don't forget it. Now, let's go have a drink."

"What about the Company?"

"They'll mind their manners for a while. Alec can see them from his post."

Together, they made their way into the keep.

Watching them go, the Company breathed a sigh of relief. Grown-ups cramped their style. Once Willie motioned that Jade and Simon were out of earshot, Maggie launched into the story of how Jael had won the Captaincy.

Seated next to her new Lieutenant, Kassandra the Sixth, listened avidly as the sun broke fully from the clouds. The shadows flitted about her face for a moment or two, then followed Simon into the keep.

In Bryholm an assassin sat out on the terrace of the Bog Pig Tavern, nursing a cup of wine and thinking about the past. The wind had risen in the night, promising rain, and it was almost too chilly to sit outside for long, but Anne liked the cold. It helped her to think. Watching a gull wheel over the Vardsa River, she was reminded of the last time she'd seen one.

It had been just over a fortnight since she'd boarded the *Ptarmigan* to liberate the Captain's payment; a payment for services to be rendered against a certain Traveler who was not to reach the Continent alive. She had reached it alive. The Captain had not been so lucky.

Afterward, Anne had returned to Beryl and her family and, true to his word, the young guardsman—whatever his name had been—had arranged for safe passage for the *Kilnmach* out of Branbridge Harbor. A week later the assassin was back in Bryholm.

The money she'd taken from the *Ptarmigan* was a quarter of what she'd been promised, but Anne wasn't complaining. It was better than a quick trip to the bottom of the Bjerre Sea, and it was enough to assure her a comfortable living for a while once she'd exchanged the heavy Gwynnethian gold into less obvious tender.

To manage this she'd gone first to Poindiers in Gallia where she knew a discreet broker who could change most of her coin to precious and semiprecious stones. Then she'd journeyed to Bachiem. For a reasonable fee, the Cousins there had given her the name of their own broker who'd exchanged the thirty-seven coins of Kathrine the Fifth for silver, at a most unreasonable fee, but then she'd expected that.

Now, with her money safely placed in her own Bryholm bank, Anne could breathe a little easier. As for the delinquent portion of her payment, she was willing to wait. She'd found that Fate often took a hand in evening the score if a person was patient. Anne was very patient. And it looked as if Fate might be moving fairly soon. All word from Branion spoke of a country in chaos; every major faction arming for civil war and the Essusiate nations preparing to take advantage of it. Delegates from the Hierarchpriest of Cannonshire and the DeMarian Duke of Kempston had both been in the capital seeking financial and military support. The former had gone to the Palace, the latter to the main chapterhouse of Danelind's powerful Mercenary's Alliance.

Anne had a nodding acquaintance with most of the Bryholm Alliance Chapter; she'd crossed the Bjerre Sea in their midst on several occasions. The talk among the rank and file was that there was lucrative, possibly long-term, work to be found in the employ of the Duke of Kempston and members were flocking to Bryholm from across the country.

Anne's Visit to Branbridge had stirred her interest in the Triarctic Capital's response and today she'd wandered down to hear the latest news at the Bog Pig. Built against the chapterhouse itself, the tavern was a well-known mercenary haunt, and the best place to gain information on political instability.

This morning the place was in an uproar, the main taproom and private chambers crowded with members and nonmembers alike. The bar already bore the evidence of several brawls even at this early hour, and bouncers lined the walls. One of Anne's acquaintances, Lieutenant Tarn Jorgen, secured her a quiet corner table out on the terrace by tipping a drunken associate onto the floor, then explained the reason for all the excitement. The Duke of Kempston's agent, Gabriel DePaula, was meeting the Alliance Executive this morning to finalize negotiations for three hundred soldiers. Word had it that the Alliance was opening space for seventy-five new members; all they needed was a patron and the initiation fee. In the Bog Pig, members were being wined and dined by dozens of people anxious for their patronage. Many were roaring drunk already.

Tarn smiled down at her, his dark eyes twinkling with more than just drink.

"Need a patron, Annie?"

The Traveler laughed. "For what, Tarn? To get myself skewered on the end of a Branion pike? No, thank you."

He sat down opposite her with a chuckle. "You could at least buy me a drink for getting you the table."

"You've had plenty to drink from the smell of you. Besides, you're going to owe Malki one when he wakes up. I think his head's stuck in a pool of half-dried vomit."

The two glanced down at the prone man under the table, and Tarn shrugged. "He won't remember a thing about it tomorrow." He prodded Malki with a booted toe. There was no response. "So what brings you to the Bog Pig? A job?"

Anne shook her head. "Just catching up on the news from Branion."

"Word is it's been turned on its arse."

"So I hear."

Tarn leaned forward. "Why don't you come with us and find out firsthand, Annie. There's good money to be made across the sea, and I'd be a cheap patron, really."

"There's plenty of money be made right here without risking life and limb, Tarn. Anyway there's two young men headed this way trying to look tough. Why don't you go and patronize them?"

Tarn turned, caught sight of the two youths and grinned widely, the sunlight gleaming off a gold tooth. "New armor, undented shields, good teeth—noble's sons. Perfect. See you 'round, Annie." He rose and, weaving expertly through the crowd, took each of the young men by an arm, and steered them toward the bar.

Anne watched in amusement until her view was blocked by a shadow falling across her table.

"Hullo, Anne."

She glanced up, saw a stocky young man she knew from the Bryholm Cousins, and gestured toward the opposite chair. "Hullo, Bill, what're you doing here?"

The youth dropped down with a thump and caught the eye of a server. "I'm going to Branion," he announced.

"What, with this lot? I heard you'd just made Cousin."

"I did." He tossed the server a silver helm. "Ale. Keep it coming."

The man withdrew and Bill returned his attention to Anne. "There are opportunities in Branion," he explained.

"Opportunities for mercenaries, not for Assassins."

"Either way. It'll be exciting."

"It'll be deadly. What, were you asleep in 'Sneak up From Behind Them' class? We're not supposed to give people a chance to hit back."

He gave an unconcerned shrug. "Where's your fighting spirit, Anne?"

Downing the last of her wine, the Traveler set the empty cup on the table. "Never had any. Where's your sense of self-preservation?"

"*I* never had any, at least, that's what Suzy says."

"What does she think about your going?"

"She's coming, too."

Anne stared at him. "Your sister's going to be a mercenary? I thought she was studying to be a physician."

Bill nodded. "She is. She got permission to go from Master Villnian. Convinced him that battlefield surgery would be good experience."

"I figured she had more sense."

"Apparently not." He grinned and accepted his drink from the server, downing it in one swallow. "I guess you're not going, then?"

"You guessed right."

"So, whatcha doing here?"

"Selling tombstones. I should make a killing."

"Oh, ha, ha."

Anne motioned at the server with her cup. "Have you found a patron?"

The Cousin shook his head. "Not yet, but I do have a name. Captain Duncan Storjen. Master Villnian says he might take us on."

"You aim high," Anne noted dryly.

"You know him?"

The Traveler nodded.

"Introduce me?"

Anne shook her head. "I'm against killing the young, Bill."

"No, you're not."

"No? Well, it's your funeral." She glanced around and then gestured at a mercenary squire leaning against the bar. He ambled over, his walk vaguely unsteady.

"Where's Captain Storjen, Axel?"

"What's in it for me if I tell you?"

"I won't kick your backside for mouthing off at me."

The squire made a show of thinking about it. "Fair enough," he said with a sloppy smile. "He's in the back playing skeans with Captain Uthaugh."

"Tell him I want to talk to him."

"Well, I was kinda hoping to avoid him for a couple of hours." He swiped futilely at the beer stains on his tunic front.

"In a couple of hours you'll be passed out on the floor and Bjorn will have rifled through your pockets. Go now while you can still walk." She tossed him a silver helm.

The squire caught it and headed off, weaving unsteadily toward the back of the taproom.

Bill toasted her with his empty cup. "Thanks, Anne."

The Traveler just shrugged.

An hour later, walking along the riverbank, the wind tugging at her hair, she turned over what she'd heard from Tarn, Storjen, and the others. The Duke of Kempston was raising an army to fight her cousin Yorbourne for the Branion Throne. The odds were one to one at this point as everyone knew the true Aristok was still alive in hiding somewhere and could tip the balance depending on who found her first.

Many of the Triarctic-raised mercenaries believed that the Living Flame was displeased with Its hierarchy and would produce her only when the traitors had been purged from Branion. Whoever they turned out to be was immaterial—at least from their point of view; they would be paid regardless. Rumors of fantastical sightings to substantiate this had circulated freely, especially after the torching of the Branbridge Flame Temple. Although the official story was that a fallen candle in a central altar room had set the tapestries alight, no one really believed it. A few thought it was an Essusiate plot, but most gave it a metaphysical origin. It was more romantic.

Anne considered it all as she made her way past a couple of mercenaries throwing up in the river. The idea that the Living Flame was taking a hand in recent events wasn't as absurd as it sounded. Anne herself had heard the voice of Essus, and if one God was involved, then they probably all were. Gods were like jealous children that way, she reflected heretically. They couldn't stand to see someone else get all the attention.

As for the Aristok's whereabouts, obviously the Essusiate artist had taken her advice to heart and managed to bury himself and the child very well. She wished him continued success.

Pausing at a stone bridge, she leaned against the railing and stared into the murky water below.

Events were certainly moving very quickly in Branion these days, she surmised. Bill was right there, it would be exciting. But it would be insanely dangerous to go back now.

Of course, she reflected, as she watched a school of small fish disappear under the bridge, if what she'd heard were true, there'd be few enough Flame Priests left to identify her.

She shook herself. It was out of the question. She'd just have to learn what was happening secondhand.

Drawing a throwing knife from its sheath, Anne began to strop it absently across the railing as she glanced along the bank. People were still hurrying into the Bog Pig, hoping to do some last minute negotiating that would see them take ship for Branion. "Fools," she snorted. Half of them were destined to die.

Still, it would be interesting to see what happened with the new Aristok, she thought idly. The child had won the protection of the Gods. She'd be a formidable ruler if she survived their attention.

Turning, she leaned her back against the railing. She wondered where the artist had taken the child. If it had been her in charge of the girl's safety, she'd have gone to the Duke of Kempston. As an enemy of Yorbourne's, the Duke would have reason to give them sanctuary and the means to raise a big enough army to enforce her will on the Branbridge nobles. Traveling by land they just might make it to Dunley Vale in a fortnight if nothing occurred on route to hinder them.

On the other hand, she mused, the whole country was on alert. The artist might have holed up somewhere closer, believing that he'd never make it there undetected. If he'd done that, they could be anywhere.

Tucking away the knife, Anne straightened and began to wander slowly back along the river bank.

No, she decided, he'd want her someplace safe, and the only safe place in Branion right now was in the center of a potentially loyal army; Terrilynne DeMarian's army. He would be making for Caerockeith. She'd bet her new fortune on it.

Passing the same pair of mercenaries, now lying prone and snoring at the base of a tree, Anne resisted the urge to rifle their pockets. If she went with them to Branion, a fortune would be the least of her risks.

Still, it could be done. The crossing would be rough, but not impossible this time of year. They should make the coast in three or four days, then a week to cross Heathland. No one would recognize her in the midst of a mercenary troop. A fortnight to prepare for war, a summer campaign, and she'd be back in Bryholm by Mean Damhar at the latest, whether the war dragged on or not.

She mulled it over.

The partial payment she'd received for the Palace Visit was large enough to ensure financial comfort for a long time. She didn't have to take a job for at least a year and could afford to go into hiding in the Mercenary's Alliance for that length of time if she were crazy enough to do it.

Pausing on the bank across from the Bog Pig, Anne shook her head in disgust. A visit to the Kempston holding in Heathland was dangerous enough, especially if the Aristok and her painter protector were there, but joining the Mercenary's Alliance was downright stupid. If she were really considering returning to Branion, she could just make the crossing in their midst for a small fee, then disappear. Actually entering their ranks was absurd.

So why was she considering it?

She frowned. Joining the Alliance would bring her reasonably close to the main action without exposing her to the scrutiny of those who might recognize her. Heathland was a small place, and strangers stood out. It would also help obscure the sight of any Flame Priests healthy enough to still be searching for her. But she'd be breaking the cardinal rule she reminded Bill of. Assassins did not give their Hosts a chance to hit back.

Of course, she could fight face-to-face if she wanted to, she admitted as she stared at the tavern sign swinging back and forth in the spring breeze. The lichen-covered hog and the sheaf of bulrushes caught the light each time the sign moved, making her suddenly restless.

It would mean joining a company, her thoughts continued. Taking orders. Anne didn't like taking orders.

On the other hand, she might be able to call in a few favors and buy herself into the officer corps. Essus alone knew she had enough money.

But then she'd be giving orders. Anne didn't like giving orders either.

Either way it would mean working with others, with strangers; relying on them for her safety and being responsible for theirs. It would never work. It was ridiculous.

She found herself at the tavern door. Ridiculous or not, it looked like Fate had decided to take a hand. She went inside.

Above her the sign stopped swinging as the wind died.

Two days later, she stood on the deck of a transport ship heading west.

It had been easier to join up than she'd expected. Captain Storjen had taken her to see the Executive right away and, with his word on her abilities and, after paying an exorbitant fee, she'd found herself an Adjutant in his Fifth Bryholm Company.

The uniform itched.

Tarn and Bill had each had a good laugh at her expense, but one jaundiced glare from the Traveler had stilled the young Cousin at least, and once they put to sea, there was plenty of work to distract them both. Tarn was a Fourth Company Lieutenant; Bill and Suzy had joined the Fifth, the Cousin as a private solder, his sister as a Physician with full rank and privileges. Healers of any kind were hard to come by in the Alliance, and she was already busy dealing with the dozen or so cases of seasickness.

Anne herself expected to spend most of the crossing with Storjen, learning the ins and outs of running the company. Not for the first time she wondered what she was doing there. One thing was certain, however; if she'd figured out what the Essusiate artist and the DeMarian Duke would be doing, then so would the Duke of Yorbourne, and he would act swiftly. Maybe Fate or Essus were taking a hand once more. There might be a need for her special talents in Branion again.

As the coastline of Danelind disappeared, Anne turned her face to the open sea and the yet unseen shores of Heathland.

In Branbridge, the Duke of Yorbourne handed a missive to a page, and then lay back. Though confined to his bed, he still maintained a steady stream of pages and messengers between his chambers, Gawaina De-Kathrine, and his various ducal holdings. Lysanda and Hadrian DeSandra had come to see him yesterday, filling him in on the events of the last week and receiving their own orders. They were simple. The two were to continue to make themselves useful to the Hierarchpriest. Ellisander himself would be attending the Privy Council in two days. In the meantime they were to be his eyes and ears.

As for the Flame Temple, the Duke might have been as surprised and impressed by Hadrian's sudden ruthless abilities as had his sister, had the Viscount not continuously professed his own innocent intent. As it was, Ellisander simply assured the younger man that he was safe from discovery, in Yorbourne's debt, and dismissed him.

Now the Duke turned his rumination to the potential this heretical act had created. Whoever had engineered it, the torching of the Flame Temple had been a crucial stroke of genius and the Duke marveled at the simplicity of the idea, knowing that even he would never have had the audacity to even think of it. With one blow, the Branion Seers had been blinded and the conspirators more securely hidden than ever Rosarion had been able to manage. He must take advantage of the corresponding chaos as quickly as possible.

The excitement of the possibilities made his head pound and he laid back with a grimace. The fire had left its mark on him as well as on the political scene. He had frequent headaches and his vision swam in bright light. When he'd returned to his senses, he'd ordered the curtains kept drawn and that had given him some relief, but he was still far from well. The irony of the situation was not lost on him. The cataclysmic event that made all things suddenly possible again had also incapacitated him on the brink of success. He seethed in frustration, but quickly quelled the feeling as his temples throbbed with increased vigor, causing his stomach to twist in nausea. In two days' time he must attend the Privy Council and win over the few powerful nobles remaining. To do so, he needed all his faculties intact and that meant resting and regaining his strength now. It would be worth it in the end.

He closed his eyes and forced himself to relax. Slowly the headache eased and his thoughts returned to his plans.

The first thing he'd done on regaining consciousness was to assure himself that his call for troops had gone out. He knew Terrilynne would move as soon as the roads dried, and he had to be ready for her. Yorbourne itself was well prepared to repel any invasion from the north, and the Duke planned to attack Kempston as soon as he was able to convince Gawaina to send the militant orders against Terrilynne's southern demesne. Meanwhile, his secretary reported that the messengers had been sent out and answers were due within the week.

As for the missing Aristok and her artistic abductors, Lysanda had informed him that there was still no word on the child's whereabouts. Due to the Flame Temple disaster, most of the searchers had been laid up indefinitely and none of his people had heard of them making themselves known to anyone.

Ellisander was not worried. He knew where they were headed. Eventually they would surface, and he would use it to his own advantage.

His head began to pound again; with reluctance, he pushed all designs of power and strategy aside for now and made his mind go blank. Time to rest.

Slowly, his rebellious mind obeyed and he slept.

Two days later, as Adrianus was helping him dress for Council, a messenger from Yorbourne with urgent news for the Duke was shown in. The woman was filthy and gray with fatigue, and she swayed dizzily as she bowed. Ellisander waved her to a chair. After Adrianus had draped a cloth over it, the woman sank down gratefully. The duke took a chair opposite as the Companion served them both wine, and steepled his fingers.

"I know you," he said, looking speculatively at her. "You're a Chandler. One of Kerry Chandler's. Arnet, isn't it?"

The messenger colored faintly behind the dirt on her face. "Yes, My Lord."

"How is your father?"

"He's well, My Lord. He's guarding the northern route with his company."

"That gives me comfort. The Chandlers have always carried out their duties to the Dukes of Yorbourne with courage and honor. You may collect yourself for a moment if you wish before discharging your message."

"Thank you, My Lord." After a quick gulp of wine, she took a deep breath. "My Lord, the Aristok Kassandra the Sixth is at Caerockeith."

The world was suddenly covered in a fine, red haze.

When it cleared, the woman was accepting another cup into shaking hands. She glanced fearfully at the Duke, but when Ellisander motioned for her to explain, she obeyed.

"Word is that the Duke of Kempston is planning on marching against Yorbourne within a fortnight in the name of the Aristok, My Lord."

Ellisander's eyes narrowed, but he stilled his rage carefully, only allowing an expression of grieved concern to cross his face.

"What is the word on my niece?" he asked, allowing the fatigue of his illness to creep into his voice. "Is she all right? Has she been . . . injured or coerced in any way?"

The messenger dropped her gaze. "Forgive me, My Lord, but I've not heard. I only know that she was brought to Caerockeith by the Essusiates who abducted her. It is said that she has named the Duke of Kempston as her Regent, but no one in Yorbourne believes it," she added stalwartly.

Ellisander rubbed at his eyes with one hand. "No, it's entirely possible," he answered wearily. "It's the first thing my Cousin would secure . . . by whatever means." He looked up. "The second would be to march against those nobles still loyal to her father's wishes. How prepared is Yorbourne to respond to an attack from the north?"

The woman swallowed. "That is the second part of my message, My Lord. We are prepared to repel a reasonable-sized force, but word is that Kempston is gathering a much greater army than we anticipated. I've heard that troops from Sorlandy and Wakeford have already arrived in Heathland."

"Wakeford. So Albion is involved as well?"

"Yes, sir. My Lord, Yorbourne fears that we may be overrun before help from Branbridge can arrive."

"Is Yorbourne afraid of the Duke of Kempston?" Ellisander asked her sharply.

She looked up, her eyes wide. "Oh, no, My Lord. Yorbourne knows the righteousness of Your Lordship's cause, and that gives us strength, but . . . we fear for the Aristok."

"As does Branbridge."

"Yes, sir." She twisted her cap into a shapeless mass. "My Lord, Steward Manderus Greydove has charged me to ask if any assistance may be hastily sent to us to help free the Aristok Kassandra from Kempston's influence as she is bound to move against us first."

"And even if she did not, you would be ordered to attack as she came south," the Duke added.

"Yes, My Lord."

"I shall send a troop of some size to escort you back to Yorbourne and I will give you a letter to present to Shannon DeYvonne, Earl of Berford, as you pass through her lands. She will give you what troops she has ready. Regardless, you may tell Manderus that as many troops as possible will be sent as soon as they may be summoned. I do not forget my people, or their plight, but as you know, I've been ill," he added dryly.

The woman bowed her head. "Thank you, My Lord." She hesitated. "Sir, I did not mean to imply that Yorbourne or Steward Manderus were hesitant in their duty. We will fight Kempston no matter how big an army she sends against us."

The Duke smiled wearily. "I have no doubt of your loyalty, Arnet, or of Manderus'. I'm tired and my words were perhaps a little sharp. Forgive me."

The woman swallowed, too overcome by her Lord's apology to speak.

"How long has it been since you rested?" the Duke continued.

"Since . . . since I set out, My Lord, three days ago."

"Adrianus will find you a place to wash and eat. In the meantime, I'm due in Council. When you've recovered some strength, say in half an hour, I want you to come to the Privy Council Chambers—Adrianus will escort you. I want you to tell the assembled everything you've just told me." He rose and the woman jumped to her feet.

"Thank you for delivering your message so promptly, Arnet," the Duke said. "When this is all over, I shall show my gratitude in more tangible ways. In the meantime, I charge you to keep up your spirit and that of your people. We have loyalty and honor on our side.

We will win, we will liberate the Aristok from her captors, and return her to her Throne where she belongs."

The messenger straightened. "Yes, My Lord. Yorbourne will not disappoint you, sir."

"I have every confidence in you." The Duke turned. "Adrianus, will you show our messenger to a chamber where she may refresh herself."

"Of course, My Lord. Shall I also send for a contingent of Shield Knights to escort Your Lordship to the Privy Council?"

"Yes."

The Companion bowed and, taking the messenger lightly by the arm, withdrew.

When the room was quiet, Ellisander sat back, his head spinning from the effort he'd just made. Yorbourne would fight. The next step was crucial and he needed all his strength to achieve it. He must now convince Gawaina DeKatherine that Kassandra was being coerced and that every proclamation issuing from Caerockeith was false, emanating not from the Aristok herself but from Terrilynne DeMarian. It would not be too difficult. That Simon of Florenz and Hamlin Ewer were in Heathland with her would be enough to rekindle Gawaina's hatred of Essusiatism and lay suspicion against anyone who associated with them. She could then be convinced to send the Sword Knights against southern Kempston and the Shield Knights to support Yorbourne.

Slowly, his head cleared of pain. He took several deep breaths and rose as there was a knock on the door. At his reply Shield Knight Lieutenant Isabelle DePaula entered with his escort. He allowed them to surround him, and with their familiar presence giving him confidence, he made his way through the palace to the Privy Council Chambers. Despite the delays, it looked as if everything was falling back into place. He would secure the loyalty of the Hierarchpriest, crush Terrilynne, be revenged upon Rosarion, and have the Aristok back under his control by the end of the summer.

At Caerockeith, the Aristok had grown bored with storytelling and had decided she wanted to see Mosswell whether that meant guards or not. Alex was sent to find adults to take them, and a few minutes later he returned with Fay, Alec Hanson and Sasha Lamb in tow. Kassandra made her wishes known, and soon they were heading down the road.

Kassandra looked up at Fay as they walked. "Jael says he lives in the village with his Granny an' his Gramma."

Fay nodded.

"How come he doesn't live in Branbridge with you an' Hamlin?"

"Because his Mother lives in Mosswell."

"But his Papa lives in Branbridge, right?"

"That's right."

"How come they don't live together?"

"Because Jade has to go where the Duke goes, because she's one of her guards, and Simon has to stay in the capital where he can find patrons for his murals."

"Patrons like my Papa an' me?"

"That's right."

"Does Simon miss Jael?"

Fay nodded. "Of course he does. He visits him when he can, and Jael comes to Branbridge to visit us, don't you, Jael?"

The boy threw a stick for Soot to chase. "Yeah, Gran, 'cause you don't come here to see me 'cause you an' Granny don't like each other."

Kassandra turned an interested gaze on Jael. "Why?"

"We don't dislike each other," Fay began, but Jael interrupted her.

" 'Cause Ma wanted a baby before she got too old, so she went lookin' for someone to help make one an' she picked Da 'cause he was handsome an' an artist, see, 'cept he's an Essusiate an' she's a Triarch, but Ma doesn't care about that and neither does Da, but Gran and Granny do, 'cause they're old-fashioned on account of them bein' old."

"Scamp!" Fay made a mock swipe at him, but he just danced away with a laugh.

"That's why, though, isn't it, Gran?"

"Perhaps," she answered primly. "I love Jade, and I love you. Alida and I don't always see eye-to-eye, but we do manage to be polite to one another. That's all that matters."

Kassandra had been silently absorbing this new information. Now she stuck a finger in her mouth as she
walked. "My Momma an' my Papa had me to make a
buncha DeMarians from a long way away come back
together," she said after a while. "Papa said. Do people
always have babies for reasons?"

"No, poppet," Fay answered. "Most of the time, the
babies are gifts from the Gods."

"Was your baby?"

Fay nodded with a smile. "Simon was a surprise gift."

"A surprise gift?"

"That's right. I'd been seeing Hamlin for a long time,
but I never thought I'd be having a baby with him."

"How come?"

"Well . . ." she paused. "When I was working for the
Earl of Guilcove, I was too busy to have a baby, so I
made sure I wouldn't."

"How?"

Fay paused. "Do you know how babies are made,"
she asked.

"Sorta. They grow in their Momma's bellies, right?"

"More or less. Well, there's a tea that women drink
so that they don't grow a baby until they're ready. I'd
been injured and I was laid up, so I couldn't take it."

"Why?"

"It didn't go with the other things I had to take."

"Oh."

"Anyway, Hamlin was trying to make me feel better,
and . . . Simon kind of snuck in then."

Jael smirked and Kassandra tipped her head to one
side, a thoughtful look on her face.

"Nan an' Jennet are trying to make Rosarion feel better," she said at last. "Will they have babies, too?"

The boy guffawed and Fay shot him a disapproving
look. "No, dear, it's different," she answered.

"Why?"

"It just is. It's a grown-up thing. You'll understand
when you're older."

"Oh."

They reached the outskirts of Mosswell. Most of the
Company ran ahead and when they reached Jael's home,

Jade's mother was standing by the door, wiping her hands on her apron.

Alida Asher was of an age with Fay, but there the similarities ended. Plump where Fay was stocky, and white-haired where Fay was gray, she had deep blue eyes that darkened slightly when she saw the other woman, but quickly grew warm when Jael ran to her.

"Granny, the Aristok wants to meet you."

Fay stood back while the boy made the introductions.

Alida bowed. "It's a pleasure, Your Majesty," she said and Kassandra nodded.

"You can call me Kasey 'cause you're Jael's Granny," she announced. "He says you make the best scones with jam of anyone."

Alida laughed. "It just so happens that I have some in the oven, Kasey," she answered. "Would you like to try some?"

"Oh, yes!" The child nodded vigorously as the Company crowded forward, looking hopeful.

Alida sighed. "Well, I suppose there's enough for everyone. Go on inside."

There was a stampede through the door and Alida shook her head when the guards looked at her hopefully.

"I can't feed the whole garrison," she said. "You two will have to wait for your own tea."

Alec gave her an aggrieved look. "But we're supposed to guard the Aristok, Alida."

"Oh, very well, I'll have some sent out to you."

She dismissed them with a gesture, then glanced at the other woman.

"Will you come in, Fay?" she asked stiffly.

Fay shook her head. "I should get back. You'll send the child with her guards when she wants to return?"

"Of course."

"Good, well, good day, Alida."

"Good day, Fay."

The two women parted company. Fay headed back up the road, and Alida turned to deal with the crowd of children in her kitchen.

"Now, settle down, or no scones!"

There was instant silence.

"That's better. Now, Jael, you and Maggie go fetch

some milk from Connie next door; I've nowhere near enough for all of you. Willie, please get the gooseberry jam from the top shelf of the pantry, and Ross, you and Alex set out cups and plates. The little ones can sit at the table, the rest of you will have to make do on the floor by the stove. Carrie, run to the workshop and tell Jem the scones are almost ready."

The older children scattered to do her bidding while Kassandra took her place at the head of the table surrounded by the others. Aggie looked up at Jael's grandmother.

"Kasey's the new Capt'n of the Company now," she said.

"Well, that's only right," Alida answered as she bent to remove a tray of scones from the stove.

"Jael don't mind."

"Jael's a good boy."

"Can I have two scones?"

"If there's enough."

Aggie settled back, her belief in the ways of the world assured. Kassandra watched fascinated.

A few minutes later the scones had cooled enough to be eaten, Jael and Maggie had returned with the milk bucket, and Carrie had come back into the kitchen with Jem in tow.

Jem Roth was a slight woman with wiry muscles and short gray hair. She kissed the top of Jael's head and bowed when the boy introduced her to Kassandra.

"Granny an' Gramma are weavers," he told her. "They make cloth from wool to make clothes."

"Do you make plaides?" Kassandra asked Jem, fixing her with a fiery stare.

Jem shook her head. "Only the Royal Weaver's Guild are allowed to make the plaides of the Branion nobility, Majesty, I mean, Kasey," she answered, "and the plaides of Heathland are made by Heathland weavers. Jael's grandmother and I make cloth for tradespeople and artisans. They don't wear plaides."

"But you could make a plaide for me if I wanted you to."

She shot her partner a worried look. "But you have special weavers to make the DeMarian plaide," she answered hesitantly. "Why would you want us to make you one?"

" 'Cause Papa's plaide is too big for me, an', 'side's, it's in Branbridge," she explained. "I need a plaide my size for when I ride in front of the army an' punish Uncle Sandi for killin' Papa. So I want you to make me one."

Jem wet her lips. "We, uh, can't, Majesty."

"Why?"

Alida came forward to kneel beside her. "We aren't members of the Guild, little one," she answered. "And only Master Weavers of the Guild are allowed to make a DeMarian Plaide. It's by Royal appointment only."

Kassandra drew herself up. "I am the Aristok," she said imperiously. "*I* make Royal 'pointments, an' I 'point you to make me a plaide an' cousin Terri will pay for it. There. Now you won't get into no trouble."

The two adults exchanged a glance, then Jem shrugged. "All right."

"Granny, I'm hungry. If I don't get a scone soon, I'm gonna die." Jael's whine cut through the silence and Alida stood. "Of course, sweetie. Here, you hand them out."

For a long time the only sounds in the cottage kitchen were those of eating. Finally the scones were gone and the plates and cups washed and put away. Kassandra expressed a desire to see the rest of the village. She thanked Alida very politely and allowed Jael to lead the way outside.

The two adults were left staring at each other. "Well," Alida said after a while. "Jade says they're leaving the twelfth day of Mean Ebril. That doesn't give us much time." She sat down. "It's a good thing she's so little."

"But how are we even going to get the right colored dye for the skeins?" Jem asked in an exasperated voice. "It's not like the DeMarian plaide is of common stock."

"I don't know, Jem, but we've just been given a Royal commission, so you'd better get on over to Val's and find out. Anyway it was originally an Elliot plaide. Maybe someone in Dunley Vale has the right dyes."

Jem left muttering darkly while Alida went into the workshop and began to remove the half-finished brown cloth from the smaller of the two looms.

Outside, the Company were involving Kassandra in a spirited game of tag while her guards looked on. They raced through the village, shrieking and laughing, and tumbled out to the west fields. There they hunted for early strawberries while Ross seated himself on a large stone and began to carve whistles from bits of reeds that the others brought him.

It was Marri who found the mud puddle.

The fields were mostly dry from yesterday's rain, but by a series of rocks there was one large puddle left. The child's shriek of glee brought the others running.

"That's a big one, Marri," Davin observed, kneeling down and poking his finger into the water.

"Yeah. It oughtta make the biggest mud pies ever."

"What's a mud pie?" Kassandra asked.

"Huh," Davin scratched at one ear. "A pie made of mud," he answered finally.

"Do you eat it?"

"No. You just, uh, make it, like."

"An' sometimes you throw it at somebody else," Jael added.

"Show me."

By the time the sun had become a great orange ball in the western sky, Kassandra and most of the others were mud up to the ears despite Alec and Sasha's attempts to keep order. The Aristok had just sent Carrie and Bella off to hunt for spotted pebbles to act as raisins for the top of the pies when they heard a woman's voice.

"Alex! Kate! Come for supper!"

The two children rose reluctantly. "I guess we'd better go," Alex said.

"Willie!" A young man dressed as a squire came into sight over the hill. "Ma says for you and the brats to come home and eat. I'm to take the rest of you lot back to the keep." He stopped in his tracks. "By the Flame, you're gonna catch it; you're all filthy!"

Jael wiped ineffectually at the mud on his leggings. "Aw, it'll flake off when it dries, Evan."

"You wish. Anyway, come on."

"Kasey's gonna eat at my house, right, Kasey?"

Kassandra nodded.

The squire caught hold of Maggie as she made a run past him. "That's fine. I'll tell Jade. Cheapes, get home, Havens and Crofts, front and center!"

Bella giggled but presented herself, holding out her hand for him to take. The others gathered around.

"Are we gonna play after supper, Jael?" Alex asked after listening to his name being called for a second time.

"Yeah. We'll meet at your house."

"We could play in the barn. Remember Dandelion, she just had four new . . ."

"Alex Potter, you bring your sister home this instant, you hear!"

"Gotta go." The two ran off toward the village behind the three Cheape children. Jael watched as Evan herded the others toward the castle, then offered Kassandra his hand. The two of them started slowly back toward his home, the guards once again in tow.

"Jael Falconer Asher, don't you dare set foot in this house looking like that! Shame on you!"

Alida stood at the kitchen door, hands on her hips, glaring at her mud-covered grandson. "And look what you've gotten the Aristok into!" She cast a scathing glance in the direction of the guards. "And shame on you, Alec Offord Hanson, for letting them." She turned back to Jael. "Honestly, child! And the pigeon pie all ready to be eaten, too. Well, there's nothing for it. Get those clothes off at once. I'll put the kettle on so you can at least wash your hands and face. Alec send Sasha back to the castle for your suppers, I haven't enough for all. Jem!"

Her partner ambled out from the parlor and began to laugh.

Alida shot her a disapproving look. "Jem, could you bring Jael's other tunic and leggings downstairs and hunt about in that chest under the eaves, there's bound to be something of the boy's that Kasey can fit into for now."

She took the pile of muddy clothes that the two children had wriggled out of and carried it to the pantry where she dropped it into a large washtub.

"Really, Jael, I don't know what I'm going to do with you," she admonished. "And don't you laugh, you'll be helping me wash them after supper."

"But, Granny, we were gonna go over to Alex an' Kate's to see Dandelion's new kittens after supper."

"Kittens?" Kassandra asked.

Alida smiled down at her. "You're welcome to go and see the kittens, Kasey, but, Jael, you're staying home until those clothes are washed. You know better than to come home looking like that at suppertime."

"But, Granny . . ."

"Don't you 'Granny' me, boy. Oh, there's the kettle." She bustled over to the stove.

Jael hung his head and Kassandra looked over at him. "You get into trouble a lot, don't you," she observed.

He grinned. "Yeah, I guess so."

"Don't worry. I'll help you wash our clothes," she offered. "Then we can both see the kittens. I've never washed clothes before. Is it fun?"

Jael scratched at a bit of dried mud on his arm. "Kinda. Yeah, I s'pose so when you've got someone to do it with."

Further conversation was interrupted by Alida's approach with the kettle and a washcloth.

After supper, Alida sent them off to get coal from the village stores to heat the water for the clothes. The sun was almost down below the horizon and the sky was a deep, dark blue. Kassandra pointed as they made their way through the village, Jael swinging the bucket as they walked, Soot running along beside them, and the ever-present guards behind.

"Look," she said. "That's DeMarian blue. It looks just like Papa's tunic."

The boy nodded. "Granny says that Braniana DeMarian reached up an' took the color from the twilight sky when she became Aristok."

"Ballentire says that the Living Flame came from the sky, too."

"Uh, huh, from the Flame Star. See there."

The two children stared at the distant speck of red light just becoming visible in the sky. Jael began to sing an old song that his mother had taught him. His sweet soprano voice lifted into the air and, one by one, the villagers came out to their doorways to listen. Finally, they reached the stores, and after filling the bucket, they headed back.

Later that night, after washing and hanging their muddy clothes by the stove, and after visiting Alex's and Kate's kittens, Jael asked his grandparents if Kasey could stay the night. Alida agreed. She sent Sasha up to the castle to tell Jade and have her and Alec replaced by the night watch.

Dressed in an old nightshirt of Jael's, Kassandra sat up in his bed in the loft with the boy and the dog tucked in beside her, while Jem told them the story of Braniana DeMarian and the Fire-Wolf. She made a good job of it, growling fiercely until Soot began to bark and Alida called up to them all to settle down.

When the story was over, she kissed them both good night and took the lamp downstairs.

The Aristok lay, staring out the loft window at the Flame Star high in the sky. It twinkled at her, and she smiled.

"Jael?"

"Yeah?"

"I had a real nice time today."

"Me, too."

"I never played with lots of children before. Back home there was only just me."

Jael raised himself up on one elbow. "That's gotta be real lonely," he said.

"Uh-huh. Jael?"

"Yeah?"

"I want you an' the Company to come with me when I gotta go home."

"Can Ma come, too?"

"Sure."

"All right."

"You'll like the palace. It has all kinds 'a rooms an' towers an' stuff."

"Has it got a dungeon?" Jael asked, his eyes wide.

"Oh, yes, hundreds."

"Hundreds?"

Jem thumped on the ladder. "You two settle down and go to sleep."

They both giggled and scrunched down under the covers.

"We are asleep, Gramma," Jael answered.

"Then do it quietly."

"We will."

There was silence in the loft for a while.

"Good night, Jael," Kassandra whispered.

"Good night, Capt'n."

Kassandra giggled. "Know what?"

"What?"

"I'm gonna make you my Consort when I grow up."

"Yeah? Will I get my own horse?"

"Oh, yes."

"A black one with white feet?"

There was another thump on the ladder, and the children hunched down in the bed again.

"Yes," Kassandra whispered a moment later. "A black one with white feet an' a soft nose."

"Thanks, Kasey."

The children grew quiet. Finally their breathing deepened and Kassandra the Sixth and her new Consort-to-be fell asleep, while outside the small cottage the garrison of Caerockeith guarded her dreams.

15. Strife

Three days after arriving in Caerockeith, Rosarion sat by Jennet Porter's hearth, wrapped in blankets. The fire was a strong warmth against his body, but his eyes were fever-glazed and his face was sheened with sweat. He barely had the strength to cough and clear the accumulating phlegm from his lungs, so he merely huddled, shivering in the blankets, his breath coming out in short, rattling wheezes.

Getting to Caerockeith had taken more out of him than he'd expected. Standing by the Aristok as ordered while she took the oaths of Innes Eathan and her Triarctic Company, he'd suddenly felt flushed and dizzy and would have fallen had Atreus not gripped his arm. After the ceremony, he'd slowly sunk to the floor behind the milling crowds of nobility. The last thing he saw was the young Knight's concerned features as he caught him.

He remembered nothing more until three days later when he awakened in a strange bed with a strange woman bending over him.

She'd smiled kindly when she saw him open his eyes.

"You're awake, then?"

He blinked and made to speak, but his lips seemed glued shut. He scrubbed weakly at the dried mucus on his mouth with one hand and managed to croak out one short sentence.

"Who are you?"

"Jennet Porter, Caerockeith's Flame Priest," she answered, running a damp cloth over his face and mouth. *"You're in my rooms. You've been delirious for three days. We were afraid we might lose you."*

"We?"

*She gave him a puzzled look as she set the cloth aside.
"Your comrades; His Lordship Atreus DePaula—he's
stayed with you every night—myself, and the Aristok.
She's been asking after you every day since you took ill,
and is extremely put out that I won't let her in to visit
her Flame Priest, I must say."*

He winced and coughed thickly. "How . . . am I?"

*"Well, since you're awake, I'd say you're better than
you've been. Nan will be pleased."*

"Nan?"

*"Nan Guilcove, the garrison physician. I'll send for her
in a minute; she'll want to know you're awake. Meanwhile, you'll be thirsty, I expect." She helped him raise his
head and sip some water from a cup. "Are you hungry?"*

"Some."

"I'll send for some broth."

He grimaced.

"What?"

"Nothing. Just . . . tired of broth."

"Broth is good for you."

*He coughed, spraying a thin line of blood and saliva
over his lips. "I know."*

Later, with the broth warming his stomach and stilling
the shaking in his hands, his senses had slowly awakened, including, embarrassingly, his need to relieve himself. Once he'd managed to bring himself to tell Jennet,
she'd been pragmatically understanding, and had helped
him rise and twist his body onto a nearby commode.
Then she'd quietly left him alone.

She'd returned a few minutes later and, with her help,
he was able to make it to a chair by the fire. She hadn't
thought he should be up so soon, but he'd explained
hoarsely that it was important that he at least make the
attempt to rise; important for his self-esteem if not for
his body. But the few feet had taken more out of him
than he'd cared to admit, and once seated with a blanket
tucked about him, he'd found himself falling asleep once
again. He didn't fight it. The room was warm and closed,
and even with his lungs slowly refilling, he felt safe and
comfortably detached.

When he awoke again, the room was empty. The fire

was still blazing in the hearth, however, and he didn't have to urinate again, so he assumed that not much time had passed.

He gazed dazedly into the flames, trying to bring his muddled senses into some order.

Three days; that would make it Di Jerdein, the last day of Mean Boaldyn. He shivered. Spring was well underway. Soon the roads would be dry and Terrilynne DeMarian would march against her cousin Ellisander, and there would be war.

He closed his eyes, the thought invoking a kaleidoscope of mixed feelings that made him extremely uncomfortable. Could he have prevented it? he wondered. If he'd never told Ellisander of his first vision, would the Duke have reached for the Throne regardless? Would Rosarion himself now be sitting wrapped in blankets before his own hearth behind a Flame Temple untouched by fire while Marsellus the Third held court in his ancient palace to the west, his loyal brother-in-law at his side? Or would it all have played out just the same, only with a slightly different cast of characters? If Fate's chosen instruments refused to act out Its version of history, did It turn to others until Its purpose was fulfilled? And did it really matter?

Before he could answer this long string of questions, the door opened and a woman, short and stocky, with nondescript light brown hair tied severely back and hazel eyes that stared frankly around the room, entered.

She paused to glance briefly down at him, then moved to the window and threw it open.

Cool, fresh air filled the room and Rosarion's head and lungs began to clear. He felt better almost immediately, and took a tentative breath as the woman came to stand in front of him.

"I'm Nan Guilcove," she said at once. "The physician here. You should be in bed, and that window should stay open."

"Rosarion DeLynne, and you're right."

She looked him up and down and then raised one eyebrow. "They say you're a Flame Priest."

"I was."

"And an Herbalist."

"Yes."

"And that you have white lung, third stage, but I could have guessed that just by looking at you."

"How am I?"

"Well . . ." She pulled up a chair and sat. "You're alive."

"I gathered."

"Right. Your breathing's not so good."

He nodded. "Wheezing."

"This last attack probably damaged your lungs some. I'll give you something to help keep them clear in a minute."

She looked him keenly up and down and, suddenly aware of his disheveled appearance, Rosarion wiped the sweat from his face with the edge of his sleeve, grimacing as his hand scraped against three days' worth of stubble.

"I need a special expectorant," he said, his voice still weak and scratchy. "Red-and-white clover, wormroot if you have it." He paused. "Wolfweed if you don't."

"Wolfweed?" She frowned at him.

"It helps calm the seizures and shaking caused by prolonged exposure to the Potion of Truth," he explained.

She scrutinized his features again, taking in the unhealthy pallor of his skin and the dark circles under his eyes, and grimaced. "You mean caused by prolonged *withdrawal* from the Potion of Truth," she replied.

"Both."

"You do know that wolfweed is a poison that can build up in your body and eventually kill you?"

"I'm already dying."

"That's the spirit."

He looked up at her sharply, and she returned the expression with a raised eyebrow. "It was all I could find on the trip up here," he found himself explaining. "Wormroot *is* preferable."

"How long have you been taking the wolfweed?"

He thought back. "A week, maybe ten days. I've been smoking it with wild lettuce," he forced himself to admit.

She stared at him again. "I'm surprised you're still alive."

"I have a strong constitution despite everything."

"You must have. Well, at least you haven't been taking it long enough to poison your blood. We'll deal with the lungs first. I'll make you up a clover-and-camomile expectorant."

He shook his head. "I can't take it. I have too many residual herbs in my system that react with camomile."

"Like?"

He hesitated. The ingredients and proportions for the Potion of Truth were a carefully guarded secret. Even he would not go so far as to betray that knowledge, but working at cross-purposes with Caerockeith's physician wouldn't help his recovery.

"Like ratroot," he said finally.

"Why, by Essus, would you take ratroot?"

"For no reason that involves Essus," he answered stiffly. When she waited for further explanation, he merely looked away.

Finally she shook her head. "Can you at least tell me how long you've been taking it?"

"A long time."

"More than six months?"

He nodded cautiously.

"More than two years?"

He nodded again.

"You're insane. Do you have any idea what kind of damage that causes?"

"I know what kind of damage it causes to go without it after prolonged use; seizures, blindness, and dementia." The sweat broke out afresh on his face. "I'm really going to need some very soon, Nan. It's been three days." He gripped his hands together to stop the sudden shaking, but she noticed anyway, her eyes narrowing.

"Very well," she said at last. "I'll bring you a clover-and-burnet expectorant for the lungs, an infusion of wormroot and dragonstail should help with the withdrawal; it's good for all kinds, and . . . I'll find you some ratroot . . . somewhere."

"What's dragonstail?" he asked, ignoring the disapproving tone in her voice.

"It's a marsh herb found predominantly in western Heathland," she answered, rising and touching the back of her hand to his forehead. "It grows wild all over this area, and doesn't react to any form of narcotic or hallucinogen . . ." When he glared up at her, she shrugged. "All right, any form of visionary herb. Better?"

He gave her a rueful half-smile. "Sorry. It doesn't have any .. religious significance, does it?"

"You mean for Essus?"

"Yes."

"Not that I know of." She handed him a handkerchief to wipe his face with. "It's only called dragonstail because it looks like one. It's actually a mild sedative and an antiemetic. It's used to calm the body and the spirit to promote healing."

"But you will bring the ratroot?"

She gritted her teeth. "Yes, I will bring the ratroot. I won't leave you to shake yourself to pieces."

At that moment the door opened. Nan turned to say something to Jennet Porter, then snapped her mouth closed, her expression affronted as Innes Eathan walked into the room.

The Senior Flame Priest had served the Branbridge Flame Temple for over thirty years. She had not actually taught Rosarion, but she had gone into vision with him and considered his defection to be more than heresy; it was a personal betrayal of his brother and sister Seers. Ignoring the physician, she came to stand before him, her arms crossed belligerently across her chest.

"Julianus is dead," she said bluntly.

He closed his eyes.

"And Bronwynne," she continued. "And Devarian, and Martina, Llewen, Bethsalan, and Talisar. A lot more, too."

He pressed his hand against his mouth as a cough began to work its way up his throat. Finally he met her eyes. "Willan?" he asked.

She pursed her lips together. "I hear he's alive," she said after a moment. "But his hands were badly burned from trying to pull others from the wreckage you caused."

"*I* caused?"

"That's right. I consider you as responsible for their deaths as Yorbourne or any other conspirator might be."

"You still don't believe he's guilty, then?"

"I believe you're guilty, and I intend to see you on trial for heresy, murder, and treason as soon as we get back to Branbridge, no matter how far you've managed to weasel your way into the good graces of the Aristok. Once we return and those of us that are left are able to go into the Prophetic Realm, we'll see just how guilty the Duke of Yorbourne is. Until then, I'm holding you primarily responsible."

Rosarion made to say something, then shook his head and closed his eyes wearily. "You have no idea," he answered finally.

"You're right there. Marsellus, I might almost be able to understand, but the Archpriest? How could you betray Julianus, Rosarion? He was like a father to you."

Rosarion pressed his sleeve against his mouth as a thin trickle of blood made its way past his teeth.

"If you don't mind." Nan pushed suddenly between them. "My patient needs rest, *Your Grace*," she grated.

Innes gave a disbelieving snort. "He should be *resting* in a cell."

"Maybe, and whatever you do about that in the capital is your concern, but here in Caerockeith I give the orders. Now if you will excuse us . . ." She met the Flame Priest's dark gaze with a stare of equal magnitude and finally Innes moved away.

At the door, she turned. "Just remember, Rosarion," she warned. "You're alive on sufferance, physician or no. Put one step wrong and I'll be on you like a gryphon on a kill."

She left.

"Bloody Flame Priests," Nan spat.

Rosarion stared into the fire, his hands gripping the arms of the chair to keep them from shaking. "I didn't cause the burning of the Flame Temple," he said quietly. "Whatever else I'm guilty of, I'm not responsible for that. Will I have to pay for every move Ellisander makes?"

Nan tucked the blanket about his shoulders with an absent gesture. "Maybe," she answered. "You know what they say, guilt through association. But as I told her, you're my patient, and you'll reach a cell when I say so, not before." She moved toward the door. "I'll get those infusions now. Don't go anywhere."

She closed the door softly behind her and Rosarion was left to stare into the fire once again.

The Aristok was in Mosswell again that afternoon, watching Alida Asher make bread. She'd fallen in love with the small cottage and its inhabitants, but today was to be the last day she could enjoy it. A scout had arrived this morning to inform Terrilynne that the troop ships from Eireon had been sighted. They would land tomorrow and, with the Sorlandy and Danelind mercenaries due the day after, they would pose too great a potential threat for the young Aristok to roam freely. She would have to confine her playing to the castle keep after today.

Used to such security measures in Branbridge, the child had not argued, although she had commanded that Jael and the Company were to have unlimited access to her. Terrilynne had readily agreed. She needed Kassandra distracted for as long as possible, and while the Aristok was holding court over the crowd of castle children she was not holding court over the adults. Terrilynne was having enough trouble managing that on her own.

The Duke of Kempston had called a Command Council the day after the oath taking, and the sides had quickly formed up. Innes Eathan was still reluctant to believe in Ellisander's complete guilt and was unwilling to commit her full support to an assault against Yorbourne. She was arguing caution and a quiet entrance into Branbridge under the protection of the Hierarchpriest of Cannonshire; a plan of action that Terrilynne knew would spell arrest for the Aristok's comrades and political suicide for herself and her own supporters, not to mention put the child in immediate danger from Ellisander and his machinations. Most of the Triarctic Company did not see this and supported Innes' ideas, however. They felt, as Kalidon did, that the danger did not justify civil war. Amanda and Gladys had their hands full keeping the DeMarian Duke from tossing the entire group into the castle dungeons.

At least Morag had sent word that the border Heaths

would not interfere with the movement of the Duke's troops across their lands as long as those troops kept their hands off the locals and their property. It had cost an exorbitant sum, especially to gain the temporary permission of the centrally located Armistones, but it had been worth it. Word was that troops from Sorlandy and Kempston had met just west of the Lindie-held town of Falkieth and were coming west without impediment, Alexius DeMarian in command.

As dusk brought word of the Aristok's return to the castle surrounded by her junior court, Terrilynne dismissed yet another deadlocked Command Council. The decisions could wait until tomorrow. Justin ap Callum would be arriving with his Eireon hirelings and the added swords would give her secular authority more weight against Innes Eathan's ecclesiastical power.

If the Flame Priest did not bow to her command then, she would be either compelled or moved forcibly aside, the Duke promised herself darkly. When they marched on Yorbourne they would marched united, one way or another. Terrilynne DeMarian was tired of arguing.

The assembled nobility took supper in the main hall again that night, but it was a subdued affair. The Aristok was tired and cranky, and Simon was closemouthed and distant, sending the child's mood spiraling down into petulance. Jordana DeLynne could barely tolerate the presence of Atreus DePaula and her distant kinsman Rosarion, even though both were present by order of the Aristok, and Innes Eathan was in a foul mood as well.

Kalidon DeKathrine managed to place himself between the two factions, but even his cheery disposition could not lighten the air of tension and suspicion.

As for Rosarion, he was up against Nan's orders. Gaunt and gray, as soon as Simon left to take Kassandra up to bed, he excused himself as well, leaning heavily on Atreus' arm. This left the Duke of Kempston to host the remains of the banquet, and she called an end to the evening as soon as possible. They would all need their rest anyway, for tomorrow was going to be a very busy day.

In Terrilynne's inner chamber, Kassandra the Sixth

was petulantly insisting that she wasn't sleepy, but her mood brightened immediately at the sight of Jael and Soot sitting on the huge four-poster bed. With a yell of pleasure, she pulled away from Simon and leaped onto the bed with a great bounce.

"I knew you would come!" she said excitedly. "I told Alida that I wanted you to come, and she promised you would! I forgot all about it till now."

Soot started barking as the two children began jumping up and down on the big eiderdown. Then Kassandra stopped bouncing and looked around. "Where're the others?" she asked.

Simon came forward. "You can see them tomorrow," he answered, drawn into her pleasure despite himself. "Twelve children tearing up the Duke's bedchamber is ten children too many, don't you think?"

"I guess, but Jael's gonna stay, right?" Kassandra began bouncing again.

"Right, if you don't destroy the bed before it's time to go to sleep."

The child dropped onto her bottom with a smaller bounce as Simon moved to turn the covers down. Jael continued to jump until a short look from his father caused him to follow his Captain's lead. Simon smiled.

"Into your nightclothes now. Did you bring a nightshirt, Jael?"

"Yes, Da. It's by the fire."

"Well, go and get it."

"Mine used to be Luis'." Kassandra said, fishing hers out from beneath one of the heavy, goosedown pillows. "An' he gived it to me 'cause I didn't have one 'cept back home."

"Granny made mine," Jael answered. "It's got dogs on it, see?"

The two children compared nightshirts until Simon sent them to wash and change. When they were both tucked comfortably into the huge bed, with Soot happily encamped between them, Kassandra glanced expectantly up at the artist.

"I'm ready for my story now," she said.

Simon sat at the foot of the bed, and laid his injured hand gently in his lap.

"What sort of story did you want?"

"One about Papa."

A shadow passed across the artist's face, but was swiftly dismissed.

"Surely you've heard every story I have to tell you about your Papa," he stalled.

"So tell me an old one."

"An old one."

"Tell me about when I was born."

"Ah. You mean a story about you."

"Yes."

He sat back against the large, wooden bedpost as Kassandra and Jael snuggled down into the covers.

"Well, it was a beautiful day in Mean Ebril," he began. "Everyone was waiting for the arrival of the Heir to the Throne, but she was late."

"Something's wrong. Curse it, what's the matter with that blistering midwife? Kath's been in labor for almost a day!"

The Aristok paced across the Royal garden and kicked viciously at a young boxwood.

Simon, his own face tight, put on a reassuring smile. "Nothing's wrong, Leary," he said. "Didn't Julianus prophesize that the child would be born whole and strong and cradled in the arms of the Living Flame, but only after many hours of struggle?"

"Maybe," Leary answered in a petulant tone.

"An' I was," Kassandra interrupted eagerly. "An' Papa always said that the Living Flame was with me strong on account of that. An' he said that I was born wif a red-an-white caul all aroun' me, an' nobody knew what that meant, 'cept then Julianus said it meant my Realm would be pros . . . pros . . . pris. Right, Simon?"

"That's right, Sparky."

Jael looked up from rubbing Soot's ears. "What's a caul?"

"Goopy stuff," Kassandra answered.

"Goopy stuff?"

He looked to his father who shrugged. "Goopy stuff."

"An' Simon painted me being born in the great hall,"

Kassandra continued. "Wif everyone standin' 'round, 'cept no one was really there."

"Artistic license," Simon explained.

"Uh-huh. Have you started drawin' for my painting of coming here yet?"

Simon looked away. "Not yet, Sparky."

"When are you going to?"

The artist's answer was cut off by the appearance of Fay at the door. He stood.

"I thought I'd come and kiss the children good night," she said coming forward. Simon nodded.

"When, Simon?" Kassandra repeated.

Fay glanced at him curiously.

Bending down to kiss the child's forehead, he paused as she curled her little fingers around the laces of his tunic. "Tonight, Sparky," he answered finally.

"Will you show me the drawings tomorrow?"

Untangling her fingers, he kissed Jael, then turned away. "Yes," he said stiffly, ignoring his mother's worried frown. He headed for the door. "Will you stay, Ma?" he asked as he opened it.

"Of course, Simon. But are you certain you're ready for this?"

He shrugged, his expression blank. "Why wouldn't I be? I'm fine," he answered as he left the room.

Two children looked silently at Fay until Jael tugged at his grandmother's sleeve.

"Is Da all right, Gran?" he asked, his voice scared.

Fay leaned over to fluff his pillow. "He will be," she answered.

Kassandra pulled at one of the silver threads in the bedspread. "Is Simon upset 'cause I wanted him to make me a picture?"

"No, poppet, that's not why he's upset."

"You said he had to start practicing again, an' that he wouldn't if we didn't push him, so I pushed."

"I know. You did the right thing."

"So why is he upset? He always loved to draw an' paint before. He made a picture of Bal an' me that he never even finished."

Sitting down beside her, Fay regarded the child, meeting her unsettlingly adult gaze with a serious expression of her own. "It's hard to explain," she began. "Simon's afraid he can't paint anymore, and painting is so very important to him that he feels lost without it. But he doesn't want us to know that he feels lost and afraid, so he pretends that he isn't."

"Why?"

"Because he feels he has to be strong for us, so we have to be very patient with him and let him know that we love him and it's all right for him to be afraid. Can you both do that?"

"Yes," Kassandra answered promptly, but Jael looked uncertain.

"Jael?"

"How can we do that?" he asked, his voice very small.

"Well, you can spend time with him and try to remind him that he has more than just the painting."

"Doesn't he know that?"

" 'Course he does," Kassandra said firmly, catching on to the boy's actual meaning. "You mustn't never think that he doesn't 'member you. But it's like when Papa lost Momma. He got all hurt an' mad an' cried an' shouted an' forgot everything until Simon an' Uncle Sandi reminded him he had me.

" 'Sides," she continued, "He's gots a lot more, too. He's my knight an' I need him, an' so do you, so I will remind him that he's gots us both an' he will remember an' be better."

"Promise?"

"I promise."

Fay nodded. "And so do I, Jelly."

"Gran!"

"Jelly?" Kassandra's eyes grew very wide.

"That's what I used to call Jael when he was very little," Fay answered, laughing at the boy's horrified expression. "And he used to call me Jam."

"Jam?"

"That's right."

"My Papa used to call me Little Gwyneth, an' Simon calls me Sparky, but 'most everyone calls me Your Majesty now."

Her voice was woeful, but Jael snorted. "At least no one ever called you Jelly."

"I don't think they'd have been allowed."

"Boy, are you ever lucky."

"Oh, stop your complaining, both of you," Fay said with a laugh, tucking the blankets up around them. "It's not what people call you that matters, it's the love behind the words. Now, it's time to go to sleep. Scoot down, and I'll sing you a lullaby."

"Do you know the one that Warrin sang for me?" Kassandra asked. "The one about the sea?"

"Yes, I do. Do you want that one?"

"Uh-huh."

"All right. You take Spotty, here, and Jael you make Soot behave—he's scratching again and it better not be fleas—and I'll sing you the one about the sea."

The two children lay back, the toy horse and the small dog held tightly in their arms.

Fay sat back against the bedpost and began to sing.

Soon the children's eyes grew heavy, and they slowly fell asleep.

As the castle settled down into night, Simon sat in the top turret of the south tower, staring out the window at the water below. It was cold and dark in the small room, a single candle flickering in the breeze, illuminating a pile of drawing materials scattered across the stone floor. After a long moment he cast a dull, empty look down at them.

It had taken some time for Alex Potter to find what he asked for, and even longer for Simon, his breathing suddenly shallow, and the sweat popping out on his forehead, to take up the charcoal stick in his left hand.

Hating the feeling of awkward uncertainty in every movement, he had begun half a dozen attempts and finally thrown the charcoal away in disgust. Now, staring out at the dark waters, the fear he had held at bay for so long overwhelmed his denial.

His right hand would never truly heal. Nan Guilcove had examined it that day, and the look on her face was diagnosis enough. He'd been unable to watch her work, keeping his eyes firmly on a spot by the infirmary door while she cleaned and rewrapped it, but he couldn't deny how it felt. Although the weeping had stopped and the various wounds had scabbed over, the palm was stiff and hard to move, the fingers either tingled or felt nothing when Nan gently pressed each one between finger and thumb. She had managed a few reassuring words, but facts were facts. The hand was useless.

As for the left, the drawings he'd struggled to make were crude and amateurish, lacking even the potential he'd shown as a small child. He'd never gained the necessary skill in that hand, no matter what Lorenzo had tried to teach him. He'd never thought he'd have to. Now it was too late.

Scattering the supplies, he stood and pressed his face against the wall's cold stone. He couldn't do it. If Kassandra ever commissioned the sort of vast murals her father had ordered to mark each event of his short reign, they would not be painted by him. His abilities had died in that cell in the Flame Temple.

Too bad his life hadn't ended at the same time, he'd thought bitterly. Then he might have left something worthwhile behind. Inside the shadows rose, drawn by his pain, but he thrust them savagely away. Turning, he stared out at the Banngate Estuary flowing darkly below the castle walls. It looked cold and very deep.

He wasn't sure how long he stood there, staring out the window. Finally a sound behind him made him turn.

His mother stood by the tower door, her face drawn and worried.

"It took me a while to find you," she said in a neutral tone. Simon shrugged.

"The children?"

"Are with Hamlin. It's cold up here."

"Is it? I didn't notice."

Fay looked down at the scattered supplies, saw the crude marks on the paper and came forward, her expression grieving.

Simon found himself shrinking away. She stopped.

"Simon . . ."

"Don't." Holding up his good hand to stop her, he pressed his back against the wall. "Just don't."

"Son . . ."

"No. I don't want your pity, Ma. I don't need it. I don't need anyone's pity."

She raised her head. "Who said I was offering pity? I'm your mother. It's my right to care."

He turned away, shaking his head. "Just go away," he said finally. "Please, just go away."

"You shouldn't have to be alone with this."

"I will always be alone with this!" He whirled to face her, his expression savage. "Always, for the rest of my life! Every day, every hour, I'll always remember what I lost on the floor of that cell! And why."

Fay expression grew still. "I see," she said quietly.

About to speak, Simon closed his mouth and turned to face the window again. They stood that way, each silent with their own guilt for a long time, until Fay finally left the tower.

Hating himself for what he'd said, Simon laid his forehead against the cool stone and gave himself over to grief.

Hours later he awoke on the cold floor to one softly spoken word.

"Son?"

Simon made no answer.

"Son, come, sit up, you'll catch your death."

The artisan lifted him, unresisting, and guided him to the window seat. Draping a blanket about his son's shoulders, Hamlin then took his own place across from him. Patting his sides absently, he drew out his pipe and pouch, and filling the bowl, he lit it from the candle and sat back. The familiar odor filled the room, and Simon's face relaxed slightly. Hamlin glanced out the window.

"Your mother's very worried about you, Son," he began cautiously. "She blames herself for your injuries, and I think she fears you blame her, too."

Simon met his father's eyes defiantly, then dropped his own gaze. After a long time, he tightened the blanket about him.

"I said something to her."

"Hm." Hamlin puffed at his pipe, waiting.

"I didn't mean to blame her. I don't blame her. It just came out." Simon fell silent.

The two sat quietly together for a long time. Hamlin did not press his son to talk after his first comments, and Simon did not offer. As the moon rose over the distant hills, the artist shivered.

"Leary's been gone, been . . . dead, for twenty-four days," he said quietly, almost to himself. "Exactly twenty-four days. I counted them off this afternoon."

"Hm?"

"It took me twenty-four days to paint the Merrone roundel piece for the Duc of Nepaline, and it took him almost that long to get around to paying for it. Leary always paid me in advance."

"Leary was a good patron, one of the best," his father agreed.

"I'm so tired," Simon whispered as if he hadn't heard him. "So tired of hurting." He stared fixedly down at the bandage on his hand. "Every day since Leary died I've missed him so much it hurt like a ragged wound. And this . . . Then . . ." He waved helplessly at the scattered supplies, unable to speak the words. Hamlin bowed his head.

"Then he came to me and it didn't hurt so much, but they tried to drive him away and the pain came back, only worse. I can't lose him again, Pa, he makes the pain go away."

Hamlin drew on his pipe, and the bluish-gray smoke curled about in the air between them. "You know Rosarion believes you won't heal as long as he keeps near?"

"Rosarion?" Simon's face twisted angrily.

"Mina, then, and your mother."

"They don't understand. They can't understand. It won't heal, not well enough, Pa, you know it and I know it. I can't lose Leary, too. I can't lose them both."

Hamlin frowned. "You know your mother believes that after this life is finished, we rejoin past loved ones in the bosom of Essus."

Simon snorted. "*Leary* was the Vessel of the Living Flame, Pa. I don't think we'll be meeting in the bosom of Essus."

Hamlin shrugged. "Don't be too sure." When Simon stared at him, he smiled a little self-consciously. "Don't tell your mother this, but I've always had my own ideas about that sort of thing, ideas I don't think she'd approve of."

"Ma's always been conservative."

"She is that."

After a moment Simon looked up again. "What sort of ideas?" he asked reluctantly.

Hamlin drew in a large puff and let it out slowly. "Well, I've always believed—and this is only my belief, mind—that the world is made up of a great, creative . . . spirit, and that everyone, people and Gods alike, dip into it like taking water from a river. Some people, great artists or musicians, can pull more from the river than most people. When we die, all that creativity and all that . . . whatever it is that makes us who we are, returns to the river to be dipped out by someone else."

Simon couldn't help but smile a little fondly. "An artist's idea of perfect symmetry," he murmured.

"Maybe."

"Why didn't you tell me this before?"

Hamlin shrugged. "Everyone has to come to their own idea about life and about death. I'm telling you now because you had your own ideas before, but you've lost sight of them." He drew on his pipe, frowned, and then held up the candle flame to the bowl again.

"So what are you saying?" Simon asked a little tensely.

"Maybe that Leary will always be with you in your art."

Simon's face grew bleak. "My art?" he asked bitterly. "I told you, my art is lost."

Hamlin frowned. "Maybe in this form," he answered. "But maybe art's a little bit more than the hand that produces it. Maybe art's in here." He tapped his breast. "This . . ." He held up his hand. "Is just one way of giving it form, but it's not the only way."

"It's the only way I know."

"Hm." Crossing his arms, Hamlin leaned back, slowly puffing on his pipe. He'd told him the words. Simon would just have to come to the belief in his own time.

The painter watched him a moment, then turned his gaze to the window.

As the night air filled the room, Hamlin sent a prayer up to Essus to help his son, and Simon closed his eyes, his spirit returning to Leary's shadowy arms.

*   *   *

The next day the Eireon troops arrived at Caerockeith under the command of Eleanor mac Mairi, the youngest of the Royal Princes. Kassandra reviewed them from the top of the gatehouse tower with Terrilynne on one side and Innes Eathan on the other. It made a formal statement of secular and ecclesiastical unity, although neither was especially comfortable with the arrangement.

Having been told that they now fought in the name of the Aristok, the Western Isle warriors sent up a great cheer as they knelt as a body—in the manner of the Eireon Triarchs—before their new Vessel of the Living Flame. Kassandra smiled beatifically down on all of them, sketching in the air the ancient blessing she'd learned from her father. Eleanor led the responding chant of loyalty.

Beside her, Terrilynne smiled darkly to herself. The highly religious Eireon soldiers had demonstrated that they were firmly on the side of Kempston and the Aristok. As a Royal Prince and a Triarctic Priest, Eleanor brought another weapon against Innes and her push for a peaceful solution. Recognizing this, the Archpriest sought Kassandra's permission to withdraw as soon as the Eireon commanders called the dismissal to set up camp to the west of the castle.

All that week Terrilynne's army began to take form. Those from her own ducal holding of Kempston arrived the next morning, the soldiers from Sorlandy swelling their ranks. The last troops from Albion's lands of Wakeford arrived the day after and, one day after that, Nathaniel DeKathrine was pleased to inform her that his own troops were prepared and waiting to join the vanguard as soon as it came through Dunmouth. Mosswell and the surrounding areas were already choked with soldiers encamped on every bit of dry land. Gerron Reed had his hands full arranging feed and fodder and could not be made to say a polite word to anyone, but his mood soon brightened as a long line of supply wagons arrived from Lanborough. Zavier DeMarian had finally been convinced to throw in with his cousins Terrilynne and Albion.

The homes of Dunley Vale were also filled to bursting with Cailein and Taggen hill fighters. The Triarctic troops were made to understand that they were to leave them strictly alone and, so far, there'd been little strife between the two groups, but Morag warned Terrilynne that the sooner they started out, the better. Branion and Heathland could not go long in close quarters without a fight. Terrilynne agreed, but told her to be patient. They were almost ready.

Then, on the fourth day of Mean Ebril, the great party of troops from Danelind arrived in Caerockeith. The army was assembled and Terrilynne sent out word. The eight hundred troops would move on Yorbourne in eight days.

That night she called for a full Council of War. The Aristok Kassandra the Sixth sat at the head of the huge main hall table, dressed in her father's Royal tunic, belted at the waist by a silver warrior's belt. The new DeMarian plaide Alida and Jem had made for her lay across her shoulder and was pinned with Terrilynne's own sapphire plaide pin. She wore a long dagger in a small, silver scabbard, proclaiming her intent to take her throne through martial force despite her youth. Her hair, now washed free of its brown disguise, glowed as red as her eyes.

Terrilynne, Albion, Zavier and Alexius made an honor guard of DeMarians around her, each dressed in formal dark blue and black, the fire-wolf of their family and the various crest animals of their holdings prominent on their surcoats. Each wore the Royal plaide, gray wool shot with dark red and black, with the fine blue thread of the subordinate plaide running through it, and each wore the silver warrior's belt and the trappings of the Knights of the Sword, the traditional order patronized by the Royal Family. Behind them, Eaglelynne stood ready to record the proceedings.

Terrilynne's Cavalry Commander, Amanda, Earl of Guilcove, came dressed for war in the formal dark green and black of the DeKathrines, as did the Viscount of Dunmouth and Kalidon DeKathrine, resigned to the fighting. So did his cousin, Viscount of Dorsley, Xaviana

DeKathrine, not so resigned, but unable to argue now that war was at hand.

Terrilynne's Lieutenant, the Earl of Radnydd, also came in the formal attire of her traditional title of High Archpriest of the Flame Champions of Gwyneth, stressing her ascension over the secular holdings and Triarctic authority of her kinswomen, the Viscounts of Porth Wells and Bothsyde, and the Archpriest of Radnydd. For their part, these other DeLlewellynnes sat surrounding Innes Eathan, in her dark red Priest's robes and Jordana DeLynne in her garb as the Captain of the Shield Knights. Eleanor mac Mairi sat beside Zavier DeMarian and the generals of the Sorlandy, Eireon and Danelind mercenaries were placed together.

At the foot of the table, placed in the position of honor, Morag Cailein sat with her uncle Sean and Gord and Eve Taggen, each wearing their families' green-and-gray or green-and-red Heathland plaides.

Finally, Simon of Florenz and Rosarion DeLynne sat just behind and to the left and right of the Aristok in the position of senior councillors. Simon had not bothered to seek out formal attire and was dressed in his usual clothes, Rosarion had carefully chosen a secular tunic and breeches of DeLynne deep purple and red. Ignoring the glare Innes Eathan shot him and Simon's stiff refusal to look at him at all, the Herbalist concentrated on the bright flag of Branion hanging above the main hall door, the dark red fire-wolf mirroring his Sovereign's fiery hair, and reminding all that carried the legacy of seven hundred years in her small frame.

It took three hours to get everything sorted out, but by the time they broke for dinner, most of the decisions were made. The army would leave on the twelfth day of Mean Ebril, the Aristok's fifth birthday. The main body would move southeast through Dunmouth and attack Yorbourne from the west, the Heaths would cross the Gildarock Hills and attack from the north. Terrilynne's scouts reported that Ellisander's Steward, Manderus Greydove, had scraped up only seventy-five troops to defend the Dukedom, most concentrated in the main city named for the Royal Shire. The fear was that they would take sanctuary behind Yorbourne's thick walls, forcing a prolonged siege, but Terrilynne put that fear to rest. They would ravage the countryside, but would not linger if Ellisander's minions could not be brought to bear. They would carry on south toward Branbridge until they met resistance. And it would come, she assured them, Ellisander DeMarian would not be taken without a fight.

Toward noon, a messenger arrived with further news of Yorbourne. She reported that fifty heavy cavalry from Pennineshire were making their way east toward Yorbourne and that one hundred more were coming up from Berford and Cambury. But that was not the news of greatest importance. Word was that two hundred Sword Knights and Flame Champions were headed north under the Archpriest of Linconford's banner. That Gawaina DeKathrine had sent troops from her own Dukedom as well as the militant orders under her control in support of Ellisander did much to quiet the dissension of Jordana and Innes. The lines had been drawn. They would fight. When Terrilynne put the question to them flat out in council, who would they support, they acquiesced. They would not take up arms against the Aristok.

Five days later a very welcome distraction arrived. Bessie Cheape sang out from the battlements that six brightly painted wagons were coming up the road from Dunley Vale. The Spinning Coins Tumbling Troupe had arrived at last.

With the jingle of horse bells and the shouted laughter of trailing children, the Troupe made its way up the road to stop at the castle's inner common. Standing on the roof of the lead wagon, Ballentire of Briery let a long blast loose from a spiral trumpet.

The Aristok fairly flew down the halls and out the castle keep. Her little feet pounded against the wooden castle bridge and Ballentire was just in time to jump down and catch her as she threw herself at the Troupe Leader.

"Bal!"

"Kasey! We haven't missed your birthday, have we? We came up as fast as we could."

"No, it's in three days!

"We're goin' to war, Bal!" The child twisted in her arms until she could see their wagon. "Where's Tam?"

"Here, Kasey."

The child accepted a hug from the tumbler and then squirmed out of Ballentire's arms and raced past the lead wagon, shouting for Warrin.

Jumping from his wagon, the big man swung the child into the air. She laughed and threw her arms about his neck.

"Oh, I missed you so much, Warrin!" she said excitedly. "I've got all sorts of new friends, an' you have to do your fire-eatin' trick for them 'cause I told them you would! An' I can juggle so much better now! You have to see me! An' Jael—he's my Lieutenant; I have a whole Comp'ny of my own now—he's gots a dog that can stand on its hind legs wif a biscuit on its nose! Its name is Soot! An' I'm getting my own pony in just three days! I'll be five, you know! An' I have a special idea, Bal! I have an idea I want you all to do!"

Unable to get a word in edgewise, Warrin just smiled and nodded as the other Coins crowded around to greet their young patron.

Turi accepted a quick hug and then tweaked her sleeve to get her attention.

"Where's everyone else, Kasey?"

She tipped her head to one side. "Hamlin, Fay, Dani, an' Luis are all comin' through the gate now, see?" She pointed. "Rosarion's been real sick, so you'd better ask Nan if you can see him. She won't let *me*." Her expression grew dark. "'An Atreus is prob'ly with him, an' Simon is making me a picture, but he's feeling scared an' lost, so you all have to promise me that you'll make him feel better."

"We will, Kasey."

The rest of Turi's words were drowned out as the garrison had now gathered and Ballentire began a shouted greeting to them all. Carrying Kassandra on his shoulders, Warrin led the Coins into the castle proper.

*   *   *

That night the Spinning Coins Tumbling Troupe prepared to give a special performance ordered by the Aristok herself. Rosarion and Simon—despite his excuses—had been brought to Terrilynne's inner chamber and had been closeted with the Coins and the Aristok all day preparing her show. Dani and Luis had been set as guards at the door and no one from Caerockeith had been allowed to enter.

Now, they set up a makeshift stage out on the castle common, for the Aristok had ordered that as many who could were to attend the performance. Torches lined the walls behind and free-standing holders beside to illuminate the stage. Enough benches had been found to seat all the castle nobility and, as darkness fell, soldiers crammed in behind them, eagerly awaiting the night's entertainment.

Intrigued, Terrilynne took her place at the front beside the Eireon Prince, surrounded by all her DeMarian cousins save one. The Aristok was not there; she had other plans for the evening.

Once they were all gathered, a lone trumpet call sounded from the top of the gatehouse tower and Warrin Fire-Eater took center stage.

He stood naked, his whole body painted with bands of fiery red, yellow and orange. He looked so much like a titan from the Triarchy texts that most of the audience gasped when he took his place. Bennie lit four torches and passed them over, and as Warrin began to throw them into the air faster and faster, the gathered were held spellbound by the whirling lights.

Next, Tamara and Turi appeared, dressed as androgynous fire-demons, tumbling and dancing to the ancient story of The Birth of the Living Flame. One by one, they were joined by others until the entire stage was awhirl with fiery shapes. Finally, Ballentire appeared, dressed as Braniana DeMarian and they all fell immediately to the floor in supplication. Tamara and Turi began to weave about her and as the music rose to a crescendo they wrapped a deep red cloak about her and disappeared. Ballentire threw her arms wide and bits of red rag flew out into the audience who scrambled to collect them.

When they'd quieted down again, a single pipe began

to play and Ballentire returned to center stage, dressed now as the traditional chorus, a fifth century Branion Herald.

"My Most Honored Lords!" she shouted. "Tonight, the Spinning Coins Tumbling Troupe is proud to present to you a new work, commissioned by none other than Her Most Regal and Sacred Majesty, Kassandra the Sixth, Aristok of Branion!" She stepped forward as the gathered began to cheer, and silenced them with a gesture. "These are troubled times, My Lords, as you all know," she said in a dramatic stage whisper. "Treachery and villainy are rampant in the land. None know who to trust or who to turn to. In this atmosphere of turmoil, on the eve of battle and of victory, we present to you *The Murder of Marsellus the Black.*"

The audience stirred uneasily as the Troupe Leader turned and disappeared behind the back curtain. A cloth painted to represent a private chapel was lowered, and Hartney, wearing a red wig, and dressed in a dark blue-and-black DeMarian tunic, took center stage, kneeling as if in prayer. Behind him, a shadowy figure slowly emerged.

Beyond the stage, the audience was frozen in silence as the murder of the late Aristok was played out before them. Coached by Rosarion, the Troupe had much of the details right and, although only one figure plunged her blade into the Aristok's chest, it was enough to cause a shiver to run through the gathered Triarchs. This is what they had come to avenge and when Hartney fell, an angry murmur could be heard.

Then Kassandra herself came to stand at stage left, with Simon beside her. As Hartney gave one final cry, she echoed it with a piercing scream that brought many to their feet. Simon himself almost looked to swoon, but at the last moment, he caught her as she fell and lowered them both to the floor. When he looked up the audience could see real tears in his eyes and on his cheeks. The lone assassin turned to confront them, then threw out her arm, calling on them to flee the wicked treachery of an uncle's hand. The audience stirred uneasily and Innes Eathan's face grew stony.

At farthest reaches of the common, an assassin in the

uniform of a Danelind soldier stood watching with her fellow officers, her own expression unreadable.

The play continued, chronicling Kassandra's run for the safety of Caerockeith and her cousin Terrilynne played by Tamara. At the finale, the Coins, dressed as soldiers, gathered around her. The trumpet sounded again as the Aristok stood, sword raised, prepared for war. As one, the gathered soldiers began to chant her name and Ballentire raised her arms.

"Long live Kassandra the Sixth!"

"ALL HAIL THE ARISTOK!"

The audience's reply was deafening, and the child turned, her arms outstretched, her eyes glowing vibrantly in the torchlight. The power of the Flame seemed to pulse from her fingers, moving out to embrace her subjects. Many fell to the ground in supplication and many more reached their own arms out to her.

Before her, Terrilynne DeMarian felt the pull of the Flame, and she, too, joined those on their knees. Innes Eathan's face was now rapt in awe and when the two looked at each other, they nodded in understanding, as Kassandra the Sixth had meant them to.

There would be war in Branion.

16. The Twelfth Day of Mean Ebril

The next three days were a flurry of activity as the army made ready to move on Yorbourne and their families made ready to follow them as far as Lanborough. Kassandra saw little of the Company, for she now spent most of her time with her cousin Terrilynne, inspecting the preparations and showing herself to the gathering troops as a living symbol of the Throne.

Of those who'd brought her safely to Caerockeith, some would be accompanying her to Yorbourne, others would be joining the Mosswell civilians. Simon was to accompany her as her primary councillor and protector, Rosarion as her representative of the Flame. As a member of the Branbridge Town Watch, Fay would be marching in Kassandra's Personal Guard, as would Atreus. Hamlin was accompanying them because he would not leave Fay's side.

Fay had protested vehemently that he didn't even know how to use a weapon, and he'd replied just as loudly that he could wield an ax as well as any man and had pulled a mean bowstring as a youth. The argument had finally been settled by Kassandra who'd wanted as many of her original protectors by her side as possible. So Hamlin Ewer, Stained-Glass Artisan of Branbridge, was to take his place among her Guard beside his wife who refused to speak to him.

Of the Spinning Coins, most were heading for Lanborough, taking Dani and Luis with them under their protection. Only Warrin Fire-Eater would be traveling with the army as Kassandra's personal bodyguard.

And so the army of the Aristok was prepared to move on Yorbourne.

On the last night, after the final banquet and the last bout of juggling and tumbling, Turi of Moleshil managed to get away and come to Rosarion in Jennet Porter's rooms. They hadn't spent a lot of time together since the Troupe had arrived, for the Duke of Kempston had kept the performers busy diverting her troops from mischief. Now, on the eve of moving out, however, they were left to pack and wait for dawn like everyone else.

Turi reached Jennet's door as the castle bell tolled ten. Waiting for the echoes to die away, he knocked.

Atreus DePaula answered. He smiled shyly at the other man and then stood aside to let him enter. Turi bent to whisper in his ear and the young Knight nodded and withdrew. Turi then went straight to Rosarion, sitting, dozing by the fire.

The tumbler searched his face, noting the lack of color and the feverish gaze, then smiled crookedly at him.

"We're all ready to move out," he said, tucking the blankets more securely about the other man's shoulders.

"So are we."

"Will you be all right to travel?"

Rosarion nodded. "Nan's given me enough herbs to stem the withdrawal. I should be fine in a few days."

Turi gave him a disbelieving look.

"All right, I should be better in a few days."

"Hm."

Settling himself on the floor by Rosarion's feet, Turi leaned against his legs and for a time neither man spoke. Then Rosarion stirred. "Where did Atreus go?"

"Atreus?" The tumbler casually picked up a taper and began poking at the coals with it.

"Yes, Atreus. You said something to him before he left, and he nodded."

Turi smiled. "I didn't think you saw that."

Rosarion shifted uncomfortably. "Was I not supposed to?"

"Are you jealous?"

"Well, no, of course not, I just . . . are you?"

"Should I be?"

"I don't know. It just . . . well, it just happened. You're not mad?"

Turi turned to lay a gentle hand on his arm. "No. I'm good at sharing. Besides, Atreus and I discussed this the first night we arrived. I think he was as worried as you about what I'd think, so relax. We just arranged a little surprise for you, that's all. Atreus has gone to steal a bite of something from the kitchen for a late night picnic, just the three of us. A jug of wine, a warm fire; who knows where it will lead." Turi waggled his eyebrows at the Herbalist who twisted uncomfortably under the blanket.

"Is it hot in here?"

Turi grinned. "Oh, yes."

"That's not what I meant."

"I know."

Shaking his head, Rosarion reached over and ran his hand through the other man's hair. "This is so strange," he murmured. "I haven't felt this way about anyone in so long, and now I have two of you."

"Essus showers his blessings on his favored children."

"Oh, is that the reason?" The Herbalist's tone was sarcastic and Turi laughed. Reaching up, the tumbler caught Rosarion's hand in his and kissed the palm. Then, leaning back against his legs, he picked up the taper once again as they waited for Atreus.

It was some hours before all three men finally succumbed to sleep. As the castle bells tolled four, the shadows about the glowing hearth stirred restlessly. Usually they were content to hover about Simon, weaving in and out of his memories, drawing strength against the ever encroaching darkness. At those times they had a kind of hazy form and identity, but tonight the painter's dreams were nightmarish, and the shadows found access to his thoughts difficult. Cast adrift, they floated on a growing tide of forgetfulness as the Shadow Realm tugged at their sense of self. But the shadows had once been a powerful Avatar and they resisted. They found themselves hovering over another man whose tie to their earthly life was strong.

The Prophetic Realm saturated this man's being, and as they drew nearer, the shadows found themselves entangled in its strands like seaweed on the waves. The Seer's Realm was in turmoil tonight, flowing over and through the Physical Realms. As the shadows absorbed this chaos, they felt swollen with possibilities, snatches of sights, sounds, feelings and smells they no longer had the senses to interpret drowning them in a sea of sensations. They touched the quiescent presence of Essus, floating as they did within the strands of the future, and drew back, confused. Then they returned to hover over the sleeping form of their one-time priest and reached out, as they had in life, for answers. As they made contact with his mind, they remembered who they'd been.

Rosarion awoke with a start. On both sides of him, Atreus and Turi slept on, undisturbed, and the Herbalist stared into the darkness, trying to decipher what had awakened him. The room was dark and quiet, offering no clue. In the hearth the coals glowed faintly, their dying light illuminating only a few inches of ashes beyond the grate. Rosarion stared at them until the coals became dancing red sparks before his eyes, and then the sparks took form.

Within the space of a heartbeat it seemed he was standing before the fire.

The flames were tall, licking against the mantel and throwing a savage heat across his body so that he flinched away. He tried to call out, to turn toward the two men in the bed, but found he was unable to move.

Before him the fire weaved and twisted in a complicated dance. Shadowy tendrils of red mist reached out from its heart, growing and changing. They touched him, entwined about his chest, grew solid, and pulled him close. The room became very quiet, even the sound of the crackling fire growing muted. All he could hear was his heartbeat overloud in the still room, and then he realized with a start that it wasn't *his* heartbeat. The shadows grew suddenly more substantial and he felt warm lips press against his neck.

"Rosarion."

The word was whispered so softly that for a moment he thought he'd imagined it.

"Rosarion."

He tried to turn, but the shadowy arms held him immobile, and he was suddenly reminded of the times he'd convulsed on the herbarium floor while the visions played out before him and Ellisander DeMarian held him securely in his arms.

The pressure suddenly increased. With a great effort, he managed to turn his head, found himself staring into the fiery gaze of Marsellus the Third, and knew suddenly whose presence had touched his mind in the Flame Temple dungeons on that fateful day.

He froze.

The specter seemed to stare beyond him, the orbs red and unfocused. Wisps of flame pooled from its nose and mouth and when it spoke it sent a shaft of heat across his face.

"Rosarion."

The Herbalist began to shake, his overwhelmed senses on the verge of collapse.

The specter did not seem to notice. *"Rosarion,"* it repeated. *"Something's going to happen."*

"Wha . . . What?" he managed to croak.

"Something. Can't you feel it?"

Despite his confusion, Rosarion reached out with his Sight and drew back with a gasp as the room spun out of focus. The Prophetic Realm pressed against his mind and he closed his eyes, willing it away.

A pressure on either side of his head made him open them again as the late Aristok turned him toward the fire. The flames took form slowly, growing solid for an instant before breaking up only to grow solid again. They began to rise, expanding out from the hearth until Rosarion felt he was standing in the midst of a crimson conflagration that blotted out all other sensations. He smelled smoke, heard screaming and the dying shriek of wounded horses, and suddenly the flames opened and he was standing in the middle of a great battle. Mounted knights thundered toward each other, while the whistle of arrows streaking toward the rear was a constant frightening whine above his head. The two groups of riders met, and then a great black warhorse loomed over him, iron-shod hooves lashing at the air. He cried out and flung himself to the ground as its rider drove a barbed lance down toward his head.

The lance buried itself in the breast of a man beside him, and the figure thundered past leaving Rosarion crouched amidst a pile of corpses. He tried to rise and found that the specter of the late Aristok was still holding him tightly about the chest.

"See!" it hissed.

The two armies milled back and forth across a bloody field. Command flags and the banners of Branion's noble families surged forward, fell back, and surged forward again as each side held the advantage for half a heartbeat then withdrew, leaving its wounded on the bloody ground before them.

Rosarion saw his own house banner fall, saw Jordana DeLynne knocked from her horse, and then the air grew chill as a great figure rose above the battlefield.

The Shadow Catcher bent and scooped up a great armful of the dead, their battle-colors leaching away as swiftly as the life in their eyes. It turned its empty sockets on Rosarion and reached out one skeletal hand.

With a cry, the Herbalist turned to bury his head in the breast of the late Aristok, like a child seeking protection from the terrible sight. A steellike chill passed over his back, but the flaming arms of Marsellus the Third held him close and the chill slowly faded away.

Rosarion glanced up and saw the Captain of the Dead move past him to take up another armload of spirits, before turning Its attention elsewhere. Rosarion felt himself grow faint with relief.

"See."

Suddenly realizing what he had turned to for aid, the Herbalist shuddered and made to pull away but the specter only let him turn so that he faced the battle once again.

"See," it repeated.

The smoke and struggling figures moved aside and Rosarion suddenly saw Kassandra on a tall horse, supported by her cousin Alexius. She was dressed for battle in plaide and surcoat, a herald and flagbearer standing beside her. Red-and-white strands of light surged about her face. He saw her eyes grow wide, and turned his own gaze in the direction she looked.

In the center of the battlefield the emotions of the dying and wounded hovered over the combatants like a fog. Slowly they rose, taking the form of a giant, misty snake that wove its blind, ugly head back and forth in a questing motion. As Rosarion watched, it rose, higher and higher, and then suddenly streaked toward the child ruler. Kassandra faced it without fear, and then it touched her.

Energy slammed into her small frame like a thunderbolt, lifting her from the saddle, and as the power of the Flame rose in response, Kassandra lost control of it.

Without thinking, Rosarion threw himself forward, trying to reach out with his mind and suck the harmful energy away from her, but her father's arms held him fast.

"What are you doing?" the Herbalist shouted, twisting so that he stared into the empty eyes of the late Aristok. "Let me go! She needs help!" He struck out at its arms and head, and the specter bared its teeth, snapping them closed an inch from Rosarion's face.

"What will you do!" It hissed.

"Go to her! I'm a Seer Priest, I can channel the emotions away from her!"

"Seer Priest? Heretic and traitor!"

"No! I'm sworn to her! I can help her! Let me go!"

The specter released him so suddenly that he staggered forward and fell, sinking his hands into the bloody, mud-churned ground. Staggering up, he scuttled forward on his hands and knees, clambering over the dead and wounded alike in his haste to reach his Avatar. He threw his mind forward, and trained for such action, it streaked out, taking the form it was most familiar with.

The amphisbane rose above the Aristok's banner.

It twisted into a circle to meet itself, striving to make the bond that gave it strength and then froze, realization almost snapping Rosarion back to himself.

He stretched above the child, above her banner, above the tide of anger and fear, stretched to make the circle, and saw that he was alone. No familiar gaze locked with his, no second head and body and mind reached out to touch his. He was alone.

"He is not here."

Rosarion jerked, as the dead voice of Marsellus the Third whispered in his ear once again.

Rosarion tried to speak, coughed a wad of phlegm and blood out onto the ground and tried again.

"He . . ."

"He is not here. He must be here. I need him. She needs him. Why isn't he here?"

The sounds of the battlefield muted and the figures, mounted and on foot slowly faded away.

"Tell me, Seer, what do you See?" the specter hissed.

"See? I see a battle," Rosarion answered irritably.

"No. You See an amphisbane standing on its tail, speaking the words of prophecy. Below a fiery tree a wyvern sleeps. It climbs the tree, its claws digging deeply into the bark . . ." The ghostly voice became harsh, the fingers digging hard into Rosarion's shoulders. He winced in pain, but remained still as the voice continued.

"The tree explodes! One tiny shoot stabs toward the darkness but is taken over by another.

"Who is the tree, Seer?" The specter clutched him about the chest again in a mock embrace.

The sudden jerk made Rosarion cough. "You," he whispered. "You are."

"And the wyvern?"

"Is Yorbourne."

"Why does the tree explode?"

"Because," the Herbalist swallowed hard against another cough. "Because you are murdered."

"By the wyvern, by Yorbourne?"

"Yes."

"Who is the tiny shoot?"

Rosarion made to speak, but hesitated, unsure.

"Who is the tiny shoot, Seer?"

The Herbalist shook his head. "I don't know. Kassandra, Ellisander. Either one. The symbolism is too vague . . . I don't know."

"Exactly." Its hot breath caressed his neck and Rosarion closed his eyes. *"The symbols are vague because the future is fluid, fragile, capable of change.*

"The Shadow Catcher draws up a great catch of the dead," it continued. *"Whose dead?"*

"Branion dead. Branion soldiers."

"No. You are too far in the future now."

The air around them grew suddenly chill despite the heat from the spectral embrace.

"See."

Rosarion found himself flung back into the Prophetic Realm so fast that he cried out as his Sight spun out of control. The visions came so quickly that he could barely discern one from another. Then they steadied, and the Flame Temple stood before him outlined in a fiery conflagration. Rosarion tried to hide from the intense heat, but could not turn away as Branion's priesthood died once again, burning and choking in a parade of anguish. He might have begun to seizure had the late Aristok not held him so tightly.

"Branion dead," the specter whispered. *"Branion priests. The priests that might have protected her are all gone to the Shadow Realm, and she is alone."*

"No."

The now familiar battle loomed up before him again. Kassandra stood in its center, the Living Flame swirling about her like a whirlwind, each death and each wound streaking from the field, to her, to the ground, like bolts of lightning. And each one took a piece of her with it.

"She cannot stand it," the specter said.

Rosarion shook his head almost violently. "No," he insisted. "She's strong. The Flame has manifested in her more than in the past eight rulers combined."

"This time is different. It's not the Flame, but the battle which fills her. The Flame is out of control and cannot protect her. It will snap her mind."

Rosarion shook his head again, desperately seeking some answer. "Then we have to keep her off the battlefield, keep her away from it all," he tried.

The specter shook its own head. *"Yorbourne will be there. Cannonshire will be there. The muster of the Realm has begun. She must stand as a buttress against chaos before her people or the Realm will suffer."*

"What can I do?"

"Complete the amphisbane that will protect her."

"But Simon completes the amphisbane."

"Where is he?"

"How should I know! He's supposed to be there!"

"Tell me, Seer, what do you See?"

"I can't . . ."

"TELL ME WHAT YOU SEE!"

Slapped by the voice of the late Vessel, Rosarion's Sight shot forward again, this time seeking an answer to Simon's whereabouts. The battle rose up before him and suddenly he saw the painter standing beside Kassandra, the white strands of light about her coming from him. Simon turned toward him, his lips forming a question. He Saw himself nod, saw the red strands which began with him stream out toward the Aristok, and saw himself reach out toward the other man. Their thoughts touched, began to merge together in a red-and-white braid of power, and then suddenly Simon jerked and cried out in pain. The link cracked.

Instinctively Rosarion sent his own strength back and the painter began to rally and then Leary was suddenly between them in the shape of a maddened fire-wolf. He tore at the fragile link, and as it fractured, Simon was flung to the ground, blood spraying the air between them. He died, his hands scrabbling at a wound Rosarion could not see.

The Herbalist twisted to stare into the fiery orbs of the specter.

"He was killed," he said in a horrified whisper. "He was killed, and you . . . you caused it."

The specter hissed and tendrils of red fire spilled out of its nostrils. *"You go too far."*

"But I Saw it! You Saw it! We were building the amphisbane and you attacked us!"

The specter paused as if in thought. *"I cannot let him go to you,"* it said finally. *"Without his memories I will fade into the Shadow Realm. You must break the bond that holds us together, or I will fight the amphisbane and so will he."*

Rosarion stared at it. "But . . . but why?" he stammered. "If you want me to do this . . . why will you fight it?"

The specter's features twisted. *"Simon's memories give me identity. Without him, I have only need. I will not want to give him up, but you must break us apart before he takes that blow, or my daughter is lost and so is the Realm."*

It gestured and the battlefield changed to become a sea of fire.

"But the garden . . ." Rosarion protested. "I saw a green garden."

"The future is fluid, fragile, changeable. It will be lost if you don't win, and you will not win if Simon falls. I'll try and aid you if I can."

"But you just said you'd fight me."

The specter hissed impatiently. *"Your mind is open to me. It seeks my forgiveness. Call on that, and you may break through my need to live, to stay with Simon. Either way, you must win.*

"There is one more thing. Essus is there. Is here. I don't know why. Perhaps to aid us, perhaps not. I don't know. Find out."

"How?"

"Just . . . do it."

The pressure about his chest lessened as the specter's voice grew faint.

"Wait. You spoke of . . . forgiveness."

"Save Simon. Save my daughter . . . maybe then."

The specter faded away and Rosarion found himself sitting up in bed, staring at the rising sun peering over the horizon. Beside him, Turi stirred and made an inquiring noise, but did not awaken. Atreus slept on. Carefully, the Herbalist began to work his way out from between them.

In the south tower Simon had spent a cold night alternately dozing and starting awake to stare at nothing. His dreams had been full of violence and anxiety and had left him with a sense of unease he could not shake. Now as the castle bell greeted the new dawn, he looked up with bloodshot eyes. It was the twelfth day of Mean Ebril, Kassandra's fifth birthday and the day the army was to march on Yorbourne. Groaning, he got stiffly to his feet. Staring down at the scattered supplies, the supplies which had lain there for three days undisturbed, he bent to gather them up and heard the door open. When he saw who it was, his face grew dark.

"What do you want?" he demanded harshly.

Rosarion stood in the doorway, clutching his robe. As the air whistled down the hall, he shivered, but met Simon's glare with an even expression.

"We need to talk," he answered.

"No, we don't."

The Herbalist came forward. "Yes, we do. I have Seen the future. You're in danger."

Simon snorted as he scooped up the pile of sketches one handed. "We're going into battle, Priest," he said scornfully. "We're all in danger."

"Not like this. I Saw you. I Saw you fall."

Simon's face grew concerned for a moment and then the expression of scorn returned.

"So?"

"So? So we have to work together to keep that vision from unfolding."

"Why?"

The Herbalist felt the blood rise to his face, and he took a deep breath.

"Because it's important that you live," he said calmly, each word spoken slowly as if he were addressing a child. "Without you, we cannot help Kassandra."

"We?"

Rosarion closed his eyes, then lowered himself onto the stone bench. This was going to require some explanation and he couldn't do it standing. "In my earliest vision I Saw an amphisbane. That's a . . ."

"I know what an amphisbane is," Simon interrupted coldly.

"Right, well, it represents you and me joined together to protect Kassandra. We need to merge in order to do that."

"She has Terrilynne and an entire army to protect her. Why would she need us?"

"Because Terrilynne won't be able to help her when she faces the dead and dying on the battlefield. She needs *us*.

"The Aristok must remain with the army as a symbol of the Throne, but Kassandra's just a five-year-old child, Simon. How do you think she'll react when she's exposed to all that bloodshed and all that pain. How do you think the Living Flame will react? It will manifest."

"Maybe."

"Not maybe. Definitely. It's so close to the surface already that the slightest pressure brings it to the fore. But this time it will meet a power too potent for it to handle. It will be like the passing of the Flame Priests all over again, only much worse, a thousand times worse. She won't survive it."

"You've Seen this?"

"Yes." Rosarion hesitated then plunged ahead as the cold began to seep through his robe. "Marsellus the Black came to me tonight. He showed me the future. When Kassandra needs us the most, we won't be able to protect her. He'll stop the merge to keep you from leaving him, and at that point you get hit."

"Hit?"

"Wounded somehow. I didn't See how. But Marsellus wants me to break the bond between the two of you, so we can complete the merge."

Simon's face grew hard. "So that's what this is all about," he said grimly. "Why you all keep coming up here. Why you just can't leave me alone. You want to banish Leary again, so you can have what you want, what my parents want, what everyone else wants, and I'm left with nothing all over again."

Rosarion shifted in the cold and pressed his fingers against his lips. After a moment he looked up. "Not nothing, but . . ." he stood. "Not Leary. If you remain linked with him, you'll die."

Simon met his eyes and the sudden crimson shadows in his gaze made Rosarion shiver.

"I don't care."

"But . . ."

"No!" Simon chopped one hand down. "By Essus, how much more do you want from me? I ran with her; I made her safe. I did everything I was supposed to do. I'm empty now, don't you understand? I have nothing left; nothing in my life left to keep going for!"

Rosarion stared at the other man and found himself growing angry. "Nothing." He repeated. "You have nothing; you? The man the very Gods themselves turned to? You have nothing? How dare you."

He stood, his expression bitter. "You have everything."

Simon glared at him. "I can't paint," he grated out, the pain inherent in the words twisting his features.

"Have you tried?"

"*Yes.*"

"And that's all that means anything in your life?"

Simon moved closer and his added three inches made him tower over the slighter Flame Priest. "Yes," he snarled.

Rosarion returned his glare. "Really? Your parents, your son, Kassandra, they mean nothing to you? You have nothing?" He straightened, his eyes flashing dangerously. "Let me tell you about nothing, you self-pitying bastard, so that when it finally does come your way you just might recognize it.

"Four years ago white lung swept through Branbridge. You might remember the outbreak, it took the Consort Kathrine DeMarian. It also took my family, not just one member, all of them, my parents my brothers, my sister. I was given up for dead. At eighteen *I* had nothing, no health, no future, no family. I wanted to die. What else was there for me? But I didn't die. I lived, somehow. And every day since then I've lived and tried to build a life, not knowing if a chill or a cold or a fall would end it all just like that!" He snapped his fingers at the other man. "So don't tell me you have nothing. That's just a lot of self-indulgent crap.

"*She* needs you, and I need you. The amphisbane can't exist on its own. Without us both together, she'll fall, and I won't allow you to let her down."

Simon looked at him, his face expressionless. "And how do you plan to stop me?" he asked.

Rosarion hit him. It wasn't a hard blow, but it snapped the artist's head backward and almost unbalanced the Herbalist himself. Simon threw a hand back against the windowsill, then flung himself at the other man. Rosarion was slammed against the other wall, the breath knocked out of him, Simon's good hand bunched in his robe.

*   *   *

*"An' you'll help Simon an' apologize to him an' let
him be mad at you if he wants.*

The Herbalist made his hands fall to his sides and as
he did, Simon's grip relaxed a fraction. He used the respite to cough his lungs free.

"I'm sorry about your hand," he gasped when he got
his breath back. "Truly sorry. If I could heal it, I would."
When Simon twisted the fabric of his robe tighter, he
winced as it dug into his ribs. "Everyone responsible for
your loss is dead, except for you and for me."

Simon's face darkened. "Me?" He jerked Rosarion
forward. "You think I'm responsible for this?"

"You knew the risks when you went to save Fay," the
Herbalist gasped, struggling to breath around the twisted
fabric. "Don't tell me you didn't; the risk of death, of
torture to give up the child's whereabouts. You went
anyway. You believed it was worth it then. What
happened?"

Simon's face sagged. "I didn't realize the cost would
be so high."

Rosarion dropped his gaze. "I know," he said softly.
"You were prepared to die, but you didn't. Now you
have to find a reason to keep living. You have to find it
because Kassandra needs you."

"What good could I possibly be to her?" Simon asked,
the pain in his voice causing Rosarion to close his eyes.
"How can I protect her with only one good hand?"

"You can stand by her, be with her when she goes to
battle. Simon, she's only five years old."

"I can't."

"You can. You have to. You were chosen."

Simon shoved Rosarion against the wall again. "Chosen," he said bitterly. "When do I get to chose?"

The Herbalist met his eyes. "Now. You can choose to
deny your responsibilities and run away, or you can
choose to face whatever life you have left. I can't tell
you what kind of life it will be; I haven't Seen it, but I
can tell you this, and it comes from the Prophetic Realm
itself. If you don't link with me on the battlefield, we'll
be lost—you, me, Kassandra, maybe the entire Realm.
Now I know you don't care about my future, your fu-

ture, or the Realm's future, but you have to care about Kassandra's. She needs you."

"Stop saying that."

"I can't, it's the only weapon I have."

Simon grimaced and let him go. Turning away, he sank down onto the window seat.

Rosarion watched him quietly.

"I never had any doubts before," Simon said after a long time. "I never doubted my talent, my ambition, my feelings. I knew who I was, what I was and where I fit into the tapestry of the world. Now . . . now I'm not sure of anything. How did my whole life suddenly turn upside down? What happened?"

Rosarion hesitantly straightened his robe. "A little girl decided she wanted to paint trees with you instead of taking her nap."

Simon shook his head. "Was it really that simple?"

"Yes." The Herbalist shivered. Wrapping his arms about him, he hunkered down on the opposite bench. His ribs ached where the specter had gripped him, and his chest felt bruised from Simon's rough handling.

"To put it in your terms, I guess you could say we all paint our own picture of how we want to live," he said, "but we forget that other people are painting their pictures, too, and they often overlap. If my sister Saralynne had never died, maybe Ellisander would never have needed the Throne to fill the empty space in his life. If I hadn't contracted white lung, maybe I wouldn't have needed Ellisander to fill mine. And if Kassandra hadn't come to you that day, you would never have gotten entangled in her story and mine and Ellisander's . . ."

"And Leary's," Simon added.

"And his, but you were already entwined with his, and so with Kassandra's, too, you see. She came to you and you had to help her and it cost you the most important treasure in your life, but it didn't kill you. The painting's not finished yet."

"So I just have to keep going, crippled and grieving?"

"Yes, until you find some purpose that makes it worthwhile. Then maybe you'll stop."

"Did you?" Simon stared at the other man with feverish intensity. "Your purpose led you to treason and betrayal; was it worth it?"

Rosarion shrugged. "Maybe not. But it also led me to redemption and love. That was worth it."

"Hm." Simon stared out the window. "It's getting light," he noted woodenly, changing the subject.

"The twelfth day of Mean Ebril," Rosarion agreed. "The day of decisions."

Simon took a deep breath. "We haven't had much sleep to march to Yorbourne on, not if we're to do some magical-linking nonsense as well."

The Herbalist felt a sudden release of tension that made him dizzy. "You'll do it, then?" he asked.

Simon nodded slowly. "I'll do it. But for Kassandra, not for you, and not now. Later, when it's closer to the time. I don't want to lose Leary any more than he wants to lose me. I hope you realize what kind of a sacrifice you're asking for."

"I realize. I loved a DeMarian, too."

Simon studied the other man's face for a long time and then nodded his head. "Well, we'd better get going. The Aristok's probably up by now, demanding her pony."

After a moment he offered his hand stiffly. Rosarion took it and stood, and the two men left the room and the scattering of materials behind. After a long time, the early morning shadows faded.

In Terrilynne's inner chamber the Aristok Kassandra the Sixth was indeed already up and demanding to see her new pony. Fay barely managed to get her dressed before the child was off flying down the halls, Jael at her heels. The two children met Simon and Rosarion at the main stairs. Kassandra gestured excitedly for them to join them, but did not pause.

Fay stopped to glance searchingly into her son's face. "Are you all right?"

Simon nodded slowly. "I will be." He paused. "Ma."

"Yes?"

"I'm sorry. I didn't mean the . . . those things I said."

Her shoulders sagged slightly with relief. "I know," she answered.

"Come on!" Kassandra's impatient voice echoed up the hall.

Fay smiled. "You go on, Simon; it's you she wants anyway. I'll get Hamlin and follow later." She looked Rosarion up and down. "And you'd better put some clothes on."

Blushing despite himself, Rosarion glanced at Simon. "Shall I . . .?"

The artist nodded.

Rosarion turned back toward Jennet's rooms while Simon moved to follow Jael and Kassandra. Looking from one man to the other, Fay raised one questioning eyebrow, but did not ask.

The two children were already at the stables by the time Simon caught up to them, and there by the main doors, just as she'd been promised, was a dapple gray pony.

With an exclamation of joy, Kassandra raced up and threw her arms around the animal's head.

The pony accepted the greeting placidly.

The Aristok turned. "Oh, Terri, it's lovely! Isn't it lovely, Jael?"

Standing off to one side with Nicholas Orren, the Duke of Kempston smiled. "She meets with your approval, then?"

"Oh, yes! Look Simon! Isn't she the most beautiful pony you ever saw? Doesn't she have the dearest, softest nose?"

The artist came forward, and stroked the pony's nose. "Yes, she does, Sparky."

The child then turned her excited gaze back on her cousin. "What's her name, Terri?"

"Whatever you want it to be."

"Um." The Aristok put her finger in her mouth. "Spotty!"

"But don't you already have a pony named Spotty?"

"Ter . . . ri." Kassandra's voice and expression was impatiently patronizing. "That Spotty isn't real, it's just a toy."

Icarus smirked.

"Oh," the Duke of Kempston said, feigning embarrassment. "Right, of course."

"So this will be Spotty the *real* pony, an' she's the prettiest pony ever," Kassandra added, turning back and stroking the animal's nose.

It nuzzled her, and she laughed.

"She's after a bit of something," Majesty," Icarus said, coming forward.

"A bit of something?"

"You know, a treat like."

"Oh." The child's expression grew suddenly anxious. "But I don't have any treats for her," she said.

"I 'spected you wouldn't yet, so I brung a bit of apple for you to give her, if it weren't too bold of me?"

"Oh, no." Kassandra's face brightened as she accepted the offered fruit.

"Now hold it out like this," the man took her tiny hand in his and laid it flat, the apple on her palm.

The pony leaned forward and plucked the fruit away.

Kassandra stifled a shriek of laughter. "It tickles. She has all these tiny hairs on her nose, Jael, look."

The boy leaned over to examine the animal's mouth.

"Now you oughtn't to get yer faces so close to her teeth," Icarus warned, moving them both carefully away. "She's a gentle one, but there're some that aren't. Best not to get into the habit."

Kassandra moved obediently to one side and put her arms about the pony's neck again, pressing her cheek into the soft side of its muzzle.

"Have you looked after lots of horses, Icarus?" she asked.

"I have, Majesty."

"Then you have to come with me an' take care of Spotty an' show me how."

He nodded. "I look after all the garrison horses," he answered, "an' I'd be proud to teach you how to take care of your'n."

The child smiled and turned to press her nose against the pony's neck.

"She smells nice."

"It's the most precious, most comforting smell in the whole world, Majesty," the Stablemaster agreed.

"Didn't you want to ride her?" her Cousin interrupted.

"What? Oh, yes!"

"Well, then let Icarus saddle her up."

The Aristok waited impatiently while Icarus got Spotty saddled and then allowed her cousin to help her mount. The Stablemaster then led the animal forward as Terrilynne reached up to support the child.

"Do you want to show Spotty to the troops?" she asked.

Kassandra considered it. "All right," she agreed, "but they must be quiet, 'cause she might spook."

"Of course."

Icarus led them from the stable yard, but Kassandra quickly turned around, almost unbalancing herself.

"Simon!"

"I'm here, Sparky."

"I want you to come, too."

"All right."

So, with Terrilynne on one side and Simon on the other, Kassandra the Sixth went out for her first mounted inspection of her troops.

The army made ready to depart soon afterward. With Kassandra at its head, it began to slowly wind its way eastward, past the now empty cottages of Mosswell and the silent lines of mounted Caileins waiting to take over the castle as agreed.

As she passed them, Terrilynne reined up beside Joan and Morag.

"Caerockeith," she said simply.

Joan nodded. "It's good to be back."

Terrilynne turned to Morag. "I'll see you in Yorbourne."

"We'll be there, if only to watch you kill your own people."

"Not my people, Morag, Ellisander's people."

The Heathland woman shrugged. "Whose ever."

It took most of the day to get the army out of Dunleyshire and across the inland ford onto Branion territory. Eddison kept a careful eye on the weather, but it

remained clear and by late afternoon they were all encamped in Northern Lanborough.

This was the last night the Mosswell civilians would
remain with the army and many of the Caerockeith garrison were excused duty to spend one last night together
with their families.

Terrilynne had the Royal tent pitched in the center of
the camp, and set up a ring of perimeter guards, most
drawn from the ranks of Eleanor mac Mairi's troops. As
the Commanders met for the day's reports, Kassandra
professed herself satisfied with Terrilynne's ability to
lead the Council in her absence. She sent for her own
Company and went off to play about the tents, blithely
waving to Terrilynne who asked her to stay within the
ring of perimeter guards. After a moment's quiet conference, Warrin trailed silently behind the young ruler.

Hamlin and Fay went to say their good-byes to Dani,
Luis, and the Coins, while Rosarion sat with Turi and
Atreus by a small creek that ran past the camp. This
would be their last night together and all those involved
sat quietly, not needing to speak, simply taking comfort
from each other's presence.

Simon, who had spent the day walking beside Kassandra, either supporting her on her pony or holding her
hand as she skipped along the road, now headed off past
the first and second ring of guards to find a quiet spot.

Sitting on a rocky outcrop on a nearby hill, he looked
down at the growing campfires mirroring the setting sun.
As the sun began its slow decent to the horizon, the
shadows lengthened.

"Well, Leary," he said to a particularly dark patch of
shadow lying under a juniper shrub, "I brought her to
Terrilynne like you wanted. Now I'm here, ready to push
you out of my life like you wanted. I hope you know
what you're doing."

A breeze rose up, rustling the nearby fauna and causing the shadows to weave back and forth. Far below
Simon saw a tiny bridge stretching over a stream that
sparkled in late sunlight, and he smiled sadly.

"Do you remember the night we stood over the River
Swift, Leary? The night those Bachiem men attacked

us? I wasn't afraid that night, not for you nor for me. We seemed invincible in those days, didn't we?"

High above, a gull called its challenge to another, while the swallows dived and danced in the wind. The surroundings were suddenly so lovely that Simon's hands twitched for a brush and paint. He clenched his left fist.

"I wasn't afraid that night, Leary," he whispered. "But I'm afraid now. Not of the battle to come, but of . . ." He swallowed. "What if it's no good? What if it really is lost forever. I'm not sure I can face losing you both."

A cloud passed over the sun, causing the shadows to merge into the landscape.

"I know what you're thinking," the artist continued. "Maybe I am a coward. Maybe I always was."

The cloud passed, and the sun shone out brightly again, causing his eyes to water painfully. "All right, so maybe I wasn't, but I'd never lost anything worth the risk before and now . . ." he trailed off.

"Now I've lost you, I've lost the painting. What do I have left?"

The shadows gave no answer, simply weaved patiently to and fro. Down below, the wind brought him the sounds of camp; whinnying horses; shouting soldiers; pots and pans banging together as the cooks prepared supper; a child's laughter.

He looked down, imagining that he could see the dozen children playing carelessly about the tents, the great events in motion paling in comparison to the game they were playing. He smiled faintly, understanding a little, comforted a little, and the shadows melted away in the direction of the camp.

Safe in the center of the army, Kassandra the Sixth had tired of hearing stories. She was stiff from her unaccustomed riding and wanted more exciting entertainment. Now, seated on Warrin's lap, she waved regally for Jael to come up with a new game.

Stretched out on the ground at her feet, the boy chewed reflectively on a piece of grass as he thought. Finally he looked up, squinting against the sun.

"You wanna play 'Leave All'?" he asked.

The other children sprawled about them murmured their agreement as their Captain considered it.

"What's Leave All?"

"It's a game."

Kassandra frowned and jabbed the boy with her toe. Jael grinned.

"It's a really old game," he explained. "It's like Hide-and-Seek and like Tag, only different."

The Aristok slid off Warrin's lap, plunking herself down beside him. "Different how?"

"Well, you got a Seeker, a Caller an' Runners, see. The Seeker hides their eyes and counts to ten, an' the rest of us hide. Then that person tried to find us an' say's *Fire an' land give us a call, give us an' answer or nothing at all!* An' then one person, the Caller, the person the rest of us chose, says *Leave All!* real quiet an spooky like. An' the Seeker looks for the Caller an' when they find 'em, they try an' catch 'em and then everyone runs for home."

"An' if the Caller gets caught," Maggie broke in excitedly, "then they both try an' catch the Runners until everyone is caught or everyone's made it home. An then whoever's left hides again, see?"

"An' you keep playing until only one Runner's left an' they win," Jael finished.

"What if there's no Runners left?" Kassandra asked, intrigued.

"Then the Caller wins."

"Oh."

"We usually make Alex the first Caller," Ross said. "On account of him being the fastest runner."

"What about you? You can't run real fast, don't you always get caught right off?"

Ross gave her a secret smile. "Runnin's not all of it," he replied. "There's hidin' an' sneakin', too."

Jael nodded. "Ross's won a few times. So has Aggie an' Bella. They use *strategy*."

The two littlest Company members grinned smugly.

"What do you use?" Kassandra asked, turning to Jael. He shrugged carelessly. "Runnin' an' dodgin'."

"Oh. I expect I should have to use *strategy*, too, like sending someone runnin' in front of me to *distract* 'em."

"That would be *strategy*," Jael agreed.

Kassandra nodded, her decision made. "We will play Leave All," she pronounced. "Warrin?" She turned to the big man.

"Yeah, Sparky?'

"You must stay here, because you are too big to play, so you must watch, but not always where I'm at or you'll give away where I hide."

"Oh, um, all right, I won't, but you won't go too far outta sight, will you?"

"No. I promised Terri that we wouldn't go past the main tents."

"We'll make the Royal Standard home, how 'bout," Jael offered. "No one goes too far from home, anyway."

Kassandra nodded her satisfaction. "That oughtta be so," she answered, " 'cause where the Standard is at is the heart of Branion. My Papa told me that."

"That's 'cause where the Standard is at, the Aristok is at," Kate added.

"Whatever," Jael said impatiently. "So!" He clapped his hands together. "We need a Seeker."

"You." Kassandra pointed at him.

"All right. I'll stand by the Standard pole an' close my eyes an' the rest of you choose a Caller an' run an' hide."

The Company all leaped to their feet, huddling into a tight circle as Jael turned his back on them.

"We'll make Davin the Caller," Arron whispered. "He's got the best voice. Maggie, you take the Capt'n an' show her how to play. That all right with you, Capt'n?"

The Aristok nodded as the company straightened.

"We've got our Caller, Jael," Arron shouted. "Go!"

The children scattered as the Seeker began to count.

Maggie took Kassandra's hand in hers and carefully tiptoed past him, while the Aristok tried not to giggle. When they were about three tents away she turned.

"Watch."

The two girls peered around the tent side as Jael shouted, "Ten!" and spun quickly around.

* * *

"Fire an' land give us a call, give us an' answer or nothing at all!"

Kassandra rubbed at her eyes as the bright sun made them water and continued to look at Jael. Around her the shadows stirred.

"Leave all!"

Davin's voice floated over to them, and Jael began to move cautiously away from the Standard pole, turning every now and then to check behind him.

"Now what?" Kassandra asked breathlessly.

"Now we wait. We have a good position here, so when the running starts, we should make it to the pole."

"Maggie, I'm kinda hot."

The older girl turned and laid her hand on the other child's forehead. "Your head's kinda warm. Maybe you overdid it ridin' today. Do you wanna sit out?"

"No." Kassandra sat and pulled off her little boots, wiggling her toes in the sudden breeze. "That's better."

Minutes later they heard Jael's triumphant shout, "Found!"

"Come on!" Maggie rose, and the two girls began sprinting toward the pole as the Company exploded from behind every piece of cover.

Jael missed Davin on that round, but he did catch Kate. Kassandra sent Warrin to retrieve her boots.

The next round Jael and Kate stood by the pole and Marri was the Caller. That round caught Ross and Aggie.

As the Company gathered about the pole again, Kassandra bounced excitedly up and down, unable to stand still.

Willie touched her on the shoulder. "How about you be the Caller this time?" he asked.

Almost out of breath, she nodded.

Jael began the count and they scattered.

Off to one side, Innes Eathan bowed to the setting sun as she began her meditation before the evening mass. Beside her, the Archpriest of Radnydd did the same. Both priests felt tense and nervous, and Innes frowned as she found herself unable to slip into the necessary state of serenity needed to commune with the Living Flame.

She glanced over at the other woman.

"Maybe her proximity," Hywellynne offered, sensing her thoughts.

"You, too?"

She nodded.

"Nine. Ten!" Jael spun around, taking his first look around the surroundings. The other Seekers followed his lead.

Beside Maggie, just past before the farthest tent, behind a great rock, Kassandra snickered. Wiping her face, she sat down and began to tug at her leggings until she had struggled out of them. She then pulled off her little belt and the ribbon in her hair. Dressed now only in her father's tunic which fell loose about her calves, she stretched up in the air, enjoying the cool freedom of the movement. She was still too hot, but at least she didn't feel all tied up by clothes.

In the Royal tent, Terrilynne paused to listen to something that had sounded just beyond her hearing, then rubbed irritably at her eyes.

"Is it getting dark in here?"

Alexius nodded and called for more light as Terrilynne bent, squinting over her map of Yorbourne. Exchanging uneasy glances, her Commanders followed suit.

By the stream, Rosarion paused in the act of getting a drink, staring into the water at the sun's reflection. Turi and Atreus exchanged a puzzled glance.

From his vantage point, Simon stood as a chill worked its way up his spine.

High above, the gull wheeled silently. The swallows had disappeared.

Jael pushed each of his fellow Seekers toward a different direction. They spread out cautiously as he raised his hands to his mouth, ready to give the call.

*   *   *

The breeze dropped as a thin cloud covered the sun. The whole camp seemed suddenly silent as if poised for some dramatic event.

"Fire an' land give us a call, give us an' answer or nothing at all!"

Simon frowned and began to move quickly down the hill. Rosarion stood, his Sight suddenly wide open, seeking the identity of the power that had awakened it. In the Royal tent, the four DeMarians grew still as if in a trance.

Maggie touched Kassandra on the shoulder and the child raised her head.

"Leave all."

The words were softly spoken, just loud enough for Jael to barely hear them, but they seemed to be taken up into the air to swirl around their heads. All about the camp, people stirred uneasily and stood.

Jael moved forward.

"Fire an' land give us a call, give us an' answer or nothing at all!'

Kassandra raised her voice. "Leave all!"

The Seekers came forward.

On the edge of the tents, Simon stared as a thin wisp of almost invisible flames began to weave their way toward the sky behind a large rock.

The two senior Flame Priests also saw it and moved slowly forward, their eyes wide.

Standing, talking to Edrud DeLlewellynne, Jennet Porter grew distant and turned toward the Royal Standard.

Rosarion waved a hand in front of his face to try and clear his vision of the red mist that suddenly covered it. He would have fallen if the others hadn't caught him.

* * *

The Seekers began the hunt and once again Jael called out.

"Fire an' land give us a call, give us an' answer or nothing at all!"

Her hair now literally standing on end as the electricity crackled through the air, Kassandra clambered on top of the rock. Maggie made an inquiring noise, but the young Aristok shook her head. Before her the sun was sinking, casting a reddish haze over the whole camp. Energy seemed to spread through her, and she felt much like she had that morning in Turi's wagon and later facing Terrilynne and Innes Eathan in Caerockeith, only now it felt under control; under her control. Only five years old, she nonetheless had still determined that the feeling came from contact with the Living Flame. She wasn't afraid. She had been the first time because she hadn't known what it was, but now the feeling was as familiar as her father's arms about her had been. Besides, *She* was the Vessel. It was supposed to come to her and do what she said, like everyone else. Standing on tiptoe, she let it fill her totally.

Unnoticed, Simon moved up beside her, his face wondering. Kassandra looked at him and smiled, then touched his arm. A shock, like a bolt of lightning ran through him and, just for an instant, he knew what it was to be born to the legacy of the Living Flame. He knew the power and the obligation of carrying the heart of the Realm in his breast and knew that he would do whatever necessary to keep its newest Vessel from harm.

Before them the flames grew brighter and Kassandra turned. If she squinted, she could just make out a shadowy figure standing in the center of the sun. It nodded its fiery head as she opened her mouth to speak.

"LEAVE ALL!"

The words rose into the air like a flock of birds, echoing across the landscape and, all around, people began to move from their guard positions, from their campfires and tents, converging on their young Vessel.

"LEAVE ALL!"

Her eyes aflame, Kassandra looked across at the gathered people and smiled, holding her arms out to encompass them all. As one, most of them knelt before her.

Innes Eathan pushed forward, her expression confused. "So many times," she breathed, her voice falling flat in the charged air. "Has there ever been a time since Braniana herself that the Flame has shown itself to us so often?"

"But why does It manifest now," Hywellynne asked, her voice hushed.

"I don't know."

Beside them, her own eyes glowing red from the Living Flame's proximity, Terrilynne DeMarian was also wondering.

Jade Asher, called to the rock with the rest, looked down to see her son pressed against her leg. "What happened, Jael?"

The boy shrugged, afraid to speak in the sudden crowd of adults.

Aggie let Eddison lift her into his arms as she looked over at them all, her face innocent. "We were playing Leave all, Jade."

"Leave all?"

"You know, the game."

"And Braniana went into the hills and wrestled with the Living Flame, and they became one."

The crowd turned to see Rosarion as he came forward, supported by Turi and Atreus.

"And when she emerged from the mountains of Gwyneth, the people saw that she had been changed, and they gave the ancient summons, *Flame of the Land give us a call, give us an' answer or nothing at all!*"

"Flame of the Land," Jade whispered. "Fire and Land."

"And Braniana answered, *Leave all you are doing and follow me,*" Rosarion finished.

"Leave all," Simon whispered.

The Herbalist nodded.

Jennet Porter glanced from the child standing patiently, one hand on Simon's shoulder, to the setting sun in the distance. "She is truly a strong Vessel. The Realm is blessed.

"Your Grace?" She touched Innes Eathan on the arm.

The other woman started.

"The sun is going down. The faithful are gathered. Time for mass." She smiled.

Innes gazed about dazedly and then suddenly returned the smile. "So it is. And the Vessel of the Living Flame called the people together, and told them all that had transpired."

"And the people of the Land and the Living Flame made a pact that day that has lasted throughout the centuries," Rosarion continued.

"That the Flame should stand by them in need, protect them from danger, and grant them peace and prosperity." Hywellynne smiled as she spoke the ancient words.

"An' that the people should come together to worship the Living Flame and Its consecrated Vessel." Kate's piping voice finished the litany, and Jennet smiled down at her.

"The Living Flame has called, and the faithful have gathered."

"Then we should worship."

Moving to stand before her Avatar, Innes Eathan, Priest of the Flame, bowed low, then moving to the child's left, she raised her arms and began the High Mass.

As the familiar words wrapped about them, Kassandra watched the fiery figure in the sun slowly disappear and then leaned against Simon contentedly. Whatever Papa had wanted, he'd got, and Simon seemed happier, too. That was enough for her.

The artist also watched the figure slowly melt away, not knowing what it foretold, but, placing his good hand against his breast, he felt the faintest tingle of his contact with Leary. He was still there. With a relieved sigh, he put his arm about Kassandra's shoulders.

17. Battle

The army reached the borders of Yorbourne four days later. They'd passed quickly through Lanborough and Dunmouth, picking up added troops and supplies and so, as the sun set on the sixteenth day of Mean Ebril, a force of just over one thousand mounted knights and foot soldiers bivouacked on Ellisander DeMarian's lands.

Terrilynne's scouts reported no alarm had yet been raised, so they moved out before dawn the next day, cutting a swift path through the countryside.

Word came that the Caileins and Taggens had crossed the Gildarock hills and were moving south, stopping only to round up cattle and horses to be sent back to Heathland. They'd met and defeated a smaller force under the command of Lieutenant Johann Chandler at the border, but reported no losses. Whether because this was so or because they didn't wish to admit any casualties to their Kempston allies was unclear, but it hardly mattered. Terrilynne sent word that they should continue south with all possible speed toward Yorbourne Town.

The Duke's vanguard was moving slowly, hampered by the rain that had fallen for the last two days. They'd had met with little or no resistance—most of Yorbourne's people fleeing at their approach—but as they came to within fifteen miles of the county capital itself, Terrilynne's scouts reported troops gathering at a stone bridge five miles north of the walled city. The Duke sent out extra scouts to assess the enemy position while the army waited in the rain.

The word came back quickly.

*　　*　　*

"They have a force of about five hundred, Captain," Fionn Griffith reported, stripping off his sodden gauntlets.

"Archers?"

"About half."

"Position?"

Fionn bent over the map of Yorbourne. "Here," he laid down one damp finger. "They're drawn up in formation across the main road, between these two wooded areas, infantry and a few mounted troops entrenched in the center, archers at the flanks."

Albion peered over his sister's shoulder.

"They must have been expecting us to give battle yesterday," he observed.

Terrilynne pushed him aside impatiently. "The rain slowed us down. Did you see any standards, Fionn?"

"Yes, Captain: Pennineshire, Berford, Cannonshire, and Yorbourne."

"Commanded by who?"

"The Duke's standard is being raised by Manderus Greydove, his Steward; but he's not in command of the army, the Earl of Pennineshire is. Berford's second son Theolynn commands her troops, I believe, but I don't know who the Hierarchpriest has sent, probably a Senior Flame Champion or a Sword Knight. Also there's a force from Danelind under the Royal Banner."

Those gathered around the command table murmured uneasily, but Terrilynne showed her teeth. "How many are there?"

"About fifty, Captain."

"It's a token. If there are any more, they've probably been rerouted to the capital."

"Or to Kempston," Alexius muttered.

"I think I also saw the banner of Seth Cannon, Captain," Fionn continued.

"Seth?" Innes frowned and Terrilynne turned to her. "Can you contact him, Your Grace?"

The priest shook her head. "Not mentally, My Lord. It takes very special circumstances to manage that, but I could send a messenger to summon him. His vows as a Priest of the Flame supersede any political or secular obligations he may have."

"Would he come?"

Innes drew herself up. "I am his superior, My Lord," she said in an indignant tone of voice. "He'd better come."

"Good, send your messenger." The Duke turned to the others gathered around her. "We march immediately. It's two hours to noon now. If we hurry, we can deal with Greydove's troops today and be at Yorbourne Town itself by tomorrow."

"What about the Danelind troops, Terri?" Eleanor asked. "Will they fight those who carry the banner of their Sovereign?"

The Duke shrugged. "My force is made up of mercenaries; they fight for pay, my pay, but I have other plans for them anyway. Now," she turned. "We move out."

They sighted the opposing force three hours later, formed up, as reported, across the main road to Yorbourne Town. Terrilynne set most of her own people about a thousand yards away, infantry in front, mounted troops behind and archers to the flanks. The Duke herself sat in the center of the third line with Eleanor mac Mairi. The Aristok Kassandra was beside them, mounted before her cousin Alexius, with Simon and Rosarion just behind. Spotty was waiting at the back with Icarus Haven. Captain Storjen and his three hundred mercenaries were drawn up in reserve to the rear of her lines with specific orders of their own.

Terrilynne gave the signal, and the Royal Standard was unfurled and raised into the air. The red-and-gold fire-wolf above the three golden oak leaf clusters flashed in the sunlight. There was an immediate stir among the Yorbourne lines.

The two groups had a good, long look at each other, then a young Cailein man was brought to the Duke of Kempston. They had a short conversation; he nodded and withdrew, and Terrilynne summoned Eaglelynne to deliver the first diplomatic volley to their enemies. *Welcome the legitimate army of the Aristok and escort them to Yorbourne Town, or be named traitor with their Lord.*

The Herald rode out and was admitted into the lines

of the enemy. A few minutes later they saw her riding back.

"They say they've word from Yorbourne and Cannonshire that we're holding the Aristok against her will, Captain. They've orders to demand we relinquish her into their care and surrender ourselves to their army or be taken by force."

Eleanor snorted and Terrilynne smiled grimly.

Kassandra looked over. "What does that mean, Terri?" she asked.

"That they've been told to fight us," the Duke answered.

"So are we gonna fight?"

"We are, My Liege. Amanda?"

The Earl of Guilcove opened her visor. "Yes, Captain?"

"Move your people forward seven hundred yards."

"At once, Captain!"

The Earl turned and called the advance.

All across the lines, the call went up and slowly the center of the army lurched forward. Behind them, the Danelind mercenaries melted away.

The Yorbourne troops tensed, the archers readying their bows.

When the Aristok's army got to within three hundred yards, extreme arrow range, they paused.

"Why aren't they charging?" Kassandra asked.

"They will, My Liege. Right now we're just playing a waiting game."

"Waiting for what?"

"For their soldiers to realize how outnumbered they are, Majesty," Alexius explained.

"That, and for our other troops to move into position," Terrilynne added.

"What other troops?"

"The Danelinds and the Caileins. You see, there's more to winning a battle than just charging, My Liege."

"I know, there's *strategy*."

Terrilynne shot the young Aristok a half-astonished, half-impressed look. "That's right. Who taught you about strategy?"

"Jael."

"Figures."

"Captain, there's movement on their flanks," the Earl of Radnydd called out.

"I see it."

The main bulk of the Aristok's army watched as the Yorbourne archers raised their bows and let off a defiant volley into the sky. The steel-tipped projectiles whistled through the air, most to fall short.

"Sound the attack."

Terrilynne's trumpeter blew one long note into the air and the Earl of Guilcove's troops charged.

They closed the gap swiftly. The Yorbourne archers got off several more volleys, many now reaching their targets, but it barely caused a ripple in the advancing troops. At one hundred yards the center of the Yorbourne line charged forward to meet them, and soon it was hand-to-hand fighting on the field, infantry against infantry.

Terrilynne now sent the Earl of Radnydd's troops running toward the flanking archers; these cast aside their bows to act as light infantry as their own people came to defend them.

They fought this way for a good hour, with both sides withdrawing, reforming, and charging again. It was clear neither side had the advantage. Then the Earl of Pennineshire went down, his banner falling beside him. The Yorbourne troops paused, wavered, and might have broken had their standard not been snatched from its bearer by a young woman who raised the rampant firewolf and wyvern high above them, shouting for them to stand fast.

The Yorbourne troops rallied and came at the Kempston infantry with renewed vigor. They pushed them back a hundred yards, and Terrilynne called for her third line to prepare to move forward. Once again the two sides met with a crash.

Then a column of thick, black smoke rose in the sky behind the Yorbourne lines. One by one the local troops turned to look.

"The bridge!" someone shouted. "They're burning the bridge!"

The cry was taken up. "They're behind us! Mercenaries and Essusiates! We're cut off!"

The Yorbourne lines began to waver. Terrilynne gave the signal for her mounted knights to charge. They reached the enemy within minutes, and the Yorbourne line started to come apart. The woman holding the banner of Yorbourne stood defiant, still calling on her people to hold. She was cut down by Eddison Croft, and the Yorbourne lines broke and ran.

Terrilynne's troops pursued them into the bulk of the opposing army. It disintegrated, troops scattering in all directions and very quickly it was over. Kempston was in possession of the field.

Throughout the fighting, Kassandra had sat composed before Alexius, quietly absorbing the action. Behind her, Rosarion had been alert to every shift and surge of the Living Flame, but it lay still, as poised and quiet as its young Vessel.

Simon glanced curiously at him, but the Herbalist shook his head and, after a moment the artist swung his attention away with a frown.

Meanwhile, Terrilynne rode forward with her commanders.

The Earls of Guilcove and Radnydd had taken a few dozen prisoners, including Manderus Greydove and the Earl of Berford's son. The woman who had rallied the troops was still alive, though grievously wounded. The Duke of Kempston gave orders that she was to be treated with all respect and left her in the care of Nan Guilcove. Seth Cannon was not to be found.

Of the Aristok's troops there were a few dead and several more wounded, but not as many as Terrilynne had feared. They were loaded onto the wagons which trundled after the army as the rest moved on toward Yorbourne Town.

They met up with the Danelinds and Caileins who'd caused such havoc behind the opposing lines. Captain Uthaugh saluted with a smoke-blackened grin, and even Morag looked grimly pleased. As well as burning the main bridge, they'd attacked the nearby village, sending the inhabitants scattering into the woods, ransacking the

few homes, and setting them on fire. It was the smoke
from the burning cottages that had risen over the trees
rather than that of the bridge. When the hostilities had
ceased, they'd allowed those inhabitants left to begin
putting out the fires.

Morag now accepted the Duke of Kempston's thanks
with an ironic salute, and her people melted away. The
Danelinders rejoined the main force as Terrilynne sent
scouts off looking for a ford to cross the Grass River
and the army encamped for the night. Tomorrow they
would march on Yorbourne Town itself, its leaders prisoners of the Aristok and the Duke of Kempston.

It took most of the day to get the army over the ford
five miles west of the bridge. They then swung back
toward the road and reached Yorbourne Town in the
late afternoon.

The gates were closed.

Terrilynne bivouacked the army before the main entrance, just out of arrow shot and Nathaniel DeKathrine
and Innes Eathan began the negotiations. It took several
hours of undignified shouting back and forth and the
parading of the prisoners before the City Mayor sent a
delegation down for a quieter conference. They were
brought before the Duke of Kempston who promised
them protection and a peaceful occupation. With most
of their military leaders either dead or taken, the city
elders capitulated.

Making the best of a bad situation, the townsfolk
cheered as the Aristok entered their city, riding her dapple grey pony and escorted by her army. The captured
nobility were made to swear their allegiance to Kassandra the Sixth and her Regent, the Duke of Kempston,
and by dusk it was over. Yorbourne had been taken
much more quickly than its Duke had hoped.

Three days after the Aristok had taken possession of
Ellisander DeMarian's city, the Royal Duke received the
news from Seth Cannon. Yorbourne had fallen, Brandius
DePaula, the Earl of Pennineshire was dead, as was the
Hierarchpriest's Flame Champion Captain Collin De-
Lynne. Theolynn DeYvonne and Manderus Greydove

were prisoners, and Arnet Chandler, the messenger who'd sworn that Yorbourne would fight for their Duke no matter what the odds, had done just that and now lay, a wounded prisoner of the Duke of Kempston, not expected to live.

A Privy Council was swiftly convened. The doors were locked, and Senior Flame Champions lined the walls as the highest nobles in the land shared what each of them had learned of the battle and its aftermath.

Shannon DeYvonne, the Earl of Berford, was the first to rise. "My son has managed to send word that Kempston had over a thousand troops from her Dukedom and from Albion DeMarian's," she said, reading from the sheaf of missives in her hand, "as well as troops from northern Dunmouth."

"That will be Nathaniel DeKathrine," Lysanda said quietly to Ellisander. He nodded. "Seth has confirmed these numbers," he agreed.

"As well as family companies of Caileins and Taggens from Heathland. He also reports that the Duke has large forces of mercenaries from Danelind, Sorlandy and Eireon; the latter commanded by the youngest Royal Prince."

"Mairi's playing it fast and loose with our treaty terms," the Duke of Lochsbridge noted grimly.

Ellisander made a conciliatory gesture. "She's simply being cautious, Eve. In civil war—as this conflict most obviously has become—it is most politically expedient to back either both combatants or neither of them."

"If it had been neither, the odds might have been less overwhelmingly on Kempston's side," Evelynne muttered.

The Duke of Yorbourne gave an eloquent shrug. "Perhaps not. Terrilynne is a seasoned General, poor Manderus was outmatched. Had I not been ill . . ." he paused, then passed one hand swiftly over his face as the gathered murmured their sympathies. "But no matter," he said, straightening. "That is the past. We must look forward to the future. My people fought bravely, knowing that they were outnumbered, but understanding that their sacrifice was of the utmost necessity. They will be honored when the time comes. Until then it has at least shown us what Terrilynne is about. She will drive

through the country, taking what towns she may until
she reaches the capital if we do not bring her to battle
farther north."

"That would be preferred," the Hierarchpriest noted.
"Battle on or near Branbridge would only serve to de-
stabilize the Realm further. It is time to rally the north."

"I agree." The Duke of Yorbourne sat back, sipping
from his glass as the others about the table nodded
their concurrence.

"I've sent troops to Kempston itself," Gawaina offered. "Soon she'll be cut off from further reserve
troops, but as Your Lordship has made clear, the Duke
of Kempston will not abide long in Yorbourne, but will
push on regardless of her numbers, likely through . . ."
She gestured for a map, and a junior Knight of the
Sword came forward and spread one out before them.

The bright colors of Branion gave them pause for a
moment, each noble staring down at the boldly drawn
political boundaries, each one searching for his or her
own demesne of power and for its position relative to
the future conflicts.

"She will likely move south through Sidbury and Samlinshire, then . . ." The Hierarchpriest squinted at the
map with a frown, ". . . swing west around the Kenneth
through Austinshire and down across the northern tip
of Lochsbridge, to Werrickshire and finally Branshire
and the capital."

Ellisander stirred. "I suggest we make our stand in
Lochsbridge, with your agreement, cousin," he added,
inclining his head toward Evelynne. "This is, after all, a
DeMarian conflict. The Lords of Sidbury, Austinshire,
and Werrickshire should not be asked to bear the brunt
of it."

Evelynne's expression suggested that she wondered
why Lochsbridge should be asked to bear it either, but
she said nothing. She hadn't become Admiral of the
First Fleet by ignoring the political power of others, especially that of her cousin Ellisander.

Meanwhile, Camerus DeSandra, the young Earl of
Austinshire, stood, his pale features flushed. "My Lord,
you mustn't think Austinshire is unwilling to do its duty.
If Kempston comes to us, we'll fight her." He banged

his fist on the table. "And I'm sure that if Sidbury and Werrickshire's Lords were here, they'd say the same," he added generously.

Ellisander gave him a solemn nod as the others about the table tried not to smile. Evelynne simply rolled her eyes.

"Thank you, Cam," the Duke of Yorbourne replied. "I did not intend for you to believe I held your loyalty in question."

"Nor do any here, My Lord. Please sit down, Cam." Gawaina added with a grimace of impatience. The Earl of Austinshire took his seat again with an embarrassed air as she continued. "But My Lord of Yorbourne is most correct in his choice. The land in northern Lochsbridge is hilly. We could be in place long before Kempston arrives, entrenched in a good position with such strength as might give her pause."

"Exactly," Ellisander agreed. "We will concentrate all our loyal forces in that place. Terrilynne will not stay long where she's not given battle—battle is her goal—so she'll come with all speed when she learns we're gathered in Lochsbridge." He glanced over at the Earl of Austinshire who was sitting back, his arms crossed, a peevish expression on his face. "Don't worry, Cam," he said with an indulgent smile. "Austinshire will not be forgotten. We'll set you in front for the first charge."

The Earl's countenance brightened immediately. "Thank you, My Lord."

Ellisander smiled graciously. The Duke of Lochsbridge just shook her head.

Terrilynne did come up fast. News of an attack against her southern holding reached her in Samlinshire, but as the Hierarchpriest had predicted, it did not split her forces. She simply sent word for her Stewards to hold fast within their strongholds and wait. Their fate would be decided in Lochsbridge by the summer's end.

Samlinshire did not stand in their way, but neither did they flock to Terrilynne's banner. The rearguard fought several inconclusive skirmishes in Austinshire with the Earl's troops harassing the larger army and generally slowing it down, but causing little actual damage. Terrilynne sent the Caileins east and a force of Danelinders west to wreak havoc on one or two towns in retaliation, but the bulk of her forces pressed on.

They reached the border of Lochsbridge on the second day of Mean Mehefin. It was a beautiful morning, the sun sparkling off the nearby river and the warm breeze rippling through the fields. The Aristok's army paused on the crest of a small valley, and the Duke of Kempston sent out her scouts. They returned quickly with news of an enemy force only ten miles distant. Terrilynne called the advance, and the army moved on, pausing on a rise where they could overlook the opposing force. More scouts were sent out, reports to be brought before the Command Council as soon as they returned.

Within the hour a steady stream of soldiers came and went, each adding more information about the force arrayed against them.

Fionn Griffin was the first to report.

"They have maybe three thousand troops, My Lords, drawn up beside the River Mouse; five hundred heavy horse under the banners of the militant orders and twice that of light infantry, flanked by archer support."

Sasha Lamb supported this count.

"All the noble families save DeCarla are present, My Lords, as well as the militant orders of Sword, Bow, and Lance. However, I saw the temple banners of only three priests including the Hierarchpriest."

And then Eleanor mac Mairi's scout chief.

"The Captains of the Orders are in command of four main blocks of troops, My Lords, archers on each side. All have one Flame Priest within their ranks, but none of name. They must be there for morale rather than for battle. Seth Cannon's banner was seen in the main as was that of Wendall DeYvonne, the new Captain of the Flame Champions and a Yorbourne supporter. He has some fifty mounted troops of that order, but they seem to be concentrated in the center with the commanders."

By the time the last scout had finished her report, they had a detailed idea of the enemy position and strength and who were involved. It would indeed be a DeMarian conflict, with Kempston, Wakefield, Lanborough, and

Cresswick taking the field against Yorbourne, Lochsbridge, Clarfield, and Wiltshire.

Kassandra's Ducal holdings of Briery and Kraburn had obviously been torn. Unsure of which Regent to send troops in aid of, they'd split their forces equally, sending a force of about one hundred light infantry under Jonathan Ryan to Kempston and an equal number to Yorbourne. Of the noble holdings of Branion: Dunmouth, Humbershire, Guilcove, Snowdon, Dorsley, and Wiltham supported Kempston while Berford, Austinshire, and Cambury, Pennineshire, Sommersdowne and Surbrook supported Yorbourne. The rest had remained at home to await the results. Gwyneth had also remained neutral as had the Branion holdings on the continent. Heathland, as was pointed out by Sean Cailein, had sided with Kempston. In all, a force of fifteen hundred would meet one twice that many.

Terrilynne dismissed her scouts and turned to the seasoned veterans in her Command Council.

"Any ideas?"

Eleanor mac Mairi spoke first.

"Well, charging right into them won't do much good. They have strong flanking archer support and a defensible position from which to repel us."

"We can't go around them either," Amanda added. "They're right across the main road. It's heavily wooded to the east, and the river's to the west."

"Our only option seems to be to make them come out from their entrenchments," Kalidon said simply.

"How?" Alexius asked him.

"We caused a distraction to the rear in Yorbourne. Can we do it again?"

Terrilynne shook her head. "We were fighting hastily mustered militia that time. We're facing Triarchy Knights and soldiers led by their own Lords now. No. I think our only option is to hit them head on, whatever losses we may take to arrow fire on the way."

Innes Eathan pursed her lips in disapproval. "Maybe not, My Lord."

Terrilynne glanced at her. "What did you have in mind, Your Grace?"

"Diplomacy, My Lord. Send myself and Hywellynne

under a flag of truce to discuss other options. I'm sure we can come to some kind of understanding that would avoid the spilling of Branion blood."

Terrilynne's supporters around the table began to murmur angrily, but the idea was negated from an unexpected quarter.

"No."

The gathered turned surprised looks on their Aristok.

Up until this time, Kassandra DeMarian had been sitting quietly at the head of the table, playing with her toy horse and kicking her feet idly in the air. Rosarion and Simon, seated behind her, would not have believed she'd been paying attention at all, but now she raised her flame-covered gaze to Innes Eathan's face.

"No," she repeated firmly.

The Flame Priest was somewhat taken aback. "Most Holy . . ." she began in a patronizing voice but the child gestured her to silence with a sharp wave of her tiny hand.

"Nobody's gonna talk wif Uncle Sandi. He can come here and say he's sorry to me, or Terri's gonna go get him wif the army, but we're not gonna 'gotiate."

"But, Most Holy, why?"

" 'Cause there's a plot against the Throne!"

The few nobles who'd been members of Marsellus the Third's Privy Council those many days ago felt a superstitious tingle run up their spines.

Kassandra stood up in her chair. "When my Papa said that, he wanted everyone that was part of it thrown out of Branion!"

"Yes, but His Late Majesty was speaking about foreign Essusiates, Most Holy."

"I don't care. My Papa didn't never 'gotiate wif traitors, an' I'm not gonna either. We can give 'em one chance to say they're sorry an' then we'll make 'em!"

She glared fiercely at the Flame Priest, and Terrilynne suppressed a chuckle. She straightened.

"The mandate of the Aristok," she said formally, "is to fight unless the opposing force dismantles and surrenders its leadership to us immediately."

Kassandra gave her a regal nod and returned to her seat.

"Now," the Duke of Kempston continued, pointedly ignoring Innes Eathan's angry sputter, "as was mentioned, with the river to one side and woods to the other, our only choice is to charge straight up the middle, regardless of how suicidal a tactic that may be. Triarchy Knights don't like to hide behind breastworks, we should be able to taunt them out into the open. But first we need to work on their morale, make it plain that they fight, not me, but the rightful Aristok of Branion and the Vessel of the Living Flame. For that, I want the Aristok's Standard as close to the front as possible, along with as many nobles as personal guard as may be fitting. I want banners, colors, gleaming armor, drums and pipes, the works, and our Flame Priests obvious beside her. By the time we charge, I want every soldier in Yorbourne's army to know their actions are treasonable."

"Where do you want my people," Captain Uthaugh asked.

"We'll line up the troops from each Triarctic Realm against each other on the flanks."

There was more murmuring around the table.

"Do you think that's wise, My Lord Duke?" Eleanor asked.

"I do, Your Highness. I want the enemy looking out across that field at their own people on the side of the Aristok."

"What about us?" Morag Cailein asked.

"I'd like you to form up in reserve if you would, Captain, ready to give support to whatever flank requires it. This will be predominantly a battle of nerves. Whatever way it falls, I'll likely need you to be there quickly."

The Cailein Leader nodded.

And so it was decided. The army would camp here, in sight of the enemy tonight, and would move into position at first light tomorrow. The council broke up, talking quietly among themselves, sorting out the smaller details.

Kassandra went under heavy guard to Amanda De-Kathrine's tent. This close to the final battle, Terrilynne did not want to take any chances with a possible kidnapping. The Garrison of Caerockeith ringed the inner perimeter and Warrin sat beside her bed, a heavy ax resting on his lap, determined to remain awake all night. Her own protectors shared the tent with them and as the night grew deep, most fell into a restless sleep.

As the moon rose over the Duke of Kempston's army, Kassandra DeMarian sat up in bed, her stuffed horse tucked securely under her arm. Her Papa had told her about war, and her experiences on the journey home to Branbridge had supported his words. Where there were battles, people died. She had felt the spirits of the dead from Yorbourne to Lochsbridge touch the Living Flame within her before melting away to the Shadow Realm and knew that the next day's battle would bring even more dead than before. She was not afraid. She was the Aristok, but a lot of the people she loved would be in the fighting tomorrow, so she passed her crimson gaze over the indistinct shape of each sleeping adult in the tent, trying to pass a little protective fire their way. It was dark, but the Living Flame, warm and bright within her, illuminated their forms with a faint red glow that only she could see.

Head tipped to one side, she watched the rise and fall of Hamlin's chest, hearing the dark rumbling of his snoring. The artisan was big and gentle and old, not at all like her Papa, but he was Simon's Papa, so she had come to think of him as a kind of grandfather. Now and then Fay would shift irritably and give him a sleepy shove and his snoring would cut off only to begin a few minutes later. The young Aristok smiled in the darkness, knowing that Fay would keep him out of danger.

To Kassandra's mind, Fay was like Gawaina DeKathrine, a fiercely loyal and powerful woman, too strong to be given the unremembered comparison to a mother, but loving enough to trusted and loved in return. The child hoped she would not be too reckless tomorrow.

Beside Fay and Hamlin, Rosarion and Atreus made one indistinct shape under their blanket. Misty tendrils of red wrapped about the Herbalist, stretching toward her and she moved her fingers through the strands, making patterns in their midst and feeling the faint touch of warmth as they touched the Living Flame. They were hers plain and simple, and with the single-mindedness of children she did not worry about their fate. If they lived they would serve her, and if they died they would wait to serve her in the Shadow Realm.

Her gaze then moved on to Warrin's comforting, ever watchful bulk. Warrin was like a mountain—huge, sturdy, and indestructible. She would not worry about him either, but beyond the tumbler, curled up in a tight ball beside her cot, lay Simon of Florenz, her Papa's dearest friend and her first defender and protector.

Even in the darkness Kassandra could see the air of fragility that surrounded him, as if the slightest touch would lay him down again, but woven about him was the shadowy presence of Marsellus the Third and a misty white fog that enveloped them both like a cocoon. The child frowned, unsure of what this meant. Her mind, heightened by the Living Flame, reached out and touched an alien, primodial presence alike yet different from the one she carried.

The Living Flame met the power of Essus, and they brushed against each other in the gentlest of caresses before drawing back. It was not yet time for them to join forces, and the child nodded, understanding the unspoken words. She yawned then, suddenly sleepy, and snuggled down into her blankets, her cheek pillowed against her toy horse and her fears about the coming day allayed.

By dawn the next morning the two armies were lined up across the road, facing each other at a distance of a thousand yards.

Terrilynne DeMarian had taken great care with the array of her own forces. The early morning sun glinted off as many polished breastplates and colorful crests as she could muster, most drawn up in the center of her heavy calvary to mirror the troops before them. The Aristok Kassandra the Sixth, dressed once again in her father's tunic and the Royal plaide Jael's grandparents had made her, sat before Alexius on her big roan. Flanked once again by Rosarion and Simon, she was also surrounded by the nobility of the Realm, DeMarians to the fore. Her ever-present bodyguard, Warrin Fire-Eater stood behind her, his ax in his hands, the strips of vibrant paints turning him once more into a titan from Triarctic legend. The rest of her personal guard fanned out around the gathered Commanders.

The Eireon troops stood to the left in the position of honor, as they did for the opposing force beyond. Eleanor mac Mairi had her banner cheerfully waved at her older brother, Ferdiad, and he responded in kind.

As Kempston's people deployed, there was a stir among the waiting troops, near the banners of Yorbourne and Cannonshire, but it wasn't until Terrilynne had the rampant fire-wolf and tyger of Kempston and the Royal fire-wolf and three golden oak leaf clusters of the Aristok raised that the stir became a buzz. Finally a group broke free from the main body and came toward them.

Beside the Duke, Eaglelynne leaned forward.

"It's a party of Heralds, My Lord; Yorbourne, Cannonshire, Branion and . . . Ptarmiganna?"

The others about Kempston stirred. "The Head of the Heraldic College?" Gladys asked.

"She's very old," Kassandra piped up.

"That she is," Terrilynne agreed. "Well, Eaglelynne, we'd better hear them out."

"My Lord."

Terrilynne's Herald made her way through the mounted knights and escorted the small group back in.

Ptarmiganna was a tall, straight-backed woman, despite her advanced years. She had once been the personal Herald of Atreus the Third himself and still carried the authority that legendary Aristok had bestowed upon her although she'd retired from active service twenty years ago. She'd been the Head of the Heraldic College for over a decade, and had presided over the training of every Herald present. Her hair beneath its dark blue cap was a smooth, milky white, as were her eyes beneath. A lifetime in the saddle had given her almost uncanny control of her mount despite her blindness, although she still allowed an apprentice to lead her.

The Aristok sat up very straight. "My Lord Herald," she said succinctly and the old woman started.

"My Most Regal and Sacred Majesty," she answered. "You are well, I hope?"

"Oh, yes."

"I am most relieved to hear so. You have been long away, and the Realm has been in turmoil."

"I know, but I am back now."

"We carry many messages to be heard, Your Majesty. Will you hear them?"

"Yes, but you can tell Cousin Terri. She's my Regent now."

"Truly, Your Majesty? There are many yonder who wonder at the legality of such an appointment."

Kassandra's eyes flashed. "I don't care about that. They'll do what I say or I'll make 'em. You can tell 'em that from me."

"Yes, Your Majesty." The most senior Herald, her expression smooth, now turned her sightless gaze in the direction of Ploverian, the Hierarchpriest's personal Herald. He advanced and was greeted by the Duke of Kempston.

"The Hierarchpriest of Cannonshire welcomes Her Most Regal and Sacred Majesty Kassandra the Sixth back to her Court," he said formally, "and expresses great feelings of relief that Her Majesty is unhurt. My Lord asks that Her Majesty return to her capital to be minority crowned and take her place at the head of the Realm. To that end, I come with messages to the Duke of Kempston from the Hierarchpriest of Cannonshire. Her Lordship demands that you deliver up the Aristok Kassandra the Sixth into her keeping and throw down your arms, placing yourself and your troops under her authority, and that you dismiss those troops brought with you from other Realms within the Triarchy. I am to give assurances that all will be treated with respect until such investigations as are necessary are completed. I am also to demand that the abductors of the Aristok, Simon of Florenz, his family, and Rosarion DeLynne be given up to Captain Lavigne of the Sword Knights at once and that Shield Captain the Earl of Wiltham come immediately to My Lord of Cannonshire for an accounting of the actions of her company gone astray from their errand.

Beside Jordana, Kalidon shifted his weight, but the Earl gave no other sign of having heard.

"I also bear an order from the Nominal Archpriest of the Flame, Roselynne DePaula, to Her Grace Innes Eathan that she too return with us, and to the troops of the Triarctic Alliance and their leaders, reminding them of their ecclesiastical oaths, and demanding that they withdraw at once to their own lands. The Hierarchpriest warns all citizens of Branion gathered here not to shed the blood of their own in this way, for only destability and destruction can ever come of such civil conflict and that the Realm is already vulnerable to its enemies which are, even now, amassing on the Continent and to the north."

The gathered Commanders began talking among themselves, but Terrilynne kept her attention on Ploverian.

"Is that the whole of your messages, My Lord Herald?" she asked politely.

"It is, My Lord."

"They are many. I shall begin my response at the end. First, know that I have already made alliance with the north and their strongest border family stands with the Aristok. As for the Continent, when we're finished here, I shall bring my troops to bear upon that threat and perhaps send those already under arms to deal with it. I expect there'll be enough left standing to be adequate for the task.

"As for the leaders of Sorlandy and Danelind, they are under contract to the Aristok and fight for her. Eireon, too, has already made its vows to the Vessel of the Living Flame and fights righteously under her banner.

"In regards to those whose presence is requested, I will not release them to the Hierarchpriest as I have need of them, and I will not dismiss my troops for I have need of them also.

"And now I have some demands of my own. As Named Regent to Her Most Regal and Sacred Majesty, Kassandra the Sixth, I demand that the Hierarchpriest of Cannonshire herself dismiss those troops gathered here in aggressive defiance of the Aristok's wishes and that she place Ellisander, Duke of Yorbourne, under arrest and deliver him up to my Lieutenant, for he is accused of regicide by the Aristok herself. At such time as this is done, the Aristok will take the oaths of those nobles gathered here and shall journey to Branbridge with her army as escort." She finished, and Ploverian bowed.

"I shall say so, My Lord."

Terrilynne now looked toward the other two Heralds. "Those with you, have they messages of their own to impart?"

"They have, My Lord."

At Ploverian's gesture, Marsellus the Third's personal Herald now came forward.

The Herald Ospreyan was a middle-aged man with the seasoned look of a veteran soldier. He'd joined the Herald's College late in life after a career of fighting on the Continent and had stood for both Kassandra's father and Kathrine the Fifth before him. Now he bowed before the new Aristok who greeted him formally.

"Most Regal and Sacred Majesty," he answered. "I come to offer my services as Herald until such time as my office is filled with one of Your Majesty's own choosing. Please forgive the lateness of my arrival as affairs of protocol have kept me overdue."

Kassandra accepted his excuses and his services with a regal nod of her head.

"You can come an' stand by me," she said.

Ospreyan moved away from the Heraldic group and took his position behind her.

The last to speak was Wrenassandra, the personal Herald of the Duke of Yorbourne. She turned to the Duke of Kempston and bowed stiffly.

"My message is to the Duke of Kempston also," she said after Terrilynne indicated she should speak. "My Lord, the Duke of Yorbourne challenges you to single combat to end this conflict at once without the spilling of Branion blood."

There was silence across the center of the army, while on the outer edges of hearing the message began to spread out in whispers.

Terrilynne raised an ironic eyebrow, but considered the offer.

Alarmed, Rosarion bent to whisper in Kassandra's ear. The Aristok straightened.

"No."

All eyes turned to her.

"I will not allow it."

Rosarion whispered something else and the Herald's eyes narrowed.

"Uncle Sandi is a traitor," Kassandra said loudly for as many to hear as possible. "An' he's not to get outta this by dying nobly."

There was a faint titter which was swiftly quelled.

Terrilynne smiled mirthlessly. "My Lord Herald, you may tell my cousin Yorbourne that the Aristok forbids me to take justice into my own hands, else I would gladly send him into the Shadow Realm. However, since he desires a lack of bloodshed, he may deliver himself up for Her Majesty's justice. I give him assurance that he will be treated with all respect and fairness until such judgment may be passed, and offer pardon to all troops amassed against the Aristok this day if they will throw down their arms and withdraw the field and their leaders swear their loyalty to the Aristok and her Named Regent."

Wrenassandra bowed. "I will deliver up your message, My Lord."

She turned her mount, and the group of Heralds returned across the field.

Kassandra turned to Terrilynne. "Now what?"

"Now we give them a chance to hear all that, My Liege."

It was some time before the Heralds moved to the rear, and the Hierarchpriest's forces began to maneuver under the blowing of trumpets and the waving of battle flags.

"I guess this won't be settled peacefully," Terrilynne noted.

Her Commanders nodded their agreement.

"What are they doing?" Kassandra asked.

"Looks like they're moving their light infantry forward," Alexius answered. "Do you think they're going to charge, Terri?"

"Maybe."

"It's stupid," Jordana DeLynne spat in disgust. "They have the defensible position. If they had any brains, they'd stay where they are."

The Duke of Kempston adjusted the strap on her breastplate and shrugged. "Like I said, those are Triarchy Knights, their commanders, anyway, and they don't like to hide behind breastworks. They like to get it over with."

"I'm a Triarchy Knight, and I wouldn't charge, My Lord."

"You're a Shield Knight. Your tradition is one of defense."

Kalidon DeKathrine laughed. "And besides, Jo, Triarchy Knights don't like to *think* either, you know that."

"*I'm* a Triarchy Knight, Kal," the Duke reminded him mildly.

"Present company excepted, of course," he responded, refusing to be contrite.

"Hm." Terrilynne frowned, her attention drawn back to the advancing troops. "Their leaders don't want to give them time to consider what they're doing. They're going to rely on numbers alone." She accepted her helmet and slipped it on. "It's as I expected, a simple slugfest. It does have a certain romantic appeal," she added.

"Shall we wait and amass arrow fire as they approach, Captain?" Eddison asked.

"No. Have your troops assembled for a charge. The rest of you stand ready. If Ellisander wants a slugfest, I think he should have one."

Her Commanders looked unsure, but obediently moved off to join their units.

"DeMarians don't like to think either," Kalidon whispered to Jordana who just sighed.

Terrilynne shot him a look, but did not chastise him for his words. Instead she turned to Eddison again. "Send for Edrud DeLlewellynne."

"Captain."

The big man, dressed for battle in the light green-and-white surcoat of the DeLlewellynnes, rode up a few minutes later and saluted. He carried a large unlit torch and his squire, his niece Gwendolynne, carried the ancient Royal Gryphon Standard of Gwyneth. Terrilynne motioned, and her standard bearer added the Aristok's banner above it.

"Give us a light, will you, Kal?" Terrilynne asked.

The Knight looked down, past his heavy plate mail, and armored war horse to the ground some distance away, but obeyed with a grunt. With Holly's help he got awkwardly off his mount and pulled out his tinderbox and knelt. After a moment's work, he got a small fire going.

"It's an ancient Gwynethian custom, My Liege," Terrilynne said in answer to Kassandra's curious glance. "Used long before Braniana's time. The throwing of the torch symbolizes the challenge of those sworn to the Living Flame."

Kalidon held the torch to the fire, and when it was lit, returned it to Edrud, then had Holly help him back into the saddle. Terrilynne showed her teeth at him before returning her attention to the field. He gave her a grudgingly admiring smile in return.

Holding the torch aloft, Edrud saluted the Aristok, then turned his mount and maneuvered it to the front of the army. He froze a moment, the torch held high for all to see, and then began to canter toward the opposing troops, his squire behind with the banners of Gwyneth and the Aristok. When he was well within arrow shot, Edrud stood in the saddle and flung the torch toward them.

It sailed through the air to land in a shower of sparks. "Charge."

The flag was lowered, a trumpet sounded, and Eddison's light infantry began to run. The light troops of Cannonshire came out to meet them.

In the center of Gawaina's second line, Ellisander DeMarian sat beside the Hierarchpriest, watching the proceedings with a carefully constructed air of dignity.

He'd listened impassively to the Heralds' words, giving no sign of concern. Kempston's reply and her demands had been no surprise. He'd known that his offer of single combat would probably not be accepted, but had been willing to carry it out if it had been. It had been a calculated risk, made more for show than anything else. His hands twitching inside his metal gauntlets, he examined the preceding feeling dispassionately. Disappointment. He'd been looking forward to killing Terrilynne with his own hands. Ah, well. She would die one way or another. He'd planned for this since before they'd left Branbridge.

He'd subtly suggested that the Hierarchpriest of Cannonshire instead of himself should lead their combined troops to Lochsbridge. On the surface to avoid the conflict becoming one of simply Yorbourne against Kempston; as Regent for Marsellus the Black in his minority and before that for his sister, Kathrine the Fifth, Gawaina DeKathrine was a good, nonpartisan choice. Mostly, however, it freed Ellisander himself from the responsibility of commanding the army. He had other things to do.

Resisting the urge to glance about him for the faces of those loyal to his cause, he allowed himself a small smile. His people were in place and knew what to do, just as he did.

Returning his attention to his gathered enemies, the fire in his eyes glowing hotly. They would all die, every last one who stood against him: Kempston, Wakefield, Lanborough, Dunmouth, Innes Eathan, and Jordana DeLynne, even the Aristok herself. They all had to die for his plan to succeed. And they would die. His people were in place and they knew what to do.

Out on the field, the two centers met with a crash. There was no strategy or finesse in it, both sides merely smashing at each other, trying to force the other to retreat. As the first casualties began to fall, Kassandra DeMarian shivered. Alexius looked down with a frown, and beside her Rosarion tensed.

On the left, the forces of Captain Uthaugh of Danelind hit the light troops of his Royal master and those of Surbrook and Sommersdowne, driving them back toward the entrenchments. They looked as if they might break, but through the sheer will of his counterpart Commander, the Duc Lief Alexsen, the latter held fast, and the advancement halted.

In the center, Eddison Croft's Kempston troops hit those of Cambury and Berford but met a serious check. His Sergeant, Nicholas Orren went down, and then the Lieutenant himself was knocked to the ground by a burly Cambury man. The center bowed back toward the Aristok's lines, and then Captain Gerry Pearson of Dunmouth came to Eddison's aid and the line stiffened. The Kempston Lieutenant rose, bloody and furious, to lead the attack once more.

On the right the Sorlandy mercenaries smashed against those of Berford and Austinshire. They'd met on opposite sides the year before in the fighting in Fenland and the ground was quickly littered with casualties as both sides fought a heated grudge match.

The two forces fell back, regrouped, and charged again, each line pushing the battle first one way and then the other. Finally, seeing no advantage in continual infantry attacks, Terrilynne called for her heavy cavalry and her light troops began their withdrawal. The Cannonshire troops used the respite to catch their breath and call their own cavalry to the fore.

The flag was raised over the ranks of the Aristok's army, and two heavily armored companies trotted out into the open.

The left was commanded by Albion DeMarian, the right by his cousin Zavier. Each had over two hundred armored knights strung out across the field. They carried their shields with their individual and militant crests embossed on the metal and as they stood to order, Albion raised himself in his saddle and began the undulating DeMarian war cry. Zavier took it up and for one long moment the two disharmonious Royal voices caused a chill to climb up the spines of all who heard them. Then Nathaniel and Kalidon DeKathrine added their own family's cry. One by one the nobles gathered in the Aristok's name sent their voices to join those of the Royal Knights, their combined howl almost deafening.

Against this force now came the mounted troops of the militant orders of Sword, Bow, and Lance under their individual Captains. They moved silently into position for they served as Triarchy Knights in this capacity and not as individual families.

The two groups stood frozen for a long time, and then a trumpet sounded, and the militant orders charged. They were met by the forces of Kempston and soon battle was joined by Lords sworn to the same oaths but now on opposite sides.

The morning wore on with both still equally matched. Early in the fray, Camerus DeSandra went down and then Sword Knight Captain Lance Lavigne. Nathaniel DeKathrine took a solid blow to the head from Lysanda DeSandra and fell to be trampled by those around him. By the time Albion DeMarian reached his lover, the Viscount of Dunmouth was dead. His face grim, Albion turned his mount and set it against Lysanda. She managed to avoid him, and soon they were both mixed back into the greater conflict.

On the left, her closer tie to the Flame giving her the advantage, Evelynne DeMarian threw her troops against those of her cousin Zavier. She dispatched Nerielle De-Paula with casual ease, and then turned on her comrade, Serus DeYvonne. The Lance Knight barely escaped her notice with a broken sword arm before she found herself face-to-face with Zavier himself.

The two cousins had never liked each other, and the opportunity to do battle made them both grin mirthlessly. Driving his charger between the DeMarian Duke and Serus DeYvonne, Zavier raised his sword as his mount lunged toward hers. Soon the two DeMarians were locked in a grim individual contest.

All this time the sky had become increasingly cloudy. Now a patter of rain began to fall, and Alexius pulled her cloak about Kassandra. The child was flushed, leaning heavily against her cousin, her little face damp.

Off to the right of the main body, Morag Cailein sat with her people beside the larger body of Danelind mercenaries. Content to earn her pay without actually risking life and limb, she watched the fighting with interest. She rarely had the luxury of observing Branion battle tactics from the sidelines and wanted to absorb as much as possible. The more she knew about them, the better she could fight them in the future.

Out of the corner of her eye she saw a tiny flash of light. Shaking her head, she concentrated on the fighting before her. Then she saw it again. Turning, the Cailein Captain stared intently into the woods some two hundred yards to her left.

Hidden among the early summer leaves, Lieutenant Tomlyn Martin of the Flame Champions readied his archers. Sent by Roselynne DePaula, Nominal Archpriest of the Flame and follower of Ellisander DeMarian, they were only twelve, but twelve was all they needed to be, for they were Seers as well as archers. They'd been set in place the night before, and covered from discovery by the junior Seer Priest in their midst, they waited for the right opportunity. Their orders were simple. To take out the leadership of the opposing force. Tomlyn's orders were even simpler and he gave them no thought as he waited. He owed Ellisander DeMarian his life. The Duke had taken him from the prisons of Fenland, had brought him to Branion, and aided him in his advancement. He had never asked anything in return. Until now. Tomlyn Martin would not fail him. Squinting through the leaves, he glanced idly at the child Aristok not five hundred yards away, no distance at all for a Seer Archer.

Morag Cailein shook her head and returned her gaze to the battle.

To her right an assassin in the Danelind Fourth Company also glanced toward the trees, a worm of unease beginning to twist in her stomach. She didn't like the look of the woods. It was too dark. It made her feel restless and exposed. Unhooking her crossbow, she began to maneuver herself toward the far left of the mercenaries' lines.

Meanwhile the battle raged unabated. As the waiting troops became restless, Terrilynne gave the signal and the second line of heavy cavalry followed the first. From

the opposing lines, reinforcements came out to meet
them as the original combatants slowly disengaged.

Throughout the battle, Kassandra had been growing
more and more flushed. Alexius gave her some water,
but it didn't seem to help. The young squire glanced
fearfully over at her Lord, but Terrilynne was busy di-
recting the movement of the cavalry and did not notice
her. Alexius wrapped her arms about the child, and
held on.

When Zavier DeMarian finally fell to his cousin Evelynne, Kassandra jerked, and the air about her began to
grow hazy. Now that a tiny pathway had been forged,
the hate and fear of the battlefield began to move
toward its small conduit.

With his drug-saturated sight, Rosarion could also see
it weave toward them, taking the form of the great snake
of his vision. He turned and caught Simon's eyes. The
painter swallowed, nodded, and Rosarion reached out
his Gift toward the other man.

With his inner sight already attuned to the Prophetic
Realm, he was not surprised to see the amphisbane rise
up. He felt it settle over him like a second skin and he
stared out from its eyes as the two squat heads arched
up over Kassandra, the one red, the other white. The
creature's other half turned to face him, and Simon's
eyes looked out at him as they had so long ago in his
very first vision. Rosarion reached out, spreading the
power of his mind like a great shield over the child.
Simon's own personal strength, still there despite his injuries to mind and body, added a tinge of refracted rain-
bows which glittered as the emotions of the battlefield
pressed against the shield and were pushed back before
the power of the Flame Priest and the Painter Knight.
Before them, the child relaxed visibly. Simon nudged his
mount slightly forward.

The link was made, but unable to watch for the blow
he knew was coming, Rosarion almost lost contact as, in
the next instant the artist jerked backward. Pain shot
across the link, and Rosarion gave an involuntary cry as
the power of the battle slapped against his mind. Suddenly bereft, he struggled to gain a hold over it and

reached out for Simon's mind again. Forcing his head to turn and his eyes to focus, he saw the artist fall, an arrow protruding from his chest. The shock of what that meant engulfed his control and the vision went spinning away as the battle rushed over him. He never noticed the arrow that caught him in the fleshy part of the thigh. He fell.

Around them a hail of missiles began to find their marks. Terrilynne took one in the arm, Alexius had another score across her neck. All the commanders about them suddenly found themselves targets and either sat gaping, or fell.

Warrin Fire-Eater was one of the first to recover. Without thinking he ran the few feet to the Aristok's mount and swept the two DeMarians from the saddle as another arrow thudded into the squire's backplate. The three of them hit the ground, the child covered by the tumbler's body.

On the left, Morag Cailein saw the movement and suddenly knew what it foretold. There were Seers in the trees. She hated Seers. Spinning about, she scanned the crowd of Branions for the Aristok, but the child was no longer in view. Cursing, Morag called her people to order and led them charging across the field.

Anne had also seen the movement. She'd been watching the woods intensely and now she raised her crossbow and fired.

A body fell from an inner tree, and then her sight was blocked by a band of screaming Heaths. She turned, and saw the confusion in the Branion ranks and began to fight her way free of her fellow mercenaries. Beside her, her two youthful comrades saw her go and struggled to follow her.

In the center of the army, Rosarion crawled toward the artist. He stretched out his hand and the sudden contact steadied his vision. Calling Simon's name, he poured strength through their link and was blocked by a blood-covered fire-wolf that rose up before his mind's eye. Leary.

Growling madly, the fire-wolf lunged toward the priest, knocking him away from Simon and breaking the contact of their minds. As a fresh gout of blood pulsed from the artist's chest, Leary and Rosarion faced each other on the new battleground of the Prophetic Realm.

On the field Jordana DeLynne traded blows with the Lance Knight Captain. Both connected, both fell, their spirits adding force to the flow of energy that rushed toward the child. Albion, too, took a blow that sent him flying from the saddle.

In Warrin's arms Kassandra began to shake, her small body too young to hold the rush of fear and hatred that battered against her. This was not like any contact she'd had before with the Living Flame; this was a suffocating ocean of thoughts and memories and feelings. She held on for as long as she could and then went hurtling off on the rush of energy. On the ground, she fell into seizure as Alexius' blood darkened her bright hair.

Rosarion felt the Aristok flung away and cried out to Simon, but the Artist was insensible, his spirit prone between the limbs of the raging fire-wolf. It howled its challenge at the heretical priest, snapping and snarling as he tried to reach the painter. All Rosarion could do was keep calling Simon's name.

On the field, the forces of Terrilynne DeMarian began to falter and were inexorably driven back as they were suddenly bereft of leaders. Then Eleanor mac Mairi's horn sounded and the Eireons entered the fray. The Kempston side hardened and pushed forward.

On the left flank of Cannonshire's army, Prince Ferdiad mac Mairi watched his sister charge the field. His commanders turned questioning faces in his direction, but he shook his head.

"We wait."

Pages were soon sent scuttling toward them from the main body. They reached the center of the Eireon ranks, but did not return.

Meanwhile, Anne had reached the Aristok's battle flag and quickly took stock of the situation. Nobles lay scattered on the ground tended by their banner carriers and what squires had been able to reach them from the back. Before her the unconscious form of the Aristok was being rocked by a large man, while another DeMarian, hair as bright as the child's, lay white-faced and bleeding beside them.

Turning she saw the two Danelind youths come running up behind her. She made a grab for the young physician.

"Sus, see to that girl. Bill, take this and cover us!" She thrust her crossbow into the youth's hands. "If you see any movement from the trees, fire at it."

Bill glanced in the direction she indicated. At five hundred yards, he'd be lucky to hit the woods rather than the mass of Heathland pony riders who'd just reached the line of trees, but he said nothing, simply raised the weapon, his hands steady, and waited.

Meanwhile, Anne turned to Simon of Florenz.

The painter had changed since she'd seen him last, his face was haggard and gray and his hand was bandaged and secured to his chest. An arrow protruded about an inch away, blood oozing out around the shaft.

She dealt with that first. Raising him up, she supported his limp weight and stuffed a handful of his cloak around the missile, then tied it firm with a strip of leather from her crossbow quiver. Then she patted him on the cheek.

"C'mon, Brother," she breathed. "C'mon, wake up, wake up."

Half in the Shadow Realm, Simon blinked and looked up. Above him the fire-wolf growled. He felt the heat from its body and winced.

"Leary," he whispered.

The fire-wolf looked down at him.

"Simon!"

The painter glanced over and saw Rosarion lying prone before him, one outstretched hand held pinned by the fire-wolf's front foot.

"Simon, the child! We have to help Kassandra!"

"Sparky?"

Far in the swirling race of colors and sounds and feelings, he heard her cry out.

"Sparky!"

He reached out, and the fire-wolf snapped its teeth at him.

"Leary, don't! She needs us!"

The fire-wolf just growled and continued to press them both down.

"Leary!"

The fire-wolf turned and, eyes mad, lunged for Simon's throat.

It was then that a blinding white light flashed before them like a bolt of lightning. It caught up Rosarion in a blast of power and flung him at the fire-wolf. He grappled it about the chest, and as they fell, they were all swept up in a whirlwind of memories.

"You protect him, you hear? Keep him out of trouble. A dozen cracked skulls and broken furniture with no one to pay for them; or worse, Leary lying knifed in some alley or brothel room would end your prospects in Branion pretty quick."

Simon and the fire-wolf flinched away from the memory, but it bore down on them relentlessly.

"Art transcends religion."

"You're a flaming disrespectful bastard, you know that? Aren't you afraid of anything at all?"
"Mediocrity."
"Liar."

"This is marvelous, Simon. I don't want the night to ever end."

"Like flames reflected in blood. How could you ever mix such a color? You couldn't, not truly. You could only experience it firsthand, and always be in danger of burning or drowning in it."

Slowly the fire-wolf relaxed its grip from the weight of the shared memories. Beside them Rosarion lay still, hushed into silence.

* * *

"They mean I'm immortal, all encompassing Flame and I can't lose."
"What?"
"Anything at all."

"Leary," Simon whispered, but the wolf shook its fiery head.

"I'm afraid that woman was right, the Aristok's been murdered. I'm so sorry, Son."

"Leary."

"The Temple dungeons. Nothing to recommend them unless you like the sound of screaming."
"Does that happen often?"
"Oh, yes. The Seer Priests can just reach in and . . . but torture softens 'em up, especially if the prisoner's Essusiate."

Simon began to shake and the fire-wolf looked down, the expression in its flaming eyes pained.

"Leary?"
"I'm here."
"It hurts, I can't use it. Help me, Leary, it hurts. Make it stop. Make it stop!"
"I will, Simon."
"Leary! Where are you? It's dark. It's . . . hot. I can't feel you. I'm so hot. I can't see you! Don't go, Leary! Please don't go."

The fire-wolf twisted, became a man with flaming red hair and grieving features. He fell to his knees and gathered Simon up as the white light grew brighter and brighter.

"Don't leave me, Simon."
"Leary?"
"Simon. It's dark, I need you. Don't leave me."

Simon looked up into his friend's pain-filled eyes. He reached up and cupped his cheek with his good hand.

"I won't leave you," the artist whispered. "I promised I wouldn't leave you."

Rosarion found his voice. "Simon . . ."

"Is it likely to tip us in the scorching drink?"

All three of them jerked as a new voice entered the swirling mists.

"Simon? Why did Papa go?"

The artist looked up. "Sparky?"

"Why did Papa go?"

Drawn to the voice, Leary also raised his head as tendrils of crimson mist began to weave toward them.

"You know your mother believes that after this life is finished we rejoin past loved ones in the bosom of Essus."

"Maybe Leary will always be with you in your art."

Simon raised his good hand and stared at it as Hamlin's voice echoed through the red-and-white fog.

"What if it's no good? What if it really is lost forever. I'm not sure I can face that."

"I'll keep her safe, Leary, I swear to you."

Taking his friend's face in his good hand, Simon raised it up. "Leary," he said gently. "I have to help your daughter. I promised you that I would keep her safe. But I won't leave you either. I have an idea. You'll have to trust me. Can you do that?"

The specter stared into his friend's eyes, then very slowly turned and looked at Rosarion.

The Herbalist nodded.

All those on the battlefield suddenly saw a bright shaft of shifting red-and-white light arch over the center of Terrilynne's line. It rose in the shape of a great amphisbane which stretched its two scaly necks out to cover the Aristok once again. Slowly sense returned to the child's face, and she struggled to rise past the arms of her protector. As she stood, the Eireon horn was sounded again.

Eleanor mac Mairi's troops charged unimpeded onto the field; on the left, the Heaths made the trees and swarmed up to engage the Seer Archers and the remainder of Kempston's heavy cavalry rallied and broke the center of Cannonshire's front line with a determined assault. Terrilynne's banner carrier galloped onto the field, waving the Aristok's standard, and suddenly it was all over. Cannonshire's mounted troops disengaged, the light troops and archers threw down their arms. The army of Kassandra the Sixth stood in command of the field, the twinned power of Essus and the Living Flame arching over it like a giant rainbow.

The Regents' War of 737 DR was over.

18. Simon of Branbridge

Ellisander DeMarian stood staring out across the field, his expression coldly indifferent. He had seen the arch of power grow over Terrilynne's lines, seen her forces gain strength from it while his own had stopped, struck dumb in their tracks. He'd known at once what it foretold, and several plans of action had come and gone in the space of a heartbeat. He could have slipped away in the confusion of the final moments and made for the Continent as his ancestor Drusus DeMarian had done when Atreus the Third had overrun the country, but Ellisander was not the running sort. He could have fallen on his own sword, but he was not the romantic sort either. Finally he had simply sat stiffly beside the Hierarchpriest as Kempston's Commanders had approached and demanded their surrender. After a long moment, Gawaina DeKathrine had thrown her sword down on the ground in disgust. Ellisander had ignored them.

They'd not attempted to wrestle his weapon from him, just flanked him with guards and waited for their Lord. When Terrilynne DeMarian finally rode over, one arm bandaged and lashed to her chest, Ellisander had smiled coldly at her.

"Pity I didn't manage kill you, at least," he said.

Terrilynne's eyes were dark coals. "No, but you did manage to kill our cousin Zavier."

He shrugged. "One more bastard get of Marsellus the Second for the Shadow Realm," he said indifferently.

"One more bastard get of Drusus will soon follow him," she replied.

He nodded toward her arm. "Who knows, perhaps that

*will turn septic and I'll see you there sooner than you
think. Then our ancestors will truly be even."*

"*Till then."* Terrilynne turned her mount and rode
back to her own lines.

Ellisander considered the conversation dispassionately. It was still possible that those he'd set in place
would carry out their mission. Tomlyn Martin had fallen
to the Caileins, and Roselynne DePaula was a prisoner,
but he had others. He might yet win the day.

His eyes glowing hotly, Ellisander DeMarian looked
out across the hills of Lochsbridge and continued to plan
for the future, irrespective of his present situation.

Terrilynne herself was busy setting her commanders
over their suddenly swelled forces. The individual armies
of the Aristok and the Hierarchpriest of Cannonshire
had merged, with most of Gawaina's troops granted a
temporary pardon. She, Evelynne DeMarian, and those
others known to be uninvolved in the plot against the
Throne had been freed on their oaths and were seeing
to the organization of the march to Lochcairen Castle,
Evelynne's seat of power. The wounded, including Alexius DeMarian, Eddison Croft, Edrud DeLlewellynne,
and Serus DeYvonne would follow in the wagons.

Kalidon DeKathrine had taken a blow to the chest
that had broken several ribs, but he grimly refused to
lie in the wagons. He was riding despite the pain and
gave a weak salute to Terrilynne as she passed him, his
indomitable spirit refusing to be bowed under the weight
of their losses. She'd nodded to him, understanding his
point, but sent Nan Guilcove to have a look at him anyway. The physician carried out her order as soon as she
was able, but there were many wounded still on the field
and the healers were all kept very busy.

Most of the dead were being buried where they'd
fallen by the archers of Cannonshire. The nobles were
being loaded onto wagons by their own people for travel
to their individual lands, but Albion DeMarian had carried the body of Nathaniel DeKathrine from the field
himself.

Cleaning the mud and blood from his lover's face, Albion had wrapped him in his own cloak and set him gently in the wagon beside the body of Zavier DeMarian. He would take him to Dunmouth so that he could be buried in his own family crypt, but in the meantime Nathaniel would ride beside the DeMarian Duke in a place of honor. Bending his head, Albion sent a prayer to Nathaniel's spirit, wishing it a safe journey to the Shadow Realm, and then turned aside.

The army slowly got itself sorted out and moving on the road to Lochcairen. Warrin carried Kassandra the whole way, refusing to give her up to any who offered. Her face wan, the child slept most of the time, only awakening to put her arms about the big man's neck.

Fay and Hamlin walked, supporting Simon on his horse between them. The artist was too weak to stay upright in the saddle by himself, but he held onto the pommel as his parents held onto him. His expression was unfocused, turned inward to something only he could see, but every now and then he blinked dazedly over at Rosarion.

The Herbalist himself was held up in the saddle before Atreus DePaula. His head ached more horribly than his leg. At one point, he'd just about given up and sent his Sight reaching out for the Shadow Catcher, but Simon's touch still lingered in his mind, its new sense of purpose giving him strength. Closing his eyes, he allowed Atreus to hold him up and slowly fell into a light doze.

The army made Lochcairen well into the night. Runners had been sent ahead by Evelynne DeMarian and the keep was ready to take in its noble guests and confine the prisoners. The surrounding town was recruited to billet the wounded. Their care went on throughout the night and it wasn't until late morning the next day that all had been seen to in some fashion.

As the afternoon sun shone through the windows of the castle's main hall, those nobles able to stand were summoned to the Aristok's presence to swear their oaths. Those Flame Priests that were on hand met to enter the Prophetic Realm and the long questioning of witnesses began as the Aristok opened the investigations of treason and regicide.

Once begun, it went quickly enough. Without Rosarion to hide their involvement, most of the conspirators were quickly discovered and the trials begun.

The first to come before Kassandra and her Court were Lysanda and Hadrian DeSandra. Almost babbling with fear, the Viscount spilled the entire story. Truly the weak tool, as Ellisander had called him, he implicated every possible conspirator, then threw himself on the Aristok's mercy, but his involvement in the burning of the Flame Temple precluded any such judgment. After a short conference with her Council, Kassandra handed him over to Innes Eathan, her Nominal Archpriest of the Flame.

Lysanda's case was as easily determined. As the highest secular authority next to the Aristok, the Hierarchpriest of Cannonshire pronounced the death sentence for treason, and she was led away, her expression scornful.

The rest of those accused were sentenced according to their level of guilt and noble standing.

Finally there was only Ellisander DeMarian left.

The Duke of Yorbourne had spent the night in Lochcairen's main tower room. He had slept and eaten well, and although he was brought in chained and under heavy guard, he walked easily, an expression of sneering indifference on his face. When he reached the traditional nine paces from the Royal dais he paused and looked off into space.

Gawaina DeKathrine stepped down from Kassandra's left side and held up a document.

"Ellisander DeMarian, Duke of Yorbourne, Earl of Greensgate and Aquilliard, you are here charged with regicide, in that you did plan and order the assassination of Marsellus the Third, Aristok of Branion; of treason, that you did plan to place yourself illegally in the Regency of Kassandra the Sixth; and of heresy that you did plan and order the assassination of the Living Flame's rightful Vessel. How do you answer these charges?"

Ellisander did not bother to change the direction of

his gaze. He smiled faintly. "I do not," he replied in an indifferent tone. "You do not have the authority to thus charge me."

Gawaina drew herself up. "I charge you by the authority granted me by the Aristok herself. I also have the authority to compel you."

The Duke of Yorbourne turned his fiery gaze on her and smiled again, but said nothing.

The Hierarchpriest turned to the Aristok. "If it please, Your Majesty, I offer two pieces of evidence to support these charges: the written confession of the Viscount Hadrian DeSandra and the written confession of the Flame Temple Herbalist, Rosarion DeLynne."

She passed a bound sheaf of papers to Terrilynne who bent down to whisper to the child. Kassandra glanced at Simon, seated beside her, who nodded. She looked up.

"We know what's in there an' we're 'pared to believe them," she said. "But we wanna know why Uncle Sandi killed my Papa."

His eyes lost in thought, Ellisander shook his head minutely, then returned the child's fiery gaze with his own.

"You are a child, Kasey," he began evenly, ignoring the glare his informality provoked from the Hierarchpriest. "You would not understand adult reasoning, and I will not seek to make you understand here in front of those unworthy of hearing. Perhaps when you're older."

"You will not have such an opportunity, My Lord Duke," Gawaina DeKathrine interrupted angrily. "Your crimes are punishable by death."

Ellisander gave a barking laugh. "My only crime that you have any involvement in, Winna, is playing you for a closeminded, bigoted fool. And I admit that with pleasure. I will also take pleasure in knowing that, however long I live, my place as Regent shall not be taken over by such a fool, but rather by a DeMarian, despised enemy though she may be. That way at least, Kasey might live to avoid the pitfalls of madness that her father and aunt fell into with your assistance."

The Hierarchpriest's face was white with rage, but she kept her temper. "Your guilt is certain," she growled. "And sentence shall be passed." She stared down her nose at him, her lip drawn up in a sneer. "If you have any final words, My Lord Duke, I suggest you say them now."

Ellisander smiled pleasantly back at her. "Do you mean I should beg for mercy, Winna? You know me better than that. I will not bend my knee to this rabble. I would rather go to my death as befitting one of the Living Flame."

"Very well," she answered, "and as you have no one here who will speak on your behalf, sentence will be passed forthwith."

"I will speak on his behalf."

The quiet words turned everyone's head as Rosarion DeLynne stood. He was pale and sickly, unable to stand long on his injured leg without Atreus' support, but he repeated his words to the growing confusion of the gathered. Even Kassandra turned to him in surprise. Gawaina DeKathrine's eyes narrowed, but Simon nodded very slowly, his face in shadow.

"You," the Hierarchpriest hissed. "You would do better to save your breath for your own trial."

"Each in its own time, My Lord," the Herbalist answered. "Will you hear me, Majesty?"

Kassandra looked at him intently for a moment, then nodded.

"Yes, Rosarion," she said solemnly.

Atreus helped the Herbalist limp to the required nine paces from the dais, but several feet from the Duke of Yorbourne. He supported his weight as Rosarion went awkwardly down on his knees.

"Majesty," the Seer Priest began. "You know my guilt. I've confessed it to you privately as well as here publicly. And you know your uncle's guilt even though he won't speak of it." He resisted the urge to glance at Ellisander, but out of the corner of his eye he saw the Duke sneer. "His crimes are punishable by death, Majesty but none here may carry out that sentence."

"Oh?" Gawaina asked hotly.

"No, My Lord Hierarchpriest, for many reasons under the law of this land, as you will remember when I speak of them." He paused for breath, wiping a sleeve across his brow and then looked up again. "First, the Duke of Yorbourne is a DeMarian. No one save a DeMarian has the right to pass judgment upon him." He turned to Terrilynne.

"You, My Lord Duke of Kempston, as Named Regent, have such a secular right, but you do not have the ecclesiastical right. Ellisander DeMarian is second in line to the power of the Living Flame. Only the True Vessel has the right to pass such a judgment." He drew a deep breath. "And, My Honored Lords of Her Most Holy's Privy Council, that Vessel is a child barely five years of age. *No* Vessel in their minority has *ever* passed a sentence of death, not in seven hundred and thirty-seven years of their protectorate. Do you want to set such a precedent here today? Do you want such an order given by this child before she's old enough to truly understand what sentence she's passing on her own uncle?

"You're her Councillors, sworn to advise her for the good of the Realm. Is this for the good of the Realm, My Lords, or simply for revenge?"

"And is it for the good of the Realm that he be pardoned the death of the late Aristok, his own cousin and brother-in-law?" Gawain replied coldly.

"No, My Lord. But none here save the Aristok herself has the right to condemn him, and she is too young."

"Then let him be imprisoned until her majority," the Hierarchpriest answered impatiently.

"That is all I ask, My Lord."

The Hierarchpriest turned to the Aristok. "If it please Your Majesty, then that is my council."

Terrilynne nodded. "And mine also, My Liege."

Kassandra looked at her uncle for a long time, and then turned to Simon. The artist's eyes were closed, his face gaunt and gray.

"Simon?"

For a moment he seemed far away, and then he opened his eyes. "Majesty?"

"What do you think?"

He met her gaze, so like her father's, with a sad expression. "I think this whole affair is tragedy enough already, Majesty."

She nodded gravely. "I will have him put in prison till I'm sixteen," she said. "An' then I will deal wif him myself."

Terrilynne coughed discreetly.

"Yes?"

"Might I suggest, My Liege, that he be guarded by the garrison of Caerockeith.

"I do not doubt the abilities of the Shield Knights," she added as the new captain bridled. "I ask this as a boon granted by the Aristok to her Regent for victory on the battlefield."

Ellisander snorted, but Kassandra nodded her head.

And so it was decided, and the Duke of Yorbourne was led away.

Gawaina DeKathrine turned to her Sovereign. "Will you hear the case against Rosarion DeLynne now, Your Majesty," she asked, her lip drawn up in a faint sneer. "He is, after all, already kneeling."

Kassandra turned her fiery gaze on the Hierarchpriest who, after a moment, averted her own eyes. Then the child turned to the Herbalist. Rosarion swallowed, his mouth gone suddenly dry.

Kassandra shook her head. "I have already heard the case an' have thought about it a long time," she replied. "I want to put it off till I'm older, too."

"But Majesty, as your Councillors . . ."

"As my Councillors, you can do what I say, an' I say I'm gonna wait till I'm older!" she snapped. "Rosarion?"

He looked up, a faintly hopeful expression on his face. "Yes, Most Holy?"

"I want you to go an' stay wif the Coins till I send for you. That way Turi can keep you all right till then an' Warrin can keep an eye on you soes My Lord Gawaina won't think you're gonna run off. An' I want Atreus to go, too. Atreus?"

"Yes, My Liege?" the Knight answered.

"I want you to bring Rosarion back when I'm sixteen, soes he can have a real sentence then."

"Yes, My Liege."

"Good. Now Rosarion, you can stand up." She waved one hand regally.

Atreus helped Rosarion to stand, and the Herbalist bowed before his Avatar, knowing, as she did, that the chances of him living eleven years on the road were remote, but they would be good years.

"Thank you, Most Holy," he whispered.

Kassandra smiled beatifically at him. Gawaina De-Kathrine frowned, but said nothing.

"Now," the Aristok continued. "I've done all the bad stuff, an' I wanna do the good stuff before supper. Terri, you remind me if I forget anything."

"Yes, My Liege."

"First. Everybody else is pardoned. Next, I don't want no more mean stuff against Essusiates. Fay an' Hamlin an' Simon are Essusiates an' they saved me, an' sides, so did Essus, so no more being mean to them. Next, My Lord Duke of Kempston is my Regent. I named her that before, but it's 'fficial now. I want her company to move to Branbridge wif me an' all be in my Palace Guard or in my Knights, whatever, Terri will do it. I want Warrin in my Shield Knights, too, even though he's gonna stay wif Rosarion an' the Coins."

There was a murmur at this, but no one dared speak openly against it.

"Next, the Coins are to have a uh . . ." she put her finger in her mouth.

"A Royal appointment, My Liege?" Terrilynne suggested.

"Yes, that, an' lots of money, too. Next. Ospreyan is my own Herald, an' Alida an' Jem are now my 'fficial weavers. Ospreyan, you tell the Weaver's Guild that I want that an' make 'em take 'em in."

The Herald bowed, showing no sign of the trouble his young new ruler's lack of diplomacy was going to cause him. Meanwhile she'd turned her attention elsewhere.

"Simon?"

"Yes, Majesty?"

"I want you an' Fay an' Hamlin to all go stand there." She pointed to the center of the room where Ellisander had stood. Mystified, they obeyed, Simon leaning heavily on Hamlin's arm.

Kassandra stood. "Good, now it's gonna be done right. 'Cause you all, but most especially Simon, went an' saved me an' brought me home safe, I wanna reward you. So I'm gonna make a new noble family. Ospreyan, you 'member an' write it all up proper, 'cause Dani and Luis aren't here an' they get to be part of it, too."

"Yes, Your Majesty."

"So, I name you all DeFays," she waved her arms to encompass the family. "That means Fay, you're Fay DeFay. I know it sounds kinda funny, but they're all named after you."

The woman blinked. "I'm honored, Majesty."

"I know. That means that Jael's a DeFay, too, even though he was an' Asher, but he's Simon's son an' it counts, so he's a noble now, an' I want him an' all my Company to be with me at the palace an' play with me 'cause I'm tired of being alone, an' a course Alida an' Jem must come, too, as my weavers an' you must get along, Fay."

"Of course, Majesty."

"Good. That's all."

And so it was. Kassandra dismissed her Council and then led the way in to supper.

That night Rosarion DeLynne went to see Ellisander DeMarian.

The Duke was seated on the room's small pallet and did not bother to look up as the Herbalist entered.

Rosarion stood uncertainly looking down at the chains about the Duke's wrists and ankles, and found himself unable to speak.

Finally Ellisander gave a short sigh.

"Yes, Rosarion?"

The younger man resisted the urge to shuffle his feet. "I, uh, came to see how you were."

Even to him the words sounded hollow, but the DeMarian merely smiled.

"I am, as you see, well enough."

Rosarion nodded. "I . . ." He paused, unsure again and Ellisander finally met his eyes.

"It's quite all right, you know," he said. "I do forgive you."

"Forgive?"

"That's what you're here for, isn't it, forgiveness?"

Rosarion opened his mouth and closed it again. "I guess I am," he said simply.

"Then you have it." Ellisander looked away again.

Rosarion turned to go and then paused. "I just didn't think we should end it that way," he said.

"With you begging for my life?" The duke smiled almost kindly at him. "I thought it was very romantic. You're a lot like Saralynne was, you know."

"Is that why you saved me?"

"Perhaps." Ellisander shook his head. "Perhaps I cared for you because of yourself, not just for her memory. Perhaps I cared for you both too much, too much for my own good.

"Will you write to me in prison?" he asked suddenly.

"Yes."

"Why?"

Rosarion looked away. "Because perhaps I care for you too much for my own good, too."

Ellisander shook his head. "You're a foolish man."

"I know."

The door opened and Briar Stone put his head in the door. "That's all the allowable time, Your Grace," he said apologetically.

"They're afraid I'll corrupt you again," Ellisander said with a chuckle. Catching Rosarion's gaze, his eyes glowed brightly. "And they're right. Run away, little priest, before you land in the fire again."

Rosarion felt himself flush.

"Good-bye, My Lord," he said quietly.

Ellisander blew him a gentle, mocking kiss, and Briar ushered the Herbalist out of the room.

The next day, Rosarion left Lochcairen in the company of Atreus DePaula and Warrin Fire-Eater, bound for the Spinning Coins and his new life.

The Court of Kassandra the Sixth stayed in Lochcairen a month. Most of the army was sent to the Continent under the Command of Albion and Evelynne DeMarian. The rest were waiting to escort their Aristok to her capital.

The day before they were to leave, Kassandra the Sixth and Simon DeFay of Branbridge walked hand in hand through the castle gardens. Mindful of Simon's injuries, they moved slowly and on reaching a plot of grass, they sat, watching the bees hard at work in the roses. Finally Kassandra looked up at the artist.

"Simon?"

"Hm?"

"Is it all over now?"

He smiled down at her. "No, Sparky, it's only just begun now, but you'll have lots of help."

"Oh. Simon?"

"Yes, Sparky?"

"Is Papa still wif you?"

"Yes."

"How come? Fay said it was bad for you."

Simon felt a tingle in his mind and sent a soothing thought to it.

"We've come to an agreement, your Papa and I," he answered. "He stayed, but he doesn't interfere . . ."

"*My* Papa?" Kassandra's voice was incredulous, and the painter laughed quietly.

"Yes, *your* Papa. In return, I promised to always remember him and keep him by me."

"How're you gonna do that?"

"I'm going to paint a little miniature of him to put in a locket and I'm going to always wear it."

Kassandra's eyes grew wide. "Can you do that?" she asked. "I mean paint so little wif your left hand?"

"Yes, I think I can. It doesn't have to be perfect, the love in it will be enough. It will take a long time before my work with the left is up to the quality of the right, but I have time to practice."

"Yes, you gots twelve years."

"Twelve years?"

"Uh-huh. Then you gots to paint my majority coronation on a wall, an' you gots to paint my adventures wif the Coins an' the Company somewhere, too."

"So I do."

"Simon?"

"Yes, Sparky?"

"What kinda bee is that big one?"

"Where? Oh, that's a bumblebee."

"Why do they call it that?"

"I guess because it bumbles awkwardly around."

"Oh. But it still flies anyway, right?"

"Right."

The artist and the child continued to sit and watch the bees until the sun began to set, and then they made their way back into the castle and the gathered Court of Kassandra the Sixth, 737 DR.

High Summer, Mean Lunasa, 783 DR
The Cathedral of the Holy Triarchy, Branbridge

The old man set his brush carefully aside and rubbed a cramp in his left hand. After forty years he'd never fully gotten used to the change, but looking up at the vast expanse of lines and forms above him, he supposed he'd done all right.

Leaning back against the scaffolding, he held up the large silver locket that rested on his chest. Rubbing his thumb and finger against the warm metal, he cracked it open and studied the small portrait inside. A fire-haired, fire-eyed man grinned back at him, not a bad likeness for all it was painted so long ago.

"Hello, Leary," the old man whispered. "Well, it's finally finished. What do you think of your Cathedral today?"

His eyes were drawn back up to the great painted panels and suddenly he wanted to impress the moment into his memory forever; the colors, the lines, the sunlight streaming in through the windows to cast multicolored light across the flagstone floor. He breathed deeply, all his senses alive to their individual sensations; the hardness of the scaffolding, the stiffness in his limbs, the scratch of dried paint on his cheek. He listened to the sounds of birds outside and his own heartbeat echoing in the silent expanse of stone. He took in another great breath, and the overpowering scent of fresh paint took him back seventy years in a kaleidoscope of memories too many to dwell on.

Finally, he looked up again to the ceiling of the Holy Triarchy Cathedral sweeping off before him. Bedecked in the most beautiful colors of his ability, depicting the early adventures of Kassandra the Sixth as she had requested so long ago. Each panel, each alcove, each border even, was a masterpiece of its own, and his eyes ached just looking at them.

"Finally, truly finished," he whispered. Holy Triarchy, the greatest Cathedral of the Living Flame in the whole of the Triarctic Realm was finished. Not a bad legacy for Essusiate-born Simon of Florenz.

"Simon DeFay," the wind whispered gently in his mind.

"Simon of Branbridge," he answered absently. His and Jade's daughter Rosemary was the first of the De-Fays now, Earl of Werrickshire and happy to be so; happy that her father never interfered with what he supposed was really his title and lands. But no, he'd given them up when she'd turned sixteen, so he could have the time to paint. He was Simon of Branbridge now. The artistic title had always been honor enough for him.

Now Jael . . . He smiled as he thought of his son. Jael had gone farther than any of them, he supposed. Jael was a DeMarian now, Consort to the Aristok Kassandra the Sixth and Earl of Essendale. Who'd have thought it so many years ago?

The old man shifted with a groan and looked back up at the final panel depicting Kassandra the Sixth's majority; the acceptance of the mantle of the Living Flame, the adult authority over the Realm, and the final death judgment over her Uncle Ellisander.

He sighed. She'd done it, he thought; coldly and rationally, knowing that as long as Ellisander was alive, she and her subsequent heirs would never be safe from his machinations. She was truly a DeMarian fit to wear the crown.

He took a pull from his jug. She had children of her own now, hers and Jael's. Quinton, the oldest, had just had his first child, a daughter, named Kassandra after her grandmother. The line was assured. As for the rest who had lived the events bedecking these walls, well, Luis and Dani were happy and prosperous, living in his parent's old house despite their noble connection. Terrilynne's old company had advanced, and Kassandra's playmates had grown and prospered also, warmed by the light of Royal affection. Kassandra had kept them by her all these years and they had repaid her with solid advice and support. Kate Potter was the Archpriest of the Flame now, and her brother Alex, the Aristok's Royal Herald. Carrie and Bella Croft were Sword Knights, and Ross was Kassandra's own secretary. Maggie was her Captain of the Shield Knights and her little sister, Aggie, was Lieutenant. Willie Cheape was the Hierarchpriest of Cannonshire and Davin and Marri were Captains in Her Majesty's navy. Who'd have thought it?

The old man shook himself. Oh, yes, Rosarion had predicted it, hadn't he?

His thoughts turned to the last time he'd seen the Seer Priest, four years after Kassandra had returned to her capital. The Coins had come to Branbridge for their annual performance before the Aristok and afterward she and Simon had gone to see Rosarion.

The Herbalist had been lying, bundled in blankets, on the cot in Turi's wagon, too weak to rise when they'd entered. But he'd made one last prophecy for his Avatar, holding tightly to Simon's hand and drawing on their old bond for strength.

The artist had felt the amphisbane rise up to slip over them both, and Seen its red-and-white-colored limbs wrap about the child. He looked into the eyes of its other half and saw it smile, then their contact slowly faded and Simon almost sobbed aloud from the surprising emptiness that rushed in as the Shadow Catcher took Rosarion's spirit up in its arms. Leary, close as always, gave him comfort, glaring at the Captain of the Dead until it disappeared with its burden, for Leary was not ready to go just yet.

Simon and Kassandra sat for a long time, unspeaking, in the tiny wagon, and then the two them went out to tell Atreus and Turi that Rosarion had finally crossed over.

The old man took a shaky breath. Rosarion DeLynne had been only twenty-four when he'd died. Only two years older than Leary had been.

"Too young," he whispered. "Much too young."

The Aristok herself was fifty-one now and as full of energy as she'd been at five. She'd wanted Holy Triarchy painted for her fiftieth birthday but hadn't commissioned it until a month before. She'd been put out when it hadn't been finished, but what could he do?

His gaze was inexorably drawn up again.

She'd be happy now that it was finished. He shook his head. She was the most impatient patron he'd ever had.

"No, she wasn't."

The shadows danced about him, blocking his view for a moment. Simon brushed his hands across his face.

"No, she wasn't Leary. That honor was always yours. So now that you've decided to grace me with your presence, what do you think?"

The shadows seemed to grow and swell.

"Beautiful. Truly magnificent, and worthy of the greatest living painter in Branion," they acknowledged. After a time there came a faint sigh. *"She surpassed me, didn't she."*

"Together they surpassed us both. New territory in Gallia and Panisha; Gwyneth happy and Heathland quiet for over two decades. Essusiates and Triarchs living in peace and respect for each other. You should be very proud."

"I am proud," the shadows whispered. *"Of both of you."*

The great building grew suddenly darker and the old man shivered.

"Is it cold in here?" he asked.

"Yes. It's time, Simon." The shadow swirled about him, taking the form of a tall, fire-haired young man. He held out his hand.

"Time?" The old man looked up, saw the silent figure standing patiently behind Leary and sighed. "Oh. Yes, I see. But . . . well, no matter."

"What?"

"There were just so many works, and so little time to realize them all."

Leary smiled his understanding as Simon closed his eyes.

He sat quiet for a long time, clearing his mind of all regrets. For a moment he seemed to sleep, and then he opened his eyes wide.

"The colors," he breathed. *"Oh, Leary, look at all the colors."*

FIONA PATTON

In the kingdom of Branion, the hereditary royal line is blessed—or cursed—with the power of the Flame, a magic against which none can stand. But when used by one not strong enough to control it, the power of the Flame can just as easily consume its human vessel, as destroy whatever foe it had been unleased against. . . .

Tanya Huff

☐ **NO QUARTER**   UE2698—$5.99
☐ **FIFTH QUARTER**   UE2651—$4.99
☐ **SING THE FOUR QUARTERS**   UE2628—$4.99

VICTORY NELSON, INVESTIGATOR:
Otherworldly Crimes A Specialty
☐ **BLOOD PRICE: Book 1**   UE2471—$4.99
☐ **BLOOD TRAIL: Book 2**   UE2502—$4.99
☐ **BLOOD LINES: Book 3**   UE2530—$4.99
☐ **BLOOD PACT: Book 4**   UE2582—$4.99
☐ **BLOOD DEBT: Book 5**   UE2582—$4.99

When Henry Fitzroy is plagued by ghosts demanding vengeance, he calls upon newly made vampire Vicki Nelson and her homicide detective lover to help find the murderer. But Vancouver may not be big enough for *two* vampires!

THE NOVELS OF CRYSTAL
☐ **CHILD OF THE GROVE: Book 1**   UE2432—$4.50
☐ **THE LAST WIZARD: Book 2**   UE2331—$4.50

OTHER NOVELS
☐ **GATE OF DARKNESS, CIRCLE OF LIGHT**   UE2386—$4.50
☐ **THE FIRE'S STONE**   UE2445—$3.95

THE GOLDEN KEY
by
Melanie Rawn
Jennifer Roberson
Kate Elliott

In the duchy of Tira Virte fine art is prized above all things. But not even the Grand Duke knows just how powerful the art of the Grijalva family is. For thanks to a genetic fluke certain males of their bloodline are born with a frightening talent—the ability to manipulate time, space, and reality within their paintings, using them to cast magical spells which alter events, people, places, and things in the real world. Their secret magic formula, known as the Golden Key, permits those Gifted sons to vastly improve the fortunes of their family. Still, the Grijalvas are fairly circumspect in their dealings until two young talents come into their powers: Sario, a boy who will learn to use his Gift to make himself virtually immortal; and Saavedra, a female cousin who, unbeknownst to her family, may be the first woman ever to have the Gift. Sario's personal ambitions and thwarted love for his cousin will lead to a generations-spanning plot to seize total control of the duchy and those who rule it.

• Featuring cover art by Michael Whelan

ALSO AVAILABLE FROM THE AUTHORS OF
THE GOLDEN KEY

MELANIE RAWN
EXILES

Michelle West

The Sun Sword:

□ **THE BROKEN CROWN** UE2740—$6.99

The Dominion, once divided by savage clan wars, has kept an uneasy peace within its borders since that long-ago time when the clan Leonne was gifted with the magic of the Sun Sword and was raised up to reign over the five noble clans. But now treachery strikes at the very heart of the Dominion as two never meant to rule—one a highly skilled General, the other a master of the magical arts—seek to seize the Crown by slaughtering all of clan Leonne blood. . . .

The Sacred Hunt:

□ **HUNTER'S OATH** UE2681—$5.50
□ **HUNTER'S DEATH** UE2706—$5.99

KATE ELLIOT

CROWN OF STARS

"An entirely captivating affair"—*Publishers Weekly*

☐ **KING'S DRAGON**   UE2771—$6.99
In a world where bloody conflicts rage and sorcery holds sway both human and other-than-human forces vie for supremacy. In this land, Alain, a young man seeking the destiny promised him by the Lady of Battles, and Liath, a young woman gifted with a power that can alter history, are about to be swept up in a world-shaking conflict.

☐ **PRINCE OF DOGS**   UE2770—$23.95
Return to the war-torn kingdoms of Wendar and Varre, and the intertwined destinies of: Alain, raised in humble surroundings but now a Count's Heir; Liath, who struggles with the secrets of her past while evading those who seek the treasure she conceals; Sanglant, believed dead, but only held captive in the cathedral of Gent, and Fifth Son, who now builds an army to do his father's—or his own—bidding in a world at war!

Prices slightly higher in Canada.   **DAW 211X**